Tom & Lucky
(and George & Cokey Flo)

Tom & Lucky

(and George & Cokey Flo)

A Novel

C. Joseph Greaves

BLOOMSBURY

NEW YORK · LONDON · OXFORD · NEW DELHI · SYDNEY

Bloomsbury USA
An imprint of Bloomsbury Publishing Plc

1385 Broadway	50 Bedford Square
New York	London
NY 10018	WC1B 3DP
USA	UK

www.bloomsbury.com

BLOOMSBURY and the Diana logo are trademarks of Bloomsbury
Publishing Plc

First published 2015

© Charles J. Greaves 2015

LIBRARY OF CONGRESS CATALOGING-IN-PUBLICATION DATA HAS BEEN
APPLIED FOR.

ISBN: HB: 978-1-62040-785-1
ISBN: ePub: 978-1-62040-787-5

First U.S. edition 2015

1 3 5 7 9 10 8 6 4 2

Typeset by RefineCatch Limited, Bungay, Suffolk
Printed and bound in the U.S.A. by Thomson-Shore Inc., Dexter, Michigan

To find out more about our authors and books visit www.bloomsbury.com. Here
you will find extracts, author interviews, details of forthcoming events and the
option to sign up for our newsletters.

Bloomsbury books may be purchased for business or promotional use. For
information on bulk purchases please contact Macmillan Corporate and Premium
Sales Department at specialmarkets@macmillan.com.

For the Tallow Lane Gang: Mike, Danny, Nancy, Roddy, and Tracey

Novels arise out of the shortcomings of history.
—Georg Philipp Friedrich von Hardenberg

THE YEAR WAS 1936.

Lucky Luciano was the most powerful gangster in America. Thomas E. Dewey was an ambitious young prosecutor determined to bring him down, and Cokey Flo Brown—grifter, heroin addict, and sometimes prostitute—was the witness who claimed she could do it. Only George Morton Levy, a courtly Long Island defense attorney, stood between Lucky and a life behind bars and between Dewey and the New York governor's mansion.

This is their story.

One

Lucky

"Six is the point. Six."

Salvatore Lucania weighs the cool dice in his hand. Small in stature, lost in the shapeless tweed of a borrowed jacket, he watches through hooded eyes as bills flutter and settle like autumn leaves on the green expanse before him, there to be sorted and matched in concordance with the shouted wagers of the sporting men who elbow and jostle, their polyglot ruckus evolving under a hazy trinity of overhead lamps into order and then, finally, into silence.

He gives the dice a slow rattle.

"Come on, kid. You jackin off or shootin crap?"

Laughter.

Lucania's eyes, cold and reptilian, search out the voice. The laughter dies.

1

He blows into his fist.

"Comin out."

He tosses the dice backhanded. They short-hop and carom off the far rail and tumble to their final, immutable rest.

Double threes.

Whoops, and jeers, and a rough hand slapping his back.

Lucania glances at his pal Meyer, who stands quietly by the side pocket. Their eyes meet and hold. Meyer's eyebrows lift.

"Hose him down, Frankie. This kid is hot!"

"Twenty clams."

"Covered."

"Abe's Cabe."

"Covered!"

"Sawbuck."

"You're off."

"Fade 'im!"

"Snake eyes!"

"Boxcars!"

"Baby needs a new pair of shoes!"

The process repeats, as it has throughout the night and into the bleary morning, with only the shooters changing in their rotation until the men by acclamation, their number winnowed by the inertial forces of loss and fatigue, finally call it quits.

At nearly five A.M., Lucania watches as winnings are counted, and outcomes assessed, and maledictions quietly uttered. A cigar is lit with a flourish. The croupier is tipped and bows obsequiously as he moves through the shadows toward the stairs leading up from their basement redoubt.

The men sort hats and topcoats, don mufflers and gloves. They stamp or pace like stallions in a tight and skittish cluster.

"Excellent evening," Meyer says as the two boys stand with hands in pockets, waiting for the alley door to be opened.

"Not too shabby," Lucania agrees.

They make for a curious pair, the young Sicilian and the younger Russian Jew where they stand flanked by older and larger men whose body odors and rancid breaths mingle in the dead basement air with the acrid smells of bleach and oil, coal dust and smoke.

Yawns are stifled. Coats open and flap.

"You boys done real good tonight." A fat man—Pazzano, the Calabrian baker from Mott Street—has turned and is speaking to Lucania. "Whatta you plan to do with all that money?"

"You see my friend here? He's savin up for college."

The man laughs. "Hey, you hear that? We got a couple college boys over here."

One of the redheaded brothers from Brooklyn, the one with the pink facial scar, shoulders his way through the men until he is standing beside Lucania.

"Nice night, kid. In case you was worried about gettin home safe, my brother and me'll walk you right to your doorstep. Safer than a police escort we are. Only cost you a fiver."

"No thanks."

"You sure about that? It's a dangerous world out there. Anythin's liable to happen, you ain't got the proper protection."

"You heard me the first time."

"Okay, kid, have it your way. Just tryin to be helpful is all. Don't say you wasn't warned."

And still they wait for the alley door to open. Connor, the Tammany man, resumes his rambling yarn about a whorehouse fire in Five Points.

"—and not a one of 'em wearin more than the smile she was born with. And Timulty, the station chief, with his wife off visitin her sister in Philly, he steps forward like the gentleman that he is and says he's got an empty bedroom at his apartment, see—"

"Christ, the wife is gonna skin me."

"What's takin so goddamn long?"

"Frankie! What the fuck are you doin up there?"

A door opens above. All heads turn to the staccato clatter of shoes on wooden stairs.

"What the—"

Three men have descended, each with his hat pulled low and a muffler covering his face. They move silently into position with their guns leveled and steady—one by the furnace and one at either end of the billiard table, the three guns forming a deadly triangle.

The room is suddenly silent.

"Let's go, cash on the table," a gunman orders, gesturing with his weapon. He wears a topcoat of gray herringbone and gloves of black kid.

None of the gamblers moves.

"I said—"

"Do you have any idea who you're talkin to, boyo?"

The gunman turns and raises his pistol and thumbs back the hammer. Connor's hands lift in slow surrender.

"Cash on the table, Micky! Let's go, chop-chop!"

This time all do as instructed, each man either emptying his pockets onto the hard green felt or turning them inside out for the gunmen's inspections. Soon, over eight hundred dollars stands in a greasy, crumpled heap.

"You too, Junior."

The gun points at Lucania, who meets it with eyes as hard and black as the muzzle staring back at him.

"Go fuck yourself."

The gunman steps closer. His hand blurs as his pistol lashes, smashing Lucania's cheek.

All the men flinch. All, that is, except Lucania, who tastes the blood as it trickles toward his chin.

"Let's go, tough guy. Cash on the table."

Lucania tosses a fistful of folded bills onto the felt. Meyer's eyes, alert throughout, watch as the gunmen stuff cash into their pockets.

4

"Thanks, boys," their leader sing-songs as he backs toward the staircase, his gun sweeping left and right. "It was nice doin business."

One by one the gunmen make their way up the narrow steps, with the leader the last to ascend, crouching as he backs until, with a whirl of gray herringbone, the door slams shut behind him.

The room erupts.

Men are shouting and swearing, and some are fumbling for pistols. The alley door is rattled and tested by heavy shoulders. Amid the heat and frenzy, Meyer offers a handkerchief to his friend, who presses it to his cheek.

"Thanks."

One of the men, his gun at the ready, has sidled to the staircase. He ducks his head for a look, then raises a hand to the others.

"Quiet!"

Above him, the door creaks open.

"Don't shoot! It's me, Frankie!"

The men crowd the staircase as the croupier descends on wobbly legs, a bloodied bar rag pressed to his head. He is swept and spun as if by a surging tide and backed against the table, where he stammers his story of how the gunmen had lain in wait and coldcocked him and left him for dead. The man who holds him by the shirt collar pulls the rag-hand free and turns him by the chin, so all can witness the bloody, purplish lump above his ear.

He is released.

"Somebody's a dead man!" bellows Connor.

"Open the fuckin door," another orders, and Frankie, his keys jingling, hurries to oblige.

Snow has fallen during the night, and the men emerge from the basement single file like hibernates smoked from a den with their greatcoats steaming and their breaths billowing frosty white in the cold light of daybreak.

They confer but briefly. Theories are advanced, and names ventured, and vengeance crudely sworn until, one by one, the men drift away, trudging heavily down the alley and into the blanketed morning.

Meyer is alongside Lucania as both boys, hurrying now, raise their collars and duck into the icy headwinds buffeting a Third Avenue whose flocked expanse is yet untracked by car or horse or man.

The boys watch over their shoulders.

"Son of a bitch, that hurt."

"Here, let me see it."

They stop, and Lucania lowers the bloody handkerchief.

"It's all right, you won't need stitches. Put some snow on it."

"Son of a fucking bitch."

They are moving again, hastening against the risen dawn.

"By the way," Meyer says, "what did I tell you about betting the four and ten?"

"Hey, I won, didn't I? And besides, what's the difference now?"

"Dumb luck is nothing to be proud of."

Lucania pauses once more to crane his neck. "Keep an eye out for that scar-faced Mick bastard."

"What for? He knows you've just been robbed. That's the beauty of it. I'll bet you nobody goes to the cops. Statistics show that crimes perpetrated against other criminals are very rarely reported."

"Whatever you say, Meyer."

"Risk management," the younger boy proclaims with a finger raised. "First you figure the odds, then you figure out how to shave 'em."

"What are the odds my old man kicks my ass when I get home?"

"Just tell him you went to the library and fell asleep in the stacks. That's what I always say."

"Yeah, right," Lucania says, examining the bloody handkerchief. "At least you been in a fuckin library."

They arrive at the corner of 12th Street, where they stop and wait, shuffling their feet and blowing warmth into their hands. Soon a figure emerges from out of the sunrise, furtive in its approach, ducking from pushcart to car, from stoop to storefront.

The boys move into a sheltering alcove and wait for the new arrival. He too is a young man, flushed and winded when he finally appears.

"Like candy from a baby," the new man says, pulling an enormous roll of bills from his herringbone topcoat and handing it off to Meyer.

"Nice work. Is everybody square?"

"You bet."

"What about you?"

"I took my cut. Count it if you want."

Meyer pockets the cash without counting it.

"Your boys are in the dark?"

"Just like you said."

"You're absolutely sure about that?"

"Sure I'm sure. I done just like you told me."

The new man turns to Lucania, eying the bloody handkerchief. "Sorry about the knock, Sallie, but I hadda make it look good."

Meyer steps between them to survey the empty street. He exhumes the roll from his pocket and peels off a pair of bills.

"Here's a little bonus," he says to the new man, "for a job well done."

Before either can react to the *snik* of the knife blade, Lucania has jumped onto the new man's back and is pounding at his neck, jabbing and stabbing as though chipping ice from a block. The man's shrieks turn to gargles, viscous and strangled, and then to silence as Meyer ducks to avoid the spurting blood and Lucania, still stabbing, rides the falling body all the way to the sidewalk.

The alcove is an abattoir, its walls spattered and running. Meyer grabs Lucania's arm with both hands and wrestles him off the prostrate figure whose body is sprawled on the sidewalk with its legs on bare pavement and its head, or what remains of it, a crimson flower blossoming in the snow.

7

"What the hell'd you do that for?"

Lucania's breath comes in heaves as he wipes his face with a sleeve. "Risk management."

"Christ, let's get out of here."

Meyer pulls him by the arm, but Lucania shrugs free and rummages the dead man's overcoat, counting out bills as he stands.

"Sorry, pal." Lucania leans forward and spits. "But I hadda make it look good."

Two

George

May 1915

HIS FIRST PROBLEM was the dictograph.

The device, purchased by Mrs. Florence Carman and installed by one Gaston Boissonnault, had allowed Mrs. Carman to eavesdrop from the safety of the marital bedroom on the conversations that her husband, Dr. Edwin Carman, had been having in the supposed privacy of his downstairs examining room. It was the discovery of this device that had changed the focus of the investigation from an assassination, dispassionately perpetrated by some unknown enemy of LuLu Bailey, into a crime of jealous passion.

His second problem was the maid, Celia Coleman. The current version of her story had Mrs. Carman tearing through the kitchen, gun in hand, on her way to the side of the house where she would thrust the weapon through the examining room window and shoot Mrs. Bailey dead, the bullet perhaps intended for the philandering doctor. In this latest, more dramatic telling, Mrs. Carman had then brandished the gun as she'd returned through the home's back door, announcing to the maid, "I've shot him!"

His third problem was the Burns Agency detective, Archer Owens, the man who'd originally been their savior. Employed by the Nassau County district attorney's office to keep watch over the maid, Owens had approached the defense team with a sensational tale in which Celia Coleman had been kidnapped by the D.A., held against her will, and browbeaten into fabricating her current testimony. This bombshell, although disputed by Coleman herself on the witness stand, was felt to have been largely responsible for the hung jury that had ended the first trial of Florence Carman. After that trial, however, Owens had visited Celia Coleman at her home in South Carolina and had, in the presence of at least two witnesses, been loudly accused by the maid of attempted bribery, effectively blunting the detective's further utility as a witness.

But all these problems paled in comparison to the one that had kept young George Morton Levy awake, tossing and turning, for the better part of a week. It wasn't so much the difficulty of the case, or the sudden resignation of John Graham as lead counsel for the defense—the first trial had, after all, taken a heavy toll on the aging barrister—but rather Mrs. Carman's adamancy that George and George alone was the one to take Graham's place.

"But I'm only twenty-six years old," George had reminded her, fidgeting in his chair.

"I realize that."

"And I've never tried a murder case. Or any major case, for that matter."

To this, the defendant had only shrugged. "You've tried other cases. Edwin told me as much."

George's imploring eyes shifted to Dr. Carman. "I really don't have the experience. And what if I make a mistake?"

"George, dear," Florence Carman told him then, her hand firm on his knee. "I'm not asking for another continuance. You know this case better than anyone. You helped with the investigation, you sat through the first trial, and you're the most capable young man I've ever met. I have complete confidence in your ability to win an acquittal."

The case, it must be said, was not without hope. The maid, Celia Coleman, had from the witness stand contradicted the very affidavit she'd signed on the day after LuLu Bailey's murder. In that document, which George himself had prepared, Celia had said nothing about a gun, or a side-yard excursion, or a dramatic back-door confession. But George had made the mistake—the rookie mistake—of obtaining her signature on only the last page of the document, which had given the maid, once in the custody of the district attorney, room in which to repudiate the first two pages of her testimony.

And then there was the gun itself. Or rather, the fact that no gun had ever been found in the Carman household, leaving a gaping hole in the prosecution's theory of the case. This was a hole that Lewis J. Smith, the dogged district attorney of Nassau County, had tried to fill with farfetched theories about gang connections and mystery accomplices. It was the missing gun, George had always believed, more so than Archer Owens's dramatic testimony, that had led ten members of the original Carman jury to cast their votes for acquittal.

The prospect of trying one's first murder case was enough to warrant any young lawyer's insomnia. Here, however, the trial's more salacious aspects—the beautiful defendant, her dashing doctor husband, and the heavy barrage of journalistic innuendo regarding the good doctor's other female patients—had turned the proceedings into a carnival sideshow the likes of which New York hadn't seen since the Harry Thaw trial of 1908. Indeed, when the first Carman trial had opened in October of 1914, more than three thousand spectators had crowded the Mineola courthouse, vying for three hundred available seats.

And now it would all fall to George. George, who'd been too busy with his semipro baseball and football careers to bother attending college. George, who'd worked his way through the night program at NYU Law School by taking odd legal jobs for three dollars a week, searching titles and serving process. George, who'd only recently taken the New York bar exam upon attaining the minimum age of twenty-one years.

But George Levy accepted the Carman case, and with it the butterflies and the lost appetite and the chronic insomnia. Really, what choice did he have?

The reporters scoffed, and the judge condescended, and the sneering D.A. ran roughshod over the earnest young lawyer in the stiff woolen suit, yet somehow George persevered. Better still, for two grueling weeks of thrust and parry, move and countermove, George Morton Levy rose to the occasion, his courtroom baptism culminating in a blistering cross-examination of Celia Coleman that had left the young maid in tears, breathing new life into the Owens version of events and, most important of all, exposing for the first time the maid's long-festering animosity toward her employer, the coldly imperious Florence Carman.

But all did not go smoothly for the defense, not by a long shot. A critical issue in the case was visibility, since all the other patients in Dr. Carman's waiting room testified that they'd seen nobody cross the front lawn after the fatal shot had been fired. This left the defense with two alternative scenarios with which to rebut Celia Coleman: Either the gunman had fled west, across the neighboring lawn, or else the falling twilight had obscured the patients' views from the waiting room's street-side window.

In the retrial, however, the district attorney slammed both doors shut with a trio of new witnesses.

The first was Dr. James Scarr of the New York Weather Bureau, who described from his record book the atmospheric conditions in Freeport, N.Y., on the night of the murder. The sun had set at 7:32 P.M., he testified, with astronomical twilight lasting until 9:31. Therefore, between 7:50 and 8:10, when the crime had unquestionably occurred, there had been more than adequate daylight by which to observe a running figure from several blocks away.

George cross-examined Dr. Scarr with a single question: "Are you the man who prepares the weather forecasts for the papers?"

"Some of them."

"That's enough," said George with a wave, and the courtroom erupted in laughter.

The other two witnesses were not so easily dismissed. May Black and her daughter Ruth had been summer renters of the house next door to the Carmans', and yet had never been questioned by police. With no ax to grind, and no reason to color their testimony in favor of either prosecution or defense, both described hearing the fatal gunshot from where they'd sat on their front porch, and both described hurrying to the fence that separated their house from that of the Carmans.

Neither saw any fleeing assailant.

This was devastating testimony on two levels. First, it corroborated Celia Coleman's version of events in which the killer—Mrs. Carman—had fled neither westward nor into the street, but rather back to the rear door of the house. Second, it sent a subliminal message to the jury that if the police had been so slipshod in their investigation as to have missed these two critical eyewitnesses, then might they also have overlooked the murder weapon hidden somewhere inside the Carman home?

Thrust and parry, punch and counterpunch, with both sides bloodied and exhausted after two weeks of mortal combat. Thus was set the stage onto which young George Levy rose with shaking knees to present his final argument. The apogee of his nascent career, his summation would be delivered to a packed courtroom, before a skeptical judge, and with the national press scrutinizing his every word and gesture. And also, as George was acutely aware, with his client's very life on the line.

George began by reviewing the evidence, both pro and con. Then he lambasted the district attorney for effectively kidnapping Celia

Coleman and forcing her to commit perjury. And then, sensing the need for a tenth-round knockout, he closed with a haymaker.

"Gentlemen of the jury," he said, "let me share with you my greatest fear. You may feel that you cannot decide between myself and my worthy opponent, the district attorney, and so might find that there has not been a major guilt, but only a minor one. Well, let me disabuse you of that notion. Mrs. Bailey has been murdered. Either Mrs. Carman killed her, or she did not. There can be no compromise on that point. You must either free Mrs. Carman," he said, his voice rising as his finger swung toward his client, "or you must send her to the electric chair!"

There occurs in all jury trials, be they criminal or civil in nature, a kind of subconscious transference in which the jurors assign to a party their like or dislike, their collective trust or mistrust of that party's counsel, who speaks on his client's behalf. And therein lay Florence Carman's salvation, because any animus those Long Island farmers and fishermen might have harbored for the icy, statuesque beauty on trial before them was more than overcome by her slight, bandy-legged counsel's inherent good nature. George Levy was not only genial; he was also sincere and trustworthy, and his voice fairly hummed with the righteousness of his cause.

"Scrappy," they would call him afterward. "A good egg. Just a regular guy."

The acquittal of Florence Carman was a national sensation, and it made George Morton Levy the talk of the New York trial bar.

Three

Tom

September 1915

THE SCHOOL BELL, muted at first behind thick sandstone walls, trilled with clamorous rapture as the doors flew wide and the children spilled tumbling and laughing down the broad concrete steps and onto the emerald lawn.

First came the younger grades—a bright terrazzo of knee-skinned boys in summer knickers and pigtailed girls in sailor dresses and shiny Mary Janes. Among the older children who followed, the girls bunched and giggling and the boys in attitudes of boredom or roughhouse, one stood apart from the rest.

Tommy Dewey strode through the throng, whistling as he went, oblivious to the tumult around him. Inured, perhaps, to the girls' stolen glances and the boys' hopeful voices raised in greeting or farewell. Secure—some might even say smug—in his role as Central High's newest and brightest young light.

His route to the train depot covered six familiar blocks that Tommy pedaled languidly, his bike carving lazy serpentines on the sun-dappled macadam. The houses he passed—the Millers' and the Jameses' and old Mrs. Pulver's—were spruce and tidy, the lawns still midsummer-green even as the elms and maples, as if sensing their incipient nakedness, were blushing their first autumnal hues.

The 4:15 from Detroit was right on schedule, and Tommy leaned his brand-new Cadillac alongside the older, rustier bikes on the north wall of the platform, where Jenks and Lacy stood waiting by the ticket window. Tommy joined his old grade-school pals just as the hulking locomotive chuffed and screeched to a halt.

"Ducky," Lacy said without turning.

"Buck up. You could be at Cadet Corps doing push-ups."

"At least I'd be home by five."

"With nothing in your pockets but lint."

"Hey," Jenks said to Tommy. "Did you get a load of Mary Watkins today?"

"Steady, man. Don't be a cad."

The boys watched in silence as the doors opened and the passengers alighted, several nodding or waving to Annie Dewey's only son while the porters handed down luggage. Then, finally, the cargo door opened and Jackson waved the boys over.

"Don't tell me you gents got all slicked up for me," the old Negro grinned as he hefted the heavy bundles and carefully handed them down. Tommy liked Jackson best of all the porters because he never tossed the bundles, scuffing or shredding the bottommost newspaper.

"Junior high," Tommy explained. "It started today."

Jackson stood akimbo, his gaze drifting toward the horizon.

"Junior high." He sighed. "All them pretty young things in itty-bitty skirts and white ankle socks."

"Steady, man," Jenks told him. "Don't be a cad."

Their bundles secured and balanced, the boys retraced their route, wobbling over the Main Street bridge before turning up Water Street, standing on their pedals and straining against the weight of their cargo, as if the grim tidings they bore from France and Belgium carried with them a palpable mass.

The others were assembled at the neat Victorian bungalow on West Oliver Street. There a half-dozen bicycles leaned against trees or sprawled haphazard below the freshly painted steps that led to where the boys themselves were already goldbricking on the porch, drinking milk and choosing cookies from a passing silver tray.

"Mater!" Tommy cried as he lowered his kickstand. "If you keep feeding them, I'll never get them to work!"

"Nonsense, dear," his mother replied as she turned toward the kitchen. "An army travels on its stomach."

By the time Tommy had divvied the papers and dispatched his minions and finished his own delivery route, a purplish dusk had settled over central Michigan, and the lights along River Street reflected a familiar constellation on the mirrored face of the Shiawassee. Inside the glowing Victorian on West Oliver, where a fire now crackled in the parlor and where Vivaldi swooped and soared from the phonograph, Tommy's father sat clucking at the day's headlines.

"They're estimating half a million Christians have been killed in Asia Minor!" George Dewey thundered, glaring over the page to where his wife and son stood watching from the doorway to the kitchen. "And now I suppose the Democrats will blame *that* on Taft!"

"Careful, George M. You'll have a thrombosis."

"The world is going to Hades in a handbasket!"

"Not here, darling. Here in Owosso we're having pot roast for dinner."

The mealtime conversation strayed only briefly from its usual fare of national politics, state politics, and local politics to include a smattering of Annie Dewey's afternoon bridge and a generous helping of Tommy's first day of school, complete with a grilling on teachers, classes, and classmates.

17

No, debate was not offered this year. Yes, he'd signed up for choir. No, he didn't think the new civics teacher was a Bull Moose. Yes, he was certain there was no junior high newspaper.

Seizing on a lull in the inquisition, his mother passed Tommy the carrots. "I ran into Glenna Watkins this afternoon."

"Oh, dear. Was she injured badly?"

"Don't be impertinent. She told me that Mary had quite the time in Chicago this summer. The symphony and the ballet and *tout* the art museums. Glenna said that she'd positively *blossomed*. That was the word she used."

"I'll bet she did."

"You bet she did what, dear? Said, in the case of Glenna, or blossomed, in the case of Mary?"

"Let the boy eat his supper."

"I was only recounting a conversation, that's all. It's not as if I were *prying* or anything."

"Might we please change the subject? Father, did the Tigers win today?"

"Five-two. Cobb went three for four."

"Hot socks!"

"We'll have no more of *that*, young man. People will think you were raised in a saloon. I'll wager that Mary Watkins doesn't go around spouting vulgarities in front of *her* parents . . ."

Tommy perched on the piano bench with his mother seated behind him, the click and clash of her knitting lapsing into unconscious rhythm with the tick and tock of his metronome. He played Chopin's "Revolutionary" Étude and Beethoven's "Für Elise." After Debussy's "Clair de lune," he noticed that the sounds of her knitting had ceased.

"Sing for me, my angel."

He sang. Bizet's "Habanera" and Bach's "Bist du Bei Mir." He closed with her favorite, Schubert's "Ave Maria," and when he'd finished "*In hora mortis nostrae, Ave Maria!*" she'd dabbed at her eyes before again taking up her needles.

"Someday," she told him, "mark my words, Thomas Edwin Dewey will sing in the great opera houses of Europe."

He turned on the bench to face her.

"Correction, Mater. Father says that someday he'll be president of the United States."

Four

Flo

VIOLET'S BROTHER RALPH looked like Joe Brooks in his best Sunday getup—a double-breasted number with a white pocket hankie and spectator shoes. We watched as he strolled past the shop window like some Ridge Avenue high-hat out taking the air, just walking and smoking and eyeballing the merchandise. Then he glanced over his shoulder and crushed out his cigarette and disappeared through the door.

We could hear the little bell go *tinkle, tinkle* from clear across the street, where we sat with the top down and our feet up on the dash.

"Don't worry," Vi said, reading the look on my face. "Ralph knows his onions. Besides, you can't cheat an honest man."

She reached into her bag and pulled out her hope chest and shook loose a couple of ciggies. I made sure my hand was nice and steady when she lit me up.

"Okay, you know the script," she said after another few minutes of slouching and smoking and me tapping my foot on the windshield. "Don't ball it up."

I took the photograph from the envelope and stepped out onto the sidewalk. It was hot and muggy and my armpits were already sweating as I peeled the dress off the small of my back. What little breeze there was came from the west, off the Allegheny, like stink off a burning tire. I fanned myself with the photo as I hurried across the street.

The shop was called Larry's Loan & Pawn. According to Ralph, Larry was a cheap kike bastard who sucked the blood out of working stiffs like him, which made it okay to pull the old fakeloo so long as we didn't get caught. Me personally, I didn't care about blood or money—all's I wanted was to get in jake with Vi and her crowd at school. That, and maybe catch a pass from Ralph, who was a swell-looking hunk but was also around twenty-five, which made him ten years older than Violet and me, so who was I kidding anyway?

Tinkle, tinkle. The shop looked like your grandfather's attic might look if your grandfather played the accordion and the saxophone and collected old typewriters and dusty sets of china. The guy behind the counter was tall and stoop-shouldered and looked like a vulture, right down to his bony neck and his Adam's apple and his great big honker of a nose. He wore a vest and a necktie but no jacket, and he give me a quick once-over before pointing the beak back at Ralph, who was all matter-of-fact while feeding him the hooey about the museum he worked for in New York and how he liked to browse around in joints like this whenever he traveled because you never know what hidden treasures, blah blah blah.

I walked up to the counter and laid the photograph on the glass.

"What's this?" Larry asked, pinching cheaters from his vest.

I gave Ralph the fish-eye and walked Larry down to the far end of the counter. I'll admit that my heart was thumping so loud I thought maybe Ralph could hear it from where he'd moved to stand behind me, pretending to study some junk up on the wall above Larry's head.

I read Larry the script about my sick mother and my dead father who collected old photographs. All of which was a yarn, because my dad was alive and usually drunk and using my mom as a punching bag, and also because the photo on the counter—which showed some long-haired Indian on a spotted horse with a rifle across his lap—had actually come from Ralph, who'd bought it for a penny at the Carnegie Library and browned it under a flatiron.

I looked up at Larry, who was glancing over my shoulder at Ralph, who, I knew without looking, was making a slicing motion with a finger across his throat.

"Uh, look here, young lady," Larry said, taking the photo and holding it up to the milky light from the window. "I'm busy just now with this gentleman, but if you'll leave this with me, I'll look it over when I have a free moment."

I reached my hand for the photo. "I can't do that, sir. Mama would kill me if I let it out of my sight. Heck, she'd kill me if she knew I'd taken it from Papa's collection in the first place."

Larry made a face like he'd bit into a lemon.

"All right then." He glanced at Ralph again before walking over to the cash register and jabbing one key and banging his fist on another. The drawer slid open with a loud *cha-ching*, which was the exact sound Ralph had made out in the car when he'd described to us the dough we'd soon be splitting three ways—half to him, a quarter to Violet, and a lousy quarter to me, who was the one taking all the risk.

I jumped when Larry slapped a dime down on the glass.

"There's a drugstore just around the corner," he said. "Go have a soda and come back in fifteen minutes. I'll be finished with this gentleman then, and we can talk about this picture business."

I was supposed to make a fuss about leaving the photo, only I didn't see the point in it anymore, so I just turned for the door and scrammed. I gave Violet the high sign after I'd passed clear of the window, and then I ducked around the corner and into the drugstore and ordered myself an egg cream, plus a second one for Ralph.

I twirled on the counter stool and waited.

"You were supposed to make a stink," Ralph said when he entered, tossing his hat onto the counter.

"Did he bite?"

He took the stool one down from mine. He picked up his drink and took a long sip and half turned to face me.

"Hook, line, and sinker," he said. "If you weren't such a little squirt, I'd kiss you smack on the mouth."

"Applesauce," I told him, turning my face to the door.

Violet appeared then, backlit in the doorway, posing like Theda Bara with a hand on her hip.

"Well?"

"Fish in a barrel," her brother said. "Corn in a can."

"How much?"

He looked down the counter to make sure the jerk was busy.

"I told him I'd pay twenty now, and another twenty if it proved to be the genuine article. I told him if it didn't, then he could keep the first twenty as a gesture of good faith."

Violet took a long drag on her cigarette and flicked it to the sidewalk. She sashayed in and sat between me and her brother and helped herself to my soda. She was always doing stuff like that—taking my magazines or my lipstick—just to show that she could.

"Okay, Flo, now it's your turn." She gestured toward the door with her chin. "Don't take any wooden nickels."

What I took was a long drink of Ralph before sliding off my stool and giving my dress a tug. The material was cotton—yellow flowers on a white background—and I imagined Ralph's eyes on my chassis as I stepped into the sunlight and paused there long enough to give him a gander.

Tinkle, tinkle. Larry was standing behind the counter with the cheaters up on his head. He was polishing some kind of a lantern, like

23

he was hoping for a genie to appear and grant him three wishes. Or like he'd already gotten one wish, and now he was hoping to squeeze out a couple more.

"That was fast," he said, setting the lantern aside. "Did you bring any change from my dime?"

I'll admit, that threw me a little. I started to answer, but he waved it off.

"Never mind. Let's have a look at this picture."

He slapped the rag over his shoulder as he walked to where we'd been standing before. He lowered the cheaters onto his nose and lifted the photo up to the light again, tilting it this way and that. Only now, I noticed, he was holding it carefully by the edges.

"I'm no expert," he finally said. "Where'd you say your father got this?"

"I don't know for certain, sir. I only know that Grandpa was an Indian scout before the Civil War and that Papa got most of his pictures from him."

Larry made a low humming sound.

"Mama's got a whole box of old pictures like that," I improvised, then immediately regretted it as Larry frowned and set the photo down and removed his cheaters and slipped them into his vest.

"I don't get customers in here looking for photographs," he said, sliding the picture across the counter. "Not my stock in trade. But I'll tell you what I will do, just this once, because I'm softheaded and I'm sorry about your mother taking ill. I'll give you two bits. That's my best offer, take it or leave it."

I took the photo and studied it. "That won't help Mama very much," I said as I turned for the door.

I got as far as the saxophone.

The apartment, Ralph said, belonged to a friend. The crowd was young and noisy, and there was phonograph music and booze for sale and a few shuffling dancers, but mostly it was some kind of a petting party with college boys curled up on sofas whispering sweet nothings into their girlfriends' shell-like ears.

"Say, what kind of a joint is this, anyway?" Violet shouted over the din.

Ralph fanned himself with his hat. "Go grab a seat. Those people are getting up."

We slid into the chairs, and Vi lit up a smoke without offering one to me. Ralph returned after a minute with three skinny glasses that he held in both hands like he'd brought us a bouquet of flowers.

"What's this?"

"Bubbly," he said, passing off the drinks. "We're celebrating!"

We certainly were. The take from Larry's Loan & Pawn had been an even sawbuck, which Ralph said was double what he'd expected. He must've made change from the bartender, because he gave us each our two-fifty, meaning he'd sprung for the drinks himself. He picked up his glass and raised it in a toast.

"The kid did all right," he said to his sister. "I think she's got the goods."

Violet didn't answer, and she practically gulped down her drink before dropping her cigarette into the empty glass and setting it on the floor. She stood to leave, brushing some ash from her skirt.

"Come on, Flo, let's ankle. This place is all wet."

"What's the rush?" Ralph said, taking hold of my hand. "We only just got here."

"Yeah," I said. "We only just got here."

"Suit yourself." Violet hiked her purse and made for the door, threading her way through the dancers and disappearing without so much as a backward glance. I felt a twinge of something—regret maybe, or guilt—like somehow I'd just scotched my initiation, until Ralph moved his chair closer to mine.

"Hey, baby, don't cast a kitten," he said, resting a hand on my knee. "She's just a little sore is all, on account of you doing so good."

So we had us another drink, and we punched the bag for a while, and then we got up and danced. The next thing I knew, we were sitting in a corner—Ralph in an armchair and me in his lap—and his tongue was playing Uncle Wiggily inside my mouth.

"You're a swell kid, do you know that?"

"Shut up," I said, "and do that again."

I know this sounds silly, but I actually thought about Larry then— just a flash of him standing behind the counter, polishing his lantern and waiting for Ralph to return. Not realizing that it was me, not him, who'd got her wish granted. Or was about to, anyway.

"I need to go iron my shoelaces," I told Ralph, slapping his hand as I stood and tugged my dress into place. "You keep the motor running."

There was a line for the bathroom, but the girl at the front took one look at me and said, "You'd better go first, honey. You look blotto."

After finishing my business, I stood for a minute with my hands on the cold porcelain, studying the glassy-eyed girl in the mirror. She looked, I thought, an awful lot like my mother. Not the tired house-wife in the frayed dress and apron, but the hopeful young bride in the photo that hung by the door in my parents' bedroom—the pretty Jewish girl in the cloud of white lace with the smile that seemed equal parts joy and terror.

A fist pounded the door. I licked my lips and gave my bubs a lift.

"Okay, kiddo," I said to the mirror. "The bank is open."

Ralph was right where I'd left him, sitting and smoking, his smile all lopsided and dirty.

"Hey, beautiful," he said, standing and taking my hand. "Let me show you something."

He led me down the hallway to one of the bedrooms, where he locked the door behind us and then disappeared into the little bathroom and returned with a towel in his hands.

I didn't resist, not even a little.

It was Ralph, in fact, who ended up saying, "Slow down, willya," and "Take it easy," and "Save some for next time." Not that I really heard him. Because what he'd shown me was a little like double-dutch jump rope, in that once you got past the tricky part at the beginning, the rest was just nothing but fun.

When we'd caught our breath and cleaned up our mess, we shimmied back into our clothes. That's when I grabbed Ralph by the lapels and pulled him close and looked him square in the eye.

"I know this is gonna sound crazy," I said, "but how's about you and me blow this two-bit town and never look back?"

Ralph met me at dawn, and helped with my bag, and watched as I took a long backward glance at the only home I'd ever known. It looked small and crummy, especially compared to what I knew was out there waiting.

"It's your fairy tale, baby," Ralph said as he wrestled the car into gear. "Where do you wanna go?"

I pointed north.

Five

Lansky's Law

December 1921

As the train lurches and rattles southbound, two men make their way toward the dining car. Both are young, and both darkly handsome in new business suits with hats in their hands and topcoats over their arms. The shorter man—the one now known to his friends as Charlie—waits as the taller man hurries forward to open the door.

A Sal or Sallie—a grown man with a little girl's name—would never command that kind of respect.

The dining car resembles a hospital ward, with its crisp white tablecloths stretching in ordered pairs along a narrow center aisle. Heads turn as the two men enter, and more than one woman's gaze lingers on the taller man's face, with its high cheekbones and its deeply cleft chin.

"There they are."

Two other men, both younger still, sit with their backs to the bulkhead at the last table on the right-hand side of the car. Meyer Lansky, the shorter of the pair, wears a suit of gray flannel, while Benjamin Siegel, his baby-faced companion, sports a garish houndstooth jacket.

Both stand to greet the new arrivals. All break into grins.

"Meyer, Benny. You boys remember Joey A."

Pleasantries are exchanged as the men shake hands and settle in, arranging themselves and their hats and topcoats on the soft leather banquettes, their high spirits contrasting with the gray parade of bare trees scrolling past the train car's rain-streaked windows. After the Negro waiter has left with their breakfast orders, Charlie Lucania twists in his seat to survey the neighboring tables.

When he leans forward to speak, his voice is barely a whisper.

"So I talked to Cousin Alphonse. He says this Gordon is a Polack named Irving Wexler used to bust heads for Benny Fein. Says they call him Waxey on account of he was a pickpocket before he fell in somehow with Rothstein, who bankrolls the whole operation. Al says they got boats, trucks, money, and muscle, and all of it in spades."

"Yeah? Then what's he need us for?"

"He don't need us, Benny, but we need him. Tell 'em, Joe."

Like his companion before him, Joe Adonis turns to study the car before leaning forward to speak.

"I'm down in Philly the day after Christmas to watch Frankie Genaro fight Kid Wolfe, see, and the promoter, this guy named Boo-Boo, he introduces me to Waxey Gordon. Says the name like he's some big shot I should know who he is. Turns out he's from the old neighborhood and we know a few people, so he invites me out to dinner after the fight. Come to find out the guy owns two or three speaks plus a legit nightclub in Philly, and get this—he's buildin a barrel house over in Jersey. Meanwhile, he's bringin in train cars of rye from Canada, he's bringin in boatloads of Scotch and gin from

Europe, and he's got more bonded whiskey stored in a warehouse in Philly than he's got trucks he can move it in."

"Al says Gordon and Rothstein are like the fuckin funnel for half the booze comin into the country," Charlie adds. "Them and this Nucky Johnson in Atlantic City, they got the whole East Coast tied up with a bow."

"Anyway, Gordon gives me a ride to the train after dinner and says to me, you put together thirty-five grand and I'll sell you a thousand cases of hundred-proof bottled-in-bond rye whiskey I gotta get rid of on account I got no place left to store it. Says it would normally go for around fifty Gs, but seein as how I'm a Genaro fan from the old neighborhood, he'll sell it to me on the cheap."

The men all look to Meyer, who composes his hands on the table. Only nineteen, and boyish still despite his sharp suit and tie, Meyer Lansky remains one of Charlie Lucania's closest and most trusted friends. Charlie remembers their very first meeting, when fourteen-year-old Salvatore Lucania had tried to extort lunch money from ten-year-old Maier Suchowljansky, a skinny little Yid from Grand Street. Although only half his aggressor's size, the younger boy's answer had been immediate and emphatic. "Go fuck yourself," he'd told Lucania, and a friendship was born on the spot.

"Thank you, Joey, for that background," Meyer now says, unfolding his hands and picking some lint from the tablecloth. "The question before us, gentlemen, is whether we want to get any deeper into this bootlegging racket. There's a lot of competition out there, and we're making good money as things presently stand. Moving booze on the scale Joey's talking about would represent a major expansion of our operations. It would require more capital and more guns and more risk. We'd need to triple the buy-money bank and get Frank and maybe Joey if he's interested to use their influence to move us into midtown in a much bigger way. I don't have to tell you that that will make certain people very unhappy. People like Dwyer and D'Aquila and Masseria, to name a few."

"Fuck Masseria. I'll piss in his fat fuckin ear."

"Thank you, Benny, for that turgid insight. The point is, we'll be crossing a Rubicon if we do this deal. And that assumes the booze is genuine and that Gordon can deliver as promised. It also assumes . . . Ixnay, here comes the dinge."

The waiter returns with a second Negro in tow. They place four silver cloches on the table and remove them with a flourish.

"Hey, Charlie, what the fuck is that?"

"It's supposed to be corned beef hash."

"Look at Rockefeller, eatin corned beef hash. What's that on top?"

Charlie pokes at his food with a fork. "What, don't you know nothin? It's a fried egg for Christ sake."

"It *also* assumes"—Meyer watches the waiters depart—"that Gordon can keep on delivering into the future, because the capital outlay we're talking about won't be recouped with a thousand cases of whiskey, no matter how good it turns out to be."

Here he pauses, looking to each of his traveling companions.

"So, gentlemen. Do we stand pat and enjoy what we have now, or do we raise the stakes and become full-time bootleggers? I put the matter to a vote. Benny?"

The youngest boy shifts in his seat. "I say fuck yes. We're already takin the risk so's other guys can make the big dough. I say we get in the game while the gettin's still good. This Volstead Act ain't gonna last forever."

"What about you, Joey? If we do this deal, it means you're in for a one-fifth share, along with the three of us and Frankie Costello."

"Heck, you guys know my vote. That's why I called Charlie in the first place. It's why we're on this train, ain't it?"

All eyes shift to Lucania.

"Charlie?"

Once again Lucania turns, his eyes sweeping the half-empty dining car.

"Don't turn around or nothin, but you see them two guys over there? The ones who look like a couple of Wall Street big shots? I'm tellin ya, that's gonna be us a year from now. Only difference is, they're the ones gonna be comin to us on bended knee to get booze for their parties and their fancy restaurants and their best out-of-town customers. But here's what I wanna make clear. If we do this thing, I don't wanna be some nickel-and-dime bum sellin watered-down coffin varnish. So I say we make a pact right here and now. We buy only the best, and we sell only the best. If we do that, then pretty soon we'll make a name for ourselves in all the right places. Between our friends in the garment district and Frank and Joey's connections on Broadway, we'll have half the fuckin city by spring. And as far as guys like Dwyer and Masseria go, I agree with Benny. Fuck them old-timers. We work with 'em where we can, and we piss on 'em when we can't."

The men grunt and nod in agreement.

"Okay, so what about you, Meyer?"

The smaller man tugs the napkin from his shirt collar and dabs at the corners of his mouth.

"I've been reading a book. It's by a Harvard professor, an econo-mist, and he talks about a concept called the law of supply and demand. It goes something like this. In summer, when peaches are ripe and plentiful, the price of peaches falls because the available supply exceeds the demand. In other words, there are more peach sellers than there are peach buyers. But come fall, when the local supply runs out, then the price of peaches rises. And why is that, Benny?"

"Because there's more people want peaches than there are peaches to buy, so people will pay more."

"Precisely. Demand exceeds supply, so prices rise. Before this Volstead Act, there was a rough equilibrium between supply and demand for beer and wine and liquor. Availability was constant, demand was constant, so prices held steady. Only now, everything's been thrown out of whack. The demand is still there, but supply has been artificially suppressed, so naturally prices have gone through the roof. Especially, as Charlie points out, for the real McCoy. And that unmet demand represents opportunity."

"Come on, Meyer, just say yes, for Christ sake."

"Patience, Charlie. I'm trying to make a larger point. This law of supply and demand operates beyond just peaches and booze. It applies to anything that the people want but that the law suppresses. Policy. Dope. Broads. If we play our cards right, this deal with Gordon could be just the beginning for us. I've been running some numbers."

Meyer removes a folded envelope from his pocket.

"If we can move a thousand cases of rye whiskey, we stand to clear over a hundred grand in just a few months' time. Think about that. That's more money than our parents will see in their lifetimes. And Benny's right about this Volstead Act—it ain't gonna last forever. So this is no time for half measures. With the connections we've already made, and with the dough we can earn from selling as much booze as we can as fast as we can, we could move ourselves into every racket in town. Diversify, in other words. Position ourselves for the long run, for after Prohibition is over."

"And get ourselves shot in the process."

"No, Joey, not if we play it smart. Look at us. Two Jews, a Sicilian, and a Neapolitan. Frank's a Calabrian. We're like the fucking League of Nations. We have our separate interests, sure, and those we'll continue to pursue. But on this Gordon deal, and on any other deals we decide to do with the money we make, we'll combine our varied resources and connections."

"Like a trade union," Joey suggests.

"I was thinking more like an all-star team in baseball. But let's not kid ourselves. This ain't gonna be easy. Our trucks are gonna get hit, and we'll have to hit back and hit back hard. But if we make the right friends and we watch each other's backs, then pretty soon we'll have chips on the table in every game in the city."

Charlie is laughing.

"What's so funny?"

"You, Meyer, you little bastard. You're startin to sound just like me."

Meyer signals the waiter for their check.

"Then God help me, Charlie, because in all the years I've known you, that's about the scariest thing I've ever heard you say."

Six

Alchemy

December 1921

HIS PUBLIC DENUNCIATION of District Attorney Lew Smith for witness tampering in the Carman case would return to haunt George Morton Levy in 1916, when Smith was appointed to the Nassau County bench and promptly dedicated himself to making George's courtroom life miserable.

Smith's revenge took many nefarious forms. During George's closing arguments, for example, the judge would descend from his bench, stroll to the windows, and ask in a bored voice, "How much longer is this going to take, counselor?" More often, however, the judge's sabotage was solely visual—rolled eyes or a shaking head during George's arguments, with smiles and nods of approval for the district attorney—all carefully calibrated to leave no record of judicial misconduct on appeal.

In response to these tactics, George developed a repertoire of tools and tricks with which to blunt the judge's influence. During the examination of jurors, for example, George would liken the jury's role as the exclusive judge of the facts to a "juror garden" in which the judge should not be allowed to trespass. Similarly, the jurors were to respect the judge's function as the exclusive arbiter of the law. "You stay on your side of the fence," George would tell them, and then, with a nod to the scowling figure on the bench, "make him stay on his."

George, you see, believed in the American jury system; he trusted in the collective wisdom and life experience of twelve ordinary citizens as a bulwark against the prejudices and peccadillos of any single jurist. He revered the concept of equal justice under law personified by the statuary image of a blindfolded lady with her scales held high in equipoise—scales on which no thumb should ever tilt the balance. And especially no thumb belonging to Lewis J. Smith.

For the most part, George's strategy worked. "We could tell the judge hated your client," jurors would tell him in confidence after a verdict, "but we didn't pay him any mind. We knew he was trespassing." But since Smith was the sort of judge who'd never met an accused he didn't long to incarcerate, George's growing string of acquittals merely served to roil the simmering animosity between the former district attorney and the affable young defense attorney.

It was thus the misfortune of Louis Enright to learn that his prosecution for grand larceny—that is, for the felonious receipt of money or property under false pretenses—had been assigned to Lewis J. Smith for trial.

The accused was a tall man, gray and solemn, some seventy-five years in age. An engineer by training and a tinkerer by profession, Enright had come to Long Island from the oil fields of West Texas with, George would later learn to his dismay, a wake of angry investors foaming at his stern.

No sooner had Enright landed in Nassau County than he'd formed a new company to exploit his latest invention, which he described as a secret process by which to extract gasoline from Long Island's abundant deposits of peat. After raising some quarter-million dollars in equity capital from a group of starry-eyed investors that included several of the county's leading citizens, Enright then proposed a second stock offering to augment the first. This latter proposal, combined with a dearth of demonstrable progress in the commercialization of Enright's invention, sent a group of suspicious shareholders to the office of then-D.A. Charles R. Weeks.

A grand jury indictment for grand larceny soon followed.

Despite the daunting prospect of yet another trial before Judge Smith, George remained hopeful. One reason for his optimism was that Professor Enright, as he insisted on being called, had been careful to make no express promises to his investors. Moreover, all the shareholders had been warned in writing both that the venture would be time-consuming and that it would be expensive. Lastly, Enright himself appeared sober, intelligent, and well-spoken—in short, credible—and could be expected to make an excellent witness on his own behalf.

But George took his greatest comfort from the professor's own resolute self-confidence. "I've said I can make gasoline from peat," he told his lawyer, "and I can prove it!"

With Judge Smith on relatively good behavior, the trial went about as smoothly as George could have hoped. The D.A.'s witnesses each conceded on cross-examination that Enright had merely opined that he could make gasoline from peat, and had candidly acknowledged never having done so in any commercial quantity. Since the crime of grand larceny required the knowingly false representation of a material fact—not merely an exaggerated opinion—the case appeared to have died a quiet death by the time the prosecution finally rested.

At the close of the state's evidence, George stood and moved for dismissal of the indictment. But no sooner had he done so than Professor Enright, greatly agitated, clamped a bony hand on George's arm.

"My professional honor has been impugned!" the old man remonstrated in a stage whisper. "That is the one thing I cannot abide!"

"What do you want me to do about it? The case is already in the bag."

"I want to perform a demonstration! I want to prove to the world that I can turn peat into gasoline!"

A frowning Judge Smith interrupted this huddled colloquy.

"Counsel? Is there something the matter?"

Against his better judgment, George rose again to his feet.

"Your Honor, Professor Enright has just informed me that he would like to demonstrate his secret process for the jury."

"You mean now? Show us the actual procedure?"

"Yes, Your Honor."

"Permission granted!"

Enright sprang from his chair and hurried to the rear of the courtroom where, from a large leather satchel, he removed a strange apparatus consisting of a glass beaker, an alcohol lamp with a hand crank, and several lengths of rubber tubing. The jurors stood with excitement as the old man carried his device past the gawking reporters and courtroom spectators—many of them skeptical investors—all the way to the witness box.

"This will only take a moment," Enright said as he lit the wick and removed from his pocket a chunk of ordinary peat, which he then crushed in his hands and sprinkled inside the lamp. Once the lamp was sufficiently heated, Enright began turning the crank. After a minute, a pale amber liquid began dripping from the rubber tubing into the beaker. After another full minute, Enright lifted the beaker and carried it to the foreman of the jury.

The foreman sniffed at the beaker and pronounced his verdict.

"Gasoline!"

Great commotion engulfed the courtroom as Judge Smith, banging his gavel, grumbled that he'd take George's dismissal motion under advisement. He then called the noon recess.

"What does that mean?" Enright asked George.

"It means we've won. Congratulations."

Satisfied, the professor returned his device to the satchel before wading out to the hallway through a pressing throng of admirers.

George was busy gathering his papers when an even greater commotion arose from the hallway door through which all had just departed.

"Judge! Judge!" came the foreman's voice as he ran back into the courtroom. "We need to see the judge!"

By now all the jurors had returned to the courtroom, and Judge Smith, hearing the disturbance, appeared at the door to his chambers.

"What is it? What's going on?"

"Judge! There's gasoline all over the hallway! The man's a fake!"

Lewis J. Smith's eye-daggers pinned George to the wall, where he stood openmouthed.

"Well, Mr. Levy? What have you got to say about this?"

"Uh, maybe it's the gasoline he'd already made?"

"Oh no," said the foreman. "He put the contraption back in his bag, but there's a trail of gasoline running clear down the hallway!"

A brief investigation proved the truth of the accusation, revealing as it did a thin scrim of yellow liquid leading down the marble corridor, down the stairs, and straight to the downstairs restroom where the professor had taken refuge. And so it was that after the noon recess, and despite the technical shortcomings of the prosecution's case, the jury returned an emphatic verdict of guilty on the charge of grand larceny.

Which wasn't, it turned out, the end of the story.

Prior to the sentencing hearing, which had been scheduled for some weeks later, George and a committee of Enright's creditors conducted a review of the old man's assets. The search confirmed exactly what the professor had long maintained—namely, that he'd actually spent all the money he'd raised on the invention, leaving only five thousand dollars of his own personal funds on deposit in a bank in Hicksville. This, plus a hodgepodge of old oil and mining stocks, was the sum total of Louis Enright's net worth.

The creditors, many now sympathetic to the chastened old man, agreed to recommend a suspended sentence in exchange for relinquishment of the professor's oil and mining stocks to the committee. Enright readily agreed, and to George's surprise, so did the judge. All was well that had ended well, until a few months later, when George received a telephone call at his office from an irate Judge Smith, who demanded George's immediate presence.

"Your man Enright is not only a crook," the judge fumed upon George's arrival, "he's also a double-eyed villain!"

"What do you mean?"

"Look here," the judge said, slapping before George a stack of bank statements for the Hicksville account. They showed over a hundred thousand dollars in post-trial deposits.

"There must be some mistake," George protested. "We went through his finances with a fine-tooth comb."

"There was a mistake all right, and it was mine for being soft-headed and suspending the old man's sentence. Now I'm sending him to Sing Sing."

"Wait a minute, Judge. Give me a few days to look into this. Something's obviously not kosher here."

On that they both agreed, but for entirely different reasons. Nevertheless, George was afforded the opportunity to visit the bank and inquire about the account. What he learned from a helpful young cashier surprised even him.

"Professor Enright said he was afraid of having his account attacked by creditors," the clerk explained. "So what he'd do is leave a hundred dollars in the account for living expenses, then withdraw the rest in a cashier's check. The first check was for four thousand nine hundred dollars. Then when he needed money again, he'd redeposit the cashier's check, leave a hundred in the account, and then withdraw the rest in another cashier's check. He did that over and over again—so many times that he'd soon deposited over a hundred grand. But it was really just the same five thousand dollars."

Relieved, George brought the cashier to Judge Smith, who listened to the young man's story with barely disguised incredulity.

"I don't believe it for a minute," the judge snapped. "But even if I did, it just goes to prove that the old fraud is up to something. I don't know what it is, but I damned well know how to stop it. I'm sending him to prison!" Which the judge did before the week was out.

George was still downcast from these events when he ran into District Attorney Charlie Weeks in court a few days later. The two men sat in a back bench, waiting for their cases to be called.

"You know, Charlie, I had a football coach once, a pretty gruff fellow, and he used to tell us that quitters never win, and winners never quit. He drummed it into our skulls." George shook his head wistfully. "Maybe that's what explains it."

"Explains what?"

"Why I never seem to know when to quit while I'm ahead."

Seven

Chicago

July 1923

ALERTED BY THE squeak of new brogans on pile carpet, Leonard Reid looked up in time to glimpse a blur of blue serge streaking past his office door.

"Tommy? Tom!"

The jug-eared law clerk appeared in the doorway, his body bent like a sapling in the wind.

"Sir?"

"For God's sake, son, where's the fire? Did you look into that title question I—"

"Yes, sir. I've dictated a memo that'll be on your desk in the morning."

"And what about—"

"I posted the court calendar in the conference room, and I pulled all the documents I think you'll want to use for the Spencer deposition."

Reid studied the earnest young whirlwind. He recalled when his cousin Annie had telephoned in May to ask him to hire her son for the summer, and that his first impulse had been to decline. After all, it was not the general practice of firms like Litzinger, Healy & Reid to employ first-year students, even top students from a top law school like the University of Michigan. More daunting still was the prospect of having to tell Annie Thomas Dewey that her only son's perform-ance wasn't up to snuff. Now Reid could only smile at the memory of that conversation.

While it was true that some in the firm thought the young man from Owosso priggish and smug, none could deny that, less than three weeks into his summer clerkship, Thomas E. Dewey had made himself as indispensable as any of the firm's junior partners.

"Where are you off to now?"

"Voice class. The studio's holding a scholarship contest tonight, and the winner gets the whole summer program free."

"I suppose that's the infernal song I've heard you humming all week?"

"No, sir. That was just me horsing around."

And like that, the boy was gone again, his rich baritone trailing him down the hallway.

"I wish I'd had time to practice! I only just heard about the scholarship contest this morning!"

Tom closed the door carefully behind him. Up on the darkened stage, her blonde curls blazing under a single white spot, stood the young mezzo-soprano from Wisconsin, Marilyn something-or-other. Or was it Marian? He crept down the aisle and took an empty seat among his classmates. They were an odd assortment of seasoned performers and starry-eyed amateurs, as varied as vaudeville, united by the singular honor of having been accepted into the Stephens Studio's traveling master class.

Once his eyes had adjusted to the darkness, Tom could make out the heads of what he assumed was the panel of contest judges seated in the front of the theater and, centermost among them, the leonine mane of Percy Rector Stephens. The piece being performed was "O Don Fatale" from Verdi's *Don Carlos*, and when the girl had finished, Tom lifted his hands to applaud.

Only nobody else was clapping.

"Thank you, Mary Ann." Stephens cleared his throat as he consulted a clipboard. "Next up is Miss Rose Winters."

Tom's performance came late in the program, and by the time he'd mounted the creaking stage, the audience had shrunk to under a dozen dark and indecipherable shapes—including the front-row quintet whose haggard faces he could barely discern beyond the spotlight's harsh radiance. He'd chosen for his recital Handel's "Hear Me, Ye Winds and Waves," which he performed in English, in G minor. And when he'd sung the final "I pray for death alone," he was startled to hear a pattering of applause waft toward him from out of the darkness.

His scholarship was awarded the following week.

"You've got it, you know."

Tom recognized the voice, and the recognition slowed his steps even as it quickened his pulse.

"Oh, hello, Frances," he said, trying for casual. "Are you walking my way?"

Frances Hutt fell into stride beside him. The petite brunette with the porcelain skin hailed from Oklahoma, Tom believed, by way of New York. As Percy Stephens's personal secretary and studio manager, not to mention a dazzling mezzo-soprano in her own right, Frances had excited the imaginations of every bachelor in class.

"This thing I have, I do hope it isn't contagious."

"Save the false modesty for amateur night. I'm from the big city, and I know about these things."

Scuttlebutt had Frances Hutt as an athlete of some sort, and a Methodist. Tom knew for a fact she was single, because that was an issue he'd already researched.

"I can assure you that any modesty I might possess, I come by honestly. Take this evening, for example. I plan a modest dinner in the city, followed by an elevated train ride to a modest little park in Lake Forest, where I'm meeting some brothers of the Phi Mu Alpha for an evening of Brahms concertos. Modestly performed, I have no doubt."

"Gosh, that sounds idyllic."

"What about you? I thought you and Stephens were yoked to the plow this week."

"Oh, Stevie's having dinner with friends from New York, and I've managed to slip the yoke for one night at least. I thought I'd celebrate by walking the Loop and doing a little shopping."

Tom stopped and turned to face her on the crowded sidewalk.

"See here. Not on an empty stomach, I hope?"

"Why, Mr. Dewey. Is that how they ask girls out to dinner in Owosso?"

"Oh, no. In Owosso we do it like this."

He dropped to a knee, taking both of her hands in his.

"Miss Frances Hutt, would you do me the great honor of joining me for an evening repast?"

The restaurant was called Raklios. It was a Greek place—a greasy spoon, really—wedged into a crowded block of storefronts whose plate-glass views of Washington Boulevard were framed by the El tracks across the street. The front door was open and the radio behind the counter bleated "Toot, Toot, Tootsie" into the rattle and rumble, the hiss and clang of a sultry Chicago rush hour.

Tom ordered a Hamburg steak. Frances ordered a salad. Both ordered lemonade. Frances insisted on separate checks. Tom objected, was overruled, and heard his appeal summarily denied.

"How are you enjoying Chicago?" he asked her—feebly, he knew—ending the silence that had hung awkwardly in the wake of the waiter's departure.

"Oh, it's all right, I guess. I love the lake, and the art museum, and watching all the sailboats. What about you?"

"Me? I think Chicago's a wonderful town for speakeasies and floozies and gangsters with tommy guns. Crooked cops and fixed baseball games, for goodness sake. For the life of me, I can't understand how the people of a city this large and sophisticated continue putting up with it."

He couldn't read her smile, or the sparkling eyes that danced behind it.

"Listen to me," he said, arranging his silverware. "I must sound like Pollyanna from Podunk."

"Is that why you're studying law, Tom? To come and clean up Chicago?"

"Not me, thank you. I wouldn't even *be* in Chicago if it wasn't for Stephens. And as for the law, well, you might say I'm conflicted on the subject."

"You mean you're impaled on the horns of a dilemma."

"Well, yes, something like—"

"For what it's worth, I think you have a wonderful voice, and a real future in opera or musical theater. And I'm not just saying that. I know plenty of singers who delude themselves into thinking they've got the goods—that they're the next Caruso or the next Jolson. In your case, Tom, it's no delusion, and you need to hear that from somebody who knows."

"You're very kind, Frances. But even if I believed you, that still doesn't solve my dilemma. A man doesn't have the luxury of thinking only about today, or next week, or the next couple of years. He's got to plan for the long haul. I enjoy performing, don't get me wrong, but the human voice is a fragile instrument. What if I were to give up the law and then lose my voice? Where would I be then?"

"Pursuing your dream. Doing what you were born to do."

Now it was Tom's turn to smile.

"Did I say something funny?"

"No, of course not. It's just that who's to say what one is born to do? Maybe I was born to clean up Chicago."

"No, that sounds awfully messy. Leave that to the police and the politicians."

"Now you *are* being funny. The police need all the help they can get, and as for the politicians, well, they're the ones most in need of a good scrubbing."

Her smile, he realized then, had vanished.

"Would you listen to me? Out to dinner with a swell girl and here I am blathering like an idiot. I'm sure you weren't expecting a hayseed civics lesson."

"Don't be silly. It's refreshing to discuss something besides music, music, music. Sometimes I think Stevie and his friends all live in a big glass bubble. All they ever talk about is this performer or that concert. After a while, it gets to be like ice cream. I enjoy ice cream, but not every day. Not every meal."

"It's just that where I come from, a man in public office would be tarred and feathered if he so much as looked the other way at corruption. Here it's not only tolerated; it's practically part of the Democratic Party platform."

"You make Chicago sound like Gomorrah."

"In some ways it's worse than Gomorrah. If there were ten righteous men—"

"Wait, I have an idea! Why don't you come to New York and clean up Tammany Hall? Then while you're at it, you can audition for the Met, or maybe a role in the Follies. There are so many opportunities for a singer in New York, Tom, you have no idea. I'm sure for a lawyer as well, what with Wall Street and everything."

"You make it sound easy. The problem is, I've got two more years left at Michigan."

"They have law schools in New York, don't they?"

"You mean transfer? I'm afraid it's not that simple. Besides, my mother would pitch a fit."

"Uh-oh. We mustn't upset Mother."

"You haven't met my mother. And besides, my father owns the local newspaper. His goal in life is to make me the governor of Michigan."

"Far be it from me to deprive the good people of Michigan. But come September, I'm heading back to New York. So if you had any ideas in that thick skull of yours about the two of us going steady, well, then you'll have no choice but to come along."

"Now hold on a minute. I didn't—"

"Careful, Tom Dewey, your Podunk is showing. Women have the vote now, haven't you heard? And I'll let you in on another little secret."

She leaned across the table.

"We have to think of the long haul as well."

Eight

The Speak

August 1923

WE NEVER EVEN gave it a name.

When we talked about it at all, we just called it the place, or the joint, or sometimes even the office. We didn't want the hoi polloi showing up at our door. Or the revenue agents, for that matter. You had to know somebody to get in, or else know somebody who knew somebody, and that somebody had to be someone we trusted.

Sure, there were classier joints in town. The Blaue Club, for instance, or the Sachsenheim. And the booze we served wasn't always bonded, but we poured an honest drink and offered beer on tap and peanuts in a barrel, plus live piano on Friday and Saturday nights. It wasn't a blind pig, I can tell you that much. Or one of those crummy shine boxes.

My partner's name was Pearl, Pearl Callahan, and she was a real tomato. I'd met her in Youngstown, just before Ralph had split back to Pittsburgh, and we got along good. We ran a picture gag together—she was the roper and I was the spieler—and after a year or so we'd banked enough kale to wash the coal dust out of our hair and make for the bright lights of the city.

Pearl was twenty-four then, and I was what she called "fifteen going on thirty." She had a bunch of funny expressions like that. She said I was slicker than snot on a doorknob, and that I could talk a hungry dog off a meat wagon. She was like the crazy big sister I never had—the one with the horse laugh who drank like a catfish and cussed like a stevedore—and ours was a partnership made in grifter heaven.

Pearl was the one who'd said there was dough to be made in bootleg liquor. So we raided our piggy banks and rented a three-story building on the east side of Cleveland for a hundred and twenty a month plus utilities. We ran the joint downstairs, and used the second floor for storage, and then me and Pearl lived on top, in what we called the penthouse. We scrubbed and painted the place ourselves, and then we hung old boxing posters on the walls. We rented our furniture and glassware from a restaurant supply store on Euclid Avenue where we paid cash and nobody asked any questions.

I kept the books and managed the inventory, while Pearl was in charge of customer relations. We paid five clams a week to the precinct captain, plus twenty a month to the Murray Hill Mob, who also sold us our hooch. The precinct captain was named Tierney, and his bag man was a great big mulligan named Quinn, who called us colleens and usually let Pearl suck his cock for the fiver.

We took turns, Pearl and me, tending bar and waiting tables and working the door, plus we had a shine in on Mondays to mop out the joint. The piano man worked for tips. Once we were up and running, we were clearing almost eighty dollars a week, and in summer we did even better. Me and Pearl split the net fifty-fifty, with a small weekly adjustment for what she called the tonsil tax.

We sent Ralph a postcard once. It said, "Who's crying now, you lousy crumb? Drop dead soon. Love, Flo." And below that, Pearl had scribbled, "Piker!" That was good for a giggle.

With Ralph out of the picture, there were always a few drunks at last call wanting to walk me home—meaning up to the third floor—only most were so splifficated they couldn't of climbed the stairs if I'd let 'em, which I almost never did. But Pearl had a regular fella, a postman named Wally Stein, who she called Wally the Whale even though on account of his job he was actually pretty skinny, if you get my meaning.

Cleveland was a boomtown then, and the fifth-largest city in America. It had auto factories and a railroad line and a baseball team called the Indians, who'd apparently won the World Series in 1920, which people there were still talking about. Sometimes it was all they talked about, that and the union riots. But all things considered, it was actually a pretty swell town.

Like I said earlier, I hardly ever dated the customers. But there was this one Saturday night in early August when the joint was jumping and we had to call in the shine, whose name was Marcus, to work the door on account of us being so busy. Well, Marcus, who was probably close to sixty and had the brains of an Irish setter, he let four bohunks into the joint who we'd never seen before and who took a table by the door and ordered beers and then sat there like bumps on a log all night and weren't dancing or playing cards or even talking, not even to each other.

Anyway, these guys just sat there nursing their beers until around midnight, when the crowd started to thin a little. Then all of a sudden they stood up, and one of them sapped down Marcus, and two of them pulled guns and came around the bar and shoved Pearl aside to open the register.

We raised bloody hell, and Pearl even jumped on the one guy's back as he turned to leave with our money, which, on account of it being a good night, was probably thirty or forty bucks. Well, two of the guys—I'm thinking they must've been Polacks—they pulled Pearl off their buddy's back and tossed her onto a table, splashing the suds and breaking a few of our glasses in the process. Wally happened to be in that night, and while he ran over to help Pearl to her feet, he didn't try to stop the robbers. I can't say as I blame him for it, but Pearl was awfully sore at him afterwards.

And that's when this funny thing happened. Just as the piano man quit playing and the rumpus settled and the bohunks were on their way out, this big guy, who I hadn't really noticed until then, stepped in front of the door and blocked their getaway.

"Scram," said the guy with the money, and to emphasize his point he poked his gat right in the stranger's belly. Only the stranger, who was maybe six foot four with a face like a side of beef, he didn't bat an eyelash.

"Turn around and put the money back," the stranger said, nice and calm, like he was ordering a cup of tea.

The gunman cocked his pistol. "Says who?"

"Says Joe Porrello," the stranger said, and then he opened a cigarette case and tapped out a smoke like a guy who was waiting for a bus.

Well, that was the end of the robbery. The gunman walked back to Pearl and handed her the whole wad of dough. "I'm real sorry, Miss," he told her, loud enough for everyone to hear, and then he gestured to his buddies, who all huddled up and shuffled out the front door like choirboys leaving the midnight Mass.

And that's how I first come to meet Big Joe Porrello.

It was also the last time our joint ever got robbed.

Nine

Wild Bull

September 1923

CHARLIE HAS NEVER seen a crowd quite like the one that greets his hired limousine as it rolls to the curb on West 155th Street. It appears to him like a rally, or a riot, or like the ninety thousand spectators expected at the evening's main event have somehow managed to swarm the Polo Grounds en masse. And indeed, the elevated ramp connecting the grandstand to the Ninth Avenue train is packed with men in coats and straw boaters, pushing and shoving, moving like prodded cattle past truncheon-wielding policemen on foot and on horseback, funneling into the vast holding pen that awaits them beyond the stadium turnstiles.

"Christ, would you get a load of this," Charlie says, parting the velvet curtains, his attention shifting from the older man beside him. "This could be a million-dollar gate."

Johnny Torrio leans to take in the sight. "You handlin any action on this thing?"

Charlie shares a smile with his honored guest from Chicago. "I'll take your action, Pops. Who do you like?"

"At three-to-one, I like the spic. Al went to that training camp up in Saratoga. He said if Dempsey's six feet tall, then so is he."

"You know what they say. The bigger they are, the harder they fall."

"You better hope that ain't true, Charlie, or else you and your pal Lansky are gonna make one helluva noise. How's about three fifty to your grand?"

"Sure, why not. What's another grand among friends?"

The car has stopped, and the driver is opening the curbside door. Charlie alights in a double-breasted suit of oxford gray paired with a crisp white shirt and a tie of navy silk. His topcoat and fedora are in matching pearl. The clothes, purchased specially for the occasion, are the brainchild of Arnold Rothstein, Charlie's friend and mentor. If you want to change your image, Rothstein told his young protégé, then start with what people can see.

Charlie Lucania badly wants to change his image.

Foolishly, Charlie was arrested three months earlier for selling heroin to a police informant while agents of the Secret Service looked on. A search of his apartment yielded a small cache of morphine, heroin, and opium. Once in the custody of federal authorities immune to the blandishments of Frank Costello's buy-money bank, Charlie Lucania—with a 1916 narcotics rap already on his record—had no choice but to bargain for his freedom. After two hours of interrogation and three hours of negotiation, a deal was finally struck: Charlie would direct the agents to a trunk full of heroin, its street value in excess of a hundred and fifty thousand dollars, in exchange for dismissal of the charges against him.

For Charlie the deal meant freedom, but at a heavy price. News accounts of his arrest labeled him a major purveyor of narcotics—an albatross that has threatened the carefully cultivated image of gentleman bootlegger that has been Charlie's entre to the private clubs and glittering soirees of New York society. Worse, despite a promise they wouldn't do so, the police had branded Charlie a stool pigeon, and even though the dope he was forced to sacrifice had been his own, its ownership could never, for obvious reasons, be publicly acknowledged.

The net result of the whole debacle was wary looks from both sides of the street. Nothing short of a biblical resurrection is required, and tonight, Charlie hopes, will be his personal Easter.

Dempsey-Firpo is the hottest ticket of 1923, which meant that Charlie had to shell out twenty-five thousand dollars to assemble his two hundred seats in the first five rows at ringside. Working with Costello and Joe Adonis, Charlie drew up a list of the hundred most influential figures in New York and beyond—a veritable who's who in politics, sports, entertainment, and the rackets—with each receiving a pair of complimentary ducats from Charlie Lucania.

"This is worse than a fucking wedding," Costello had groused as the roster of invitees was winnowed from the original list of five hundred.

"Tell me about it," Charlie replied. "At a wedding, at least you get cake before the fightin starts."

Torrio takes the lead as the men wend their way through the crowd. Heads do not turn and fingers do not point as they approach the clubhouse turnstiles, because they, unlike some of their less reticent contemporaries, are men who understand the value of anonymity. Understand that the tallest trees in the forest are the first to get cut. Which is why Charlie's arrest and its attendant publicity had been all the more vexing.

The ticket taker hesitates as he tears the stub and returns the rain check to the man in the new pearl fedora.

"Row A, Seat One," he says. "Mister, you must really be somebody."

The empty ring stands like an altar near what would normally be second base; and like an altar, it exerts an invisible magnetism to which all heads in the vast, open-air stadium orient. The crush of bodies only intensifies as the men are escorted to their ringside seats by a stoop-shouldered usher, who parts the surging multitude with a practiced repertoire of prods and pleas, shrugs and sidling shuffles.

A dozen patrons stand to greet the pair's arrival as the usher whisks their seats and then bows, newly fawning, at the younger man's proffered twenty.

"Charlie!"

"Hey, Charlie!"

"Hiya, Charlie. How ya doin, Johnny? How's Chicago?"

The men are surrounded. Hands are shaken, and shoulders grabbed and squeezed. Benny Siegel and Frank Costello are already there, as are Joe Adonis and Vito Genovese. There's Charlie Murphy and Jimmy Hines from Tammany Hall, along with Flo Ziegfeld and Earl Carroll from Broadway. Ben Gimbel is there, and John Ringling, and the dapper Kenny Sutherland. The men form a bright constellation of disparate stars whose gravitational pull captures the awestruck and the merely curious along with a healthy smattering of showgirls and flappers who crowd in closer, vamping and giggling, to bask in the reflected glow.

A bell rings, and an announcer appears. Charlie takes his seat and is handed a flask as the crowd settles down for the preliminary bouts. Cigars are proffered, and another flask, and soon a purple twilight has settled over Coogan's Hollow.

Others, meanwhile, continue to arrive. King Solomon from Boston, and Waxey Gordon from Philly. Al Capone and his entourage from Chicago. Police Commissioner Enright, along with Chief Inspector Lahey. All stop to pump the hand of their front-row benefactor.

"I gotta hand it to you, Charlie. I never seen nothin like this," Torrio says after Babe Ruth has paid his respects. "You got this whole fuckin town in your pocket."

"Supply and demand," Charlie says, turning to eyeball the seats behind him. "Life is sure funny, ain't it Johnny? When I was in grade school, I had this teacher, Mrs. Goldfarb. I didn't speak English so good, and I missed a lot of classes, and I got sent to this truant school over in Brooklyn. Mrs. Goldfarb, she's the one who done it. Told my parents I was a bad influence. Said I'd never amount to nothin and that someday I'd wind up in jail. Made my mother cry."

"What a cunt."

"Then maybe a year ago I'm comin out of the Copa with Rothstein and Joey A. We got these girls from the Follies with us, and we're on our way to this party on Long Island. Anyway, I stop to get my coat, and guess who's workin the hatcheck counter in back? It's Mrs. Goldfarb. She's an old lady by then, but I recognize her plain as day."

"So what did you do?"

"I called her over. I said, 'Mrs. Goldfarb, do you remember me? I'm Sal Lucania from First Avenue.' I said I wanted her to know she was absolutely right about me. I said I been in trouble my whole fuckin life, and I been in jail, and I've caused my parents nothin but grief. And then I gave her a C-note and kissed her on top of the head and said she'd have to excuse me, because Mr. Rothstein and I didn't want to keep Mr. Whitney waiting."

Darkness thickens, blanketing the main event. In the glare of the overhead lights, amid the oompah brass of a marching band, the gladiators finally arrive. First comes Firpo, the massive Argentine, looking every inch the Wild Bull of the Pampas—a circus animal snared and tamed and gaudily costumed in silks of yellow and purple. He is followed by the champion, Gentleman Jack, the Manassa Mauler, whose muscled neck and shoulders are wrapped in a simple white sweatshirt.

"Care to double that bet?" Torrio shouts over the bellicose roars of the crowd.

"You're on, Pops. Don't ever underestimate the little guy."

As the crowd quiets and the fighters and seconds gather for their final instructions, a rotund figure rises from his seat and moves through the shadows on the far side of the ring. Giuseppe Masseria is trailed by two bodyguards as he circles the apron, and most of the sportswriters and all the policemen at ringside turn to watch as the fat man waddles in Charlie's direction.

"Christ," Costello leans forward to whisper. "Get a load of what's comin."

Masseria stops before Row A, Seat 1. He nods to Johnny Torrio, then offers a meaty hand to the dapper young Sicilian seated beside him.

"Salvatore Lucania," the fat man says, his grip an iron vise. "I think it's high time you and me had us a little talk."

Ten

The Devil They Knew

October 1924

LIKE ALL MEN, George Morton Levy had his fair share of vices. Cuban cigars, for instance, were a habit to which he'd taken as a kitten takes to string. Also, try though he might, the sight of a well-turned ankle never failed to slow his step. And since George, unlike many of his colleagues at the trial bar, was never much of a drinker, he often sought refuge from the toils and stresses of the courtroom at the poker table.

Stud was his game, and George soon fell into a weekly contest with a group of his old Freeport cronies. These included George Loft, the candy man, and Victor Moore, the actor. Steve Pettit, a real estate broker and the former sheriff of Nassau County, and George Bennett Smith, the local Cadillac dealer. The men would meet on Saturday nights at the Elks Lodge, and their games would last into the wee hours of Sunday morning, whereupon sums as large as two thousand or three thousand dollars would ultimately change hands.

Beatrice, George's second wife, viewed these weekly conclaves with an increasingly jaundiced eye—to the point that, when her hints gave way to objections and her objections to ultimatums, she became downright creative in demonstrating her displeasure. She would, for instance, show up at the Elks Lodge after midnight with her knitting—and later, with her infant son, George Jr.—nestled in her lap. After a while, these antics forced George to accept a difficult but necessary truth.

He needed a new place to gamble.

Jack McDermott was a lawyer from Manhattan who'd long been urging George to try his hand at craps. George had resisted at first—as Exalted Ruler, he'd even barred dice games from the Freeport Elks Lodge—but McDermott persisted, telling George he had a line on a big floating game in the city. So one day George relented, and the two men, joined by a younger partner of McDermott's, planned a clandestine reconnaissance outing for the following weekend.

The location, it turned out, was a furnished loft over a garage on East 48th Street. McDermott somehow knew the password. George had arrived for the evening with two hundred dollars in his pocket, while McDermott and his partner brought less. A lively crowd surrounded the brightly lit table, and it was through a bluish haze of cigarette smoke that the wide-eyed lawyers recognized such notable high rollers as Subway Sam Rosoff and Nick the Greek Dandolos shouting and laughing and clutching fistfuls of bills like bridal bouquets.

The rules of the game were deceptively simple. The point to be made by the shooter determined the odds. If another customer took your action, then you had a bet, either for or against the shooter. If nobody wanted your action, then you could play against the house for a nominal fee of 5 percent of your winnings.

The lawyers wormed their way to the table, where they were welcomed, and introduced, and given free drinks. Then, before the ice in their glasses had even melted, they were relieved of all their cash. As they thanked their hosts and began shuffling for the door, they were stopped by a shouted voice from the other side of the table.

"Counselor! Hold on a minute! Are you short of money? Here."

A thick roll of bills hit the felt with a thud. George returned to the table and retrieved it, counting out five thousand dollars as he circled the table to address his would-be financier.

"I don't believe we've met. I'm George Morton Levy."

"Sure we have, Counselor. Earlier this year, at Max Hirsch's house."

Now George remembered. Max Hirsch trained thoroughbreds at Belmont Park, and George recognized Arnold Rothstein as the man whose horse Sporting Blood had won the 1921 Travers Stakes. Rothstein had requested that George represent two of his nephews who'd been charged with stock fraud. George had taken the case, had won a quick dismissal of the indictments, and had promptly forgotten the whole affair.

George, of course, knew Rothstein's reputation as a high-dollar gambler, and that his nickname, the Big Bankroll, derived from his alleged investments in bootlegging and bookmaking and any number of dubious ventures.

And then there was the small matter of the 1919 World Series.

"Listen. Don't let a run of bad luck send you boys home early," Rothstein told the men in a low, silken voice. "You fellows are smart. Think of gambling not as random chance, but as a rough kind of science. Like a sine wave that oscillates within a limited range of probabilities. You'll win a few and you'll lose a few, but in the end it'll all even out. And if you're adequately capitalized, then you'll be the ones—not Lady Luck—who decide when to call it a night."

The lawyers elected to stay, each borrowing five hundred dollars from Rothstein. Eventually, their collective fortunes—waxing and waning in accordance with their benefactor's mathematical hypothesis—reached a post-midnight apex that found them up over five thousand dollars.

In deference to both the lateness of the hour and the amplitude of their positions, they huddled to discuss an exit strategy.

"This looks like a pretty rough place to take your money out," McDermott said, eyeing the other players, several of whom were shadowed by bodyguards.

George nodded. "Let me talk to Rothstein."

The Big Bankroll laughed, clapping a hand on George's shoulder. "Tell you what, Counselor. Leave your winnings with me, and when you're ready to pick them up, they'll be waiting for you at Lindy's."

George knew the restaurant-deli, which was just around the corner on Broadway. He also knew that it served as a kind of unofficial headquarters for Rothstein, who was known to stand out front on the sidewalk most evenings, paying and collecting his manifold wagers.

The lawyers conferred again. Concluding that the devil they knew was preferable to whatever might be lurking outside, they voted to leave their money with Rothstein.

Two weeks later, George found himself back in Manhattan, at a sheriff's department smoker with his Long Island friends Steve Pettit and Grover Walsh. It was Walsh, short on cash, who hit George up for a loan.

"I haven't ten dollars on me," George said, patting his pockets. And then he remembered. "But let me make a call."

The cashier at Lindy's confirmed that he was, indeed, holding an envelope bearing George's name, so George arranged for its delivery by messenger. This transaction completed George's introduction to a stratum of New York society whose conduct, George thought, well illustrated the distinction he'd learned in law school between that which is *malum in se*, or inherently wrong, and that which is *malum prohibitum*, or "wrong" merely because it's forbidden by law.

And so, George Levy became a regular at Saturday night craps. What right had the state, he reasoned, to govern a man's private vices? Besides which, the men he was meeting and the friendships he was forming might well open new and lucrative vistas for a man in his line of work.

Beatrice took a somewhat different view. "It's unbecoming for a man of your stature to go around consorting with hoodlums and gangsters."

"But criminals are my stock in trade," George reminded her. "They pay the bills around here."

"We should be mixing with a better class of people. Long Island society people."

"I'll mention that to Willie Vanderbilt the next time I see him. He generally plays on alternate Saturdays."

One night George was leaving a game near First Avenue and 49th Street with over four thousand dollars in his pocket when he heard footsteps on the sidewalk behind him. The street ahead was dark and empty, and George felt his heart beating faster.

Spying no taxis on First Avenue, he proceeded to Second Avenue at a somewhat brisker pace, but the footsteps did not slacken. And so it went—past Third Avenue and Fourth Avenue, and then finally to Fifth Avenue, where, to his enormous relief, a taxi had pulled to the curb to disgorge a laughing young couple.

George dove into the backseat of the cab, and as it merged into traffic, he turned to see through the rear window the receding figure of a man, tall and powerfully built, with a flattened potato for a nose.

George's pulse had returned to normal by the time he reached Pennsylvania Station, where he proceeded down the stairs to his platform. The platform was wide and mostly empty, with only scattered newspapers and a few snoring drunks to keep him company. He chose an empty bench by the staircase, where he lit a cigar to calm his nerves.

Soon the Long Island train rumbled into view. George snuffed his cigar and had just started toward the track when a pair of ragged men appeared from behind a tiled pillar.

"Hey, pal, what's the hurry?"

"Yeah, where's the fire?"

George halted. He sidestepped, but the men did likewise. Ahead of him, he noticed, the train doors had opened and swallowed the eastbound passengers. The platform, George realized with growing alarm, was now otherwise deserted.

George backed as the two men advanced. He knew he couldn't fight them, and he doubted he could outrun them in his suit and wing-tipped brogues.

For the second time that evening, he felt a shadow pass over his heart.

"Now hold on, fellows," George said, still backing up, but the men had stopped in their tracks. Their gaze, George realized then, had shifted over his shoulder.

He spun around to look.

The large man with the flattened-potato nose was hurrying down the stairs with a hand thrust into his overcoat. As George turned again to confront his assailants, the platform before him was empty.

The big man, his breathing labored, skidded to a halt beside him.

"Who are you?" George demanded. "Why are you following me?"

"I'm sorry if I frightened you, Mr. Levy," the big man said, removing his hat, "but you usually leave your money with the house, so I was sent to protect you."

"Sent? Sent by whom?"

"Why, by Mr. Rothstein, of course."

The man trotted ahead to the waiting train and held the door for George.

"You can never be too careful, Mr. Levy," he said as George stepped on board. "This town is full of crooks."

Eleven

Tammany Hall

EVEN THE MAYOR was a songwriter.

James J. Walker, a grinning, glad-handing son of Greenwich Village, had already penned such popular ditties as "There's Music in the Rustle of a Skirt" and "Will You Love Me in December as You Do in May?" before dipping a cap-toed brogan into the murky waters of elective politics. He was soon a Democratic assemblyman and then a popular state senator, and he took the oath of mayoral office in January of 1926 amid a national economic boom of historic proportions.

With Al Smith in the governor's mansion and Democratic strangle-holds on the city's legislature and judiciary, its public works and public safety departments, the New York into which Tom Dewey graduated from the Columbia University School of Law was a testa-ment to the strength of the Tammany Hall political machine at the height of its storied powers.

Uptown, they'd dubbed it the Harlem Renaissance. Downtown, in the windswept canyons of Wall Street, they were calling it the Roaring Twenties. And in a midtown bathed in the golden footlights of Broadway—in its nightclubs and speakeasies, its theaters and dance halls—it was known as the Jazz Age. But whatever you called it, and from whatever vantage you witnessed its glittering abundance, the second decade of the twentieth century had found in New York a host city of unique incandescence.

Ever dapper in his silk hat and spats, Mayor Jimmy Walker played the strutting drum major to this trombone parade of enterprise and decadence that roused New York from its postwar doldrums and led it, high-stepping, to its manifest destiny as a world capital of art and culture, industry and finance—a city of six restless million whose skyscrapers tickled the heavens, whose stages hung the stars, and whose hustling, bustling streets carried more automobile traffic than all of Europe combined.

But the roar of the steam shovel and the syncopated din of Tin Pan Alley masked another, darker sound in a city where the raking claws of graft were audible to all but the willfully deaf. It was a city in which a police captain's bars might be bought for a few thousand dollars, or a magistrate's robes for ten. A city in which the population grew by 15 percent as the municipal budget swelled fourfold. Where the mayor, dubbed Beau James by an adoring press, held court at the Central Park Casino—refurbished at a taxpayer cost of over $350,000—with bootleggers at his table and a showgirl on either arm.

Meanwhile, in the ground-floor apartment of a modest brown-stone on West 22nd Street, the mustachioed young lawyer newly associated with the Wall Street firm of Larkin, Rathbone & Perry rubbed a circle on his bathroom mirror. Tom Dewey paused a moment to listen, razor in hand, to the bright, tinkling melody emanating from the piano in the parlor. But when Frances Hutt's delicate etude was joined by a reedy vocal tenor, Tom's smile morphed into a frown. Grabbing a towel, he threw the door wide and stalked, fully lathered, into the carpeted hallway.

"For God's sake, man, put some guts into it!"

The music stopped as Frances shielded her eyes. "Goodness, Tom, put some clothes on."

"I told you that'd smoke him out of his hole." Marland Gale dropped to a knee and splayed both hands over his heart. "*If you knew Dewey, like I know Dewey, oh, oh, oh, what a guy!*"

Frances's hands clapped to her ears as she pivoted on the bench. "Now see what you've gone and started?"

"What do you say, Tom? How's about a little Eddie Cantor for old time sake? *Yes, we have no bananaaas*—"

"C'mon, knock it off." Sewell Tyng, the third man in the room, squared a thick stack of handbills as he rose from the couch. "Let's get going. We've got a governorship to win."

The three lawyers were soon striding eastbound toward Fifth Avenue with their overcoats buttoned, the gauzy lights of the Flatiron Building guiding them like a beacon. The night was damp and unseasonably cold for the first Tuesday of November, and the side-walk would have stretched dark and empty before them save for a lone pedestrian, stooped and shuffling, on whom the three men rapidly gained.

Sewell Tyng held a gloved fist to his throat. "You're a damn lucky man, Dewey. When are you going to make an honest woman out of that songbird back there?"

"Not so fast," Marland Gale protested. "What are you trying to do, get me evicted?"

"I can't evict you, Marty—Frances needs the piano. Besides, she's been offered a part in the *Scandals*, only this time for the road show."

"What?" Gale grabbed his roommate's coat sleeve, spinning him to a halt. "Any guy who'd let a classy dame like that ride the rails with a bunch of clowns and chorus girls ought to have his head examined!"

"You're preaching to the choir, Marty. Only women have the vote now, haven't you heard?" Tom shrugged free, and the men were moving again. "I've told her I don't like it—either the work or the company. But she's no shrinking violet, in case you haven't noticed. She says she has her *future* to think of. If he didn't know any better, a fella'd think she was trying to send him a message . . . Excuse me, sir? Have you voted yet?"

The shuffling pedestrian started, backing a step at the younger man's proffered handbill.

"I most certainly have. For Ogden Mills."

"That's a good fellow. Here." Tom stuffed a handbill into the old man's jacket. "If you've got any Republican neighbors, remind them the polls close at eight!"

The lawyers were hurrying now, cutting across the empty street.

"A million more like him and we'll send the Happy Warrior back to the Second."

"Don't kid yourself," Tyng said. "If we could find a million like him, Tammany would find two million more."

"That's a damn cynical thing to say."

"I'll forgive your naïveté, Tom, but only because you're new at this. Let me tell you a little story. I was working the polls two years ago, right here in the Tenth, when all of a sudden a bunch of hood-lums showed up—great big apes with hairy knuckles and guns stick-ing out of their jackets. They hung around for a while, making everybody nervous, and then a bus rolled to the curb and maybe two dozen floaters came strolling in. None of them registered, of course. Probably all from out of state."

"What did you do?"

"What could we do? We called the police, but they never came. Heck, it was probably a cop who was driving the bus. All we could do was protest the votes, which earned us a horselaugh from the hoodlums. Then once the bus pulled out, they all moved on to the next precinct. Those guys on the bus must have voted a dozen times that day, and do you want to hear the corker? Someone filed a complaint with the Board of Elections saying *we* were the ones intimidating voters. Can you beat that?"

"You make it sound worse than Chicago."

"Chicago? Chicago's for amateurs, brother. There's a saying in these parts you'll do well to remember, and that's that nobody's ever lost a nickel betting on Tammany Hall."

"If you believed that for a minute, Sewell, you wouldn't be out here tonight. You wouldn't have spent the last six weeks knocking on doors and passing out handbills. And for that matter, neither would I."

"Maybe we're just a pair of cockeyed optimists."

"We're Republicans, damn it. We think the people of this city deserve decent, honest government. We think it's a crime the way public projects come in at twice over budget, and the way government payrolls are padded with hacks and cronies, and the way every loaf of bread sold in this city carries a ten-percent kickback to union gangsters and the crooked politicians they pay to look the other way."

"Start printing the campaign signs." Marland Gale made a frame with his hands as he walked. " 'Dewey for Attorney General.' "

"Not me, friend. I've got a living to make. Maybe Sewell here should run for assembly. 'A war hero who's too rich to be corrupted.' Now there's a slogan for you."

"I heard when they probated Boss Murphy's estate it was worth over two million simoleans," Gale said as the men turned north into the headlights on Fifth Avenue. "Not bad for a guy who hadn't held a job for twenty years."

"You mean the man who elected three mayors and three governors? I'd call that a job well done."

The men divvied their handbills and took up positions on the corner, waiting for prospective voters.

"The fellow I don't understand is this Buckner," Tom said. "He's the United States attorney for God's sake, with all the power of the federal courts on his side. He's got the FBI, the Intelligence Service of the Treasury, the Secret Service, the Postal Inspection Service, and the Narcotics Squad all at his beck and call. He should be busting these rackets and blanketing this town with grand jury subpoenas. Come to think of it, he should be posting federal marshals at every polling place in the city."

"Easy, Dewey. You've got a chorus girl to support."

"Tell you what, Tom. Why don't you tell that to Buckner in person? He's invited some of us to lunch at the Lawyer's Club on Thursday. Sam Koenig will be there, and so will Tom Desmond and some younger fellows from Buckner's staff. We're getting the Young Republicans back together, and we all think you should be part of it."

"Thank you, Sewell, but the last time I checked, there were only twenty-four hours in a day."

"Suit yourself," the older man said as a clutch of shoppers approached. "But Desmond will be very disappointed. He and Koenig both made a point of asking for you by name."

Twelve

Broad Shoulders

May 1927

THE WAY I figured it, three was my lucky number. I left Cleveland in March of '26—that's the third month, see?—and headed for Chicago with the three grand I'd cleared after selling my share of the speak to Pearl. Big Joe Porrello had set me up in a suite on the third floor of the Hotel Metropole, and he'd promised to visit me whenever he was in town, which he said was usually around three times a month.

Lucky three, get it? But it wasn't too long before three didn't seem so lucky after all.

I liked Big Joe, don't get me wrong, and I know he was sweet on me. More than his other girlfriends, that's for sure, and maybe more than his own wife even. But after a while, a girl comes to realize that sweet only gets you so far, and that she needs to have certain things in a city like Chicago that she don't necessarily need in a place like Pittsburgh or Youngstown or even Cleveland.

Take food, for instance. Do you have any idea what a room service meal costs in a joint like the Metropole? A girl could go broke without leaving her room! And then there's dinner out, and let me tell you something, you don't go out to dinner in Chicago wearing any old thing you pull out of your closet. You need gowns, not to mention hats and gloves and a half-decent fur, or else you look like some kind of a crumb.

I tried to explain all this to Big Joe, and at first he bought me a few nice things like lingerie and stockings and frilly girl stuff he wanted to see me wearing. Or not wearing. Or putting on and then taking off again. Or leaving on, in the case of the stockings. But when it came to going out, what did he care if I wore the same lousy dress I wore the last time we went out together? *Ish kabibble*, that's what he cared.

Plus I was getting bored. I know, you'd think lying around in bed all day listening to the radio and farting through silk underpants would be the elephant's eyebrows after running that joint in Cleveland for three years, working ten, twelve hours a day waiting on tables and washing glasses and scrubbing up other folks' puke. But you'd be wrong. The truth of it was, I was going off my nuts. I felt like that bird you hear about, the one that lives in the gold-plated cage.

I needed to stretch my wings.

I met Jack Zuta on one of Big Joe's visits around Christmastime. Big Joe and me went to this club on the south side where Al Capone was supposed to be, and Frankie Rio, but instead it turned out to be a bunch of third-rate palookas sitting around smoking cigars and getting drunk on their own bootleg hooch. I was bored out of my skull, and pretty soon Big Joe and me had us a humdinger of a row.

It started over Big Joe taking lip from this guy half his size about some deal involving a boat and who it was that was supposed to have registered it. I asked Big Joe how come if he was such a big shot now he didn't just tell the pipsqueak to chase himself. Big Joe got all sore and told me to dry up. I said he should dry up, 'cause I was only asking a question, and then he told me I didn't know from nothing and I should go downstairs and powder my nose.

So that's what I done. And when I came back to the dining room, instead of going to the table where Big Joe was waiting, I walked over to this guy at the bar who'd been giving me the big eye all night, and I asked if he wanted to dance.

Now, normally I wouldn't of done something like that, on account of it making Big Joe look like a heel in front of his gangster friends. Also on account of Big Joe being the jealous type as far as his nature goes, and a baby grand as far as his size goes. But I was madder than a wet hen by then, and I'd had a couple of drinks too many, and I suppose, looking back on the situation, I was only trying to get some kind of a rise out of the big galoot.

At first I thought this guy at the bar was a Jew, but then he told me that his name was Jack Zuta, which sounded Italian, and that he worked for Capone. Now if I had a nickel for every guy in Chicago who claimed to work for Capone, I could of bought myself a Duesenberg. Only this guy seemed on the level, and if he was even the slightest bit afraid of Big Joe, who was staring pitchforks at us the whole time we were dancing, he sure as hell didn't show it.

He wasn't the best-looking guy in the joint, this Jack Zuta, but he had real nice manners, and he wore a flower on his lapel, and he cut a rug like Oliver Twist. I guess you could say he had class, and it'd been years since I'd been around any of that. Plus he had these long, dark lashes like Valentino that made my knees a little wobbly when we danced up close and he looked me straight in the eye.

I could see Big Joe at the table getting madder and madder, swelling up like an overpumped tire, and so I told Jack Zuta I'd better get back to my date. He asked me where I was staying, and I before I could stop myself, I told him the Metropole. Then he asked me what room, and I told him to slow down a little, and that made him laugh. He said, "Okay, the Metropole then," and he went back to the bar, and I went back to Big Joe.

Big Joe, of course, burned like a fuse for the rest of the evening, until we got out to the car, and then he really exploded. Called me a bitch, and a slut, and an ungrateful little whore. Said he should slap me silly and make me walk back to the hotel. Said that the guy I was dancing with used to run a string of five-dollar houses and that my even talking with him in public made me look like a quiff and made him, meaning Big Joe, look like some kind of a sucker who had to pay cash for his nookie.

To which I was about to make a smart-ass remark, but then thought the better of it under the circumstances. The circumstances being that I was in a speeding car with two hundred and forty pounds of angry Dago with a gun under his arm and a straight razor strapped to his ankle.

Big Joe always carried that goddamn razor. I'd asked him once what it was for, and he said it was for when he ran out of bullets.

Big Joe had cooled down by the time we got to the hotel, and by the time he finally went to sleep, we'd already kissed and made up. But in the meantime, I'd found out a few things about this Jack Zuta fellow. Like that he wasn't really Italian but a Polak. And that he really *did* work for Capone, as some kind of a fixer. And that the Guzik brothers had run him out of the whorehouse business a few years earlier, before he'd somehow managed to catch on with the Capone outfit.

So anyway, Big Joe went back to Cleveland the next morning, and I went back to my radio. Then in the afternoon, at around three o'clock, a bellboy knocked on my door and handed me a bunch of flowers with a note that said, "Pick you up at six. We'll dance. Jack Z."

I gotta tell you, it made me a little sore, that note, but it also made me smile. Jack Zuta had moxie, and I liked a man with moxie. Besides, I figured, if he worked for Capone, then I'd be doing Big Joe a favor by making connections he could use someday in his rackets. At least that's what I told myself. But the main reason I was smiling was on account of this whorehouse business, because there was this idea I'd been chewing on even before I'd met Jack Zuta, and here was my chance to finally do something about it.

We went to dinner at the Blackhawk. Carlton Coon was there with his Kansas City Nighthawks, and me and Jack danced a few waltzes with both of us laughing and me all the time keeping an eye out over his shoulder for any of Big Joe's bootlegger friends.

When we finally sat down to eat, I told Jack what Big Joe had said about the Guzik brothers and Jack laughed it off, saying it was the best thing that'd ever happened to him, what with him connecting first with Johnny Torrio and then later with Capone. He said he was a bookkeeper now and was strictly legit, which I thought was sweet of him, thinking he had to appear legit in order for me to be interested.

"Let me ask you something," I said once the food had arrived. "How hard would it be to set up a whorehouse in this town? And not some two-dollar crib, but a swanky joint with real booze and clean sheets and girls who know how to behave?"

"What?" he said, acting all surprised.

"Look honey," I told him, "I think you're a swell guy, so let's not kid each other and get off on the wrong foot. I'm no debutante, and you know it. I ran a drum in Cleveland, and I worked the short con in Youngstown before that. That's how I met Big Joe, during a robbery at my speak. Only now he's got me squirreled away in that hotel all day with nothing to do but stare at the wallpaper, and I'm starting to go buggy."

Jack shook his head as he lit us a couple of smokes.

"You're buggy all right," he said, handing me my cigarette. "To run a house in Chicago you'd need the okay from the cops and the outfit both, and you'd never get either one, so forget about it. Believe me, I know. And if you tried to go independent, you'd still need a booker and a bondsman, and you'd never get either of those."

"What's a booker?"

He rolled his eyes. "A booker is sort of like an employment agent. Every week he sends fresh girls to the houses—like shuffling a deck of cards. It mixes things up for the customers."

"So what if I didn't use a booker? What if I found my own girls and I was smart about it and never got pinched?"

"Then I'd still say no dice. If the outfit ever found out, you'd get your joint robbed or wrecked or both. Maybe that pretty face of yours, too. This isn't beanbag, kiddo. There was one guy I heard about who tried to muscle in on the Guziks, and they found his body in the bathtub. They found his head in the sink. I hope you're getting the picture here. And I've yet to meet the pro skirt whose mouth wasn't bigger than her handbag. So, like I said, don't even think about it."

If there was one thing that got me sore, it was some mug telling me what I could and couldn't do. It was my mother who used to say that if she wanted me to do something, all's she had to do was tell me not to.

"But you'd know how, right? Even if we're just beating our gums, you'd know how to set one up?"

His head was still shaking, but at least this time he was smiling.

"Yeah, Flo, I'd know how to set one up. And I'll tell you all about it, but first you gotta promise me two things."

"Anything."

"First you gotta promise you ain't serious, 'cause even loose talk like this could get us both killed."

I nodded. He reached a hand under the table and rested it on my thigh.

"Second, you gotta promise me you'll ditch that goon Porrello, because I ain't in the habit of sharing my girlfriends with nobody, understand?"

So that's how I came to be dating two guys at the same time. It was also about then that lucky number three walked into the picture.

I explained to Jack Zuta that if I was gonna break it off with Big Joe, then it had to be real gentle-like, on account of Big Joe being a hothead. Jack said that if Joe Porrello ever gave me any trouble, he'd personally cut Joe's balls off with a butter knife and feed 'em to his goldfish. Which, sweet though it was, I knew to be strictly patter, on account of while Big Joe carried a gun and a razor, the only weapon I'd ever known Jack Zuta to carry was a gold fountain pen.

As far as Big Joe was concerned, I never saw Jack Zuta again. And as far as Jack was concerned, I'd broken it off with Big Joe for good. So when me and Big Joe spent New Year's together, Jack thought I was in Pittsburgh visiting family. And when Big Joe called the hotel after midnight and found out I was gone, I'd say I'd been sitting up with some girlfriend's elderly mother. Best of all, whenever the rent was due on my suite at the Metropole, I got two checks every month, and both for the full amount.

Things, as the man said on the radio, were copacetic. And then all of a sudden they weren't.

Joe Sussman was a friend of Jack Zuta's who used to run a whorehouse on Madison Street. Jack introduced me to Suss with the idea, I think, of getting me to quit talking all the time about going into the business, on account of Suss getting roughed up pretty good by Mike Heitler and having to lam it up to Duluth. Only there were two things Jack didn't see coming, and come to think of it, neither did I. The first was that Suss wanted back into the business and was actively looking for a partner. The second was that Suss fell for me like a sack of rolled oats, and the truth of the matter was, I fell for him just as hard.

Pretty soon I had what you might call a romantic triangle on my hands. Or maybe it was a rectangle. Whatever it was, I was the one who had to work out the angles.

The nice thing about Suss was that he wasn't so full of himself. Most of the guys I'd met in Chicago, they were either hard-boiled or else they wanted you to think they were. Guys who all they ever talked about was this big shot they knew, or this racket they were part of, or this boss they were gonna bump off. But never Joe Sussman.

For one thing, he didn't weigh more than a buck sixty, so who was he gonna kid? Plus he liked to poke fun at himself for being yellow, or being slow on the uptake, or having a tiny dick, when in fact he turned out to be braver, smarter, and better in the feathers than Jack Zuta and Big Joe Porrello put together.

The first time me and Suss made it, even the guests in the adjoining rooms lit up cigarettes.

But the best thing of all, Suss wasn't the jealous type. He knew all about me and Big Joe and, of course, all about me and his pal Jack Zuta. Yet he never asked stupid questions, even when he knew I'd spent the night with Joe or I'd just come back from a weekend out of town with Jack. All's he'd say was that he was glad I'd had a swell time, and that he was happy I'd made it home safe. Also that for a big ape from Cleveland, he thought Big Joe had excellent taste in women's underwear.

At first we debated whether to open our house in Chicago or Duluth. Suss's argument was that Duluth was a wide open city that was full of good-looking blondes and had easy access to Canadian booze. My argument was that Duluth might as well be the North fucking Pole, and what good would it do us to run a first-class joint only to freeze to death or get eaten by wolves?

In the end, we settled on Duluth. Not on account of Suss winning me over, but because we had no other choice in the matter, given what happened next.

It started in April, when Big Joe had the bright idea to surprise me for my twentieth birthday, which I'd forgot he even knew about. And because I forgot, I'd made a date to meet Jack at the Hotel Sherman for dinner. And because I'd also made plans to meet Suss later that night, I left word at the Metropole as to where I was gonna be.

Geometry, I'm sorry to say, was never my strong suit.

The evening got off to a good-enough start when Jack and me got back to our table from the dance floor and the waiter came over with one of those fancy plates with a silver dome on top. And when he lifted up the dome, there was a pair of sapphire earrings with little diamond sparkles staring me smack in the kisser. I squealed and ran around the table and gave Jack a big hug. Even the eggs at the other tables were smiling, and some even clapped like we'd just gotten engaged or something.

After that we had our dinner. Then the band started up with a slow number, and we were back on the dance floor cheek to cheek when over Jack's shoulder I seen Big Joe come charging into the dining room, looking around like he wanted to rip somebody's head off.

That somebody being me.

"Uh-oh," I said.

"What?"

"Don't look now, but Big Joe Porrello's standing over there by the doorway."

Jack spun me around to get a gander at Joe. I felt his body go limp in my arms.

"Jesus Christ," he said. "What're we gonna do?"

"I don't know about you," I told him, "but I think I'll go powder my nose. If he does happen to see you, watch for that razor he wears on his ankle."

I made for the powder room posthaste, while Jack went the other way, toward the big swinging doors to the kitchen. Big Joe saw me first and headed to cut me off. Then Jack must've reached the doors just as a waiter was coming out, because there was this loud crashing sound, and everybody in the joint—Big Joe included—turned their heads to look.

"Son of a bitch," I heard Joe say as he started across the dance floor.

Jack, who by then had soup all over his shirtfront, saw Big Joe coming and hightailed it into the kitchen. I changed directions and made for the hotel lobby. I figured if I could catch a taxi, I could get to the Metropole and maybe pack a bag before Big Joe'd finished dicing Jack Zuta into chicken à la king.

Then I heard, "Flo! *Pssst*. Over here!"

Joe Sussman was standing by a door off the lobby with that crooked grin on his face. He had one hand on the crash bar and was waving me over with the other.

"Suss!" I said. "What're you doing here?"

"Never mind that," he said. "Let's go, baby."

He grabbed my wrist and yanked me onto the sidewalk. We stumbled around the corner onto 23rd Street, where Suss had parked his old Buick near the rear entrance to the hotel. Then, just as he'd opened the passenger door, we both heard a familiar voice calling from back near the loading dock.

"Flo!" Jack was hollering and waving his arms like a castaway who'd just spotted a passing freighter. And then . . . "Joe?"

Suss circled the car, tipping his hat to his old pal Jack Zuta just as the rear doors to the hotel flew open and Big Joe Porrello came charging out like a train that had jumped the tracks.

Suss fell in behind the wheel. He turned the ignition, and the engine sputtered and caught, and then he paused long enough to give me the once-over.

"Nice earrings, baby," he said, throwing the car into gear. "They'll be the bee's knees in Duluth."

Thirteen

The Ride

THE TROUBLE BEGINS, as it always does, with his father. Antonino
Lucania had not been forewarned that his middle son, Salvatore—
or Charlie, as the boy now calls himself—would be joining the
family for dinner. When Charlie arrives, late as usual, with a bagful
of gifts and is promptly swarmed by his mother and siblings,
Antonino does not rise from the table to join them. Instead the old
man opens his newspaper and finishes his meal in silence, then stands
without speaking to grab his coat and hat and head for the door to the
stairwell.

"What's the matter, Papa? First no hello, and now no goodbye?"

Antonino pauses without turning. Then the door slams shut
behind him.

What else does Charlie expect? His father, who'd been a sulfur
miner in their Sicilian hometown of Lercara Friddi, believes in three

things above all others: the infallible mercy of Our Lord Jesus Christ, the virtues of honest labor, and the honor of his family's name. This was a man who'd paid for their passage to America by saving his centesimi for years in a glass jar under his bed. A man who'd come to America with neither a dollar in his pocket nor a word of English to his name, but who'd managed to feed and clothe and house his wife and their five children by the sweat of his brow and the sheer deter-mination of his fifteen-hour workdays.

To Antonino Lucania, his son Salvatore's life is a mockery of all he holds dear. Godless, the boy had quit attending Mass when, at age fourteen, he'd quit attending school to hang around with the neigh-borhood Jews. Lazy, the boy had chosen the gaudy flash of hoodlum life over the value of an honest day's wages. But worst of all to Antonino Lucania is the way in which his son has tainted the family name with his drug dealing, and his arrests, and his criminal reputa-tion in the neighborhood. And thus it was no insult to Antonino when he learned through a friend that his son Salvatore was calling himself "Luciano" now.

Good, the father thought. Maybe now their neighbors would forget that the thug named Charlie Luciano is the flesh and the blood of Antonino and Rosalia Lucania.

Charlie, for his part, laughs off the old man's performance. If not for Charlie's money, and his gifts, and the respect he's accorded in the neighborhood, the Lucania family would still be living in that squalid cold-water flat on First Avenue. His mother would still be working in rags, and his siblings mocked and taunted for their hand-me-down clothes. Instead of ignoring him, the old man should be thanking Charlie—or better yet, kissing his feet—for all he's done for this family. For their comfort, and for the deference they're rightfully paid. Because he, Charlie Luciano, is the one risking life, limb, and prison to provide for the family as his father never could— for the family who's so-called reputation the old man so worries about.

Someday his father would own up to the truth. Someday he'd have no choice, because someday Charlie Luciano would be too damn big for even his father to ignore.

An hour after the old man's departure, Charlie stands at the kitchen window, a damp dishcloth cooling in his hands. Tenth Street yawns dark and cavernous below him with its sidewalks empty and its curbside automobiles quietly slumbering. To the east he can see the cars on Avenue A, their headlights revealing the tall gothic arches of the corner church and, on the sidewalk beyond, the figures passing in dark silhouette—the nightly promenade of junkies and whores, toughs and downtown hustlers.

This is Charlie's old neighborhood, and his lips curl into a smile.

Charlie excuses himself when the telephone rings. He touches his mother's arm as he exits the kitchen, plucking a grape from the fruit bowl and lifting the heavy receiver to the sound of a familiar voice.

"Salvatore, *a cussi tardu!*" his mother cries as he emerges moments later from his parents' bedroom, shrugging into his overcoat.

"*Nun ma aspittari,*" he tells her, kissing her forehead while palming a wad of folded bills into the pocket of her housecoat. "*Ci sta nu problema a putia ca u devu risolviri.*"

Outside his parents' apartment the night is crisp, the air redolent of wood smoke and coal smoke and a hint of rotting garbage. Charlie pauses for one deep breath before continuing westbound along 10th Street. He turns into the colder air on Second Avenue, where the comforting thrum and bustle of flaring headlights and laughing pedestrians bathed in storefront neon restore a spring to his step. Instinctively he scans for patrol cars up and down the avenue, his right hand hefting the .38 revolver in his overcoat pocket, easing the weight that would otherwise break the perfect line of his lapel.

He turns west again at 15th Street, his pace quickening, and by midblock he is eyeing the curb line, searching for the car that will carry him uptown. Farther ahead, at the corner of 15th and Third

Avenue, he spies a familiar form, hunched and smoking, loitering under a streetlamp.

"Let's go!" Charlie calls, still walking, still checking the sidewalks front and rear.

The man stamps out his cigarette. He steps to the curb and opens the rear door to an idling Packard with darkened headlights.

Charlie knows in an instant that everything is wrong. The car is unfamiliar, and the Irishman in the backseat is a stranger, hatless and hulking. But before Charlie can react, the hard muzzle of a pistol jabs into his spine, forcing him inside the car as another, smaller man appears from the shadows and shoves into the backseat beside him.

"What the fuck is this?"

As Charlie's hand closes on the revolver in his pocket, the pistol presses at his skull, forcing his head sideways and down to where the Irishman grabs him, pinning his arms. From the front seat, the twin barrels of a sawed-off shotgun swing into view.

The rear door slams, and the car is already moving.

"Okay, wise guy, show me both hands." The shotgun barrels dip. "Nice and easy."

The speaker is hidden in shadow. Charlie releases his grip on the revolver and frees his hands from his pockets. Fingers claw into his overcoat, his suit jacket, his pants, removing his gun and his cigarette case and lighter.

The shotgun withdraws.

"Relax, Charlie. Everything's gonna be fine." The front-seat voice is calm, reassuring. "*Nun ti preoccupari*. If we wanted you dead, you'd be dead already. Just sit back and be quiet and we'll have you home before midnight."

The car reeks of men long at close quarters—of body odor and garlic and gun oil. It stinks of stale cigarettes and, from the slab-faced Irishman seated beside him, of cheap rotgut whiskey.

Charlie settles into the seatback. He recovers his hat and rests it on a knee.

Although he is outwardly calm, Charlie's mind is racing wildly. Is this a hit, or merely a summons? Are these the men in charge, or are they flunkies? Do they want information, or something more tangible?

There are only two things that Charlie knows for certain. The first is that the men who surround him are cops. The second is that wherever it is they're taking him, it's not to any station house.

"Joe the Boss ain't gonna like this," Charlie says. He is addressing the Italian in the shotgun seat, but it's the Irishman beside him who responds.

"Is that a fact? Well, that's too fucking bad for—"

"Shut up, both of you."

The big man glares at the front-seat voice but, Charlie notices, does as he is told. And so they ride in brittle silence, west at first and then south along the river, their progress slowed by traffic snarls and construction barriers and the tweet and shriek of police whistles.

It takes them twenty minutes to reach the Battery.

"You guys are makin a big mistake," Charlie tries again, probing. "If I knew where he was, I'd give him up in a heartbeat. I got no reason to protect that crazy son of a bitch."

The man in the front seat turns. Although his face is backlit by the oncoming headlights, Charlie can detect the outlines of a smile.

"Listen to you, already squealin like a baby. I guess it shouldn't surprise me, a stool pigeon like you. And here I heard you were a big shot now, you and your pals down in Atlantic City. Well, guess what, big shot? Ain't no pals around to help you tonight. And none of your payroll coppers neither. So do like I said and shut your yap. You'll do plenty of squealin before the night is over."

Charlie is focusing now, marking time in his head. It takes them fifteen minutes to load the Packard into the belly of the ferryboat. The men remain inside the car, cramped and hot in their woolen overcoats, shrouded behind windows raised and fogging. All around them, doors are slamming and voices are trailing away toward the iron stairs to the deck.

"I can't fuckin breathe," Charlie finally says, and the leader rubs a circle on the shotgun window with his fist. The ferry engines are rumbling as the window cranks open and a cooling combination of salt air and diesel fumes floods into the car.

Charlie can hear seagulls somewhere above them as the boat shudders and lurches into motion.

"Hey, wise guy. Is it true you know Al Capone?" asks the little guy on Charlie's right.

"Yeah, sure. Gimme your address and I'll have him pay you a visit."

"I said shut up, all of you."

The passage takes twenty minutes. Then on the Richmond County side the process is reversed as voices return and the window cranks closed and the surrounding car engines stutter and catch. Soon they are part of a long procession of headlights that climbs and levels and wends its way through the ferry terminal and thence onto Bay Street, where the Packard pulls to the side to allow the other cars to pass.

The shotgun reappears.

"Now," says the leader, and Charlie is shoved forward with his face pressed into the seatback as his arms are twisted behind him. He feels rope scratching, burning, biting into his wrists.

"You fucking bastards," he says. "I'll tear your fuckin heads off. I'll cut your fuck—"

Zip, zip, zip. A roll of adhesive tape is passed from man to man beside him. Three, four times it circles his head, trapping the words in his mouth.

"All right, let's go."

The car is moving again, merging onto a Hylan Boulevard that's deserted at this hour, the roadside houses dark and abandoned. Charlie struggles against his bonds, testing at first, then thrashing and flailing in earnest. What he feels in that instant is neither fear nor panic, but a hot, blinding rage that overwhelms his reason and sends his legs kicking and his body crashing over the seatback like an errant torpedo.

Rough hands yank him backward, and Charlie catches the glint of the brass knuckles only in the final instant before the big man's fist slams the side of Charlie's face, shattering his cheekbone in an explosion of swirling embers.

Charlie's last memory inside the car is of blood—his own blood—running in thin rivulets down the seatback, the image playing to a score of shrieking seagulls that circle and descend, hundreds of gulls, their cries growing louder and louder until he hears nothing but the gulls and then he hears nothing at all.

"Wake up!"

Charlie wakes to find that there are five men now, with a porcine newcomer in a vested suit standing slightly apart from the others. The new man keeps his hands in his pockets and is rocking on the heels of his polished brogans. The others stand in a square around Charlie where he lies in the mud with a cold wind at his back and the putrid stink of dead fish and rotting garbage filling his nostrils.

Charlie tries to stand, but his wrists remain bound and he only manages to extend one leg and roll awkwardly to a seated position. His breath comes in short, clotted snorts. His face, he knows, is badly swollen and he notes with his one sighted eye the piles of windswept trash and the angled cars behind the men that block his view of the street and the wooded hillside rising above it.

"Help him up," says the fat man.

Charlie is hoisted to his feet and stands weak-kneed and wobbling before his captors.

"Ask him nice, just the one time."

The Irishman from the backseat grabs Charlie by the lapels and lifts him onto his toes.

"Jack Diamond! You tell us where to find him, and you go home tonight on the boat. Clam up, and your body washes up tomorrow in

87

Jersey. You hear me, wise guy?" He shakes Charlie as if he were weightless. "You hear me? Nod once for yes."

Charlie knows now they are homicide dicks—a special squad of some sort, tasked with finding Legs Diamond. In July, the night that two men were killed in his Hotsy Totsy Club on Broadway, Legs had mysteriously vanished. Now eyewitnesses to the murders have been disappearing, and the cops are growing desperate. They are tearing the city apart, searching for the loudmouthed bootlegger who'd once been Arnold Rothstein's bodyguard and therefore, in the minds of the police, Charlie Luciano's ally.

Since he can neither curse nor spit at the man who holds him, Charlie arches his back and thrusts his head forward, targeting the Irishman's nose. The blow connects with a satisfying *crunch* that leaves Charlie once again heaped on the muddy ground.

He waits for it. He is kicked once, twice in the ribs before a shoe presses down on his shattered cheekbone, grinding his head into the mud. The embers return, orange and dancing, and he is screaming beneath his gag.

Voices burble, then a sharp command. Charlie can see on Hylan Boulevard the lights of a passing car. He struggles at his bonds, his hands balled into fists.

He is lifted again by his overcoat, and a fist is driven into his belly. But he remains standing because, he realizes now, another man is behind him, holding him upright.

The Irishman is back, only this time with a knife.

The blade is short and sharp and jagged along its cutting edge. It sways hypnotically in the reflected lights off the bay. The face behind the blade is flushed and bloody and the blood has soaked the Irishman's shirtfront.

Whiskey breath comes at Charlie in gusts.

"You dirty wop bastard," the Irishman wheezes. "You'd better talk to us. Nod once and I cut the tape." The blade is cold on Charlie's cheek, where it lingers for but a second before inching higher. "If not, I swear to Christ, I'll carve your fuckin eye out."

"For God's sake," says the fat man. "It's not like we wanna be out here freezing our asses any more than you do. Speaking for myself, I'd rather be home in front of a fire. And what do you owe Jack Diamond, anyway? I hope he ain't your bodyguard, 'cause he didn't do too great a job for your pals Rothstein and Little Augie, did he?"

The fat man stops talking and rocking long enough to light a cigarette.

"Besides, it seems like every hoodlum in New York is trying to kill the guy, so stop and think for a minute. Is it really worth losing an eyeball to protect some trigger-happy asshole who's already as good as dead? Come on, Charlie, don't be a sap. It's only a matter of time. Be a smart boy, and go ahead and nod."

The men wait, all looking at Charlie.

The Irishman turns. The fat man shrugs.

"Okay, tough guy. Have it your way."

The blade digs into his face. Charlie screams under his gag while his blood spurts as from a burst balloon onto the Irishman's sleeve, his pants, the ground under his feet.

"Jesus," says the smaller man behind him.

Charlie slumps again, his knees turned to jelly, but still he is held upright. He cannot tell whether his eye is gone, on the ground along with the trash, but he knows that in order to live, he must do something and do it quickly.

His fists ball and twist, the rope cutting deeper into his wrists.

Charlie nods, with grunts meant to approximate speech.

The fat man flicks his cigarette to the ground.

"About time. Here, give me that."

The fat man takes the knife from the Irishman. He wipes it clean with a handkerchief, then runs his fingers along Charlie's face, probing for the edge of the tape.

The man behind Charlie loosens his grip. Charlie balls his numbing hands and twists again and feels for the first time that the rope is beginning to slacken.

The tape is ripping free. Then it stops, and Charlie sees the heads of the men turning one by one toward a sound that he recognizes as the whine of a distant siren.

"Shite," the fat man says.

The other men are anxious, pacing now as the fat man switches the knife to his right hand. He feints toward Charlie's abdomen, then slashes upward so that, although Charlie has jerked his head backward, the blade catches the underside of his jaw.

Charlie is gagging now, sprawled on his side, choking on mud and blood. He sees the fat man's polished brogans, then feels the heavy thud of a body blow, the blade plunging deep into his back.

"So long, tough guy. You shoulda talked when you had the chance."

The brogans are gone. Charlie hears two automobiles starting. His hands, although still tangled in the rope, have come unbound.

The sirens are several, and they are growing louder.

Somehow Charlie is on his knees, then on his feet, and he is making his way toward the roadway like a man wading in heavy surf. He himself feels heavy, and his clothes are stiff as oilcloth. First he sheds the rope, and then the tape, which, as he rips it from his head, is sticky in his hands.

Headlights rake his body, and he raises a shielding hand. The cherry strobes and the garbage stink and the banshee scream of the sirens blend together, disorienting him, turning him in a circle.

He is seated on cold, hard blacktop.

Running feet and flashlights.

"Hey, are you all right? Jesus, look at this guy."

Charlie lies back, freezing now, longing for sleep. His head lifts from the pavement and a light shines in his eye.

"Call an ambulance!" one voice shouts, while another says, "See if he's got a wallet."

More fumbling hands. Squinting into the headlights, Charlie can see the shapes of running men. He hears the crackle of a two-way radio.

He tries to speak.

"What's that? What'd he say?"

Charlie licks his lips and starts again.

"Fifty bucks."

"What?"

He shields his eye with a hand. "I said call me a cab, and I'll pay you fifty bucks."

The patrolman turns away. "Can you believe this guy? He wants us to get him a taxi."

"Lucania," reads a patrolman with a flashlight. "Salvatore Lucania."

"Hey, Sal. What happened here? Who did this to you?"

Charlie waves them off. "Go on, scram. Take a day off. I'll handle this myself."

Another car arrives and then, finally, the ambulance. Charlie is numb by now, light-headed and empty, the warmth drained from his body. A stretcher lies on the cold pavement beside him.

"You're lucky to be alive, mister," the ambulance driver tells him.

"Yeah, sure," Charlie says, the scene blurring again, fading to white. "That's me. I've always been lucky."

Fourteen

Word of Honor

As THE THUNDERING roar of the 1920s echoed across the American landscape, George Levy found to his surprise that his courtroom exploits had made him a modestly wealthy man. And like other wealthy men living on a still-rural Long Island suddenly booming both in population and prosperity, George decided to dabble in real estate.

With his growing circle of well-heeled friends and a reputation for honesty and sound judgment, George had little trouble finding other speculators eager to reap the rewards of turning the day's bucolic duck and potato farms into the morrow's bustling residential suburbs.

In May of 1928, George purchased a 557-acre tract of farmland in Massapequa for $306,000—or roughly $550 per acre—with the notion of subdividing the land for homes. He paid $32,000 down and signed a promissory note for the balance. He then put the word out to his wealthier friends in Manhattan.

William Fox, the studio mogul, jumped at the opportunity to invest. Fox, in fact, agreed to repay the $32,000 George had advanced, and further agreed to put up, along with two other investor-partners, whatever funds were required to develop the property. Under the terms of this handshake proposal, a corporation was to be formed in which George would own 25 percent of the capital stock while risking none of his own money. Saul Rogers, an attorney for the Fox Film Company, was tasked with drafting the papers that would memorialize the parties' agreement.

Enter Edward West Browning, husband of the notorious Frances "Peaches" Browning—a man whose personal life had left him a national laughingstock but whose real estate acumen had made him one of Manhattan's largest and wealthiest landlords. Browning caught wind of the deal with Fox and approached George personally, offering $2,000 per acre for the Massapequa property, 50 percent of which would be payable in cash.

At a time when a Steinway grand piano cost $400 and a new Cadillac $2,000, the Browning offer represented a profit to George Levy in the life-altering sum of one million dollars. And since New York law required that any agreement concerning real property must first be reduced to writing before it could be enforced, George had every legal right to accept the Browning offer for his own personal benefit. All it would have taken was George's signature on the confirmatory letter from Browning.

Despite having no legal obligation to Fox or his colleagues, and despite the urging of friends who questioned his sanity, George nonetheless presented the Browning proposal to his prospective partners. Even under the terms of their oral agreement, George still stood to net a cool quarter-million dollars if they accepted the offer from Browning—not bad for a $32,000 investment.

William Fox, however, had other ideas.

"We'd be crazy to accept this offer," Fox harrumphed, tossing the Browning letter aside. "If he wants the property this badly, it means it's worth a hell of a lot more than he's offering. I say no deal!"

George, nonplussed, pointed out that none of them was really a real estate developer in the first place and that a profit, after all, was a profit. He refrained from explaining that he could, as a matter of law, not only accept Browning's offer without their approval but also cut them out of the deal entirely.

The men put the matter to a vote. George lost 3-to-1.

Enter the stock market crash of 1929. With a suddenness that was all but unimaginable only a few months earlier, many of the nation's largest fortunes were lost in October of that year, leaving rich men nearly poor and poor men newly destitute. Soon half the nation's banks failed, and fifteen million Americans lost their jobs. Unemployment swelled to 25 percent, while crop prices fell by half. Foreclosures skyrocketed, and displaced families flooded the homeless shelters and soup kitchens of every American city.

The Browning offer evaporated, of course, along with the personal fortune of William Fox, who soon declared bankruptcy. By the time the tangled tendrils of the Massapequa real estate deal were finally unraveled, George was out over one hundred thousand dollars, a sum that represented almost the entirety of his life savings.

According to Saul Rogers, Fox's lawyer, "It was the most honorable thing I've ever seen in my life. I told George so at the time, and I also told Fox he was taking advantage of George. It almost cost me my job with the Fox Film Company, but it was true. Instead of making a million dollars or a quarter of a million dollars, George Levy ended up owing a hundred thousand. How nuts can you get?"

George, for his part, was more sanguine. "Saul was wrong," he later said. "I'd promised Fox and his partners seventy-five percent of the deal, and that was that. A man is only as good as his word."

If adversity reveals the true character of a man, then the Great Depression served as a kind of national litmus test—a test that George Morton Levy passed with highest honors.

Prior to October 1929, George had been hired by the Paraiso Realty Corporation to handle the mortgage transactions from another real estate development, this time in the Long Island hamlet of Wantagh. While George had no ownership interest in Paraiso and no control over its operations, he did deal directly with the buyers of the subdivided lots, each of whom came to George's Freeport office to sign their mortgage documents. So when the Great Depression hit and the buyers were unable to obtain deeds to the lots for which they'd been faithfully paying on installment, George became angry. And since most of the mortgage transactions had been handled by his office, George felt an obligation to do something about it.

"A lot of those contracts went through my firm," he explained to an incredulous colleague. "Those people didn't know Paraiso from pineapples. They depended on me."

George called the Long Island Title Company to inform them that, beginning immediately, he would assume personal responsibility for all the unpaid mortgages. Ultimately, George paid out more than thirty thousand dollars—effectively the rest of his dwindling nest egg—to assure that his clients received their titles.

Nor was that the end of the affair. George had also recommended a friend—a contractor named Arthur Hendrickson—to perform grading work on the Wantagh project, and by the time Paraiso went under, Hendrickson had been paid only half of his fourteen-thousand-dollar contract. George pledged to pay him the balance.

"But you don't owe it, George," Hendrickson told him, flabbergasted. "Paraiso owes it."

"Can you handle the loss if you don't get paid?"

"No," said Hendrickson. "If we don't get it, then we'll have to close up. We're through."

"Well then, stop talking about it. You wouldn't be in this mess if I hadn't put you there. Let's go to the bank and work something out."

To the bank they went, where George signed eleven promissory notes of seven hundred dollars each, all payable to Hendrickson. Why eleven? The extra note, George explained, represented interest for the delay in full payment. Thereafter, as Hendrickson would present a note to the bank, George would scramble to deposit funds from his law practice to cover it. Eventually, all the notes were paid in full.

"The Hendrickson Company is now one of the largest heavy equipment contracting firms in the country," Hendrickson would later tell an interviewer, "and we wouldn't be here at all if it hadn't been for George Levy. We were absolutely down and out when he took on that obligation that didn't belong to him. I don't know of any other case like it, and we've been in business a long time."

For George, the explanation was simple. To a man who'd never ventured far from his boyhood home, friendships were more important than the material trappings of success. This was a man, after all, who still drove the same Abbott-Detroit roadster he'd bought on his thirtieth birthday. A man who used scissors to cut the sleeves off his dress shirts because he felt they restricted his arm movements in court.

But George had another, perhaps more philosophical rationale for behaving as he did. Unlike ordinary tradesmen such as the butcher, the baker, and the candlestick maker, a successful lawyer depended almost exclusively on his reputation for integrity and trust. Pro bono work—cases undertaken with no expectation of payment—was an honored tradition as old as the law itself. George Levy believed in the lawyer's unique and privileged place in American society. He felt that the awesome powers conferred by admission to the bar—the powers to subpoena, to sue, and to prosecute—came with commensurate responsibilities.

And so every evening after dinner, old pals in distress—George's so-called parishioners—began appearing at the Levy home, and few if any ever left empty-handed. George could still work, he told his fretting wife, Beatrice, and he could still borrow money, and what was the point of it all if their neighbors were homeless and hungry?

"How he did it, I don't know," George's third wife, Margaret, later recalled. "At one point during the Depression it seemed as though George was keeping just about everybody in Freeport afloat. If you ask me, George invented Social Security before Congress ever heard of it."

Fifteen

Uncle Sam

THE YOUNGER OF the men could barely hide his disappointment.

"If only he'd taken the time to read the papers," Tom Dewey groused to George Medalie as the two lawyers trudged the four frigid blocks from Foley Square—the downtown plaza crowded with apple hawkers and chestnut vendors and a young girl playing the accordion—to the office building their law firms shared at 120 Broadway.

"Juries are complex organisms, Tom. Never forget that. At best, they're the conscience of the community. At worst, they're an angry mob with torches and sharpened pitchforks. In this economic climate, defending a firm like Empire Trust against a widow claiming she'd been swindled was no easier task than slaying the Nemean lion."

"Yet Heracles somehow managed it."

The older man smiled. "That he did. And the Appellate Division, unless I'm greatly mistaken, will be our avenging Zeus."

The widow in question, one Nanny Glover Kaufman, had sued the Empire Trust Company alleging that, without her knowledge or consent, it had exchanged certain preferred stock she'd owned for common, with disastrous consequences come the crash of October 1929. Empire Trust was a client of McNamara & Seymour, the litigation boutique to which Tom had migrated in 1927 after a volatile exit from the Augean stables of Larkin, Rathbone & Perry. George Z. Medalie, age forty-seven, was a respected courtroom veteran whom Stuart McNamara had retained to guide his firm's newest associate through his first jury trial.

"What was that phone call this morning?" Tom asked as they turned the corner onto Broadway. "It must have been important for the clerk to interrupt like that."

"It was Bill Mitchell."

"As in William D. Mitchell, the attorney general?"

"The same."

"My God, what did he want?"

Medalie sighed. "It seems that President Hoover, in an appalling lapse in judgment, has just appointed me to be the next United States attorney for the Southern District of New York."

Tom stopped and clapped a hand on the older man's shoulder.

"Why, that's fantastic! Congratulations!"

Medalie turned away as he sneezed, pulling a handkerchief from his pocket. "I won't lie to you, Tom. It's an honor to be following in the footsteps of men like Elihu Root and Henry Stimson." He blew his nose. "But it's also a damnable business."

Medalie was moving again, with Tom hurrying to catch up.

"Why? What do you mean?"

"I mean that with Tom Crain as the district attorney, it'll be up to the Justice Department to tackle Tammany Hall single-handed, and that's just what I plan to do. This Seabury investigation is going to open a whole new front in the war on public corruption, and I'm going to need fresh troops to mount an offensive. At least a dozen or more talented, dedicated young men willing to perform public service for their Uncle Sam at great personal sacrifice. Men like your friends in the Young Republican Club. Lawyers from the best schools and the biggest firms on Wall Street."

"But I thought the federal prosecutors were already top-notch."

"One would hope so, but then let's face the facts. The U.S. attorney's office hasn't been as proactive or as effective as the times require. Graft is eating at this city like a cancer, and bootleggers like Waxey Gordon and Dutch Schultz are operating in broad daylight without the slightest fear of arrest or prosecution. It's nothing less than a civic disgrace. When times were good, the public was willing to laugh and look the other way. But the public mood is changing, Tom, I can sense it. Meaning now is the time to act."

"I'll be happy to put the word out. I know a few fellows who'd be perfect candidates for the job."

"I was hoping you'd say that. Perhaps you could ask around and work up a list for my consideration. Then we could meet for lunch next week sometime, assuming I'm not at death's door with this infernal cold."

"I'd be honored."

"Oh, and there's one other thing." Medalie turned to Tom as they reached the building entrance. "I'll be very disappointed if the name Thomas Dewey isn't at the top of that list."

"*Leave* McNamara and Seymour?"

Frances Dewey twisted on the piano bench.

"Why, Tom, you've only just started there! And after all Mr. McNamara's done for us. He's promised to make you a partner!"

"I didn't say I'd apply. I only said I'd think it over."

"And?"

"And that's what I'm doing. What *we're* doing. It's not my decision, you know. We're in this together now."

"And what does your mother say?"

"Who says I consulted with Mother?"

Frances, her arms folded, tapped the toe of her slipper.

"All right, so I cabled her on the ship. If you want to know, she's against it. She said if I stay with McNamara, then at least I won't be sending men to Sing Sing."

"And what about Mr. McNamara? Have you even talked to him?"

"Not yet, but I know he thinks the world of George Medalie. You should have seen him in that courtroom, honey. Seen the respect he commands. And not just from the judge, but from every one of those jurors. Did you know that his father's a rabbi? And that he speaks fluent Greek?"

"But it's a political appointment, isn't it? What will happen if Hoover is defeated next year? They'll bring in a Democrat to replace Medalie, that's what. And you'll be out of a job."

"You're right, and that's one for the minus column. Along with the pay cut, and the longer hours, and the not-so-incidental fact that I've never tried a criminal case in my life."

To Tom's relief, Frances hadn't flinched at the words "pay cut." After turning down offers from the "Scandals" and the San Francisco Light Opera, both at Tom's insistence, she'd have been well within her rights to veto the whole idea of his leaving McNamara & Seymour. Over two thousand banks had failed in the United States that year. Times were harder than ever, the future never less certain, and Tom had promised his new bride that he alone would be the family's breadwinner.

"So what's in the plus column?"

"Lots of things. Foremost is the opportunity to get some real trial experience, and plenty of it. That'll give me a leg up in the long run, no matter how the job market tightens. Plus, the men George will be hiring are some of the very best in town. Columbia, Yale, and Harvard men. I've already talked to Barry Ten Eyck, and he's going to apply. Even if the job lasts only a couple of years, connections like those will last a lifetime."

"You mean political connections."

"But most important of all is the work, honey. Medalie's got his sights set on the big game—the top crooks like Dutch Schultz and Waxey Gordon. Not just to grab a few headlines, but to smash the criminal rackets once and for all."

Tom knelt beside Frances where she sat.

"Don't you see? This is more than just a political opportunity. It's a chance to clean up this city before the Democrats are back in office and things return to business as usual."

Frances ran a hand through her husband's hair.

"What?"

"Nothing. I was thinking about our first dinner together, do you remember? About how you didn't want to clean up Chicago, and how I was the one who said you should come and clean up New York instead. I guess I have no one to blame but myself."

Tom edged closer, wrapping her in his arms.

"I know this would be a huge sacrifice, honey. I wouldn't even consider it unless you were behind me all the way."

"I'm not worried about me, you silly man. I'm only concerned that it's the right move for my husband and his career. A very wise boy once told me that a man's got to think of the long haul."

Tom kissed the crown of her head. "I'm supposed to meet Lowell for dinner this evening. I have a hunch Medalie's recruited him to twist my arm. Why don't you come along? We'll listen to what he has to say, and then we can make an informed decision. Together, the two of us, and Mother can mind her own business."

The car was on its third pass through a Central Park growing steadily whiter in the still-falling snow. Lowell Wadmond, one of Tom's Young Republican colleagues and the chief assistant to outgoing U.S. attorney Charles H. Tuttle, was hunched behind the wheel, his head bobbing in time with the wipers.

"If this is such a great opportunity, Lowell, then why aren't you staying on?"

Wadmond glanced at Frances Dewey in the front seat beside him.

"For one thing, Mary would brain me with a poker. Four years of public service were three too many, as far as she's concerned. Plus there's that office at White and Case with my name on the door. But for a fellow like Tom, this could be the chance of a lifetime. I know George Medalie, and I think he's capable of great things. Tom would be crazy to miss out on it."

"What do you mean, 'a fellow like Tom'?"

"I mean a bright-eyed bulldog with his sights set on elective office. Do you know what we call him down at the Young Republicans? Among other names best unspoken in mixed company, he's known as Governor Dewey."

"I'll tell you my greatest fear, Lowell." Tom leaned his chin on the seatback. "I'm worried I'll get lost in the shuffle down there."

"Hold on a minute. Tom Dewey afraid? Not the same Tom Dewey who told Albert Stickney to go sit on his thumb."

"Tom!"

"And got himself fired for it. I'm serious, Lowell. What have you got there now, fifty assistants?"

"Closer to sixty. And when Medalie's finished his hiring and firing, they'll be sixty of the best young lawyers in this city. And when he's finished training them, they'll be the top prosecutorial agency in the country. With no disrespect to McNamara and Seymour, Tom, this is like being called up from the sandlot and offered a starting spot with the Yankees."

"So how's a bright-eyed bulldog to distinguish himself in a crowd like that? I could wind up trying bankruptcy frauds or mailbox burglaries."

Wadmond's eyes found Tom's in the mirror.

"Not if you're head of the Criminal Division you won't."

"What are you talking about?"

"You lunkhead. I'm saying Medalie's prepared to make you head of Criminal. He'd of made you the offer himself but he's flat on his back with the flu. I don't know what you did in that courtroom, but you'll be pleased to know you impressed the hell out of him. He called you a force of nature. Said he'd never seen a harder-working or a better-prepared young lawyer in all his years of practice."

"For all the good it did us."

"Heck, Tom, losing is part of the game. Nobody bats a thousand, not even a federal prosecutor. Not even Governor Dewey."

"Who's never tried a criminal case in his life."

"Never mind that. After a year in that office you could try a case in your sleep. Besides, when you're head of Criminal, your responsibilities are mostly administrative. You've always talked about opening your own firm someday. What better preparation than running a sixty-lawyer division of the U.S. Department of Justice?"

"Last I checked, they don't accept experience at the grocery store. The fact is, I'm earning eighty-five hundred this year at McNamara, with a promise of partnership next year. And being the bluebeard that I am, I made Frances give up her singing career with the promise that I'd provide for the both of us. I'd be nuts to even consider the kind of pay cut you're talking about, and besides—"

"All right, you drive a hard bargain. Medalie told me if you didn't go for head of Criminal, I was authorized to offer you my job."

"*What?*"

"You heard me. And if you turn this down, I'm making you walk the rest of the way home."

Again his eyes found Tom's in the mirror.

"Congratulations, my friend. You're the new chief assistant United States attorney for the Southern District of New York."

Sixteen

Kicking the Gong

March 1931

THE GUY AT the end of the bar had heavy sugar written all over his cashmere suit and his onyx cuff links and the gold chain he wore on his vest. An older gent with a ferret face and a pencil mustache, he looked kind of like that movie actor—what was his name?—Warner Baxter. He wore no wedding ring, but from clear across the room I could see the band of lighter skin on the third finger of his left hand.

If he were a book, he'd be one I'd already read a hundred times before.

He'd been eyeing me like cotton candy ever since I'd walked through the door. I gave him a few minutes to make his move, but when the time was up and he still hadn't budged, I took up my coat and my Scotch and I walked them over to where he was sitting.

"You'd better be careful, mister," I told him, setting my drink next to his. "You look any harder, they might burn right off me."

He leaned back to take in my dress. It was mostly silk, and mostly thin, and it showed a lot of leg.

"That would make for an awfully small fire," he said. "Barely enough to warm a man's hands."

"You got cold hands, I know a nice warm place you could put 'em."

"Say, there's nothing bashful about you, is there?"

"Oh, I can be shy all right, if that's what you like." I peeked down the top of my dress. "Heck, I can blush all the way to my garters."

"I suppose you realize you're young enough to be my daughter."

I leaned in close to whisper. "I'll bet when your daughter was naughty, you used to give her a spanking. Nothing too hard. Just enough to turn her bottom all pink and hot."

Like I said, I'd already read the book. I figured him for a banker, or maybe a judge. Straight as a ruler on the outside, but inside wound tighter than that gold watch in his pocket.

He took a sip of his drink, and his hand was practically trembling.

"Have you been a naughty girl?"

"Not yet I haven't, but the night is young. Let me make a phone call first and see if the coast is clear."

We left in my car, with weasel-face holding his hat in his lap, twisting the brim in his hands. It was dinner hour, and uptown traffic was light. We made small talk until around 79th Street, when he surprised me and asked me my name. I said it was Brown, Flo Brown, but he could call me Smith if he wanted, or maybe Jones. Whatever was easy to remember.

My apartment was on the ground floor, left off the lobby. I knocked shave-and-a-haircut, and when the door swung inward and weasel-face got both barrels of Dolly in her black negligee, he took a step backward.

Men tended to do that. It was like seeing Grand Central Terminal for the first time. Big, and breathtaking, and full of possibilities.

"Relax, Professor. This is my friend from Chicago," I told him, prying his hat loose and tossing it onto the divan. "She's a nice girl, and I think the two of you are gonna get along swell."

Fifteen minutes later and I was back in midtown, this time at the Three Hundred Club, one of my regular haunts. The joint was so busy I had to elbow my way to the bar. Right away this old Jew in a shabby raincoat appeared out of nowhere and offered to buy me a drink. He was an odd-looking bird with heavy spectacles and eyes that kind of crossed. I had to pick which one to look at when I thanked him for the Scotch.

"Pleasure's all mine," he said, having to shout over the music. He raised his glass. "That's what I like about this place, it attracts all the best-looking dames."

The guy was strange all right, and he dressed like a brush salesman, but I could see he was no Rube. I cut the baloney and got straight down to cases.

"It's too loud here," I told him. "You seem like a sport. How's about you and me go find someplace a little more quiet?"

"You read me like a meter, sister." He knocked back his drink. "I'm right behind you."

I offered to drive, but he wanted to take his own car, so I waited around the corner on Seventh Avenue until he pulled up behind me and tooted his horn. He was driving a Cadillac that looked like it had just rolled off the assembly line. So maybe he wasn't a salesman. Maybe he was some kind of eccentric millionaire, out mingling with the common folk. That was one thing about this racket—you never knew who you were gonna meet next.

The uptown traffic had grown heavier, and it took us another thirty minutes to get to Yorkville. That gave Dolly plenty of time to finish with the professor, because nobody lasted more than forty-five minutes with Dolly. It was a matter of professional pride with her. She was real dependable that way.

I stood outside the apartment building while four-eyes parked his car someplace that it wouldn't get scratched. When he finally appeared on the sidewalk, I took his arm and we walked together up the steps and into the lobby, where again I knocked shave-and-a-haircut.

Only when the door opened this time, it was Dolly who took a step backward. And she kept on backing all the way to the sofa, where she plopped on her ass with folded arms and a crooked slant to her mouth.

"Cockeyed Louis," she said.

The old Jew was turning a circle, eyeballing the joint like he might make an offer to buy it.

"Nice," he said, nodding his approval. "Real classy."

"What's going on?" I asked Dolly. "Who's Cockeyed Louis?"

"Louis Weiner," she said, "meet Flo Brown."

"Is Dolly your only girl?" the guy asked me, already knowing her name.

"Who wants to know?"

"What's the matter, you got wax in your ears? I'm Louis Weiner. I book all the best girls in this town. I used to book this *nafka* here, only I ain't heard from her for four whole months, and now I see why. What're you charging these days, Dolly? Two dollars? Three?"

"Five!"

"Listen, cockamamie, you're wearin out my carpet. I'd hand you your hat, but it looks like you already got it, so why don't you scram before I call somebody."

He laughed at that, tossing his hat onto the coffee table and making himself comfortable on the divan.

"Ain't you the live wire," he said, feeling the fabric with his fingers. "The thing is, we need to have a little talk, you and me. But first, how's about that drink you promised?"

"Sure thing," I told him. "Arsenic or strychnine?"

"Don't get sore about it. You seem like a smart girl. How long did you think you could operate like this with nobody being the wiser?"

"What're you gonna do, call the cops on me?"

"The cops? Sister, the cops are the least of your problems. Sit down, relax, and let Uncle Louis tell you what's what. But first, how's about that drink?"

I went to the kitchen and made us three highballs, all the time muttering under my breath. The old Jew was right—I did know this day was coming. I just didn't think it was coming today.

When I returned with the drinks, me and Dolly sat like schoolgirls with our knees to our chins while Cockeyed Louis Weiner explained the ways of the world, starting with how we should be grateful it was him who'd found us first and ending with how, from that day forward, I had to book all my girls through him.

"So today's actually your lucky day," he concluded, finally tasting his drink.

"I'm pinching myself."

He had blondes and brunettes, he told me. Black girls and white girls, two-way girls and three-way girls, with over a hundred to choose from. He made it sound like he ran the doll department at FAO Schwarz.

When he finished his pitch I said, "Thanks all the same, but I don't need help from you or anyone else."

Cockeyed Louis thought that was funny.

"Listen, *bubbala*, I'd soft-pedal that if I was you. Or else maybe you'd like a visit from Jimmy Fredericks?"

I looked at Dolly, whose face told me that was one visit I definitely didn't want.

"All right, so what's it gonna cost me, this service of yours?"

"Ten percent of the action. Not your half, but the whole shebang. And from now on, you gotta keep track. I'll send over some punch cards in the morning. And don't give me that look, because it'll be easy to make up my cut. You go on a weekly schedule, see? You charge each girl two bucks for the maid, plus eighteen for board and five for the doctor. The doctor comes on Mondays. Also, you pay an up-front deposit of two hundred and fifty for fall money."

"Don't make me laugh."

"Please, this isn't a negotiation. You want my five-dollar girls, you gotta bond. I use Jesse Jacobs, who's the best in the business. Ask

Dolly, she knows. If your place gets hit, you pay half and the bonding pays half."

"Let me guess. And if I don't pay bond, then my place gets hit."

He shrugged. "Cost of doing business. Everybody bonds."

"That's a lie. I know for a fact that Polly Adler don't bond."

"That's because she's been around, sister, and we know she's good for it. You we don't know from bupkes. We won't place a girl in a house that can't bail her out within twenty-four hours."

"You mean so she won't rat you out."

"I mean so she ain't out of commission all week on account of some greenhorn madam tried to save herself a few bucks."

"And who's this 'we' I keep hearing about? All's I see is a cross-eyed creep in a cheap raincoat."

"That's right, sister. And if you mind your potatoes, that's all you'll have to see."

"Tough guy, is that it?"

"Not me. I'm just a small businessman trying to weather the hard times like everyone else. But I'll tell you what I am willing to do, because I'm a mensch. We'll start you off with a clean slate and forgive what you already owe."

He reached into a pocket and pulled out a pad and a pencil.

"Here's my phone number. Memorize it, then throw it away. I'll bring the punch cards tomorrow, and you can pay your deposit then. From now on you'll call that number on Fridays and I'll send you the pick of the litter. And just to be clear, this bitch over here is back in my kennel. Ain't that right, Dolly?"

Dolly nodded.

"Good," he said. "I was afraid we'd have to send out the dogcatcher, but now I can see that we all understand each other."

He stood and collected his hat. To me, he said, "Cheer up, sister. You've got protection now, plus you won't have to schlep all over the city trolling for suckers. My five-dollar girls, they bring their own trade. You can stay home and put your feet up. Listen to the radio, or read a good book. And eat more, you're too skinny."

What I was too much of was tired—too tired to drive downtown again. Besides, I had a lot to think about. Me and Dolly both. We needed a jag. After Cockeyed Louis left, I went into the bedroom and got down my hat box and broke out the opium pipe.

"Well, kiddo," Dolly said, "it was fun while it lasted."

"The nerve of that guy, sayin he'd send out the dogcatcher. So what are you gonna do now?"

She shrugged, lighting the lamp and blowing out the match. "Go back to booking with Louis, I guess. It beats working a sewing machine."

I opened the can and prized out a thick wad of gum. I made the pills extra big on account of my nerves being jangled like they were.

"Who is this Fredericks character anyway? Some kind of a leg-breaker?"

"Jimmy Frederico. He's Italian, and a real gorilla. He wrecks the houses that hold out their girls. You ever see him outside your door, honey, don't let him in."

"Who does he work for? And don't tell me it's Cockeyed Louis, 'cause that guy couldn't lead a dog on a leash."

"I don't know exactly. Some wiseguys downtown. You want my advice, you don't want to go asking too many questions."

I closed up the can and took up the lamp and made a small adjustment to the flame. My hand, I noticed then, was shaking.

"There was a time I could've snapped my fingers and had a mutt like Cockeyed Louis put in his place," I told Dolly. "You ever heard of Jack Zuta? He was my sugar daddy in Chicago until that rat bastard Capone had him killed. The same with Big Joe Porrello in Cleveland, only it was the Mayfield Road Mob that rubbed him out. It's always the goddamn Italians. They're like the cockroaches that show up whenever you turn off a light."

Dolly got up and closed the street-side curtains. Then she got a towel from the bathroom and laid it at the base of the door. She was real careful like that. It was one of the reasons we got along.

"Whatever happened to that nice Jewish boy from Duluth?"

"You mean Joe Sussman? After Zuta got killed, Joe went back to Chicago. Said New York had him all balled up. Last I heard he was doin okay, but things are pretty rough in Chicago these days. Ain't nobody's safe, not even little kids on the street. I told that to Suss, but he just laughed. Said if I found a place that was safe, to be sure and let him know. Now I hear they're gonna put Capone on trial, and do you know what for? Not paying taxes. Ain't that a scream."

I gave Dolly the first go with the pipe. She worked the pan over the lamp and took the smoke in short, jerky puffs. She coughed and passed it to me, then laid down on the divan.

"You could always close up and move," she said. "Just tell Louis you're quitting the game. I know madams who do it all the time. Sometimes they just move across the hall. But if Jimmy finds out, there'll be hell to pay."

I took my turn with the pipe and then set it back on the table. I stretched out on the divan next to Dolly, who scooted over and pulled me into her bosom.

"You know that last creep with the mustache?" she said, already sounding sleepy. "He told me he was the principal, and I was a naughty schoolgirl for talking in class. Asked if we had a ruler anywhere."

"What'd you tell him?"

"I said sure, King George was in the other bedroom."

We both giggled.

"I ain't gonna run like a rabbit," I told her after a while, snuggling my head on her arm. "I'm finished running from guys like Cockeyed Louis."

"What'll you do?" she asked, her voice barely a whisper.

"I'm gonna find this Jimmy Fredericks, that's what. And then I'm gonna become his special girl."

Seventeen

Ace of Diamonds

April 1931

DESPITE THE HOUR, Lucky cannot sleep. He lies on his back and studies the high ceiling, listening to the traffic sounds and the human sounds and the torpid castanet-clatter of horses' hooves on cobblestone. There are no crying babies here on 59th Street, no shouting wives or drunken husbands, breaking glass or screaming sirens. And yet the night sounds of the city still find a way, like rats in a tenement wall, to claw into his head.

The telephone on the nightstand rings, jolting Lucky upright. It is the front desk calling to announce a visitor.

The clock reads three A.M., and he is not expecting visitors.

"Who the hell is it?"

"I'm terribly sorry, Mr. Lane. It's a Mr. Adonis. He says he knows you. Shall I have him call tomorrow, or—"

"No, no, it's okay. Wait. Ask him what cigarette he smokes."

Lucky holds the line.

"He says Chesterfields."

"Okay, send him up."

Lucky dons slippers and a silk robe from the closet. From the bar in the sitting room he retrieves a bottle of King's Ransom and two crystal glasses and arranges them on the breakfast table. Then he sits, listening for the chime of the elevator.

Abruptly he stands, returning to his bedroom and removing a .38 revolver from the drawer of his nightstand. He goes back to the kitchen and places the gun on the table.

The knock, when it comes, is loud and urgent. Lucky takes up the gun and crosses to the door and peers through the peephole. He slips the gun under a sofa cushion before returning to the door.

"Joey, come on in."

"Thanks, Charlie. I'm sorry to call so late."

The men repair to the table, where Lucky pours them each two fingers of Scotch.

"I got news," Adonis says, swirling his drink, "and I'm afraid it ain't the good kind. Joe the Boss called me tonight around midnight. Said we hadda talk right away over at his place. As soon as I get there, the fat bastard sits me down and says he's got proof it was you behind the Morello hit. Says you're a dead man, and on account of us goin way back and everything, he says I'm the guy's gotta take you out. To demonstrate my loyalty, he says. Says I gotta 'remove that stone from my shoe.' "

"Shit!"

"I'm tellin ya, Charlie, the guy's off his nut. First he starts this thing with Maranzano, and now that we're all in the trenches, he wants to whack his best soldier? What kind of a fucking strategy is that?"

Lucky stands and crosses to the window. The dark oblong of Central Park stretches before him like a tombstone.

"That ain't why I said 'shit,' Joey. Listen. I'm gonna tell you somethin, and I'm sorry you're only hearin it now, but believe me, it was for your own protection. Me and a few of the guys, Albert and Vito and some others, we been studyin this thing for a while now. The truth is, we backed the wrong horse. This Maranzano is tougher and smarter and better organized than Masseria, and now it's to the point where he's got more muscle to boot."

Lucky turns to face his would-be assassin.

"We're on the wrong side of history, Joey. And if we don't do somethin soon, we stand to lose everything we been workin for."

"Christ, I been waitin to hear you to say that, Charlie, and I ain't the only one. What can I do to help?"

Lucky returns to stand by the table. He pats his friend on the face.

"You helped already, Joey, comin straight here. I won't forget that."

"Hell, Charlie. Everything I got, I owe to you."

Lucky collects his drink and returns to the window. His voice, when he speaks again, is distant, contemplative.

"Everybody wants this thing to be over. Business is lousy, the cops are crawlin up our asses, and nobody can take a crap without lookin over his shoulder. At first it was just two Mustache Petes fightin over who's got the biggest dick. Only it's been eighteen months now and everybody's been pulled into it, not just the Sicilians. We all know it's gotta stop, but nobody can figure out how to stop it, right? Well, I know how to stop it. Maranzano's gotta know that with the Clutch and Mineo dead, there's only one guy that can get close enough to Masseria, and that's me."

"What are you sayin, Charlie?"

Lucky turns again to his friend.

"We've already made the arrangements, Joey. Me and Benny and Tommy Lucchese are gonna meet Maranzano on Monday. The deal's gonna be real simple. I kill Joe the Boss, and Maranzano becomes top dog. In exchange, Maranzano guarantees our safety. I get Masseria's rackets, and we get a free hand again in runnin our business."

115

"Geez, Charlie. What about the others? What about Capone?"

"Al's on board, and so are Meyer and Frank. So are Ciro Terranova and Frank Scalise."

"Holy crap."

"For a minute there I thought maybe you'd dropped a turd in the punchbowl, on account of if Joe don't trust me no more, then maybe I missed my chance to take him out, and that puts the kibosh on the whole deal. But the more I think about it, this is exactly the break I been lookin for. So if you really wanna help, Joey, here's what you can do."

"Name it, Charlie."

"I want you to go back to Masseria. Tell him you got a meet set up for Wednesday. Let's make it on Coney Island, at Jerry Scarpato's place. That fat bastard loves the food there. You tell him he's invited to come and witness my execution."

"What time?"

"Make it one o'clock for lunch."

"And what about his bodyguards?"

"Don't worry, I'll handle them. And if he asks who you're usin for the hit, you tell him Vito and Albert. But whatever you do, don't say nothin about Benny. You mention Benny, he'll smell a rat."

"What if he don't wanna come?"

"Then we'll find another way. But if he thinks I killed his pal Morello, then this is one show he won't wanna miss."

Adonis nods without speaking. Lucky lays a hand on his shoulder.

"Joey A. You sure you're okay with this? 'Cause if it works out like I think, word's gonna get around."

"What, you think I'm scared? You think I've gone soft or somethin?"

Lucky tousles his old friend's hair.

"You might get them manicured fingernails dirty."

"Fuck you, Charlie. Go look at your face in the mirror. That's what happened the last time I wasn't there to cover your back."

★   ★   ★

The children have returned to their buses, and the Monday afternoon crowd, generally small to begin with, has thinned to a handful of stragglers, leaving few to witness firsthand the four men in gray fedoras as they pass through the Bronx Zoo's squeaking wooden turnstile.

"It's over this way," Benny Siegel says, tilting the map he'd received at the ticket booth.

"This way's faster," says Tommy Lucchese. "Trust me, I practically grew up in this place."

They follow a winding blacktopped path in which benches are set at regular intervals. In their hats and overcoats, the four men draw looks from the mothers still shepherding their children, fussing and dragging, toward the exit.

"Hey look," says Joe Adonis as they pass the elephant exhibit. "It says right here, Giuseppe Masseria."

"Smells just like him."

"Hey, Charlie. This guy's got bigger balls than you do."

"Knock it off you guys. Come here and listen up."

The men cluster around Lucky as he removes a map from his pocket.

"The lion cage is right around this corner, so remember what we talked about. Everyone know what they're supposed to be doin?"

Hands pat overcoats or dip into pockets. One by one, the men nod.

"Benny? Do me a favor and don't shoot nobody who don't shoot you first, okay?"

"Sure thing," Siegel says, rolling his shoulders. "I'll be on my best behavior."

"That's what I'm worried about. Okay, any questions? No? All right then, let's do this thing."

The men are moving again, strolling now, affecting a careless ease as they round the next corner. Ahead of them the pathway stands empty save for a seated man on a bench.

"I count three," Lucchese says.

Behind the seated figure and flanking him on either side stand two men with their hands in their pockets. They are stationed out of earshot, their backs to an iron railing.

Salvatore Maranzano turns his attention from the sleeping lion. He does not stand to greet the new arrivals. Siegel, Adonis, and Lucchese fan out with their backs to the lion cage, each man facing his counterparts who guard the Castellammarese leader.

Maranzano pats the bench beside him. "*Buon giorno*, Salvatore. Come and sit. You must be tired, carrying such a heavy burden."

Lucky sits. The lion lies on open concrete, its body striped by the canted shadows of the tall iron bars. It is a male, old and dirty, and its mane is flecked with flies.

"Behold the king of beasts," Maranzano says, following Lucky's gaze. "Reduced to a life of captivity and humiliation. If he had known this to be his fate, I venture to guess he would have chosen instead an honorable death. At least, I prefer to imagine so."

Benny Siegel tenses as Maranzano removes a silver case from his pocket. He selects a thin cigar and lights it as Lucky watches.

"That is one important difference between man and beast," Maranzano continues, shaking out the match. "The beast is difficult to capture, but he is very easy to kill. With man, the opposite is true. *Nun si d'accordu?*"

Lucky shrugs. "I wouldn't know. I ain't never tried to capture nobody."

Maranzano chuckles. "No, of course you haven't. Today we associate the lion with gladiatorial contests held in the Coliseum, but it was actually the elephant that symbolized Roman power and privilege. Do you know your Roman history, Salvatore?"

"Can't say that I do."

"Indulge me, then, in a little story. When Caesar returned triumphant from Egypt in 46 B.C., he arrived at nightfall in the company of forty trained elephants bearing torches in their trunks. They marched alongside him, right up the steps of the Roman capitol. Caesar, you see, understood the power of spectacle. The power of symbols."

Maranzano turns to face the younger man. He takes hold of Lucky's chin. Siegel's hand moves into a pocket, but Lucky stops him with a look.

Maranzano is examining Lucky's scars, his drooping eyelid.

"Charlie Lucky," he says, withdrawing his hand. "The man who went for a ride and lived. That is powerful symbolism right there. Maybe the stuff of which legends are made. One should never under-estimate the power of symbols, Salvatore. They are invaluable to men like us—men who were born to command."

"If you say so."

"But of course, you already know this. Bringing the Jew, for example. That is making a statement. Do not for one minute imagine it is lost on me."

Lucky gives the man a second look. Maranzano is smart—maybe even as smart as they say. Although his accent is heavy, his command of the English language is impressive for so recent an immigrant. Charlie has heard that Maranzano once studied for the priesthood in Sicily.

"When this war is over, Salvatore, I intend impose a new order among our Sicilian brethren, all patterned after Caesar's Roman legion. *Decini* led by a *capo*. Each *capodecina* reporting to a *sottocapo*. Five *capo famiglia* in total, myself included, and no more of this nonsense where dozens of independent outfits are fighting each other for turf. Discipline and organization will be the new order of things. What do you think of such an idea?"

"I'm all for organization. Like the man said, the business of America is business."

"Precisely. And that would make you, Lucky Luciano, one of the five most powerful mafiosi in New York. Truly a man to be reckoned

119

with. A man to be respected, and a man to be feared. What are you now, thirty-five years of age?"

"Thirty-three."

"Thirty-three. So young. Do you believe you are prepared for that kind of responsibility?"

"Does that mean we got a deal?"

Maranzano smiles. He takes a final draw on his cigar before stamping it underfoot.

"What it means is that I've considered your proposal." Maranzano's eyes return to the lion. "I accept all of your conditions, but I also impose one of my own."

"What's that?"

"You, Salvatore, must be the one. As much as Giuseppe Masseria and I have disagreed, it simply would not do to have a Jew or an Irishman pull the trigger that ends his miserable life."

"What's that, another symbol?"

"No, my young friend, it is much more than that. Call it a question of honor. Me honoring him, and you honoring me. His death will come as a mercy. Don Giuseppe may be my enemy, but he is also Sicilian, and in his own way, he is a lion."

Maranzano nods to the cage.

"Even he deserves a better fate than this."

Nuova Villa Tammaro is crowded when Lucky arrives on Wednesday afternoon, but still Anna Tammaro hurries forward to greet him. She grabs a menu from the rack and leads her honored guest to a table in the rear of the restaurant, where Joe Adonis and Giuseppe Masseria have already tucked into heaping plates of antipasti.

Adonis stands, wiping his mouth with a napkin.

"Sorry I'm late," Lucky says as he sits, his eyes searching the surrounding tables for Masseria's bodyguards. "Geez, boss, I didn't know you was gonna be here too."

Masseria chews as he speaks. "When Joey told me where he was goin, I sez to myself Joe, you can kill two boids with one stone. You can eat at your favorite restaurant, and you can spend a little time with your most trusted soldier. Joey, pour Charlie Lucky some wine."

"No thanks, I got a long day ahead."

"Come on, Charlie. Piddu Morello and me, we used to sit for hours, just eatin and drinkin and talkin things out. Plannin for the future. I miss them conversations, so humor a lonely man and have a glass of wine."

The meal lasts over two hours, the antipasti followed by clams casino, and linguini with red clam sauce, and lobster Fra Diavolo. The dishes are served family-style, with the largest portion—the lion's share—taken by Masseria, who washes it down with a second bottle of nero d'Avola. The conversation ranges from Benito Mussolini to Gaspare Messina to the murder of Joe the Baker. By the time the cannoli arrive, the restaurant is almost empty.

"I gotta get goin soon," Lucky says, reading his watch.

Adonis grabs hold of his arm. "C'mon, Charlie, what's the rush? How's about a little cards?"

"Yeah," Masseria tells him. "You're always in a hurry. Relax a little. It's good for the digestion. And besides, we still got business to discuss."

Masseria unbuttons his vest as he leans back in his chair. He belches. One of the bodyguards is sent to procure playing cards from the kitchen.

"Hey, I just realized somethin," Masseria says as he shuffles. "You and me, Charlie, we ain't never played poker before. What kind of stakes you like?"

"Whatever you say, boss."

"I say nickels and dimes. You, Charlie, you're a big-shot gambler, but me, not so much. I don't trust things to chance. I think chance is for suckers. Ain't that right, Joey?"

Masseria deals. Lucky gathers his cards and fans them. He holds a pair of queens.

"Arnold Rothstein taught me one thing about poker," Lucky says, opening with a dime. "He said the mistake most guys make is that they only play the cards, but the cards even out in the end. The thing to do, if you want an edge over the long run, is to play the man."

"Call," Joey says.

Masseria slides two nickels into the pot. "What does that mean, 'play the man?' "

Lucky discards three.

"You know how some guys are. Set in their ways. Scared to take a chance. Easy to bluff. Or else too pigheaded to know when to fold."

Masseria nods. "Sure, I get it. Or maybe too cocky for their own good."

Lucky gathers his cards again. He frowns as he squeezes a peek at queens and sixes.

"Cocky's the worst of all," Charlie agrees. "Guys that get cocky, they're the ones who never know what hit 'em. I'll check."

"Check," Joey says.

"Dime. So what kind of gambler are you, Charlie? I think you play it close to the vest. Never give too much away."

"You read me like a book, Don Giuseppe. Dime and dime again."

"Hey, you can't check and raise!"

"Sure I can. I just did."

"Fold," Joey says.

"Okay then, fuck you. I call," Masseria says, slapping down three aces. "Read 'em and weep."

Charlie mucks his cards. Masseria cackles, his belly quivering under his vest.

"I'll always remember this day, Joey. Beatin Charlie Lucky in the first poker hand we ever played together."

Lucky checks his watch. It is three fifteen.

"I gotta take a leak. Go ahead and deal me in."

Lucky stands, and suddenly time seems to slow, as it will in a dream. He is crossing the empty dining room, his footfalls echoing on the polished hardwood as his gaze slides to the picture windows in front. There he sees Masseria's armored limousine, huge and black in the afternoon sun, while at the curb opposite he sees car doors opening and three men stepping into the street. Behind him, chairs are scraping. In the kitchen, the muffled clatter of pots and pans has ceased.

The bathroom is new, the tiles white and gleaming. Lucky steps to the toilet and unzips. Over the stream of his own water he hears the front door jingle, and then hurried footsteps, and then a shout.

Lucky pulls the chain. Four shots puncture the sound of swirling water as he steps to the sink and carefully washes his hands, shaking them once and running them through his hair, patting it into place. He tilts his head this way and that, studying his face in the mirror.

"Too big to ignore, Papa," he says aloud.

Lucky exits the bathroom. In the street beyond the windows, Masseria's limousine is gone. Benny Siegel, Vito Genovese, and Albert Anastasia are waiting for him at the table.

All have guns in their hands.

Masseria is slumped forward, moaning, his head resting on the table. Blood trickles down his chair, wetting the floor at his feet.

Using a napkin, Joe Adonis hands Lucky a revolver. It is a .38, snub-nosed and nickel-plated, heavy in Lucky's hands.

Lucky takes the gun and the napkin and stands directly behind Masseria. He places the muzzle at the back of the groaning man's head.

"So long, pal."

He fires a single shot.

Lucky steps back to examine his handiwork. Blood and brains spatter the tabletop while the rest of Masseria's body, toppled by the final bullet, lays faceup on the hardwood with the dark blood pooling around him in a kind of saintly aura. Lucky pictures the image in black-and-white, as it will appear on the front page of every evening newspaper.

Lucky wipes his prints from the gun. He flaps the napkin once, draping it over the dead man's face.

"Okay, let's go," he says, stealing a final backward glance at Joe the Boss. The dead man's hand, Lucky notices then, still clutches a playing card.

It is the ace of diamonds.

Eighteen

Saratoga

PERHAPS IT WAS inevitable that George Levy, a gambler by nature, would discover the twin diversions of golf and thoroughbred horse-racing, and that he'd find the ideal setting in which to pursue both these pastimes in the verdant, neo-Victorian ambience of Saratoga Springs, New York.

The historic Saratoga Race Course, America's oldest, officially opened for business on August 2, 1863, less than a month after the Civil War battle of Gettysburg. Known as the Graveyard of Champions, Saratoga was where Samuel D. Riddle watched his great steed Man o'War suffer its only lifetime defeat at the thundering hooves of the appropriately named Upset in 1919. And it was in the Travers Stakes of 1930 that America's second-ever Triple Crown champion, Gallant Fox, lost by eight lengths to the upstart Jim Dandy, an incredible 100-to-1 longshot.

After years of cajoling by his friend and client Mortimer Lynch, a professional bookmaker, George was finally persuaded to visit Saratoga in 1932 for what was promised to be a weekend of golf and relaxation in the mineral springs that had made the resort town famous. His guide for the occasion was to be Oscar Rhodes, a fellow Elk's Lodge member and the son of Walter Rhodes, who was a successful Freeport hotelier and the rear commodore of the South Shore Yacht Club.

Flamboyantly eccentric, with his signature monocle and walking stick, dandy young Oscar was only too happy to show Uncle Georgie the ropes, and George—having just emerged, exhausted but victorious, from the second of the notorious Dubert Armstrong vote-rigging trials in Queens—was only too happy to be shown. And so the unlikely pair made plans to meet that Friday evening at Throggs Neck to catch the last car ferry to Albany.

It was during the overnight boat passage that George had his first inkling of what he'd gotten himself into when, close to midnight, he was awakened by an urgent rapping on his stateroom door. Opening it, he faced an ashen Oscar Rhodes, who informed George that he'd been involved in a game called Spin the Top with "a couple of rough characters," and could he possibly borrow ninety-seven dollars until they made it to Saratoga?

At the racetrack the following day, Oscar led George past the queues and the touts and the ticket takers—all the way to the special clubhouse entrance, where, removing and fogging his monocle, he breezily inquired whether the guards there had received the fish he had sent them. One responded that he'd received no fish and, more to the point, where were Oscar's clubhouse passes? To which Oscar responded by flapping his gloves in the direction of the admissions supervisor.

"Harry, this is George," Oscar announced. "Don't worry, he's with me."

The day proceeded without incident, and George found himself captivated by the pageantry and excitement of the program. It was only after the seventh race that Mortimer Lynch, George's old client, pulled George aside to ask in a low voice how far Lynch should go in extending credit to this Rhodes fellow. Startled, George replied that as far as he knew, Oscar hadn't two nickels to rub together. In fact, George explained, he'd been lending Oscar five or ten dollars per race throughout the day, just to keep him occupied.

Lynch's face went as white as Wonder Bread.

"What's the matter?" George demanded.

"Hell, George. We figured if he was a friend of yours, he must be good for it."

"Good for what?"

"Why, the guy's been betting big all day. He's into us for around forty thousand dollars!"

As George looked on in horror, Lynch convened a hasty conference with his fellow bookmakers. In the midst of the shouting and finger-pointing, Oscar Rhodes blithely strolled in from the clubhouse bar, pulling up short in the doorway.

"Georgie," he said, eying the melee, "I think you've been talking . . ."

Sunday morning found George lighting the week's first cigar alongside three of his newer golfing buddies up to Saratoga from the Lakeville Club in Great Neck. Dave was a lawyer, Lou was a vaudeville actor, and Frank was a former bootlegger. The men had planned an early start to their round in order to make it to the track for the first post. They kicked off the day's wagers with a $250 Nassau as George regaled them with the tragic saga of Oscar Rhodes.

"Jesus Christ," Lou said, once the laughter had died. "What'd they do to the guy?"

"Nothing, I hope. He checked out of the hotel last night, and I haven't seen or heard from him since."

"That's the problem with on-track bookmaking," Frank said in his graveled voice, lighting his own first cigar. "Between the long shots and the welshers, those guys take a terrible risk. It's why we need pari-mutuel wagering in New York. I hear they're installing a tote board at Arlington Park in Chicago."

"Pari-mutuel wagering will never be legal in New York," Dave declared. "Hell, even Jimmy Walker couldn't fix that."

"Maybe," George replied, bending to tee up his ball. "Then again, maybe it's already legal."

"What do you mean, already legal? It's right there in the state constitution, plain as the nose on your face."

"I have a client who's running a dog track at the Mineola Fairgrounds," George informed the men as he took his practice swings. "He wants to install a totalisator for pari-mutuel wagering. He's got a scheme to make it work, and there's a Florida appellate court decision that says he might just succeed."

"Come on, Levy. What's the angle?"

"It's ingenious, really. You see, you don't *bet* on the dog, but rather you purchase an option to *buy* the dog. The option certificate costs two dollars, but if the dog wins, of course, then its value increases. In that event, the house will buy back your option certificate at a premium that's determined by the odds on the tote board."

Frank roared, a meaty hand on his belly. "You fucking lawyers. I gotta hand it to you."

"Why, that's a blatant subterfuge!" Dave sputtered. "It's not only illegal, it's . . . it's borderline unethical!"

"Is it? I contend it's no different than the commodities markets, where people buy options on things like soybeans and pork bellies all the time. They have no intention of ever taking possession. They're just betting the price will rise."

"Maybe so, but I still say it's illegal."

"You'll be pleased to know you're in good company, Dave, because that's what the district attorney thinks. I've invited him to settle the question in court."

George had caddied in his youth, and he'd been a star shortstop and quarterback in high school. Although relatively new to golf, his native athleticism had translated seamlessly from the diamond and the gridiron to the rolling links of his new country club.

George and Lou were two-handicaps, while Dave was a solid five. Frank, on the other hand, although known as a heavy gambler and a hail-fellow-well-met, was actually a terrible golfer—a fact that never diminished his enthusiasm for the game.

As the men teed off and the round progressed, their bets became ever larger and more exotic. By the time the foursome had reached the seventeenth tee, Frank stood to win over three thousand dollars if he only could break 99—a feat he'd never before accomplished but that, thanks to a front-nine score of 42, was well within his sights.

The seventeenth was a par three, with the tee box fronting a lake. The distance to the flag was only 170 yards, but the carry to a dry landing was over 130. George, Lou, and Dave had all reached the green safely. Frank was laying 89 for the round, with just the par-three seventeenth and the four-par eighteenth standing between him and a healthy payday.

Bogey-bogey was all it would take. For his tee shot, Frank had chosen a four iron.

"Press?" Lou inquired as Frank took a practice swing and then turned to the grinning men on the bench.

"Hell, yes. And I'll press you right back."

Higher mathematics ensued. All eventually agreed that the total bet was now $7,500.

Frank plucked some grass to test the wind. Licking his lips, he gave his club a final waggle as he stood over the ball, his hands fumbling for the perfect grip.

"Hundred bucks says it's in the drink."

"Geez, Frank. Sure you don't wanna use a practice ball?"

"Don't forget to breathe."

Frank stepped away. He took another practice swing as the lake before him grew to the size of the Great South Bay. Again he addressed his ball as the bench behind him fell mortally silent.

Thwack!

Frank had swung with everything he had. Swung so hard, in fact, that his clubhead had barely grazed the ball, which squibbed a few feet to the side. His four iron, however, rose in a majestic arc, rotating as it soared, eventually finding the center of the lake with a towering splash.

The laughter carried all the way to the clubhouse.

It was on the eighteenth fairway, after Frank had carded his triple-bogey six and then sliced his final drive into the rough, that Dave sidled up to George as the two men trailed after their caddies.

"I don't know if I've mentioned this," the lawyer said, his voice discreetly lowered, "but I have an application currently pending for a seat on the Supreme Court bench."

"Why, that's splendid, Dave! You'd make a wonderful judge."

"Thanks, George. It's something I've wanted my entire life. And not to be a burden, but I was wondering if you might put in a good word with Frank. I don't know him that well, but I know he respects you an awful lot."

"Frank? What's Frank got to do with it?"

"Come on, George. Quit kidding."

George stopped, turning to face his colleague.

"I'm not kidding. You have a fine reputation, and I'm sure the bar association will support you a hundred percent. What's Frank got to do with anything?"

"My God," the younger lawyer said, placing a hand on George's arm. "You really don't know, do you?"

"Know what?"

"Frank Costello is the power behind the throne at Tammany Hall. Rumor is he controls every patronage job and every public official in the state of New York."

Nineteen

Waxey Gordon

November 1933

THE OTHER MEN sprang to their feet as George Medalie entered the long conference room. Without speaking, the United States attorney for the Southern District of New York strode to the end of the twenty-foot table and sat. Two easels had been set up at the far end of the room, one on either side of a rolling blackboard covered with names and numbers, all written in a tight, precise hand.

Medalie checked his wristwatch. "Go," he said.

The other men sat as Tom Dewey stepped to the head of the table. He cleared his throat and pointed a pencil toward the blackboard.

"The defendant, Irving Wexler, was born in New York City in January of eighteen eighty-eight. His first arrest, for picking pockets, came at the age of nineteen when—"

"Stop," Medalie said. "That's backstory. Save the backstory for later, if you need it at all. Right now I'm a juror. Tell me why it's so

131

important that I'm here at the courthouse today instead of working to feed my family."

Tom swallowed. He turned to study the blackboard for a moment, and then he began again.

"The evidence in this case will show that the defendant, known among his underworld associates as Waxey Gordon, earned over four-and-a-half-million dollars during the years nineteen thirty and nineteen thirty-one from his various criminal enterprises, and yet he paid less than one hundred dollars in federal income taxes."

"Much better," Medalie said, shifting in his chair. "But let me ask you a question, Tom. Forget your opening for a second. You've been preparing this case for how long now?"

"I don't know. The better part of thirty months."

"You started with a single deposit slip, and since then you've had an army of lawyers, accountants, and T-men working two shifts per day for almost three years. How many bank records would you say you've examined during that time?"

Dewey looked to the seated men. "Over two hundred thousand, I'd guess."

"All for accounts under phony names. You've painstakingly matched deposits and withdrawals, following a paper trail from here to New Jersey to Pennsylvania and back again. You've interviewed a thousand witnesses, and traced over a hundred thousand telephone calls. You've reviewed letters, bills, receipts, loan records, truck registrations, insurance policies, and God knows what else until your eyes were practically bleeding. In short, you've been hacking your way through a forest of paperwork for so long that it's all you can see at night when you lay your head on the pillow."

"All right, so what's your point?"

"My point is, you've got to put a ruby-red nose on it. You've got to give the jurors something meaty, something juicy they can sink their teeth into. Something that sits in their gut and stays there for the rest of the trial. For example, how many cars does Wexler own?"

"Personally? He's got three Pierce-Arrows and a Cadillac limousine."

"There you go. I drive a Ford. Where does his kid go to school?"

"Staunton Military Academy."

"Mine goes to P.S. Nineteen. You see what I'm driving at? You're a bona fide savant, Tom, not to mention the most meticulous human being I've ever met. But in front of a jury, you need to forget all the hours you've logged and all the facts and figures you've gathered and collated and committed to memory. You need to step back for just a moment and ignore those trees and take a good, hard look at the forest. If you start out with numbers and dates and documents, you'll have the jury asleep before the first recess. What's the girl's name? That waitress who worked across from the brewery?"

"Helen Denbeck."

"Helen Denbeck. I even like the name. Okay, how about this? Gentlemen of the jury, we will prove that the accused, Irving Wexler, is the biggest bootlegger in America, and that he heads up a criminal enterprise that includes a dozen speakeasies, two hotels, five nightclubs, three warehouses, four garages, sixty delivery trucks, and at least three breweries in New Jersey alone. And do you know what else we'll prove? We'll prove that in the year nineteen thirty, when his income was nearly two million dollars, Mr. Wexler paid only ten dollars and seventy-five cents in federal income taxes. Why, that's barely enough money to fill the tanks of his three Pierce-Arrow automobiles, let alone his chauffeur-driven Cadillac.

"Now, in order to prove all this, we're going to show you a whole bunch of documents, and you'll be hearing from experts in the fields of accounting and banking, voice recognition and handwriting analysis. But you don't need a mountain of documents and a team of expert witnesses to know that a man who has two hundred bank accounts, a man who can afford to send his son to the Staunton Military Academy, a man who lives in a ten-room apartment on the Upper West Side and who maintains a luxury penthouse at the

Piccadilly Hotel, is cheating Uncle Sam when he declares eight thousand dollars in annual income. Oh, and by the way, we'll also prove that Mr. Wexler owns the Piccadilly Hotel.

"Now, Mr. Wexler, he's going to deny that he owns all this, because you know that a man who's crooked enough to be a big-time bootlegger is too crooked to put things in his own name, let alone to be bothered with paying taxes like the rest of us working stiffs. And that's where the documents and the experts will come in. But you'll also be hearing from ordinary folks like Helen Denbeck, who used to wait tables across the street from one of Mr. Wexler's breweries. She'll tell you how Mr. Wexler's employees used to come into her restaurant for lunch soaked in beer. She'll tell you about the truckers and armed bodyguards and keg rollers who came and went from Mr. Wexler's plant at all hours of the day and night, and about the lookouts who waved handkerchiefs in the street whenever the coast was clear for the beer trucks to roll.

"Once you've heard all this evidence, you gentlemen will be afforded a great privilege. You'll get to do what no crooked cop or feckless politician has been able or willing to do for the past dozen years. You'll get to act as the conscience of this community and throw the book at Mr. Wexler and send him to jail, where he belongs. So I'm going to sit down now and let Mr. Wexler's lawyer do his little dance, and then we can all get to the business we came here to do. I'm looking forward to it, and I know you are too, so thank you in advance for your service, and let's roll up our sleeves and get busy."

The room was silent. Then, one by one, the men began to clap.

"Gentlemen," Medalie said, showing his hands for quiet, "if you'll excuse us for a moment, I'd like to have a word with my chief assistant."

Chairs scraped and papers rustled as the other men stood and filtered out, closing the door behind them.

"Am I in some kind of trouble?"

"No, Tom, not at all. In fact, just the opposite. I wanted you to know how proud I am of the work you've done on this case. I don't think you realize how extraordinary it is for one man to have the tenacity it's taken to accomplish what you've been able to accomplish here. Never before, not even in the Capone trial, has a prosecutor faced the kinds of obstacles you've had to overcome. I'm talking about forged and altered bank records, and murdered witnesses, and local cops arresting federal agents. Do you remember what Wexler said to us that day we first questioned him?"

Tom smiled. " 'When you get your figures together so they prove something, come back and we'll talk again.' "

"He could afford to be cocky then. He had the D.A., the New York Police Department, the banks, and even the magistrate's court in his pocket. Everything he owned he'd hidden behind false names and dummy accounts. He was virtually untouchable—a crown prince living safely within the fortress of Tammany Hall, waving at the poor folks down below. But the thing he didn't count on was that there was one man standing among them with the patience and the fortitude to penetrate his castle keep."

"And the resources, thanks to you."

Medalie stood. He removed a silver dollar from his pocket and, as was his habit, worked it through his fingers as he paced.

"I have news, Tom, and I wanted my chief assistant to hear it first. I'm stepping down as United States attorney, effective at the end of next week."

"*What?*"

"I know it's sudden, but it can't be helped. In any event, I've done what I came here to do. I've hired new personnel, instituted new policies, and inculcated what I hope has been a renewed sense of purpose and determination. Our conviction rate is up to eighty-two percent, with nineteen of twenty-one verdicts affirmed on appeal. But this kind of trial work—this exhaustive, round-the-clock racket busting—is a young man's game. That's why next week a special panel of judges from the Southern District will appoint Thomas E. Dewey as the acting U.S. attorney until the A.G. chooses my replacement."

"Me? But . . . but what about—"

"The trial? Don't worry about that. I've timed it so that nobody can derail this case, even if they wanted to. You'll convict Waxey Gordon, Tom. And if we ever get our hands on Dutch Schultz, you'll convict him as well. A few months from now, you'll not only be the youngest man ever to hold the office of United States attorney for the Southern District of New York; you'll also be the most feared crime-buster this town has ever known. And if you play your cards right, you'll ride that reputation all the way to the governor's mansion."

Tom felt a little dizzy. He groped for the table, sinking into a chair.

"I don't know what to say."

Medalie laughed. "I'd suggest you say, 'I accept.' That way I can make a formal announcement tomorrow."

"You know I do. And George, I also want—"

"Stop. You don't need to say another word. This isn't a gift, you know. It's a promotion that you've earned, and you've earned it in spades. There's just one thing I'd ask you to keep in mind after I'm gone."

"What's that?"

"Seneca taught us that those who hold great power must wield it lightly. I've watched you these past few years, Tom—the sixteen-hour workdays, the obsessive perfectionism, the demands you've placed on the others. That's all fine for a chief assistant, but as the acting U.S. attorney, you'll need to be a leader as well as a commander, and those are very different roles. I don't think it would surprise you to hear that there are some in this office who think you're a pompous son of a bitch. 'The only man who can strut sitting down.' You've already won their admiration, Tom, grudging or otherwise. But starting next week, you'll also need to earn their respect."

"Yes, of course. I won't let you down, chief."

"I know you won't. I wouldn't be doing this if I had any doubts. But I also want you to remember something else. The only thing standing between order and anarchy in our society is the law, and the law is only as effective as the men who are charged with enforcing it. I'm not talking about the law that's found in statutes and casebooks. I'm talking about the verdicts that are rendered by juries every day in America's courtrooms."

He placed a hand on his young protégé's shoulder.

"In law school they teach us metallurgy, but in practice we learn how to weld. It's time to take up the blowtorch, Tom. Silver medals are great in track and field, but inside the courtroom, all that counts is the gold. You remember that, my boy, and the world will be your oyster."

Twenty

The Combination

"WHAT DO YOU mean you're on salary now?"

I was standing in the open doorway to the bathroom watching Jimmy shave his neck with my safety razor. You know how a guy will get sore when his girlfriend uses his razor on her legs? On account of the way it dulls the blade? With me and Jimmy, it was just the opposite, and I had the nicks on my shins to prove it.

"You heard me," he said. "Nick Montana's out. Charlie Spinach and Cockeyed Louis are on the way out. There's a new combination taking over their books."

"Says who?"

"Says Little Davie and Tommy the Bull."

"Tommy Pennochio? I thought that guy peddled dope."

"They both pedal dope. Only now they're moving into prostitution."

Jimmy told me this all matter-of-fact, like he's reading a weather report in the newspaper. Like there's a cold front moving into the area and I better drip my faucets so the pipes don't freeze.

"What the fuck are you even talking about?"

He rinsed off the razor and set it down on the sink. He took up his brush and painted more soap on his face.

"I told ya, Tommy and Davie are taking over. The bookers are going on salary, and everything's getting organized."

This was great. First Chicago, I thought, and now New York. And it figured it was the Italians who were the ones behind it. It was always the fucking Italians.

"So what's it mean for us, this new combination?"

"For one thing, it means you gotta start bonding again. Only now it's a regular thing. Ten dollars a week for each girl, and no exceptions for nobody."

"That's bullshit and you know it. Peggy Wild and Jenny the Factory ain't gonna pay no ten dollars a week."

"That's where you're wrong, Flo. Anybody tries to hold out, me and Little Abie, we pay 'em a visit. That's why we're on salary now."

I nudged him over and got my works out from under the sink. I kept them in an old Kotex box. I sat on the toilet and got out the spoon and lit the candle stub with a match. I broke off a quarter cube, on account of that cold front was moving in fast.

"How am I supposed to find girls if I gotta start charging 'em ten dollars a week and I got no booker?"

"That's the thing. Davie says that if everybody bonds, then after a while it becomes normal and nobody squawks. But if some madams hold out, then it ruins it for everybody. That's where me and Abie come in. And there's still gonna be bookers, just some new guys is all."

"What new guys?"

"Dave Miller and Pete Harris. And a guy named Jack Eller."

I fixed myself a shot while Jimmy watched in the mirror. It gave him the heebie-jeebies, he said, when the needle went in, but I noticed he always watched. I usually shot myself in the leg, up over the knee. That way it didn't show, and I could move it around. Taking three shots a day, my thighs looked like I had the chicken pox.

"What kind of a salary?"

"What's it to you?"

"What's it to me? First you were gonna be my butter-and-egg man, and now you tell me you're on salary to a couple of Mott Street hoodlums? Oh, and by the way, I gotta start bonding again? I ought to start charging you rent. I'll bet you wouldn't like that, would you?"

"How would you like I take that junk and flush it down the goddamn toilet?"

"I'd like to see you try it."

Most people who dealt with Jimmy Fredericks thought he was just a big ape. And while it was true that Jimmy could be a loud-mouth, and that ruffling feathers was part of his job description, the Jimmy I knew was more like a coconut—all hard and hairy on the outside, but actually soft and sweet once you cracked him open and got inside.

We had a lot in common, me and Jimmy. He'd had it pretty rough as a kid, and then he'd quit school when he was fourteen and started living on his own, just like I did. Only Jimmy wasn't real bright, so he'd done a few stretches in places like Elmira and Sing Sing and Dannemora. Most of his life, in fact, he'd been in and out of the slammer. In Dannemora, he told me, on account of him being so big, the bulls made him fight with the niggers. They'd bet money on him, like he was some kind of a dog. Then when he finally got paroled a few years ago, they just dumped him off at Grand Central where he wound up sleeping for weeks on a dirty mattress in a subway tunnel.

What did they expect a guy like Jimmy to do, get himself a job on Wall Street?

They're hypocrites, every last one of 'em. I've had clients who were lawyers and doctors and even a politician once I recognized from the newspapers. The same teetotaling bluenoses who talk all day about the evils of vice and corruption, then grab their high hats and stop by the local cathouse on the way home to the wife and kiddies.

It's enough to make you puke. Give me a choice between a hypocrite and an honest crook and I'll take the honest crook every day of the week.

And it ain't like jobs was growing on trees, even for the Ivy League college boys. So Jimmy done what he had to do, lifting himself up by his own bootstraps, and I respected him for that. He had moxie. It ain't like he enjoyed being a leg-breaker, but he had a wife to support, and that Lillian of his was a real piece of work. That's why he spent most of the week at my place. That's why I had nicks all over my shins.

"I need a lift uptown," Jimmy said, drying his face with a towel. "I'm meeting Tommy and Davie."

"At three in the morning?"

"You want I should take a cab, go ahead and say so."

Jimmy never did learn to drive, on account of him being either broke or behind bars for most of his life. But before you get the wrong idea about Jimmy, and think maybe I was soft in the head for putting him up and driving him around and everything, there's a few things you need to understand. For instance, when word gets around that you're Jimmy Fredericks's girl, ain't nobody gives you any trouble. Like that time Cockeyed Louis refunded my two hundred and fifty bucks bond money, and included an extra sawbuck for interest. You think anyone else ever got a refund, let alone interest? Or like whenever Cockeyed Louis or Charlie Spinach tried to send me some girl who was hopped up or on the rag, all's it took was one phone call to straighten things out.

Little things like that, believe me, they made a difference in this business.

Oh, and there's one other thing you should know about Jimmy Fredericks. You remember Wally the Whale, Pearl's old boyfriend from Cleveland? Well, I'm sure you get the picture.

My latest joint was a two-story brownstone on West End Avenue where I had a colored maid named Addie who changed the sheets and didn't steal the silver and kept her big mouth shut. I lived upstairs and usually used both the downstairs bedrooms for business, but they were empty right at that particular moment on account of business having ended an hour ago. So my choices were to drive Jimmy uptown to his meeting or else to lay in bed and listen to Jack Armstrong on the radio.

I grabbed my keys off the dresser.

"Thirty-five bucks," Jimmy said after we'd rounded the block and turned uptown onto Broadway.

"What?"

"My salary. You wanted to know. It's thirty-five a week."

I started to say something but decided to hold my tongue. Back when he was working with Jerry Bruno, Jimmy was making fifty, sometimes even a hundred bucks a week.

"Go ahead and say it."

"Say what?"

"You think I'm a sap for sticking my neck out for a lousy thirty-five bucks."

I looked over at Jimmy. His face was turned to the sidewalk, and his fists were balled in his lap. Maybe it was the morphine, or the hour, or the wounded expression I pictured on his face, but I didn't have the heart to tell him that was exactly what it was I'd been thinking.

"Listen, honey. At least you're still in the racket. That beats selling apples in the park."

One of his fists opened up, and he reached over and patted my knee.

The drive was seventy blocks, and when we pulled to the curb outside a Chinese joint near 130th Street, Jimmy leaned over and gave me a peck on the cheek.

"Don't wait up, Flo. Sleep tight, and don't let the bedbugs bite."

The joint was dark inside, and a Closed sign hung in the door. I watched Jimmy walk into the restaurant and take a seat by the window. It looked like there were three other guys in the booth.

None of them stood. None of them offered to shake his hand.

Twenty-One

Boss of Bosses

May 1934

CHARLIE LUCKY AND Frank Costello watch from the shade of the open-air terminal as the Sikorsky S-40 flying boat trims its engines and glides like an overfed goose toward the crowded passenger dock. Men scramble and shout as fenders are readied and lines tossed and the hulking seaplane is captured and turned and lashed to its moorings.

"Right on time," Costello says, reading his watch.

A floating platform is lowered into the water just fore of the dockside wing. Only then does the passenger door open and a uniformed hostess alight. She is young and blonde and wearing the smart blue uniform of Pan American Airways. She steps to the auxiliary platform and helps the other passengers as they duck their heads and descend from the still-rocking aircraft into the blinding Florida sunshine.

"There he is."

Costello nods to the tanned little man in the white guayabera shirt who is stepping down from the plane. Once on the dock, the man sways his hips and with his free hand twirls the laughing hostess in an impromptu cha-cha step.

"Christ. Guy's been gone for a week and he thinks he's Xavier Cugat."

From his dockside rhumba and from the smile still lighting Meyer Lansky's burnished face, the men know that their friend's mission to Cuba has been a success. It's only the details that concern them now as they stroll toward the baggage claim area.

"Somethin tells me that's an empty briefcase you got in your hand," Lucky says as Lansky stops amid the throng of arriving passengers and draws a cigar from his shirt pocket and runs it under his nose.

"Not exactly. I got my dirty laundry inside."

"We'll take your word on that one."

The old friends embrace. Meanwhile, two men from the Santo Trafficante's outfit in Tampa are pacing, watching them from the curb. Charlie raises a finger, indicating they'll be ready in a moment, and then guides Lansky to a quieter corner of the terminal.

"We want any privacy, now's the time to talk."

Lansky lights the cigar, turning it slowly over the flame.

"Gentlemen," he says, shaking and tossing the match, "if there was a mirror on that wall over there, you'd be looking at the new casino managers of the Hotel Nacional. We also have the gaming license, the rights to develop our own luxury hotel and casino, and an island-wide exclusive on slot machines and pari-mutuel wagering. I tried for the parking meters, but you know what the colonel told me? He said if he gave those away, even the president would notice."

"You beautiful bastard. So what's Batista's end?"

"Three million down, with a credit for our little gift. After that it's a percentage of our gross against a sliding-scale guarantee. I'll lay it out for you later. But the important thing is, we need to have the three mil on deposit in Zurich by the first of July. Once that happens, we can start moving our people into the casino. And Frankie's slots, of course. That is if La Guardia hasn't impounded them all by then. Excuse me, Tracey?"

The hostess in the blue uniform turns at the sound of her name.

"Tracey, these are my friends Frank and Charlie from New York. We're having a little celebration tonight at the Biltmore. We'd be delighted to have you join us as our special guest."

"Why, thank you Mr. Meyers, but I lay over tonight in Havana."

"Such a shame. Next time, perhaps."

Costello holds his tongue until the girl is out of earshot.

"Okay, so Batista gets our money. But what do we get besides a greasy handshake?"

"Don't worry, Frankie, it'll all be nice and legal. Better than legal. It'll be backed by the full faith and credit of the Cuban army."

Once the luggage is ready, Lucky signals to Trafficante's men, one of whom turns and whistles. Within moments, three black Cadillac Fleetwoods pull forward to the curb. While one man opens the trunk of the middle car, another hurries for Lansky's suitcase. A third man holds the rear door open for the three honored guests from New York.

The drive from Dinner Key to the Biltmore Hotel is fifteen minutes, and after some terse and coded conversation, the three friends lapse into a shared silence, each lulled by the rush of ocean air and the steady drone of the Cadillac's powerful V-16 engine.

Lucky finds himself, as he often does lately, dwelling on the past. In this case, on how the imperial reign of Salvatore Maranzano had proved to be so short-lived, its downfall hastened by an ill-considered ceremony in which the newly crowned Caesar, addressing a blue-ribbon assembly of the nation's top mafiosi, declared himself *capo di tutti capi* to which all in attendance must pay homage. He then unveiled his new organizational plan, further alienating the hard-eyed men who'd been led to believe that their two bloody years of street combat had been a war of independence.

It wasn't long before these same men were turning to Lucky Luciano for counsel. Not just Masseria loyalists like Vito Genovese, Tom Gagliano, and Carlo Gambino, but also those who'd fought on the Maranzano side. Men like Joe Bonnano, and the estimable Joe Profaci.

What had been touted by Maranzano as the dawn of a new era of peace and prosperity had proved to be a summer of disillusionment and anger, in which men already bent by the twin hardships of Depression and gang warfare were soon bowed by the heavy thumb of yet another imperious Mustache Pete. Adding to that burden was Maranzano's ill-conceived battle with Louis "Lepke" Buchalter over control of the Amalgamated Clothing Workers, a fight in which civilian casualties were again garnering unwanted newspaper headlines.

For Lucky, the penultimate straw came in May of 1931, at a meeting called to prepare for a planned national crime summit in Chicago. When Lucky mentioned that Meyer Lansky would be part of his delegation, Maranzano replied, "The Jew can come, but he can't be in the room when we meet." The final straw came soon after, when rumors of a Maranzano hit list that included Luciano and his so-called Broadway Mob of Vito Genovese, Frank Costello, and Joe Adonis began making the rounds.

It was, Lucky concluded, either kill or be killed.

While the impetus came from Lucky, the final plan was vintage Meyer Lansky. Maranzano, Lansky had learned, was the subject of an ongoing Internal Revenue audit, thus presenting a perfect ruse by which to separate the new boss from his omnipresent bodyguards. Lansky hired Red Levine to assemble a team of Jewish hit men to pose as revenue agents. On the appointed day—Thursday, September 10, 1931—four briefcase-wielding torpedoes arrived at Maranzano's headquarters in the New York Central Building, where they retired to an inner office and then butchered the Boss of Bosses with carving knives.

A fittingly symbolic end, Lucky thought, for a man who aspired to be Caesar.

Only later did Lucky learn that while Red Levine's men were making their getaway, they'd passed Vincent "Mad Dog" Coll in the stairwell. Coll, a notorious killer for hire, had apparently been given the Maranzano contract on Luciano. Upon learning that his employer had been killed, Coll coolly turned around and followed Levine's men down the stairs, pocketing his twenty-five-thousand-dollar advance.

"What're you smiling at?" Lansky asks.

"Elephants with torches."

"What?"

"Nothing. I was only daydreamin."

With Maranzano out of the way, Lucky moved quickly to consolidate power. He embarked on a national goodwill tour in which he personally assured both friend and wary foe alike that Charlie Luciano harbored no sovereign ambitions, but instead sought to foster real cooperation, and regional autonomy, and the establishment of a national crime commission to demark territories and settle disputes.

Styling himself as the anti-Maranzano—as a modern American businessman working to create an environment in which all might prosper—Lucky managed to achieve in a few short months of suitcase diplomacy that which had eluded three generations of Sicilian strong-men with their stilettos and their garrotes and their interminable bloodshed.

And so the son of Antonino and Rosalia Lucania from First Avenue was now the de facto head of organized crime in America.

While Charlie is lost in his memories, Frank Costello, his gaze out the driver's-side window, is also deep in thought. Frank has the utmost respect for Meyer Lansky, but he worries about his old friend's naïveté when it comes to Fulgencio Batista. It was Frank, after all, who'd slapped the backs and greased the palms of every city alderman and state assemblyman in New York. It was Frank who rubbed elbows with the judges and congressmen, who broke bread with the governors and senators, and whose name appeared in the little black books of every political operative working this side of the Mississippi.

Meyer is smart all right, Frank thinks, and maybe he's even a genius, but what does he know about politics?

Take the FDR debacle as an example. With Hoover on the ropes and the Oval Office just waiting for whoever could win the Democratic nomination for president, it was Meyer and Charlie who'd wanted to back Al Smith. Frank could still recall their first discussion at the Hotel Claridge, when he'd explained to his friends that with two New Yorkers as the Democratic front-runners, the road to the White House ran straight through Tammany Hall. At the Democratic National Convention in Chicago, the New York delegation would hold unprecedented sway and could, he'd told them, if they played their cards right, actually decide the outcome.

Smith, it was true, had been a longtime friend and ally. A machine pol of the old school, the Happy Warrior had carried their water in Albany for years, and had a mattress full of their money to show for it. But Smith was a Catholic, Frank had argued, which all but disqualified him in a national contest. Even if Roosevelt was a gimp and a high-hat, Frank was certain that the Harvard man and fifth cousin of Teddy Roosevelt would be the preferred candidate of the other states' delegations.

As the convention approached, both camps pleaded for Frank's endorsement. They would, as he told Meyer and Charlie, suck his cock in Macy's front window if that's what it took to win the support of Tammany Hall. Now was the time, Frank argued, to dump Smith and strike a deal with Roosevelt. They could bargain for an end to the Seabury investigation, or for replacing George Medalie as U.S. attorney, or for keeping Jimmy Walker as mayor.

But Charlie and Meyer were loyal—Frank has to give them that—and so when they all arrived in Chicago, it was at the Drake Hotel, Smith's campaign headquarters, that they took their six-bedroom suite. And while the hookers ebbed and the booze flowed, Frank watched with quiet resignation as the national delegates moved inexorably toward Roosevelt. It was a once-in-a-lifetime opportunity to expand their reach all the way into the White House, and now it was lost forever.

They were still weathering the fallout. The Seabury Commission's crusade against public corruption had ushered in a new wave of reform politicians, from Herb Lehman in Albany to Butch La Guardia in New York. "Good government" was all the rage, and organized crime the national bogeyman. Worst of all, in a direct rebuke to Tammany Hall, a Democratic president had allowed Tom Dewey, an unabashed Republican, to remain in office as acting U.S. attorney for the Southern District of New York.

So what does Meyer really know about the political situation in Havana? Nothing, that's what. Betting the house on Batista is like betting on Masseria in the Castellammarese war, another Lansky blunder. Thank God Charlie had bailed them out of that one. But even Charlie Lucky couldn't shoot his way out of a malarial rat-hole like Cuba.

"Everything okay?" Meyer asks, patting Frank's knee.

"Sure. Just tired is all."

Meyer Lansky nods. He, too, is tired—exhausted, in fact, after a solid week of breakfast meetings, working lunches, cocktail summits, and ceremonial dinners. If only his friends could be made to fully appreciate the importance of what they've just accomplished—what *he's* just accomplished—in being the first foreign investors to wet their beaks in the heady nectar of Cuban tourism.

"Diversification" is the watchword now, and with Prohibition ended, gambling is the locomotive that will pull their gravy train. Frank, of all people, should understand that. He'll soon have his slots—thousands of them—in every hotel in Havana, just as he recently moved into Louisiana, thanks again to Meyer's efforts.

Come to think of it, Batista isn't very different from Huey Long. Both are personally ruthless, and politically adroit, and as greedy as Old King Midas. Not only will they make millions in Havana, Meyer is certain, but they'll also launder millions more from their various stateside interests. Instead of sitting there fretting like an *alter cocker*, Frank should be thanking him on bended knee.

Diversification. They have carpet joints in New Orleans, Palm Beach, Hot Springs, and Saratoga. In New York they have the unions and the industrial rackets, as well as loan sharking and protection. They have hotels and, of course, they have nightclubs. Plus they have stakes in dozens of legitimate businesses, from dairies and bakeries to real estate and trucking. And they have drugs and the Italian lottery. Each of the men sitting beside him is clearing over five million a year and, once Dutch Schultz is dead or behind bars, they'll move into the uptown policy, which represents another fifty million gross.

On a cash-flow basis, they'll soon be bigger than U.S. Steel.

As far as booze goes, Meyer and his friends part company. Charlie seems to think that once they liquidate their inventories, they'll be out of the game entirely. To Meyer, this is shortsighted. Although legally barred from the liquor business, they could still parlay their old alliances and distribution channels into profits, since bootleg booze is cheaper than liquor that's taxed. Frank understands this, and so does Joey. Charlie will soon come around. But Meyer has another idea—one that will take it even further.

It's like the California gold rush, Meyer has told his father-in-law. Some prospectors got rich and some went bust, but none did better than the men who sold the shovels.

In November Meyer formed Molaska Corporation, and thanks to the side deal he's just negotiated with Colonel Batista, Molaska will soon be importing Cuban molasses by the boatload. They'll open a factory in Cleveland, in Moe Dalitz's territory, and while the front room is making table sugar, the loading dock will be delivering raw material to every distillery in the country.

This is diversification of another kind—the first salvo in Meyer's own little war of independence. He has repeatedly warned Frank and Charlie to keep their names out of the newspapers. Look what happened to Legs Diamond, he's told them, and to Waxey Gordon, and will soon be happening to the Dutchman. Think of Icarus, he said, and then, of course, had to explain the allusion.

It's obvious to Meyer that the national mood is changing. Gangsters, once viewed as modern-day Robin Hoods, are lately considered crumbs—and worse, as leaches sucking the lifeblood from a newly anemic nation. Nowadays the public wants scalps, and the politicians want headlines. And when they come for Lucky's scalp, Meyer is planning to be ready.

The cars are passing under a double row of palm trees, approaching the hotel entrance. When they pull to a stop at the curb, Trafficante's men alight.

"If you'll wait here, gentlemen," their captain says, and the three friends sit and watch as the bodyguards enter the lobby of the same hotel where, just five years earlier, their old friend Fatty Walsh famously met his maker.

A signal is given, and the rear doors open wide.

"Meyer! Don Luciano!"

Santo Trafficante stands in the cavernous lobby, his arms thrown open in greeting. Forty-three years old, Trafficante is short and powerfully built, with the rugged face of a prizefighter. He embraces his old friend Meyer, then bends to kiss the hand of Charlie Lucky.

"All right, Santo, I ain't the fuckin pope. I don't think you've met my consigliere, Frank Costello."

The men shake hands. "It's good to finally meet you, Frank. I've heard so many good things. And this is my son, Santo Junior. Santo, may you always remember the day that you met the Boss of Bosses, Charlie Luciano."

Trafficante's kid doesn't look like much to Lucky. He's around twenty, taller than his old man, but softer too—like a college boy, with thick eyeglasses and a limp handshake. Charlie wonders why Santo has brought him all the way to Miami.

"My men will check you in and bring your keys to my suite. Come, it's this way, right next to the swimming pool."

Two of the bodyguards fall in beside them as they make their way through the lobby and out a glass door and down an open-air loggia echoing with laughter and the sounds of water splashing. Soon Charlie is gazing over the largest swimming pool he's ever seen, the turquoise oblong studded with emerald and sapphire and ruby swimsuits.

"I have a cabana reserved for the weekend," Trafficante says, waving toward the pool, "and I made starting times for tomorrow morning if you'd like to play golf. The room is just ahead."

Once inside the luxury suite, Trafficante dismisses his bodyguards. He latches the door and lowers the window blinds. The four men are alone now, with Junior in the kitchen wrestling the cork from a bottle of French champagne. They take seats in the spacious living room, the sofas plush and white. Stacked on the coffee table is a pyramid of bundled C-notes totaling fifty thousand or so by Lucky's estimation.

"It sure was a shame about Waxey," Trafficante says, waiting for Junior to finish topping the men's glasses before raising his own in a toast. "I know you had your differences, Meyer, but he sure made a lot of guys rich. *Salute!*"

They all touch glasses, the euphonic chime of crystal filling the suite.

"Waxey was already history," Meyer says, draining his glass and setting it on the table. "If Dewey hadn't nailed him, then the Dutchman certainly would have. The feds could've saved themselves the trouble."

"The fucking Dutchman." Trafficante shakes his head. "I was just telling Santo he is . . . what's the word again?"

"Anachronism," Junior says.

"Exactly. A man out of place with his time. Like your man Maranzano, all bang-bang and rat-a-tat-tat. Good for headlines, but not so good for business."

Lucky sets down his glass and takes up a packet of bills. He riffles it with his thumb.

"Some guys when they was kids, Santo, they never learned to play nice. Take Charlie Wall for instance."

Trafficante's glass pauses halfway to his mouth. He sets it back on the table.

"So, you've heard of my little problem."

"Your problem ain't so little, Santo. Wall has friends on the commission. I can't come down here and wave a magic wand."

"But my father thought—"

"*Zittite*! Never question Don Luciano!"

The kid goes white at his father's outburst. He sets the bottle on the table and crosses to the windows, where he pinches the blinds and looks out toward the swimming pool, his toe tapping impatiently on the carpet.

"You know I'll do what I can, Santo, but there's interests on both sides of this. If I go around sayin Wall's out and Trafficante's in, then I'm no different than Masseria or Maranzano. And to be perfectly honest, I don't have that kind of juice."

Lucky tosses the packet of bills to Trafficante, who catches it and sets it back atop the others. The older man sighs.

"I understand, of course. When Iggy Antinori and I disagreed, we sat down like gentlemen and worked out our differences. But this Wall, he is like your Dutchman, who knows only the gun. I'm not afraid for myself, Charlie, you know that. But if we start losing shipments, I'm worried that our friends in Corsica might begin to have second thoughts."

"That would be a problem," Meyer agrees, lighting a cigarette.

"You want my advice, Santo? I say let Antinori and Wall shoot it out. If you're lucky, maybe they'll knock each other off. Meanwhile, you keep your head down and your powder dry, and just be ready when the time comes to step in and pick up the pieces."

"The same strategy you used in the Castellammarese war?"

"Somethin like that. Only do me a favor, willya? Don't get your ass caught in the cross-fire. We're gonna need a friend we can trust when things heat up in Havana."

At the sound of the knock, Trafficante stands and crosses the room. He squints through the peephole, then slides the latch and throws the door open.

"*Surprise!*"

The girls wear skimpy swimwear and very high heels. They are tanned and long-legged, and each has a room key tied with a ribbon around her neck.

"Ladies," Trafficante says, taking one on either arm. "I'll trust you to escort my special guests to their rooms. And when you get there, be sure to show them everything there is that Miami has to offer."

Twenty-Two

Madman

June 1934

"YOU HEARD ME. I demand that you try my client for murder."

Elvin Edwards, the district attorney of Nassau County, already knew he had one madman on his hands. Now, it appeared, he was dealing with two.

"What the hell are you talking about?" he demanded of his old friend and nemesis, George Morton Levy. "Your man's an escaped lunatic who's lucky he isn't on death row. Now you want me to put him there?"

"I want to exonerate him, and to clear his name, and that means you putting him on trial for murder."

George's client, the notorious Joseph Ustica, was indeed an escapee from the King's Park State Hospital for the Criminally Insane, to which he'd been committed in 1928, thereby avoiding trial for the bludgeoning murder of William Gilbride, a wealthy Long Island sport fisherman. That sensational killing, the legal wrangling that followed, and his dramatic escape from the asylum in 1930 had made Ustica both a household name and a kind of regional bogeyman to whom several subsequent murders had been attributed. For years, Long Island parents had coerced their recalcitrant children with the threat that "Ustica will get you if you don't behave!"

The peculiar saga of Joseph Ustica had begun in July of 1928, when Gilbride's burlap-wrapped body was discovered near a wooded lane in Bellmore, four miles from the Freeport restaurant in which he'd last been seen alive. That waterfront dive was jointly owned by Ustica, a shell-shocked veteran of the Great War, and Anthony D'Apolito, a petty criminal and suspected rum runner. Ustica's car had been found abandoned two miles from the body, with Gilbride's bloodstains on the backseat. When an eyewitness—Lucille McDermott, the owner of a Freeport employment agency—placed all three men together at lunch on the day Gilbride went missing, police arrested Ustica and D'Apolito and charged them both with Gilbride's murder.

After days of coercive questioning, Ustica became unstable. His attorney, Peter Beck, promptly moved for a trial continuance and a mental evaluation of his client. This led to Ustica's involuntary commitment at King's Park until such time as he might be deemed competent to stand trial.

D'Apolito, meanwhile, had hired Fiorello La Guardia as his attorney, and La Guardia had retained Charlie Weeks—the same Long Island lawyer who'd been district attorney back in the Louis Enright peat-to-gasoline case—as D'Apolito's local counsel. To Weeks, D'Apolito admitted having struck Gilbride with a rolling pin, but insisted that it was Ustica who'd then delivered the fatal blow with a tire iron. Together the men had wrapped Gilbride's body in burlap, dragged it to Ustica's car, and deposited it in the woods.

With Ustica institutionalized and unable to testify, Weeks and Edwards struck a deal by which D'Apolito would plead guilty to a lesser charge of manslaughter, thereby avoiding the death penalty, and would be sentenced instead to a maximum of twenty years in state prison.

And so with D'Apolito in Sing Sing and Ustica safely at King's Park, the case of the William Gilbride bludgeoning murder was finally and officially closed.

That is, until Ustica escaped.

During his years as a fugitive, Ustica's name would crop up in connection with every unsolved homicide on the eastern seaboard, or so it seemed, garnering headlines from Plattsburgh, New York, to Pittsburgh, Pennsylvania. As his notoriety grew, so, too, did the tales of his savagery and cunning. So imagine George Levy's surprise when, on a blustery afternoon in February, Joseph Ustica's elderly parents appeared in George's office, begging him to take their son's case.

"How can I," asked George, "when nobody even knows where he is?"

"We know where he is."

"Well, then, either bring him in or stop talking about it. Otherwise we'll all be arrested for harboring a known criminal."

And so Ustica surrendered. To George's surprise, his new client appeared to be a gentle soul—a little fragile, perhaps, but as sane as any man. Even more surprising was that when Ustica professed his innocence in connection with the murder of William Gilbride, George actually believed him.

And therein lay a dilemma.

"You can avoid trial and return to King's Park," George explained, "or you can stand trial for murder and risk the death penalty."

"Then let's go to trial, Mr. Levy, because I'd rather die than go back to that loony bin."

George's first order of business was to have Ustica examined by experts and declared by a court to be mentally competent. His next hurdle—the one that found him in Elvin Edwards's office—was to convince the district attorney to prosecute Ustica for the Gilbride murder.

"George, you're as crazy as he is," Edwards said. "This case is closed. Why not leave well enough alone?"

"Because the man's reputation is at stake, not to mention his freedom. What's the matter, Elvin? Are you afraid that if Ustica's found innocent, your deal with D'Apolito won't look so good with the voters?"

"But Ustica's not innocent. Hell, everybody knows that. D'Apolito will say so, and an independent eyewitness will corroborate him. And besides, Gilbride's blood was all over Ustica's car!"

"There you go," George said, lighting a cigar. "Now all you have to do is prove it."

The trial of Joseph Ustica for the 1928 murder of William Gilbride finally began on June 6, 1934, before the Honorable Cortland A. Johnson and a packed courtroom on Franklin Avenue in Garden City. And no sooner had the trial begun than matters took a strange and unexpected turn.

Transported from Sing Sing to appear as the star witness for the prosecution, Anthony D'Apolito, Ustica's erstwhile partner and co-defendant, flatly refused to testify.

"But you can't plead the Fifth!" an angry Judge Johnson thundered at the witness in chambers. "Double jeopardy precludes your retrial for murder!"

"I don't care," said D'Apolito. "I ain't talking."

"Then you'll leave me no choice but to hold you in contempt. That means prison!"

"I'm already in prison."

"I'll add time to your sentence!"

"What, an extra six months? C'mon, Judge, don't make me laugh."

So while the prosecution lost a key witness, George Levy gained a valuable insight. If D'Apolito had nothing to lose, yet remained unwilling to testify, then who, George wondered, was he still trying to protect?

Undaunted, the district attorney called as his next witness the estimable Lucille McDermott. A proud woman of regal bearing, Mrs. McDermott described to the jury her visit to the Freeport restaurant on the day of the murder, where she'd seen both Ustica and D'Apolito eating lunch with William Gilbride. Ustica's car, she testified, had been parked just outside the restaurant. Gilbride had been drinking heavily, and with each drink order would produce from his pocket a thick wad of cash.

George began his cross-examination of Lucile McDermott gingerly, working purely from an instinct honed by nearly twenty-five years at the bar.

Why had a woman like her been at such a seedy restaurant in the first place? She'd come, McDermott testified, to upbraid the owners for constantly firing waitresses she'd sent from her employment agency.

Wasn't it unusual for a customer to pay cash for each drink as it was ordered? That was the policy D'Apolito had instituted at the restaurant.

How did she know the restaurant's drink policy? It was one of the issues about which the waitresses had complained to her.

How did she recognize Ustica's car? She assumed it was his car because Ustica had been sitting in it when she'd first arrived at the restaurant by taxi.

The woman seemed to have a ready answer for each of his questions, and the longer she testified in her stiff and imperious manner, the louder the alarm bells sounded inside George Levy's skull. Something wasn't right, but George couldn't put his finger on exactly what it was. Finally, he asked an innocuous question that provoked an unusual response.

"Where do you currently reside, Mrs. McDermott?"

"That's none of your business. I don't have to answer that."

After the judge informed her otherwise, she grudgingly replied, "Franklin Avenue."

George raised an eyebrow.

"Where on Franklin Avenue?"

She shifted uneasily in her chair. "Fifteen hundred."

"I'm sorry?"

"I said fifteen hundred!"

Now both eyebrows were up.

"Why, that's the Nassau County Jail, isn't it?"

Lucille McDermott didn't respond.

"And you're an inmate at the jail, isn't that correct?"

Again no reply.

"For what crime are you presently incarcerated in the Nassau County Jail?"

This time the judge required an answer.

"Check forgery," the witness sobbed, collapsing forward in her chair.

The dam was broken then, and the truth poured out with the tears. Yes, she'd gone to the restaurant that day. No, it wasn't on business. Yes, she and D'Apolito had been lovers. No, Ustica wasn't present when she'd arrived. Yes, she'd witnessed Anthony D'Apolito murder William Gilbride. No, Ustica had not been involved. Yes, D'Apolito had taken Ustica's car to dispose of the body.

George's acquittal of the notorious madman was a tabloid sensation. Doubly satisfying, in light of the Louis Enright debacle, was that George had won the case without having to put his vulnerable client on the witness stand.

Twenty-Three

Runaway Jury

June 1935

WHILE FEDERAL PROSECUTORS working first under George Medalie and then under Thomas E. Dewey grabbed national headlines with their high-profile racketeering and public corruption convictions, their state counterparts under Manhattan district attorney Thomas C. T. Crain seemed almost moribund by comparison.

While Crain had convened grand juries to investigate both the 1928 murder of Arnold Rothstein and George F. Ewald's 1930 purchase of his own magistrate's robes, neither grand jury returned an indictment. Meanwhile, the extent of Crain's efforts against the policy and industrial racketeers who were terrorizing the city and draining an estimated half-billion dollars each year from the local economy was to post a "Complaints" box in the hallway outside his office door.

The janitors emptied the box every evening at six.

But this institutional indifference to organized crime ended with a bang once the March 1935 New York County Grand Jury was impaneled.

The grand jury, a British gift to American jurisprudence, is an assembly of twenty-three ordinary citizens tasked with hearing evidence and, if they believe the evidence so warrants, voting indictments against criminal wrongdoers. Because grand jury proceedings are conducted in secret, both to protect the innocent and to confound the guilty, no judge is allowed in the grand jury room, nor are counsel for the witnesses or the targeted malefactors. The purpose of a grand jury proceeding is not to adjudicate guilt or innocence, but simply to determine whether probable cause exists to bring a person to trial.

At the state level, evidence is presented to the grand jury by an assistant district attorney, who serves as the jury's gatekeeper and adviser. A grand jury also has the power to conduct independent investigations, write reports, and issue subpoenas to compel the testimony of witnesses.

Lee Thompson Smith, the pugnacious president of the New York County Grand Jurors Association, was elected foreman of the March 1935 grand jury. William Copeland Dodge, another Tammany Hall stalwart who'd succeeded Thomas Crain as district attorney in 1934, assigned his youngest and least-experienced deputy, Lyon Boston, to serve as the grand jury's adviser. When Boston suggested that prostitution and Communism—rather than, say, racketeering or public corruption—might be worthy subjects for the grand jury's attention, the enraged Smith took the unprecedented step of barring Boston from the grand jury room and instead hired Samuel Marcus, the former counsel for the Society for the Prevention of Crime, to act as the grand jury's attorney.

Unmoored from both the constraints and cooperation of the district attorney's office, the Smith grand jury sought to undertake an independent investigation into the twin scourges of policy—

the so-called numbers racket—and corrupt bail bonding. Dodge, incensed by Smith's impudence, actively obstructed the grand jury's efforts, at one point even refusing to authorize the payment of twenty dollars in travel expenses requested by a witness whom the grand jury had subpoenaed.

The situation quickly devolved into an acrimonious stalemate, with attorney Marcus resigning his unofficial post in frustration.

As this very public standoff between district attorney and grand jury foreman dragged into its third month, newspapers and civic groups, churches and bar associations joined in the chorus decrying Dodge as the stooge of Tammany assemblyman Jimmy Hines. Dodge, for his part, railed against the "runaway grand jury," proclaiming, "I don't intend to surrender!"

Having exhausted all other remedies, foreman Smith finally pleaded his case directly to Governor Herbert H. Lehman, requesting the appointment of a special prosecutor "of unusual vigor and ability" to act independently of Dodge in investigating and prosecuting New York public corruption.

Bending to this shift in the political winds, Lehman announced in early June his intention to call an extraordinary term of the state supreme court and to appoint an independent prosecutor whose task it would be to root out organized crime and civic corruption in New York County. And to blunt any suggestion of whitewash, Democrat Lehman appointed a staunchly Republican jurist to preside over this extraordinary term, in the person of sixty-three-year-old New York Supreme Court Justice Philip J. McCook.

McCook, a flinty New Englander, was a veteran of the Great War and a scion of the famous "fighting McCooks of Ohio" who'd burnished his crime-busting credentials as the presiding judge in the Westchester County land fraud scandals. McCook had also, just eighteen months earlier, administered the oath of mayoral office to his close friend and political ally, Republican Fiorello La Guardia.

More problematic for Lehman was the question of whom to select for the role of special prosecutor—the man whose task it would be to work hand-in-glove with McCook and a newly empaneled special grand jury. Lehman's decision was freighted with considerations more political than practical. The chosen candidate could, for example, demand enormous resources, and any parsimony on Lehman's part would be criticized as protectionism on the part of the Democratic governor. So while it went without saying that the man selected to act as special prosecutor would have to be independent of Dodge, Hines, and the Tammany Hall political machine, there was a corollary risk in naming an ambitious young Republican who might one day aspire to occupy the governor's own office.

In consultation with his political advisers—as well as with bar leaders, La Guardia, and Police Commissioner Lewis Valentine—Lehman compiled a list of four candidates who he felt met his exacting criteria. The men Lehman selected were George Z. Medalie, Charles H. Tuttle, Charles Evans Hughes, and Thomas D. Thacher. All were prominent lawyers. Each was over fifty. And while all were Republicans, none was viewed by Lehman as a likely political threat.

In Washington, meanwhile, even larger forces were at work. William O. Douglas, a Yale Law School professor newly appointed to the Securities and Exchange Commission, was urging the candidacy of one of his Columbia Law School classmates. Tom Dewey's painstaking prosecution of Waxey Gordon, Douglas argued to President Roosevelt, was the very example to which the office of special prosecutor should aspire.

But whither Thomas E. Dewey?

Eighteen months earlier, following FDR's appointment of Democrat Martin Conboy as U.S. attorney for the Southern District of New York, Tom had at last returned to private practice. Spurning offers from the big Wall Street firms, he'd instead taken over his mentor George Medalie's old lease at 120 Broadway, hung out his shingle, and immersed himself in a succession of lucrative civil cases.

On the domestic front, Tom and Frances had moved to an eight-room apartment at 1148 Fifth Avenue—a home large enough to accommodate Tom Jr., then age two, and the second child the happy couple was expecting in October. On weekends, the Dewey clan decamped to a modest country home in Tuxedo Park, where Tom kept a sailboat. Alongside his manifold professional and personal obligations, Tom continued his work with the Young Republican Club, even leading a successful campaign to depose the hidebound Samuel Koenig as New York's Republican county chairman.

Only thirty-two years of age, Tom Dewey was already a man of reputation and substance. A real comer, it was said within Republican Party circles. "He has the sizzle, and he's got the steak." What he lacked, however, with the Republicans out of power both in Washington and Albany, was a high-profile platform from which to launch his quiescent political ambitions.

"The world is full of lawyers, Tom," George Medalie told his young friend in one of their many back-channel telephone discussions, "but it's critically short of leaders."

"But I'm not even on the short-list of candidates."

"Never mind that. I need to know whether you'd accept if the opportunity presented itself."

"I don't know, George . . ."

"This won't be a political appointment. And by that I mean no change in administration will affect you once you've been named. The governor's over a barrel, Tom, with the president sitting on his chest. You can set your own budget, hire your own team, and run your own show. Best of all, you can see it all the way through to the end, and politics be damned. My God, son, an opportunity like this comes along once in a lifetime."

"So why aren't you taking it?"

"We've already had that conversation. The fact of the matter is, there's nobody better qualified than you. Hell, you know it and I know it. And besides, I feel like I owe you one."

"Don't be ridiculous. Owe me how?"

"I once promised you that the U.S. attorney's office would be your ticket to the governor's mansion. Well, Roosevelt had other ideas. So think of this as a do-over. A second bite at the apple, for both of us."

By late June of 1935, all four men on Governor Lehman's list of preferred candidates had declined the appointment, each citing personal or professional obligations. Then, in a show of unity that even the governor couldn't ignore, all joined in a public announcement urging Thomas E. Dewey for the role of special prosecutor. Lee Thompson Smith, the grand jury foreman whose obstinacy had ignited the controversy, soon joined in the motion to draft Dewey. The press followed suit, demanding, "Make it Dewey!"

June 29, 1935, was a Saturday. In Boston, Tom was taking the place of his late uncle Edmund in giving his cousin Elizabeth away in holy matrimony. In Manhattan, meanwhile, Governor Lehman had convened a special meeting at his Park Avenue apartment in a last-ditch effort to change the mind of at least one of his handpicked candidates for the post of special prosecutor.

The meeting lasted two hours. The wedding ceremony was shorter. Both ended at approximately one o'clock in the afternoon.

For his part, Tom danced at the reception that followed the nuptials, and offered a toast, and even joined the band in a ballad he dedicated to the young bride and groom. Meanwhile, on the broiling sidewalk outside his apartment, a weary Governor Lehman addressed a small group of reporters to announce his final choice for the post of special prosecutor.

Later that evening, still in his tuxedo, Tom stepped off the train at Grand Central. As he walked through the bustling terminal, the headlines of a dozen evening newspapers screamed for his attention, all featuring the same blockbuster announcement.

He couldn't suppress a smile.

Twenty-Four

The Cure

January 1936

AIN'T THAT A hot sketch? The one time I ran upstairs and left Addie in charge of the show, she let a couple of dicks in the joint.

The next thing I knew, there were men shouting and girls screaming and a fist pounding on the bathroom door. I turned around to lift up the toilet seat just as the door frame splintered and one of the dicks grabbed my arm and dragged me into the hallway. Pretty soon we were all lined up in the parlor downstairs, all of us facing the wall and waiting for the paddy wagon, and they had my works and all my junk laid out like tchotchkes on the coffee table behind us.

Rhatz!

And you want to hear the screwiest part? With all the things I should've been worried about at that moment—getting booked, and making bail, and maybe doing time—what I was actually thinking was, wait till Pete finds out. That's because Pete Harris had already been calling me Cokey Flo behind my back, and here I went and got myself pinched with a needle in my leg and a pair of his three-dollar girls downstairs in the sheets.

Shit!

And then, of course, there was Jimmy. I knew he'd start right away on the dope angle, on account of me having only a grand or so left in the bank. Like it was my fault I was the one who paid for every little thing around the house while he bought his wife a mink coat for Christmas and didn't even send me so much as a penny postcard, the big cheapskate, let alone money for rent or food or gasoline.

"Think we should call an ambulance for this one?" one of the dicks said to the other.

"How about it, sweetheart? You gonna be okay to ride down-town?"

I told him, "If it's all the same with you, I vote for Coney Island."

He didn't even smile. "Couple hours from now," he said to his partner, "she won't need to go to Coney Island. The walls of her cell will be spinning all by themselves. Ain't that right, dopey?"

"Go chase yourself."

They both had a laugh, but from where I was standing there was nothing funny about it. Even if everything went exactly like it should, it'd still be hours before Pete and Jimmy could bail me out. And then I'd need to score right away, which Jimmy wouldn't like one little bit, especially if I had to borrow his money to do it.

"Okay, let's go."

They led the four of us—me, Addie, and the two girls, Kitty and Joan—out to the wagon in handcuffs. The johns, of course, they'd already cut loose. A lady I recognized from across the hall was standing on the sidewalk with her mouth hanging open, and I was tempted to kick it shut but instead just lowered my head and looked the other way.

At least Addie and me were dressed for the weather. The girls they didn't let change or put on an overcoat on account of the nightgowns were some kind of evidence, I suppose. They weren't even wearing underwear, the two girls, and both of 'em were hugging themselves in the back of the wagon, their teeth already chattering.

Pretty soon I'd be the one whose teeth would be chattering.

They took us down to the Jefferson Market Women's Court, where they booked us and split us up and dumped me in a cell in the basement. It was only my second pinch in New York, and I gave 'em the name Frances Martin, which was the name I'd used on the lease. They said the night session began at eight, which was more than two hours away, and that I should relax and make myself comfortable. And when I asked about making a telephone call, the matron with the key ring laughed as she walked down the corridor.

It seemed more like two days before they finally came to get me, and by then I was already feeling the hunger. Somehow Jesse Jacobs was waiting in the courtroom, and so were Jimmy and Pete Harris, and I'd never been happier to see either of them in my life. Together they posted a $2,800 bond for the three misdemeanor counts, which were maintaining a house of prostitution, possession of a hypodermic syringe, and possession of a cube and a half of morphine. So while I was out on bail, I was also in hock to the combination for their half of the bail money, and Jimmy or no Jimmy, I knew I'd have to pay that back at the rate of six for five.

Jimmy, bless his heart, had brought along a morphine tablet that I chopped up and snorted right there on Pete's dashboard. After that, everything got kind of fuzzy, and I told Pete to pull over to where I stepped out on Sixth Avenue and puked my guts in the gutter in front of maybe a dozen bystanders. Then the sidewalk started spinning, like I'd gone to Coney Island after all, and that was the last thing I remembered.

My first thought when I awoke in the morning was that the whole episode had been a bad dream. But then I smelled bacon frying downstairs, and coffee, and when I tried to sit up in bed, my stomach did a back somersault.

I made it to the toilet just in time, and after I'd finished puking and I'd sat down on the floor, I opened the cabinet under the sink and saw that my Kotex box wasn't just empty—it was gone altogether.

And then I knew it wasn't a dream.

Meanwhile, silverware was rattling in the kitchen, and pretty soon Jimmy's voice was calling up the stairs.

"Flo? C'mon, Flo! Time to rise and shine!"

I started bawling then, sitting on the cold tile floor and wiping my face with my arm.

"In a minute!"

First I brushed my teeth, then I grabbed a robe and held on to the bannister all the way down to where I saw Jimmy in the kitchen wearing Addie's ruffled apron. He hadn't shaved yet, and his suspenders were hanging down to his knees, and he had a chewed-up cigar stub sticking out of his craw.

I had to smile, despite how lousy I felt.

"There's my princess. Sit down, I'm makin pancakes."

"Thanks all the same, honey, but I ain't hungry."

Truth was, the smell of the frying batter was making me sick all over again. But I sat and watched his back, as broad as an icebox. He was humming like my mom used to do, after my dad had left home for the day.

"I need a shot, baby," I told him. "I need it awful bad."

He didn't answer. After a while he turned around with two steaming plates and set one down in front of me. Pancakes and bacon were usually my favorites, but I shoved it away.

"You gotta eat, Flo. You're already thin as a dime."

"I will. I just need to settle my stomach first."

Jimmy ate, and it didn't take long. I used to tell him to count his fingers when he got up from the table.

"Look, honey, we need to work this out," he finally said, wiping his mouth and carrying his plate to the sink, where he turned on the water tap.

"Don't I know it."

"You owe a grand to Jesse now, and they ain't gonna send you no more girls until you pay it back with the interest and then start bonding again."

"How am I supposed to pay it back if I can't open a new joint?"

Jimmy looked at me over his shoulder. I was in a jam. At least he understood.

"Can't you talk to somebody?" I asked him.

"I can try, but it ain't gonna do no good until you get yourself off the junk. People are sayin you can't be trusted, Flo. Plus you'll probably do time on the pinch, and you don't wanna take the cure in jail, do you?"

I shook my head, still staring down at the pancakes.

"I been askin around. There's this place on Central Park West. They say the doctor's okay, and he don't ask too many questions."

"Oh yeah? And who's gonna pay for that, do you suppose?"

He turned all the way around to face me.

"I will, that's who. You can pay me back after you've paid off Jesse Jacobs."

I started crying again. Jimmy walked over to the table and stood beside me.

"I know it ain't gonna be easy, baby, but you really got no other choice. So what do you say, will you give it a try? For me?"

I nodded. Jimmy fished something from his trouser pocket and set it on the table next to my plate.

It was another morphine tablet.

"Last one, Flo. After this, you're getting straight."

Twenty-Five

The Dutchman

January 1936

"THAT COCKSUCKER IS comin after me? After *me*? Don't he know I'm the one saved his fuckin life?"

"He knows," Frank Costello tells Charlie Lucky. "And you know what he said? He said, 'Tell Luciano that someday I'll show my gratitude in court.'"

"Yeah? You think maybe that's good?"

"No, Charlie. I think that's a threat."

Lucky throws up his hands. He retreats to the bar and returns with an open bottle of wine. He fills the trio of glasses that flank the still-steaming bowl of pasta in tomato sauce.

"Okay you mugs. *Salute.* To Mama Castiglia."

Meyer Lansky and Frank Costello raise their glasses just as a knock sounds from the hallway.

Lucky peers through the peephole, then swings the door wide for a nervous little man in a flawless blue suit, who leans over the threshold without setting a toe in the suite.

"*Buona sera*, Mr. Ross. I just wanted to make sure everything turned out to your satisfaction."

"Everything's jake, Henry. I hope I ain't hurt nobody's feelins. It's just that a guy's gotta get some home cookin every once in a while."

"Of course, Mr. Ross."

"You tell the boys in the kitchen not to take it personal, okay?"

"Of course, Mr. Ross. Have a wonderful evening, and call downstairs whenever you're ready."

Frank is dishing up the pasta. "Charlie, you're the only guy I know who lives in the fucking Waldorf and still sends out to Brooklyn for tagliatelle Bolognese."

"I'd eat your mother's tagliatelle if I lived in the fuckin White House."

"You could of been eating in the White House if you'd listened to me about Roosevelt."

"Please, Frankie," Meyer says, "do we have to hear this again?"

"Instead you've got Dewey back on the scene, and now he's crawlin up your ass like a bedbug."

Dewey. It's all Lucky's been hearing of late, ever since the Dutchman's string of banner headlines has finally reached its end.

Arthur "Dutch Schultz" Flegenheimer has been the white whale to Tom Dewey's Ahab ever since the special prosecutor's days as an assistant U.S. attorney under George Medalie. It was Schultz, in fact—the Bronx beer baron turned industrial and numbers racketeer—who was Medalie's first target back in 1931. But no sooner had the Medalie team indicted Schultz for income tax fraud than the Dutchman went into hiding, and he remained in hiding until both Medalie and Dewey returned to private practice.

Far from sitting idle during his self-imposed exile, Schultz instead used the opportunity to consolidate his bloody grip on both the numbers racket in Harlem and the city's restaurant service unions. He fought shooting wars with Legs Diamond and Mad Dog Coll, and he embarked on a protracted territorial struggle with Waxey Gordon that ended, ironically enough, with Gordon's own federal income tax conviction by Dewey. By 1934, the ephemeral Dutchman was declared the nation's "Public Enemy No. 1" by J. Edgar Hoover, and reform mayor Fiorello La Guardia staked his personal reputation on finding Schultz and finally bringing him to justice.

Then, with the noose tightening, Schultz did a curious thing. After sending out feelers through lawyer Dixie Davis, the Dutchman offered to settle the tax charges against him for the princely sum of one hundred thousand dollars in cash. When U.S. Treasury Secretary Henry Morgenthau Jr. flatly rejected the Davis offer, Schultz finally surrendered himself to the authorities. Not in Manhattan—where the felony indictment had been handed down, and where a thousand Wanted posters bearing Schultz's doe-eyed image were blanketing the city—but rather in Albany, where the delinquent taxes should theoretically have been paid.

Free on bail while awaiting his trial upstate, Schultz was forced to manage his Harlem interests from a distance. So when Jules "Julie Martin" Modgilewsky, a fearsome enforcer for Schultz's restaurants racket, was alleged to have shorted the Dutchman some seventy thousand dollars in protection money, Schultz summoned Martin to the Harmony Hotel in Cohoes, New York. During the course of their heated meeting on March 2, 1935, Martin denied having skimmed the seventy grand, but eventually admitted to taking twenty thousand, a sum to which he'd claimed a moral entitlement.

With a horrified Dixie Davis looking on, Schultz yanked a gun from his waistband, forced the muzzle into Julie Martin's mouth, and pulled the trigger. Afterward, Schultz apologized to his lawyer for having murdered a man in his presence. Later still, when Martin's body was found in the snowy upstate woods with deep and grisly chest wounds, Schultz explained the tableau to Davis over breakfast.

"Oh, that," the Dutchman said, digging into his oatmeal. "I cut his fucking heart out."

The trial of Arthur Flegenheimer for the willful evasion of U.S. income taxes began on April 16, 1935, in the United States Courthouse in Syracuse, New York. Using the very documents amassed by Dewey and Medalie back in 1933, attorney John H. McEvers—a veteran of the Capone prosecution team who'd been brought to New York as a special assistant to Attorney General Homer Cummings—presented indisputable evidence of the Dutchman's undeclared income totaling $2.8 million over the three-year period from 1928 to 1931.

Employing an ingenious defense strategy, Schultz acknowledged the nonpayment, but blamed the oversight on erroneous legal advice he'd received, to the effect that no taxes were owed on income derived from an illegal activity—namely, bootlegging. He further claimed that once he'd been properly advised, he'd made a good-faith effort to resolve the matter, only to be rebuffed by Henry Morgenthau. As defense attorney James Noonan told the jurors, "It shows he was on the level, and that there was no willfulness in his heart. The government wouldn't take his money!"

The jury hung, 7-to-5.

A retrial was scheduled for July, but with venue now moved to the small Canadian border town of Malone, New York, where the prosecutorial baton was passed to Martin Conboy, the man who'd succeeded Thomas Dewey as U.S. attorney for New York's Southern District.

In a cynical bid to ingratiate himself with the local citizenry, Schultz and his entourage arrived in Malone several weeks in advance of the trial date and proceeded to spend lavishly, replenishing local coffers badly depleted by the Depression. This continued until the pastor of Malone's First Congregational Church cried foul from the pulpit after Schultz was seen at a semipro baseball game in the company of the town's mayor. The resulting public outcry forced District Judge Frederick H. Bryant to revoke the Dutchman's bail.

By then, however, the proper tone had already been set.

The Malone trial was, in essence, a reprise of the earlier trial in Syracuse, but with a very different outcome. This time, the jurors voted unanimously to acquit Arthur Flegenheimer on all counts. Judge Bryant spoke for many stunned observers when he said that the verdict "shakes the confidence of law-abiding people in integrity and truth," telling the erstwhile jurors, "You will have to go home with the satisfaction, if it is a satisfaction, that you have rendered a blow against law enforcement and given aid and encouragement to the people who would flout the law. In all probability, they will commend you. I cannot."

Downstate in Manhattan, a furious Mayor La Guardia was even more succinct. "Dutch Schultz won't be a resident of New York City," he vowed. "We have no place for him here." To which the Dutchman responded, "So there ain't room for me in New York? Well, I'm goin there anyway." And go there he did, to reassemble the pieces of his shattered criminal empire that rival mobsters had already begun to collect.

Months before the Dutchman's acquittal, and with a view toward preserving his own lucrative sinecure, Bo Weinberg, Schultz's chief enforcer, had met with New Jersey crime boss Longie Zwillman to prepare for life after Arthur Flegenheimer. Zwillman called in Charlie Lucky, and a summit was held at the Waldorf Towers. They drafted a blueprint for the division of Schultz's rackets should the Dutchman—as was universally expected—join Al Capone and Waxey Gordon as guests of the federal government. Weinberg, in exchange for retaining his usual 15-percent override, agreed to disclose to Zwillman and Charlie Lucky all aspects of the Dutchman's operations.

And so it was that, upon his Lazarus-like return from upstate, Schultz made a beeline to Charlie Lucky. The two men discussed not only the business at hand but also, surprisingly, the Catholic religion. Schultz, a lifelong Jew, confided to his astonished host a promise he'd made to himself while in the Malone city jail, to the effect that if he were to be acquitted on the income tax charges, he would convert to Catholicism. Jesus Christ, the Dutchman told Lucky, had been the one who'd answered his prayers.

There was nothing Christian, however, about the Dutchman's appraisal of Bo Weinberg. Correctly suspecting his chief lieutenant's disloyalty, Schultz ordered his men to stake out Longie Zwillman's house in New Jersey. In September, the stakeout finally paid a deadly dividend. Informed that Weinberg's car had just pulled into Zwillman's driveway, Schultz personally rushed to the scene, and when Weinberg emerged from his meeting a few hours later, the Dutchman was outside waiting.

Bo Weinberg was neither seen nor heard from again.

As the newly appointed special prosecutor of organized crime in New York, Thomas E. Dewey was all but salivating at the prospect of finally getting his crack at the Dutchman. Because double jeopardy precluded a prosecution for felony income tax evasion, Dewey instead focused his army of twenty all-star lawyers, twenty stenographers, ten accountants, four process servers, four clerks, four messengers, two grand jury reporters, and seventy-five specially recruited police detectives on Schultz's policy racket—the so-called numbers game or Harlem lottery—which by Dewey's estimation was grossing some twenty million to fifty million dollars annually.

But before Dewey could secure a state grand jury indictment, a federal grand jury in October of 1935 accused Schultz of eleven misdemeanor counts of failing to file income tax returns for the very same years—1929 through 1931—for which the Dutchman had already been acquitted in Malone on the more serious felony counts of willful income tax evasion.

Schultz, who'd moved his headquarters to Newark while fighting extradition across the Hudson, was enraged at the prospect of having to re-wage a legal battle he'd thought was already won. Blaming Dewey for his ongoing woes, the Dutchman devised a crude but effective solution to his problems.

He would simply murder the special prosecutor.

Dewey had already been receiving death threats, including one call to his Park Avenue apartment in which Frances, then eight months pregnant with the couple's second child, was asked to come to the morgue to identify her husband's body. Those threats—together with an ominous warning letter from J. Edgar Hoover—had convinced the special prosecutor to accept two full-time bodyguards, whose job it was to shadow him everywhere in public.

Could a gunman bypass the bodyguards and get to Thomas Dewey?

Schultz hired contract killer Albert Anastasia, of Murder Inc. fame, to undertake surveillance of Dewey's daily routine. A week later, Anastasia reported that Dewey had a habit of stopping at the same drugstore every morning on the way to his office in the Woolworth Building. Convinced that an assassination could succeed, Schultz requested approval for his plan from the new national crime commission. At a meeting held in mid-October, the commission, chaired by Charlie Lucky, rejected Schultz's plan, fearing the backlash that such a high-profile execution would almost certainly engender.

To an increasingly isolated and embattled Dutch Schultz, the commission's vote was further proof of Lucky's personal designs on the Dutchman's rackets. Furious, Schultz decided to defy the commission and proceed with his plan. When word of that decision got back to Charlie Lucky, a second, emergency commission meeting was held, this time to approve the assassination of Dutch Schultz.

And so the race was on.

Responsibility for the Dutchman's murder was delegated to Lepke Buchalter, who assigned the actual hit to his lieutenants Bug Workman and Mendy Weiss. On October 24, 1935, the two assassins entered the Palace Chop House in Newark, where Schultz was eating dinner alongside henchmen Otto Berman, Abe Landau, and Lulu Rosenkrantz.

The ensuing bloodbath left Schultz and his three lieutenants mortally wounded. All succumbed within hours, with Schultz receiving last rites from a Catholic priest at Newark City Hospital.

And that's how Lucky Luciano saved the life of Thomas E. Dewey.

In Lucky's suite at the Waldorf Towers, the three friends tuck napkins into shirt collars as they sit down to their steaming plates of tagliatelle.

"Anyway, I ain't losin sleep over Dewey," Lucky is saying. "What's Dewey got on me? I pay my taxes like a good American."

"Come on, Charlie. You paid six years of back taxes in July."

"Ain't that what you told me to do?"

"Yes," Meyer says, "but don't you think that looks a little fishy? I mean, six years is the statute of limitations. And what did you claim by way of income, twenty grand a year?"

"Somethin like that. Maybe a little less."

"That's your first problem. And what about state taxes?"

"Come on, Meyer. You didn't say nothin about that."

"All right, Charlie, relax. All I'm saying is that Waxey paid some taxes too, but that didn't stop Dewey from nailing him."

"Jesus Christ. Maybe I shoulda let the Dutchman kill the little cocksucker after all."

"Or maybe you should take a page from the Dutchman's playbook and lam it for a while. Take Gay and go to Miami until things settle down. The way it is now, you've got a big red target on your back. Some actress gets killed in California, and they blame it on Charlie Lucky. It's got to the point where every stink-bombing or drugstore holdup, the papers say you're the one's behind it."

"Maybe you're right, Meyer. Or maybe I'll go to Cleveland and inspect your little molasses operation."

Meyer sets down his fork.

"What, you thought I wouldn't find out? Christ, I knew about it before the first boat ever left Cuba."

"My molasses deal has nothing to do with you, Charlie. Molaska was a legit partnership between me and Anna's father."

"And your pal Moe Dalitz. Relax, I ain't mad or nothin. But the thing is, you made that deal while you was in Havana on our business, and that makes it part of our business. I don't care about the sugar end, because that part's legit, but on the liquor side, everything goes into the kitty. You know the rules, Meyer. Hell, you're the one helped me to make 'em."

"All right, Charlie, if that's how you feel about it."

"How I feel's got nothin to do with it. It was up to me, I'd let you do whatever the fuck you wanted, you know that. But then word would get around that Lansky's gettin special treatment, and pretty soon every wise guy would think it was okay to cut their own side-deals."

"You're right, Charlie. I'm not arguing with you."

"You're goddamn right I'm right. Look at us, Meyer. We're a couple of shits from First Avenue livin like Morgan and Rockefeller. We're in the fuckin Waldorf, for Christ sake. But you know what? So was Cousin Alphonse, and so were Rothstein and Waxey and the Dutchman. All of 'em up to their eyebrows in booze and broads and cash. But you know what the difference is between them guys and us?"

"What's that?"

"Enemies. Them guys made enemies like that lady from Canada makes babies. Us, we just make other guys rich, and we treat 'em fair, and we play by the same set of rules. That's why we're on top, Meyer, and that's why Molaska goes into the kitty. And you wanna know somethin else? It's why we're gonna stay on top for as long as we fucking feel like it."

"*Salute*," Frank says.

"And as for Dewey," Lucky says, touching his glass to the others, "he can suck my cock, because at the end of the day, he ain't got nothin on Charlie Lucky."

Twenty-Six

Loss and Memory

January 1936

IN THE FALL of 1931, at the intersection of Southside and Roosevelt Avenues in Freeport, nine-year-old George Levy Jr., the only child of the noted Long Island defense attorney and his second wife, Beatrice, lost the brakes on his soapbox derby racer and veered into the path of an oncoming car.

The accident occurred late on a Thursday afternoon, and by the time George and Bea arrived at the hospital, their beloved son's body, horribly crushed and mangled, was undergoing a complex surgical repair that even the county's top orthopedic specialists were hesitant to undertake.

It was nothing short of a miracle that George Jr. survived his crippling injuries. It was less of a surprise, at least to those who knew them, that his parents' already rocky marriage did not.

Further surgeries and hospitalizations would leave George Jr. wheelchair-bound for life, his symptoms mirroring those of cerebral palsy. His mother would throw herself into the role of full-time caregiver, even trading her smart frocks and butterfly blouses for a nurse's starched white uniform. Even feeding and bathing her son, and changing his bandages, and tending to his most intimate physical needs. Even taking the boy with her to Reno when she filed for the divorce.

Although George Levy continued to provide financially for his son and namesake, the divorce and custody orders marked the end of their daily interactions, leaving a gap in George's life that would only grow larger as the boy over whom he'd once so fiercely doted—the boy he'd taken to Lourdes in his frantic search for a cure—matured into adolescence.

That void was very much on George's mind when, less than a year after his son's near-fatal accident, he stood at the foot of yet another hospital bed, this one in Hempstead, where young Ormond LeMaire lay battling for his life.

"Are you a family member?" asked the duty nurse, startled to find a pre-dawn visitor in the young man's private room.

"No. Just a concerned well-wisher."

"I'm afraid visiting hours don't begin until nine," the nurse said, reading her watch as she consulted the boy's chart. "If you'd like, you can wait . . ."

But the man was already gone.

On Saturday night of the previous weekend, Ormond LeMaire had attended a party near his home in Rockville Center that was hosted by the parents of his old high school friends Emily and Irma Groesbeck. There were twenty or more of his former classmates in attendance, the bright young collegians laughing and chatting and dancing to the phonograph even as a furious thunderstorm lashed the Groesbeck home on Capitolian Boulevard, the wind-driven rain and the loud, syncopated music combining to muffle an urgent pounding on the front door that only LeMaire, as he passed through the foyer from the kitchen, happened to hear.

LeMaire opened the door. He then backed into the crowded living room with his hands held high in surrender.

First the laughter died, then all conversation as the guests, one by one, took notice of the dripping figure holding a gun.

"Frank? Frank, is that you?"

Jack Wulforst stepped forward to stand beside LeMaire as the other guests crowded behind them. All now recognized Frank Murphy, their old high school classmate, beneath his hat and shimmering slicker.

Murphy's eyes were dark and hollow as they scanned the faces in the room. And then without warning, his gun burst to life.

Three shots punctuated the ragtime piano still playing on the phonograph. The first and second caught Jack Wulforst in the arm and thigh, while the third hit Ormond LeMaire squarely in the back when the young man turned away from his assailant.

As girls screamed and boys dove for cover, the gunman then turned and strode through the still-open doorway, disappearing into the storm.

It was after midnight by the time the police arrived. William Groesbeck, a sobbing daughter under each arm, urged the investigating officers to perform their duties quickly. Since the witnesses were many and their conditions ranged from fatigue to shock to outright hysteria, all were allowed to leave without giving formal statements. No crime-scene photographs were taken, no spent bullets were recovered, and no effort was made to identify or trace the assailant's weapon.

Murphy was arrested the following morning, the Rockville Centre police finding him asleep in his bedroom at his parents' house on Princeton Road, one block north of the Groesbeck residence. Belligerent, Murphy denied ever owning or possessing a firearm, and further denied having visited the Groesbeck party, claiming instead to have spent the night drinking bootleg whiskey at the Turf Inn in the nearby village of Hempstead.

Despite his protestations, Murphy was arrested and booked on a charge of felonious assault with a deadly weapon. The clothing he'd worn on the previous night, however, was never collected as evidence or tested for powder burns.

It wasn't until Monday afternoon, some forty hours after the shooting had occurred, that Elvin Edwards, the district attorney of Nassau County, first learned of the events on Capitolian Boulevard. Incensed both by the delay and the slipshod investigation, Edwards nonetheless sprang into action, dispatching Assistant District Attorney Martin Littleton Jr. to track down and interview all the young men and women who'd been present at the Groesbeck party.

Sixteen of the eyewitnesses said they'd gotten a clear look at the assailant. All identified Frank Murphy, whom they'd known since childhood, as the silent gunman.

It was three days after the shooting that the telephone rang in the law office of George Morton Levy. Later that afternoon, during an emotional face-to-face meeting with the distraught parents of the accused, George learned how young Frank Murphy had fractured his skull as a child and had thereafter suffered from epilepsy and various mental illnesses requiring a series of hospitalizations at Bellevue and other psychiatric facilities. Worse, George learned that the boy had been aware of the Groesbeck party and had, just before leaving the Murphy home on Saturday evening, vowed revenge at not having been invited.

"It's all our fault," his mother concluded, burying her face in a hand.

"Don't be ridiculous!" snapped her husband, a prominent Wall Street broker. "You can't blame yourself for something like this. Nobody could have anticipated—"

"I wasn't blaming myself."

"Oh, I see. I suppose it's *my* fault that—"

"Perhaps if you'd been more involved. Perhaps if you weren't holed up in your office at all hours of the day and night."

"And how do you propose that we pay for all these doctors and headshrinkers? Do you think money grows on trees? Do you think that—"

"All I'm saying is that if you'd been around more often, if you'd spent more *time* with the boy, then perhaps . . ."

George listened to the familiar argument in silence. Then, once the combatants had arrived at a weary détente, he agreed to represent Frank Murphy to the best of his abilities.

His first order of business was to visit Mercy Hospital to witness firsthand the crippling injuries that the shooter had inflicted. His second was to visit his new client at the Nassau County Jail, where, to George's dismay, Frank Murphy continued to deny any role in the Groesbeck shootings. George's third and final destination was the office of Martin Littleton, the assistant district attorney assigned to handle the prosecution.

As this would be his first actual exposure to the storied George Morton Levy, Littleton asked Elvin Edwards, the veteran D.A., what kinds of tricks and sharp practices he might expect to encounter.

"None whatsoever," Edwards told him. "You can trust George with your life."

"I beg your pardon?"

"You heard me. Just don't let him light one of his damned cigars in the conference room."

Despite the young prosecutor's wariness, the meeting proved surprisingly cordial. Levy, Littleton quickly discovered, was more interested in learning the facts of the matter than in probing for any sort of advantage. At the end of the day, Littleton agreed to turn over copies of all the sworn statements he'd amassed, and also to arrange for the sixteen eyewitnesses to return to his office the following day to be personally questioned by George.

"The police investigation was fairly well bungled," George later informed the Murphys, "and we might make some hay out of that. Make the police look like monkeys, and embarrass the district attorney with a few scathing headlines. And make no mistake, there are plenty of lawyers out there who'd be only too happy to take your money and put on that kind of a show. But the unavoidable fact is that sixteen of your son's closest friends will all testify without reservation that it was Frank who shot Ormond LeMaire."

"Then what are our options?"

"There's only one option. Hire an alienist and plead temporary insanity. Try to keep your son out of prison and get him into a hospital setting where he'll receive some proper treatment."

The trial, which lasted a week, quickly devolved to a battle of experts. Littleton recalled, "The very fact that [Levy's] record of wins was so large predisposed me against him. He might be a pretty clever customer, I thought to myself, but he wasn't going to take me in. Gradually it occurred to me that he had no tricks at all. It was an extraordinary trial, and the judge might as well have stayed at home around his fire. There was no dispute about the facts and not a single objection was raised during the trial; it was strictly a dispute between medical experts."

In his closing, Littleton echoed the state's medical expert in arguing that the planning involved before and after the shooting—specifically, Murphy's acquisition and disposal of the weapon—evidenced premeditation and a clear state of mind. To this George countered, also consistent with his medical experts, that young Murphy's medical history, coupled with his amnesia on the night of the shooting, were themselves the best evidence of his mental incapacity.

On July 7, 1932, after five hours of deliberation, the jury returned a guilty verdict, with an express recommendation for mercy.

Two lives ruined; two families left fractured and grieving. But the case had become personal to George, whom Littleton would describe as having "the tenacity of a toy bulldog when he got hold of a pertinent fact." George continued to pursue the Murphy case through a maze of post-trial motions and appeals until, almost four contentious years after the verdict, George finally won an order of executive clemency that saw his client transferred from state prison to the bucolic Matteawan State Hospital in Fishkill, where Frank Murphy could finally begin receiving the medical attention he desperately needed. It was, in practical effect, the same outcome that would have resulted had the jury's verdict been one of acquittal.

It was only a small victory, to be sure, in a career of greater triumphs. But to a parent who was himself no stranger to the lingering effects of personal tragedy—to the loss, and the estrangement, and the gnawing recriminations—it was an outcome well worth the effort.

Twenty-Seven

The Roundup

February 1936

IT ALL BEGAN with Eunice Carter.

The only woman, and the only African American, on Tom Dewey's handpicked team of courtroom sluggers, Carter had been an assistant district attorney under the feckless William Copeland Dodge but had distinguished herself as a tireless and incorruptible Women's Court advocate. Tom had originally recruited her in the hope that, as a black woman, Carter might prove useful in his planned extirpation of the Dutch Schultz numbers racket in Harlem. But when the Dutchman's brutal murder left Lucky Luciano as the special prosecutor's primary target of interest, it was Carter who'd first suggested a means by which to breach the walls within walls of stony silence that seemed to surround the Sicilian mob boss.

It was a tried-and-true formula for prosecutorial success: start at the bottom by arresting and flipping the small-fry in order to land the bigger fish. At the U.S. attorney's office, both Medalie and Dewey had employed it to perfection in building their painstaking cases against Legs Diamond and Waxey Gordon. But the Italian gangsters, in contrast with their more colorful Irish and Jewish forebears, had proved an opaque confederation whose insularity, discipline, and strict code of silence frustrated even a cursory understanding of its structures and methods, let alone its leadership and inner workings.

Employing tips and phone taps, the special prosecutor's team of crack assistants soon focused its attention on the familiar territory of the Women's Court and its revolving-door cast of madams and prostitutes, bookers and bondsmen. Word on the street, which had reached the attuned ear of Eunice Carter, was that a new downtown combination was using violence and intimidation to organize and centralize the formerly freelance world of New York prostitution. Here, then, was the toehold—the first rung on a rickety ladder that might, with luck and perseverance, lead all the way to Luciano's Waldorf-Astoria penthouse.

Tom, at first, was skeptical. "I didn't take this job to go after prostitutes!" he'd snapped when Carter and fellow assistant Murray Gurfein first broached the vice-racket angle. But then Frank Hogan signed on to the investigative team, as did Charlie Grimes and Harry Cole. Before long, a succession of aggrieved madams was giving grand jury testimony about a shadowy combination involving up to two thousand prostitutes, three hundred disorderly houses, and a menacing cadre of bookers and bondsmen, enforcers and loan sharks—a veritable "NRA of prostitution," as Tom came to describe the rapidly unfolding landscape.

"But it still doesn't get us there," he told his assembled team of assistants. "Who's going to believe that the head of the Unione Siciliana, the so-called Boss of Bosses, is taking pocket change from two-dollar prostitutes?"

"A jury will believe it," Cole replied, "when we prove that Tommy the Bull Pennochio and Little Davie Betillo, two known Luciano associates, are in charge of the whole operation."

It may have taken a while to convince the special prosecutor as to the merits of the Carter approach, but once he was on board, Tom translated his conviction into immediate action.

From the outset, secrecy had been a central tenet of the special prosecutor's office. Adopting the guidelines first laid down by his mentor, George Medalie, Tom had forbidden private practice by any assistant, or discussion of any pending investigation with the press or public, or fraternization of any kind with the criminal element. His assistants were to live as Caesar's wives, he'd told them, avoiding even the appearance of impropriety. Cases were to be tried in court, not in the newspapers. He'd even forbidden assistants working on one case from discussing their efforts with their colleagues within the office, except on a need-to-know basis.

It was not surprising, then, that the great vice raid of 1936 bore all the hallmarks of a covert military operation.

In the waning hours of Friday, January 31, undercover detectives arrested Betillo and Pennochio, along with combination enforcer Abie Wahrman and loan shark Benny Spiller, as the four men left a party on 16th Street in Manhattan. Elsewhere in the city, detectives were descending on restaurants and nightclubs, sidewalks and apartment houses, hauling in enforcer Jimmy Fredericks, bondsmen Jesse Jacobs and Meyer Berkman, and bookers Al Weiner, Jack Eller, and Dave Miller. In Philadelphia, they arrested booker Pete Harris. In total, sixteen key members of the vice combination were held incommunicado at various precinct houses throughout the city in what proved to be but a preliminary bout to the next night's main event.

Saturday, the first of February, was cold and overcast in Manhattan. At precisely 8:55 P.M., at eighty different locations throughout the city, plainclothes officers opened sealed envelopes bearing only the addresses to which they'd been dispatched. Following the instructions inside, the 160 officers descended on the suspected disorderly houses at nine o'clock sharp, arresting any prostitutes or madams they found working within.

Preferring unmarked cars and taxicabs to conspicuous paddy wagons, the arresting officers delivered their haul of 87 prisoners to the Greenwich Street police station, where the protesting women were booked and then transported, again by taxicab, to the Barclay Street side entrance to the Woolworth Building. There the entire Dewey team of twenty lawyers, twenty stenographers, and dozens of aides and clerical assistants were waiting on the fourteenth floor, ready to take their statements.

It was an extraordinary tableau. Brightly rouged women in silk evening gowns and little else slouched and smoked, paced and slept while awaiting their turns to be interviewed. The special prosecutor's offices reeked of cigarettes and cheap perfume. The women, inured to the revolving door of the Women's Court, were defiant—even dismissive. They were from out of town, they told their interrogators, just visiting a friend. They were only playing bridge. They were models or manicurists, shopgirls or dressmakers. Virtually all, it seemed, claimed to be virgins.

The worldlier of the madams—Polack Frances and Sadie the Chink among them—counseled the younger, more skittish girls. "Keep your yap shut and everything will be fine," they instructed. "Remember, you don't know from nothin."

Tom patrolled the crowded hallways alongside John Lyons, his chief of detectives, assuring the agitated women that it was the higher-ups he was after, not the prostitutes or madams. "Cooperate," he told them, "and the charges against you will be dropped. Moreover, you'll receive complete immunity for your grand jury testimony."

But his assurances fell on calloused ears. "So, you're Dewey," one of the prostitutes sneered, towering over the special prosecutor in her patent leather heels. "Run along, Boy Scout, and peddle your papers."

As gray dawn broke over Manhattan, frustratingly little progress had been made. At noon, Philip J. McCook, his Sunday brunch interrupted by a call from Tom Dewey, appeared on the fourteenth floor of the Woolworth Building, where the jurist and the special prosecutor, joined by his chief assistants Bill Herlands, Murray Gurfein, Jake Rosenblum, and Barent Ten Eyck, huddled to strategize in Tom's private office.

"So that's where matters stand," Tom concluded, lighting a cigarette. "We've got close to a hundred suspects in custody, but none of the girls is talking. They assume this is business as usual, and that they'll be back on the street by Monday. I've told them we've got their bookers and their bondsmen in custody, but either they don't believe it or they think someone else will be coming to their rescue. We need to send them a message that will really get their attention."

"What did you have in mind, Tom?"

"I want all the girls held as material witnesses, each on a ten-thousand-dollar bond."

McCook was skeptical. "The usual bond on a prostitution charge is something like three hundred dollars."

"Usual is exactly our problem. If these girls make bail, which is what *usually* happens, then we'll lose them forever. They'll either disappear or else their lives will be threatened and all of our effort will have been wasted. We need time to work on them, Judge, and they need to understand that this is no laughing matter."

"With bail that high, you're practically inviting a constitutional challenge."

"Which is all the more reason why the girls should be held incommunicado, without access to lawyers."

"What?"

"Hear me out a moment. If these girls have access to counsel, we'll be up to our necks in habeas petitions before the week is out. And once they're back in the hands of the gangsters, our case will go right down the drain. I'm telling you, this is the only way we're going to get to Luciano."

Still frowning, McCook found a chair and sat.

"Let's not lose sight of the bigger picture, Judge. We've got a lot riding on this extraordinary term, and as you well know, our initial focus was on Schultz. We can't afford another false start. The public expects results, and so does the governor. So does the mayor. We need to give them something tangible, and we need to give it to them soon."

McCook grunted, filling a pipe.

"If word gets around that we hauled in a bunch of prostitutes and nothing comes of it, I'll be a laughingstock, which is exactly what Hines and Dodge have been hoping for. I can already see the headlines, Judge. Not to mention our pictures, yours and mine, side by side on page one."

McCook lit his pipe. He watched the bluish smoke waft and curl toward the ceiling.

"All right, Tom. I know you're in a tight spot. If you're quite certain this is our only avenue . . ."

"Thanks, Judge. I promise you won't regret it."

The arraignments, conducted there in Tom's office, took most of the afternoon. Seventy prostitutes pleaded not guilty, and each was remanded to the custody of the Women's House of Detention on a material witness bond of ten thousand dollars. For the combination men, each charged with the crime of compulsory prostitution, justice was even harsher. Little Davie Betillo's bail was set at twenty-five thousand. For Jimmy Fredericks it was forty, and for Tommy the Bull Pennochio, a whopping seventy-five grand. All were returned to the Raymond Street Jail in Brooklyn to await trial.

In the elevator lobby of the Woolworth Building, as prostitute Nancy Presser waited to descend to the idling paddy wagons now lining the curb downstairs, she caught the eye of Ralph Liguori, her former boyfriend and now a stickup man for the combination. Liguori ambled over, hands in pockets, with an easy smile on his face. Looking left and right, he leaned in close to whisper.

"If you squeal," he told her softly, "I'll kill you myself."

Twenty-Eight

Rock Bottom

May 1936

TO THIS DAY, I swear to God, I blame the fucking dogs.

Mrs. Calvit—that's Dorothy Russell to you—had a pair of furry monsters that were too big for her old apartment, let alone for the crummy two-bedroom she was leasing at the Hotel Alamac on West 71st Street. So when I moved in to live with her, well, let's just say things got a little too close for comfort.

I got the job through Dr. Gardiner from the sanitarium. Dorothy Russell, he told me, the daughter of actress Lillian Russell, was an old patient of his who was looking for a caretaker that could also act as a stenographer, and could I type worth a damn? I told him, "If I could practice a little," and so he let me bang away on a brand-new Underwood that he kept at one of his nurse's desks. The quick brown fox jumped over that same lazy dog three hours a day for two solid weeks, and the faster I typed and the more accurate I got, the more I started to think that maybe I was that quick little fox and that Dewey was the lazy old dog who, while he may have gotten Jimmy, would never lay a paw on me because from now on, brother, I was strictly legit.

That was a laugh, I realize now, but don't forget this was right after I'd heard about Jimmy getting pinched along with everybody else, and what with all the bookers and most of the girls in town cooling their heels in jail, it was a cinch I wasn't opening up a new joint even if I had the money to do it, which I didn't. Besides which, I'd jumped my bail on the misdemeanor charges back in January, so I couldn't very well risk another fall or else I'd be looking at some serious time in prison.

I needed to keep my head down and my nose clean. I needed to go legit. That was the plan, anyway. And what looks more legit than a girl with her very own dog?

I named her Pearlie, after my old pal from Ohio. I'd found her in the park one day, all skinny and dirty and shivering, and I knew right away that she'd been abandoned. She had no collar, and at first she wouldn't even come to me when I called her. Finally I bought some caramel nuts off a guy on the street and used those to gain her trust. I'd leave one and walk away, and then another, and pretty soon Pearlie was following me through the park with her little tail wagging, and I had myself a pet.

Mrs. Calvit didn't mind, at least not at first. She was a real dog lover, she said, and Pearlie was such a cute little thing. The other beasts would chase her around the apartment, drooling and slobbering, and I had to close her up in my bedroom until they all got used to each other, but after a while they let Pearlie play with them, and sleep with them, and even eat her little meals in a bowl right next to theirs.

More than once I thought to myself that Pearlie was kind of like me, small and scrappy, while the big dogs were more like Jimmy, all gruff on the outside but really more bark than bite.

Poor Jimmy. I missed him something awful, locked up in that crummy old jail. He'd hired a lawyer named Siegel, who I went to visit a few times, just to see what I could do to help with Jimmy's case. But every time I went down there, Siegel would give me the brush-off. Too busy, he was, to even sit with me. Like I had some kind of disease or something, and he didn't want it going around his fancy office.

Word on the street was that five of the girls who'd been arrested had already cut deals with Dewey and were ready to rat out the others. Word also was that if you spun a good enough yarn to Dewey, you got out of jail free and they put you up in a hotel and paid for your room and board with cigarettes and candy and trips to the movies included. They even took you out drinking and dancing, with everything on the house.

That's some system of so-called justice, ain't it? With times being hard like they were, I knew girls who'd rat out their own mothers if it meant getting three hot squares and a roof over their head, never mind movies and cigarettes.

I walked the big dogs twice a day, once in the morning and once before dinnertime. Every now and again I'd pop into one of the fancy hotels along 59th Street and pinch a few pieces of stationery from the lobby. Then I'd type these long letters to Jimmy when Mrs. Calvit was taking one of her naps. Here's one that I sent to him back in April:

My Dear Cousin:

Well, it's the day after Easter and everything is still the same. There is nothing new. I feel very melancholy to-night. Very blue. I'm disgusted with the whole world. There is no justice at all. I wish Uncle Dee would die of cancer, the louse! He should of died from leprosy when he was a baby.

I think it's terrible to make a person do time before they are even convicted. Its not fair. They let lousy murderers go free. But a person that never did anyone any harm in their life, has to rot in jail. Look at that Vera Stretz case. A confessed murderess! She even admitted doing it, on the witness chair, yet she is freed. But a person that hasn't even been convicted yet has to stay in jail, until some louse gets good and ready to bring them to trial! Look at all the money that was spent on Hauptman! The Governor himself intervening for a filthy foreigner of a baby-killer. The worst kind of killer there is. That's why I say there is no justice in this world.

Gee, I'm so blue, and lonesome for you. I don't know what to do. Believe me, if I had about five minutes, with a few certain people, alone, I'd know what to say and do. There would be just five rats less, to bother people.

Well, it's no use wishing. I'm going down to see Siegel Wednesday, I guess. I want to know what he intends to do. What defense has he worked out? I want him to get busy, and try to get his head to working. Not to think he is going to get money for nothing. He should never mind bull shi--ing so much, but get something done. I can't stand this suspense and inactivity much longer.

Well, don't worry, old pal, everything will be O.K. Just have faith and courage. That's the main thing. Maybe you'll thumb your nose at all these louses that are lying like hell, just to save their own skin.

Take care of yourself, and ask them if they will allow you to buy some linement, so you could rub your legs. Maybe if you massaged them with something, you'd get a little releif, so you could get some sleep. I worry about your legs an awful lot. I wish I could rub them for you.

Regards from all, and all my love,
> your Faithful,
> Cousin

So yeah, I missed my Jimmy something awful. The one silver lining to my situation was that Jesse Jacobs was in jail too, and so were Pete Harris and Benny Spiller, so I didn't have to go around looking over my shoulder, worrying about getting my nose broke on account of my so-called loan, which, with the vig still running, was now somewhere north of three grand and counting.

I'd become Mildred Nelson—the name Jimmy and me'd used when I checked into Dr. Gardiner's sanitarium. I was Mrs. Calvit's personal assistant, earning twenty-five dollars a week and living on the Upper West Side and typing her book and story manuscripts. I even gave her a few story ideas of my own, about a "friend" who was tied up in the rackets, with the understanding that if she sold one to *Liberty* magazine, we'd split the take fifty-fifty. I had a dog and, after a few weeks on salary, I had a little money put aside. Which was good, because the so-called cure I'd taken at Dr. Gardiner's sanitarium hadn't worked worth a damn, and I'd taken to using heroin on account of morphine being so expensive and all.

Still, things could've been worse, believe me, and things might have actually worked out in the end except, like I said, for the fucking dogs.

Pearlie had energy, see, and she was getting on Mrs. Calvit's nerves. She needed a yard, only we didn't have one. But there was this basement apartment on West 75th that came on the market real cheap that had a little fenced yard out back, and I told Mrs. Calvit that if we went in as partners we could rent it and park all our dogs over there during the day and get more work done without tripping over ourselves all the time. She thought that was a "grand idea." But then she must've forgotten, because after I'd signed the lease, she said she couldn't possibly afford "such an extravagance" and was "quite contented" to have her dogs with her at the hotel like she'd always had.

Joe Sussman used to say that if life gives you lemons, the first thing you need to do is make a little lemonade, then go out and find someone who life gave vodka and have yourselves a party. So I decided that the new apartment wasn't a problem, really, but an opportunity. As in, what if I took the money I'd been saving and bought a bed and a dresser and moved into the new place myself? And better yet, what if I used the new apartment to make a little lemonade on the side?

The way I figured it, with most of the working girls still in jail and the rest of 'em running scared, there was a whole bunch of johns out there with nothing to do and nobody to do it with. So I started calling some old numbers I had. Nice guys mostly, none of the creeps. "Want to meet for a drink?" I'd ask them, and most of them did. I figured they might have an extra five dollars to spend, even if times were tough. And I was right about that too.

Only now if I brought a guy back to the apartment, I was the one who had to do Dolly's old job. Chief cook and bottle washer, that was me. Which is why I'd started buying an extra cube a week, just to settle my nerves. What the heck, I had the money. Meanwhile, as far as Mrs. Calvit was concerned, the reason I was busy most nights was because I was working in a dance studio.

So all in all, things were going okay. Until all of a sudden when they weren't.

He had dark hair, thick and wavy, and dreamy blue eyes and no wedding band. I'd seen him once before, hanging out on the sidewalk near the new apartment. He'd made a joke about the dogs, about who was walking who. I made him for a drugstore cowboy— just a single guy who was bored and restless and liked to take the air.

On the night in question, which was May 8, three days before Jimmy's trial was scheduled to start, I was walking to the new apartment with Pearlie on her little leash. When I saw my drugstore cowboy, he was standing on the corner under a streetlamp, smoking a cigarette. I didn't know if he remembered me or not, but I stopped and bummed a smoke.

"Pretty night, ain't it?" I said, just to chew the rag.

"I'll say."

"What's the matter, your girlfriend stand you up?"

He smiled. "Nah. I just like to be outside is all. Can't stand being cooped up. It makes me squirrely."

"You live around here?"

"Close by."

We stood there smoking, watching the cars.

"Well," I told him, "thanks for the ciggy."

"You bet."

I started on my way, and then I stopped and turned around.

"Hey," I said. "You like lemonade?"

"What?"

"What I mean is, if you're lookin for a little company, I might be available."

"Available how?"

"Come on, honey," I told him, offering my arm. "We'll discuss that part later."

His smile turned into a grin as he took my arm and spun me around and shoved my face against the building. Then he slapped the handcuffs onto my wrists while Pearlie circled around us, back and forth, barking her little head off.

Twenty-Nine

Hot Springs

April 1936

OUTSIDE THE SOUTHERN CLUB, the sidewalk on Central Avenue is crowded with lunch-hour strollers, the men in white ducks and boaters and more than a few of the women shouldering brightly colored parasols. Lucky waits while Dutch Akers, his local body-guard, stands and stretches and sucks a final drag from his cigarette before grinding it out underfoot.

"How'd it go?"

Lucky dips a hand into the pocket of his trousers. Discreetly, he fans five C-notes for the bodyguard's inspection.

"I'd be impressed if I didn't know you'd started with two grand."

Lucky laughs. "Tell you what. If it wasn't for suckers like me, smart guys like you'd be forced to retire on your pensions."

The men walk slowly, taking the air and eyeing the women. They soon make their way over to Bathhouse Row where, behind them, the towers of the Arlington Hotel rise from the Valley of the Vapors like the twin spires of some mythic Moorish citadel.

"Hey, Charlie. Is it true what they say about Mr. Madden? Did they really used to call him the Killer?"

Akers, Lucky knows, loves to hear the old Prohibition stories of the rum runs and rubouts that put Hot Springs, Arkansas on the national map and made men like Owen Madden and Charlie Luciano rich.

"It's no secret that Owney done time for murder," Lucky tells him, "but that ain't what made him a legend. It took more than balls and bullets to make it in them days. Lots of guys had both in spades, but the ones who come out on top were the guys who had the smarts to go with it. I'll tell you a little story, only you didn't hear it from me, understand?"

"Sure, Charlie."

"During Prohibition, Owney had this gin joint up in Harlem."

"The Cotton Club."

"That's right. And one day his partner, Frenchy DeMange, got himself kidnapped by Vincent Coll. You ever heard of him?"

"Sure. Mad Dog Coll, the baby killer."

Lucky nods. "Coll was a torpedo for hire, with over fifty notches on his gun. One was almost mine, but that's another story. Anyway, Owney pays fifty grand to ransom Big Frenchy, who's like a brother to him. Meanwhile, Coll and Dutch Schultz are fightin it out like it's the Marne, and pretty soon the bodies are pilin up like cordwood all over Harlem and the Bronx."

"What year are we talking about?"

"I don't know. Thirty, thirty-one. Anyway, Coll needs money, see, to pay for his war with the Dutchman, and he figures Owney for a soft touch on account of him payin so quick on his pal Frenchy. So Coll kidnaps Owney's brother-in-law and then calls Owney up on the phone. Sure, Owney tells him, not a problem, just don't hurt the poor guy. But while Owney's talkin to Coll with his left hand, he dials Dutch Schultz with his right and holds the two phones together so's the Dutchman can hear what they're sayin. The Dutchman, who's got a fifty-grand bounty on Coll's head, he gets the picture, see, and he has an inside man at the phone company put a trace on Owney's line. Ten minutes later, just as they're makin the final arrangements for the drop, Owney hears a Chicago typewriter on the other end of the phone, rat–a–tat–tat, glass flyin and tires squealin, and that was the end of Mad Dog Coll, shot to ribbons in a phone booth. Fuckin Owney freed his brother-in-law, got revenge on Mad Dog, and got his fifty grand back, all without leavin the chair he was sittin in. And that's what I mean about smarts."

Farther down the promenade, amid the crush of ambling couples and baby strollers and tourists hurrying to catch the daily double at Oaklawn Park, Lucky spies a pair of men. The big one is Irish, he figures, and the other Italian. They're wearing wool suits and fedoras, and might as well have "New York City Police" tattooed on their foreheads.

"Uh-oh," Lucky says. "Get ready for trouble."

"Pardon me," the Irishman says, wading through the crowd and blocking Lucky's advance, "but aren't you Charles Luciano?"

Akers steps forward. "There some kind of problem here?"

"Detective Brennan," the big man says, opening his coat to display a badge he wears on his belt. "This is Detective Di Rosa. We're with the New York Police Department. I'm afraid we'll have to ask you to come with us, Mr. Luciano."

"Come with you where? What for?"

"There's a magistrate's warrant outstanding for your arrest."

"Magistrate's warrant? What is this, some kind of a joke?"

"No, sir. I'm sure a judge will explain everything in due course."

Brennan reaches for Lucky's elbow, but Akers clamps a hand on the policeman's wrist.

"Hey, pal." Di Rosa rushes forward like a bulldog. "You don't wanna be doin that. Just mind your own business and nobody'll get hurt."

Lucky is chuckling, shaking his head.

"This is Arkansas, gentlemen," Akers reminds them. "You're out of your jurisdiction, and you're not taking anyone anywhere."

Di Rosa leads with his chin, getting up in the bodyguard's grill. "What are you, some kind of wise guy?"

"No, sir," Akers says, pulling a thin leather case from his pocket and dropping it open. "I'm Herbert Akers, and I'm the chief of detectives here in Hot Springs."

"Can you believe this fuckin bullshit?" Lucky calls from his hotel bathroom over the sound of running water. "Them guys is in town lookin for Al Karpis, and who do they find? That Dewey, he oughta come down and shoot craps, the luck he's got."

Galina Orlova is like a yearling filly, Akers thinks as he watches the New York showgirl pace in her short flapper dress. Gay All Over, he knows they call her, and here she is in the flesh, striding and turning, all legs and arms, pausing only when Lucky emerges from the bathroom freshly shaved and shrugging into a linen suit jacket.

"Okay, let's get this over with. What's the judge's name?"

"Garratt, Sam Garratt. My boys went to fetch him from the track. Sonny Davies is already at the courthouse. This shouldn't take but half an hour."

"Zat's good," the girlfriend says, straightening Lucky's tie, "because he promised to take me shopping."

"Don't worry, baby, I'll be back before three. Ain't that right, Dutch?"

"Yes, sir," Akers says. "But first we need to swing by the club and pick up the bail money."

"If Owney gives you any shit, you remind him I dropped fifteen hundred at roulette this morning."

"But Lucky, you told me zat you alvays vin," Orlova purrs, rubbing up against Lucky like a housecat.

"In the end, baby," he tells her, patting her bottom. "I said in the end I always win."

The courtroom is empty, save for the five silent men seated three on the left and two on the right in the hard wooden benches up front. When the door finally opens, four of the men stand as Samuel W. Garratt, chancellor of the Circuit Court of Garland County, enters while buttoning his robe.

The judge is tall and stoop-shouldered and sports a toupee that is slightly askew. He carries a folded newspaper under his arm that Lucky, smiling where he sits, recognizes as a copy of the *Daily Racing Form*.

"Pleasant afternoon, gentlemen," the judge says as he takes his place on the bench and spreads the paper open before him. "Mr. Davies, what trouble have we gotten ourselves into today?"

Allen T. Davies, the city attorney of Hot Springs, is a fleshy man with thinning blond hair and a suit of rumpled seersucker. He steps forward and hands a document up to the judge.

"Good afternoon, Your Honor. It seems these gentlemen here were part of that cock-up down in Malvern yesterday, and as if they haven't done enough damage in our community for one visit, today they've accosted Mr. Luciano on the promenade. They have in their possession what they claim is a warrant from a magistrate judge in New York charging Mr. Luciano with trying to extort—and I'm paraphrasing here, Your Honor—trying to extort a hundred bucks from a pimp. Do I have that right, gentlemen? A hundred dollars? In any event, Mr. Luciano wishes to put this matter behind him and get back to enjoying the fine weather we're having. As such, he's agreed to appear voluntarily and do whatever is necessary to allow these gentlemen to get home to their jobs and their families as soon as possible."

The judge frowns, first at the warrant and then at the fidgeting duo in the pew.

"Officers? Is there anything you'd care to add to Mr. Davies's remarks?"

The men share a look. Brennan, the Irishman, stands and clears his throat.

"Your Honor, the warrant you're holding compels the arrest of Charles Luciano for extortion accompanied by threats of violence and flight from prosecution. Specifically, it charges a violation of the Federal Kidnapping Act, which makes it a federal crime to avoid giving testimony in a proceeding—"

"I can read, Officer. But let's cut the bullshit, shall we? Y'all didn't travel a thousand miles just to serve paper on a chicken-shit charge like this. So how's about one of you tells the court what the hell is really going on here?"

Brennan looks to his partner for help. Di Rosa shrugs.

"Uh, we're not real clear on the underlying facts, Your Honor. Only that Mr. Dewey, the special prosecutor in New York County, heard we were coming to Arkansas and asked us to look for Mr. Luciano while we were here."

"I see." The judge is nodding now. "Mr. Dewey's reputation precedes him. A regular Dick Tracy, or so it's been said. Mr. Davies, what do the people have in mind, exactly?"

"Well, Your Honor, it seems to me that bail"—and here he glances at Akers, who splays five fingers next to his hat—"in the sum of five thousand dollars ought to suffice under the circumstances. That should buy us some time to clear up this whole misunderstanding."

The judge bangs his gavel. "So ordered. Mr. Davies, I'm sure you can handle the paperwork. Mr. Luciano? The court thanks you for your cooperation and hopes this hasn't been too great of an inconvenience. But since we're all here, and if you'll forgive my impertinence in asking, who do you like in the seventh today at Oaklawn?"

Lucky stands and tugs at his jacket. "Tomahawk, across the board."

"Tomahawk." The judge licks a finger and turns the page of his paper. "By God, maybe this wasn't such a waste after all. Very well, gentlemen. Y'all skedaddle back to New York. Our docket gets a bit crowded this time of year, but I'm sure Mr. Davies here will let you know as soon as your matter comes up for hearing."

On Friday afternoon, two days after his court appearance, Lucky sits in his usual box at Oaklawn Park with Gay Orlova beside him, her blonde waves tucked into a fetching new sunhat. Both are watching through heavy binoculars as the horses in the third race round the clubhouse turn and thunder into the stretch. Both rise to their feet as the co-favorites, dueling neck and neck, gallop for home.

"Come on, Eastport! Come on, baby! Eastport! Eastport! Yeah!"

They whoop and hug, the showgirl bouncing like a cocktail shaker inside of Lucky's embrace. Over her shoulder, Lucky frowns at the sight of the three suited men picking their way down the steps of the grandstand.

"Here, baby. Run up and cash these like a good girl."

As the showgirl shoulders her way past the new arrivals, Lucky stands and braces himself for the blow that the sullen face of Allen T. Davies is already telegraphing.

"Hello, Charlie. You remember Rich Ryan and Jimmy Campbell."

"I don't suppose you boys are here for the fourth race?"

"No, Charlie," Davies says, scanning the seats around them. "I'm afraid we've got ourselves what you might call a situation."

A rap on the heavy oak door quiets the conference room chatter. James Campbell, the Arkansas state assemblyman, opens it to a breathless Dutch Akers.

"Is she okay?" Lucky asks Akers, turning from where he stands at the window.

Akers nods as he takes a seat at the table. Lucky returns his gaze to the street as Richard Ryan, the criminal defense attorney, resumes his interrupted narrative.

"The point is, Carl Bailey is no friend of ours. He ran for attorney general on a law-and-order platform whose first plank was cleaning up Hot Springs. Hot Mess, he likes to call us in the press. Says we're a pustular pimple on the face of the great state of Arkansas. Which means this is exactly the kind of fight he's been itching to have."

"What fight?" Akers surveys the faces at the table. "What's going on?"

"Dewey," Davies tells him. "He's flown one of his Harvard boys down with a grand jury indictment and an extradition warrant signed by the governor of New York. It seems they plan to try Charlie on some sort of a prostitution rap. The A.G.'s gotten wind of it, and he's driving from Little Rock with the capitol press corps in tow. That kind of attention will limit our options, gentlemen, and means we'll have to fight this thing out in public. But at least we've got Sam Garratt in our corner."

Again Lucky turns from the window.

"C'mon you guys, what am I payin ya for? Dewey must be out of his fuckin gourd. I expected income taxes, but prostitution? The bastard's just grabbin at straws."

"Sounds like a rap you can beat, Charlie."

"Normally, I'd say sure, but here's the thing about Dewey. From what I hear about this judge he's got in his pocket, he could convict the pope of bein Jewish. Which means we gotta fight this extradition with everything we got. At least buy ourselves some time so we can figure out what the hell's goin on."

Campbell turns to Ryan, the defense attorney. "What are you thinking, Rich?"

"I don't know. This Dewey's been making a hell of a racket. Sam's gotten telegrams from the governor in Little Rock and the police commissioner in New York. He'll have to increase the bail; that much is certain. Which means you might have to spend a couple of nights in jail, Charlie, but that might be the safest place for you with those two detectives running around. Meanwhile, maybe we can make some hay out of these competing warrants. One's a federal rap and one's state, right? So Al, how's about if you issue a fugitive warrant for Charlie's arrest on the federal charge, and on that basis we oppose extradition on the state warrant? Take the position we plan to put Charlie on trial for the federal rap right here in Hot Springs. That should buy us some time to plan our next move."

"Sorry, Charlie, but you're under arrest."

The men laugh.

"Once the hubbub quiets down and Bailey gets his headlines, then we'll arrange bail for Charlie and see if we can't get him acquitted on this extortion charge. How does that sound?"

The men fall silent as Lucky moves from the window. Ryan steps aside, ceding his place at the head of the table.

"All right you guys." Lucky's palms are flat on the tabletop. "If that's the plan, then here's what I wanna see. Al, you call Moe Polakoff in New York and tell him to get his ass down here on the next available plane. Dutch, go tell Gay we're havin dinner tonight at the jail, and have her bring some decent chow and some clean sheets from the hotel. And my shaving kit. And my pajamas—the blue ones with the piping. As for you, Richie, you and Al get in there and kick the shit out of Dewey's Harvard boy—what's his name again?"

"McLean."

"You kick the shit out of McLean and send a message back to New York that Dewey's bullshit don't wash down here in Arkansas. And last of all, Jimmy"—here Lucky turns his attention to the Arkansas assemblyman—"I still don't know what the fuck I'm payin you for."

Again the men laugh.

"Okay, that's it. And don't screw this up, 'cause there's a horse I really like in the feature race on Sunday."

★　★　★

Lucky is still in his pajamas on Saturday morning when he hears the distant commotion. Sheriff Roy Ermey of Garland County lays down his cards and hurries through the open door of the cell. Dutch Akers and Jimmy Campbell share a puzzled look.

"What the hell is that?"

Ermey returns at a run, his key ring jangling as he bypasses the cell and heads straight for his office without so much as a sideward glance.

Now all the men lay down their cards.

"Dutch, go see what the fuck is going on."

But before any can move, a squadron of men—at least a dozen by Lucky's count—darkens the narrow hallway. All have shotguns or rifles, and all are wearing the belted blue uniform of the Arkansas State Police. With them are the two New York detectives, Brennan and Di Rosa, along with Dewey's redheaded assistant, Edward McLean.

"Charles Luciano?" the police captain reads from a blue-backed document. "By order of Governor Junius Marion Futrell and the Circuit Court of Pulaski County, you are hereby under arrest as a fugitive from justice in the state of New York."

"Get dressed, Lucky." Brennan removes a cigarette and taps it on the pack. "We're takin a ride to Little Rock."

"Habeas corpus. It means to deliver the body—your body—back to Hot Springs so they can try you on the federal charge."

Moses Polakoff sits opposite his client at a wide wooden table, his pin-striped suit and bow tie in sharp contrast to Lucky's work shirt and jeans of matching blue denim with the words "Pulaski County" stenciled over the breast pocket. A guard stands at attention behind him, cradling a short-barreled shotgun.

"I've heard that song before, Moe. Richie Ryan sang it to me in Hot Springs. Then the National Guard came along and broke up the show."

"That was just a stunt by Futrell, the Arkansas governor, repaying some favor to Lehman. Dave Panich is the best appellate lawyer in Arkansas, Charlie. He says we've got a good judge here who's not in anyone's pocket. We have a ten-day stay to pursue an appeal, and Panich is on his way up to Kansas City as we speak. What's not helping matters is that Bailey, the attorney general, is running around claiming Owney Madden tried to bribe him with fifty grand."

"Fuck the attorney general. Our problem ain't the politicians or the judges down here, Moe. Our problem is Dewey. What are you hearin about this pandering bullshit?"

Polakoff lowers his voice. "Dewey's got something like a hundred prostitutes already in custody, and some of them are pointing the finger at Little Davie. I guess the theory is that Davie answers to you, so it must be your racket."

Lucky swears in Italian. The guard frowns.

"That's bullshit and Dewey knows it. He couldn't lay a glove on me, so he tries to pull a freshman stunt like this."

"I know, Charlie, I know."

"I've never taken a dime off a skirt in my life! And anyway, who's gonna believe a bunch of junked-up whores in the first place? Somethin ain't right here, Moe. Dewey wants to be governor so bad he can taste it. He wouldn't be stickin his neck out like this unless the fix was already in."

"Here's something else you're not going to like. As we speak, Dewey and Lehman are ramming a bill through the New York legislature that will allow the trial of multiple defendants for a series of related offenses under a single indictment."

"Try that again in English."

"It's called a joinder law. It means he's planning to put you, Davie, Tommy Pennochio, the bookers, the bondsmen—this whole so-called vice combination—on trial together. He wants to sit you all at the same table, then let the girls throw mud at the bookers, and get the bookers to point the finger at Tommy and Davie. Then he'll ask the jury to return a verdict against everyone, including you."

"Jesus Christ."

"Dewey held a press conference the other day and said you were the biggest gangster in America, in charge of the worst vice racket in New York history. He basically made his opening statement to every potential juror in the city, with nobody around to contradict him."

"That little cocksucker."

"And that's not all. According to Chappie, Tommy and Davie were dropping your name all over town, trying to get the madams and bookers in line."

"Why the fuck didn't Chappie say anything to me?"

"I don't know. Maybe he figured you'd given Davie the okay."

"Jesus Christ, it's like a bad fuckin dream. What are we gonna do about it?"

"For right now, we sit tight and hope that Panich can find a sympathetic judge to hear our appeal."

"And what if he can't?"

Moses Polakoff shrugs. "Then we'll find you the best criminal defense lawyer in the state of New York."

Lucky wakes at midnight to the *clang* of an iron door. He lifts his head on an elbow. Footsteps echo in the corridor of the Pulaski County Jail. Three, maybe four men are heading his way.

"Now what?" he grumbles, reading his watch.

He is seated and scratching at his head by the time they arrive. There are four men in total, three of whom he recognizes by their backlit silhouettes.

"Here you go, Lucky." A pile of folded clothes hits the floor at his feet. "Time to go home."

They are hurrying in darkness. Down the polished corridor, past the cells of the slumbering inmates. Through the guard's room, and then down a carpeted hallway past the sheriff's office.

"Where are you guys takin me? My ten days ain't up till tomorrow."

"Wrong, Charlie. Your ten days expired at midnight."

One detective is on each of Lucky's arms. They guide him through the intake area and to the front desk, where a jailer is already waiting.

"Cuff him," Brennan tells Di Rosa, and Lucky feels the cold embrace of metal on his wrists.

A clipboard is signed, and the jailer opens the outside door. The cold air meets Lucky's face like a slap.

"Where's my lawyer? You guys can't just yank me outta here. This is America, for Christ sake."

Nobody responds. Down at the curb, a patrol car is idling. McLean claims the shotgun seat, while Lucky is wedged between the detectives into the middle seat in back.

He feels a sickening sense of déjà vu.

The patrol car travels without lights or siren. It is a short drive to the train yard. The car stops well short of the platform, where the men haul Lucky onto a graveled sidetrack. A train is waiting, hulking in the darkness, and Lucky can see lights filtering through the steam. Ahead, a cluster of men has gathered on the platform.

"Jesus," McLean says. "Fucking Bailey."

As the four men march past the caboose, a cry echoes from the platform. The waiting reporters surge to the railing.

"Lucky! Hey, Lucky! Any last words for the people of Arkansas?"

A camera flashes. Lucky is lifted and placed on the first iron step of the train car. He twists in the grip of his captors and manages a single shouted plea as the door slams closed behind him.

"Help! I'm bein kidnapped!"

Thirty

Mouthpiece

May 1936

GEORGE LEVY HAILED a taxi outside the courthouse and took it straight to his hotel. He'd arrived in Albany on Thursday evening, just fourteen hours earlier, and he had every intention of returning to Freeport in time for Friday night dinner. He'd packed but a single change of clothes—the very suit he was wearing as he paid the cabbie and bounded up the steps and entered the hotel lobby.

If George had been a drinker, he'd perhaps have detoured into the bar for a celebratory cocktail. As it was, his plan was to check out immediately, grab a quick bite at the little sit-down deli across the street, then catch the two fifty train for Grand Central. That left him an hour for lunch and, with any luck, enough time for a victory cigar on the platform at the railway station.

Celebration was certainly in order. Earlier that year, George had obtained a declaratory judgment from the New York Supreme

Court that the dog racing purchase-option scheme employed by his clients at the Mineola Fairgrounds, while clearly an avoidance of the state's gambling laws, was not a violation of them. In a judicial opinion that was still being chuckled over in New York legal circles, Judge Paul Bonynge had waxed philosophical about the small hypocrisies that the law endures in order to attain the ends of justice:

> Does not the Supreme Court grind out thousands of divorces annually upon the stereotyped sin of the same big blonde attired in the same black silk pajamas? Is not access to the chamber of love quite uniformly obtained by announcing that it is a maid bringing towels or a messenger boy with an urgent telegram? Do we not daily pretend to hush up the fact that an offending defendant is insured when every juror with an ounce of wit recognizes the defendant's lawyer and his entourage as old friends?
>
> More than half a century ago P. T. Barnum recorded the fact that the American people delight in being humbugged, and such is still the national mood. Nowhere is this trait more clearly shown than in the field of gambling. A church fair or bazaar would scarcely be complete without a bevy of winsome damsels selling chances on bed quilts, radios, electric irons, and a host of other things. If the proceeds are to be devoted to the ladies' sewing circle or the domine's vacation, no sin is perceived and the local prosecutor, whoever or wherever he may be, stays his hand. But if a couple of dusky youths are apprehended rolling bones to a state of moderate warmth, blind justice perceives the infamy of the performance and the law takes its course.

Following the morning's oral arguments, the Appellate Division in Albany would at last lay the matter to rest and would, George was confident, uphold the legality of pari-mutuel wagering in the Empire State—a small victory for his clients, but one whose benefit to New York's horse racing industry would be measured in millions of dollars.

"Mr. Levy!" the receptionist called to George as he strode through the carpeted lobby.

"Yes?"

She waved a slip of paper. "There's an urgent message for you. A Mr. Polakoff has telephoned several times."

George carried the message slip to the phone booth in the hotel bar.

"Mr. Levy?" Even with the poor connection, George could hear relief in the stranger's voice. "Thank God I caught you. Your office gave me this number. I hope you can spare me a moment."

"What's this about?"

"My name is Moses Polakoff. I'm the attorney for Charles Lucania, better known as Lucky Luciano. As you're probably aware, my client has recently been indicted on multiple counts of compulsory prostitution. That's the crime of having placed women in houses of prostitution with the intention—"

"Yes, I know what it is. But what can I do for you?"

"My client needs a trial lawyer, Mr. Levy. A lawyer of impeccable reputation, but one with the guts to stand up to the special prosecutor and his army of Ivy League whiz kids. You've come highly recommended by Frank Costello and Lou Clayton, among others, and of course your reputation precedes you. But I'm not going to sugarcoat it. You've seen what Dewey's been doing to us in the newspapers. We're in a jam, George, and we need help. And just so you know, money is no object to Mr. Lucania."

"Now hold on a second. If I were to take the case—and I'm not saying I will—my rate is five hundred a day during trial. That's what I charge everyone."

"That's fine, obviously."

"And you'll have to forgive me, but I haven't been following the case all that closely. How much time would I have to prepare?"

Static filled the silence on the line.

"That's the other thing," the voice finally said. "The trial opens Monday, and there's no chance in the world of putting it off."

Saturday noon found George in a well-appointed office at 475 Fifth Avenue sitting opposite a small conference table from Moses Polakoff, age forty, and another, younger lawyer named Mezansky. Both men watched as George finished reading the sixty-one-page indictment. Both noted the furrows deepening on their visitor's forehead as he reached the final page.

"Ninety counts," George said, squaring the onionskin pages and sliding them across the table. "My God, all Dewey has to do is wave this thing in front of the jury. They'll figure Luciano must be guilty of something."

Polakoff nodded. "That's exactly what I've been saying."

"Do you have a list of the prosecution witnesses?"

"No. Dewey won't give us one, and the indictment, as you can see, fails to identify who testified before the grand jury."

"That's the new procedure, I suppose, with the repeal of section two seventy-one."

Polakoff shared a look with his colleague. "I can see you're up to speed. We've filed a motion arguing that the old procedure should apply, since the charged offenses predate the repeal. We've also demurred to the indictment on a similar ground—that the joinder law's application to the charged offenses would be ex post facto."

"That will turn on whether the joinder law is considered one of procedure or substance."

"Exactly. We think the trial of multiple counts and multiple defendants under a single indictment is both procedural and substantive in nature. That's our argument, anyway."

"Tell me about this judge."

Polakoff sighed. "Philip McCook is a clergyman's son from Connecticut—a law-and-order, God-and-country Republican. He and Dewey were appointed together and given the same marching orders: to convict the top racketeers, come hell or high water. Anything less will be seen as a black eye for both the mayor and the governor. McCook, who's close friends with La Guardia, knows that better than anyone. So far, he's let Dewey get away with murder. Have you heard about Luciano's bail?"

"No."

"Three hundred and fifty thousand, the highest in New York history."

"I see."

"Thanks to the pretrial conference, we've had some insight into Dewey's trial strategy. Basically, the prostitutes are innocent lambs, and the defendants are wolves and vultures growing fat on their degradation."

"And you take issue with that?"

"At least allow me to play devil's advocate. Assume for a moment that these girls are prostitutes by choice, for the simple reason that they can earn three to four hundred dollars a week compared to the eight or ten they'd be making as waitresses or cigarette girls. But one of the problems with prostitution is that if a girl gets arrested, no legitimate bonding company will post her bail. The default rates are simply too high. So the girls need cash, which they often don't have because many of them are also drug addicts. By those lights, Jacobs and Berkman, the two unlicensed bondsmen, were simply filling a need, to the benefit of all concerned. And at ten dollars a week, or roughly three percent of the girls' gross earnings, their rates were actually quite reasonable."

"But if a girl is never arrested, that's all profit to this so-called bonding combination."

"Just like any insurance premium. As for the rest of them, well, they're all part of the machinery that makes the system work.

Madams, bookers, lenders, upper management. If it wasn't illegal, and to some people immoral, you might say it's a fair and efficient system designed to protect the girls by keeping them off the streets and out of jail."

"And Luciano is part of it?"

"No, of course not. But we've been hearing rumors ever since that raid back in February that Dewey's putting tremendous pressure on the girls. They've been held for months now under constant threat of prosecution. Many were addicts who've gone through withdrawal, and God only knows what they've said or signed. Dewey's message seems to be, 'Tell us what we want to hear and the charges against you will be dropped and you'll be given immunity for your testimony.' And what he wants to hear, of course, is the name Charlie Lucky. Those who refuse are left in jail. Those who agree to finger Luciano are released from custody and moved to swanky hotels, where they're wined and dined by the handsome young lawyers from Dewey's office."

"That sounds a bit far-fetched."

"Except that it's true. We've had private operatives tailing the few we've been able to locate. Several of Dewey's assistants—Gelb, Cole, and Ten Eyck—have been taking the girls out for food and drinks on a regular basis. Dempsey's, the Villanova, Keane's Tavern. And not just one or two drinks, from what we can determine."

"If all that's true, then there's a defense right there: undue influence of witnesses. Witnesses, I have to assume, who weren't very credible to begin with. Have you tried talking with any of them?"

"Tried, yes, but Dewey won't allow it."

"What do you mean he won't allow it?"

Polakoff laughed. "Welcome to our world, George, where Dewey's word is law. We don't know how many will actually testify, but the indictment lists thirty prostitutes as potential witnesses. Dewey's got at least forty more stashed away, plus a handful of madams and low-level functionaries—the bookers and bondsmen and strong-arm types. If he can get even a few to say that Charlie Lucky's the boss, then we've got ourselves a hell of a problem. And the maddening thing is that other than David Betillo, who's an acquaintance from his old bootlegging days, Lucky doesn't know any of his co-defendants. He couldn't pick them out of a lineup."

George settled into his chair and pushed up his coat sleeves to reveal his bare forearms beneath. He'd heard of D.A.s woodshedding witnesses, of course—Lew Smith in the Carman case came to mind—but nothing on the scale of what Polakoff was describing.

"With thirteen defendants and a ninety-count indictment, it'll be a three-ring circus in that courtroom. Who are the other lawyers?"

"Ten defendants," Polakoff corrected. "We have it on good authority that three of the bookers will be pleading guilty. And there'll be no public spectators allowed—just the defendants, the lawyers, and a large pool of reporters. We'll ask that witnesses be excluded, of course, and McCook has hinted that he'll sequester the jury. As far as the lawyers go, they're all pretty solid. You know Jim Murray, I'm sure, and Maurice Cantor, who was Arnold Rothstein's lawyer. But I've made it clear to them that if you come on board, then you'll be the captain of the ship. As far as trial strategy is concerned, whatever you say goes, as long as their clients aren't prejudiced. And, of course, that you'll take the lead in jury selection."

Polakoff's look was imploring. To avoid it, George directed his gaze to the windows overlooking Bryant Park.

The time had come to decide. Undertaking to represent America's most notorious gangster in one of the most ballyhooed trials in history was no trifling matter. It was, in fact, a life-altering proposition. Until now, George had been known, where known at all, as a competent, affable barrister from Long Island. Should he take the Luciano case, he'd henceforth be called a mob lawyer—a mouthpiece. The label would follow him into every courtroom, every client meeting, and every social function he'd ever attend. It would shadow George Jr., his son and namesake, into an already difficult adulthood. It would appear in George's obituary.

And then there were the practical hurdles. This extraordinary session of the New York State Supreme Court involved two dedicated grand juries, a special prosecutor, a judge, and a so-called blue-ribbon panel of "experienced" petit jurors—meaning, George suspected, white businessmen who'd previously voted to convict—all of whom had been convened and constituted for the singular purpose of taking down Luciano.

Dewey, the special prosecutor, had spent untold taxpayer dollars, had tapped telephones and offered indulgences, and had run hundreds of witnesses through the two grand juries. He had, as Polakoff suggested, a small army of lawyers, accountants, and police detectives at his beck and call. He had a judge in his corner who seemed more of a co-prosecutor than a neutral referee, and he'd even enlisted the state legislature to tip the scales in his favor.

Never before in New York history had multiple crimes against multiple defendants been combined into a single trial. And to make matters worse, it would be a trial by surprise, with no foreknowledge as to who the witnesses would be, let alone what they might have been coached or coerced into saying.

Those were the downsides. George, on the other hand, was a lawyer and an officer of the court. He believed that every defendant, no matter how unsavory his reputation or heinous the crime alleged, was entitled to his day in court. All were innocent until proven guilty. To George, who'd aspired to the trial bar ever since his early teens, these were neither bromides nor hackneyed clichés, but rather the twin pillars upon which stood the greatest system of criminal justice the world had ever known.

George turned to Polakoff, who still was watching him, hanging as if on tenterhooks.

"Tell me the truth, Moe. Is Luciano really innocent?"

"Innocent?" Polakoff shook his head. "No, George, he's not innocent. He's a convicted drug dealer, a former bootlegger, and a notorious bookmaker and gambler. He's got his fingers in any number of murky deals with some very dicey characters. I don't ask, because I don't want to know. But he's no whoremonger, I can tell you that much. And he'd like the opportunity to tell you so himself."

"All right then, let's go see him."

Polakoff straightened. "Does that mean you're taking the case?"

"I may be crazy," George said, standing and gathering up the files, "but I wouldn't miss this thing for the world."

Thirty-One

The Wire

May 1936

"ALL RIGHT, PEOPLE. Listen up."

Tom leaned with his back to the desk, his fingers tracing the carved mahogany inlay. Of the twenty men and one woman crowded onto the chairs and couches hastily arrayed in a semicircle before him, it was Sol Gelb, Barry Ten Eyck, Jack Rosenblum, Stanley Fuld, and Harry Cole who appeared the most anxious. Which was only natural, since it was they, more so than the others—Charlie Grimes, Frank Hogan, Bill Herlands, Murray Gurfein, Thurston Greene, Paul Lockwood, Ed McLean, Vic Herwitz, Milt Schilback, Jack Grumet, Ed Joseph, Harry Steinberg, Livy Goddard, Manny Robbins, Charlie Breitel, and Eunice Carter—who'd be the ones standing shoulder to shoulder with the special prosecutor in the courtroom battle set to begin in less than an hour's time.

All the lawyers present, however, thanks to six solid weeks of fifteen-hour workdays, had an intensely personal stake in what was to come.

Outside the office where the prosecutorial team had gathered, the fourteenth floor of the Woolworth Building was a beehive of last-minute activity. Telephones rang and typewriters clattered. Stenographers and clerks, detectives and accountants bustled along a carpeted hallway glimpsed only in slatted fragments through the lowered window blinds.

"Is it just me," Tom began, affecting the tone of breezy confidence he'd learned from George Medalie, "or does this feel a little bit like Christmas morning? Some of you know what I mean. The shopping is done, the packages are wrapped, and now it's only a matter of tearing them open. We're down to the fun part, people! Especially when we know that somewhere in that pile of boxes is the one special gift we've been waiting the whole year to receive. The one we pestered our parents for. The one we wrote to Santa about."

"A Lucky doll!" someone warbled in falsetto, and the room erupted in laughter.

Tom waited for the merriment to subside.

"Allow me to be serious for a moment. I don't have to tell you how important the next three weeks are going to be. Not just for this office and the careers of those working here, but also for the people of New York and the cause of justice and decency in these United States. Because nothing less is what's at stake in this trial."

He paused there for effect, scanning the room, meeting the eyes of his audience.

"It's been a long road we've traveled, and God knows, it's been a rocky one. We've had to overcome frightened witnesses and drug addictions and threats from thugs and gangsters. We've had one of our own, Ray Ariola, prosecuted by a district attorney who's made it perfectly clear he'll do anything in his power to thwart us in our mission. And we've had to fight an epic extradition battle just to get our star defendant back in the jurisdiction. At times it's seemed as though we were twenty lawyers against the world. But all of that is behind us now, and our eyes must be focused from this moment forward on the task that lies ahead."

He circled the desk and perched on the edge of his swivel chair.

"An hour from now, jury selection will begin. We have a preliminary list of seventy witnesses, and as to those witnesses, each of you knows your assignment. Frank will be in charge of matters at this end. We have a dedicated wire running from the courtroom to the investigators' office, which will allow us to coordinate the transfer of witnesses from custody. Judge McCook is counting on us to monitor the proceedings and avoid any delays or interruptions due to the unavailability of witnesses."

Tom risked a glance in Gelb's direction. Little Sol, his chief trial strategist, was studying his shoelaces.

"With a venire of two hundred talesmen, I'm expecting voir dire to last at least two days, possibly three. The only witnesses we'll need for today are Weiner, Balitzer, and Marcus, each of whom will enter his guilty plea before jury selection begins. In front of the whole panel, I might add, which ought to give our esteemed colleagues for the defense a little something to think about."

Chuckles and murmurs rippled through the room.

"Speaking of defense counsel, I understand we have a new face in the crowd. Murray?"

Murray Gurfein flipped a page on his legal pad. "Sam Mezansky called on Saturday afternoon to say that George Morton Levy will be appearing as trial counsel for Luciano. Levy's a Long Island defense attorney with a sterling reputation and a hell of a track record. He's currently in partnership with Elvin Edwards, the former Nassau County D.A. You may recall that Levy represented Joseph Ustica in that Gilbride murder case a couple of years ago."

"Against Edwards, if memory serves."

"That's right, which tells you something right there. I spent most of Sunday asking around about Levy. Word is he's a quick study, good on his feet, and that juries love him to death. He tried his first capital murder when he was all of twenty-six years old. George Medalie even used him once in a union-busting case in Rockville Centre. It's no stretch to say that Levy's the best defense lawyer on Long Island. He's also a member at the Lakeville Club, where he's golfing buddies with Frank Costello and Frank Erickson, which probably explains his connection to Luciano."

"Thank you, Murray. We've wondered whether Polakoff was going to try the case, and now we have our answer. If they hired Levy this late in the game, then I'm guessing he wasn't their first choice. Or maybe they've had him up their sleeve the whole time. In any event, it doesn't change anything we're planning to do."

Herwitz raised a hand. "What about peremptories?"

"What about them?"

"With ten defendants, is the judge going to limit them to twenty per side or twenty per defendant?"

"That's outside your bailiwick, Vic, and it's also beyond our control. In any event, we've already briefed it. Now if there are no other stupid questions, I'll conclude by thanking you all for your hard work to date, and for the even harder work I'll be expecting from each of you in the days and weeks ahead. It won't be easy, people, but nothing worth accomplishing ever is. Break a leg, gentlemen. You too, Mrs. Carter. And Sol, will you and Frank stick around for just a second?"

Chairs scraped as the lawyers stood and gathered their papers. When the hallway door opened, the tumult of the outer office gusted across Tom's desk until the door closed again, leaving the three men alone in the muted quiet.

Tom checked his watch. He stood and crossed to the hallway windows, where he adjusted the half-open blinds, further dimming the room.

"Don't go weak in the knees, Sol," he said without turning. "This is the part where we all need to stand our tallest."

"My knees are fine, chief."

"Even if McCook orders the witnesses excluded, we'll be in full compliance with that order."

Gelb didn't respond.

"Right?"

"I said I was fine with it, okay? Let's leave it at that."

Tom turned to face the two seated men.

"Look. McCook knows we have the wire. He knows we'll be monitoring the proceedings, and he knows we have witnesses here to prep. He can add two and two."

"But you're not going to tell the defense."

Tom removed a silver dollar from his pocket and worked it through his fingers as he returned to his desk.

"Come on, Sol. That bunch would object if I asked permission to use the men's room. You want to talk about cheating? Cheating is sending hoods to stand outside the House of Detention and shout threats up at the women. Cheating is offering money and drugs to those who don't cooperate. These aren't choirboys we're dealing with, and let's not forget it. These are vicious thugs who terrorize young women and live off the sweat of their disgusting, degrading labor. Young women who, but for the grace of God, could be our own sisters or daughters. These are the lowest of the low, Sol, and I, for one, am not going to apologize for the fact that hearing the others testify might stiffen their spines a little. Not to mention give us a few insights that will help us put Luciano behind bars where he belongs."

The telephone rang, the sound slightly muffled, and Tom yanked open a drawer.

"Yes? All right, Mrs. Rosse, just give us five more minutes."

He replaced the receiver and removed a cigarette holder from his pocket.

"Frank? Where do we stand with Presser and Balitzer? Other than a boat load of hearsay, they're our entire case against Luciano."

"Don't forget Bendix and Good-Time Charlie."

Tom tapped out a cigarette. "Neither of whom I'd trust to take out my garbage. Neither would you, and neither will the jury."

"Well," Hogan said, tipping back in his chair, "I think Nancy is pretty solid. As for Mildred, she'll do anything to help Pete, so as long as we have the one, we have the other. What we could really use is a witness who isn't a convict or a prostitute."

"You can't expect to see clergy testifying in a prostitution case. You like that? It's a line I'll be using in my opening."

Tom lit a match and leaned forward into the flame.

"Hell, I'll settle for another prostitute. I just hate going into that courtroom with only four eyewitnesses. For all the evidence we've got against the others, that's really all we have against Luciano—two prostitutes, one pimp, and a serial stool pigeon who's heading up the river for life. I feel like I'm walking into that courtroom half-naked."

"We'll keep working the others," Hogan said, "but at this point I wouldn't count on anything new. Not that you'll need it, chief. We've got Luciano in the bag."

"We'd better, or I'll be the national poster boy for prosecutorial incompetence."

Tom stood. He tugged at his lapels, then took his new hat down from the rack.

"How do I look?" he asked, tapping the bowler into place.

Frank Hogan smiled. "From where I'm sitting, you look an awful lot like the next governor of the great state of New York."

Thirty-Two

The Kite

May 1936

I FELT LIKE DEATH warmed over.

My head was throbbing, and my side was aching, and I hadn't kept down so much as a mouthful of food for nearly three days. I was burning a fever, sweating like a pig while shivering with the chills. I was too weak to stand, and I couldn't sleep, and my stomach felt like I'd swallowed a quart of battery acid.

And the next day, I knew, was going to be worse. That evening, at least, the nurse had come and given me a shot. But that was the last one—the end of my five-day cure—and from then on it would be strictly cold turkey.

After my pinch on 75th Street, I'd telegrammed Mrs. Calvit and asked her to call Sam Siegel to come and bail me out. But Siegel, the dirty bastard, never raised so much as a finger to help me out. So then I asked Mrs. Calvit if she'd at least come to the courthouse and testify, but a fat lot of good that did. Siegel eventually sent some snot-nosed kid to handle my trial, and by the end of the day I'd been convicted of solicitation.

The only thing I had going for me was that I'd given my name as Fay Marston, and even though Mrs. Calvit testified that she'd known me as Mildred Nelson, the court never connected me with my first arrest as Florence Newman or the outstanding fugitive warrant for Frances Martin. That, and the fact that Mrs. Calvit agreed to take care of poor little Pearlie until I got out of jail.

So there I was, Fay Marston, convicted prostitute, awaiting sentence in the medical unit of the Women's House of Detention. The torture unit was more like it—a dungeon full of drunks and junkies screaming and crying and begging for one thing or another they knew perfectly well they were never gonna get.

And I was playing my part, curled up in my bunk, shivering and moaning, too weak even to use the toilet. I still hadn't heard from Jimmy, even though Siegel's kid must've told him where I was, and as bad as I felt physically, it was the silence from Jimmy that maybe hurt me most of all.

A bunch of the girls from the Dewey vice trial, which had started on Monday, were on the same floor as me, and I figured it was only a matter of time before word got around. That afternoon, sure enough, I got a kite from Gracie Hall, a girl who'd worked at my joint on West End Avenue.

Dear Flo: Some of the girls have seen you and reported you to the D.A.s. They will probably want to question you. Why don't you take the bull by the horns and send a note down to the D.A.s and tell them who you are? Mr. Ten Eyck and Mr. Hogan come to the building every evening. They are very nice and it won't hurt you to talk to them. Maybe it will be better that way. Grace

Gracie and her friend Judy came to see me that night. That was on Wednesday, the third day of the trial. From the expression on Gracie's face, I could guess what I must of looked like. I'd weighed around a hundred and ten pounds when I was arrested, and now, with nothing but a few mouthfuls of cereal over the past five days, I felt like a scarecrow. Like a stiff breeze could have lifted me up and blown me right through the bars.

They found me groaning under a pile of blankets.

"My God, Flo, look at you," Gracie said, laying a hand on my forehead. "You need to be in the hospital. Or at least over with us in the witness block. We get all kinds of special treatment."

"I'll bet you do. You and the other rats."

"Don't be like that. Just be quiet and listen."

She sat on the edge of the bunk, stroking my hair.

"Everything's changed, honey. All them guys, Jimmy and the rest of them, they're all going to prison. You need to talk to Mr. Ten Eyck. We all talk to him. He'll explain everything. If you help them, they'll take care of you. We get special food, and we wear our own clothes, and they take us out to the movies twice a month. Out to dinner too. We even get to go shopping once in a while."

"Tell it to Sweeney."

"It's true, I swear! Some of the girls have even been sprung. Helen Kelly, Irene Smith, Thelma Jordan—they're all living in hotels. Peggy Wild too, and Jenny Fischer. As a reward for being cooperative. Some of the other girls like Mildred Harris and Nancy Presser, the ones who were girlfriends with the combination guys, they're getting the deluxe treatment. I heard Thelma and Nancy are getting a cruise when the trial is over. As close as you were to Jimmy, I'll bet you could get all kinds of stuff. So don't be bullheaded. Here. Take this."

She pressed a pencil stub and some paper into my hand.

"Write a note to Mr. Ten Eyck. T-E-N E-Y-C-K. He'll want to see you, I know he will. And do me a favor, willya? Tell him I'm the one who said so. That'll help me out a little bit too."

Thursday came and went, again with no word from Jimmy. That's when I started to get angry. Angry about the sappy letters I'd written him. Angry about Siegel. Angry about the two of them leaving me here to rot in jail. Angry about little Pearlie, roaming around Mrs. Calvit's apartment, wondering where Mommy had gone. Feeling abandoned again, the poor little thing, and me with nothing I could do about it.

I knew exactly how she felt.

I thought about Christmas then—about when I'd given Jimmy that card with the C-note inside, only to find out he'd given his wife a fur coat. So what did I owe Jimmy Fredericks, anyway? I practically supported the big ape when times were tough for him. I cooked for him, and cleaned up after him, and drove him around like a coolie. And now that the shoe was on the other foot, what do I hear from him? Nothing, that's what. The big kiss-off. He didn't know if I was dead or alive, and I guess he didn't care.

If what Gracie said was true, and if all the combination guys were going down anyway, then I was a first-class sap for lying there with my mouth shut. I had leverage now, but once the trial was over, I'd have nothing but a sentence to serve and a record to live with for the rest of my life. And what was I gonna do then? There were no jobs out there, and even if there was, I'd never get a reference from Mrs. Calvit. I'd be back on the street, that's where I'd be, just another two-dollar whore with no Jimmy Fredericks to protect me. And every time some smelly creep was breathing hot in my ear, I'd be thinking about that one chance I'd had, and how I'd let it slip right through my fingers.

But what if Gracie was wrong? What if I ratted, and then Dewey rolled snake eyes? My life wouldn't be worth a ten-cent slug. I'd wind up in the river, or worse, and who'd take care of Pearlie then? There was no place you could hide from a guy like Charlie Lucky, and even if you could, you'd spend the rest of your life looking over your shoulder.

Goddamn fucking Jimmy. If only I could talk to him, or to Siegel, and get the inside dope. If I met with this Ten Eyck, he'd try to sell me a bill of goods about how great the trial is going and how the train is leaving the station without me. But for all I knew, that was a bunch of hooey. I needed to get my hands on a newspaper and see what the press was saying. Maybe that way I could make up my mind.

I used her pencil and paper to send a kite back to Gracie. I asked for a newspaper, and for another chance to talk.

The paper came with my dinner, which I still couldn't touch, and Mildred Curtis, one of the other girls I knew, came by and read it to me. She told me that June Gary, who was using the name Joan Martin in the trial, had gone on the stand and ratted out Jimmy, saying how he'd wrecked her joint and sapped her down and threatened to shoot her dog.

Shoot her little dog! I knew that was a lie because Jimmy would never do something like that. And then I was hopping mad all over again. Mad at June, who was a big troublemaker and was always moving her joint around, trying not to bond. Mad at Dewey for letting her spin a yarn like that on the witness stand. Mad at myself for lying there in my cell like a pile of dirty rags, unable to make up my mind.

That night, when the matron called the girls to the commissary wagon, I managed to get on my feet and walk, all weak and doubled-over though I was. Then when I saw June Gary standing there buying cigarettes, I couldn't help myself. I called her a dirty, lousy rat for what she'd said about Jimmy.

"I warned him I'd get even," she said, not backing down. "He didn't have to get rough like that. He didn't have to threaten my dog."

"You're a goddamn liar."

"Look at my head!" she said, bending forward and parting her hair. "Look what he done to me with his lead pipe. Go on, look!"

I had a different idea, and grabbed a fistful of hair.

"Owwww! Help! Guard!"

I yanked and twisted as hard as I could, and then Gracie jumped in and tried to pry my fingers loose, but June kept right on screaming. Pretty soon I heard running feet, and then I felt someone grabbing me and lifting me clear off the ground.

"All right, break it up!"

I ended up on the floor with the matron pinning me down with her knee.

"I guess you ain't so sick as you look," she said. "Not so sick you can't spend a little time in the hole."

They carried me there on a stretcher, with guards in front and back and the matron walking alongside. The other women laughing, or clapping, or hooting as I went by.

The cells in solitary were small, and they had only a narrow slot high up in the door for food. It was cold inside, and it smelled like piss, and when the door slammed shut behind me, everything went dark.

Only then did I start crying again.

I cried for a long time, and when I finally stopped crying, I fumbled in my pocket for the pencil and paper. I started to scribble, unable to see what I was writing through the darkness and the tears.

Mr. Ten Eyck

Dear Sir, I would like to see you on a matter of great importance in the Dewey Vice Case . . .

Thirty-Three

The Dock

May 1936

LUCKY IS KEEPING his head down.

He imagines that he is invisible and that the judge and all the lawyers and witnesses who are talking and arguing, swearing oaths and shouting objections, cannot see him. That he could simply stand up and walk, ghostlike, past the guards and reporters—down the stairs and out of the courthouse, where he could hail a cab and return to the Waldorf and slip into a silk robe with a drink in his hand and open up a newspaper and read all about the vice trial of Lucky Luciano, all with nobody being the wiser.

Except, of course, for the jury. Because while Lucky pretends he is a block of ice in a cold and flowing river, invisible and unmoved by the currents surging around him, the fourteen men in the jury box keep careful watch on the trial's star attraction with stares and side-long glances, as if checking to make sure he doesn't disappear from the courtroom like an ace that vanishes up the gambler's sleeve while the other players are distracted.

It is Saturday, the sixth day of the trial, and except for Dewey's opening statement, in which the special prosecutor branded Lucky "the czar of organized crime in this city" and called defendant Davie Betillo "the active general in the army under Luciano," not a single lawyer or witness has so much as mentioned Lucky's name. The whores and madams have instead been content—no, make that eager—to use their moment in the spotlight for settling old scores with the bookers and bondsmen and the strong-arm enforcers who'd fleeced them and intimidated them and in some cases beat them bloody in an effort to turn their loose amalgamation of independent houses into a kind of citywide chain.

Jimmy Fredericks, as far as Lucky can tell, is already sunk. Wahrman and Liguori too, if the jurors buy what the girls are selling. The girls, who are salesmen by nature, have been rehearsed to a fare-thee-well and are staging a bravura performance in their roles as fallen angels in calico dresses peddling sob stories of broken homes and broken lives and a final, miraculous shot at redemption thanks to their savior, Thomas E. Dewey, the great and incorruptible crime buster. The same girls who, as soon as the trial is over, will be back in their two-dollar houses posing as virgins, or as nymphos, or as whatever avatars of sweaty male lust will earn them their next cube of heroin.

Some of the lawyers—Siegel, for example, and Carlino—are rough on the girls, demanding the lurid details of their drug addictions, their sex lives. Scorning them for their aliases and their vagrancy and their lengthy records of arrest, implying that the girls will say or do just about anything to further their own interests. Lucky believes that this, while undeniably true, is also a mistake. A gentler approach, a more respectful tone, would stand them in better stead with the bluenosed jurors, who fidget and frown at the lawyers' bullying tactics.

It's a tricky business, Lucky admits, and the strategy that Polakoff and Levy have settled on is to let the others scuffle and brawl in the gutter while they remain above the fray. To portray Lucky as a gentleman gambler unfairly tarred by an overzealous prosecutor. And while it was Polakoff's idea to subpoena various witnesses who could attest to Lucky's gambling, it was Lucky himself who'd urged upon Levy that, with the exception of Davie Betillo from the old curbside liquor exchange, Lucky had never laid eyes on a single one of his co-defendants.

Dewey has placed a poster before the jury, a cast of characters, with the original thirteen defendants appearing above the line and other names—presumably witnesses or people whose names will otherwise be mentioned—appearing below. The poster reads:

Charlie Lucky	**Charles Luciano**
Tommy Bull	**Thomas Pennochio**
Little Davie	**David Betillo**
Abie	**Abraham Wahrman**
Bennie Spiller	
Jimmy Fredericks	**James Frederico**
Ralph Liguori	
Jesse Jacobs	
Meyer Berkman	
Pete Harris	**Peter Balitzer**
Jack Eller	**Jack Ellenstein**
Dave Miller	**David Marcus**
Al Weiner	

Cockeyed Louis	**Louis Weiner**
Nick Montana	
Binge	**Anthony Curcio**
Chappie	**Santos Scalfani**
Teddy	

Yoke	
Jo-Jo	**Joseph Weintaub**
Andy Coco	**Andrew LeCoco**
Charlie Spinach	**Charles Pisano**
Spike	**Spike Green**
Danny Brooks	**Daniel Caputo**
Billy Peluso	**William Peluso**
Joe Levine	
Abe Karp	**Abraham Karp**
Max Rachlin	
Vito	

Levy has objected to leaving the poster in sight of the jury, but this objection, like all the defense motions before it, has been promptly overruled.

Still, Lucky thinks, Levy was the perfect choice for the job. The little Jew is courtly but commanding, radiating an invisible magnetism that others in the courtroom can feel. Lucky is reminded of Meyer Lansky in the way that Levy fills the room when he enters, the way that others fall silent when he talks. Even McCook, who lets Dewey run roughshod over the other lawyers, is deferential to Levy, listening when he speaks and even sustaining one or two of his infrequent objections.

This is not to say that Lucky has grown overconfident. He knows from Dewey's opening statement that the special prosecutor plans to call witnesses who will claim that Lucky attended meetings with his various co-defendants, actively managing the day-to-day affairs of the so-called vice combination. But Dewey was vague, or probably just cagy, in never disclosing who would actually testify to what. Worried, perhaps, that Lucky might try to influence the witnesses. Or worse, make them disappear. The way he'd made Dutch Schultz disappear, saving Dewey's miserable life.

From where he sits at the defense table, Lucky can read Polakoff's hastily scribbled notes. Dewey had told the jury that in late summer of 1933, all the old bookers were summoned to a meeting downtown at which Lucky had walked into the room and announced, "You guys are through. I'm giving the business to Little Davie." This had turned the jurors' heads and, for that moment at least, Lucky was visible again. The story, however, is a complete fabrication, and Lucky wonders who Dewey has coerced into telling it on his behalf.

As for Tommy Pennochio and Davie Betillo, while not yet sunk, both are taking on water. Before jury selection even began, three of the four bookers named in the indictment—Dave Miller, Pete Harris and Al Weiner—stood before the judge and the roomful of prospective jurors and pleaded guilty to all ninety counts. These are the men who dealt with the whores on a week-to-week basis; the men who, having turned state's evidence, would soon be pointing their fingers up the so-called ladder that Dewey described, right at Little Davie's skinny behind.

But all in all, the trial is going well. Indeed, Dewey has overplayed his hand in at least one respect that he'll soon come to regret. Lucky knows, from reports of the private detectives Polakoff has hired, that Dewey's assistant prosecutors are taking the girls out to bars and restaurants on a regular basis. Yet when Siegel broaches the subject with a witness named Muriel Ryan, Dewey can't jump onto his high-horse fast enough. Again Lucky leans to read the handwriting of Moses Polakoff:

Q: *Were you out in the evenings from the House of Detention?*

A: *Twice.*

Q: *Twice in the evenings? With whom? Any of Mr. Dewey's assistants?*

A: *With a police officer and a matron.*

DEWEY: *I think that is a most offensive question. I object.*

COURT: *What do you object to?*

DEWEY: *The implication that my assistants were going out with these women held as prisoners.*

COURT: *Maybe the noise prevented me from hearing the exact words. If there was such implication, it should not be.*

So while certainly not cocky, Lucky is growing ever more comfortable where he sits. None of the bookers can claim to have met him, and neither Tommy Pennochio nor Davie Betillo will ever dare mention his name. Meanwhile, Dewey has marched into the first trap Polakoff has set for him, and there will be other traps waiting down the road.

The water will rise, Lucky thinks, drowning the Abie Wahrmans and the James Fredericos, submerging the Ralph Liguoris and the Benny Spillers. But it will stop just short of his own battle-scarred chin. And if by some combination of bad luck and perjury the water should engulf even Charlie Lucky, then George Morton Levy, the charismatic little Jew, will be there to rescue him.

In the meantime, Lucky sits and watches, content with being invisible.

Thirty-Four

Stacked Deck

May 1936

GEORGE LEVY WAS no stranger to crowded courtrooms or high-profile cases. He was inured to reporters and photographers, to police escorts and gawking spectators. But even he had never seen anything quite like the Luciano vice trial.

From the mobs thronging the barricades outside the Supreme Court building to the police snipers perched on the adjacent rooftops in Foley Square, the air outside the courthouse fairly crackled with electricity. Inside the second-floor courtroom, where a squadron of uniformed guards accompanied the defendants as they arrived from the jailhouse each morning in handcuffs and shackles, the daily ritual of chains and locks, truncheons and shotguns reminded George of a Dixie chain gang, or maybe a political show-trial held in the concrete bowels of some grim Baltic gulag.

However one might choose to describe it, it was definitely not an atmosphere conducive to the principle of presumed innocence. And if any fading ember of that glowing ideal had somehow managed to rekindle itself after the previous day's proceedings, it was extinguished each morning at ten o'clock sharp by the arrival of Philip J. McCook.

The old judge had set an early tone for the trial when, on the first day of jury selection, he'd summarily denied each and every one of the defense's pretrial motions. The grand jury was improperly constituted? Denied. The defendants are entitled to separate trials? Denied. The joinder law shouldn't apply retroactively? Denied. The defense was entitled to know the names of the witnesses who'd appeared before the grand jury? Denied. The so-called blue-ribbon venire panel had been improperly chosen? Denied. Each defendant is entitled to the same number of peremptory jury challenges as were accorded to the prosecution? Denied. Each defendant is entitled to know with which of the ninety alleged offenses he is specifically charged? Denied, denied, denied.

Next came the voir dire, at the outset of which Harry Kopp, veteran co-counsel for defendant Thomas Pennochio, had requested that the special prosecutor reveal the names of the witnesses he intended to call. This, Kopp argued, would allow the prospective jurors to identify in advance any potential conflicts that might arise if, for example, a witness personally known to a juror might later appear to give testimony, and would obviate the danger of jurors having to disqualify themselves in mid-trial. That motion was also denied.

McCook then allowed the special prosecutor to give a précis of his case—in effect, a preliminary opening statement—to the entire venire panel, on the theory that doing so would help "expedite the selection of jurors." Dewey used this unprecedented opportunity to tell the packed courtroom that which he'd already told the rest of the nation in newspaper and radio interviews: namely, that Charles "Lucky" Luciano was a vicious thug and gangster who "sat way up at the top in his apartment at the Waldorf as the czar of organized crime in this city."

So much for the presumption of innocence, George thought as he sat, dumbfounded, watching the scene unfold. And so much for limiting the people's proof to only those matters charged in the indictment.

While defense counsel were still pissing blood from these early kidney punches, another, graver problem became apparent to George on the trial's third day. It happened during the course of Dewey's formal opening statement, the one given after the twelve trial jurors and two alternates had finally been seated and sworn.

As George understood it, the whole rationale of the joinder law was one of convenience, in that it allowed a prosecutor to charge and try multiple felonies against multiple defendants under a single indictment. In making his case to the legislature, Dewey had argued that the crime of conspiracy—which allows a similar outcome, but constitutes only a misdemeanor—was inadequate to deal with the growing scourge of organized crime in New York. The legislature agreed, and New York's Code of Criminal Procedure was amended accordingly, just in time for the Luciano trial.

An attribute unique to the law of conspiracy, however, is that the hearsay statements of one co-conspirator are admissible as evidence against the others, even if the original speaker is unavailable to testify as a witness. Thus, what would otherwise be inadmissible hearsay— for example, when Wilma Witness testifies that Mike Missing told her that Danny Defendant said such-and-such—is admissible in a conspiracy case against the speaker's co-conspirators as long as the hearsay statement was made during the course of and in furtherance of the conspiracy.

Acting as a counterweight to this liberal rule of evidence is the requirement that, before a conviction can be had, the testimony of a co-conspirator must be corroborated "by such other evidence as tends to connect the defendant with the commission of the crime." In other words, the mere hearsay statements of co-conspirators are insufficient, by and of themselves, to uphold a conspiracy conviction.

But during his second opening statement, Dewey had described to the jurors threats allegedly made by unindicted individuals like former bookers Nick Montana and Cockeyed Louis Weiner—speakers who, Dewey acknowledged, he had no intention of ever calling to testify. When objection was made that such hearsay testimony would therefore be improper if offered at trial, since no conspiracy was alleged in the indictment, it was again overruled by McCook.

Thus, George realized, Dewey had chosen not to plead conspiracy in order to avoid the sentencing limitations of a misdemeanor prosecution, but now wanted the benefit of the liberal rules of evidence as they pertain to a conspiracy case. Moreover, Dewey wanted those rules to apply without the risk of the jury acquitting the defendants on the conspiracy charge—for example, due to lack of corroboration—which would ordinarily render all the co-conspirator testimony retroactively inadmissible. And McCook, it appeared, was perfectly willing to oblige him.

The ramifications of this development were profound. Dewey could, for example, claim that all the dozens of madams, bookers, bondsmen, and managers of the so-called vice combination were co-conspirators, even though no conspiracy had been alleged in the indictment. This meant that any of the madams, for example, could take the stand and say something like, "Cockeyed Louis told me I had to bond because Charlie Lucky said so," and that McCook was prepared to allow such rank hearsay into the record as evidence against Luciano.

George had played against stacked decks before. He'd survived a dozen trials before Lew Smith, for example, and he'd often come out on top. But this was a horse of a different color. George had had no role in the pretrial skirmishing and no chance to anticipate the prosecution's strategy. Indeed, he'd had no opportunity to even meet with the judge until the first day of trial, and it seemed to him now that whatever impressions his co-counsel had already made, they had served only to stoke McCook's innate hostility toward the defense side of the courtroom.

Polakoff, at least, was proving to be a competent, dignified trial attorney. The same could be said of Sam Siegel, Frederico's lawyer, and Maurice Cantor, who represented the fourth and final booker-defendant, Jack Eller. James Murray, appearing on behalf of the unlicensed bondsmen Jesse Jacobs and Meyer Berkman, and David Paley, counsel for the shylock Bennie Spiller, both seemed to be taking a page from the Levy-Polakoff playbook and keeping as low a profile as possible. As for Caesar Barra, who represented both Pennochio and Betillo, and David Siegel, who represented Abie Wahrman, George had yet to form an opinion.

The main burrs under McCook's saddle appeared to be Kopp, who also represented Pennochio, and attorney Lorenzo Carlino, counsel for defendant Ralph Liguori. Both lawyers were brash and outspoken and openly antagonistic toward Dewey, and both were irritating the judge with a steady stream of interruptions and talking objections. McCook, for his part, was tempering his anger and maintaining a clean appellate record. This, George knew from experience, was a sign that the old judge expected the case to end in conviction. George wondered if Kopp and Carlino could see this as well.

As for the man they called Charlie Lucky, George had to admit to actually liking his notorious client. Most men in Luciano's position would have been frightened, or angry, or some combination of both. They'd have blustered and bellowed, fulminated and fumed. But Luciano proved to be gracious and soft-spoken and showed a keen interest in his lawyers' discussions of trial strategy and tactics. It was Luciano, in fact, who'd first commented on Liguori's lawyer, saying, "McCook is like God to them guys on the jury, and that puts horns on that loudmouth Carlino."

"He's only protecting the record," George told him. "We all may burn in hell before this is over."

"Not you, counselor. Them jurors might worship McCook, but it's you they'd bring home to dinner."

"You think so?"

"Listen. If there's one thing I know, it's people. While you're watchin the judge and the witnesses, I'm studyin them guys in the jury box. As far as they're concerned there's only three people in that courtroom, and that's McCook, Dewey, and you. McCook they respect like a father. Dewey gets on their nerves a little, like a know-it-all kid brother, but at least they admire his moxie. You, Levy, you're like their favorite Jewish uncle."

"I wouldn't put too much stock in the lawyers, Charlie. Remember, what we say isn't evidence. If the jury likes Dewey's witnesses, then they'll believe Dewey's case. It's our job to see that they don't."

"I can't see 'em likin that bunch of sleazy pimps and whores."

"I hope you're right, and that the cumulative effect will work in our favor. I only wish we knew who Dewey plans to call about that supposed meeting downtown."

"It has to be one of the old bookers," Polakoff said. "Charlie Spinach, or maybe Spike Green. They're both up on the poster board."

"Don't lose any sleep over them guys," Lucky assured them. "They know better than to rat. Prison's a tough stretch to begin with, but it's hell for a guy who's a rat."

"It's clear that our friend Mr. Dewey has somebody up his sleeve. If he didn't, he wouldn't have said what he did in his opening."

"Yeah, well, you know what, counselor?" Lucky stretched his legs, lacing his hands behind his neck. "What Dewey's got and what Dewey thinks he's got might turn out to be two different things."

Thirty-Five

Cold Feet

May 1936

TOM STOOD, FISTS on hips, towering over the fidgeting man.

"What the hell are you trying to say?"

Charles Burke, the former whorehouse booker known in the trade as Good-Time Charlie, was hunched forward in his chair. Again he ran a hand over his face.

"I can't do it, Mr. Dewey. I won't do it."

"You haven't any choice, you ninny. You're under subpoena. We have your witness statement right here. You signed it under penalty of perjury!"

Tom snapped his fingers. Sol Gelb dug the document from his briefcase and handed it to the special prosecutor.

"You said right here . . . you were called to a meeting downtown . . . all the bookers were there. Then Little Davie came in . . . and when Charlie Lucky walked into the room, all the Italians stood up.

Lucky said, 'You guys are through. I'm giving the business to Little Davie.' Then Lucky walked out again, and all the Italians were still standing. Do you deny saying this?"

"I don't deny saying it. It's just that it ain't true, that's all."

"You testified before the grand jury!"

"Okay, so sue me. You asked me for a story and I gave you one. You put me on the stand now and that's exactly what I'm gonna say."

Barent Ten Eyck had entered from the courtroom. When he saw the look on his boss's face, he halted in the doorway.

"Listen, you. I'll put you on that stand, and if you so much as change a word of your sworn testimony, I'll prosecute you for perjury. I'll handle your trial myself, do you hear me?"

Good-Time Charlie shrugged. "Do what you gotta to do, Mr. Dewey, but I ain't gonna say what you want me to say."

Tom's face had turned crimson. He looked to Gelb, who gestured toward the doorway with his head.

"We'll be right back. Officer, keep a close eye on this man."

Tom stalked into the vacant courtroom, trailed by Gelb and Ten Eyck. The main doors to the hallway were closed and locked for the lunch recess, but the clerk and the court stenographer were still inside, still busy shuffling papers. Tom strode toward the door to the empty jury room.

"What?" Ten Eyck asked when the door had closed behind them.

"It's a run-out," Gelb told him. "He says he won't testify."

"Nuts."

"He's obviously been threatened." Tom was pacing now, slapping the witness statement against his thigh. "Luciano's boys got to him somehow. But how, Sol? How did you let this happen?"

"That's one possibility."

"What do you mean by that?"

Gelb shrugged. "I mean, maybe he's telling the truth. Maybe he made up the whole downtown meeting story. No one else has ever corroborated it."

"Damn it, Sol! I used that testimony in my opening! We've promised it to the jury!"

Gelb hiked his hip onto the conference table. He flipped a page on his legal pad, studying the list of witnesses.

"The whole point of calling Peluso was to set up Good-Time Charlie. Now what should we do?"

"Recover, that's what. We'll need another witness and pronto. Who's available?"

"We can move up a few of the girls. Betty Baker, Helen Hayes, Gussie Silver, and Helen Walsh. Run the clock out today and then start strong tomorrow with Pete Harris."

"Damn it all!"

Ten Eyck cleared his throat.

"What?"

"I was going to save this until later, but . . . I've got news. Good news, I think."

"Well?"

"I got a note the other night from a girl in the drug ward at the House of Detention. Fay Marston is her name, but she's known as Cokey Flo Brown."

"That's your good news? Another junkie inmate?"

"This junkie I think you're going to like. She wasn't part of the original sweep. She was picked up for solicitation on May the eighth. Turns out she's Frederico's girlfriend. That part's on the level. She ran a house that got busted in January, and she skipped bail on three misdemeanor counts. You remember those 'Dear Cousin' letters to Frederico?"

"Yes?"

"Well, she's the one who wrote 'em. Only now she's sore at the big guy and says she wants to cooperate."

"She's a plant," Gelb said. "A ringer."

"Could be, but I don't think so."

Tom had stopped pacing and stood with his fists on his hips.

250

"Can she give us Luciano?"

"I don't know. She's playing it cute for now, and she's still pretty sick from the cure, but she's dropping some pretty broad hints. Says she spent a lot of time with Frederico. Lived with him, talked with him, even drove him to his meetings."

"For God's sake, Barry. When can we get her to testify?"

"I'm meeting her again tonight. We'll have to promise her something, that much I know. She's weak as a kitten, but she's no bunny."

"What's her status on the solicitation charge?"

"Guilty and awaiting sentence."

"Good. Get the sentencing postponed. Do it now, before we go back. Then tonight you tell her she's facing time on the misdemeanors, time for the bail violation, and five to ten for solicitation. Twenty years in total. Give her the hard sell, Barry. Make her come around."

Ten Eyck looked to Gelb, who grinned. "Tell her you'll marry her."

"Whatever you do," Tom said, poking Ten Eyck's chest with the rolled-up witness statement, "close the deal tonight. We just lost half our case against Luciano. Use good judgment, but for God's sake, do whatever it takes!"

Thirty-Six

The Hard Sell

May 1936

IT WAS SOME BIG shot's office where we met, with wicker chairs and a comfortable leather couch and a carved wooden desk. On the desk were pictures I couldn't see in heavy silver frames, and a fancy inkwell in some kind of greenish jade or marble. More important, there was a half-full bottle of brandy standing open next to the inkwell.

That's why I was laying down as I talked, resting a coffee mug on my stomach, and why Mr. Ten Eyck, who said to call him Barry, was pacing back and forth, back and forth, on the other side of the desk.

"So that's how I come to meet Jimmy," I said, finishing my story. "Charlie Spinach was there, and they gave me their spiel on the bonding, and I agreed to play along."

"But really you just wanted to meet Frederico?"

"I guess. I mean, I knew I had to bond if I wanted to stay in the business. But yeah, I wanted to meet this Jimmy Fredericks everybody was talking about. I figured if he was the muscle, then he was the guy I should get to know."

"And then what happened? You actually fell for him?"

I shrugged. "I guess you could say I fell for Jimmy. He was a hard-luck story, just like me. We were both a couple of mutts. Turns out we had a lot in common."

"And since Jimmy didn't drive, you chauffeured him around?"

"Sometimes. Like if it was late, and if his pal Danny wasn't around, and if taxis were hard to come by."

"So you must have driven him to some of his meetings with the other combination guys—Tommy the Bull and Little Davie and Charlie Lucky."

It was funny, lying on the couch like that and talking to the ceiling. Like visiting a headshrinker. It made you really focus on what you were saying. And the brandy didn't hurt one bit. In fact, it was the best I'd felt in over a week.

"There you go again with Charlie Lucky," I said to the ceiling, which had a wicker fan with a pull chain. "If that's what you're after, then why don't you say so?"

"I'm only after the truth."

"Yeah, sure. You're like that old man with the lantern."

"I'm certainly not going to put words in your mouth."

"Relax, Barry, you don't have to. I get the picture. Dewey's the monkey, and Charlie Lucky's the weasel. But just out of curiosity, what does that make you?"

I snuck a peek at Ten Eyck. When he wasn't pacing, he was bent over the desk, scribbling notes on a pad. Only this time he was just standing there, watching me where I lay. Even checking out my legs.

"I guess you could say this monkey has coattails."

"Let's hope so, for both our sakes."

"So about Charlie Lucky . . ."

"I read the newspapers. For example, I read where your boss called him public enemy number one."

"But you know him, right? You know what he looks like?"

"Sure I know Lucky. He's tall, but he's kinda short. Thin, but a bit on the heavy side."

"You've seen his picture, haven't you?"

"I said I read the newspapers."

"Do you think you could pick him out of a lineup?"

"I know I could."

"How about a crowded courtroom?"

I propped myself on an elbow and took another sip of the brandy.

"I don't know about a courtroom. I suppose that depends."

"Depends on what?"

"On what kind of a deal I was offered. My memory is fuzzy these days. Sometimes I remember things, and sometimes I don't."

"Look, Flo. All the girls who've testified have gotten the same deal. You'll receive immunity from prosecution for whatever you say on the witness stand. As far as the pending charges go, we'll do everything in our lawful power to get them dismissed. On the prostitution conviction, we'll appear at your sentencing and inform the court that you've been a cooperating witness. We can't guarantee it, but that usually means a suspended sentence."

He was a funny bird, this Ten Eyck. Tall and thin, and though he didn't look that old, he was already losing his hair. Attractive, if you go for the type that looks like he's just stepped down from his sailing yacht. Fair-haired, I guess you might call him, with a long nose and a pointy chin and rimless eyeglasses. He looked a little like Violet's brother Ralph.

"I heard a different story, Barry. I heard girls got out of jail and got taken places."

"Yes, but they're being held as material witnesses, whereas you've been convicted and remanded into custody. I'm afraid there's only so much we can do in your case."

"And I'm afraid my memory is starting to fade again."

"Come on, Flo, you're a smart girl. Maybe the smartest of the bunch. Why don't you quit chewing gum and put your cards on the table?"

I half rolled on the couch to look at him.

"You want cards? Okay, here's a card. Like I said, I read the newspapers. So far as I can tell, you and your pal Dewey ain't had a single witness who could put Lucky in a room with any of them other guys."

"We've got witnesses. We just haven't called them yet."

"Oh yeah, who? Nancy Presser? Thelma Jordan? Good luck with them. A couple of dumb Doras. Either one would sell her own sister for a half cube of morphine."

"Sure, like you wouldn't."

I relaxed onto my back again, the coffee mug resting on my stomach like a whispered promise.

"Oh, Barry. You think I'm just some two-dollar bag, but I got news for you. When you were learning your algebra, I was running my own speak. When you were pinning your first girlfriend, I was fucking two of the biggest gangsters in Chicago. I been around the block, honey, and I learned some things."

"We were talking about cards."

"Okay then, here's another. A little birdy told me that Nancy and Thelma are getting a trip to Europe after the trial. Me, I could use a vacation. Especially if Lucky and Little Davie walk, which it sounds like they might. And if that happens, we'll all need to disappear. Maybe even you. Maybe even your boss."

"What you've heard is nothing but gossip and rumor. Nobody's getting any trips. And if you're worried about reprisals, we can protect you."

"Yeah, right. But you know what worries me most? How I'm gonna live when this thing is over. Times are hard, in case you ain't noticed. Oh, I can type all right, but who's gonna hire me? I don't suppose Mr. Dewey is looking for a secretary?"

Barry stopped his pacing and sat. He screwed the cap onto his pen and set it down next to the pad.

"All right, Flo, we don't have all night. What did you have in mind?"

"That's more like it."

I sat up and swung my feet to the floor. I had to wait for a second until the room quit spinning around.

"I know you can't write me a check or anything, so I got to thinking about all those reporters over at the courthouse, all scrapping over the same lousy story like dogs over a bone. And then it came to me that the girl who sends Charlie Lucky to prison is gonna have her name in every newspaper in the country. Maybe even in newsreels and magazines. She could be bigger than Mae West if she plays her cards right."

"Funny you should say that."

"Why?"

"Never mind. Go on, I'm listening."

"So what I figured is, that's gotta be worth something, right? Her life story, I mean. Her exclusive life story should be worth a pretty penny to a magazine or even a movie studio. Especially if someone with coattails were to put in a word to someplace like, say, *Liberty* magazine."

Barry didn't say anything at first. He just sat there with his mouth tight, spinning his pen around like a propeller. And then:

"You understand I can't make any promises. If I did, and the defense were to ask you what we talked about, then you'd have to tell them the truth. So let's speak hypothetically for a second, just you and me."

"That's what I thought we were doing."

"You're right that Mr. Dewey knows a lot of important people, and you're also right that the magazines and the studios have been pestering us, looking for the inside dope."

"There you go. Now you're on the trolley."

"From everything I've heard so far, yours is exactly the kind of story that a magazine might pay good money for. But it needs the right ending, Flo, and it won't have the right ending unless Charlie Lucky is convicted. And that means you taking the stand and tying him directly to the others in the combination."

"I understand."

"Good. Now we're both on the trolley. So go ahead and tell me a story. If I think it's any good, then we'll get a stenographer in here and we'll put it down on paper. After that, I'll take it to Mr. Dewey. He'll want to question you himself, which means that the story you tell now and the story you tell Mr. Dewey have got to jibe. That means no loose ends and no contradictions. Then if he gives the okay, you'll get to tell that story on the witness stand."

"In front of Jimmy and Charlie Lucky."

"And all those hungry reporters. And it better match exactly the story you told in writing, because their lawyers will be getting a copy of the transcript, and they'll turn you upside down looking for inconsistencies. If you do all of that, then after the trial is over, we'll talk again about magazines and movie studios."

"But you can't make any promises."

He didn't answer, so I just sat there for a minute, studying the angles. For something like the twentieth time.

"You really think you can nail Charlie Lucky?"

"We *will* nail Lucky, with or without your help."

"Which means you've got somebody else besides me who'll testify against him?"

"We have several witnesses, only one of whom you've even mentioned."

"And how much do you think a magazine or a movie studio might pay for the exclusive rights to a story like mine? Hypothetically speaking, of course."

"I can't say for certain. I would think a few grand at least."

"At the very least?"

"At the very least."

I nodded. I was feeling tired all of a sudden, and brandy or no brandy, the shakes were coming on.

"Can I have a night or two to think it over and give you my answer then?"

He stood and began gathering up his things.

"You can have one night. After tomorrow, all bets are off. With the bail violation and now the solicitation conviction, that means twenty years, Flo, and Mr. Dewey will see that you serve every day of your sentence. And believe me, when you hear that iron door slam shut behind you, you'll rue the day you let this opportunity pass."

I believed him all right, and I knew he knew I believed him.

"Okay, Barry. You'll have my answer tomorrow."

"That's a smart girl. And just to be clear, I've made no promises about any magazine or movie deal, or about anything else for that matter. I'm going out on a limb for you, Flo, so don't saw it off and leave me hanging."

"I understand. I'd never do that."

"Okay, then. Now the ball's in your court."

Thirty-Seven

What Goes Around

May 1936

LUCKY HAS BEEN counting the witnesses on a yellow legal pad, marking with a series of vertical lines and slashes their halting procession from the side doorway of the courtroom to the elevated witness chair—five witnesses to a group, seven groups in total, the marks evoking ordered sheaves of wheat, or maybe pencils brimming from a row of beggars' cups.

Thirty-six pencils so far, and not a single witness who has directly tied Lucky to the so-called bonding combination.

Some, it is true, have mentioned his name. Bookers Dave Miller, Danny Brooks, and Pete Harris have all testified to conversations they'd supposedly had with others—Fredericks, for example, or Wahrman—in which each had been convinced of the combination's legitimacy on the ground that it was backed by Charlie Lucky. While distressing to hear, these statements, or so Lucky has been assured by both Polakoff and Levy, are not enough to support a conviction.

"We knew there'd be hearsay linking you to the others," Levy tells Lucky after another day of testimony, "and it's unfortunate that the judge is letting it in. But it's meaningless without corroboration from an actual eyewitness who wasn't part of the conspiracy. That means one of the prostitutes, or else maybe a third party. That's what we need to worry about."

"What witnesses? I'm fallin asleep out there, listenin to them whores pile dirt on these other guys' coffins."

"Don't worry," Levy says, "they're coming. If they weren't, you wouldn't have been indicted in the first place."

Then, just as Levy has predicted, the first of them finally appears. It is Thursday morning, the ninth day of the trial, and the witness in question is a recidivist hotel burglar named Joe Bendix.

Under direct questioning by Dewey, Bendix claims to have known Lucky for eight or nine years, and says he was looking for work as a collector for the combination in May or June of 1935 when he was introduced to Jimmy Fredericks by a man named Charlie the Barber. Fredericks supposedly told Bendix that he'd have to run the matter past Lucky Luciano. A few days later, Bendix was instructed to come to the Villanova Restaurant on West 46th Street to meet with Lucky in person. Bendix arrived with his fiancée and found Fredericks and Lucky sitting at a table. After a few minutes, Lucky came over and sat with Bendix, telling him, "If you're willing to work for forty dollars a week, that's okay with me. I'll tell Little Davie to put you on."

Two weeks later, according to Bendix, he again met with Lucky at the Villanova, where Bendix reiterated his interest in the job. Lucky instructed Bendix to report to a man named Binge at the Hotel Wolcott, saying, "He'll take care of you." He then added cryptically, "When you go around to collect, once you get wise to things, you can make yourself a little extra on the side, from the madams."

Bendix concludes his testimony by stating that he'd never managed to connect with Binge, that he'd found other work instead, and therefore that he'd never actually gone to work for the combination.

Dewey then tenders the witness.

"This bastard is so fulla shit his eyes are brown," Lucky whispers to Levy, a vise grip on the lawyer's arm. "Not one fuckin word of what he said is true!"

Lucky's hands, at first balled under the table in rage, begin to loosen once Levy rises and steps to the lectern and begins his gentle cross-examination of Joe Bendix.

He starts with Bendix's criminal history. It is an exhausting recitation of burglaries, arrests, convictions, and incarcerations that begins at the Bridgeport, Connecticut, city jail at age seventeen, ends at Sing Sing prison at age thirty-eight, and includes intermediate stops at the Elmira Reformatory, Sing Sing, the Welfare Island Workhouse, the Ohio State Prison at Columbus, three more visits to Sing Sing, and a penultimate incarceration at the Welfare Island Penitentiary. With Levy's seamless repertoire of questions, asides, vocal inflections, and facial expressions, Bendix is gradually transformed from an earnest volunteer witness into an unrepentant and calculating thief who might very well steal the judge's gavel should the bailiff make the mistake of turning his head.

With the stage thus set, Levy next probes Bendix's claim to have known Lucky for many years. Bendix says he was first introduced to Lucky by a man named Captain Dutton at the Club Richman back in 1928. Only Bendix cannot describe this Captain Dutton—Tall or short? Fat or thin?—and further cannot describe the mutual friend, a Mrs. Casner, who allegedly introduced them. Then Bendix makes his first critical mistake.

Q: How old a man was Captain Dutton, about?

A: A man about 38 or 39 years old.

Q: Give us a good description, will you please, of Captain Dutton?

A: I don't recall. I met the man—that is almost eight years ago, and I met him for a half hour.

Q: Yes. But you remember Luciano in great detail, don't you?

A: I know him longer than I know Captain Dutton.

Q: What is that?

A: I know him longer than I know Captain Dutton.

The witness, clearly rattled by Levy's probing, is soon stumbling over other aspects of his story.

Q: Were some extra chairs brought up to the table?

A: There were chairs at the table.

Q: Did you expect somebody?

A: No, that is the way the table was situated.

Q: I beg your pardon?

A: That is the amount of chairs that were at the table. There were four or five chairs at the table.

Q: Just a moment. Richman's Club is a pretty crowded club, is it not?

A: That is right.

Q: And you were sitting at Richman's Club with a party of three and you have got five chairs at the table, have you?

A: The only table available.

. . .

Q: About how many extra chairs were there?

A: There were four or five. The place was not crowded.

Lucky is watching the jury, watching their faith in Joe Bendix evaporate like dew on a hot summer sidewalk. Watching Dewey's face redden, like that of a cartoon thermometer on the verge of exploding. Watching Bendix, shifting and fidgeting in the witness chair, growing ever more combative and insolent as Levy peels his story apart like an onion.

Then, as Levy is examining Bendix about his failed second marriage, Dewey finally does explode, bursting the bubble of cool confidence that had theretofore enveloped the special prosecutor, and for the first time in the course of the trial, Dewey is gently admonished by Judge McCook.

Q: And how long before January first, 1935, were you giving your wife and child nothing?

A: I didn't have much time to give her anything; a short time—

Q: How long before January first, 1935 were you giving her nothing?

A: Will you let me answer that question the way you wanted it?

Q: How long? That calls for time, please.

A: I was only out of prison a short while, and the woman had left me while I was in prison. What do you expect me to do, support her during the time I was in prison and she left me?

MR. LEVY: I am sorry I cannot answer that, but the Court does not permit it, you see.

THE WITNESS: Well then, you asked for it and you got it.

THE COURT: I think instead you had better answer the counsel's question.

Q: You like to volunteer, do you not?

A: In what way?

MR. DEWEY: I object to that, because the witness has been amazingly free from that.

THE COURT: Sustained.

MR. LEVY: I object to the characterization of Mr. Dewey. The witness has been just to the contrary, I maintain, and—

MR. DEWEY: Just as I object to counsel's voluntary statements.

MR. LEVY: Will you kindly show the courtesy of listening for once, until counsel is finished? And remember you are not running this courtroom?

263

MR. DEWEY: I have listened for long, and I am tired of being bullied by counsel for Luciano, just because he is counsel for Luciano.

MR. LEVY: Now may it please the Court, I resent that statement, I except to it, and I ask your Honor to rebuke the learned Special Prosecutor for the remarks he made.

THE COURT: That is a little too much like what was said the other day, Mr. Dewey. I do not think you ought to say it. Proceed.

MR. LEVY: I thank your Honor.

Levy next moves to the first of the two alleged meetings, in May or June of 1935, at the Villanova Restaurant. He begins by establishing the presence of Bendix's soon-to-be third wife, a woman named Joy Dixon, at the first of those meetings.

Q: Were you standing up at this particular time?
A: Sitting down.
Q: You remained sitting down?
A: That is right.
Q: At a table with your wife?
A: Yes, not when Luciano walked over.
Q: Wait a minute. What did you do with your wife?
A: I asked her to excuse me when Fredericks came over to the table.
Q: And then she left the table?
A: That is right.
Q: Where did she go?
A: She sat at another table a few tables away.

Then Levy moves to the second meeting and to Bendix's decision to take the job that he, in the final analysis, never performed.

Q: Had you made up your mind at that time whether you wanted to go into the whorehouse business?

A: Yes, sir.

Q: You had made up your mind you wanted to go in the business?

A: Yes, sir.

Q: So the second time you met Charlie Lucky, you were ready to become a collector for whorehouses, is that right?

A: That is right.

Finally, Levy moves to Bendix's last arrest and the circumstances under which he became a witness for the prosecution.

Q: Did you start your sentence in Sing Sing before you wrote to anybody in connection with any crime?

A: I wrote before I got my sentence.

Q: You wrote before you got your sentence. And whom did you write to then?

A: I wrote a letter to Mr. Dewey.

Q: You wrote a letter to Mr. Dewey. Had you previously written a letter to Mr. Dodge, the District Attorney of New York County?

A: I did.

. . .

Q: Where were you when you wrote Mr. Dewey a letter?

A: Tombs Prison.

Q: New York City?

A: That is right.

Q: You wrote and indicated to Mr. Dewey you might know something about this case, is that right?

A: I did.

. . .

Q: What hotel did you operate in the last time?

A: Hotel Madison.

Q: New York City?

A: Right.

Q: Do you remember the room that you got into?

A: I do.

Q: Do you remember the name of the man?

A: I do.

Q: What was his name?

A: Sackett.

Q: Mr. Sackett, the hotel manager?

A: That is right.

Q: And you entered his room, did you not?

A: That is right.

Q: And nobody was there when you got in, was there?

A: That is right.

Q: And you robbed the room of certain things, certain possessions, did you not?

A: That is right.

Q: And that was the last case in which you were involved?

A: That is right.

Q: I will return to that in a moment. What was the last sentence in connection with that crime?

A: Fifteen years to life.

Q: Life is what is called for under the Baumes Act, is it not?

A: No, not life. Fifteen years to life.

Q: Fifteen years to life. That is your final conviction; is that true?

A: That is true . . .

Q: Did Mr. Dewey promise you that if you told the truth as he thought the truth was, that he would try to help you in connection with your troubles?

A: He did, yes.

Q: He did tell you that much?

A: Yes.

Q: And you believed him, did you not?

A: I did . . .

Q: And you were reading the newspapers pretty carefully at that time, were you not?

A: I was.

Q: And you knew about this alleged charge of prostitution at that time, did you not?

A: I did.

Q: And you read in the papers that Charlie Lucky was supposedly the head of it, did you not?

A: I did.

Levy passes the witness. He sits and confers with his client while Sam Siegel takes over the lectern.

"That was fuckin beautiful," Lucky whispers, peering over Levy's shoulder. "The jury ain't buyin a single thing this lousy crumb is sellin. And for that matter, neither is the judge."

"I hope you're right. But we need to find this Captain Dutton, and we need to find Bendix's wife."

"If this guy claims to know me for so many years, then how come he had to go through Fredericks to ask me for a fuckin job?"

"Exactly. A job he decided to take, yet somehow never got around to performing. The whole thing reeks to high heaven."

Lucky nods to the prosecution table, where Dewey, still red-faced, huddles with his assistants.

"Get a load of the Boy Scout. He looks like a kid who just lost his birthday balloon."

" 'They have sown the wind,' " Levy quotes from Scripture, " 'and they shall reap the whirlwind.' "

"You mean what goes around comes around?"

"Just a moment," Levy says, laying a hand on Lucky's arm. Siegel has concluded his questioning, and Levy now stands to address the judge before Bendix can be excused.

"May I also say this? We shall make an effort to locate this man's wife, and if we do—I do not know with what success—we would like to have the opportunity of recalling this man as a witness."

"You want me to reserve your right in case you do?" McCook asks Levy.

"That is right."

"Very well," the judge says, bending forward and making a note.

Thirty-Eight

Wondering

May 1936

GEORGE KNEW THAT his client had dodged a bullet. Only an exceptionally bright and personable witness can get away with back-talking and wisecracking on cross-examination, and Bendix was neither bright nor personable. As a result, he'd alienated both the judge and the jury and had, for the first time since the trial had begun, even rubbed a little tarnish onto the sterling-silver facade of the learned special prosecutor.

All of which raised the question of what, exactly, Dewey had been thinking. Surely he'd known that the testimony of an eight-time loser desperate to avoid life in Sing Sing would carry little weight to begin with. Add to that the man's improbable story, which, not incidentally, contradicted the entire prosecution narrative of Luciano as a hands-off overlord working only through layers of intermediaries. Lastly, Bendix had made the mistake of including at least three

269

eyewitnesses in his story—his wife, Mrs. Casner, and Captain Dutton—and if any of them could be located, then he'd opened himself up to devastating collateral impeachment.

Was that Dewey's best punch? If so, then what did it say about the rest of his case against Luciano? As an experienced trial lawyer, Dewey surely knew the cardinal rules of primacy and recency—that you start strong and you finish strong if you want to have the maximum impact on a jury. If Bendix was, in fact, the prosecution's biggest weapon against Luciano, then what was left in Dewey's arsenal?

Not all George's thoughts, however, were so upbeat. As he'd turned from the podium after cross-examining Bendix, George had noticed Luciano sharing a look with Tommy Pennochio. In fact, George had noted over the course of the trial's first week a disquieting familiarity between Luciano and some of his co-defendants—particularly Betillo, Pennochio, and Liguori. It could, of course, be a simple matter of ethnic affinity. But the ease with which Pennochio and Liguori seemed to greet Luciano each morning and their tendency to huddle and whisper at the end of each day's testimony were ringing familiar bells inside George's head—bells he knew from experience he could ignore only at his peril.

These and other thoughts were racing through George's mind as Dewey assistant Harry Cole led yet another young prostitute—this one a pretty little girl named Shirley Mason—through a direct examination that appeared to be aimed at Jack Eller. Eller was the client of Maurice Cantor, and was the only one of the booker-defendants who hadn't yet taken a guilty plea. George had tuned out the witness and was focused instead on Dewey, watching him slip out of the courtroom and return again through the side door that led to the witness room.

The jurors, too, were watching. If George had learned anything in his twenty-plus years before the bar, it was to never underestimate the observational powers of jurors. For example, George had always worn a wedding band in court, even when between marriages. Once, in the middle of a lengthy jury trial, he'd been running late for court and had slipped the wrong band—a similar one, but the one from his first marriage—onto his finger. The trial had lasted for over two weeks, and once it was finished and George was speaking with the jurors about their verdict, one of them had said to him, "Mr. Levy, we were all wondering why you wore a different wedding ring to court last Thursday."

George was also wondering. Wondering what was so special about the next witness that she merited the personal attention of the special prosecutor. Wondering why Dewey and Gelb were huddling again, their conversation animated, both of them ignoring Cole as he droned on about Shirley Mason's finances, and her stolen wristwatch, and her positive Wasserman test. Wondering why the spring seemed to have returned to the special prosecutor's step.

Moe Polakoff also returned to the courtroom, interrupting George's reverie as he eased into his seat on the other side of their client. After a moment, Polakoff passed a folded slip of paper to George, who, after checking that none of the jurors was watching, held it under the table as he read.

George Paul Dutton
State Police Captain

It was six thirty P.M., and Shirley Mason was just stepping down from the witness chair when Dewey rose to his feet, his gaze pausing on the jury before turning to the bailiff who guarded the side door of the courtroom.

"Flo Brown!" he announced with a flourish.

Thirty-Nine

First Impressions

May 1936

SHE ENTERED THE COURTROOM in a baggy blue dress and a tilted hat with a veil. Her gait was shuffling, her body caved to one side, and she used the rail of the jury box to steady herself as she walked. As she laid her hand on the Bible, Tom half turned to the door through which Eunice Carter and Barry Ten Eyck had quietly entered behind her. Mrs. Carter nodded. Ten Eyck, poker-faced, moved to his place beside Sol Gelb at the prosecution table.

Still standing, Tom cleared his throat and took a long drink of water. This, he recognized, was the trial's critical moment. It was George Medalie's ruby-red nose. It was the cadenza to the final aria that would evoke either jeers or bravos from the special prosecutor's captive audience of blue-ribbon jurors.

Good-Time Charlie had been a run-out, and Joe Bendix had laid a sulfurous egg whose stench still permeated the highest corners of the

272

courtroom. All of which had left but two crooked arrows in the witness quiver Tom held in reserve for Lucky Luciano: the call-girl Nancy Presser and Mildred Balitzer, the blowsy wife of booker Pete Harris.

Both women were prostitutes, and both were heroin addicts. Neither was what you'd call Phi Beta Kappa material. And then, as if by some golden miracle of providence, Cokey Flo Brown had appeared in his office like Venus in a clamshell, thanks to Barry Ten Eyck's nightly forays into the Women's House of Detention.

Thank God, Tom thought, for Barry Ten Eyck.

Tom watched as the wraithlike figure—his unlikely diva—settled into the witness chair. Cokey Flo was dirty blonde and hazel-eyed and, despite her medical condition, actually looked younger than her given age of twenty-nine years. Best of all, her dissipated appearance, Tom could tell, was already arousing the paternal sympathies of the gray-haired gentlemen of the jury.

Sympathy was exactly what Tom had been hoping for, while its corollary—that Cokey Flo would be unable to withstand the grueling rigors of direct and cross-examination—remained his greatest fear. That she would break down or, worse yet, recant her story under the menacing gaze of Charlie Lucky, or the pleading eyes of Jimmy Fredericks, or the exhaustive, surgical probing of George Morton Levy.

If you'd asked him that morning, Tom would have set the odds of his calling Florence Brown to the witness stand at no better than even money. Although she'd seemed credible last night, when Tom had grilled her for two solid hours, there was still the possibility—as Sol Gelb had repeatedly cautioned—that Cokey Flo was a Trojan horse: a time bomb planted by Luciano to detonate inside the courtroom, blowing what remained of their case against him to smithereens.

And this wasn't the only cautionary note sounded by little Sol. "What if Mildred Balitzer and Nancy Presser are bald-faced liars?" he'd asked Tom in private. "What if they're fingering Luciano just to save their own skins? And what if Cokey Flo is doing the same?"

"You don't really believe that, I hope."

"I don't know, chief. It's gotten to the point where I don't know what to believe."

Tom had maintained an even keel, but Sol's words—his fretful skepticism—had hit him like a tidal wave. If his own men were starting to doubt the case's merits, then what did that say about the prospects for a guilty verdict?

Doubt was like a slow drip that, if left unchecked, could undermine a foundation and bring down an entire building. What if there'd been no downtown meeting as described by Good-Time Charlie, and no job interview at the Villanova as Joe Bendix had testified? What if they and the other key witnesses were simply inserting Luciano into their own life stories, like one of those novelty photos you could take on Coney Island that showed you sparring with Jack Dempsey?

Had Tom and his men leaned too heavily on the witnesses? Had they promised too much for their cooperation? A week ago, Tom would have dismissed such questions out of hand. Of course Lucky was behind the combination! Nearly a dozen witnesses had said as much. But now, after Bendix and Good Time Charlie . . .

They'd had no time to investigate Cokey Flo's story, and they had no eyewitnesses to corroborate it. Worse, they had no grand jury transcript with which to impeach her should she pull a double-cross. Her very appearance in the case was anathema to every guiding principle of the special prosecutor's office—Tom's consecrated temple of meticulous preparation, exhaustive fact-checking, and scrupulous background investigation.

He was, in short, taking a huge gamble. But any qualms he'd felt that morning had been erased by Levy's slashing cross-examination of Bendix. So poor was the hotel thief on the stand that Tom had hastily scrapped his plan to call Joy Dixon, Bendix's wife, who'd been waiting in the adjoining room, as his next witness. Instead, he'd had Mrs. Carter spirit her out of the building—let Levy find her himself, he'd whispered to Sol—forcing Cokey Flo, with whom they'd hoped to share at least one more night of preparation, into the witness box with only half an hour left in the day.

In practice we learn how to weld, Tom reminded himself. There was no room for doubts, and now that Cokey Flo was on the witness stand, there was no turning back.

Q: Is Florence Brown your right name?
A: Yes, it is.
Q: Have you sometimes been referred to as Cokey Flo?
A: Yes.
Q: A name which you very much disliked, as I understand it?
A: That is right.
Q: You are now in the House of Detention?
A: I am.
Q: How long have you been there?
A: Twelve days.
Q: Do you know the defendant Charles Luciano in this case?
A: I do.

Tom paused for a moment, allowing the jurors to glance at Charlie Lucky. Letting them see his icy stare and appreciate the courage it must be taking for this feeble young woman to face down the most fearsome mobster in America.

Cokey Flo actually seemed weaker than she'd been last night, her voice lost in the *whoosh* of rush-hour traffic flooding through the open windows of the courtroom. The judge admonished her to speak up. Defense counsel, like jackals scenting her frailty, eagerly joined in the request.

Tom kept one eye on the clock. Court adjourned at seven, which meant he could cover some background information that evening, end with a modest cliff-hanger, and use the overnight hours to regroup. After preemptively eliciting Cokey Flo's criminal record, her various drug addictions, and her first meeting with Jimmy Fredericks and Charlie Spinach, he moved to his improvised ending.

Q: Now did you, after this event concerning which you have testified, become the mistress of Jimmy Fredericks?
A: Yes.
Q: Did you live with him?
A: I did.
Q: When did you first start living with Jimmy Fredericks?
A: Two years ago.
Q: And you continued to live with Jimmy Fredericks until the time of his arrest on February first of this year?
A: Yes.

Seven o'clock. Tom breathed a quiet sigh, now that the die had been cast. Better still, he sensed that the appearance of Cokey Flo, and the high drama it portended, had rinsed from the jurors' mouths, at least in small measure, the lingering bad taste left by the smirking, smarmy testimony of Joe goddamned Bendix.

Forty

Cokey Flo

May 1936

You should've seen the look on Mrs. Calvit's face when she opened the door and saw me standing in the hallway with a hunky detective on either arm. Her jaw practically hit the floor, and the cigarette she was smoking *did* hit the floor, and she had to bend over in her ratty bathrobe to pick it up quick before one of the dogs tried to eat it.

"Where's Pearlie?" was the first question I asked her, and even before she could answer, I knew that little Pearlie wasn't there, and that her promise to look after my dog had lasted about as long as it took her to get home from the courthouse and put an ad in the newspaper. At least that's what she claimed she'd done, but for all I knew, she'd just shoved little Pearlie out the door in the middle of the night and left her to fend for herself.

I could've strangled her right then and there, and probably would have except for the detectives and the fact that we were on a tight schedule and had only enough time to grab a couple of dresses and hats, which, thank goodness, were still in the closet and hadn't yet been tossed out in the gutter along with my dog, and then only because Mrs. Calvit, the little cheapskate, was probably planning to sell them.

Life had been one big blur ever since my meeting with Barry Ten Eyck on Tuesday night. First came my formal statement on Wednesday, followed by a grilling from Mr. Dewey and a bunch of his assistants—Sol Gelb, Harry Cole, Frank Hogan, and a nice Negro lady named Mrs. Carter—which had lasted over two hours and had been every bit as tough as Barry said it would be. After that, we'd gone to the Hotel Alamac for my things, then back to the House of Detention for a couple hours of sleep, then over to the Woolworth Building again on Thursday afternoon.

The plan, or so I was told, was to have me testify on Friday morning. But then all of a sudden there was a schedule change and I was rushed to the courthouse in a squad car with the lights flashing and the siren screaming and I was parked in a room with Barry and Mrs. Carter, who'd arranged to have a cot there for me to lie on. I was visited by Mr. Dewey, who told me that I shouldn't be nervous and who handed me yet another copy of my statement and told me I should read it over again for what must have been the fourth or fifth time in the last twelve hours.

I shouldn't be nervous! I was weaker than a day-old kitten, and I was about to see Jimmy for the first time in nearly four months, not to mention go eye-to-eye with Lucky Luciano, and he says I shouldn't be nervous! I asked Mr. Dewey if I couldn't at least have a little brandy, but he said he'd have to ask the judge first, and that it wouldn't be today, so I'd just have to tough it out for the half hour or so that I'd be in the witness chair before the evening recess.

Then, just as Mr. Dewey was leaving he said, "You're a brave girl, Flo, and you're doing the right thing." To which I told him, "I'm counting on you, Mr. Dewey. If Jimmy and Charlie Lucky go free, my life won't be worth a plugged nickel." He didn't respond to that, and he left the room with kind of a queer look on his face that told me maybe he wasn't as confident about his case as Barry said he was, and that made me feel even worse than I already did. And that was saying a lot, believe you me.

It was exactly six thirty when they finally called my name. I sat up on the cot and waited for my head to stop swimming. Then I stood, and with Mrs. Carter's help I walked through the door next to the jury box and into the courtroom.

Everything was silent, like I'd walked in on a funeral. I tried not to look at Jimmy, but I could feel his eyes and Lucky's eyes and the rest of the eyes in the courtroom burning holes in my back as I wobbled past the jury to the witness chair.

Like I was walking to the electric chair, that's what it felt like. Like I was the one on trial, and it was my life that hung in the balance, and whether I lived or died depended entirely on whether the jury believed what it was I was about to tell them. Which, as a matter of fact, it probably did.

I barely remember that first half hour on the stand. All's I know is that Mr. Dewey was asking me questions and the judge and the other lawyers kept telling me to speak up. I tried not to look directly at Jimmy, but of course I couldn't help myself, and anyway I had to find Charlie Lucky so I could point him out when the time came. Then when I finally recognized him sitting between his lawyers at one of the tables, this chill ran down my spine and into my legs, and I swear I almost wet myself right there in the courtroom, that's how scared I was to see that beetle brow with that one droopy eye glowering at me with nothing but pure and perfect hatred.

Then, just like that, the day was over. All the jurors were standing, and the reporters were shouting questions, and that's when I finally allowed myself a good, long look at Jimmy, who was staring straight back at me and shaking his head in little back-and-forth movements, as if to say that he couldn't believe I'd actually done this to him, or maybe to warn me that I was making the biggest mistake of my life.

It was Barry Ten Eyck who came and got me and led me by the elbow past the defendants, who were almost all of them leaning over and whispering to their lawyers. He led me back to the witness room, where Mrs. Carter was waiting, and then together they helped me down a staircase to that same squad car that was parked out back of the courthouse.

Back at the Woolworth Building, Barry got me a glass of brandy and made me promise not to tell anybody, especially Mr. Dewey. I was told to wait in Mr. Dewey's private office, which also had a couch and comfortable chairs and its own private elevator. I laid down on the couch for a minute, and I must've fallen asleep, because when I woke up again, it was dark outside and Mr. Dewey and some of his other assistants—Gelb, and Cole, and Charlie Grimes—were just returning from court, and pretty soon all of them were congratulating me for doing such a great job.

"I was scared out of my wits," I told them, but they said that was okay, and was to be expected, and generally tried to make out like I'd hit a home run when I knew the truth was that I'd barely even stepped up to the plate.

"That worked out perfectly," Mr. Dewey said as he took a cigarette and fitted it into a holder like he was President Roosevelt. "You got your feet wet, and you got the lay of the courtroom. Now it won't feel so foreign tomorrow morning."

"I'm sorry about keeping my voice up," I told him. "It's hard with me being so weak and with all that noise outside and all those people trying to hear me."

He waved it off as he lit his cigarette. He didn't offer me one, but that was okay. I realized that for the first time I could remember, I was actually feeling hungry. The enthusiasm and the confidence those men all seemed to share was rubbing off on me. It felt good to be part of their team—the prosecution team—meeting after hours to plan our next move. Like I was their equal, and like I was finally doing something good for a change, something positive to make the world a better place.

I didn't feel like a rat at all. More like I was walking the right side of the street for maybe the first time in my life.

Mr. Dewey took me through my testimony again, then at around ten o'clock they drove me back to the House of Detention, stopping on the way for tea and a small bite to eat. It was hot that night, but I got a few good hours of sleep, and in the morning actually ate a whole bowl of cereal for breakfast. I was nervous, sure, but like Mr. Dewey had said, it was all familiar to me now, which made it okay. Lots of things in life are scary just because they're unfamiliar, but once you do them and they don't kill you, then all of a sudden you realize they're not so scary anymore.

We got to court at nine thirty, and by ten o'clock I was back in the witness chair. Only this time I was able to look both Jimmy and Charlie Lucky straight in the eye. Siegel was there as well, and I gave him a look that said maybe you should of been a little nicer to me when you had the chance, you fat little prick. And then Mr. Dewey stood up and walked to the little podium and his booming voice brought me back to the present.

"In the spring of nineteen thirty-four," he said, "do you remember going up to some Chinese restaurant uptown with Jimmy Fredericks?"

This was it—the moment we'd been rehearsing for two days straight, and that I'd been practicing on my own even before that. I took one last look at Jimmy and swallowed hard.

"Yes, I do."

Forty-One

Flo's Story

May 1936

COKEY FLO BROWN, who couldn't have weighed more than ninety pounds in her shoes and silly hat, looks more to Lucky like a schoolgirl playing dress-up than the hard-boiled madam she claims to have been. But Lucky could tell from her appearance yesterday that there was steel behind those blinking eyes, and that the blade is aimed straight at Charlie Lucky's heart.

Siegel warned them as much, predicting that whatever loyalty Cokey Flo might once have owed Jimmy Fredericks would have been forgotten ten minutes after her arrest. According to Siegel, Cokey Flo is brassy and shrewd, with a wharf rat's instinct for self-preservation. Too wised up to be testifying without some deal with the special prosecutor, but too crafty to have left her fingerprints on whatever that deal might be. Her only vulnerability, Fredericks had confided to Siegel, was the junk she either shot in her legs or snorted up her nose.

Levy and Polakoff have arranged for a doctor to be standing by in the hope of disqualifying Cokey Flo as a witness on the ground that she's still using dope. If not disqualify her, then at least expose her as a liar right out of the gate, since she has already testified to having been clean for over a week. Also, Levy has asked Maurice Cantor to track down the lawyer whom Cantor recalls having once represented Dorothy Russell Calvit, the daughter of Lillian Russell and the woman who'd testified at Cokey Flo's solicitation trial in general sessions.

According to Levy, the fact that Cokey Flo never appeared before the grand jury makes her dangerous for both the defense and the prosecution, because, unlike the other madams and prostitutes who've been in custody for nearly four months now, her story hasn't been rehearsed and vetted and was reduced to writing only on Wednesday, with the ink barely dry on the paper. Also, Levy said, the fact that she was the girlfriend of Jimmy Fredericks and may still try to protect him means that she might contradict some of the other witnesses, and that that alone could be enough to cast doubt over whatever story she's come to tell about Charlie Lucky.

Now, at the start of her second day in the witness chair, Cokey Flo's story begins with a four A.M. meeting at some Chinese restaurant uptown in the spring of 1934, where she claims that she and Fredericks arrived to find Little Davie, Tommy the Bull, and Charlie Lucky all seated at a table eating noodles. Fredericks introduced her to the others as his girlfriend. The dinner conversation that followed was in Italian, but once they'd all piled into a car to head downtown, the discussion had shifted to English.

Q: Now as best you can, tell us who said what, will you do that?
A: Well, Jimmy spoke up and said, "Gee, I think some of the bookies are holding out joints on us." And Charlie spoke up and said, "Well, can't you get them all together?" And Davie answered, "Well, yes, we can get them all together; naturally it takes a little time." And Jimmy said, "If the bookies wouldn't

hold out the addresses, then we could get more of the joints together." And Charlie says, "Well, I'll tell you what you do. Bring all the bookies downtown tomorrow, I will put them on the carpet, and we will see that that doesn't happen again." And Jimmy said, "Well, Nick is the worst offender; he collects bond and keeps it, and then when the places get pinched they run to me, and I don't know anything about it, I am not able to take the girls out, because I didn't know they had been paying bond." And Charlie said, "Well, have them all come down and we will straighten the matter out." And then they started talking in Italian, and that was about all at that time.

Lucky has to restrain himself from laughing out loud. As if anyone would believe he'd incriminate himself like that in the presence of a total stranger, and a junkie no less, and would conveniently switch from Italian to English to do it. But as Lucky turns to the jury box, his smile dissolves at the sight of thirteen stone-faced jurors scribbling in their notepads.

Q: Now do you recall after that occasion, Jimmy told you about the meeting which was referred to in that conversation?
A: Yes, he did.
Q: What did he tell you about it?
A: He told me that they had all the bookies down and bawled the devil out of them for holding out, and that they would be fined if they were caught holding out any places; and that Nick Montana thought he was smart, because he had a brother that was supposed to be a big shot, and he thought he could get away with things like that, gypping people; and they told him he couldn't do a thing like that.

Again Lucky is watching the jury, looking for skepticism, searching for some acknowledgment that of all the cooperating bookers who've testified in the trial thus far—Al Weiner, Dave Miller, Danny Brooks, and Pete Harris—not one of them has mentioned such a meeting. Looking for recognition that if such a meeting had actually happened, it would have been the centerpiece of Dewey's case from day one. But all Lucky sees in the jury box are the same attentive and sympathetic faces, the same furious note-taking.

Q: Now do you recall driving with Jimmy Fredericks and Benny Spiller down to a garage on one occasion in the fall?

A: I do.

Q: Do you recall now where that garage was?

MR. BARRA: Will you fix the date a little bit? The fall of what year?

Q: I said the fall. We have been talking about 1934, haven't we?

A: Yes.

Q: Do you recall now where that garage was?

A: It was on the Lower East Side.

Q: Do you remember the street?

A: No, I don't. I don't know much about the East Side.

Q: When you got there, where did you go, when you got to the garage; where did you go?

A: Well, I sat in the car, I didn't go in.

Q: And did Jimmy Fredericks and Benny Spiller go inside the garage?

A: They did.

Q: Did you wait outside?

A: Yes, I did, for a while.

Q: Then what did you do?

A: Well, I got tired of sitting in the car, and I got out and started walking around a little, and wondered what they had to say inside, and I thought I would listen for a while; and I listened, and all I could hear was—

Q: Now, as I understand, you cannot tell us whose voices you heard?

A: No.

Q: Well, then you cannot tell us what you heard.

A: All right.

Q: After the meeting was over, who came out?

A: Jimmy came out and Charlie and Davie and Tommy, and Jimmy and I got in the car and drove away.

Q: Where was Benny Spiller?

A: He must have still been inside. I didn't see him come out.

Q: He did not come out?

A: No.

Q: Although he went in with Jimmy Fredericks?

A: Yes, he did.

Q: Whom did you drive away with?

A: Just with Jimmy.

Q: Just with Jimmy?

A: Yes.

Q: Do you recall sometime around Easter of 1935 going down to that garage again?

A: Yes, I do.

Q: Whom did you go down with that time?

A: Well, I went down with Jimmy alone.

Q: And when you got there, did you see anybody immediately?

A: No, I didn't.

Q: Where did Jimmy go when you got there?

A: Into the garage.

Q: I beg your pardon?

A: Into the garage.

Q: Where did you stay that time?

A: In the car for a while.

Q: And then did you wander around again?

A: I did.

Q: You heard voices, but you cannot identify who was speaking, can you?

A: No, I can't.

Q: After the meeting was over, who came out of that meeting?

A: The same people.

THE COURT: Tell us the people.

A: Davie, Jimmy, Charlie, and Tommy.

Lucky has stopped watching the jury and is instead now focused on Levy, who is scribbling notes on a legal pad. Lucky leans over to read. Levy has written ADDRESS?? and TWO VISITS! and OWNER? and WHY HASN'T HE TAKEN HER THERE?

Q: Some time last summer did you go down with Jimmy to a restaurant in Chinatown?

A: I did.

Q: Do you recall the address?

A: It is 21, and it is in the Chinatown district, but I don't know the exact name of the street.

Q: You know that there was a street number 21 on the place?

A: Yes, I do.

Q: Do you remember which of several streets it was?

A: I think it was either Pell or Mott. I know they called the place "Twenty-One" anyway.

Q: "Twenty-One" was the name of it?

A: It was also the number.

Q: Oh, I see. Whom did you find when you got down there with Jimmy Fredericks?

A: I found Charlie and Davie and Tommy sitting at a table eating.

Q: And did you go up and join them, you and Jimmy?

A: Well, we walked in, and they asked us to join them.

Q: And were they talking in English or Italian on this occasion?

A: Italian.

Q: Did they at any time talk in English?

A: Yes, they did.

Q: Do you remember any conversation in English about—I withdraw that. When they talked in English, did they talk about anything other than prostitution?

A: No, they didn't.

Q: They switched to English when they talked about prostitution?

A: Yes.

. . .

Q: What did you hear about the subject of prostitution?

A: Well, I heard Charlie say that he was disgusted and didn't like the idea of it at all; that there wasn't much money in it; and they were speaking of—it was getting tough.

Q: All right. Go ahead.

A: It was getting tough, and the joints were getting difficult to manage. A lot of the women—

Q: Will you tell us who it was that was speaking, as best you can?

MR. LEVY: Pardon me, Mr. Dewey. I am sitting a few feet away and cannot get answers. May we have that read, your Honor?

(Answer read.)

Q: "A lot of the women?"

A: (Continuing)—didn't want to pay the bond. Jimmy mentioned that Peggy Wild was being very difficult; that he had sent—

THE COURT: Who besides Peggy Wild did he say?

MR. DEWEY: Nobody, your Honor.

A: (Continuing) No one—that he had sent a collector up to collect the bond, and she wouldn't—she would open the door on a chain and tell him she wasn't doing anything, and he found out later that she was in an apartment across the hall from the apartment that she claimed not to be running in.

Q: Did anybody make any comment on that?

A: Charlie said, "Oh, I suppose she is a wise guy." So Davie said, "Well, we will take care of it; don't worry."

Q: Did Charlie Lucky say anything about what they should do?

A: He said, "Why don't you"—oh, yes, he said, "Why don't you get the madams together, Jimmy?" He said, "You know, I told you before that being nice to them isn't any good." And Jimmy said, "Well, you know how it is; it is tough now, and I thought that if I could talk to them, it might be better."

Q: What did Charlie Lucky say to that?

A: He said, "Well, you can't talk to them; they are too stubborn anyway." He said, "Get after them; step on them a little bit." And Davie said, "We will take care of it. We will see."

By now Lucky has stopped watching the jury and stopped watching Levy and is focused instead on the witness, this Cokey Flo Brown. Although her voice remains weak, her entire demeanor has changed from yesterday's fear and timidity to today's confident self-possession. While yesterday she was unwilling to take her eyes off Dewey, today she is half turning toward the jury during her answers, as if drawing them into her confidence. And the jurors are responding in kind, leaning forward and hanging on every word.

Q: Do you remember an occasion when you went down with Jimmy to another or the same restaurant on the Lower East Side?

A: The same restaurant.

Q: The same restaurant?

A: Yes.

Q: Do you remember about when that was?

A: That was in about October.

Q: Of what year?

A: '35.

Q: Last October?

A: Yes.

Q: And whom did you see when you got there?

A: There was just Charlie and Davie.

Q: And Jimmy Fredericks?

A: And Jimmy Fredericks.

Q: Tommy Bull was not present at that time?

A: Not present at that time.

Q: And what conversation was there at that occasion about prostitution?

A: Well, Charlie said that he was disgusted, and he wanted to have the bonding combination stop bonding altogether. He said there wasn't any money in it, and it was all a big headache, and his name was getting mentioned in it quite a bit, and he didn't like it; and Davie said, "Well, why don't you give it a chance a while? We will see that we straighten things out."

THE COURT: Who said that?

A: Davie. And Charlie said, "Well, I don't know; this Dewey investigation is coming on and it may get tough, and I think we ought to fold up for a while."

MR. LEVY: Pardon me. This is October, Mr. Dewey?

MR. DEWEY: Yes. What else was said as you recall it?

A: He said—so Davie argued for it. He said, "Well, why don't you let it go a while and see how things go? It might pick up. I admit it is slow now because there were quite a few pinches, and naturally that takes money out of the combination, but it may quiet down and get better." Well, Charlie said, "Well, it would be better if we quit a while, and started over again at some other time when things were quiet." He said, "We could even syndicate all the places like they do in Chicago, and instead of three or four combinations having the syndicates, as they do in Chicago, there would be only one in New York, us." So Davie said, "Well, why don't you let it go for a while? I don't think it will be very tough. Even if the Dewey investigation does start on us, they will only pick on phony bonding, that is all. They will probably grab two or three of the bondsmen, and that is all there will be to it." So Charlie said, "Well,

290

all right, then let it go. I will let it go for a couple of more months, and if things are the same, you will have to let it drop."

Q: Was there any mention by—I withdraw that. Do you recall Charlie Lucky saying anything about the A&P?

A: He meant syndicate the places on a large scale, the same as the A&P stores are a large syndicate.

The clock reads ten forty-five when Dewey finally sits. Cokey Flo Brown, her voice now barely a whisper, has finished casting her spell over the courtroom.

Forty-Two

In Chambers

May 1936

"THE WORST OF it is, they believe her."

George patted his pockets as he paced, wishing he could light a cigar. Behind a screen that had been set up in the judge's chambers, two doctors—Milton Bridges for the defense, and Peter Amoroso for the prosecution—were examining Cokey Flo Brown for evidence of recent narcotics use. Eunice Carter stood with Dewey in the opposite corner of the room, both of them chatting with lowered voices, while Judge McCook read the newspaper as he ate a sandwich at his desk.

Polakoff turned his back on Dewey and spoke to George in a whisper.

"Siegel says that she came to his office a couple of times, looking for ways she might help Frederico. He gave her a copy of the indictment, and she sat with it for over an hour, making notes. When he asked her about Luciano, about why his name had been added, she said she'd never heard of him."

"I wish he'd hurry up and get to that. All this business about drugs is trying the jury's patience."

"Siegel and Kopp want you to keep her on the stand as long as possible, to see if she breaks down. I told them I'd run it past you."

George frowned. "That runs the risk that the jury will tire of me before she does."

"Have you got a better idea?"

"I have ideas, but I wouldn't say they're any better. For example, why would the learned special prosecutor put Miss Brown in the witness chair without first driving her to that East Side garage in search of at least one corroborating witness? That would have taken an hour at most—less time than it took to fetch her pretty blue frock. The answer is, he doesn't believe her story any more than we do."

George paused to glance over Polakoff's shoulder.

"He prefers an unknown garage and no corroboration to a real establishment with a real owner staffed by real mechanics who've never laid eyes on Luciano. The same goes for these damned Chinese restaurants. He's learned a lesson, Mr. Dewey has, from our friend Mr. Bendix. The hazier the details and the fewer the eyewitnesses, the less vulnerable a story is to impeachment."

The matron stepped from behind the curtain, followed by the two physicians. Dr. Bridges caught George's eye, giving his head an imperceptible shake.

The judge set down his sandwich. "Gentlemen? We await your verdict."

"Doctor Amoroso and I are in accord," Bridges said, returning a stethoscope to his satchel. "The witness presents as being in the late-middle stages of opiate withdrawal. We can't say for certain, of course, without a blood test, but it appears unlikely she's ingested any narcotic substances in at least the past seventy-two hours."

"Just like I told you," chimed a voice from behind the screen.

"As did I," Dewey said, crossing the room to McCook's desk. "This whole examination has been a cheap circus stunt with no purpose other than to unnerve and intimidate the witness."

"The witness," McCook said, folding his newspaper, "appears to be doing just fine. Wouldn't you agree, Mr. Levy?"

"It's been my experience that most prosecution witnesses do well on direct."

"Yes. Speaking of which, you know I hate to limit your cross-examination, Mr. Levy, but I do hope you'll be more expeditious with this witness. We're down to our last alternate, and I know you feel as I do that we don't want to risk a mistrial."

"Perhaps if the learned special prosecutor tried looking elsewhere than the state's jails and prisons for his witnesses, there'd be less material for defense counsel to cover."

Cokey Flo emerged from behind the screen and was working a pin in her hat.

"Be that as it may," the judge said, "let's try to keep things moving, shall we? Mr. Dewey, is there anything further we need to discuss?"

"There is, Your Honor. Miss Brown, as we all know, is in somewhat fragile condition due to the reduction cure about which she's already testified. I'm told, however, that a small measure of brandy sometimes helps to fortify women in her state, and I of course wouldn't dream of administering same without the court's permission and supervision."

"You've got to be joking," Polakoff said. "You want to let her *drink* on the witness stand?"

"I'm simply proposing that at appropriate intervals throughout the day, the court might wish to allow the young lady a small sip of brandy here in chambers. To keep her strength up, that's all. We can barely hear her as it is, and this constant rereading of her answers is slowing matters to a crawl."

"Yes, I agree with Mr. Dewey," the judge said, standing and brushing bread crumbs from his vest. "Anything to speed matters along. Are there any objections?"

"That is a most unusual request from my learned friend," George said.

"You've seen how they drag out their questioning, Judge, trying to wear down our witnesses. Trying to turn the trial into some kind of a dance marathon. If Miss Brown is too weak to continue, we'll have no choice but to request a recess, and possibly an adjournment. I want to get her on and off the stand as quickly as possible, that's all."

"An occasional sip of brandy seems perfectly reasonable, Mr. Levy. I suppose I could, as an alternative, place a time limit on cross-examination, although I'm loath to do it. But I'll leave that to your discretion."

George could see where this was heading, but he also sensed an opportunity. If he acceded to Dewey's proposal, then the judge would be less likely to sustain an objection to the length of George's cross. It was a trade-off worth considering.

"Might I have a moment to confer with my colleague?"

"By all means," said McCook.

George and Moses Polakoff retired to the corner for privacy while Dewey shared a silent look with McCook, who raised a bushy eyebrow. After a minute of hushed discussion, the huddle finally broke.

"Under the circumstances," George said, "the defense has no objection to our friend's suggestion. Miss Brown has proved herself to be a liar on opium, to be a liar on morphine, and to be a liar on heroin. We shudder to think of the strain she must be under, attempting to lie while totally sober."

"Go chase yourself," said Cokey Flo.

"I have other intentions, Miss Brown. What I propose to pursue is the truth."

Forty-Three

The Letter

May 1936

IT WAS LIKE a hot coal burning a hole in Tom Dewey's pocket.

Albert Unger, an assistant district attorney under William Copeland Dodge, had appeared during the lunch break and had left behind a letter written by Joe Bendix to his wife, Joy Dixon. The letter was dated April 21 and had somehow been misdelivered to Morris Panger, another assistant district attorney with whom Bendix was negotiating for clemency. Scripted in what Tom recognized as the hotel thief's florid hand, the letter urged Dixon to "think up some real clever story" by which to gain the confidence of the special prosecutor's office.

The letter was an explosive piece of exculpatory evidence that, if it found its way into Levy's hands, would destroy whatever remained of Bendix's credibility. The first question confronting Tom was whether Panger had taken the time to make photostats of the letter. The

296

second, of course, was the extent of Tom's obligations as an officer of the court now that he knew of the letter's existence.

Although he was known colloquially as the special prosecutor, Tom's official title was actually deputy assistant district attorney of New York County. That title—the lowest possible rank in the D.A.'s office—was itself a pointed barb from Dodge. But as an assistant D.A. himself, Panger and Tom were theoretical colleagues—partners in the Luciano prosecution—even if, in reality, Dodge and his Tammany Hall cronies were Tom's greatest antagonists.

So where, exactly, did Panger's loyalties lie? If not with the defense, then had he shared the letter with Dodge? Would he? If so, would Dodge use the letter to sabotage the prosecution? Would he take it to the press? Or was this all some kind of a setup—a test to see what the special prosecutor would do of his own accord?

Tom needed time to consider both his options and their ramifications. Thank God he hadn't called Dixon as a witness! But first there was the not-so-small matter of Cokey Flo's cross-examination, which had already resumed.

It had been Siegel and Kopp asking the questions before the lunch recess, each of them like roadside crows, strutting and pecking at the rawer aspects of Cokey Flo's testimony—her drug addictions, her hypodermic injections, her reduction cure. These were, Tom knew, mere pinpricks. Because Cokey Flo's direct testimony had been aimed at Luciano, it would be Levy wielding the carving knife on cross.

Thank God the brandy seemed to be helping. When she'd returned to the witness chair, Cokey Flo's color was better and her voice, as she parried Sam Siegel's final thrusts, was stronger and clearer than Tom had ever before heard it.

Q: How many times were you at my office?
A: Twice.
Q: How many times?
A: Twice.

Q: Twice. It was three times, wasn't it?

A: Yes, three times, that is right.

Q: Three times. You haven't got a very good memory, have you?

A: Yes, I have.

Q: You came to my office without any solicitation from me, didn't you?

A: That is right.

Q: Yes. You came to my office and you told my telephone operator to announce you to me as Flo, didn't you?

A: Yes.

Q: Yes. And when you came in, I asked you who you were, didn't I?

A: Yes.

Q: And you wanted to know what James Frederico was charged with, didn't you?

A: That is right.

Q: Didn't you tell me that the only thing Frederico has to do with this whole matter was in connection with bonding the girls?

A: That is right.

Q: That's right. And that was the truth, wasn't it?

A: It was the truth.

Q: Yes. You were trying to tell Frederico's attorney the truth, to help Frederico, weren't you?

A: Yes.

Q: Yes or no?

A: Yes.

Q: When I showed you that indictment, the last indictment containing ninety counts, it was very late in the evening, wasn't it?

A: Yes, it was.

Q: Yes. I didn't talk to you until you started to go home, isn't that so?

A: That is right.

Q: Didn't I put you in my library and tell you I didn't have time to talk to you, and that you could look at the indictment and make yourself comfortable and make notes from it?

A: Yes.

Q: Yes; and you sat there for how long in that library?

A: Quite a long time.

Q: Over an hour, wasn't it?

A: I didn't measure the time.

Q: Well, you didn't leave until around 6:30, did you?

A: No.

Q: No. And as you left I talked with you, I walked with you a distance of about ten feet from the library to the elevator, didn't I?

A: Yes.

Q: Yes. That is, the elevator opens directly into my law offices, doesn't it?

A: It does.

Q: The elevators of the building?

A: Yes, it does.

Q: And I stood there waiting, signaling the elevator and waiting until it would stop and let you go downstairs?

A: Yes.

Q: Yes. Now you tell me what was said about any of these defendants at that time by you.

A: Nothing was said about any of the defendants.

Q: You don't recall saying anything about Luciano?

A: No, I don't.

Q: Do you remember anything I said about a man named Luciano?

A: No.

Q: Didn't you tell me you had never heard of him, and I wanted to know from you how he was connected in this case, and how he came to be indicted with the others in this last indictment?

A: No, you never spoke of Luciano at all.

Tom knew enough not to smirk at Gelb or Ten Eyck, but was having a hard time restraining himself. So far, at least, Flo Brown had been a perfect witness—smart, poised, and always two steps ahead of her questioner. How a girl with her looks and intellect had ended up in the gutter was one of life's little mysteries.

Siegel was angry now, having effectively been called a liar, and Tom decided to goad him a little as Siegel returned to the subject of Dorothy Russell Calvit, Cokey Flo's last employer.

Q: When did you ask her to get in touch with me after your conviction here about a week or ten days ago?

MR. DEWEY: Objected to. I think we have gone so far afield, your Honor, as to be utterly useless in this cross-examination.

THE COURT: I will not say so yet. I do not know what is in counsel's mind.

MR. SAMUEL SIEGEL: If your Honor please—

THE COURT: I said I will not say so yet. I do not know what is in counsel's mind.

MR. SAMUEL SIEGEL: But I do object to the district attorney making an objection on the ground that the question is utterly useless. I do not know what he is talking about, but he should know that that is not a proper objection.

MR. DEWEY: I consider it—

MR. SAMUEL SIEGEL: If he wants to sum up while he is objecting, I would ask your Honor to tell him not to.

MR. DEWEY: If I did as much summation as my friends, we would never get anywhere.

THE COURT: I suggest you go on, since I have sustained your objection, Mr. Siegel.

MR. SAMUEL SIEGEL: Could I wait until Mr. Dewey takes a glass of water, your Honor?

THE COURT: You may always do that.

MR. SAMUEL SIEGEL: I find it terribly disconcerting when he walks up and down there.

THE COURT: You may always do that. You will not be disconcerted.

MR. SAMUEL SIEGEL: If he thinks he is disconcerting me by doing that, he can lay off his ears.

MR. DEWEY: What a lot of silly nonsense. If he cannot examine when I get a drink of water, then counsel ought not to be at the Bar.

THE COURT: You have intimated that it was and that it was not disconcerting. So please go on.

MR. SAMUEL SIEGEL: What was the last question after Mr. Dewey's remark?

Siegel's cross-examination limped to a close with a parting shot at Cokey Flo's motives.

Q: I ask you, what was the day you were convicted of prostitution?

A: I was convicted May 13th.

Q: What day of the week was that?

A: On a Wednesday.

Q: Wednesday. Did you see Mrs. Calvit that day?

A: Yes.

Q: What?

A: Yes.

Q: Was that the day you asked her to get in touch with me?

A: I do believe I wrote her a letter to that effect.

Q: When?

A: That evening.

Q: Wednesday evening?

A: Yes.

Q: Wednesday evening you wrote her a letter to get in touch with me to help you when you came up for sentence on Tuesday following?

A: Yes.

Q: And two nights later, Friday, you became disgusted with everything and wrote the letter to Mr. Ten Eyck?

A: Yes.

Q: What happened between Wednesday night, can you tell us, and Friday night to cause you to become disgusted with everything?

A: Well, it was something that had been going on a long time in my mind.

Q: What?

A: I said it was something—

THE COURT: Read that, please. We will have it read. There was a little noise at that time.

(Answer read.)

Q: That is, rehabilitation?

A: That is it.

Q: Your desire to go straight?

A: That is it.

Q: It culminated in your mind, and induced you to write a letter to Mr. Dewey on Friday night?

A: That is it.

Q: You thought that "now is the time, two charges pending against me, and I am now coming up for sentence," that this would be a grand and glorious time to go straight?

A: No; I thought I might—as long as I was going to be punished, I might as well be punished and clear my conscience, and when I left the House of Detention, be free.

Once Siegel, still visibly agitated, had returned to his place at the defense table, it was Levy's turn at the podium. Tom braced himself. The jurors, who'd come to view the clash between Tom's punctilious direct and Levy's gentlemanly cross as a kind of grand spectator sport, all shifted forward in their seats.

Forty-Four

Cross

May 1936

HE DIDN'T LOOK like much, the little Jew with the rimless eyeglasses and the sleeves pushed up to his elbows to expose his hairy forearms. But he was the one to look out for—both Barry and Mr. Dewey had warned me as much—and he was the one they'd pretended to be when they'd cross-examined me in Mr. Dewey's office, saying things like, "Don't let him lull you to sleep," and "Don't let him get you talking."

He seemed like a kindly uncle when he first started out in this soft and reassuring voice, like we were having a fireside chat over tea, him asking me about my background, like he was concerned for my well-being. But I knew better. I could see right through his little act, and the barbed insinuations he was making. Like that I'd have to be pretty hard-boiled to run a speakeasy when I was fifteen, and that I'd have to be a damned good liar to keep three guys on the string in

303

Chicago. Of course, knowing what he was doing and stopping him from doing it were two different things.

The problem with cross-examination was that you couldn't explain anything. He'd ask questions like "Isn't it so that—" and "You did so-and-so, did you not?" And if I tried to answer with anything other than a simple yes or no, he'd cut me off with his next question and make it look like I was arguing with him in front of the jury. It was frustrating, I'll tell you that, and after a while I started to feel faint again and asked the judge for a recess. The judge had a matron accompany me into his office, where they gave me another small sip of the brandy. Afterward—this was around three forty-five or so—Mr. Dewey had to tell the jurors that I'd had my little drink, and of course Levy made a big show of how he didn't object, like he was the one who was worried about my fragile condition.

Levy resumed with a bunch of questions about my drug habit, and how I ran my houses, and after a while I got the impression that maybe he was stalling, either to run out the clock or to tire me out before he moved in for the kill. It was weird having thoughts like those, right there in the witness chair, like you were standing outside yourself and analyzing what was happening to you even when you were answering questions and trying to make a good impression on the jury. It wasn't easy, I'll tell you that, and I was getting fuzzier and fuzzier as the afternoon wore on and my side started hurting again, and when I looked over at Mr. Dewey, which he warned me I shouldn't do, I had a pained expression on my face.

Levy, meanwhile would make these little jabs, and then he'd kind of half-turn to the jury and raise his eyebrows, as if to say, "Can you believe this woman?" Like when he was asking me about the effects of opium, trying to imply that it impaired my memory, and when I wouldn't admit that, he'd turn it around against me.

Q: Didn't find any change in your memory at all?
A: None at all.

304

Q: When you awakened in the morning you would have a clear-cut recollection of what took place the night before, would you?

A: I had to; I had to remember over three thousand customers by name and face.

Q: You had three thousand customers?

A: Yes.

Q: In your house of prostitution?

A: Yes.

Q: And when they called up, you had to remember their voices?

A: Their voice, name and the face.

Q: I see. This is by the year 1933?

A: Yes.

Q: Your memory was sufficiently acute that you could remember three thousand customers?

A: Yes.

Q: By name, voice, and some by telephone number?

A: Yes.

Q: Well then, really—

A: Not by telephone number.

Q: No?

A: By voice over the phone.

Q: And then when they came in, by appearance, isn't that true?

A: That is true.

Q: Three thousand different people you kept in mind?

A: Yes.

Q: And really, Miss Brown, the problem of remembering the details of the story you told today is very small compared to what you needed in your own business; isn't that true?

After sparring like that for over an hour, Levy finally moved to the real issues in the case, and he started out with Jimmy's role in the combination. Again, like I was standing outside myself, I thought, this guy is awfully clever because he knows I'm not gonna dump all over Jimmy. I could see his strategy plain as day, getting me to defend Jimmy and in the process contradict the testimony of the other girls. And while I was happy for Jimmy that someone was finally asking the questions Siegel should have asked, I knew Levy didn't care a rat's ass about Jimmy, and that all he cared about was undermining my story about Charlie Lucky by making me out as a liar.

But like I said, what choice did I have? As angry as I'd been with Jimmy, I wasn't about to hammer another nail in his coffin like that bitch June Gary had done and paint him as some kind of a goon running around with a blackjack threatening to shoot people's dogs.

Q: At that time you were paying—during the year 1934—you were paying bonding fees, were you not?

A: Yes, I was.

Q: Entirely with your satisfaction?

A: Yes.

Q: You were only too glad to do it, weren't you?

A: Yes, I was.

Q: You realized from your standpoint it was very necessary in your prostitution business, did you not?

A: Yes, it was.

Q: And you could not see any reason why any madam in the City of New York should have any objection to paying the small sum of ten dollars to bond; isn't that true?

A: That is true.

Q: And Jimmy would tell you that some madams did not want to bond; isn't that true?

A: Yes.

Q: And didn't he tell you if they did not want to bond, he tried to coax them, but he never wanted to use any force?

A: That is true.

Q: That Jimmy never wanted to hurt anybody?

A: That is true.

Q: That Jimmy never had a gun, as far as you saw, did he?

A: No.

Q: Or never carried any weapon, as far as you saw, did he?

A: No.

Once he'd got me to contradict what the other girls had been saying about Jimmy, Levy then started in on the Chinese restaurants, and on the fact that I couldn't describe where they were, and the fact that none of Mr. Dewey's men had taken me there so that I could identify them better. I could see that Mr. Dewey and Barry were starting to fidget, and so I got a little rattled, and when Mr. Dewey saw I was getting rattled, he tried to come to my rescue.

Q: Can you give us any better address of this so-called Chinese restaurant, except that it is near Mott Street and near Pell Street in an old dilapidated building?

A: No, that is the number of the restaurant, twenty-one.

Q: And the number of the restaurant is twenty-one?

A: Yes.

Q: When were you last in that particular restaurant?

A: In October.

Q: Of what year?

A: 1935.

Q: And since you told Mr. Dewey's assistant that story, did they ask you to point out that restaurant in any way to them?

A: No, they did not.

Q: Did you go back to look over that restaurant in any way at all?

A: No.

Q: At the time you claimed you last saw Charlie Lucky there, can you tell us who ran the place?

A: No.

Q: Was it a Chinaman or an American?

A: I have no idea.

Q: You have no idea. Don't you know who waited on you at that time?

A: A Chinaman.

Q: A Chinaman. Did you know that Chinaman before?

A: No.

Q: Is that all there is on the outside of it, the word twenty-one or the number twenty-one?

A: Well, I didn't pay much attention to it.

Q: You had been there before, you say, had you not?

A: Yes, I had been there twice.

Q: Yes.

A: I don't take notice of every detail of every restaurant I go into.

Q: Oh, you are getting a little angry now?

A: And I don't think anyone ever does.

MR. DEWEY: I object to counsel's remark.

THE COURT: Sustained.

MR. LEVY: It is a question, your Honor, not a remark. I say, are you getting a little angry?

MR. DEWEY: I object to it as a question.

THE WITNESS: No, I am not getting angry.

MR. DEWEY: Excuse me. I object to counsel badgering the witness.

MR. LEVY: And I object to you trying to badger me.

THE COURT: I overrule the objection. She has answered anyhow, so it is all water over the dam.

Q: Now you say on that occasion that you went in, what month did you put it in?

A: I put it in October.

Q: What month are you talking about that you were in this Chinese restaurant, twenty-one?

A: October.

Q: When in October were you there?

A: 1935.

Q: 1935?

A: Yes.

Q: And that is the last time you saw Charlie Lucky?

A: Right.

Q: How many times before that in your life do you claim that you saw him?

A: I saw him twice in that restaurant.

Q: Yes, any other place?

A: Twice coming out of the garage.

Q: I beg your pardon?

A: Twice coming out of the garage.

Q: Twice coming out of the garage; that is five times?

A: Yes; once uptown.

Q: Up where, uptown?

A: In a restaurant uptown.

Q: Just give us the name of the restaurant uptown.

A: That is also a Chinese restaurant. I couldn't give you the name of it.

Q: Also Chinese, located where?

A: Around One Thirtieth or Fortieth Street and Broadway.

Q: You know that is a big territory, Miss Brown, don't you?

A: Yes, but I could point the place out.

Q: You could?

A: Yes.

Q: Have you tried to with any of Mr. Dewey's assistants?

A: No, I have not.

It got to the point where I felt like Levy was making fun of me, like the story I was telling was so unbelievable that it amazed even him, who thought he'd heard everything. But unlike the other lawyers, Levy never smirked or rolled his eyes. He was always the perfect gentleman, even when he was signaling to the jury by his tone of voice that he thought everything I was saying was a load of hooey.

Q: Now what time did you leave the restaurant at Broadway and One Thirtieth or thereabouts?

A: Well, we left there about quarter of five.

Q: Yes. And you drove without any stop, right on downtown, is that true?

A: Yes.

Q: And during the time you were riding in the car you were listening to the conversation, were you?

A: I was listening—

Q: Is that true now? Kindly answer.

A: Yes.

Q: All right. You had met Charlie Lucky for the first time in your life?

A: Yes.

Q: And on your direct testimony, and on your cross, you have been telling the Court and jury what Davie Betillo supposedly said, what Charlie supposedly said, and what Jimmy Fredericks said, have you not?

A: Yes.

Q: Do you mean to tell the Court and jury that, meeting two strange men or three strange men for the first time, with your attention directed toward driving the car, you could tell the respective voices of the people in the backseat?

A: There was a mirror in front.

Q: Yes.

A: And I could see these three men in back through this mirror.

Q: See through the mirror?

A: Yes, I could see their lips moving.

Q: And through the mirror you could notice their lips moving?

A: Yes, sir.

Q: And you watched them very keenly through that mirror, in order to know which one said which, is that right? Is that true or not?

A: Well, now and again I would glance into the mirror and see them.

Q: You were not inquisitive as to what they were talking about, were you?

A: Well, it was interesting.

Q: Oh, it was, I see. And being interested, you watched them very keenly through that mirror, in order to know which one said which, is that right? Is that true or not?

A: Yes, I watched them.

Q: Now, was it dark around quarter of five in the morning or thereabouts, when you left this place?

A: It was dawning.

Q: I beg your pardon?

A: It was just dawning, just starting to break daylight.

Q: Just starting to break daylight?

A: Yes.

Q: But you could see clearly enough through that mirror the different lips moving, could you?

A: Yes, I could.

I stole a peek at the clock, even though I knew better. Court recessed at seven, and I was dying to get out of there and have another drink and even return to my cell if that's what it took to get away from Levy and all his questions. I'd long ago quit looking at the jury, like Mr. Dewey had told me I should on direct, because Levy kept my answers so short that there wasn't any time to do it, and it would've looked phony-baloney if I tried. But just the one time, after he'd asked me about the backseat voices and I'd said that I could see their lips moving in the mirror—that one time I peeked over to check how my story was going over.

God, I couldn't wait for seven o'clock.

Forty-Five

Reasonable Doubt

May 1936

LUCKY IS DYING a slow death, sitting and listening to the testimony of Cokey Flo Brown. Even on cross-examination, even when Levy is batting her around like a cat with a wounded mouse, Lucky can see that the jury is sympathetic. See that they care about her, and feel sorry for her, and want to protect her from the clutches of Charlie Lucky and his swarthy gang of downtown thugs who've bullied and threatened and reduced this poor, wayward girl to the shivering shell that sits before them in the witness chair.

It's all Lucky can do to control his temper. But a flash of anger, a sudden outburst, is exactly what Dewey is hoping for. Betillo had exploded during the testimony of Danny Brooks, forcing his lawyer, Caesar Barra, to physically restrain him. It had looked bad—like Little Davie was the frightening, hair-trigger thug of Dewey's narrative. Lucky understands this, and Polakoff and Levy have already warned him about it.

The problem, Lucky thinks, is that Levy is taking too damned long with his cross-examination, dwelling on things he's already covered over and over again. Probing for inconsistencies, Lucky supposes, but finding few and boring the jurors in the process. Plus he's burying the good points he's already made and giving Cokey Flo too many chances to repeat her ridiculous story. Worse, he's overlooking all kinds of opportunities to paint her as the dirty rotten liar she obviously is.

Take the fact that she seems to use a different name every time she appears in a courtroom. That should have been central to Levy's cross, but instead of hitting her with it, Levy's passed right over it, even though Cokey Flo herself has said that she'd never commit perjury for anyone.

Or take the fact that she claims to remember everything she'd ordered, right down to what she'd had for drinks and dessert, at some Chinese restaurant where she'd eaten dinner over two years earlier. And yet here she is five minutes later, claiming to have spent hours parked in front of some East Side garage—not once but twice—but still can't describe where the hell it's located.

It's easy, Lucky knows, to watch from the front row and criticize the guys in the ring. But still, Levy is supposed to be a pro. He should be knocking this girl senseless, not treating her with kid gloves. And if his strategy is to wear her down by keeping her on the witness stand, it clearly isn't working. If anything, Levy himself seems to be wearing down, and getting punchy, and putting the judge and the jury to sleep.

Lucky can't wait for the recess, so he can read Levy the riot act. Tell him to make his points and get out again, like a boxer throwing a jab. That's all he has to do—in and out—not spend hours going over every last detail of the direct examination.

And the jury, what are they thinking, sitting there like men around a campfire, hanging on every word and gesture from this lying little hophead? Talk about receiving money from the proceeds of a woman engaged in prostitution! This Cokey Flo is the one who ought to be on trial, not Charlie Lucky.

This whole case, in fact, is ass-backward, with the whores and the pimps and the bookers—the real offenders of public morals—throwing stones at the bondsmen and the shylocks for taking a small piece of their action in order to keep the girls off the city's streets and out of the city's jails. For performing a public service, for Christ sake! Come to think of it, this whole trial seems to be geared toward freeing the whores and madams while cutting their overhead and making their business more profitable.

That's some use of public money!

Finally, thank God, seven o'clock rolls around, and the judge puts Lucky out of his misery. The jurors stand and stretch, and the other defendants hunch to huddle with their lawyers. Lucky waits, ignoring the reporters who shout questions to him over the railing while Levy and Polakoff and Polakoff's kid Mezansky have a powwow by the lectern. Dewey, meanwhile, sits cool as a cucumber as his man Ten Eyck helps Cokey Flo from the witness chair and leads her like the father of the bride through the side door next to the jury box.

Heading straight for the brandy bottle, Lucky figures, or maybe the needle, and soon it's just the defendants and the lawyers left in the courtroom, plus the omnipresent guards, who busy themselves with their shotguns and handcuffs.

"We need to talk!" Lucky calls to Levy, who nods and seeks out the captain of the guard.

Once the four men are alone in the privacy of the wood-paneled jury room, Lucky lets them have it. Too long, too soft, and too goddamned boring! In and out, like throwing a jab. Get the crowd behind you. Bring some electricity into the arena!

"You've got to step on her a little," he tells Levy, knowing even as he speaks them that his words make him sound exactly like the Charlie Lucky of Dewey's narrative—the callous overlord ordering Jimmy Fredericks to beat the madams bloody.

Surprised by his client's outburst, Levy says, "I thought you were the one who said Carlino and Siegel were being too hard on the girls."

"Yeah, but that was before."

"Before they were talking about you, you mean."

"I mean before they started lying, goddamn it!"

"I think you're overreacting, Charlie," Polakoff intercedes in a soothing voice. "In fact, I think it's going rather well. What about you, Sam?"

The Mezansky kid shrugs. "I only caught the tail end, but I'm not buying a word she says."

"What about the jury?" Levy asks him. "Could you get a read—"

"Listen you guys," Lucky interrupts, again raising his voice. "I got ringside tickets to the Louis-Schmeling fight, and the way things are goin out there, I might as well give 'em away. We need to quit dancin around and knock this broad on her ass."

Neither Polakoff nor Levy responds.

"What's the story with this Captain Dutton?" Lucky turns on the kid, who seems to shrink under his gaze.

"We talked to him. He says he's never met Bendix in his life. But here's the best part. He says he knows the wife, Joy Dixon, which is probably why Bendix pulled Dutton's name out of his hat."

"Subpoena?"

Mezansky nods to Polakoff. "He said he'll be available whenever we need him."

A knock sounds at the door. Maurice Cantor, counsel for Jack Eller, sticks his head into the room.

"Sorry to interrupt, George, but I thought you'd like to know. Dorothy Calvit's lawyer is named Samuel Kornbluth. He's got an office in the Continental Building on Broadway."

"Can we talk to her?"

"I haven't called him yet, but I have his number. I figured you'd want to be in on that conversation."

Forty-Six

Kornbluth

May 1936

IT WASN'T UNTIL midnight that George and Maurice Cantor were able to repair to Cantor's office and place the telephone call. Samuel Kornbluth's voice, thick with sleep, answered on the second ring.

"Hello?"

"Mr. Kornbluth? This is attorney Maurice Cantor calling. I'm terribly sorry to disturb you at home, and at such a late hour, but I'm wondering whether you're still counsel for Dorothy Calvit, Lillian Russell's daughter?"

"Is something wrong with Dorothy?"

"No, nothing like that. But I have an associate here, Mr. George Morton Levy, and he'd like to have a word with you."

Cantor passed the receiver to George.

"Mr. Kornbluth? George Levy here, counsel for Charlie Luciano in the Dewey vice trial. First of all, let me join in my colleague's apology for the lateness of the hour, but I'm afraid it couldn't be helped."

"What is it, Mr. Levy? What can I do for you?"

"Well, Sam—may I call you Sam?—we have a witness on the stand right now who claims she used to work for Mrs. Calvit, and that Mrs. Calvit came to court not long ago to testify on her behalf. This witness, who goes by the name Cokey Flo Brown, claims that she knows my client, Mr. Luciano. My client says she's lying, and we were hoping that your client could help us shed some light on the situation."

"But why would you need to bother Dorothy—"

"Because they lived together, as we understand it, at the Hotel Alamac. We haven't attempted to contact Mrs. Calvit directly, since she'd only refer us to you, so we thought it prudent to contact you in the first instance and try to speed matters along. This is extremely important, as I hope you'll understand, and tomorrow is our last chance to cross-examine this witness. That means we need to know by tonight anything that Mrs. Calvit can tell us about her."

George held the receiver from his ear so that Cantor, leaning across his desk, could hear the sounds of squeaking bedsprings and rustling fabric. When Kornbluth's voice returned, it was louder than before.

"I understand your problem, gentlemen, but my goodness. You don't expect me to call her up and interrogate her at this late hour, do you?"

"Actually, Sam, we were hoping you could meet with her in person. I've taken a room at the Waldorf tonight, and Mr. Cantor and I are heading there in a moment. We'd like you to meet us in Peacock Alley so that we can give you all the details. Then we'd like you to visit Mrs. Calvit and ask her a few questions on our behalf, all within the purview of the attorney-client privilege. Then we'd like you to return to the Waldorf and fill us in. That means you'll have to call her now, as soon as we hang up, to make the necessary arrangements."

"Now hold on a minute—"

"Please understand that there's nothing untoward that we're asking you to do. The only thing out of the ordinary is the lateness of the hour and the urgency required."

"Yes, but—"

"I can't overemphasize how important this is, Sam. An innocent man's freedom is at stake."

"I understand, but—"

"And needless to say, you'll be compensated for your time."

The line fell silent as George held Cantor's gaze.

"Compensated how?"

Smiling, Cantor swung his feet onto the desk.

It was nine A.M. on Saturday morning when George descended to the Waldorf's lobby. He'd stopped only at the cigar counter on his way to the Park Avenue entrance, where Samuel Kornbluth, looking rumpled in blue seersucker, waited by the stairs.

"Thank you for being so punctual," George said as he offered the lawyer his hand and continued down the steps to the street. "I'm sorry about last night, but I simply had to get some sleep."

"Of course," Kornbluth said, hurrying to keep up. "I understand perfectly."

The traffic on Park Avenue was light. The bellman blew his whistle, hailing an approaching cab.

"As I told Mr. Cantor last evening—"

"Yes, we spoke on the phone. I hope you don't mind riding with me to the courthouse. I want to hear Mrs. Calvit's story firsthand, as it were."

"Foley Square," George told the cabbie as the men settled, shoulder to shoulder, in the roomy backseat, each with a briefcase in his lap.

"I understand you took notes."

"Yes, of course." Kornbluth unlatched his satchel and rummaged inside. He removed a yellow legal tablet and flipped to a page that

George could see was covered with hasty scrawl. "I'm sorry she can't be of more help to Mr. Luciano."

The cabbie's eyes jumped in the rearview mirror.

"Why not let me be the judge of that? If you would, just tell me what she said."

Kornbluth reclined into the seatback, balancing the tablet on his satchel.

"First of all, she's never heard the name Cokey Flo Brown. But she did read the newspaper last evening, and was quite surprised to learn that her name had been mentioned in connection with the Luciano trial, which she found quite disturbing, as you might imagine. She assumes this Brown person is actually Mildred Nelson, the young lady she hired to act as her personal typist back in February. Miss Nelson had been recommended to Mrs. Calvit by her physician, Dr. Gardener, who happened to treat Miss Nelson for a gall bladder condition."

"Gall bladder condition?"

"That's what Dr. Gardener said. Miss Nelson seemed pleasant enough, and she confided in Mrs. Calvit up to a point, telling her that she was sweethearts with a man named Frederico, who was one of the defendants being held in the Dewey vice case. She said she loved him and wanted very badly to help him. Mrs. Calvit didn't pry, of course, but one day she was reading in the newspaper that Luciano had been arrested out west somewhere, and she commented on that fact to Miss Nelson. Well, Miss Nelson grabbed the newspaper right out of Dorothy's hands and said the photo in the paper didn't look like Luciano. Dorothy asked whether she'd ever met this Luciano before, and Miss Nelson said that she'd seen him, but that the photo didn't look like him."

"Seen him? Not that she'd actually met him?"

Kornbluth shrugged. "Seen him. That's what my notes say."

"All right, go on."

"Having completed the typing work for which she'd been hired, Miss Nelson began looking for her own apartment. On May the seventh, at approximately four thirty P.M., Miss Nelson returned to the Hotel Alamac and told Dorothy that she'd found a room at 140 West Seventy-Fifth Street, and that she'd be moving there shortly. Dorothy wrote down the address. Miss Nelson also mentioned that she'd been picking up extra money in dance studios."

"Dance studios?"

"Yes, exactly. Then two days later at around noon, Dorothy received a telegram from Miss Nelson stating that she'd been arrested for prostitution and was being held under the name Fay Marston on a three-hundred-dollar bond. She asked if Dorothy would communicate that fact to an attorney named Samuel Siegel, which Dorothy did. When the case came up for trial, Dorothy agreed to testify that she'd been Miss Nelson's previous employer, which she also did, but Miss Nelson was convicted anyway. And I'm afraid that's all there is to it."

"No more communications after the conviction?"

"Not until Thursday of this week, when Miss Nelson returned to the apartment with a pair of detectives to pick up some clothes. Dorothy said that Miss Nelson was railing against Frederico and his associates for letting her rot in jail for twelve days."

"And that's it?"

"I'm afraid so. Dorothy is not a well woman, Mr. Levy, and as the daughter of Lillian Russell, she's something of a public figure. I don't think it would be in her best interests to be caught up in this Luciano business. For one thing, it might affect the salability of the book she's working on. And frankly, given the state of her knowledge, I don't see how her testimony would be of any help to anyone."

The taxi had stopped at the courthouse mall. A handful of reporters and photographers approached the vehicle as George leaned to reach into his pocket.

"All right, Sam. I think I agree with your assessment, but give me some time to consider it. Out of curiosity, what's this book Mrs. Calvit is writing?"

"It's her mother's biography. But now that you mention it . . ."

"What is it? What's the matter?"

"Oh, it's nothing, I'm sure. I just remembered that Dorothy said she'd written a story once based on something Miss Nelson had told her. About her life, I presume. Dorothy submitted it to Macfadden Publications, but it was rejected as being too much like fiction. Miss Nelson apparently asked about the story when she came to the apartment on Thursday. Wanted to know if it was going to be published. Dorothy thought it was odd, but Miss Nelson seemed pleased to learn it had been rejected."

Forty-Seven

Missed Connections

May 1936

LEVY OPENED THE Saturday morning session with what struck Tom as a very unusual question.

Q: Miss Brown, did you ever go under the name of Florence Nelson?

A: No, I never did.

Q: Did you ever give your name as Florence Nelson to anyone?

A: No, I never did.

Q: What is the name of the lady that you claimed you worked for up at the Hotel Alamac?

A: Mrs. Calvit.

Q: Calvit?

A: Yes.

Q: And did you tell her that your name was Florence Nelson?

A: No, I didn't.

Tom looked at Sol Gelb, seated to his right. Gelb scribbled something on his pad. It was a question mark.

Q: And when you read about the arrest of Fredericks, did you tell anybody that you were very much in love with him, and that you would do anything in the world to help him?

A: If I did, I don't recall it.

Q: Did you tell the lady you were working for up at the Hotel Alamac, either in the month of February or March, anything to that effect?

A: No, I don't think so.

Gelb was scribbling again. This time his entry read, *They've talked to the Calvit woman*!

Q: You wrote Jimmy Fredericks over in the jail, did you not?

A: I did not.

Q: At no time?

A: No.

Q: Never wrote him a letter?

A: An inmate of one institution cannot write to another inmate.

Q: No, I don't mean that. Before you got into jail, did you write him a letter?

A: Yes.

Q: Write him more than one?

A: A number of letters.

Q: You use the typewriter, do you not?

A: Yes, I do.

Q: May I show you this letter and ask you if you wrote that to Jimmy Fredericks on or about April twenty-third of this year?

(Examines letter.)

A: I don't believe I wrote this letter.

Q: You don't believe you wrote that letter. Now look at it very carefully.

A: I don't believe I wrote it. I would not make that many mistakes on it.

Q: You would not make them? Well then, your statement to this Court and jury is, then, is it, that you did not write that letter?

A: I did write a typewritten letter.

Q: Did you write that particular letter you are now looking at, please, yes or no?

A: I will say yes, because it looks a good deal like it.

Q: Well, a moment ago you didn't think you wrote it, isn't that right?

A: I don't think it is the same letter I wrote.

Q: Well then, which is it? Do you think it is the letter you wrote, or do you think it is not? Please, look at it again if you wish.

(Again examines letter.)

A: I always signed the letters. There is no signature to this.

Q: Yes, that is right. And it is also addressed "Dear Cousin," is it not?

A: Yes, it is.

Q: And that is the customary way you wrote to Jimmy Fredericks, is it not?

A: Yes.

Q: You knew the mail was censored over at the prison, did you not?

A: Yes.

Q: And so therefore you were trying to create the impression that you were his cousin, were you not?

A: Well, I was not trying to create any impression.

Q: Well, you wrote that way, didn't you?

A: Yes.

Q: And you knew when you wrote that way and addressed him as "Dear Cousin," that some of the jail officials would examine the letter, did you not?

A: Yes.

Q: Now look at it again, please, and tell us, one way or another, did you write it or didn't you?

A: Well, I will say I wrote it.

Q: Just a moment. What do you mean, "I will say I wrote it," if you don't think you did?

A: Well, I couldn't say I wrote this letter for sure.

Q: Well, look. Read the contents of that letter, if you will, and see if they do not refresh your recollection that that is your type of language.

(Again examines letter.)

A: All right, I wrote it.

Cokey Flo was dithering, Tom thought, and losing her composure. It was futile to deny that she'd once loved Frederico and had written of her willingness to help him. Why would she even try?

Levy would argue that her willingness extended to perjuring herself to assist the special prosecutor. So be it. Tom would simply counter that her ardor for Fredericks had cooled as she'd cooled her heels in jail. That was a wash at worst, leaving her important testimony—the five in-person meetings with Luciano—intact. What vexed Tom was that they'd already covered the Dear Cousin letters in her preparation sessions. More than once, in fact. She was a silly girl for letting it rattle her.

Having made his point, Levy then moved in a new and unexpected direction.

Q: You knew at the time that you wrote that letter to Mr. Ten Eyck that no defense lawyer intended using you as a witness, did you not?

A: Yes, I did.

Q: There is no question about that in your mind?

A: No, there is not.

Q: And you had read of this sensational case, had you not?

A: I had read of it, yes.

Q: Did you have any desire to get any notoriety out of this case?

A: None at all.

Q: Did you have in your mind that you might get some notoriety which you might be able to commercialize in some way later on?

A: I don't see how I could commercialize that.

Q: Did you, yes or no, please?

A: No.

Levy, Tom thought, was grasping at straws. A bid for publicity? Could he really be serious? What kind of an idiot would want the notoriety that comes with admitting she's a drug addict and a madam, a prostitute and a fugitive? Why, it was laughable on its face. Tom, his eyebrows raised, turned away from the jury toward Ten Eyck.

Who looked like he'd just seen a ghost.

Forty-Eight

Judas

May 1936

AND JUST LIKE that, it was over.

First Levy sat down, then two of the other lawyers—Barra and Paley—asked a few questions each, and then Mr. Dewey stood up and said, "No questions," and the judge said, "You can step down from the stand."

At first I just sat there, still kind of dazed, waiting for the next lawyer, kind of the way that guys in a bar fight wait for the next broken bottle. Then I realized that no more were coming, and that the fight was finally over, and only then did the judge's words finally sink in.

I was a free woman!

Mrs. Carter was waiting for me in the witness room, and she patted my arm and said I was a hero. Some hero! My knees were practically knocking, that's how weak I felt, or how relieved, I couldn't tell which. All's I knew was that it was over, and that I'd survived, and that I wanted out of that building like I'd never wanted anything in my life.

We left by the back staircase again, and again I was driven directly to the Woolworth Building. It was almost noon when we arrived, and this time I was led not into Mr. Dewey's private office but to a larger room with desks and chairs that was used, I think, by the detectives. When I stepped into the room, a dozen heads turned to face me, and some of the people started clapping.

"Here she is, ladies and gentlemen!"

It was Frank Hogan, one of Dewey's men who the girls called Father Frank. He crossed the room to greet me, and then he led me by the arm to an empty swivel chair.

"Just sit back and relax, Flo, this won't take very long."

There were others in the room I recognized, like Dopey Al Weiner—Cockeyed Louis's kid—and Andy Coco. They were all listening to what I thought at first was a radio program, from a loudspeaker sitting on a desk, until I recognized Mr. Dewey's voice.

Pete Harris's wife, Millie, was there, and I changed seats to take the chair next to hers.

"What's going on?" I whispered.

"We're listening to the trial. This is some bath maid from the Waldorf."

"Bath maid at the Waldorf?"

"Where Lucky lived. She says Little Abie and Davie and Meyer Berkman used to come to Lucky's apartment all the time."

"So what?"

"So Levy, Lucky's lawyer, told the jury that Lucky didn't know any of those guys from Adam. So either the maid's lying or he is."

"Shhh!"

Hogan had turned with a finger to his lips, and so I sat back with Millie and just listened. It occurred to me that if Millie knew what Levy had said to the jury, probably in his opening statement, then she must've been listening to the whole trial from the beginning, like it was some kind of radio drama.

It was weird, sitting around like that, listening to what was happening in the very same courtroom where I'd just spent three days spilling my guts. And then I realized that all the people in that room had probably been listening to me the whole time I was on the stand, and I started replaying that testimony in my head: all the lousy things I'd had to say about shooting dope and jumping bail and getting pinched for streetwalking. Sounding like a dumbbell for not remembering the places I said I'd met Charlie Lucky. Sounding like a rat for putting the finger on Charlie and Tommy and Little Davie.

I'm no dumbbell, I wanted to tell them—I'm smarter than you'll ever know. If I'd mentioned exact locations, then people could've gone there and asked questions. And I'm no rat either, because I owed nothing to Charlie Lucky or Little Davie or Tommy the Bull, and I tried my level best to take care of the only man in New York who'd ever taken care of me.

Poor Jimmy, I thought, still sitting in the courtroom with that dazed look on his face, acting like I'd sold him up the river. But I hadn't, had I? I said he'd handled the bonding, and there was no denying that, but I'd made it perfectly clear that he'd never got rough with the madams and that he'd had nothing to do with the booking. I'd done him a favor, the big oaf, even if doing it had made me look like a liar.

Someday Jimmy would understand that, and maybe he'd even thank me. But even if he didn't, then what of it? I had myself to look out for, and my own future to think of, with no combination muscle or fancy lawyers to help me out when I needed it.

I was on my own now, and what was done was done. But I'd been on my own ever since I was fourteen, and you know what? I liked it that way. I always did and I always would, with no man underfoot telling me how to act or what to think. So screw Jimmy, I thought—I didn't need his approval or anyone else's. I was plenty smart, and

I was plenty tough, and I was the one who was gonna be famous when this thing was over. More famous than Mae West even, and who'd be laughing then? I would, that's who. Laughing all the way to the bank.

"Geez, honey," Millie whispered, pressing a handkerchief into my hand. "Don't start bawlin on us."

Forty-Nine

Golem

May 1936

ON FRIDAY, MAY 29, the prosecution finally rests. Dewey moves to dismiss twenty-six of the ninety counts in the indictment, stating that proof as to those matters would be redundant. He has called sixty-eight witnesses, forty of them prostitutes or madams, but only a handful who really matter to the question of Lucky's guilt or innocence.

Joe Bendix was a joke, of course, but Cokey Flo was no laughing matter. Then, perhaps smelling the blood in the water, Dewey followed Cokey Flo with seven employees from the Waldorf and Barbizon-Plaza Hotels who each identified, with varying degrees of certainty, the co-defendants they claimed to have seen visiting Charlie Lucky's apartment.

Next came Nancy Presser, the former girlfriend of defendant Ralph Liguori. A higher class of call girl before her withering descent into heroin addiction, Presser was the third of Dewey's bombshell eye-witnesses, but, as with Joe Bendix before her, the bomb went off in the special prosecutor's face. After testifying to over a dozen professional liaisons with Lucky at both the Barbizon-Plaza and the Waldorf Towers—visits at which she claimed to have overheard Lucky discussing the bonding combination—Presser was eviscerated by Levy on cross-examination when she proved unable to describe Lucky's Waldorf apartment—Was there a piano? Was there a fireplace?—or how to reach it from the hotel lobby, or even whether it had twin or double beds. So flustered was Presser that at one point, claiming sudden illness, she attempted to bolt from the witness chair.

The implosion of Nancy Presser revived Lucky's spirits after the staggering one-two punch of Cokey Flo and the hotel employees. But Lucky was soon back on the canvas with the appearance of Mildred Balitzer, the wife of booker Pete Harris, whom Dewey was saving to deliver his final knockout.

Big and buxom, with the hardboiled demeanor of the prostitute, madam, and drug addict she long had been, Balitzer testified to pleas she'd allegedly made to Lucky, both in Miami and New York, that Pete be allowed out of the combination. As with Cokey Flo's before her, Balitzer's testimony proved difficult to impeach, its impact depending entirely on her credibility with the jury. The only silver lining after her nine hours in the witness chair was Balitzer's admission to a night of revelry at Leon and Eddie's nightclub in the company of Sol Gelb, Dewey's right-hand man—testimony that finally gave flesh to Levy's frequent insinuations of undue witness influence.

Now Memorial Day weekend would mark a sea change in the trial—a shift from the prosecution's case to that of the defense. It would be a time to lick wounds, and take stock, and prepare for what lay ahead.

"Between Cokey Flo and them hotel people," Lucky tells his lawyers after court adjourns on Friday, "this jury's got me fitted for striped pajamas. It ain't a question of whether I testify anymore; it's only a question of when."

"Now hold on a minute," Polakoff tells him. "There's no cause for panic. We've still got Captain Dutton, and now we've got this mis-delivered letter from Bendix to his wife."

"You ain't listenin, Moe. Fuck Bendix. Nobody believed a word he said anyhow. You got a witness who can answer Cokey Flo?"

"Sam Siegel said he'd testify."

"Yeah, well good luck with that. He practically testified already, and them jurors believed every stinkin lie she told 'em. The same with that Balitzer bitch."

"We've got police officers coming from Pittsburg to say that Davey Miller lied when he denied running a disorderly house. Then Gus Franco will testify that he never introduced Mildred to Tommy or Davie like she claimed. Liguori will testify that Dewey's men threatened to indict him unless he fingered you, and that they gave your photo to Nancy Presser and Thelma Jordan to memorize. He'll also say that Dewey promised to send him and Nancy to Europe as a reward for their cooperation. Then Chappie will testify that Gay Orlova's your girl, and that he's never laid eyes on Presser or any of the others before in his life. Plus we've got a dozen witnesses lined up to testify as to your gambling history and habits. In short, we've got more than enough evidence to raise a reasonable doubt in the minds of these jurors."

"But nothin that puts the lie to Cokey Flo."

Polakoff turns to Levy, his look imploring. Levy removes a cigar from his pocket and studies it as he speaks.

"Look, Charlie, I understand how you feel, I really do. But it kills me to put a client on the witness stand, even in the best of circumstances. Here there's no telling what McCook will let Dewey get away with. If you think all the hearsay he's allowed into evidence has been damaging, wait until he lets Dewey examine you about your arrest record, and your income sources, and all your business associations."

"I already told you. I'm a gambler, and I can prove it."

"You also told me that except for Betillo, you'd never laid eyes on any of your co-defendants. And I told that to the jury."

Lucky shifts in his chair, a hand mopping his face. He, at least, can see where this thing is heading, even if Polakoff and Levy can't. Or else they can, but don't want to admit it. But it isn't their necks in the noose. They'll get paid whatever happens to Charlie Lucky, and they'll be out playing golf while he sweats in the prison laundry.

"So maybe I seen Tommy and Ralph around town now and again. So what? That don't mean we done any business together. But if I admitted that to Dewey, he'd make it out like we're peas in a pod."

"If you'd leveled with me, I could have fronted the issue and minimized its impact."

"You fuckin lawyers," he tells them. "You live in your ivory tower and you can't even see what's goin on right in front of your fuckin noses. 'May it please the court, my learned friend for the prosecution.' This ain't the church social, boys. This is a carny, and the game's been rigged from day one. Only a sucker plays fair in a rigged game, and Charlie Lucky is nobody's sucker."

"I'd say this is more like a turkey shoot," Levy counters, pointing his cigar for emphasis, "and you're the one wearing the feathers. We don't want to give them a clear shot at you unless it absolutely can't be helped. We've already given Cokey Flo a black eye, and Mildred Balitzer as well. And we'll argue that by the time the hotel employees were finished looking at Dewey's photographs, they'd have said Santa Claus was in your apartment. Like Moe said, now is no time to panic."

"Listen to him," Polakoff urges.

"Plus I've been talking with some of the reporters," Levy says, trying a change of tack. "We were odds-on for acquittal before Cokey Flo and the bath maid, and now we're back to even money. Given all we've been up against, those are still pretty good odds. Now is no time to put a joker in the deck."

Lucky stands and runs a hand through his hair as he paces a tight circle.

"Okay, here's what I think. First of all, I'm sorry for losin my temper just now. I got nothin but respect for the job you guys done, so let's get that off the table. Second, if you think I'm runnin scared, then you don't know me very well. I ain't afraid of Dewey, and I ain't afraid of what he'll do to me if I testify. So if you think I'm just gonna sit there and let that cocksucker put me in a frame and not do nothin about it, then you got another think comin."

Lucky stops pacing and faces Levy head-on.

"If there's one thing I learned from Arnold Rothstein, it's that scared money can't win. You and me, George, we both know all that innocent-until-proven-guilty stuff is a bunch of bullshit. Only the guilty don't testify, and everybody knows it."

"I knew Rothstein as well, Charlie. And the most important lesson he ever taught me was to quit while you're ahead."

"Only we ain't ahead. You just said so yourself. No, I been givin this thing a lot of thought, and unless you've got an ace up that sleeve of yours, I'm takin the stand and that's all there is to it."

"Then you'll be making a big mistake," Levy tells him. "Believe me, I've seen it before. You have very little to gain by testifying. The jury already knows you deny the allegations. I've told them once, and I'll tell them again. But you have everything to lose by opening the door to your past. In fact, that's exactly what Dewey's been hoping for. Right now, Charlie, I think you beat this thing. But once you get in that witness chair, then all bets are off."

"I'm sorry, George, but I can't let that cunt get away with it. And the old lady's out of the picture, right?"

"If you mean Dorothy Calvit, she's been threatened with arrest if she even talks to us. Sam Kornbluth, her lawyer, has already been arrested for attempted subornation of perjury."

"See what I mean about a rigged game? So look at it this way. If I don't testify, and I get convicted, I'll spend my whole stretch kickin myself in the head for not takin the stand. But if I testify and go down in flames, then what the hell, at least I'll know I gave it my best shot."

Lucky rests both hands on the chair back where he stands.

"I get one chance to look them jurors in the eye and tell 'em the honest truth. I done a lot of bad things in my life, but takin money from whores ain't one of 'em. I gave, sure, but I never took. And if Dewey calls me a crook and says I'm public enemy number one, then so be it. That ain't what I'm on trial for, right?"

"You're wrong about one thing," Levy tells him. "The presumption of innocence is not so lightly dismissed. It's the bedrock of our legal system, and the lynchpin of the closing argument I'd planned to make on your behalf. Right now there are four eyewitnesses against you, and two of them have been thoroughly discredited. Or will be, by the time we rest. Their lies have hurt Dewey's case and hurt his credibility. But if you take the stand and let him bring Al Capone and Dutch Schultz into this courtroom, the jury will forget all of that. Trust me, I've seen it before. They won't give a hang about Bendix or Presser or the charges in the indictment. All they'll want to do is slay the golem Dewey will have created."

"Slay the what?"

"The golem. Like Dr. Frankenstein's monster."

Lucky lays a hand on the older man's shoulder.

"Look, George. I'm sorry if I haven't always played straight with you. But even you've gotta see that Dewey's already made me out a fuckin monster. Now it's up to me to show them jurors I'm human."

Fifty

Faceoff

UNDER THE PERTINENT rules of evidence, proof of a defendant's bad character—for example, that he is dishonest, or violent, or has committed crimes in the past—is inadmissible to show that the defendant is more likely to have committed the crime with which he is presently charged. Only if the defendant himself places his character in issue by offering evidence of his good reputation—his honesty, for example, or his peaceful nature—may contrary evidence be offered by the prosecution.

When an accused chooses to testify in his own defense, however, the evidentiary landscape changes. In that case, evidence of prior crimes or misconduct, and especially crimes involving moral turpitude, is admissible to attack his character for truthfulness. But this rule of automatic admissibility is subject to a very important limitation. Where the prior crime is only collateral to the matter on trial—where, for example, it is offered for the sole purpose of impeaching the defendant's credibility—then the prosecutor is bound by the answers given by the witness, and may not waste time or confuse the issues at trial by offering extrinsic proof as to the prior crime or misconduct.

George, of course, explained these rules to his client. If Lucky took the witness stand, then Dewey could question him as to the facts and circumstances of every crime he'd ever committed. This, George told him, would inject a litany of otherwise irrelevant and highly prejudicial material into the case, all to Lucky's detriment. And George concluded his lecture with a final warning:

"The trial court has broad discretion in determining the admissibility of prior bad acts. That means if you do take the witness stand, you're all but putting yourself at the mercy of Judge McCook."

And the quality of McCook's mercy, George was certain, would be strained indeed, dropping more like a steel hammer than any gentle rain from heaven.

The defense presentation had begun well enough, with twenty-one of Lucky's scheduled twenty-five witnesses having already testified. These included the ephemeral Captain Dutton and assistant district attorney Morris Panger. They included Lorenzo "Chappie" Brescio, and Gus Franco, and the police contingent from Pittsburgh. And they soon would include NYPD patrol officer George Heidt, who would provide a damning eyewitness account of Sol Gelb's and Mildred Balitzer's night of drunken revelry at Leon and Eddie's nightclub.

George tried one last time to dissuade his client from taking the witness stand, only to find himself talking to stone. If anything, Luciano had been energized by the defense witnesses and was more eager than ever to testify.

"Don't worry about me," Lucky told his lawyers when the fateful day arrived. "I can handle that little prick."

Thus was the stage set for the moment that the jury, and the reporters, and most of the American public, had been so breathlessly waiting. The moment that George had so thoroughly dreaded. The moment when, in the trial's fourth week—on Tuesday afternoon, June 2, 1936—Lucky Luciano crossed to the witness chair and raised his hand to be sworn.

George's direct examination was short and to the point. Lucky denied the allegations of the indictment, and he denied any involvement in the business of prostitution. He was a professional gambler and bookmaker, Lucky testified, whose only prior convictions had been for selling narcotics in New York in 1916 and for maintaining a gambling establishment in Miami in 1930. Specifically, Lucky denied ever meeting any of the eyewitnesses—Joe Bendix, Cokey Flo Brown, Nancy Presser, or Mildred Balitzer—who had testified otherwise. With the exception of the hotel employees, he said, "There has not been a witness that got on this stand of Mr. Dewey's that I ever saw in my life." And with that firm denial finally on the record, George sat and braced himself for the coming onslaught.

He didn't have long to wait.

Q: How old were you when you were convicted of selling narcotics?

A: Eighteen, around eighteen.

Q: How long were you selling narcotics before you got caught?

A: Oh, around three weeks or a month.

Q: It was not the first transaction, however, was it?

A: What?

Q: You did not get caught on the very first ounce of morphine that you handled?

A: No.

Q: Was it the second, perchance?

A: No.

Q: Was it the third?

A: I told you, about three weeks after.

Q: I am asking you, how many transactions had you before you got caught?

A: That I can't remember.

Q: Had you as many as a hundred, or just two or three?

A: I didn't have no hundred, and I had more than three.

Dewey then shifted his focus to Lucky's driving record. Reading from a stack of official documents, the special prosecutor reviewed a dozen citations Lucky had received between 1922 and 1931, in each case quizzing the witness as to the story he'd told the arresting officer. While George had instructed his client that on such collateral matters, Dewey would have to accept Lucky's answers and could not impeach him with the written records, Lucky either forgot what he'd been told or else was determined to answer the questions truthfully.

Yes, he might have told patrolman Clay in August of 1922 that he was a chauffeur. Yes, he might have told patrolman Harris in August of 1924 that he was a salesman. While he could not recall telling patrolman Hunt in December of 1924 that he was a fruit vendor, he may have told patrolman Carter in June of 1925 that he was a salesman.

And so it went. All of these answers, of course, belied Lucky's claim to having been employed only as a gambler, a point that Dewey hammered home in a single question:

Q: You lied about things, didn't you?

A: Yes. I probably told them that I had an occupation and I didn't have it.

Dewey then segued from white lies told at a traffic stop to ever more serious falsehoods.

Q: On how many occasions did you perjure yourself when you were trying to get a pistol to carry around?

MR. LEVY: That is objected to, if it please the Court. The word "perjury" under the law is ambiguous.

THE COURT: It may be so.

MR. LEVY: It depends on a great many situations.

THE COURT: Better be more specific. I have heard of such things.

Q: On how many occasions did you lie under oath in order to get a gun to carry around the streets of New York?

A: Once, I think.

Q: Only once?

A: I think so, yes.

Q: Did you get the gun?

A: Yes.

Dewey, George saw, was sketching a picture of the younger Luciano as a bodyguard and gunman, rather than a gentleman gambler. And with his next series of questions, he added color to that portrait.

Q: On July 27, 1926, were you with a man named Joseph Scalise?

MR. LEVY: Again objected to as irrelevant, immaterial, incompetent.

THE COURT: Overruled.

MR. LEVY: Exception.

Q: Were you?

A: That is right.

Q: And did you have two guns and a shotgun and forty-five rounds of ammunition in the car between you?

MR. LEVY: Just a moment. That is objected to as irrelevant, immaterial, incompetent, and improper cross-examination.

THE COURT: Overruled.

MR. LEVY: Exception.

Q: Did you or didn't you?

A: I just come back from the country, and I had a hunting outfit in there.

Q: Yes?

A: Yes.

Q: You had two revolvers?

A: Yes.

Q: And a shotgun?

A: Yes.

Q: And forty-five rounds of ammunition?

A: And a couple of boxes of cartridges.

Q: Yes, and what were you shooting on that day?

A: What?

Q: What were you shooting on that day in the country?

A: On that day, I wasn't shooting nothing.

Q: What were you doing out in the country?

A: I wasn't up the country. I just come in.

Q: Come in from where?

A: From the country.

Q: What had you been doing in the country that day?

A: Shooting.

Q: Shooting what?

A: Birds.

Q: What kind of birds?

MR. LEVY: That is objected to.

A: Pheasants.

Lucky pronounced the word "peasants," and the courtroom erupted in laughter.

MR. LEVY: This is back ten years.

THE COURT: Overruled.

MR. LEVY: Irrelevant, immaterial, incompetent. Exception.

Q: Shooting pheasants?

A: Yes.

Q: In the middle of July?

A: That is right.

Q: Shooting pheasants in the middle of July?

A: Yes, that is right.

Q: Is that your answer?

A: That is right.

Dewey then moved to another occasion on which Lucky had been arrested but never prosecuted.

Q: Do you recall a little incident on June 6, 1923? Does that mean anything in your life?

A: I don't remember what you mean.

Q: No recollection at all?

A: No.

Q: All right. Do you remember first, on June 2, 1923, selling a two-ounce box of narcotics to John Lyons, an informer for the federal Secret Service?

MR. LEVY: Objected to as irrelevant, immaterial, and incompetent.

THE COURT: Overruled.

MR. LEVY: Exception.

A: Nineteen twenty-three?

Q: Yes, sir.

A: I was arrested—

MR. LEVY: Now I object.

Q: I did not ask you that. I asked you whether on June 2, 1923, you did not sell a two-ounce box of narcotics to John Lyons, an informer in the Secret Service.

A: I was arrested, but I never sold anything like that.

Q: I am asking you whether you did not on June 2—I ask you for a third time.

MR. LEVY: I submit it has been answered, if it pleases the Court.

THE COURT: He answered him something else. He may have included that, but I will allow it again so that we get a sole answer to that.

MR. LEVY: Exception.

Q: I want to know whether—

THE COURT: Yes or no is the answer.

Q: —whether on June 2, 1923, you did not sell a two-ounce box—

THE COURT: If you will take the negative out of it, it will be a little better, Mr. Dewey. Then we can get an answer yes or no.

Q: Isn't it a fact that on June 2, 1923, you sold a two-ounce box of narcotics known as diacetyl morphine hydrochloride to John Lyons, an informer for the Secret Service of the United States?

A: I don't know who they were, but I was arrested, and if I was charged with them, that I didn't do.

Q: I did not ask you anything except: Didn't you sell the dope to John Lyons on that date?

A: No.

Q: You deny it?

A: No.

Q: Flatly?

A: I don't deny that I was arrested.

Q: I did not ask you anything except whether you did not sell dope on that day.

A: I didn't sell it to him.

MR. LEVY: It has been answered, your Honor, that he did not.

THE COURT: We finally got an answer.

Q: Your answer is no?

A: No.

Q: Positive? Isn't it a fact that, three days later, on June 5, 1923, you again sold one ounce of heroin to informer John Lyons of the Secret Service of the United States?

A: No, sir.

Q: You did not sell him anything?

A: No, sir.

Q: Isn't it a fact that at 133 East Fourteenth Street in the city of New York, narcotics agent Coyle saw you sell narcotics to John Lyons?

MR. LEVY: That is objected to.

THE COURT: Sustained.

Q: Isn't it a fact that on that date your apartment was searched?

MR. LEVY: Objected to as irrelevant, immaterial, and incompetent.

THE COURT: Overruled.

MR. LEVY: Exception.

Q: Was it or was it not?

A: It might have been.

Q: Was it or was it not?

A: Yes.

Q: Why did you say "might have been?"

A: I wasn't there when they searched it.

Q: You are not quite sure about whether it was searched or not, is that it?

A: That is right.

Q: Isn't it a fact that in your apartment were found two one-half ounce packages of morphine, and two ounces of heroin, and some opium?

A: No, sir.

Q: Absolutely false?

A: Absolutely.

Q: Isn't it a fact that, thereafter, you gave to Joseph Van Bransky, narcotics agent in charge of New York City, a statement that at 163 Mulberry Street they would find a whole trunk of narcotics?

MR. LEVY: That is objected to as irrelevant, immaterial, and incompetent.

THE COURT: Overruled.

MR. LEVY: Exception.

Q: Didn't you give such a statement to Mr. Van Bransky?

A: Yes, I did.

Q: And isn't it a fact that, thereafter, a whole trunk of narcotics was found by the Secret Service at 163 Mulberry Street, New York City?

A: Yes, sir.

. . .

Q: And you still testify under oath before this Court and jury that you have not dealt in narcotics since the year 1919?

A: That is right.

Q: And that is your testimony now?

A: That is right.

Q: That is all on the subject. What were you—a stool pigeon?

A: I told him what I knew.

Q: Were you a stool pigeon?

A: I says, I told him what I knew.

Dewey had struck a nerve, and Lucky was squirming in the witness chair. Changing subjects, Dewey then produced telephone records from the Waldorf Towers switchboard. Why had Lucky made calls to Moe Ducore's drugstore, where Joe Bendix claimed to have visited him? Why had he made calls to Celano's Gardens, where combination meetings were allegedly held, and to Dave's Blue Room, where Nancy Presser said she had met him? Why had he called notorious mobsters like Louis "Lepke" Buchalter, Jacob "Gurrah" Shapiro, Ciro "the Artichoke King" Terranova, and Benjamin "Bugsy" Siegel? And apropos of the testimony of Cokey Flo Brown, why had he made several calls to the Standard Garage on the Lower East Side?

Dewey then returned to the subject of perjury, in the form of statements Lucky had made to the authorities following his 1929 kidnapping.

Q: Do you recall that you were found on Staten Island?

A: That is right.

Q: By a police officer?

A: That is right.

Q: You had been pretty badly beaten up and cut up?

A: That is right.

Q: Tape over your eyes and mouth?

A: That is right.

Q: And you told the police officers you did not want to give any information; that you would take care of that your own way?

MR. LEVY: That is objected to—

A: I did not.

MR. LEVY: —as irrelevant, immaterial, and incompetent.

THE COURT: Overruled.

MR. LEVY: Exception.

A: I gave them all the information I knew about it.

. . .

Q: Isn't it a fact that on or about October 18, 1929, you told Detective Gustav Schley of the New York police force to forget about it, and you would take care of it yourself?

A: I did not. I gave him all the details, how I got picked up, how they grabbed me, and everything.

Q: You were questioned before the grand jury, weren't you?

A: Yes.

Q: Under oath?

A: That is right.

Q: Do you still want to say the only times you lie under oath are when you are getting pistol permits?

A: Yes.

Dewey closed with Lucky's tax returns—a subject dear to the special prosecutor's heart—and specifically with the fact that Lucky had filed his federal returns for the years 1929 through 1934 as a group only eighteen days after Dewey's investigation had begun.

Q: Six years is the statute of limitations on indictments, isn't it?

A: Yes.

. . .

Q: Your rush of conscience is only with respect to the federal government, isn't it?

MR. LEVY: That is objected to.

THE COURT: Read that question again.

(Question read.)

THE COURT: Sustained.

Q: You have not paid a dime to the state government in income taxes yet, have you?

A: That is right.

MR. LEVY: Objected to as irrelevant, immaterial, and incompetent.

THE COURT: Overruled.

MR. LEVY: Exception.

. . .

Q: Your answer was, you have not paid a dime to the state government yet, right?

A: That is right.

Q: And that is because the federal government prosecutes big gangsters and the state does not, by income tax, isn't that so?

MR. LEVY: That is objected to.

THE COURT: Overruled.

MR. LEVY: Exception.

Q: Isn't that so?

A: I don't know.

Q: You do not know?

A: No.

Q: That is all.

And so it was. Over the course of four tension-filled hours, Dewey had managed, with an assist from Judge McCook, to depict George's client as a gunman, a dope peddler, a perjurer, and a tax cheat. What he'd failed to do, however, was connect Lucky in any way to the so-called bonding combination that was the subject of the prosecution.

Which, George knew from experience, didn't matter a whit.

Fifty-One

Verdict

June 1936

THE JURY CAME back on Sunday.

Tom, exhausted by his seven hours of closing argument, had retired to the judges' dining room on the fifth floor of the courthouse shortly after midnight, searching for an empty couch on which to collapse and close his eyes. To rehearse, perhaps, what he soon might say to the press. And what he hoped he'd not have to say.

That was his plan, at least. But what instead confronted him in the silent darkness were a month's worth of regrets and recriminations. Over witnesses lost, and gaffes committed, and opportunities badly squandered. If Luciano were to walk because a dolt like Joe Bendix or a conniving syphilitic like Nancy Presser had been caught in a lie, or because Tom had failed to deliver on the promised testimony of Good-Time Charlie Burke, or because Sol Gelb had foolishly bought a drink or two for a witness who needed them, then what was the

349

point of all the hours, all the effort and energy, that had gone into staging what amounted to the most complex and meticulous criminal prosecution in New York history?

The jury *had* to have seen the truth, he told himself. Seen how the other defendants and even their lawyers had fallen on their swords for the Boss. Seen how policemen from jurisdictions both within and beyond the subpoena power of the court had flocked to Foley Square on Luciano's behalf. Seen the terror in the faces of the witnesses who'd been brave enough to take the stand and meet his baleful stare.

The combination men were only using Luciano's name, Levy had argued in his closing, to achieve their nefarious ends. But if Luciano were simply a gentleman gambler, as he'd tried to portray himself on direct, then what were the Jimmy Fredericos and the Benny Spillers and the Pete Harrises of the underworld hoping to achieve by invoking his name? Why would a recalcitrant madam or a reluctant booker of women find fear or succor under the shadow of a mere gambler? Surely the jurors, each experienced as such, had to see the logic of that. See that Luciano was no mere gambler. See that he was and is precisely what Tom had labeled him: the greatest gangster in America.

And what of Marjorie Brown from the Waldorf-Astoria, the young girl who'd stood in the hotel hallway five afternoons per week, waiting to clean Charlie Ross's room? Little Molly, they called her, who'd stepped bravely from the witness chair to touch the shoulders of Wahrman, Betillo, Berkman, and Frederico. And why would a two-bit thug like Frederico have visited Lucky's apartment twenty or more times, as Molly had attested, if not to discuss the bonding combination that was Frederico's only possible connection to the Boss?

And then there was Cokey Flo. Sick, frail, and yet brave beyond measure, she had answered every disgusting question, endured every leering insinuation the defense had hurled in her face. But never once, despite nine hours of the most grueling cross-examination Tom had ever witnessed, had she given an inch of ground in her depiction of Luciano as the heartless mastermind of the combination, ordering that houses be wrecked and madams beaten. If there had been no other testimony in the case—no Mildred Balitzer or Molly the bath maid—surely that of Florence Brown alone should have been enough to win conviction on all counts.

But wait. Levy had cajoled Cokey Flo into admitting that she'd voluntarily bonded, and had been only too happy to do so. Tom had thought nothing of that testimony when given, but now he realized its import. If the jurors considered Cokey Flo to be an accomplice or co-conspirator, then her testimony would require independent corroboration. If so, and if the jury disbelieved Bendix and Presser, then they would need both to believe Mildred Balitzer's testimony and to categorize her as a victim . . .

Confounded by these ruminations, vacillating between glorious victory and crushing defeat, Tom finally dozed. Dozed while the defendants played pinochle in the witness room downstairs. While bleary-eyed reporters, chatting and smoking, clustered in the courthouse stairwell. While the wives of the defendants sought fitful sleep on folded newspapers in the hallway outside the courtroom. While over a thousand anxious spectators—mostly neighborhood Italians—stood candlelight vigil in nearby Mulberry Park.

All of them waiting for the jury's verdict.

A poll of the reporters, taken just after closing arguments, had Luciano acquitted by a vote of thirteen to one. Inside the witness room, the atmosphere was similarly optimistic, even ebullient. The defendants joked and wagered and roared with laughter when Ralph Liguori gave Jimmy Fredericks, stamping and cursing, a hotfoot. Reflecting the upbeat mood of their clients, the defense attorneys had gathered at an all-night restaurant across the square, where, like soldiers after a battle, they recounted each sortie and skirmish of their righteous campaign with hyperbolic bravado.

Only George Morton Levy, still brooding over his client's testimony, was absent from the celebration. Once McCook had completed his charge to the jury at approximately nine thirty on Saturday evening, Levy had slipped quietly through the hallway crowds and down the staircase and out into the square, where, ignoring the flashbulbs and the shouted questions that had followed him onto the courthouse steps, he'd lit a cigar and melted into the crowd.

Meanwhile, inside the jury room, a ballot was taken. And then a second.

Philip McCook switched off his desk lamp and removed his glasses and pinched the fatigue from his eyes. He pushed up from his chair and crossed to the little bathroom, where a new shaving kit, purchased for the occasion, had been laid out on the shelf above his sink. He ran the tap and, while waiting for the water to warm, removed his tie and collar.

Outside the bathroom, where the thin light of dawn was just filtering through the curtained windows of his chambers, a buzzer sounded three short bursts.

Tom woke with a start, as though heeding some silent alarm. It was Sunday, he realized, the seventh of June. It was five o'clock in the morning. He sat upright on the couch and ran a hand through his hair before swinging his feet to the floor. He stood and straightened his clothes and started for the hallway door, where he was met by a breathless court attendant.

"Mr. Dewey," the young man said, "the jury's returning!"

Judge McCook was already on the bench when Tom arrived in the courtroom, and the jurors, looking tense and exhausted, were waiting in the box. Tom sought their eyes as he walked down the aisle and passed through the gate and took his usual chair, but none found his in return. That fact, combined with the relative speed of the verdict, weighed heavily in his stomach.

There followed agonizing minutes of delay and confusion as first the defendants and then their various lawyers returned to the courtroom. The scene was an incoherent jostling of bodies and briefcases, knees and elbows, made doubly strange by the total absence of conversation—as though all present had been summoned to some solemn and hastily called requiem.

Finally, as the last of the newspaper reporters took his seat beyond the railing, the hallway doors were locked and a sepulchral silence settled over the courtroom.

Mr. McNamara, the head clerk, stood and cleared his throat.

"Edwin Aderer," he began, reading the roll of jurors.

"Present."

"Theodore A. Isert . . . "

The wait was interminable. Tom glanced over at Levy, who was studying the jurors with focused intensity, and took small comfort from the fact that the veteran trial attorney appeared to be just as anxious as he was.

The roll completed, the clerk set down his roster. He then intoned, "The foreman will please rise."

Mr. Aderer, Juror No. 1, stood.

"Gentlemen of the jury, have you agreed upon a verdict?"

"We have," the foreman said, unfolding a paper from his pocket.

"How say you, gentlemen of the jury? Do you find the defendant Luciano guilty or not guilty on count one?"

Tom held his breath as the foreman, his face without expression, half turned to Luciano, who was gripping the edge of the table.

"Guilty," he said.

The word sang like a bullet, its twin syllables the entrance and exit wounds that felled Luciano where he sat.

A communal gasp had sucked the air from the courtroom. Tom lowered his head. A hand was slapping his back. To his right, somewhere at the defense table, he heard a pencil snap.

The rest of the verdict took forty-five minutes to read. Forty-five minutes of liturgical call and response punctuated by murmurs from within the courtroom and muffled screams from without.

By the time the entire verdict was read, the word "guilty" had been pronounced 558 times.

Fifty-Two

Aftershocks

June 1936

I KNEW THIS girl from California once, her name was Jean, and she told me all about earthquakes. About how they happen all of a sudden, with no warning or anything, and how they can knock your plates off the shelf and your food right out of the icebox. And just when you think they're over and you've cleaned up the mess, how another one comes along and does it all over again.

The verdict in the Dewey vice trial was kind of like that. We got the news during Sunday breakfast at the House of Detention. It was a great win for the prosecution, the warden announced, with all the defendants found guilty on all counts. That shook the ground, believe you me, and for a lot of the girls at our table it called into question the basic laws of nature.

The ones who'd cooperated were relieved, as you might expect, and the ones who hadn't probably felt like saps. I wouldn't know.

I was too busy making plans for what I was gonna do once the dust finally settled.

Then around two weeks after the verdict came the first aftershock. Twenty-five years for Tommy the Bull. Twenty-five to forty for Little Davie. Thirty to fifty for Charlie Lucky! Even the bookers who'd cooperated got knocked off their pins. Pete Harris and Dopey Al Weiner each got two to four years, and Davey Miller three to six.

But the worst aftershock came when I heard about Jimmy's sentence. Because this was his third felony conviction, Judge McCook had thrown the book at poor Jimmy and given him twenty-five years in prison. Twenty-five years! For a low-level schnook who'd been earning all of thirty-five dollars a week!

I have to admit, I cried when I heard that bit of news. But I didn't cry for very long.

He could've turned state's evidence, I told myself, and cooperated like I did. Or he could at least have taken the stand and testified in his own defense. But no, not Jimmy. Instead he just sat there like a puppy dog and let Siegel run the show for him, never understanding that his lawyer was more concerned about saving Charlie Lucky's skin than he was about saving Jimmy's.

I'd tried to warn Jimmy about Siegel, but would he ever listen to me? No, of course not. And now look where it had landed him.

After the verdict, but before the sentences had been handed down, Judge McCook had ordered all the girls who'd testified back to the courthouse and then, one by one, into his office. There, right in front of Dewey or one of his assistants, he'd made them all swear on the record that their trial testimony had been true and voluntarily given.

In my case, he and Barry Ten Eyck and a court stenographer made a special trip to the House of Detention. That was on Monday, the day after the verdict. The judge, when I saw him, seemed almost sheepish, like he was asking me for a favor. He wanted to know if I'd told the truth on the witness stand, and whether I'd been coerced in any way, and even whether I'd been "plied with liquor," as he put it.

No sir, Judge! Now can I get my stuff and go home?

But where was home, exactly? Technically speaking I was still awaiting sentencing on the solicitation charge, not to mention trial on the other charges from back in January. What was worse, I realized then, was that all I had to show for my cooperation with Dewey was a handshake agreement with Barry Ten Eyck that nobody else had witnessed. So now it was my turn to put my trust—my faith, my future—in the hands of somebody else's lawyer.

Say what you will about Dewey, but as far as I'm concerned, he was a man of his word. First Mrs. Carter took me to court in general sessions, where she told the judge how I'd cooperated with the big vice investigation and where I was given a suspended sentence on my solicitation conviction. Then Barry Ten Eyck himself came with me to special sessions and had a word with the judges in private, after which I pled guilty to the earlier charges and received another suspended sentence.

That could've been you, Jimmy. Hell, that could've been both of us, together.

When I was down at the Woolworth Building that last time before going to court in special sessions, Barry explained to Mr. Dewey that I'd lost my job on account of Mrs. Calvit being sore at me for dragging her name into the trial. Then Barry told Mr. Dewey that he wanted to include me in that magazine and film deal that he and Dewey were negotiating for Mildred Balitzer. Well, that was the first I'd heard anything about Millie being part of the deal, but it was okay with me on account of I liked Millie and figured there'd be more than enough green to go around. Besides, Millie had had it pretty rough—she'd had a miscarriage while in custody—and what with Pete heading for at least two years in the slammer, she'd need some help getting back on her feet.

So one day this man named Doherty, Edward Doherty from *Liberty* magazine, came and met with me and Millie at the House of Detention. We talked for over an hour about the kinds of stories we could write—about running a house, and shooting dope, and living with wise guys like Jimmy and Pete. I have to admit, we laid it on pretty thick. Then, just before I got sprung, Millie and me went with Barry to the Macfadden Publications offices in the Chanin Building and met with the head honcho there, a man named Fulton Oursaler, who said that while the movie deal hadn't come through just yet, we shouldn't worry about it because he knew the business and thought that once the articles got published starting in December, we'd have the studios begging us for the exclusive rights to our stories.

The actual deal Barry cut with Macfadden was that Millie and me would each get fifty bucks a week for ten weeks, as an advance against a total payout of $1,250 each. And while that wasn't quite as much money as Barry had promised, it was still okay with me on account of Millie getting her share and the movie deal being just around the corner. Plus it meant that Mrs. Calvit would see my name in the magazine every week for two or three months running while she, a so-called professional writer, couldn't sell her pathetic stories or her stupid book proposal for love or money.

I only wished I could be there to see the look on her face when she opened her precious *Liberty* magazine and saw my name in black and white. But I planned to be in Hollywood by then, lounging at poolside and sipping daiquiris under a palm tree. Hoping there wasn't an earthquake that might shake a coconut loose!

Things were happening so fast by then my head was practically spinning. It was only that first weekend after I'd been sprung from jail that I finally had a moment's peace and quiet to put my feet up and think about all that had happened. About how I'd gone from being carried to solitary sick and crying, abandoned by Jimmy and suffering from the five-day cure, to sitting in a plush leather chair in the editor's office at *Liberty* magazine. And all of it happening in the space of just five crazy weeks!

Only in America. If you used your noggin and played your cards right, it really was the land of opportunity.

Or so I thought at the time.

Fifty-Three

True Colors

"Your honor, I have nothing to say outside of that—I want to say it again—that I am innocent."

Simple and straightforward, these are the last words Lucky will ever speak to Judge McCook, although they're not the exact words he personally would have chosen. What he wanted to say—what he *would* say if Levy and Polakoff would only let him—is more along the lines of "Judge, you're crookeder than I'll ever be, you sorry fucking hypocrite. First you let the whores and the madams go free—which makes you the patron saint of New York prostitution—and then you railroad me into jail for what's probably the only crime on the books I ain't never committed. And the worst of it is, you know goddamn well that I'm innocent, and that your boy Dewey would never have laid a glove on me if you'd refereed a fair fight. So fuck you, Judge, and fuck the mayor and the governor too. And if I was all of you, I'd start watching my backs from now on."

This is what Lucky aches to say, but with sentencing imminent and post-trial motions yet to be made, there is no profit to be had in antagonizing the old man. Or at least that's what Levy and Polakoff have told him. So Lucky says what he does—defiant, yet measured—then waits for the hammer to fall.

While Lucky is livid at McCook, and even more so at Dewey, he recognizes that the weight of the sentence, whatever it is, will rest squarely on his own shoulders. Levy and Polakoff had warned him—had all but begged him—not to testify, but rather to let the lies and the slanders wash over him like so much rain on a stone. To place instead his trust in Levy's high-minded notions of reasonable doubt and presumed innocence. But Lucky was never one for trusting the law, let alone its fictions and constructs, and he'd vowed to himself that if he did testify and rolled snake-eyes, he'd at least leave the game with his head held high.

And that's what he plans to do.

McCook, for his part, has shed his veneer of judicial politesse and offers instead a scathing pronouncement before imposing sentence.

"The crimes of which you stand convicted are of placing females in houses of prostitution, receiving money for such placing, and knowingly accepting money from their earnings without considera-tion. An intelligent, courageous, and discriminating jury has found you guilty of heading a conspiracy or combination to commit these crimes, which operated widely in New York and extended into neighboring counties. This makes you responsible, in law and morals, for every foul and cruel deed, with accompanying elements of extor-tion, performed by the band of co-defendants whose records and characters will shortly be discussed, or some of them. I am not here to reproach you but, since there appears to be no excuse for your conduct or hope for your rehabilitation, to extend adequate punishment."

And then the hammer falls.

Afterward, on the steps of the courthouse, the special prosecutor joins the judge in abandoning pretenses.

"This, of course, was not a vice trial," Dewey tells the throng of waiting reporters. "It was a racket prosecution. The control of all organized prostitution in New York by the convicted defendants was one of their lesser rackets. The prostitution racket was merely the vehicle by which these men were convicted. It is my understanding that certain of the top-ranking defendants in this case, together with other criminals under Lucania, have gradually absorbed control of the narcotics, policy, loan-shark, and Italian lottery syndicates, the receipt of stolen goods, and certain industrial rackets . . . "

When Lucky reads Dewey's remarks in the evening papers, he is livid all over again. This is precisely the point that Levy had tried to make, first to the jury and then to the judge when objecting to Dewey's closing argument: That Lucky has been prosecuted not for the crimes charged in the indictment, but for his suspected associations and his criminal reputation.

With Lucky's stay request having already been denied, he is soon to be moved: first to Sing Sing for processing and then farther up the river to Dannemora. But first he holds a series of private meetings with selected visitors to the Raymond Street Jail.

With his brother Bartolo, Lucky plans for the future of his family. With Moe Polakoff, he makes arrangements both for Gay Orlova and for the new legal team that will soon be handling his appeal. Finally, with his old friend Meyer Lansky, he weighs the fate of his newly uncertain empire.

"It was a rotten business from the get-go," the little man says, settling into his chair in the visitor's room, where he and Lucky face each other through a screen of wire mesh.

Lucky shrugs. "Not much you can do when the fix is in. Or maybe it's just that Dewey's Jews were better than my Jews."

Meyer smiles at this. "That's what you get for listening to Frank. You wanted the best Jews, you should have come to me."

"And you wanna know the funny thing? Four fuckin weeks I sat there lookin at them broads, maybe fifty of 'em, one whore after another, and not one of 'em you'd screw without a bag over her head. Two bags, in case the first one fell off. I mean, gettin convicted is one thing, but my rep with the ladies may never recover from this."

"I must say, Charlie, you're in better spirits than I expected under the circumstances."

Lucky checks to be sure that no guards are within earshot before leaning forward in his chair.

"That's because we got new evidence that all of Dewey's witnesses were lyin through their teeth."

"What evidence?"

"It ain't important. The point is, I'm hopin this jail thing is only temporary. Meanwhile I got motions and appeals and appeals from my motions, so it looks like I'll be inside for a few months at least, no matter what happens. Plus they're sendin me to Siberia, so communication won't be easy. What I need to know is that somebody's got my back down here and is takin care of my end. And by that I mean someone I trust."

"Relax, Charlie. I've already talked it over with Frank and Joey and Vito. They send their regards, and they want you to know that everything will be business as usual. It'll be just like you were still at the Waldorf. If you want, I'll personally move everything that's yours to Zurich, so it'll be waiting for you when you get out, which we all hope will be very soon. Meanwhile, I'll handle your day-to-day banking like I already do for Benny."

"Like you already do for Batista."

Meyer shrugs. "Like I would for all my good friends. You'll have to sign a few papers, that's all. I'll send them up with Moe. Now what about your family?"

"That's already taken care of. If Bart needs money, you see that he gets it. Moe too. I'm figurin on a hundred grand for the appeal. Jesus Christ, Meyer, you shoulda been a lawyer. I was just thinkin this morning, I could've put every whore in Manhattan on my payroll, had all of 'em waitin for me when I got home at night, maybe eight or ten girls to a shift, and still come out ahead. Instead what I got was this."

Lucky gestures to his surroundings. To the industrial gray walls and the cold iron bars.

"We've got people at Dannemora, Charlie. They'll take good care of you. However long it is, it'll be easy time. Only I can't promise any showgirls."

"Jesus Christ, Meyer. And here I thought you was connected."

Lucky is smiling again when he stands and places a hand on the screen. Meyer mirrors the gesture, so that their palms are pressed together.

"We had a helluva run."

"That we did."

"With your brains and my balls, we nearly took every trick."

"If only for that damn wild card."

"Hey, what was that guy's name again, the one with the wings made of wax?"

"You mean Icarus?"

"Yeah, that guy. You watch yourself, Meyer. Especially down in Cuba, you keep your wings out of the sun."

"I will, Charlie."

"And one last thing. Tell Bennie if he wants to bake me one of them cakes of his, to be sure to put a hacksaw inside."

"We'll do better than that. We'll have a cake waiting for you at the Waldorf, with Gay Orlova inside."

"Good thing we both know a guy in the sugar business."

"That we do, Charlie. Only don't keep her waiting too long, you hear me? Even sugar won't sit on the shelf forever."

Fifty-Four

Wild Card

July 1936

ON TUESDAY, THE ninth day of June, just two days after the Luciano verdict, the intercom buzzed in George Morton Levy's Mineola office. It was lunchtime, and George hesitated before lifting the receiver, fearing yet another reporter or, worse, another publicity-seeking crank.

"Who is it this time?"

"He won't give his name, Mr. Levy, but he says he has important information about the Luciano trial."

"Take a message, Miss Dooley. I don't think I can take another—"

"I think you'd better take this one, Mr. Levy. He seems on the up-and-up."

George looked at the clock. He was due at his club in twenty minutes.

"All right, put him through."

George could hear voices in the background, and the musical clatter of dishes and glassware. A restaurant, he thought, or a maybe a tavern.

"Mr. Levy?"

"This is George Levy."

"My name is Marr, Mr. Levy. I've got a letter for you, a very important letter from one of the witnesses in that Luciano trial."

"What witness?"

"I don't know, some broad. All's I'm doin is a favor for somebody else, that's all. You want the letter or not?"

"Yes, I want the letter. Where are you now? Can you deliver it here?"

"I'm in the city. At the Villanova, on West Forty-Sixth. Can you come here?"

"No, I'm afraid that isn't possible."

There was silence on the line as a hand covered the mouthpiece.

"Okay, look. I'll come as far as Jamaica. We can meet at the station."

George again eyed the clock.

"I have a lunch engagement I can't get out of, but I can send someone from my office. And forget the station. There's a lawyer named Vollmer, Henry Vollmer, who has an office at one sixty-one Jamaica Avenue. Why don't you wait there, or better yet, why don't you just leave the letter there and—"

"No can do. I'm supposed deliver it personally."

"Deliver it for whom, exactly?"

"Never mind that. Who should I be lookin for?"

"A young man by the name of Weil, Harold Weil. He works for me, and you can trust him to bring the letter straight here."

"Henry Vollmer. One sixty-one Jamaica Avenue. Harold Weil. How about we say one o'clock?"

"That will be fine. And listen, where can I reach you in case something goes wrong? Is there an address or a telephone—"

"Look, I don't want nothin to do with this, okay? Like I said, I'm just doin a favor for a friend."

George went ahead to his meeting, and when he returned to his office at two thirty, an envelope bearing his name was waiting on his desk. He opened the envelope carefully. Inside were two handwritten notes, one folded inside the other. The outer message was written on a sheet torn from a legal pad, and while it was not signed, George recognized Harry Weil's neat, slanting hand.

Mr. Levy:

A Mr. Mar gave me this note at Vollmer's. He said it was given by Helen Kelly to the wife of the owner of Monroe's Tavern on 76th St. in N.Y.C. Helen Kelly was escorted by a cop and somehow managed to slip this note to the woman. Mar received it yesterday. The girl will try to phone you today between 5 and 6, but he does not know if she has your office number, and she will have to slip away from the cop to phone. He will try to call you today around six o'clock, and will see you tomorrow if he does not call.

The second note appeared to have been hastily scrawled. It covered the entire front and back of a plain white envelope.

My name is Helen Kelly. I am a Dewey witness. I have some important information which I believe could help to clear C. Lucky. The evidence against him from N. Presser + T. Jordan + M. Harris was perjured. I can swear to that. I should be glad to testify for him at the appeal if it could be held over until the case against Gypsy Tom Petrovich is over and I am released. I shall call Geo. Morton Levy's office Tuesday evening about 5 or 6 P.M. Please believe I am sincere in trying to help Charlie Luciana. I can't stand seeing a man go to jail on perjured evidence without a fair trial.

For Charlie's sake please don't tell Dewey about this. I'd do time if he found out I got in touch with you people.

Sincerely,

Helen Kelly

Please don't notify Dewey. It would mean big trouble for me.

George was standing by his desk as he read the letter. He looked at the clock. And then he sat down.

He remembered Kelly, but only vaguely, and so had to consult his notes from the trial. She was a prostitute who'd been called by the prosecution early on, right before Joe Bendix. Harry Cole had examined her, and Cantor and Murray had crossed. George hadn't paid her much mind and had made no notes of any substance during her testimony.

George dug the city phone book from the bottom drawer of his desk. He dialed the number for the Villanova restaurant. It was the same restaurant, he recalled, at which both Bendix and Mildred Harris claimed to have met Charlie Lucky.

It took a while, but George finally spoke with the owner, a Mr. Joe Carroll. Yes, he was the one who'd asked Marr to deliver the letter. No, it was all on the level. The Kelly girl, Carroll explained, had written the letter there, in the ladies' room at the Villanova, and had wanted to pass it to Carroll but hadn't the chance and instead had slipped it to the bartender at Monroe's Tavern. She knew plenty, she'd told Carroll, and wanted to talk to George. Carroll didn't know all the details, but he thought it involved Dewey's men taking the girls out and getting them drunk.

After he hung up with Carroll, George phoned Moe Polakoff and alerted him to the letter's existence. Then he sat watching the telephone, which, to his growing consternation, never rang again.

At seven o'clock, George put the letter in his office safe and went home for the night.

There were several phone calls over the next two weeks: cryptic and furtive messages that, in each case, had caught George out of the office. Then the sentences were handed down, and the calls stopped altogether. Polakoff, who seemed conversant with the inner workings of Dewey's office, said that the Kelly girl was still being held as a material witness in respect of this Petrovich character, a notorious pimp. He said he would monitor her status and advise George when and if she was ever released from custody.

Another week passed. Then on a Friday afternoon, the third day of July, George was stuffing his briefcase for the Independence Day weekend when the intercom buzzed. The woman's voice when it came over the wire sounded young yet surprisingly poised.

"Mr. Levy? My name is Helen Kelly. I'm terribly sorry it's taken this long for us to finally talk."

Fifty-Five

Risk Management

July 1936

IT HAD BEEN McCook's idea to bring the girls back to the court-house in order to refer them out to various social service agencies. But it was Tom who'd suggested that the judge put them under oath again and make all of them reaffirm their trial testimony. Winning a verdict was one thing, Tom knew, but keeping it was another story. And when it came to protecting this particular verdict, the judge and the special prosecutor needed to be singing from exactly the same hymnal.

Given the nature of the prosecution, Tom recognized that the case had certain vulnerabilities on appeal. Did the joinder law, for example, really apply retroactively? Were the defendants entitled to know who had testified before the grand jury? Did failure to charge a conspiracy vitiate the wholesale introduction of hearsay evidence?

But the biggest vulnerabilities by far were the witnesses them-selves, for the simple reasons that few were educated, most had been drug addicts, and all would soon need money on which to live outside of jail. For many, despite their heartfelt vows of sobriety and chastity, that would mean a quick return to drugs and prostitution. And if a girl was willing to sell her body for a couple of greasy dollars or a shot of heroin, then how cheaply might she be willing to sell her word?

Tom knew that the moment the girls were released from the House of Detention, Luciano's minions would descend on them like gnats on an open wound. Beyond the protective custody of the court, and with the sword of prosecution gone from over their heads, the girls were liable to say or do just about anything. Which meant that, whether the inducement took the form of money, drugs, or simple threats, many were likely to recant.

Such was the gossamer of which the prosecution had been woven.

Compounding this dilemma was the inconvenient fact that none of the girls had cooperated when first arrested. Since it had been the practice of the special prosecutor's office to make a stenographic record of every witness interview, that meant most of the girls had already given at least one sworn statement denying any knowledge of the bonding combination or, ipso facto, the involvement of Charlie Lucky.

Thus the fact of a girl's recanted testimony, combined with her initial denials, gave at least a numerical advantage to the appellants in urging reversal of the verdict. This was the edge that Tom, with McCook's cooperation, was hoping to neutralize.

"Think of it as a firewall," Tom had told the judge. "A way to contain flare-ups before they burn down the entire house."

"What about the defense?"

"We just want statements, Judge. We don't want to retry the case."

It was no coincidence, therefore, that the first witness to be interviewed, in her case at the House of Detention, was Cokey Flo Brown. It was important to question her, Tom had urged McCook, before Frederico was sentenced, and while her own charges were still pending. And so, with Barent Ten Eyck at his side and a court steno-grapher seated between them, McCook settled into the warden's chair and again faced the slender young woman who had all but single-handedly slammed the prison door on Lucky Luciano.

Q: May I congratulate you on looking better than you did in court?

A: Thank you.

Q: And I congratulate you also on the way that you seemed to be able to stand the strain of the court. I heard you testify. Did you tell the truth?

A: I did.

Q: If you had to go on the stand again—which I don't think you will, certainly not before me—you would tell the same story, except perhaps add something more that you might remember or something less that you might forget, you would tell the same?

A: I would.

Q: Were you ever intimidated or threatened or frightened or anything of that kind?

A: No.

Q: By either District Attorneys or anyone here?

A: Never.

. . .

Q: Did they say what they would do for you if you did tell the truth? Did they say anything of that sort to you?

A: No; they said that they would help me as much as legally possible.

Q: In the troubles that you were already in?

A: Already in.

Q: Were you properly treated by them at the Woolworth Building and here?

A: I was.

Q: And you have no complaints to make; nothing you think that could help other people who get into trouble here, or jacking them up and make them do different?

A: Not at all.

Q: All right as far as you know?

A: All right.

Q: And you have no criticism of the District Attorney's office either?

A: None at all.

Q: Did you see anybody plied with liquor, or were you plied with liquor yourself or anything of that kind?

A: No.

Q: All that happened to you was that when you were sick once or twice, they gave you liquor by my directions?

A: Yes, that is right.

Q: That is all you know about it?

A: That is right.

Q: Did anyone ever make improper advances to you anywhere, either there or here?

A: No, sir. Absolutely not.

Q: I realize that your situation is quite different from that of the others here, a good many of them, most of them, and all I can say is that I believe the District Attorney will continue to help you by keeping his promises to you in every way that he can, and if anything goes wrong or you think that it is not being done right for you, send for me, will you?

A: I will, thank you.

And so the process began, and before it was over, all seventy-seven of the women still in custody as material witnesses faced the same obsequious jurist conducting the same gently solicitous interrogation—all without the knowledge, consent, or participation of counsel for the defense.

The girls for the most part affirmed the truth of their trial testimony while denying any coercion or undue influence by the office of the special prosecutor. All, that is, until a breathless Stanley Fuld, the chief legal scholar on Tom's staff of all-star assistants, returned to the Woolworth Building on Saturday morning, June 20, and made a beeline for his boss's office.

He entered without waiting for an answer to his knock.

"Stanley? What's going on?"

"It's the Kelly girl, Helen Horvath. I just came from McCook's chambers."

Tom closed his file and set it aside. Helen Horvath, or Helen Kelly as she was known in the trade, had been a minor witness for the prosecution who was fast becoming a major pain in the neck. She'd lived with several of the key witnesses before the trial, including both Mildred Harris and Nancy Presser, and she'd told Paul Lockwood after the verdict that both Mildred and Nancy had perjured themselves, and thus that Luciano had been convicted on what she'd called "a pack of lies." Alarmed by her allegations, Lockwood and Jake Rosenblum had immediately put her under oath and taken yet another detailed statement.

"You look as though you ran the whole way here, Stanley. Please, sit down. Here, have a glass of water. I thought Harry was the one handling those things."

"He was, but he had a conflict this morning, so I agreed to pinch-hit."

Fuld dragged a chair directly opposite Tom's desk while Tom, his pulse quickening, struggled to hide his irritation at Harry Cole for delegating what was probably the most sensitive of all the post-verdict interviews to poor, bookish Stanley.

"Okay," Tom said. "Tell me exactly what happened."

"I met with McCook beforehand to explain the situation, and I showed him the witness statement she'd given to Jake and Paul. He read it through, then asked if that was still the girl's position. I said it was. He said not to worry, and that he'd try to finesse it as best he could. He also said that Petrovich, the girl's boyfriend, was coming up for sentencing, and that he'd remind her of that fact."

"And? For God's sake, man, what did she say?"

Fuld unfolded a document from an inside jacket pocket and slid it across the desk. Tom recognized it as a "daily"—a rough transcript of the morning's interview prepared by the court stenographer but not yet proofed or certified. Tom tore through the pages, looking for the relevant passage, and he found it starting on page five.

Q: These various things that you say that you discussed with the women that were with you around in different places and hotels—I suppose you don't know why they said to you the different things they said to you?

A: No.

Q: You have no way of knowing whether they said various things to you by the instructions of the office or some other way?

A: No, your Honor.

Q: And therefore, you have no way of knowing whether these women knew any of the people who were on trial before me; that is, you have no way of knowing of your own knowledge.

A: No.

Q: How did they go about questioning you, in respect to your knowledge of various individuals, at the District Attorney's office? Some of these girls testified that pictures were shown them. Were pictures shown you?

A: Yes.

Q: And what was said to you when you were shown pictures?

A: Mr. Lockwood asked me to look through a bunch of pictures and see if I could identify anyone.

Q: Did he give you any names, or indicate to you whom he wanted you to select?

A: No, I selected—

Q: Did Mr. Rosenblum either?

A: No.

Q: Did anybody?

A: No, nobody.

Q: All they did was to show you about how many pictures?

A: Oh, I don't know; I must have looked through several hundred on different occasions.

Q: And out of those, you selected some of the people that you knew?

A: Yes.

Q: And you testified about those or some of them before me, I suppose, and my jury?

A: Yes.

Q: Who were some of the people that you picked out as looking like people that you had seen, do you remember? Did you find out afterwards who some of those people were?

A: Yes.

Q: And who were some of the people that you afterwards found out the names of that you picked out at trial as people that you had seen?

A: Jo Jo Weintraub, Jack Eller, Jesse Jacobs. I thought I knew Davie Betillo, but I wasn't sure, and I picked out Charlie Luciano's picture, but I didn't know his name at the time. I thought I had—

Q: What did you tell him about the person whose name you afterwards found out was Lucky? Where did you say you had seen him, and in whose company?

A: I met him in Gypsy Tom's company two years ago, before I became a prostitute.

Q: Did you hear Gypsy Tom and him talk?

A: No, there wasn't any conversation between them.

Q: Did you hear any name used?

A: I just heard him referred to as Lucky.

Q: By Tom?

A: By Tom, but, your Honor, I am not sure it was that man.

Q: I did not ask you whether you were sure; that is, I did not ask you whether you were sure.

A: Yes.

Q: Did anybody at that office ask you whether you were sure?

A: Yes; they asked me if I was sure, and I said I couldn't be sure; he just merely looked like a man that I had seen two years before.

Q: Yes, exactly. And that the name called was Lucky?

A: Yes.

Q: You saw a man in the court—you saw plenty of men in the court?

A: I did.

Q: Did you recognize one of them as the same man that you heard called Lucky?

A: The man that I saw was heavier; he had the same sort of an eye, a drooping eye, but he seemed to be a little bit heavier-set.

Q: Is there any more difference in weight than would naturally result from a month or two in jail?

A: Well, I don't know.

Q: You realize, I suppose, that Gypsy Tom has pleaded guilty before me?

A: Yes.

Q: And I am going to sentence him later on . . .

Tom leaned back and relaxed. The old man, he thought, could still cross-examine. He slid the transcript across his desk.

"Well, Stanley, now that the judge has covered these matters in such detail, I suppose we can destroy that last witness statement, wouldn't you agree?"

Fifty-Six

California

December 1936

WE SPENT THE rest of that summer up in New Rochelle, Millie and me, living in a hotel and writing down stories and meeting with Mr. Doherty, who lived nearby in Larchmont. According to Barry Ten Eyck, Judge McCook had warned the defendants that if any harm came to any of the witnesses, he'd personally make sure that each defendant served every last day of his sentence. So while we weren't afraid of getting bumped off or anything like that, we were still being pretty careful, keeping our eyes open and our ears to the ground.

We went into the city once a week to pick up our paychecks, which were mailed to Barry's office at the Woolworth Building, and to get a read on the situation. We'd been warned by both Barry and Mr. Dewey that Lucky's people might come looking for us, pestering us to change our testimony, and so we used phony names and colored our hair and generally snuck around like thieves in the night, avoiding the old hangouts and always checking to make sure we weren't being followed.

It was actually kind of fun in a way, or maybe it was just silly, us acting like spies or lamsters when all we were really doing was going to the drugstore or visiting the hairdresser.

Come fall, once the writing was finished, Millie and me moved back to the city full-time and took a room together at the Park Crescent Hotel. I was Gloria Moore, and she was Norma Gordon. We tried to visit Barry a few times, but it seemed like he was always too busy to see us, and that maybe he was giving us the brush-off. Pete was up in Sing Sing, but they were holding him in solitary for what they said was his own protection and they wouldn't even let Millie visit. We were still avoiding the people and places we'd known before, and we were trying to watch our money, so when we weren't out to the movies, we'd spend most nights in the hotel just reading magazines or playing cards or listening to the radio.

Pretty soon we were bored stiff, and I knew that if we kept on going like we were, we'd wind up in trouble again. Since there wasn't any more dough coming in from Macfadden, and since I had my bail money back and still had a little nest egg stashed away from before I'd been pinched, me and Millie decided to buy ourselves a car, a used Chrysler, and head out to California to wait for the *Liberty* articles to appear. That way, we figured, when opportunity knocked, we'd be right there to answer the door.

Neither of us had ever driven that far before, so we made a vacation of it. We took the southern route, stopping for three days in Hot Springs, which is where Charlie Lucky had been arrested, and from there we sent a letter to Barry Ten Eyck letting him know that we'd blown town.

Millie was good company. We talked about buying ourselves a little business when we got to California, like maybe a millenary or a lingerie shop, but then as we put the miles behind us, we got an even better idea. There was money to be made, we decided, in the tourist court business, and it seemed like something we could afford. And when I say "we," I really mean me, because Millie had only her *Liberty* money and her witness fees, most of which she'd already blown by the time we left New York.

We arrived in Los Angeles the week of Thanksgiving, and by that time we'd watched carefully and asked questions and learned how to pump our own gas and check our own oil and tires. So we looked in the L.A. newspapers and found a small filling station for lease with an attached motor court called White's Auto Camp in Pomona, which is around thirty miles east of Los Angeles proper.

They had orange and lemon groves in the Pomona Valley, and palm trees, and daytime temperatures that were still in the upper eighties at a time when New Yorkers were already wearing their furs. You could wear short pants and sandals practically year-round, and you could walk down the street and pick an orange right off of somebody's tree and eat it on your way to the post office. I must've eaten a crate of oranges that first week we were there, and except for the dry desert air taking all the curl out of my hair, I hadn't felt or looked better in years.

We told Mr. White, the owner of White's Auto Camp, that we were Gloria Moore and Norma Gordon, magazine writers who'd been working for Macfadden Publications but had left New York in search of warmer weather and a steadier paycheck. We listed Barent Ten Eyck, Esq., as our lawyer and financial manager, which was practically true, and then we sent Barry a telegram letting him in on the gag.

I ended up putting five hundred down for the station, plus another hundred for stock and sixty bucks to improve the lighting. We renamed it the Rooster, on account of a hot dog stand next door that was called the White Hen and was shaped like a giant chicken. I'm not kidding, they had some crazy buildings in California.

Once word got around that a couple of girls were running a filling station, well, people started coming by just to see for themselves.

Millie would top off the gas while I'd look under the hood and check the oil and water and clean the windshield. We had business cards printed up, and we flirted shamelessly with the cops and the truck drivers, making sure everyone got a card and sometimes a peck on the cheek before they left. As far as the locals went, we told 'em we were new in town and just getting started, and that we'd sure appreciate it if they'd keep buying their gas from us. And it worked too, because pretty soon we were selling more gas than both of the other stations in town put together.

I wrote a few letters to Barry, always as Gloria Moore, updating him on our progress and pestering him for news about the movie deal. Warner Bros. had passed, he finally wrote us, but there was still hope that one of the other studios might be interested. But then the first article appeared in *Liberty* in early December under the title "Underworld Nights," and I for one thought it was a real stinker, and so did Millie. No wonder the studios weren't interested!

Around mid-December we got hit with a double dose of bad news, in the form of two letters from Barry that arrived on the same day. The first said that the movie deal was probably kaput because none of the other studios seemed to be interested, although there was one that might be willing to buy the title "Underworld Nights," for all the good that did us. The second letter said that Addie, my former housemaid, had just contacted Dewey's office claiming she wanted my address so she could send me a fur coat that I'd left at Dorothy Calvit's.

What made the movie news so lousy wasn't just that we weren't going to be rich and famous—that was bad enough—but that Millie, who by then was flat as a flitter, couldn't pay back any of the money I'd been fronting for the business. I mean, it was one thing to help her get back on her feet and all, but that didn't mean I had to carry her for the rest of my life, did it? And to make matters worse, Mil was a real city gal who'd never liked getting her hands dirty in the first place, and now she was all the time bellyaching about this crummy job, and this two-bit town, and how her clothes were always smelling of gasoline.

But all of that was peanuts compared to the other news, because there was no way that Mrs. Calvit would have tracked Addie down on her own, and certainly not to return a fur to the likes of me. No, someone had put Addie up to it—someone who wanted to know where Millie and me were hiding out—and I wrote Barry right away to tell him so.

By around Christmastime the situation with Millie had finally come to a head. We were barely talking by then, even when she bothered to show up for work, which wasn't very often, and the business was suffering. Then I got another letter from Barry, this one telling me that Millie had sent him a telegram, and couldn't we work something out to keep the business running and keep Millie happy in California? Well, that tore it as far as I was concerned, her whining to Barry behind my back, and so I really let her have it, telling her she either had to straighten up or else hit the bricks.

It was the very next morning that a truck driver walked over from the White Hen to talk to Millie, telling her that he'd overheard some guy at a Texaco station down the road asking the attendant if he knew anything about two women from back east who'd come out here to go straight and were running a filling station. I'd seen Millie and the trucker talking, so I asked her what was up, and she told me what he'd said. She was all matter-of-fact about it, but I said maybe we ought to buy ourselves a gun. She said that was crazy, and that I needed to calm down because it was probably nothing, and I was left with a nagging feeling that Millie knew more about the situation than she was letting on.

So I slept on that, tossing and turning, and the very next day I sat Millie down again over breakfast. I told her this was no time for secrets, and that whatever had happened between the two of us was water under the bridge, and that what we needed now more than anything was to stick together, because we were in a jam, and how! And that's when it all came out—the tears, the confessions, the truth.

It turned out that even before we'd left New York, Millie had been in touch with a private dick named Dunn who'd been hired by Moses Polakoff, one of Charlie Lucky's lawyers. Dunn was out visiting from Los Angeles, but he'd told Millie he was working with another shamus from New York named McCarthy. Millie said she'd admitted to this Dunn that all of her trial testimony about Charlie Lucky had been a lie to help Pete, but she'd also told Dunn that she wasn't ready to do anything about it just yet, and then she'd skipped town with me and had never gotten back to him.

But that was only the beginning. Millie then confessed that when the movie deal fell through and things had started to go sour between the two of us, she'd wired Jo Jo Weintraub in New York to ask for Dunn's address in Los Angeles, and in the process might have told Jo Jo where it was we were hiding out.

Let me tell you, it was a good thing I hadn't bought that gun, because if I had, I'd have shot Millie right between the eyes! And when I asked her how she could possibly be so stupid, she started bawling again and finally admitted what I'd come to suspect; namely that she'd scored some junk off a trucker a couple of weeks back, and that she was using again. She said she had no money now and no husband and nowhere else to go, and that she'd figured she could maybe sell her story to Dunn or, if not that, then at least get a train ticket back to New York, where she knew people and wouldn't feel like such a stranger in a strange land.

"I know what I done was wrong," she said between sobs, "and that I should've told you before. But I'm lonely and homesick, Flo, and I was afraid you'd think I was a no-good rat and toss me out in the street."

"So you think the guy who's been poking around is this Dunn character?"

She nodded. "He's on the level, Flo, I swear he is. He used to be a G-man. He just wants our statements, that's all."

"*Our* statements? You think I'm gonna stab Barry in the back after all he's done for us?"

"Oh, yeah?" she said, smearing her face with a wrist. "What's Barry done for us that was so great? He got us a few lousy bucks for a whole summer of work, and then when it came time for the big payoff, all's we got was the air. Face it, Flo—they played us for suckers. Look at poor Pete. He cooperated, and what did he get? And all so Dewey could be a big man and get his picture in the newspapers. Some deal that was! And never mind what happened to Charlie Lucky."

I went to the bathroom and brought her some tissue paper.

"It's always the same old story," she said when I came back. "The high-hats get the cake, and we get the crumbs. We're holed up in Podunk, while they're strolling down Park Avenue. They're gonna make Dewey the next governor, and we can't get ourselves arrested. As far as I'm concerned, your pal Barry can kiss my ass, and that goes double for his boss."

She blew her nose and put the tissues aside and took hold of my hands.

"Tell me I'm wrong, Flo. Go ahead. Tell me we wouldn't be better off cooperating with Dunn and going back to New York. There's nobody gunning for us there. In fact, it's just the opposite. Think about it. They need us more than ever. Lucky's lawyers, I mean. We're their only hope. If Hollywood won't pay for our stories, then why shouldn't we sell them to Dunn and McCarthy?"

She got up and went to a drawer in the kitchen and came back with a great big lump of Mexican brown.

"New York, Flo. New Years in Times Square. Champagne at the Stork Club. A couple of months and we'll be back on our feet again, with gowns and furs and clean fingernails."

"And what are we supposed to do for money?"

"What we've always done! With the girls all free and the combination guys in jail, it'll be just like old times. We can run a house and hire our own girls and never have to worry about bookers or bonding or any of that bullshit. The town is wide open, honey!"

I picked up the lump and studied it. I held it under my nose.

"What have we got to look forward to here?" Millie said as she stood again and crossed to the kitchen and came back with an old cigar box. "Selling more fan belts? Maybe someday buying the White Hen? Whoopee! You may call that living, honey, but I'd rather wake up tomorrow in a pine box. At least that way I wouldn't stink like gasoline."

Fifty-Seven

Siberia

December 1936

INMATE 24806 OF the Clinton Correctional Facility spends most of his days in the prison library, where he finds respite from the sweltering heat or the teeth-chattering cold that seasonally afflicts Dannemora, New York, only ten short miles from the Canadian border. It is there that he sits and quietly reads—his lips moving, a stubby finger tracing the words—cloistered from the stink and noise, the squalor and brutishness that are the lot of the ordinary prisoner.

He is no ordinary prisoner. He does not, for example, wait in line at the mess hall, or at the barber shop, and when he enters the communal shower, the other inmates quietly depart. When he approaches a group of men playing at cards or checkers, they all stand to greet him. He is on a first-name basis with the warden, and when the guards—those burly French-Canadians with their steel-tipped canes and perpetual scowls—see him coming, they step aside and solemnly nod.

His privilege, however, comes at a price. He makes no trouble, and sees to it that no trouble occurs. At exercise time he is besieged by inmates seeking his advice, his opinions, his personal benediction. He serves as a counselor, and a conciliator, and as the final arbiter of all disputes within both the Italian and Jewish populations. And as an inmate's discharge date approaches, he even acts as a kind of referral agent, sending written recommendations 320 miles south to Manhattan, where the word of Charlie Lucky still carries the weight of a papal edict.

He receives visitors. Meyer Lansky and Frank Costello, or Vito Genovese and Joe Adonis. Men whose mere presence within the prison walls sends whispers down the hallways, through the units, and into the cell blocks. Usually it is Moses Polakoff who accompanies these visitors, according them the privacy of attorney-client conferences at which Polakoff sits in the corner while Lucky conducts the clandestine commerce of the Broadway Mob or the Unione Siciliana.

But all this is background, just as the hum of the laundry or the din of the mess hall is background to the daily life of the prison. For what concerns Lucky most—what commands his attention from sunup until sundown—is getting out of Dannemora and returning to the bright lights of the city after five long months behind bars.

And on that score, at least, things are looking up.

The first break comes when one of the prostitutes still in police custody, a girl named Helen Kelly, kites a note to George Morton Levy. Kelly then meets with Levy in person, providing an affidavit that not only blows the lid off the inner workings of the special prosecutor's office but also obliterates the trial testimony of Nancy Presser and Mildred Balitzer.

And this, Polakoff reports, is only the beginning. In mid-November, Joe McCarthy, a private detective hired by Polakoff, lured Nancy Presser and Thelma Jordan—both recently returned from Dewey's European junket—to the Hotel Belvedere, where he'd planted a Dictaphone and recorded Jordan's admissions that she'd never even heard of Charlie Lucky before her arrest, that Lucky had nothing whatsoever to do with the bonding combination, and that she'd lied on the witness stand when testifying to the contrary.

The dominos, Polakoff tells Lucky, are starting to fall.

The next to topple is Nancy Presser, who, again thanks to McCarthy, agrees in early December to provide Frank Adams and Martin Conboy—the heads of Lucky's new appellate team—with an affidavit recanting her trial testimony.

"That's two down," Polakoff says, snapping his briefcase closed, "and two left to go."

Then, in what looks to be the biggest break so far, McCarthy receives a visit from Jo Jo Weintraub—the erstwhile errand boy for booker Pete Harris—who reports that Harris's wife Mildred has wired him from California and is apparently ready to talk. That, Polakoff tells Lucky, means that Cokey Flo herself might be in play, and if Cokey Flo recants, then there's nothing left of Dewey's case but hot air and yesterday's headlines. And very possibly—once the Kelly affidavit hits the courtroom—a state ethics investigation into prosecutorial misconduct.

"But we need to proceed with caution," Polakoff warns his client. "Remember what the judge said. If either Mildred or Cokey Flo spooks, and if word gets back to McCook, you could be stuck up here until doomsday."

"Caution? Fuck caution! I just turned thirty-nine in this shithole! Whether I do thirty years or fifty years, I still walk out of here an old man, and that's if I walk out at all. No, you tell Adams and his boys I want those affidavits, no matter what it takes to get 'em."

"All right, but don't forget—"

"And here's another thing! You tell Jo Jo there's a payday for him if he delivers. Then tell him you got a private message, straight from me. Tell him Charlie Lucky says he should go after them two broads as though his life depended on it."

Fifty-Eight

Helen's Story

March 1937

HER REAL NAME, it turned out, wasn't Kelly at all, but Helen
Horvath. She was a comely girl in a big-boned sort of way, and she
wore the same floral dress that George remembered from the trial. If
she was at all nervous, she certainly didn't show it, but rather entered
George's office with an air of self-possession that seemed preternat-
ural for a girl of nineteen, accepting George's proffered hand with a
grip that was firm and warm.

She'd arrived in the company of Luciano's brother Bartolo and a
man from Monroe's Tavern, both of whom, at George's insistence,
were made to wait outside in reception. George introduced her first
to the stenographer he'd hired for the occasion, and then to Edward
Thompson, a local attorney and notary whom George had asked to
act as a witness.

"Can I offer you anything, Miss . . . "

"Horvath, please."

"Horvath. Coffee, for instance?"

"No thank you, Mr. Levy. If it's all the same with you, I'd just as soon get this over with. I'm afraid it's a rather long story."

The story began in Kentucky, where Helen was born the youngest of four children to a couple named Nemeth. Her mother died when she was two, Helen said, at which point her father moved the family to New York and boarded her with a family here, then promptly stopped paying the board and disappeared from her life altogether. Helen entered foster care and was eventually placed with John and Anna Horvath, who raised her from ages three through fifteen—by which time she'd completed two years of high school—and then took her with them to Europe in 1932.

Her foster parents settled in Hungary, in Vesperin, but she became pregnant there and returned to the United States, alone, in October of 1933. She'd found work as a hostess in New York at a restaurant on St. Mark's Place, when she was raped by a co-worker and pressed charges against her assailant. She was held in the Florence Crittenden Home for two months as a material witness until, after the trial—a conviction—she entered the Guild of the Infant Savior, a home for pregnant girls. Her daughter Margaret was born in April of 1934, at City Hospital on Welfare Island, and was placed with the Godmothers' League in July of that year, when Helen was just seventeen years old.

With her baby in foster care, Helen was able to work a succession of menial jobs that included stints as a pantry maid and a waitress. Then, in October of 1934, she met Gypsy Tom Petrovich, a handsome Yugoslavian, who soon put her to work as a prostitute. She became ill after several weeks on the job, which engendered a severe beating from Gypsy Tom, and she found herself back on the streets again, homeless and destitute.

She soon met a man named Jack Kelly and became his live-in girlfriend. She returned to restaurant hostessing and taxi dancing, at which she earned up to twelve dollars per week in salary and tips.

Then Kelly became ill, forcing Helen to return to prostitution, again through the dubious offices of Gypsy Tom.

In November of 1935, while working at the house of a madam called Hungarian Helen, she was arrested for prostitution and advised by bondsman Jesse Jacobs to jump her bail, as there was no defense to the charge. This she did, becoming a fugitive from justice. She then contacted Pete Harris, who began booking her into various houses around the city, including those of Cokey Flo and Jenny the Factory, where she earned two dollars per assignation. This lasted for approximately nine weeks, until she again switched bookers. Under Jack Eller she began earning three dollars per customer at houses run by Gussie Silver, Morris Stein, and Jimmy Nusso.

She wasn't picked up in the great raid of February 1, 1936, but, upon learning that Mr. Dewey was offering immunity for cooperating witnesses, voluntarily appeared at the special prosecutor's office, where she was interviewed by Dewey assistants Paul Lockwood and Jake Rosenblum. She gave a sworn statement that day, and another a few days later, following which she was formally arrested as a material witness and brought to Judge McCook's home on 57th Street, where her bail was set at twenty-five thousand dollars.

She spent two weeks at the House of Detention, in a cell opposite that of Mildred Harris, before complaining to Lockwood about her treatment. She was soon released from jail and moved to the Hotel Albert, at 10th Street and University Place, on February 21, 1936. She lived there with another witness named Irene Smith for approximately one week, whereupon both were moved to the Concourse Plaza in the Bronx, where they remained for another week before moving again, this time to the Hotel Margaret in Brooklyn. Irene Smith was then released from custody altogether, and Helen was moved to the home of a policewoman named Margaret O'Dell on Staten Island for a few days while the special prosecutor's office awaited an infusion of fresh funding from the Department of Finance.

Helen said she was under the direct supervision of one policewoman or another throughout this entire period.

together in Jackson Heights that Mildred told Helen it had taken her six weeks before she'd finally agreed to cooperate, that she didn't know Charlie Lucky "any more than I knew Thomas E. Dewey," and that she was cooperating solely to help her husband, Pete. Since Peggy Wild actually *did* know Lucky, who'd been an occasional customer, Mildred would pepper Peggy with questions—How old is Lucky? How tall? How much does he weigh? Does he limp? Does he have a gold tooth?—to which Peggy tartly replied, "I never opened his mouth to look at his teeth!" Peggy Wild—one of New York's more notorious madams—also confirmed to Helen that, as far as she knew, Lucky had nothing whatsoever to do with the prostitution racket.

Helen and Mildred lived together at three different locations over the course of the last three months leading up to the trial. Mildred repeatedly told Helen that she'd never met Charlie Lucky in her life. Like Nancy Presser before her, Mildred would visit the Woolworth Building on an almost daily basis and return to the apartment drunk. On one occasion, Helen accompanied Mildred and NYPD officer William Grant to Joe Conway's Tavern at 95th Street and Amsterdam Avenue, where they'd stayed until seven A.M. with Mildred getting so drunk that she refused to climb the stairs at the apartment, making them all wait until the elevator operator reported for work.

As the trial date approached, Mildred told Helen, "I have them where I want them—I do what they say, and they're going to do something for me," and "I won't be given money directly, but I'll be given ways to get it." When pressed, Mildred explained that she was going to write the story of her life and that Dewey's people were going to help her sell the movie rights. Mildred also told Helen that Nancy Presser and Thelma Jordan were being given a cruise in exchange for their cooperation.

Helen's own trial preparation consisted of mock direct and cross-examinations conducted by Harry Cole, who would coach her on how to respond, telling her, "When I ask how you came to be a voluntary witness, come out proudly and say you wanted to salvage the remains of your self-respect. Lay it on good and thick." It was Cole, in fact, who suggested—she presumed at Mildred's urging—that Helen should testify that Pete Harris told her, "You're too nice a girl to be in this line of business."

Helen was shown photos and asked if she recognized Charlie Lucky. She remarked that the photo of Lucky resembled a man she'd once seen while in the company of Gypsy Tom. Cole and Gelb both pressed her to say that the man in the photo was Charlie Lucky, and that he was mixed up somehow with Gypsy Tom. She refused, stating only that she thought she'd once seen the man in the photo, but that she didn't know his name, and knew of no connection between the man in the photo and Gypsy Tom.

On the day of her testimony—Wednesday, May 20—Helen finally saw Charlie Lucky in the flesh and knew immediately that the man in the courtroom was not the man she'd seen that night she was with Gypsy Tom. She said as much to Gelb, who nonetheless spent an hour with her in the witness room trying to convince her to testify otherwise before finally giving up.

A few days later, after both she and Nancy Presser had testified, Helen saw Nancy again at the Woolworth Building while the trial was still in progress. Nancy was sitting in the investigator's office as part of a crowd that included Pete and Mildred Harris, Cokey Flo Brown, Danny Brooks, Al Weiner, and several others whom Helen did not recognize. All of them—a group that included both witnesses who had testified and those who had not—were listening to the trial on a direct wire that had been run from the courtroom to the office of the special prosecutor.

Nancy Presser was reviewing the transcript of her trial testimony when Barent Ten Eyck entered the room and asked, "How do you like your testimony?" to which Nancy replied, "Gee, I did pretty well, didn't I?" Helen later asked Nancy when she and Thelma were leaving on their cruise, to which Nancy replied, "As soon as they release me."

The day after the verdict, Helen found herself back in the Woolworth Building, where the atmosphere was celebratory. Paul Lockwood asked her, "What do you think of our success?" to which Helen replied, "I'm afraid you won't like my answer." She told Lockwood that the verdict was the result of perjured testimony, reciting what she'd been told by Nancy Presser, Mildred Harris, and Peggy Wild. "Luciano," Helen concluded, "was convicted on a pack of lies."

Lockwood huddled with Rosenblum, and together they hustled Helen into an office where, before a stenographer, they took yet another lengthy statement in which Helen repeated exactly the story that she'd just finished telling to Lockwood.

Shortly after the sentencing, Helen was taken back to the courthouse in Foley Square to get, she thought, her release papers signed. Instead she was told to wait in the courtroom while Stanley Fuld, one of Dewey's assistants, met privately with Judge McCook. After around five minutes, Helen was ushered into McCook's chambers. A stenographer was present, and McCook was reading the transcript of the latest statement Helen had given to Lockwood and Rosenblum. The judge then questioned Helen angrily about the statement, trying to establish that she had no firsthand knowledge as to whether the testimony of Nancy Presser and Mildred Harris had been truthful. Helen had to concede that she did not, and was relying solely on what she had been repeatedly told by Nancy, Mildred, and Peggy.

Helen concluded her statement in George's office by describing her efforts to make contact while still in police custody, and the note that she'd slipped to the bartender at Monroe's Tavern, and her motive in now coming forward, which was to help correct what she believed to be, in her words, an "unjust conviction."

From the stenographic transcript of Helen's statement, George prepared a detailed, twenty-three-page affidavit. Helen returned to George's office the next day—Wednesday, July 8, 1936—and signed the affidavit after making only a few minor corrections on both the original and the carbon. George made sure that Helen initialed every page of both documents before thanking her for her candor and watching through the open doorway as she left his office in the same way that she'd come, with her head held high.

His interview with Helen Horvath was, for all intents and purposes, George's last involvement in the defense of Lucky Luciano. He would deliver the Horvath affidavit to Polakoff, and then it would fall to others to pursue Charlie Lucky's post-trial remedies. These, George knew, would include a motion for a new trial and, failing that, a series of appeals.

George continued to follow the case, of course, and soon learned through the grapevine that Nancy Presser, Mildred Balitzer, and Cokey Flo Brown had all recanted their trial testimony in sworn affidavits, effectively corroborating the allegations of young Helen Horvath.

George wasn't so much elated or even surprised by these events as he was profoundly saddened. If the Horvath girl's story was to be credited—and George was convinced that it should—then Thomas E. Dewey, aided by an overzealous cadre of white-shoe assistants and Justice Philip J. McCook himself, had perpetrated what amounted to one of the greatest miscarriages in the history of American justice.

And now, George was relieved to know, the truth would finally come out.

Fifty-Nine

Going to Towns

March 1937

CHARLES LUCIANO'S MOTION for a new trial based on newly discovered evidence—which included the affidavits of Helen Horvath and Nancy Presser, as well as affidavits and post-trial interview transcripts from Mildred Balitzer and Cokey Flo Brown—had landed like a bomb on the fourteenth floor of the Woolworth Building, and like a bomb it had left its intended targets both stunned and covered with dirt.

Three days later—on Sunday, March 14—the still-smoldering ordinance sat before Tom Dewey as he surveyed his inner circle of assistants from the head of a long conference table. The group, which included Sol Gelb, Barry Ten Eyck, Bill Herlands, Paul Lockwood, Jake Rosenblum, Harry Cole, and Frank Hogan, had assembled at Tom's summons on what would otherwise have been a rare morning off from their ongoing restaurant rackets case, then in its ninth week of trial before Judge McCook.

The mood in the room was gloomy, with a possibility of thunder.

"This motion," Tom began with a tremor in his voice, "represents nothing less than an assault on the integrity, reputation, and career of every man in this room. It accuses this office not only of suborning perjured testimony but also of outright bribery, and, by logical extension, of conspiracy to obstruct justice. It goes without saying, therefore, that every resource at the disposal of this office must be mobilized to oppose and defeat this disgusting and libelous work of fiction!"

Tom stood and pressed his fists into the tabletop.

"I want affidavits from every man in this room! I want an affidavit from every police officer whose name appears in that Horvath declaration! I want affidavits from every officer who ever guarded, transported, or spoke with any of these women! I want affidavits from every social worker who interacted with them, and from every employee who worked where they lived while still in custody. I want the certified transcript of every contrary statement these women ever gave, and an affidavit from the stenographer who took it. And for God's sake, don't forget those one-on-one sessions they each had with McCook after the verdict was rendered. Bill!"

Herlands jumped in his chair.

"We need to delay the hearing on this motion for as long as possible. Use the pending trial as an excuse. We need time to assemble an opposition so thorough and so convincing that it leaves no room for even the slightest doubt as to the integrity of this verdict, not to mention the integrity of this office. Remember, gentlemen, our audience isn't just McCook, but also the press and the Court of Appeals. What is it, Sol?"

Gelb lowered the hand that he'd raised.

"I've read the motion twice now. If you look at the transcript of the interview that Mildred Balitzer gave in New York, which is attached to the McCarthy affidavit, you'll notice she says that she stopped taking dope a year earlier, just after the raid on February first, and she swears she's been clean ever since. Also, both Mildred and

Cokey Flo swear they received nothing of value in exchange for their recanted testimony."

"What of it?"

"Well, I was talking to one of my sources up in Sing Sing yesterday, and he told me that Pete Harris had dropped a stray remark to the effect that Mildred and Cokey Flo took a cure together at some private hospital in New York. Recently, was the impression I got. If that's true—"

"If that's true," Tom interrupted, his fist pounding the table, "then we've caught her in a bald-faced lie! Sol, get up to Sing Sing and talk to Harris. And I mean now, this afternoon. Harry, I want every available detective working on this, even if it means double overtime. We need to find this hospital and subpoena their patient records. Make that our number-one priority."

"But is it really that important, Chief? Who cares if Mildred's on dope or she isn't?"

Tom sat again. The tremor, they all noticed, was gone from his voice.

"You don't get it now, Harry, but you will. Trust me on this. As George Medalie used to say, the smallest fact is a window through which the infinite may be seen."

Tom returned to his rackets trial, but his mind was never far from the Luciano verdict. It was his greatest achievement in a career of outsize achievements, not to mention the source of his national reputation, and he wasn't about to let a pair of drug-addled prostitutes snatch it from under his nose.

The break came a few days later, when police detectives visited the Towns Hospital on Central Park West. Towns was a private sanitarium that specialized in the treatment of drug and alcohol addiction—a drug mill, Tom had no doubt—and while no records reflected the treatment of either a Flo Brown or a Mildred Balitzer, both women were known to change their names about as often as Tom changed his socks. So it wasn't until the detectives flashed booking photos of Mildred and Cokey Flo that they finally hit the jackpot.

"They were admitted on February twenty-fifth under the names Marion Wilson and Florence Stern." Barry Ten Eyck tossed a folder onto the special prosecutor's desk. "The rate was a hundred dollars per week per patient, with payment coming from a 'Mr. Stern.' We showed them a few more photos, and just like we figured, 'Mr. Stern' turns out to be Jo Jo Weintraub, Pete Harris's lobbygow, which explains how Pete knew all about it. And get a load of this."

Ten Eyck laid another Photostat atop the hospital records.

"The Sing Sing visitor's log. It seems our friend Jo Jo tried to visit Pete on September eleventh, but was refused entry. He then returned as Simon Balitzer and visited Pete fourteen different times between October of last year and February of this. The last time in the company of Maurice Cantor."

"Cantor? That makes Jo Jo an agent of the defense attorneys." Tom leaned forward, a finger stroking his mustache. "First Jo Jo steers Mildred and Cokey Flo to this Dunn character in Los Angeles, then the next thing you know he's checking them into a hospital in New York. All on Luciano's dime, I'm sure of it. By God, I'd love to put Polakoff and Adams under oath."

"Wait till you hear the best part. Mildred and Cokey Flo were signed up for a three-week cure, but they both checked out a week early. On Monday, March the eighth to be exact. And what's the significance of March the eighth? Why, it's the same day they signed their recanting affidavits."

Tom slammed his fist on the records.

"It's perjury, plain and simple! Worse, it's a deliberate fraud on the court! Knowing Mildred, she's been doping since the day we cut her loose. Then she and Flo go out to California, where Mildred runs out of money. The film deal stalls, so she wires Jo Jo and offers to sell her story to Luciano's boys in exchange for God-knows-what. Money, or dope, or maybe Pete's safety in Sing Sing. In any event, she gets a trip back to New York and a paid stint in the hospital. Then they rush her straight from the hospital to Adams's office to sign an affidavit in which she swears she hasn't taken drugs for over a year!"

"And that neither received anything of value for her testimony."

"By God, when we bring this to McCook's attention, he'll bounce them right out of the courtroom. Maybe straight into a holding cell."

"I assume you'll want an affidavit from this Dr. Towns who owns the hospital?"

"I want affidavits from every doctor, nurse, receptionist, orderly, and janitor who ever saw them there. Don't you get it, Barry? This is our ruby-red nose. Instead of a she-said-then, she-says-now contest between a couple of hopheads, we'll put the lawyers on trial for suborning perjured testimony!"

Tom grabbed his cigarettes and leaned back in his chair, propping his feet on the desk.

"McCook won't even *read* the recanting affidavits once he hears how they were obtained. In fact, here's a better idea. What do you say we submit our opposition in camera and not even serve it on the defense? We'll ask McCook to hold a preliminary hearing into whether Polakoff and Adams are trying to perpetrate a fraud. Then we'll invite the press to the hearing and cross-examine the lawyers in open court. Just sandbag the hell out of them. Instead of recanted testimony, the headlines will read 'Lawyers Lie for Luciano.' "

"I like it, Chief. I like it a lot."

Tom lit his cigarette.

"Silver medals are nice in track and field, but inside the courtroom, all that matters is who takes home the gold. You remember that, my boy, and the world will be your oyster."

Sixty

Marked Woman

November 1937

IT WAS BARELY sunrise when I reached El Paso and stopped at the first open hash house I could find. Two rusted-out trucks sat in the parking lot along with a skinny brown dog that stood and raised its hackles as I stepped onto the broken asphalt.

"Get! Go on, shoo!"

A bell tinkled over the door as I entered, and the four cowboys at the counter all looked up just in time to watch me trip over the threshold and nearly fall flat on my face.

"What're you gawkin at?"

They all returned to their coffees. I slumped into a booth by the window where I could keep an eye on my car and watch the highway beyond. There was a late-model Buick I thought had been tailing me ever since Las Cruces, but then again, maybe it was just my nerves.

My car had steam drifting up from the radiator, and now the dog was circling it, sniffing at the air. I rubbed my eyes and was looking over the menu when the waitress came from around the counter with a pad in one hand and a coffee pot in the other.

"Just scrambled eggs and toast," I told her.

I sat watching the highway, and the odd passing car, and the sun climbing cold and white over the bare treetops. One by one the old cowboys finished their coffees and dipped into their pockets and slid some coins onto the counter. They mumbled goodbyes to the wait-ress, and shrugged into their coats, and then the last of them tipped his hat in my direction as the door swung closed behind him.

The joint was empty then, and after another minute of sputtering engines and belching smoke, so was the parking lot. Even the dog was gone. As the sun rose higher, it shone through the window like a spotlight casting shadows across the tabletop—the ketchup bottle and the creamer and the salt and pepper shakers. I pawed through my bag and put my sunglasses on. I finished my coffee and raised my cup to the waitress.

I'd started thinking by then—daydreaming, you might call it—like I always did when things got too quiet. And like always, what I thought about first was the trial. Not just the courtroom part of it—I'd already worn that memory bare—but that whole crazy year that began with me running my own house and living with Jimmy Fredericks and ended with me being, well, whatever it was I'd become.

Joe Sussman used to say that you can't really understand a thing until you've put it far behind you. But I think Suss was wrong about that, because the more time and the more miles I put between me and that goddamn trial, the more I realize I'll never fully understand what it was that actually happened.

Take how it ended. Here were me, and Millie and Nancy Presser, all of us swearing that what we'd said on the witness stand was a lie, and here was Helen Kelly giving the judge chapter and verse about the boozing and the coaching and all the promises that had been made to me and Millie and Nancy and Thelma. And yet with all that evidence going for him, what was the iceberg that sunk Lucky's ship?

Millie, telling a little white lie about dope.

Like it mattered whether we were using or not, or when we'd started or stopped. And that, I guess, was the part I'll never understand. When I was Dewey's witness, it was okay that I'd just taken the cure and could barely see the nose in front of my face, let alone that I needed a belt or two just to keep from falling out of the witness chair. Same thing with Millie. But once we were Lucky's witnesses, then all of a sudden we couldn't be trusted anymore? All of a sudden we were hopheads and therefore vulnerable to what the judge called "undue influence?"

Gee, Judge. What do you call being threatened with twenty years in state prison?

And who, for that matter, was the one who shouldn't be trusted? Dewey swore up and down that he'd never promised Nancy or Thelma a cruise, yet when it turned out he gave 'em one, that was okay. Dewey swore he'd never promised a magazine deal for Millie or me, but when it turned out we both got one, well, that was okay too. Dewey swore that his men had never taken the girls out drinking, but when a cop no less finally testified that they did, that was just hunky-dory. But let Mildred Balitzer tell a tiny fib about dope and all of a sudden our affidavits "reek with perjury" and we're not even allowed to get on the stand and tell the world what really happened?

So here's how I look at it now. Lucky and Dewey, they were like two heavyweights battling their way up the ranks and knocking out every opponent they faced. Then fate played matchmaker and put them both on the same card. Neither had seen the other fight, but each thought he had his man measured. Dewey, he figured Lucky for a barroom brawler with a horseshoe hidden inside his glove. And Lucky, he figured Dewey for a gentleman boxer who fought by the Queensberry rules.

403

Except that one of them figured wrong, and a whole lot of people got spattered at ringside.

But the world turned, and people moved on, and after a week or two nobody gave a hang about what did or didn't go down on the fourteenth floor of the Woolworth Building because now there was a civil war in Spain, and the Japs had invaded the Chinks, and that cute Amelia Earhart was still missing somewhere in the Pacific.

So Charlie Lucky rots in a prison cell, thanks to the testimony of four or five witnesses who were either proven to be liars or who came right out and admitted it. And Dewey, the little crumb, is hailed by the press as some kind of great and incorruptible crime-buster and gets portrayed on film by Humphrey Bogart and then gets himself elected district attorney, all while climbing over the backs of guys like Lucky and Jimmy and Pete.

Then again, maybe I was just sore. Sore at Dewey and McCook for what they done to Jimmy. Sore about the lousy deal Ten Eyck had cut with Macfadden, letting them sell our stories to Warner Bros. and gyp us out of our cut. Sore that I had to buy a ticket like all the other suckers just to watch Bette Davis play me—me, Flo Brown!—up on the silver screen. Sore that when I told the guy sitting next to me in the theater that I was the girl who the picture was really about, he moved over a seat, like I had two heads or something.

All of which explains why I'm broke now, and on the move, and down to my last quarter cube. But don't get me wrong, I ain't complaining. I've got hot grub in my belly and just enough gas to get me where I'm heading—to where this girl in L.A. told me the dope was cheap and the houses were legal and the action was hot and heavy twenty-four hours a day.

So you see, I can take care of myself. Hell, I been taking care of myself ever since I was fourteen. I don't need any Ralph or Big Joe, any Jack Zuta or Joe Sussman, any Jimmy Fredericks or Barry Ten Eyck to be holding my hand. I'm like that cat who, no matter which way you drop her, she always lands on her feet. And like that cat, I've got a few more lives left to live.

I signaled for the check, and with my very last dime bought a pack of cigarettes for the road.

"Which way to Juárez?" I asked the waitress, tapping out a smoke.

She pointed south.

Author's Note

On October 27, 1907, Salvatore Lucania, the nine-year-old son of an impoverished Sicilian sulfur miner, arrived in New York City. By 1931, he'd grown to become Charles Luciano, a.k.a. Charlie Lucky, the most powerful gangster in New York and the reputed head of organized crime in America.

In June of 1935, Governor Herbert H. Lehman, under pressure to combat organized crime and its corrupting influence on New York politics, chose as his weapon a politically ambitious, thirty-three-year-old former assistant U.S. attorney named Thomas E. Dewey. Appointed special prosecutor for New York County and armed with expansive new legal powers, Dewey set out to do what many considered impossible: bring down the nation's most powerful mobster.

On a Friday afternoon in May of 1936, a forty-eight-year-old Long Island defense attorney named George Morton Levy received an unexpected telephone call. Moses Polakoff, counsel for Lucky Luciano, needed a trial lawyer of unimpeachable reputation to handle his client's defense against ninety counts of compulsory prostitution.

"How much time would I have to prepare?" Levy asked, to which Polakoff replied, "The trial opens Monday."

Florence Newman left Pittsburgh at age fourteen, quickly embarking on a downward spiral of crime, drugs, and prostitution. By the time she settled in New York at age twenty-two, she was Cokey Flo Brown, an addict and a madam and, as the Luciano trial commenced, a pseudonymous inmate suffering through agonizing heroin withdrawal on the fourth floor of the Women's House of Detention.

Four colorful lives, each on its own incandescent trajectory. Dewey would go on to become governor of New York, would nearly become president of the United States, and would ultimately lead one of the world's largest and most powerful law firms.

Levy would retire from practice to found Roosevelt Raceway in 1940, briefly returning to the national spotlight as the first witness called before the U.S. Senate's 1951 Kefauver Committee hearings in New York, famously depicted in *The Godfather, Part II.*

Luciano would serve ten years in Dannemora before winning a pardon from then-governor Dewey for his role in assisting the U.S. war effort in Europe. Deported to Italy, he would briefly reside in Havana, Cuba, from which he—along with boyhood chums Benjamin "Bugsy" Siegel and Meyer Lansky—would finance construction of the famous Flamingo hotel-casino in Las Vegas.

For her part, Cokey Flo Brown would move to California, would see herself portrayed on screen by Bette Davis, and would ultimately disappear into obscurity and addiction in the brothels of Ciudad Juárez, Mexico.

But for four short weeks in the spring of 1936, the intersection of these four lives—in their respective roles as defendant, prosecution attorney, defense attorney, and star witness—enthralled the nation, introducing America to the violent and darkly glamorous world of organized crime and leaving our culture, laws, and politics forever changed.

★   ★   ★

For thirty-five years, the definitive account of the Luciano vice trial was Hickman Powell's *Ninety Times Guilty*, first published in 1939 and later reprinted under various titles. An investigative reporter for the New York *Herald Tribune*, Powell covered the trial as it occurred and personally interviewed many of its key participants. Described by his colleague Charles Grutzner of the *New York Times* as "an admirer and close friend and confidante" of Thomas E. Dewey, Powell went on to serve as a staff assistant to Governor Dewey and as a speechwriter for both of Dewey's presidential campaigns. Dewey also appointed Powell to positions on the New York State Power Authority, the Legislative Commission on Industrial and Labor Conditions, and the Joint Legislative Committee on Wiretapping.

Given his close personal relationship with the special prosecutor, it is perhaps not surprising that *Ninety Times Guilty* reads as a sycophantic paean to Dewey, depicting him as an intrepid and incorruptible reformer battling the dark forces of moral corruption personified by Luciano, a sinister whoremaster. Then in 1974, Doubleday posthumously published the first of a planned two-volume Dewey memoir titled *Twenty Against the Underworld*, which, for the most part, embraced and affirmed the Powell version of history. That same year, however, another, more remarkable book was published, shining a new and very different light on Luciano the man and on the vice trial that ended his criminal reign.

The Last Testament of Lucky Luciano was written by *New York Times* reporter Richard Hammer from notes provided by Martin A. Gosch, a modestly credited Hollywood producer who claimed to have collaborated with Luciano, then living in exile, on a film version of Luciano's life. When that project was abandoned, Luciano instead proposed that Gosch turn the notes of their meetings into a definitive biography, but with one important proviso: The book was not to be published until ten years after Luciano's death.

Luciano died on January 26, 1962, of an apparent heart attack at Capodichino Airport in Naples, Italy. Gosch, tantalizingly, was at

Luciano's side when he died. Gosch himself, however, died on October 20, 1973, before *The Last Testament* was published. Hammer, the book's author, never met Luciano. Moreover, the notes from which the book was purportedly written were subsequently lost by Gosch's widow.

Given *The Last Testament*'s murky provenance, it is only natural that its authenticity has been questioned. Further complicating matters are the numerous instances in which events described in the book conflict with demonstrable historical fact. (For an excellent analysis of these conflicts, I direct readers to Richard N. Warner's "The Last Word on 'The Last Testament,' " which appeared in the April 2012 issue of *Informer* magazine.) On the other hand, *The Last Testament* is rich in intimate life details that preclude its facile dismissal as a clumsy fabrication.

Is *The Last Testament* a hoax, as some suggest, or is it a genuine oral memoir whose defects are fairly attributable to the frailties of human memory and to Gosch and/or Hammer's sometimes clumsy efforts to fill in the narrative gaps? While I don't purport to know the answer, I do know that the book provides a compelling counterweight to the Powell and Dewey portraits of Luciano as imperial overlord of the 1930s New York prostitution bonding combination.

Other books, of course—not to mention films, television series, articles, essays, websites, and blog posts, all seemingly without number—have been written about Luciano, his trial, and the milieu in which it occurred. These include *Five Families* by Selwyn Raab, *The Luciano Story* by Sid Feder and Joachim Joesten, *The Case Against Lucky Luciano* by Ellen Poulsen, and *Boardwalk Gangster* by Tim Newark, to name a few. All were influential in my confection of *Tom & Lucky (and George & Cokey Flo)*, as were *My Partner-in-Law*, Martin Littleton and Kyle Crichton's 1957 biography of George Morton Levy; *Thomas E. Dewey and His Times*, Richard Norton Smith's exhaustive 1982 Dewey biography; and *Little Man*, Robert Lacey's immensely readable biography of Luciano friend and confidante Meyer Lansky.

My own interest in the demimonde of New York organized crime
can be traced to two extraordinary conversations to which I was a
party, almost twenty years apart. The first occurred in the mid-1980s
when a friend told me the story of a strange little man who had lived
in their rural upstate community near Interlaken, New York. "Danny
King" was a virtual hermit who was notably evasive about his origins
and personal history. When King was hospitalized in the late 1960s,
he gave my friend's father a box for safekeeping that contained what
King described as his "most prized possession." Following his neigh-
bor's death, my friend's father opened the box and found that it
contained a book, *Women for Sale* by Chile Acuna, which had been
published in 1931.

Acuna, it turns out, was the star witness in Judge Samuel Seabury's
1930 investigation into New York public corruption, and the book is
a memoir of Acuna's role as chief stool pigeon in a Kafkaesque
scheme by which vice officers, bondsmen, paid informants, lawyers,
and judges all conspired to free the guilty, jail the innocent, and
generally subvert justice in the New York Magistrate's Court. It was
these shocking revelations of the Seabury Committee that led to the
resignation of Mayor Jimmy Walker and, indirectly, to the appointment of Thomas E. Dewey as special prosecutor for New York
County. Acuna himself, who lived under heavy police guard after the
trial and who legally changed his name to Charles Mason, was alleged
to have died during routine surgery at a Brooklyn hospital in 1932—a
death that some regarded as too convenient by half.

I first met Elise "CeCe" Levy, the daughter of George Morton
Levy, in Los Angeles in the late 1990s. At the time, I'd never heard of
CeCe's father, although I later came to appreciate that he was one of
the best-respected trial lawyers of his day. One afternoon in 2004,
CeCe casually mentioned that after her father's death in 1977, she'd
packed up fifteen locked file cabinets from his law office and moved
them to a friend's barn in upstate New York. Intrigued, I asked if she

would allow me to review the files. She agreed, and I immediately hopped a plane to JFK.

The file cabinets were there, as advertised, rusting under a moldering tarp. My brother and I spent an entire day combing through every drawer, every file, until we found what we were looking for: George Morton Levy's sixty-eight-year-old case file in the matter of *People v. Charles Luciano*. Inside the file were Levy's correspondence, his trial notes, his annotated motions and briefs, and a whole assortment of original, never-before-seen documents from one of the most notorious criminal trials in American history. With CeCe's permission, I took possession of the file, vowing that if ever I were to trade my own law practice for the writing life—which I finally did in 2006—I would one day devote myself to the Luciano trial.

Was Lucky Luciano really guilty of the crimes of which he was convicted on June 7, 1936? It's a question that's been debated to one degree or another ever since the day the verdict was rendered. Powell and Dewey present strenuous arguments for the affirmative, while *The Last Testament* paints a starkly different picture—of another kind of conspiracy, in which an overzealous, politically ambitious young prosecutor and a compliant judge worked hand in glove using the unlimited resources of the state to achieve a preordained result.

The gist of the case against Luciano was that he actively oversaw and profited from a criminal conspiracy that sought to organize the previously independent purveyors of New York prostitution. That such a conspiracy existed, that it was overseen by Luciano co-defendants Little Davie Betillo and Tommy the Bull Pennochio, and that its edicts were enforced by co-defendants James Frederico and Abraham Wahrman are beyond reasonable dispute. But was the Boss of Bosses himself—a man whose multimillion-dollar empire encompassed liquor, drugs, and gambling—really stooping so low as to skim the meager earnings of two-dollar prostitutes?

One thing that becomes clear to any who study the trial and appellate records is that it was Cokey Flo Brown's eleventh-hour appearance in the proceedings that turned the tide for the prosecution, breathing new life into what had been a moribund case against Luciano and forcing a reluctant George Morton Levy to put his notorious client on the witness stand, with foreseeably disastrous results.

Prior to the advent of Cokey Flo, the only direct evidence linking Luciano to the so-called bonding combination were (a) the testimony of hotel thief Joe Bendix, (b) the expected testimony of prostitutes Nancy Presser and Mildred (Balitzer) Harris, and (c) the identification testimony of a half-dozen hotel employees. Indeed, Justice McCook ultimately instructed the jury:

> As a matter of law, if the jury disbelieve the testimony of the witnesses Bendix, Nancy Presser, Cokey Flo and Mildred Harris, they must return a verdict of not guilty for the defendant Luciano on all counts charged in the indictment.

For a number of reasons, however, this eyewitness testimony was deeply suspect, particularly when viewed in the context of all that transpired both before and after the verdict was rendered.

Let's start with Genevieve Flesher, a.k.a. Nancy Presser. Nancy was a prostitute, a heroin addict, and the former girlfriend of defendant Ralph Liguori, the alleged holdup man for the combination. Once she'd been arrested in Dewey's vice raid on February 1, 1936, Nancy was held as a material witness on a bond of ten thousand dollars. At first she denied any knowledge of the man called Charlie Lucky. Then, after two months in the Women's House of Detention, she asked to meet personally with Dewey. Shortly after that meeting, she was moved to a hotel and, like the other cooperating witnesses, was allowed to visit movie theaters, restaurants, and even nightclubs, all on the government's dime.

In her trial testimony, Nancy claimed to have first met Luciano in 1928, and to have visited him professionally on numerous occasions at both the Barbizon-Plaza and the Waldorf Towers. She testified to several incriminating statements allegedly made by Lucky in or near her presence, all pertaining to the bonding combination. But Nancy's credibility was eviscerated by Levy on cross-examination when Nancy was unable to describe Lucky's hotel rooms—even, for example, whether they had twin beds or double beds—or the way in which a visiting guest must gain access to the Waldorf Tower from the lobby of the hotel.

Next came Mildred Balitzer, a.k.a. Millie Harris. Mildred was a prostitute, an addict, a madam, and the wife of booker Pete Balitzer, a.k.a. Pete Harris, a Luciano co-defendant who'd pleaded guilty and who, in a package deal with Mildred, had agreed to testify for Dewey in exchange for leniency in his sentencing. Once moved from the House of Detention to a comfortable hotel, Mildred was allowed to visit restaurants and nightclubs multiple times in the company of police officers and, on at least one verified occasion, assistant prosecutor Sol Gelb, a particularly embarrassing fact that NYPD officer George Heidt would later confirm on the witness stand at trial.

Mildred testified that she went to Florida in January of 1935 and there saw Luciano at the Paddock Bar and Grill. She allegedly asked Lucky to allow Pete to quit the bonding combination, a plea that Lucky rebuffed. She also testified to a second, similar conversation with Lucky outside New York's Villanova Restaurant in May of 1935.

On cross-examination, Mildred repeatedly denied having received a promise of immunity from prosecution for her trial testimony:

Q: I was referring to any promise concerning immunity or a reward to you for your testimony. Did you receive any such promise in writing?

A: No.

Q: Did you receive any such letter to that effect?

A: No.

Like Nancy Presser before her, Mildred was badly impeached at trial, both by a written statement she'd given on March 5, 1936, in which she'd denied ever having met Charlie Lucky, and later by the testimony of her former boyfriend, Gus Franco, who described a conversation in which Mildred admitted she "didn't know Lucky from beans," but that she "had to back up Pete." Then, after the trial had concluded, her credibility was further damaged by the disclosure of a pre-trial, handwritten letter of immunity signed by Dewey assistants Tom Hogan and Sol Gelb—the latter of whom was present in court but had sat mute even as Mildred denied the letter's existence.

The third and final witness to directly link Luciano to the combination—and the first to so testify—was Joe Bendix, a serial stool pigeon, who, following his eighth hotel-burglary conviction, was about to begin serving a prison sentence of fifteen years to life. When Bendix learned of the big vice trial, he wrote to Dewey's staff and offered to testify against Lucky in exchange for a recommendation of executive clemency. Bendix claimed to have known Lucky for more than seven years, having first been introduced to him by a man named Captain Dutton, and to have been personally hired by Lucky as a collector for the bonding combination—a job he admitted he never performed. Bendix then testified to several incriminating statements allegedly made by his new employer.

As with the other purported eyewitnesses, Bendix was impeached in myriad ways, both before and after he'd left the witness chair. First and foremost, the premise that Jimmy Fredericks had to take Bendix to meet Charlie Lucky before Bendix could be hired on as a forty-dollar-per-week collector both beggars the imagination and contradicts the entire prosecution theme of Lucky as the hands-off mastermind of the bonding combination.

Second, if Bendix really had known Lucky for so long—the unstated implication being that Lucky acted as a fence for items Bendix had stolen—then why did Bendix need to go through Fredericks to gain an interview with Lucky?

Author's Note

Third, once the defense finally located Captain George Paul Dutton—in charge of regulating nightclubs for the state police—Dutton testified that he'd never met Bendix in his life, but that he did know Bendix's third wife, a showgirl named Joy Dixon, which might explain why Bendix had invoked his name.

Finally, Joy Dixon herself, whose real name was Muriel Weiss, and whom Bendix repeatedly claimed was present at the Villanova Restaurant when Bendix met with Lucky about the combination job, later denied having attended any such meeting and even proved by her own passport that she'd been out of the country at the time the alleged meeting occurred.

The final nail in the testimonial coffin of Joe Bendix came when a letter he'd written to Joy from the Tombs prison was mistakenly delivered to the office of Assistant District Attorney Morris Panger, with whom Bendix had also been negotiating for executive clemency by offering to testify for the prosecution in a different high-profile case. In that letter, Bendix stressed the importance of gaining Dewey's cooperation and urged his wife to "think up some real clever story" to tell. Dewey, not incidentally, had the Bendix letter in his possession for over a week before it finally came to the attention of the defense via Morris Panger.

It is also worth noting that at the time Bendix was testifying for the prosecution, Joy Dixon was, unbeknownst to the defense, waiting in the adjoining room and was scheduled to be Dewey's next witness. Levy, in open court, stated to McCook, "We shall make an effort to locate this man's wife, and if we do—I do not know with what success—we would like to have the opportunity of recalling this man." Yet Dewey and Gelb sat silently at the prosecution table, even though Dewey assistant Eunice Carter was sitting in a room with Dixon not fifty feet from where Levy stood.

There were other instances, it should be noted, in which perjured testimony was either presented by Dewey or allowed to go uncorrected into the record. One example of this was the testimony of

David Marcus, a.k.a. Davey Miller, one of the bookers who'd begun the case as a co-defendant before turning state's evidence. On cross-examination, Miller—a former Pittsburgh police constable—denied having ever run a disorderly house, thus forcing the defense to call detectives from Pittsburgh to prove that both Miller and his wife had, in fact, previously been convicted of doing precisely that—a fact that Dewey's team, ever scrupulous in their due diligence, almost certainly knew.

As for the hotel employees who were called by Dewey as identification witnesses—that is, neutral corroborating witnesses able to place Lucky in the company of co-defendants Betillo, Pennochio, Wahrman, and Fredericks—all were brought to Dewey's office and shown photographs of the thirteen defendants on multiple occasions before testifying. Marjorie Brown, for example—a bath maid at the Waldorf—testified that she'd spent no fewer than five sessions with the photographs before being called to the witness stand, which naturally raises the question: If she was able to recognize the defendants from their photos the first time, then why were four additional sessions necessary?

Despite these serial rehearsals, the hotel witnesses actually performed rather poorly in court. Frank Brown, an assistant manager at the Barbizon-Plaza, took the witness stand and failed to identify a single person in the courtroom. Marjorie Brown identified George Levy as a visitor to the Waldorf before correcting herself. Waldorf employee Henry Woelfle misidentified attorney Moses Polakoff as defendant Abie Wahrman. William McGrath, a night bellboy at the Barbizon-Plaza, identified attorney Maurice Cantor as having visited Lucky. Barbizon-Plaza elevator operator Lawrence Overdriver first identified defendant Jack Eller from his photo, then switched in court and identified Jimmy Fredericks as the man he'd once taken to Lucky's room.

Between the dubious testimony of Nancy Presser, Mildred Balitzer/Harris, and Joe Bendix and the shaky identification testimony of the various hotel employees, Dewey had to have known that his case against Luciano—which he was required to prove beyond a reasonable doubt—was headed for serious trouble. And thus the eleventh-hour appearance of an intelligent, attractive eyewitness who claimed she could personally tie Lucky to the others in the vice combination must have seemed like manna from prosecutorial heaven.

So what are we to make of the testimony of Cokey Flo Brown?

Cokey Flo—also known as Florence Newman, Frances Martin, Mildred Nelson, Fay Marston, Gloria Moore, and Florence Stern—first testified to a meeting that occurred in the spring of 1934 at four A.M. in a Chinese restaurant on Broadway near 130th Street. The restaurant, the name of which she could never seem to recall, was some seventy blocks from her apartment at 333 West End Avenue. She and Jimmy Fredericks had left her apartment at approximately three A.M. with the stated intention of going to meet Luciano. Cokey Flo drove, as Fredericks did not have a license. Present when they arrived at the restaurant were Lucky, Tommy Pennochio, and Davie Betillo. Fredericks introduced Cokey Flo to the others as "a girlfriend of mine."

After some nonsubstantive dinner conversation in the restaurant, conducted mostly in Italian (which she—unlike the others present—neither spoke nor understood), Cokey Flo then drove Fredericks, Lucky, Betillo, and Pennochio to 121 Mulberry Street, an address she somehow remembered clearly. Again, the men spoke mostly in Italian. It was during this drive downtown that Cokey Flo claimed that the bonding combination was discussed, in English, with Fredericks complaining about bookers withholding addresses and with Lucky telling Fredericks, "Bring all the bookies downtown tomorrow, I will put them on the carpet, and we will see that that doesn't happen again," and then, "Have them all come down and we'll straighten the matter out."

The second event to which Cokey Flo testified is alleged to have occurred in the fall of 1934. She claimed on that occasion to have driven Fredericks and a loan shark named Benny Spiller to a garage somewhere on the Lower East Side, where she parked on the street and waited while Fredericks and Spiller went inside. Growing bored, she left her car and entered the garage, where she overheard the men's voices. Fredericks later emerged with Lucky, Betillo, and Pennochio, at which point she drove Fredericks home.

The third event occurred around Easter of 1935, when she again drove Fredericks to the same garage, again grew bored and entered the garage, and again saw Fredericks exit in the company of Lucky, Betillo, and Pennochio.

The penultimate event occurred in the summer of 1935, when she and Fredericks went to a restaurant in Chinatown that bore the street number "21." There they encountered Lucky, Betillo, and Pennochio at a table eating, and were invited to join them. As at the previous restaurant meeting, the conversation took place mostly in Italian, with Cokey Flo testifying that "the conversation switched to English when they talked about prostitution." Lucky is alleged to have complained to Fredericks that the racket wasn't producing sufficient income to continue because the houses were too difficult to manage and the madams too resistant to bonding. When Fredericks urged patience, Lucky is alleged to have said, "Why don't you get the madams together, Jimmy? You know, I told you before that being nice to them isn't any good."

The fifth and final event occurred in October of 1935, at the same Chinatown restaurant, where Lucky is alleged to have again complained about the problems with the bonding racket, and also complained that his name was being mentioned too frequently in connection with its operation. "This Dewey investigation is coming on," Lucky is alleged to have said, "and it may get tough. I think we ought to fold up for a while." Ultimately, after listening to Betillo, Lucky decided, "I'll let it go for a couple more months, and if things are the same, you'll have to let it drop."

Now let's analyze Cokey Flo's testimony in light of other facts adduced both during and after the trial.

First, we must consider the extent to which Cokey Flo's various addictions must have affected her ability to recall the alleged events and conversations to which she testified in such detail. By her own admission, she began smoking opium in 1931, with her habit growing from four or five pills per month to five or six pills per day. She began injecting morphine in January of 1935 at the rate of one-quarter grain, three times per day. This gradually increased to one and a quarter grains per day. Then, in mid-February of 1936, she switched from morphine to heroin, which she used at the rate of one ounce per week until her arrest for solicitation on May 8, 1936.

They didn't call her "Cokey Flo" for nothing, and all her testimony must be viewed through the compound lens of narcotic impairment, addiction, and withdrawal.

Dewey contended in his opening statement—before he knew of Cokey Flo's existence—that Lucky Luciano was the secret mastermind behind the vice racket, that Lucky took great pains to insulate himself from those who actually booked, bonded, and operated the so-called disorderly houses, and that Lucky was careful to limit knowledge of his involvement to only a small handful of trusted lieutenants.

This characterization is significant because, at the first meeting about which she testified, Cokey Flo was a total stranger to Lucky. Is it credible that Fredericks would have felt it appropriate to bring his girlfriend to such a meeting, or that Lucky would have allowed it? That Lucky would discuss intimate details of the vice racket in her presence? Or that when the others present all spoke Italian, he would switch to English for that part of the conversation, and for that part only?

This incriminating conversation, moreover, took place in a car not her own that Cokey Flo was driving, with her back turned to Lucky, Betillo, and Pennochio—three people whom she'd only just met. When asked how she could distinguish the voices of these three strangers, Cokey Flo testified that, despite the pre-dawn hour and the

420

absence of any artificial light in the car, she could see their lips moving in the small rearview mirror.

Substantively, Lucky is alleged to have instructed Fredericks to bring all the bookers downtown to be called on the carpet. Cokey Flo testified that, according to Fredericks, this had indeed happened shortly after the conversation in the car. Yet despite their plea bargains and agreements to cooperate with Dewey, not a single one of the booker defendants—Dave Miller, Al Weiner, Jack Eller, or Pete Harris—ever corroborated such an occurrence. Indeed, none of them claimed to have ever met Luciano in person.

The other two restaurant meetings about which Cokey Flo testified carry the same fishy taint. Would Lucky, in English, really discuss incriminating matters in front of a woman who, if no longer a stranger to him, was by then well known to be an unreliable drug addict?

Cokey Flo's testimony regarding the two meetings alleged to have taken place in a Lower East Side garage is similarly suspect. While she was able to remember verbatim conversations from the restaurant meeting in the spring of 1934—not to mention the exact time of her arrival, and even the food that she'd ordered and eaten—as well as the specific address to which she allegedly drove the men after the meal, she was somehow unable to describe the location of a garage she'd more recently visited not once but twice, having parked there long enough on both occasions to grow bored and exit the vehicle to wander.

Dewey assistant Barent Ten Eyck had been in negotiations for Cokey Flo's testimony since May 16, and after multiple meetings had finally obtained her signed witness statement on May 20, at a time when no fewer than twenty-eight prosecution witnesses were still scheduled to testify. With his army of attorneys and detectives, Dewey had ample opportunity to undertake an investigation to corroborate some of what he knew Cokey Flo would say. He could, for example, have sent detectives to drive with her to find this alleged garage and in the process might have talked to the owner and his employees and perhaps have located other valuable eyewitnesses.

Given Dewey's meticulous nature and his penchant of leaving no stone unturned, this was an opportunity he could scarcely have resisted. His failure to do so suggests either that he knew Cokey Flo was lying, making such an expedition pointless, or that he suspected as much and didn't wish to provide the defense with an address at which exculpatory witnesses might be found and subpoenaed.

Cokey Flo's selective memory is perhaps the most damning of all her shortcomings as a witness. So shaky was her appearance on the witness stand that Justice McCook—incredibly—allowed her to take periodic sips of brandy during breaks from her testimony. When asked the day on which she first communicated with Dewey's staff only a week before her testimony, she first said that it was on Friday, then later that it was on Saturday. When asked how much of her own money she'd put up for bail when she was arrested in January of 1936, she first said $900, then later said "over $2,000." When asked to identify the bank account from which the funds were drawn, she said "Central something or other" at Broadway and 94th Street, where no bank existed. Yet when asked on cross-examination to repeat the incriminating conversations she claimed to have overheard, she did so almost perfectly, with a rehearsed, word-for-word precision.

Which brings us to the blandishments Dewey offered to obtain the testimony of Cokey Flo and the other key prosecution witnesses. Defendant Ralph Liguori, the former boyfriend of witness Nancy Presser, testified that Dewey's office had offered him an expense-paid trip to Europe with Nancy in exchange for his cooperation in testifying against Luciano—an offer he'd refused. Affronted, Dewey ridiculed the very idea, and in his closing argument stated:

Oh, and the trip to Europe? That invention was just a little too funny. I mean, some of these lies you cannot analyze, but some of them—who in heaven's name is going to pay for a trip to Europe?

I, on the City's salary? My assistants, or the City of New York? When you get through with this case, gentlemen, I would like to have you look at my appropriation. I would like to have you analyze it, and the contingency fund. Trips to Europe! How utterly impossible and ridiculous! And that is the kind of things they invent in desperation.

Yet at the trial's conclusion, Nancy Presser and fellow cooperating witness Thelma Jordan did find themselves first-class passengers aboard the S.S. *Samaria*, en route to a three-month European tour, all compliments of Dewey and his assistants.

Helen Horvath, a.k.a. Helen Kelly, was a prostitute who, while being held as a material witness for the prosecution, lived in hotels and apartments with both Nancy Presser and Mildred Balitzer. In a detailed, exceptionally compelling post-trial affidavit, Helen adverts to a conversation she'd had with Mildred in April of 1936, before the trial had begun, in which Mildred bragged that in exchange for giving false testimony against Luciano, "she would not be given money directly, but would be given ways to get it," and specifically that "she was going to be given a chance to write a story of her life and they were going to obtain movie rights for her story."

After the trial, Cokey Flo and Mildred Balitzer did, in fact, sell their life stories to Bernarr Macfadden, the publisher of *Liberty* magazine, in a deal brokered by Dewey and Ten Eyck. The articles appeared in serial form during 1936 and 1937, whereupon Warner Bros. purchased the movie rights. In the 1937 film *Marked Woman*, Humphrey Bogart plays a crime-busting Manhattan prosecutor who persuades a reluctant "nightclub hostess" played by Bette Davis to testify against the city's biggest gangster.

Helen Kelly first attempted to contact George Morton Levy on June 9, two days after the verdict, while she was still in police custody. They finally met on July 6, when, in the presence of witness and notary Edward Thompson and a court stenographer, Helen gave a lengthy statement that Levy then reduced to a twenty-three-page affidavit, which Helen corrected, initialed, and signed on July 8, 1936. This affidavit was never filed with the court because Moses Polakoff, wary of further antagonizing Justice McCook, felt its contents were too inflammatory. Instead he prepared a sanitized version of the affidavit, which he eventually filed along with his motion for a new trial.

Helen's original affidavit—a copy of which (together with several other never-before-seen case documents) can be viewed on my website, www.chuckgreaves.com—describes a sorority-house atmosphere in which the arrested prostitutes, once they'd signaled some willingness to cooperate with the special prosecutor, were released from custody, moved to various hotels around the city, and taken to movies, restaurants, and nightclubs. Nancy Presser is described as getting drunk on a regular basis with Dewey assistants Harry Cole, Sol Gelb, and Barent Ten Eyck, while Mildred Balitzer is reported drinking with Gelb and her various police escorts.

Dewey, again, took umbrage at these allegations and offered rebuttal affidavits from various police officers who'd been assigned to guard the three women. NYPD officer William Grant, for example (with whom Mildred was later alleged to be having an affair), submitted an affidavit that is almost comical in its attempt to rebut the charge that Mildred—a recovering addict—was repeatedly plied with liquor:

> At no time was any one of the witnesses above named, while in my custody, in an intoxicated or other condition which necessitated assistance to said witness . . . On many occasions at meals Mildred Balitzer would partake of drinks of liquor, sometimes as many as five or six, but in no instance was she so affected by those drinks of liquor as to lose control of herself or be incapable of conducting herself with usual and normal facility . . . My attention has further been directed to a portion of said Helen Horvath's affidavit on page 15 thereof in which it is stated that I went with Helen Kelly

and Mildred Balitzer to Joe Conway's Tavern, 95th Street and Amsterdam Avenue, remaining there until 7 o'clock in the morning, and with the result that Mildred Balitzer became extremely drunk. There was one occasion when I, Helen Kelly and Mildred Balitzer went to Joe Conway's Tavern at the address stated. We remained there until 4 o'clock in the morning, approximately. Mildred Balitzer had about six drinks and she was the only one who drank as much as that. She did not show in any apparent manner that she was drunk, intoxicated or otherwise seriously affected by the liquor. We then left Joe Conway's Tavern and went to a Child's Restaurant nearby for some food. Thereafter we returned to the house. It is true that Mildred Balitzer insisted upon waiting for the elevator operator who was not on duty at that time, and finally consented to walk up, but this was an invariable practice and routine of Mildred Balitzer's.

Justice Philip J. McCook merits special attention for his role in Luciano's conviction. McCook was a political animal—a sponsor of the New York Young Republicans and a close friend and ally of Fiorello La Guardia's, with whom he'd run for public office in 1919. It was McCook, in fact, who'd administered the oath of office at La Guardia's mayoral inauguration in 1934. While ostensibly acting as a neutral referee of the Luciano vice case, the judge's actions in many respects more closely resembled those of a co-prosecutor. Here are but a few illustrative examples:

The U.S. Constitution prohibits "excessive" bail, meaning bail in a sum that is punitive, and the typical bond for a charge of prostitution in 1936 New York was approximately three hundred dollars. Dewey, frustrated by the arrested prostitutes' initial unwillingness to cooperate, asked McCook to come to the Woolworth Building and arraign them all as material witnesses and to impose bonds in unprecedented sums ranging from ten thousand to twenty-five thousand dollars, effectively guaranteeing that none of the women would ever

go free. The judge agreed, and the women were held incommunicado in the House of Detention while Dewey and his assistants
worked for several months to turn them into cooperating witnesses.

Before the trial commenced, McCook issued a standard pre-trial
order barring witnesses from the courtroom lest they collude or
conform their testimony. But he'd already given Dewey permission
to run a direct wire from the courtroom to the special prosecutor's
office at the Woolworth Building, where, unbeknownst to the
defense, Dewey had assembled many of the prosecution witnesses—
both those who'd already testified and those waiting to do so—to
provide a running commentary to Dewey's assistants, who would
then relay any insights or ideas to Dewey by telephone during breaks
in the trial.

When Norbert Gagnon, one of the sequestered jurors, learned
from his wife that "Italian-looking" strangers had appeared at their
apartment building while the trial was in progress, he reported the
incident to McCook, who assured him that all steps would be
taken to protect his family. McCook then assigned a police detective
to guard the juror's home—an inflammatory fact that was known
to and discussed at length among the other jurors. The defense,
however, was never apprised of either the incident itself or the judge's
actions.

The record is replete with instances in which Dewey and his assistants had ex parte communications with the judge. A telling example
of this occurred when attorney Samuel Kornbluth—counsel for
Cokey Flo's former employer Dorothy Russell Calvit—agreed to
meet with George Levy following the second day of Cokey Flo's
testimony. When Dewey's detective team got wind of Kornbluth's
cooperation with Levy, they arrested Kornbluth in his home. On the
evening of May 26, with the trial still in progress, Dewey assistant
Thurston Greene accompanied Kornbluth and the arresting officers
to McCook's apartment at 57th Street and First Avenue, where
McCook anointed himself a "committing magistrate" and, with no

notice to the defense, charged Kornbluth with "attempting to suborn perjury" and ordered him jailed. The next day's banner headline in the evening edition of the *New York Post* screamed LAWYER HELD AS VICE RING PLOTTER, and Samuel Kornbluth, an attorney of twenty-five years' standing with an otherwise impeccable reputation, saw his life and his livelihood ruined.

After the trial, and despite knowing that post-trial motions and appeals would be pursued, McCook nonetheless called all the women who'd testified as prosecution witnesses back onto chambers and quizzed them, under oath and in the presence of one or more prosecuting attorneys, as to the veracity of their trial testimony. This was an obvious effort to insulate the verdict on appeal and was undertaken, once again, without the knowledge, consent, or participation of the defense.

Later, once the key trial witnesses had all recanted, the defense filed a motion for a new trial with the recanting affidavits attached. Dewey prepared a 450-page opposition but, rather than serving it on the defense, he submitted it to the court in camera with a request that McCook conduct a "preliminary inquiry" into whether the recanting affidavits constituted "a fraud upon the court." McCook acceded to Dewey's request and summoned attorneys Moses Polakoff and Lorenzo Carlino to court on April 20, 1937, placed Polakoff under oath, and, over his strenuous objections, allowed Dewey to cross-examine him as to the affidavits he'd filed and the manner of their preparation.

Despite repeated pleas from the defense, McCook never allowed any of the recanting witnesses to give live testimony in support of the motion for a new trial, which he "heard" on April 23, 1937—after giving the defense less than three days to reply to Dewey's opposition—and which he denied on May 7, 1937.

Finally, at the conclusion of the trial, McCook approved the payment of approximately $450, or $3 per day, to each material witness who'd fully cooperated with Dewey's staff. Those whose cooperation was less than total received $1.50 per day. Those who'd refused to cooperate received nothing.

The post-trial recantations of Mildred Balitzer/Harris, Nancy Presser, and Cokey Flo Brown completed a disturbing pattern in which these three witnesses, whose testimony had effectively slammed the prison door on Lucky Luciano, seemed willing to swear to whatever facts best suited their present interests. Immediately following the raid of February 1, 1936, when both thought a return to business as usual was imminent, Nancy and Mildred claimed ignorance of Lucky's involvement in the vice combination. Once it became clear that the combination had been broken and that their own liberty was at stake, both women changed their tunes and implicated Lucky. Once the emoluments of their testimony ran dry, however, all three witnesses returned to their original positions. Each contradictory version was, of course, offered under penalty of perjury.

At the end of the day we are left with two competing but equally compelling narratives that underlie the trial and conviction of Lucky Luciano. In one, an intrepid prosecutor's dogged persistence overcomes fears of mob reprisal to expose the sordid truth. In the other, a zealous prosecutor and a sycophantic judge mount a reckless crusade to win conviction at any cost.

In rendering its verdict, the jury made its choice. With this novel, I invite readers, and historians, to make their own.

A word or two on methodology. In undertaking to write *Tom & Lucky*, I tried to adhere to the true historical record in all material respects. All of the testimonial excerpts that appear in the book, for example, are taken verbatim from the official court record, with only a few minor corrections for punctuation or spelling. As for the careers of Thomas E. Dewey and George Morton Levy, each unfolds along an accurate timeline, even if the individual scenes employed to depict them—the authorial devices of setting, dialogue, and internal monologue—are fictionalized. And while little is actually known about the woman who became known as Cokey Flo Brown, I've employed scattered clues from her testimony and her few extant writings to construct what I hope is a plausible, albeit largely fictitious, life story.

With a character like Lucky Luciano, however, fact and fiction have an unhappy proclivity to blend. Take, for example, the events of October 16, 1929, when Staten Island police officers found a beaten and bloody Salvatore Lucania staggering along Hylan Boulevard. That Luciano survived being "taken for a ride" is such an integral part of his personal legend that no biographer can possibly avoid it. But why did it happen? And who, exactly, was responsible?

There are at least five different versions of this story, three of which are attributed to Luciano himself. The first, which he told to police at the time, was that three unknown assailants had kidnapped him from a Manhattan street corner, taped his mouth shut, then beat and stabbed him before dumping him, unconscious, near Huguenot Beach. Years later, Luciano told a different version of the story to an undercover narcotics officer. In that iteration, it was the police who had kidnapped him, seeking to learn the whereabouts of the fugitive Legs Diamond.

Other versions followed. In *The Last Testament*, Luciano tells Martin Gosch that his assailant was none other than Salvatore Maranzano, who ordered him strung up and tortured for refusing to kill Joe the Boss Masseria. An even more colorful variant of this story appears in Hank Messick's 1971 biography of Meyer Lansky and features Lansky and Bugsy Siegel shooting it out with Maranzano's henchmen to rescue Lucky. Then there's the story told by a former FBI agent in which Lucky is kidnapped by different police officers for the crime of dating one of their daughters.

What's a writer to do? I went with the Legs Diamond version of the story, both because it seems the most plausible—Diamond was, after all, the object of an intensive manhunt at the time—and because it was corroborated by Frank Costello in George Wolf and Joseph DiMona's 1974 biography, *Frank Costello: Prime Minister of the Underworld*.

Here's another example. There are many different versions of the events of April 15, 1931, when Giuseppe Masseria was gunned down at Nuova Villa Tammaro, ending the Castellammarese war and installing Salvatore Maranzano, however briefly, as the Mafia's undisputed Boss of Bosses. And while it is generally agreed that Lucky was the man behind that murder, some versions have him actually pulling the trigger, while others have him hidden in the men's restroom when the shooting occurs. Still others have him many miles away.

Nearly all versions of the story, however, agree on one aspect: that the murder occurred during a card game that had followed a sumptuous multicourse meal. After all, Joe the Boss was a legendary glutton, the murder occurred at approximately three twenty P.M., and Nuova Villa Tammaro was reputed to be one of his favorite restaurants. In *The Last Testament*, the meal was "antipasto, spaghetti with red clam sauce, lobster Fra Diavolo, [and] a quart of Chianti." *The Luciano Story* tells us that "from antipasto to zabaglione, everything had been as delicious as the Old Country." In *Boardwalk Gangster*—billed as "the true story" of "the real Lucky Luciano"—the meal was "spaghetti with red clam sauce and lobster, all washed down with some Tuscan red wine."

There's only one problem with each of these accounts. In Masseria's autopsy report, dated April 16, 1931, medical examiner G. W. Ruger confirms that the victim's stomach was "practically empty," containing "about 2 ounces of thin, greenish bile."

You get the point. The fact is, Luciano's was a life lived mostly in secret and chronicled mostly in hindsight. Where the truth ends and the myths begin, none can honestly say. And while I've tried my best to sift the chaff from the wheat, even I couldn't resist that damned lobster Fra Diavolo.

Author's Note

★ ★ ★

I'll conclude with some well-deserved thanks. First, to all the authors whose work I've previously mentioned, and especially to Littleton and Crichton, from whose Levy biography certain quotations appearing in chapters 14 and 26 of *Tom & Lucky*—those of Saul Rogers, Arthur Hendrickson, Margaret Levy, and Martin Littleton—are taken. Second, to Elise "CeCe" Levy, not only for allowing me access to her father's files but also for sharing with me an invaluable series of autobiographical essays that George Morton Levy dictated during his lifetime. Third, to Sally Dickinson of the Watkinson Library at Trinity College in Hartford, Connecticut, for facilitating my access to the *People v. Luciano* trial and appellate records, which were gifts to the college by Trinity alumnus Philip J. McCook. Fourth, to L.A. super-lawyer Steven G. Madison for his guidance on certain questions of criminal procedure. Fifth, to Darienne Oaks—the granddaughter of George Morton Levy—for her assistance with a few odd matters of Levy family history. Sixth, to my wife, Lynda Larsen; my brother Dan Greaves, and my niece Katie Thomas Greaves for reading *Tom & Lucky* while still in manuscript and providing much-valued feedback.

Finally, I would like to thank my literary agent (and Sicilian translator), Antonella Iannarino of the David Black Agency, and my intrepid editor, Anton Mueller of Bloomsbury USA—along with Rachel Mannheimer, Marie Coolman, Laura Phillips, Helen Garnons-Williams, Maureen Klier, and the rest of the Bloomsbury team, both here and abroad—for their input and their ongoing faith and support, without which this book would not have been possible.

Grazie a tutti.

C. Joseph Greaves
Cortez, Colorado

A Note on the Author

C. Joseph Greaves is a former L.A. trial lawyer now living in Colorado. His first novel, *Hard Twisted*, was a finalist for the Oklahoma Book Award in Fiction and was named Best Historical Novel in the SouthWest Writers' International Writing Contest, in which Greaves was also honored with the grand prize Storyteller Award. Writing as Chuck Greaves, he is a Shamus Award finalist for his Jack MacTaggart series of legal/detective mysteries.

THROUGH THE
Z⊗MBIE GLASS

Books by Gena Showalter
available from Harlequin TEEN

The White Rabbit Chronicles

(in reading order)
ALICE IN ZOMBIELAND
THROUGH THE ZOMBIE GLASS

The Intertwined Novels

(in reading order)
INTERTWINED
UNRAVELED
TWISTED

THROUGH THE
ZⓍMBIE GLASS
GENA SHOWALTER

Recycling programs
for this product may
not exist in your area.

ISBN-13: 978-0-373-21077-0

THROUGH THE ZOMBIE GLASS

Copyright © 2013 by Gena Showalter

Printed in U.S.A.

To three bright lights in my life—Shane, Shonna and Michelle

"THE BATTLE LINE BETWEEN
GOOD AND EVIL RUNS
THROUGH THE HEART
OF EVERY MAN."
—ALEKSANDR SOLZHENITSYN

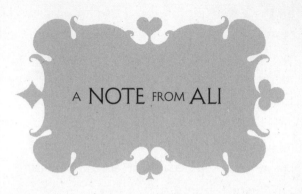

A NOTE FROM ALI

Where should I begin?

With travesty? Heartache?

No. I don't want to begin with where I am now.

I don't want to end that way, either.

We'll start with this. A truth. Everything around us is subject to change. Today is cold. Tomorrow, heat will come. Flowers bloom, then wither. Those we love, we can grow to hate. And life...life can be perfect one minute and in shambles the next. I learned that lesson the hard way when my parents and beloved little sister died in a car crash, shattering every corridor of my heart.

I've done my best to weld the pieces back together, but—*tick, tock.* Another change.

A change that cost me everything.

The respect of my friends. My new home. My purpose. My pride.

My boyfriend.

And it's my fault. I can blame no one else.

One mistake gave birth to a thousand others.

I knew there were monsters out there. Zombies. I knew they weren't the mindless beings movies and books portrayed them to be. They exist in spirit form, unseen to the ungifted eye. They're fast, determined and, at times, smart. They hunger for the source of life. *Our* spirits.

I know, I know. That's laughable, right? Invisible creatures determined to feast on humans from the inside out? Please. But it's true. I know, because I became an all-you-can-eat buffet—and offered my friends as dessert.

Now I'm not just fighting the zombies. I'm fighting to save the life I've grown to love.

I will succeed.

Tick, tock.

It's time.

BEGIN AT THE BEGINNING

A few months earlier

More and more I'd been dreaming about the crash that killed my parents and younger sister. I relived the moments as our car flipped end over end. The sounds of metal crunching into pavement. The stillness when everything was over, and I was the only one awake…maybe the only one alive.

I'd struggled to free myself from the seat belt, desperate to help little Emma. Her head had been twisted at such an odd angle. My mother's cheek had been slashed open like a Christmas ham, and my father's body had been thrown out of the car. Panic had made me stupid, and I'd hit my head on a sharp piece of metal. Darkness had swallowed me whole.

But in my dreams, I watched my mother blink open her eyes. She was disoriented at first, moaning in pain and trying to make sense of the chaos around her.

Unlike me, she had no problem with her seat belt, freeing herself and turning, her gaze landing on Emma. Tears began to rain down her cheeks.

She looked at me and gasped, reaching out to place a trembling hand on my leg. A river of warmth seemed to rush through me, strengthening me.

"Alice," she shouted, shaking me. "Wake up—"

I jolted upright.

Panting, my body dotted with perspiration, I scanned my surroundings. I saw walls of ivory and gold, painted in swirling patterns. An antique dresser. A furry white rug on the floor. A mahogany nightstand, with a Tiffany lamp perched next to a photo of my boyfriend, Cole.

I was in my new bedroom, safe.

Alone.

My heart slammed against my ribs as though trying to burst free. I forced the dream to the back of my mind and moved to the edge of the bed to peer out the large bay window and find a sense of calm. Despite the gorgeousness of the view—a garden teeming with bright, lush flowers that somehow thrived in the cool October weather—my stomach twisted. Night was in full bloom, and so were the creepies.

Fog that had brewed on the horizon for hours had finally spilled over, gliding closer and closer to my window. The moon was round and full, set ablaze with orange and red, as if the surface had been wounded and was bleeding.

Anything was possible.

Zombies were out tonight.

My friends were out there, too, fighting the creatures

without me. I hated myself for falling asleep at such a critical time. What if a slayer needed my help? Called me?

Who was I kidding? No one would call, no matter how badly I was needed.

I stood and paced the room, cursing the injuries that kept me tucked inside. So I'd been sliced from hip to hip a few weeks ago. So what? My stitches had been removed and the flesh was already scarring.

Maybe I should just arm up and head out. I'd rather save someone I love and risk another life-threatening injury than do nothing and stay out of harm's way. But…I didn't know where the group had gone, and more than that, if I did manage to track them down, Cole would freak. He would be distracted.

Distraction killed.

Dang it. I would do as I'd been told and wait.

Minutes stretched into hours as I continued to pace, a sense of unease growing sharper with every second that passed. Would everyone come back alive? We'd lost two slayers in the past month alone. None of us were prepared to lose another.

The hinges on my door squeaked.

Cole slipped inside the room and threw the lock, ensuring that no one would bust in on us. Relief plucked the claws right out of the unease, and I thrilled.

He was here. He was okay.

He was mine.

His gaze landed on me, and I shivered, waiting for a vision…hoping for one.

Since the day we'd met, we'd experienced a small glimpse

of the future the first time our eyes locked on any given day. We'd seen ourselves making out, fighting zombies and even relaxing in a swing. Today, like almost every day since my stabbing, I experienced nothing but crushing disappointment.

Why had the visions stopped?

Deep down, I suspected one of us had built up some sort of emotional wall—and I knew it hadn't been me.

I was too entranced by him.

Always he threw off enough testosterone to draw the notice of every girl within a ten-mile radius. Though he was only seventeen years old, he seemed far older. He had major experience on the battlefield, had fought in the human/zombie war since he could walk. He had experience with girls, too. Maybe *too* much experience. He knew just what to say…how to touch…and we melted. I'd never met anyone like him. I doubted I ever would again.

He wore all black, like a phantom of the night. Inky hair stuck out in spikes, with leaves and twigs intertwined in the strands. He hadn't bothered to clean his face, so his cheeks were streaked with black paint, dirt and blood.

So. Danged. Hot.

Violet eyes almost otherworldly in their purity shuttered, becoming unreadable, even as his lips compressed into a hard, anguished line. I knew him, and knew this was his let's-just-burn-the-world-to-the-ground-and-call-it-good face.

"What are you doing out of bed, Ali?"

I ignored the question as well as the harshness of his tone, understanding that both sprang from a place of deep con-

cern for me. "What's wrong?" I asked. "What happened out there?"

Silent, he disarmed, dropping daggers, guns, magazines of ammo and his personal favorite, a crossbow. He'd come to me first, I realized, not even bothering to stop at his house.

"Were you bitten?" I asked. Suffering? Zombie bites left a burning toxin behind. Yes, we had an antidote, but the human body could take only so much before it broke down.

"I saw Haun," he finally responded.

Oh, no. "Cole, I'm so sorry." A while back, Haun had been killed by zombies. The fact that Cole had seen him again meant only one thing. Haun had risen from his grave as the enemy.

"I suspected it would happen, but I wasn't ready for the reality of it." Cole's shirt was the next to go.

The blade-sharp cut of his body always stole my breath, and now was no exception, regardless of the horror of our conversation. I drank him in—the delightfully wicked nipple ring, the sinewy chest and washboard abs covered with a plethora of tattoos. Every design, every word, meant something to him, from the names of the friends he'd lost in the war to the depiction of the grim reaper's scythe. Because that was what he was. A zombie killer.

He was total bad boy—the dangerous guy monsters feared finding in *their* closets.

And he was closing the distance between us. I buzzed with anticipation, expecting him to draw me into his arms. Instead, he bypassed me to fall onto the bed and cover his face with scabbed hands.

"I ashed him tonight. Ended him forever."

"I'm so sorry." I eased beside him and brushed my fingers over his thigh, offering what comfort I could. I knew he understood that he hadn't actually ashed Haun, or even the ghost of Haun. The creature he'd fought hadn't had Haun's memories or his personality. It had had his face and nothing more. His body had simply been a shell for unending hunger and malevolence.

"You had to do it," I added. "If you'd let him go, he would have come back for you and our friends, and he would have done his best to destroy us."

"I know, but that doesn't make it any easier." He released a shuddering sigh.

I looked him over more intently. He had angry cuts on his arms, chest and stomach. Zombies were spirits, the source of life—or afterlife in their case—and had to be fought by other spirits. That was why, to engage, we had to force ours out of our bodies, like a hand being pulled out of glove. And yet, even though we left our bodies behind, frozen in place, the two were still connected. Whatever injury one received, the other received, as well.

I padded to the bathroom, wet several washrags and grabbed a tube of antibiotic cream.

"Tomorrow I start training again," I said as I tended him, distracting us both.

He glared up at me through lashes so thick and black he looked as if he wore eyeliner. "Tomorrow's Halloween. All of us have the day and night off. And by the way, I'm taking you to a costume party at the club. I'm thinking we'll stick with the whole battered and bruised theme and go as a naughty nurse and even naughtier patient."

My first outing in weeks would be a date with Cole. *Yes, please.* "I think you'll make a very sexy naughty nurse."

"I know," he said without missing a beat. "Just wait till you see my dress. Slutty doesn't even begin to describe. And you will, of course, require a sponge bath."

Don't laugh. "Promises, promises." I tsked, then tried to continue more seriously. "But I never mentioned hunting." Too many people would be out, and some would be dressed as zombies. At first glance, we might not be able to tell the real deal from the fake. "I only mentioned training. You *are* working out tomorrow morning, aren't you?" He always did.

He ignored my question, saying, "You're not ready."

"No, *you're* not ready for me to be ready, but it's happening whether you like it or not."

He scowled at me, dark and dangerous. "Is that so?"

"Yes." Not many people stood up to Cole Holland. Everyone at our school considered him a full-blown predator, more animal than human. Feral. Dangerous.

They weren't wrong.

Cole wouldn't hesitate to tear into someone—anyone—for the slightest offense. Except me. I could do what I wanted, say what I wanted, and he was charmed. Even when he was scowling. And it was strange, definitely something I wasn't used to—having power over someone else—but I'd be lying if I claimed not to like it.

"Two problems with your plan," he said. "One, you don't have a key to the gym. And two, there's a good chance your instructor will suddenly become unreachable."

Since *he* was my instructor, I took his words as the gentle threat they were and sighed.

When I'd first joined his group, he'd thrown me into the thick of battle without hesitation. I think he'd trusted his ability to protect me from any kind of threat more than he'd trusted my skills.

Then I'd proved myself and he'd backed off.

Then he'd accidentally stabbed me.

Yep. Him. He'd aimed for the zombie snarling and biting at him; I'd stepped in to help, and, with a single touch, ashed the only thing shielding my body from his strike. Cole had yet to forgive himself.

Maybe that was why he'd built a wall.

Maybe he needed a reminder of just how wily I could be.

"Cole," I said huskily, and his eyelids lowered to half-mast.

"Yes, Ali."

"This." A slow smile spread as I circled my hands around his ankles—and jerked. He slid off the bed and thumped to the floor.

"What the hell?"

I leaped on top of him, pinning his shoulders with my knees. The action caused the scar on my stomach to throb, but I masked my wince with another smile. "What are you going to do now, Mr. Holland?"

He watched me intently, amusement darkening his irises. "I think I'll just enjoy the view." He gripped me by the waist, squeezed just enough to make sure he had my full attention. "From this angle, I can see your—"

Choking back a laugh, I took a swing at him.

"Shorts," he finished, catching my hand just before impact. I wasn't given the chance to tug free. He rolled me over, stretched my arms over my head and held me down.

Tricky slayer.

"What are you going to do now, Miss Bell?"

Stay just like this and enjoy? I could smell the pine and soap of his scent. Could hear the rasp of our breath intermingling. Could feel the heat and hardness of his body pressing against me.

"What would you like me to do?" I met his gaze, and the air around us thickened, charged with electricity.

Would he touch me?

I wanted him to touch me.

"You're not ready for what I'd like you to do." He searched my face as he reached between us, his actions belying his words...*please, please*...until he slowly pushed the hem of my tee over my navel, revealing every inch of damaged flesh.

He looked me over, and my stomach quivered. Heck, all of me quivered. He crawled down, down, and kissed one edge of the wound, then the other, and a moan left me.

Please. More.

But a moment passed, then another, and he merely returned to his former position, driving me crazy with his nearness but never doing anything to relieve the tension spiraling inside me.

"One more week of rest," he said, his jaw clenched as if he'd had to force the words to leave his mouth. "Doctor's orders."

I shook my head. "I'll ask Bronx and Frosty to train me."

His eyes narrowed to tiny slits. "They'll say no. I'll make sure of it."

"At first, maybe." Definitely. Everyone always followed

Cole's rules. Even other alpha males recognized a bigger, badder predator. "However, I have a secret weapon."

He arched a brow. "And what's that?"

"Sure you want to know?" I asked, rubbing my knees along his hips.

"Yes. Tell me." His tone had gone low, gruff.

My knees slid higher, higher still, and he went utterly motionless, waiting to see what I would do next. I had two options. Try to seduce him into making out with me—*the way he's looking at me…I might actually succeed this time*—or prove I wasn't out for the count.

Sometimes I hated my priorities.

I planted my feet against his shoulders and pushed with all my might. He propelled backward, catching himself on his knees.

"With you? Distraction," I purred.

Laughing, he stayed where he was and lifted my leg to place a soft kiss on my ankle. "I must be seriously disturbed, because I like when you rough me up."

Heat spilled into my cheeks. "You make me sound like some kind of he-woman."

He laughed again, and oh, it was a beautiful sound. Lately, he'd been so somber. "I also like when you blush."

"Yes, well, I'll bug Frosty and Bronx until they say yes." Apparently my inquisitive personality was *not* charming to everyone. Go figure. "They'll be so irritated by their lack of fortitude, they'll throw me around like I'm a meat bag."

"So? You'll get a boo-boo I'll have to kiss and make better. Problem, meet solution."

I swallowed a laugh of my own and had to concentrate to

adopt a stern expression. "I'll let you kiss me better—if the boo-boo is on my butt."

"Hmm. Kinky. This is a plan I can get behind… It's a very nice behind."

Tease! "Cole," I said with a pout. "You can't flirt with me like this and then do nothing about it."

"Oh, I'll do something about it." The gruff, wanting tone was back. His gaze locked on my mouth, heating with awareness. "Once you've been cleared."

So, seven more days of Cole's china-doll treatment? *Don't whimper.* "Mr. Ankh would have cleared me already if not for you and your protests." I sat up and shifted my fingers through the silk of his hair. "I'm better now. I swear!"

"No, you're finally on the road to better. But if you start training, that could slow your progress. Besides, you're mine, Ali-gator, and you're precious to me. I want you better. I *need* you better. And okay, yeah, I don't like the thought of my friends putting their hands on you."

Ali-gator? Really? I think I would have preferred something like, I don't know, cuddlecakes. Anything was better than a comparison to an overgrown lizard, right?

And had he just called me *his?*

See? Melting…

"Bronx is secretly into Reeve and Frosty is bat-crap crazy for Kat. They wouldn't try anything." And really, before Cole, no boy had *ever* tried anything with me. I had no idea what made me so irresistible to him.

"Don't care," he said, leaning forward to nuzzle my neck. "I will put my boys in the hospital if they come near you. I don't share my toys."

I had to swallow a snort. "If anyone else called me their toy, internal organs would spill."

"Agreed. Like I said, you're mine. And, Ali, I'd love to be called your anything, especially your toy. I *reeeally* want you to play with me."

Okay, I did snort. Hello, mixed signals. "I'd really like you to prove that, Cole Holland."

His response? A groan.

I sighed. There was nothing mixed about that, was there? "Back to the pimp hand you're planning to throw around." I had no doubt he could put people in the hospital—he had before—but his friends? Never. I opened my mouth to tell him so, only to gasp. He'd just bitten the cord of my shoulder, and the most delicious lance of pleasure had shot through me. *"Cole."*

"Sorry. Couldn't help myself. Had to do a little proving."

"Don't stop," I breathed. "Not this time."

"Ali," he said with another groan. "You're killing me." He stood with me in his arms and gently laid me on the bed. He stretched out next to me but didn't pull me into his side.

I swallowed a shriek of frustration. I wasn't sure if he was punishing himself for what he'd done to me or if he really was afraid he would break me. All I knew was that I missed the feel and taste of him.

I rolled toward him and rested my head on his shoulder. His skin was warm and surprisingly soft as I traced a circle around the piercing in his nipple. *Bad Ali.*

Smart Ali. His heart kicked into a faster rhythm, delighting me.

Disappointed Ali. He remained just as he was, here but set apart from me.

"When you're better," he finally said.

His ability to resist me was *so* not flattering.

"I wouldn't be able to forgive myself if I caused you any more harm," he added, and I lost my ire.

His concern for me was *beyond* flattering.

"Look, I have to help you guys in some way, King Cole." The moment the nickname left my lips, I knew I'd made a mistake. He'd embrace that one a little too tightly. "Doing nothing is *destroying* me."

He pushed out a heavy breath. "All right. Okay. You can come to the gym tomorrow morning. We'll see how you handle things."

I kissed his jaw, the shadow-beard he sported tickling my lips. "I think it's cute that you thought I was asking for permission."

"Thank you, Cole," he grumbled. He cupped the back of my neck, tilting my head. My gaze met his. "I just want to take care of you."

"You will...just as long as you keep your swords to yourself."

His eyes darkened. "That's not funny."

"What? Too soon? My near-death experience and your part in it aren't something we can joke about yet?"

"Probably not ever."

I nipped playfully at his chin. "Okay." Taking mercy on him, I changed the subject. "Will you finally tell me what's been going on these past few weeks?" Boss's orders. Busi-

ness wasn't to be discussed. "As you can see, if it's bad news, I can take it."

"Yeah. All right," he replied, his relief obvious. "To start, Kat and Frosty broke up again."

I made a mental note to contact her first thing in the morning.

"Also, Justin's sister is missing."

Justin Silverstone used to be a slayer. Then his twin sister, Jaclyn, had convinced him to switch sides and join Anima Industries; the Hazmats, we called them. They wanted to preserve the zombies for testing and studying and planned to one day use them as weapons, uncaring about the innocent lives that were lost along the way.

"She probably ran off, afraid we'd come after her," I said. She and her crew had helped bomb my grandparents' home. I owed her.

Cole nodded. "Then there's my search. We need more slayers. I know there are kids out there as confused as you used to be, unsure why they see monsters no one else can see, and they have no idea what to do about it."

"Any possibles?"

"Not yet. But two slayers from Georgia came to help us out until we've rebuilt our team."

For a while, I'd thought the zombie problem existed only in my home state of Alabama. I'd since learned differently. There were zombies all over the world. Slayers, too.

"You should have shared this info long before now. You are such a pain, Coleslaw," I said. Better, but that nickname wasn't the winner, either.

"I know, but I'm *your* pain."

And just like that, my irritation drained away. How did he do it?

"Does Mr. Ankh know you're here?" Since my grandfather had died and my grandparents' house had been torched, Nana and I had moved in with Mr. Ankh and his daughter, Reeve.

Mr. Ankh—Dr. Ankh to everyone outside his circle of trust—knew about the zombies and did all the medical work on the slayers. Reeve had no idea what was going on, and we were supposed to keep her in the dark. Or else. Her father wanted her to have as normal a life as possible.

What was normal, exactly?

"I gave Ankh's security the finger," Cole said with a twinge of pride. "He would feel the need to tell your grandmother, and I don't want to be kicked out and have to sneak back in. I just want to be with you."

"So you're planning to stay here all night and hold me, Coley Guacamole?" Ugh. I shouldn't have gone there. That one reeked.

He barked out a laugh. "I liked King Cole better."

"That's not actually a surprise."

"It just fits me so well."

"I'm sure you think so." I gave a gentle tug on his nipple ring.

"I doubt I'm the only one. And yes, I'm staying." He curled his fingers over mine, pried my grip loose and brought my knuckles to his mouth for a kiss. A second later, there was a flash of panic in his eyes. One I didn't understand

and must have misread. Because he said, "Just so you know, you can call me anything you want—just as long as you always call me."

ON YOUR MARK, GET SET—STOP!

I woke up alone, drenched in sweat and gasping for breath, another dream of the accident hovering at the back of my mind. I'd seen my mother reaching for me. Felt the unusual heat of her touch. Heard her yell at me. Then I'd watched as the zombies finished eating my dad, glided to our car and jerked her out, ready for dessert.

She'd fought against their hold, her expression panicked. She'd called my name again. "Alice! Alice!"

I'd struggled to reach her, begging the creatures not to hurt her.

Then nothing.

Now I wanted to cry.

Why was I seeing this? It hadn't happened. Not really. Had it?

Had I woken up in the car and just didn't remember? Could this be my mind's way of reminding me?

Mom *had* ended up outside, next to my dad, even though she'd been in the car when I'd lost consciousness.

"Cole," I said, patting the space next to me. I needed his arms around me, strong and sure. He would comfort me, whatever the answers.

The mattress was disappointingly cold. He was gone.

I thought…yeah, I remembered hearing him speak to me before he'd taken off.

"I'm supposed to believe you? Just like that," he'd said, his tone angry.

No, he hadn't been speaking to me. There'd been a tense pause before he'd snapped, "Stop calling me, Justin. I told you a long time ago I'm done with you. There's nothing you can do or say to change that." Another crackling pause. "No, I don't want to hear the info you've got."

I knew of only one Justin. Either Cole had been on the phone with a boy he'd sworn never to speak with again, or my mind had played tricks on me. Right now I wasn't exactly in a mind-trusting mood.

Gingerly I sat up to gaze around the room. Bright sunlight slanted through the window. The ice-blue comforter draping the four-poster bed was wrinkled, and one of the pillows was stained with flecks of black from Cole's face paint. Oops. I'd have to clean that off before I left.

His weapons were no longer piled on the floor, and neither were his clothes. In fact, the only other sign that he'd been here was the note on my nightstand.

I'm at the gym. Call me and I'll come for you. X C

Humming with sudden happiness, I brushed my teeth, showered and dressed in my winter workout clothes. I dialed his cell, and…went straight to voice mail.

"I'm awake and ready," I said. "You can come get me anytime." I didn't have a car. Or a license. Only a permit. If I didn't hear from him soon, I'd walk. The gym was at a barn a few miles away. "I hope you're prepared to have your butt handed to you."

When I hung up, I noticed there were eleven texts waiting for me. All from my best friend, Kat. I grinned as I read.

One: Frosty SUCKS!

Two: Have I mentioned Frosty sucks it raw??

Three: How do U feel about murder? 4 or against?? Before U answer, know that I have good reason!

Four: If 4, do U know good place 2 hide body??

The rest described the many ways she'd like to kill him. My favorite involved a bag of Skittles and a silk scarf.

Mmm. Skittles.

My stomach rumbled, and I set my phone on the nightstand. I'd call Kat after breakfast, when she was more likely to be awake and I was more likely to be lucid, and find out what happened. There was a good chance Frosty had simply failed to call her after the fight last night, and she'd worried. I wasn't sure how to comfort her about that. She'd made it clear the zombies weren't a topic of conversation she welcomed.

First, though, I cleaned every inch of my room. I refused to let Mr. Ankh's housekeeper do it for me. I wasn't a sponge and wasn't going to take anything for granted. I was deter-

mined to give back, somehow. Thankfully, water and hand soap removed the paint from the pillow.

"Alice."

Emma's voice.

I turned, and oh, glory, there she was. My eight-year-old sister. Her spirit anyway. What she'd taught me: death is never the end. "You're here," I said, my heart soaring. She'd visited me before, but every time felt like the first time—shocking and unreal.

She smiled at me, and I wanted so badly to hug her close and never let go. "I only have a moment."

She wore the clothes she'd died in: a pink leotard and tutu. The dark hair she'd inherited from our mother was pulled into two pigtails, swinging over her delicate shoulders. Golden eyes that had always watched me with adoration were bright.

She'd once told me she wasn't a ghost, but a witness. Ghosts—not that they existed—were spirits of the dead that retained their memories and haunted. A myth probably born from zombie sightings. Witnesses were spirits that aided.

"I wanted to warn you that you'll be seeing less of me," she said, the smile slipping. "Visiting you is becoming more difficult. *But.* If you call for me, I will find a way to reach you."

"More difficult how?" I asked, concerned for her.

"My tie to this world is fading."

Oh.

I knew what that meant. One day I was going to lose her for good.

"Don't be sad," she said. "I hate when you're sad."

I forced my features to brighten. "No matter what, I'll

know you're out there, watching over me. There's no reason to be sad."

"Exactly." Beaming, she blew me a kiss. "I love you. And seriously, don't forget to call for me if you need me." Then she was gone.

My features fell and, I was sure, dimmed. I could have curled into a ball and cried, but I refused to let myself worry about any tomorrows without her. I'd deal with her loss when it came.

Pulling my hair into a ponytail, I headed to the kitchen. I expected to find the housekeeper. Instead I found Reeve, Nana and Kat seated at the table, sipping from steaming mugs of coffee.

"—something's going on," Reeve was saying, twining a lock of dark hair around her finger. "Dad put more security cameras in both the front and backyard—and we already had a thousand to begin with! Worse, he's put up so many lamps, my blackout curtains are no longer able to do their job."

Nana and Kat shifted uncomfortably.

"Has he said anything to either of you?"

"Well…" Nana hedged. She moved her gaze through the room, as if hoping a distraction would present itself.

One did.

"Ali! You're out of bed a week early." Her chair skidded behind her as she stood. She closed the distance between us and drew me in for a hug. "I'm not sure I approve."

Kat buffed her nails and smiled, not looking at all like a girl on the verge of committing a violent crime. She did look tired, though. There were dark circles under her eyes, and her cheeks were hollowed, as if she hadn't eaten in days. "I

would have been up *two* weeks early, but we can't all have my amazing bounce-back, can we?"

I kissed Nana's cheek and returned Kat's smile. The girl had a healthy (and justifiable) ego and wasn't afraid to show it. Me? I'd always been the girl with her head ducked as she questioned her worth.

I'd faced death and won, I reminded myself—I should probably get over that.

But...just then, I kind of thought Kat was using her ego as a shield to hide her physical weakness. She suffered from degenerative kidney disease.

"What are you doing here?" I asked her. "Not that I'm not thrilled to see you. I so am." More than thrilled, actually. From the very beginning, she'd never cared what I looked like or how socially awkward I could be. She'd just accepted me and rolled. "I thought you preferred to sleep till two on weekends."

"I came to see you, naughty girl that you are. You never answer your phone or respond to my mind-blowing texts anymore. My plan was to lecture you until you promised to have your phone surgically attached to your hand, but I decided to have some coffee first."

Speaking of coffee... "I'll take that." I confiscated her mug as I eased into the seat beside her. I wouldn't allow myself to eat or drink anything from the Ankhs, which made coffee a luxury. But I didn't mind taking from my best friend.

"Hey!" A second later, she confiscated Reeve's.

"Hey," Reeve said, then confiscated Nana's.

Musical coffees.

Nana shook her head, but I could see the gleam of amusement in her eyes.

"No need for a lecture," I said to Kat, flattening my hand on my side. "There'll be no more surgeries for me."

Her features softened. "My poor, sweet Ali."

"I don't understand how you fell down our stairs and received such a life-threatening injury," Reeve said. "You're not the clumsy type, and there's nothing sharp on the railing or the floor."

"Of course she's clumsy," Kat exclaimed, covering for me as I stuttered for some type of response. "Ali could get tangled up in a cordless phone."

I nodded and tried not to look miserable—the claim was only a lie if I failed to believe it. Maybe I *was* clumsy. Once, I'd stepped into Cole's ankle trap and dangled upside down from a tree. Another time, he'd been teaching me how to work a sword and I'd nearly removed his head.

So…yeah.

"Anyway," Kat said, quickly changing the subject, "I'm sure everyone will be pleased to know we won the football game last night."

"Go, Tigers!" we said in unison, and burst into peals of laughter.

An alarm sounded from Reeve's phone. "Crap!" She jumped up. "Sorry, guys, but I've got plans for Halloween and they actually start this morning. See ya!" She raced out of the kitchen.

Nana stood. "I've got to go, too. I want to lecture that girl's father about the importance of being well informed. Oh, and, Ali, Cole called me a little while ago and told me

you were in need of a costume, but that you'd be too busy training to shop. I thought he was kidding, like some kind of Halloween joke I just didn't understand, since only yesterday he'd been so adamant about you staying in bed. But if he thinks you're ready, you're ready—and I won't ask how he reached that conclusion."

Please don't!

And Cole had actually called *Nana?* "That's sweet of you, but I don't want us to spend money on an article of clothing I'll only wear once. I can make something I already own work."

Smiling, she patted my hand. "Darling, we're not destitute. We have the insurance settlement."

"But we *are* saving for a house of our own." There were conditions for living here, and with conditions came an expiration date. I wanted Nana taken care of for the rest of her life, no surprises. In fact, I should probably find a job… though that might prove impossible, considering I would need to take time off for school and slaying.

No. There had to be a way.

"I'm getting you a costume, young lady, and that's final. I'm looking forward to this."

I sighed. "All right, but something from the thrift store will work just fine."

She kissed the top of my head and followed the same path Reeve had taken. Without agreeing, I realized too late.

My phone vibrated, and I checked the screen.

Cole McHottie (as Kat had dubbed him): I can't leave the gym 2 get U, Ali-gator, I'm sorry. But we R still on 4 2nite. I miss U

I wondered what had happened to keep him trapped at the gym.

Disappointed, I looked to Kat.

"So, where are you and Cole going?" she asked.

"Hearts, I'm sure." It was the only nightclub the slayers frequented. "Now, about your phone calls and texts. I wasn't ignoring you, I promise. It's just strange, knowing you now know what I know, yet trying to buffer you from the worst of the details."

"It's not strange. It's terrible! I hate knowing, but I've decided to girl up and finally discuss the...you-knows from now on. And just so we're clear, girling up is far better than manning up."

"Good. About the you-knows." Knowledge was power, and I wanted her safe. Always.

The housekeeper bustled into the kitchen, spotted me, and asked if she could fix me something to eat. I declined, and she loaded a tray with croissants and cappuccino to take to Mr. Ankh. The fragrance of yeast and sugar mingled, filling the room and making my mouth water.

The moment she was gone, I hopped up to wipe the crumbs from the counter. Then I grabbed the bag of bagels I'd bought with my allowance and offered one to Kat.

She shook her head. "So...I'm sure you surmised from my oh so subtle texts that Frosty and I are over. Or is it Frosty and me? I always forget. Anyway, it's for reals this time."

"What happened?" I devoured the bagel in record time, and though I craved a second one *so* bad, I resisted. The longer these lasted, the fewer I would have to buy, and the less I'd have to spend.

"Last night," she said, looking miserable, "I wasn't feeling well—not that Frosty knew that part. I asked him to stay with me, and he refused."

"When the you-knows are out, he has to fight. We all do, if we're well. It's our duty." Our privilege.

"A night off wouldn't have killed him," she grumbled.

"But it might have killed his friends. They need all the backup they can get."

She frowned at me. "Do you have to be so reasonable, tossing out such intelligent responses?"

"I'm sorry. I'll try to do better."

"Thank you."

I studied her. She was such a beautiful girl. Petite, but curvy. Fragile, yet resilient. Her mom had suffered with the same kidney disease most of her too-short life. Kat was militant about keeping her declining health from Frosty and the boys, and so far she'd succeeded.

She lived for the moment. She never held back—in words or in action. She had no desire to fade from the world, but wanted to make an impact, a difference, and go out swinging. I could help her with that.

"How would you feel about learning to defend yourself against the you-knows?" I asked. My dad had trained me to fight them before I'd possessed the ability to see them, and that training had been invaluable when my circumstances changed. Maybe Kat would see the zombies one day. Maybe she wouldn't. Either way, I could equip her to make smarter choices.

"I'd feel...great. I think."

"That's good enough for me. Cole has a gym, and it's

loaded with all the equipment we'll need. I can show you how to shoot a gun and use a bow and arrow."

She waved a hand through the air, probably trying for dismissive, but I saw the gleam of fear behind the action. "No need for that part of the training."

"You've used both weapons before?"

"No, but the unaimed weapon never misses. I'd rather stick with that method."

I rolled my eyes.

"Will Frosty be there?" She nibbled on her bottom lip as she waited for my answer.

"Maybe."

I couldn't tell whether that pleased her or upset her; the chewing never stopped. "Well, today's, like, the biggest holiday of the year, so I'll pencil you in for noon sharp tomorrow. Or maybe sometime next week would be best. Yes. Definitely next week."

"Nope. You'll pencil me in for now *and* tomorrow *and* next week. I'm not letting you put this off. We're going to turn you into a rabid, frothing-at-the-mouth fighting machine. You'll be so hard-core, you'll be able to knock Frosty on his butt as easily as breathing."

A scary kind of anticipation lit her features. "Okay, I'm in. But only because I know I'll look good with biceps. True story." She drained what remained of her coffee and slammed the mug onto the table. "Let's go before I change my mind."

I left my grandmother a note, telling her not to expect me back until after lunch and that I loved her. I thought about texting Cole, but quickly discarded the idea. I'd surprise him.

"You want to drive?" Kat asked as I made a beeline for the passenger side of her Mustang. "You have a permit."

Acid burned a path up my throat. "No thanks. You're not old enough to be my escort or whatever."

"But you need the practice."

"Another day," I hedged.

"That's what I said about training, and you shot me down."

"Do you want to reach the gym in fifteen minutes or fifteen hours?" I asked. If I had to pick between driving and bathing in manure, I'd pick the manure. Every time. "You know how slow I go."

"True." She settled behind the wheel.

"Did Frosty ever take you to Cole's gym? Not the one in his garage, but the gym several miles from his house?" The seat belt rubbed against my wound, and I shifted uncomfortably.

"Nope. According to Frosty, the high and mighty workout station for stallions—his words, not mine—is off-limits to nonslayers."

Not any longer. I gave her the address without a qualm. The boys had brought Kat into this treacherous world of secrets, and they could deal with the consequences.

As we soared down the highway, I checked the sky for the rabbit-shaped cloud Emma used to warn me about coming zombie attacks. Today, there wasn't one, and I breathed a sigh of relief.

Kat swerved to avoid hitting another car, and I yelped.

"Is my driving making you nervous?" she asked. "I mean, you're supertense. Which is silly, considering the fact that I've only been in, like, three wrecks since you were confined to

a bed, and, when you think about it, none of them were my fault. I mean, sure, I was in the wrong lane, texting, but the other drivers had plenty of time to move out of my way."

How was she still alive? "Mad Dog, you are the best worst driver I know."

She preened. "That might be the sweetest compliment anyone's ever given me. Thank you."

A car honked as she swerved across four lanes to exit the highway, and she seemed utterly oblivious. "So, you and Cole are at the stage where he's comfortable enough to call your Nana, huh?"

"I know. It's kind of weird, right, and…" Wait. I knew Cole. He'd always been a guy with a plan. A purpose. He never did anything without a rock-solid reason. But what reason could he possibly have had to—

The answer slammed into me, and I nearly liquefied in my seat. I'd lost my family, and this was my first Halloween without them. He was trying to reduce the number of memories I'd have to battle.

He didn't know that I'd never before celebrated Halloween. My dad hadn't allowed us to leave the house at night, so there had been no reason to buy a costume, and opening the door to strangers to pass out candy had been just as big a no-no.

"Yeah," I said to Kat, wishing I could crawl into Cole's arms and never leave. "We are."

"You're so lucky. My dad has never been a Frosty fan. I'm pretty sure he's only ever threatened to castrate the boy."

Had to be those serial-killer eyes. Sometimes, when Frosty looked at you, you just expected to die horribly. "Your dad still lets you guys date, though."

"Yeah, and he always will. When I was first diagnosed with defunct kidneys, he promised to let me make my own decisions and live my life the way I wanted."

Good man. "So, what have you decided to do tonight?"

"The same thing you are. And I didn't mention it before now because I didn't want you drowning in jealousy knowing I was out having the best time ever while you were still languishing in your sickbed." She gripped the steering wheel so tightly her knuckles bleached of color. "I'm trying not to be nervous. I mean, I know all the slayers will be there, but the night will be filled with all kinds of creepers, so how will I know who's dangerous and who's not?"

"You aren't able to see real zombies," I reminded her.

"That doesn't mean they aren't there. First, I told Frosty no, but then he said, 'Would I ever put you at risk, woman?' And I said, 'How would I know? You've been living a double life since we started dating.' And he said, 'You want me to apologize again, don't you?' And I said, 'Every day for the rest of your life.' He had the nerve to laugh as if I was joking."

I smothered a laugh of my own. "So…what's your costume?"

"A too-sexy-to-handle Little Red Riding Hood."

"Let me guess. Frosty's going as the Big Bad Wolf."

"What else? I have a feeling he thinks it'll be hilarious to snap his teeth at me and say, 'I'm going to eat you up, my dear.'"

Picturing it, I shook my head. "You're going to tell him to prove it. Aren't you?"

"I like that you know me so well."

She turned onto a winding gravel road nestled between rows of trees in the process of shedding their fall coats. When the trees finally gave way to fields of wheat, Cole's "work-out station for stallions" became visible—a big red barn that looked ready to topple over. Actually, the thing could withstand a military invasion.

"This place is in the middle of nowhere," Kat remarked as she eased to a stop.

"For many reasons." Slayers coming at all hours of the day and night. The sheer number of weapons kept here. The condition we sometimes left in.

There were more cars than usual in the driveway. I frowned as I stepped into the coolness of the day. Grunts, groans and even cheers seeped from the crack in the door. "Come on." I quickened my pace.

I stopped just inside the entrance and could only gape. I'd assumed Cole, and maybe the überdedicated Frosty and Bronx would be the only guys willing to forgo a country-wide day off.

Kat bumped into me and froze. "Oh, spank me," she whispered, her tone reverent.

Here they were, all of the slayers in all their glory. There was enough testosterone in the air to jump-start the deadest of hearts. Most of the boys were shirtless, displaying bronzed muscles honed from more than just weights—honed from hacking at the enemy. I saw wicked scars, sexy tattoos and piercings, and even a few house-arrest anklets.

The blond and scarily beautiful Frosty pounded his fists into a poor, defenseless punching bag. The rough-and-tumble Bronx held the thing in place, his feet planted firmly

on the floor. There was no force on earth that could move him, even one as violent as Frosty. Collins ran on a treadmill, and Cruz lifted weights.

And Cole, well, he was in the boxing ring with a girl I didn't recognize.

There was an unfamiliar boy standing at the side, watching the pair. The only other females in the room were Mackenzie—Cole's very feral ex—and Trina, a girl Kat had yet to forgive for *not* having a summer fling with Frosty.

Don't ask.

Trina waved at me, and I waved back, but my attention quickly returned to Cole. He swung lightheartedly at the unknown girl, and she ducked before straightening and swinging at him. He ducked, too, and when she swung again, he caught her fist and jerked her against the hard line of his body, effectively disabling her.

She grinned up at him, all cocky assurance and feminine wiles—and she stayed right where she was, clearly happy to be there. A boy with a girlfriend should have released her and stepped back. Although Cole stiffened, the gleam in his eyes turning granite-hard, he remained just as he was, returning her grin with one of his own.

I wasn't sure what any of that meant. I only knew I didn't like it.

Time for Pep Talk Ali. *He's trained other girls. He's even smiled at other girls. This isn't romantic. This isn't sexual.*

Of course, Downer Ali wasn't fully convinced (yes, there are many sides to me). *He didn't pick you up because he didn't want to leave this girl's side.*

I shook my head. He was mine, my toy, and I wouldn't share.

But what if he wanted me to share him?

No! Stupid insecurity. Cole wasn't like that.

"Kitten," Frosty called, sounding more than a little surprised. "How'd you find me?"

Kat lifted her chin, the picture of female pique. "Don't flatter yourself. I'm not here for you. But just so you know, I used my phenomenal detective skills, coupled with Ali's mediocre directions. No offense," she said to me.

"None taken." Mediocre was actually better than I deserved.

"Don't be that way, baby," he replied, unwinding the tape from his fists. "You know I would have given you a ride on the Frosty Express. You just had to ask."

Bronx rolled his eyes. Several of the other guys groaned.

Cole's attention arrowed in my direction. Our gazes locked, and guilt filled those violet irises.

Guilt? Why guilt? Whatever the answer, it couldn't be good.

I will not stomp into that ring.

I will not pull the pair apart.

I will not beat them both into pulp.

He set the girl away from him. Once again I found myself waiting and hoping for a vision. I was back on my feet. Things should go back to normal. But a moment passed, then another.

Normal remained at bay.

A dash of dread joined a pinch of jealousy, a recipe for trouble.

The new guy whistled under his breath, and my attention shifted to him. Our gazes collided. A second later, the world washed away, just as I'd wanted it to do with Cole—

—we were in my bedroom, standing beside my bed. No, we were lying on my bed. I'd just pushed him down. I tilted his head with one hand and pulled at his clothes with the other. Then I licked my way down his throat. I was making strange little growling noises, as if I'd never enjoyed a taste so much and had to have more—

"—Ali!" Cole shouted.

I blinked, and the vision evaporated.

Cole appeared, his features tense. "What just happened?"

"Dude," Frosty said to the new guy. "Your brain just checked out for a bit. I haven't seen anything like that since Cole first met Al—and uh, yeah, never mind."

New Guy stared at me, looking suspicious and angry.

I stumbled back a few steps. I couldn't believe I'd just mind-cheated on Cole. Like, big-time.

"Cole asked a good question," New Guy croaked. "What just happened?"

So he'd had the vision, too. *No. No, no, no.* What did that mean? That strong of a connection had never happened with anyone but Cole. Why here? Why now? Why *this* guy?

"I have a better question," the new girl said with a sweet Southern drawl. "Will someone please introduce me to the newcomers?"

I had to make sure the vision never came true. It *couldn't* come true. It would mean Cole and I were over. It would mean the new life I'd carved for myself had crashed and burned.

A muscle ticked in Cole's jaw. "Veronica, meet Ali. Ali, Veronica. She's one of the slayers from Atlanta. Ali's friend is Kat."

"My girl," Frosty added, proudly thumping his chest.

"In your dreams," Kat replied.

They launched into a heated argument.

"Veronica is another of Cole's exes," Mackenzie piped up.

Oh, good glory, no!

"Not just any ex," Veronica added, offering me a grin as sweet as her voice. "I'm his favorite."

I stiffened, waiting for Cole to say the words *Actually, Ali is my favorite—and she's not an ex.* He didn't.

"Nice to meet you," I whispered, fighting panic.

Once I hadn't thought there was a girl more beautiful than Mackenzie. Now I knew how wrong I'd been. Veronica was. By far. She had perfectly tanned skin, dark glossy hair that was iron-board straight and fell to her shoulders and light green eyes.

Mackenzie had dark hair, though hers was curly, and dark green eyes. Put the three of us side by side, and you wouldn't have to ask who didn't belong. I had wavy hair so pale it could have been classified as old-granny white, and eyes so blue they bordered on freaky.

One of Veronica's perfect brows lifted. "So you're the infamous Ali Bell, huh? The girl with abilities no one can explain."

I could see the Blood Lines we poured around our homes, a mix of chemicals the zombies couldn't bypass. My body sometimes became a living flame, ashing every zombie I touched in seconds, while other slayers could only light their

hands and needed several minutes to achieve the same results. I could sometimes see into the future.

I wasn't sure why I could do these things, or what made
me different. My slaying genes were no more special than
anyone else's.

"Yes," I said. Cole wouldn't look at me. Why wouldn't
he look at me? "That's me."

Veronica's head tilted to the side as she scrutinized me
more intently. "Did you use one of those abilities on my
friend?"

I stuttered for a response, but came up empty.

"So what if she did?" Kat called, always my backup. "She's
got the boss man wrapped around her little finger. She can
do what she wants, to whomever she wants."

How much did I love that girl?

Venom leaked into Veronica's sweetness. "No one wraps
Cole Holland around their finger."

Cole left both comments alone as he hopped out of the
ring. "Later, Ronny. Practice without me."

Ronny? He had an affectionate nickname for Mackenzie,
too. Kenze, he sometimes called her. I hated both.

He stalked to an open treadmill, motioned me over and
pushed a few buttons. "Before you hit the ring, you need
to build your stamina back up. Do not—I repeat—do not
overwork yourself."

I closed the distance between us. "You're right about the
stamina, and I can tell you I have no plans to overwork myself, but first we need to talk."

Still he refused to look at me. "Clearly, you had a vision
with Gavin."

Gavin. The name of the boy I'd just mind–molested. "Y-yes. But that's not what I want to talk about. This Veronica girl—"

"What did you see?" he said.

"I, well, uh…" I couldn't tell him, and I wouldn't lie. So, where did that leave me? "Does it really matter? It won't come true." I wouldn't let it.

"It matters. It will come true. And we both know it." Cole walked away without another word—without ever looking back at me.

I watched him until he disappeared inside the locker room, my heart creating a staccato beat in my chest. Veronica— Ronny—followed him. She paused at the door, and *she* did look back at me.

To smirk.

CAN'T GO BACK TO YESTERDAY

While Kat and I had run the treadmills side by side, and I'd tried not to worry about the vision with Gavin and Cole's behavior before and after, Nana had been out buying me a big, puffy blue gown. *Not* from the thrift store. The shiny monstrosity had a lacy corset top, stripes on the skirt and a black hat to top things off.

I wasn't sure what I was supposed to be—other than a Southern belle magician on crack.

Normally, I wouldn't leave the house at night wearing anything with colors. And never anything this fantastical. I liked to blend with the shadows. Needed to. Tonight, however, I was making an exception.

I wanted Cole to see me in something other than the tee and shorts I'd sported the past few weeks, and the workout clothes from this morning. I wanted his eyes to light up, and for him to spend the night complimenting me, unable to

keep his hands off me. We'd dance. We'd laugh. He'd kiss me. I'd kick myself for worrying about him and Veronica-slash-Ronny.

We weren't allowed to fight tonight, but I wrapped a utility belt around my thigh anyway, my daggers hanging from the attached sheaths. I never left home without them.

I wondered what costume Cole would be wearing. He hadn't said. Well, other than the naughty nurse, but I knew that had been a joke.

I stepped into the dress, hooked everything together and studied myself in the mirror. Not bad. Quite fancy. I wished my parents were here to see me. They'd—

I cut off that thought before it could fully form. I'd cry.

Something warm and wet trickled down my cheek. Great. I was already crying.

My cell phone chirped, signaling a text had just come in. I wiped the tears away with the back of my hand.

Cole McHottie: Sorry, Ali, but making plans w/U was a mistake. I need a break. Stay in & we'll talk 2morrow

I had to read the words three times before reality set in. He needed a freaking break? Seriously?

From what? I wanted to scream. And what, exactly did "need a break" mean?

My anger and disappointment were as sharp as a blade.

Me: WHY? What's going on w/you? Respect me enough 2 talk 2 me! Apparently that's how relationships WORK.

A minute passed. Two, three. He didn't respond.

I threw my phone across the room, and then had to rush over to make sure I hadn't cracked the screen.

What the heck was he planning to do on this "break"?

And whom was he going to do it with?

This can't be happening.

My cell phone chirped. Heart racing, I checked the screen.

Mad Dog: Where are U?

Me, pressing the keys a little too forcefully: Home.

Mad Dog: U ditched Cole??

Me: No. He ditched me.

Mad Dog: UH, HE'S HERE. Just walked in.

Wait, wait, wait. He'd meant he needed a break from *me?*

Yeah. He must have. He had to know Kat would contact me. He had to know I would find out he'd gone to Hearts without me.

He just didn't care.

I trembled as I typed What's he doing?

Mad Dog: He's talking w/Lucas, Veronica & that hobag Trina & get this: he's wearing a costume that says he's a bad mofo—meaning, he's not in costume.

Veronica again.

Me, grinding my teeth: He told me he needed a break from me.

Mad Dog: WHAT? Oh, I'll give him a break—in both of his legs!! 1st, of course, I'll spy.

For the next hour, I received nearly fifty texts from Kat.

He's talking w/Frosty now.

Just came out of shadows w/Justin S—what's up w/THAT?? Altho, he just had Frosty kick JS out of club & it wasn't pretty (4 JS).

Just rubbed his knuckles in2 Veronica's hair. She laughed, & I almost punched her teeth down her throat (don't 4get my fighting lesson 2morrow!).

Handed hobag Trina a drink.

Handed Lucas a drink.

Talking heatedly w/Gavin.

Walking away from Gavin (I hate the C-man right now, I really do, but he sure does have a nice butt).

Telling me 2 stop following him.

Telling me he knows what I'm doing & getting ticked when I ignore him.

Walking away as I flip him off.

Telling Frosty 2 control me (like that's really possible).

Becoming more agitated by the second, I stomped downstairs. I trusted Cole; sometimes I trusted him more than I trusted myself. But that didn't mean I was going to stay here and let him take a "break" without talking to me about it.

Nana was at the front door, handing out the last of the candy to a ghost, a cowboy and a Smurf.

"Nana," I said as soon as the door was shut. "This is probably the first time in history a teenage girl will pose this

question to her grandmother, but, will you drive me to a nightclub? Cole's there," I rushed to assure her. "And Frosty and Kat."

She frowned at me. "I thought Cole was picking you up."

"I thought so, too," I said a little bitterly.

"What about the—" her voice lowered to a frightened whisper "—the creatures?"

"You don't have to worry. To my knowledge, they aren't out tonight. And even if they do make an appearance, your car is protected with a Blood Line. They can't get to you."

Her smile was sad and affectionate at the same time. "I wasn't worried about me, dear, but my inability to help you."

Oh. "Nana, it's my job to protect *you.*"

The sadness drained from her, leaving only the affection. "No, that's not how things are supposed to be, but we won't get into that tonight. Will there be drinking at this club?"

I wouldn't lie to her. "Yes, but I won't be doing any and neither will Cole." Alcohol impaired judgment, and he took his responsibilities as leader seriously. Me? I'd watched alcoholism destroy my dad and was determined to avoid a similar fate.

"Well, I did buy you that..." She motioned to my dress.

What adjective was she looking for? Ginormous? Unforgettable? Behemoth?

"...unique costume," she finished, "and I want you to be able to show it off. You look so beautiful."

"Thank you. But, uh, what am I supposed to be, exactly?"

"Alice in Wonderland, silly. And you're supposed to give the hat to Cole so he can be your Mad Hatter."

"So you'll take me?"

She sighed, nodded. "I'll take you."

I threw my arms around her. "Thank you, thank you, and thousand times thank you!"

Fifteen minutes later, I was stepping out of her car, and she was driving away. I approached the club's entrance and gave the guards at the door Cole's name. They let me inside without a hitch—if you didn't count the people in line desperate to get in, complaining about my lack of wait.

Multicolored strobe lights flashed, and smoke wafted through the air. There were people everywhere, each in costume. For the girls, there was clearly a theme: slutty. A slutty devil. A slutty fairy. A slutty witch. I felt seriously overdressed. For the guys, there was no rhyme or reason. A shirt made out of cardboard. A toga with pictures of grinning waffles. Clown trousers paired with riding boats. Loud music blared, fueling the frantic motions of the dancers. I navigated up the stairs to the VIP lounge, the width of my skirt only tripping three people. I considered the low number of casualties a major win.

I scanned the top floor and saw all the faces I'd seen at the gym, plus a few extras.

Where was Cole?

Mackenzie Love caught my eye. Wearing a skimpy black dress with colorful peacock feathers stretching over her shoulders, she strutted over. "Well, well. Ali Bell. I'd like to tell you how awesome you look, and if I can figure out a way to sound sincere, I will. What *is* that thing?"

My cheeks flashed white-hot with embarrassment. "You can't guess?" I asked, using a scathing tone that suggested she was an idiot. "Wow. How sad for you."

She paled and stomped away.

"New drinking game, everyone," the new guy, Gavin, called. Blond and handsome—and dressed as a pimp—he was surrounded by a bevy of hot brunette vampires. "Anytime someone speaks, down a shot!"

Cheers abounded.

"And meanwhile, if anyone wants a free make-out session," one of the vampires shouted, "I'm giving them away."

More cheers as a laughing Gavin kissed her.

Then he kissed the girl next to her. He used tongue with both.

I watched, reeling. For once, a vision just had to be wrong. There was no way I'd be into a guy like him. He was beautiful, yes. I'd give him that. But no. Just no.

"Ali!" Kat rushed over and threw her arms around me. She had to be the cutest Little Red Riding Hood I'd ever seen. Her barely there dress was red, black and white, and hugged all of her curves. The tulle skirt flared at the waist and stopped a few inches below her panty line. Long white socks stretched to her knees. "You made it!"

Before I could respond, Cole stalked past us, grabbed my hand and tugged me away from her.

I tossed her a he's-going-to-get-it-now glance. She gave me a thumbs-up before Cole pulled me into a shadowed corner, and I lost sight of her. He crowded me against the wall, his arms at my temples, caging me in. His heat and scent surrounded me, drugged me.

Oh, no. I wasn't going to melt this time.

"What are you doing here?" he demanded.

How dare *he* use that tone with *me?* "I am so mad at you," I said, beating at his chest.

His aggressive stance softened in the slightest degree. "I know. And you have every right to be."

"You ditched me. You want a break from me."

"Yes. No." He scrubbed a hand down his face. "Not from you. You don't understand."

"Of course I don't! Moron! You haven't explained it to me. You ignored my text."

He glared at me, his anger heating back up. "I wanted to be with you, I did, but I couldn't not come here since I'm the D.D."

"And you couldn't bring me with you? Because, and I quote, making plans with me was a mistake?"

"It was. I don't want you here because I know…"

"What?" I demanded when he paused. I hit him again.

"Gavin is here, all right?" He flashed his teeth in a scowl. "I don't want you around him, okay? Get it now? I need a break from the jealousy. As long as you're near him, I can't get past it."

How could I want to slap him and kiss him at the same time?

But then, I already knew the answer. I'd been battling the green-eyed monster, too. "I promise you have no reason to be jealous."

His shoulders drooped. "I know that, in theory, and I'm sorry for the way I've acted. I've never felt this way, and I'm not handling it well. If you have another vision with him…"

I slid my hands to the nape of his neck and toyed with the ends of his hair. "It wouldn't make a difference. My feelings

won't change. But I guess we need to talk about what I saw, even though I'd rather forget it."

"It's bad, isn't it?" he croaked.

I nodded, suddenly unable to speak.

"Then I'm not ready."

He faced monsters on a daily basis, but this was too much for him? *Oh, Cole. What am I going to do with you?* "Will you trust me, then? Trust my feelings for you?"

A moment passed before he nodded. It was a stiff acceptance, but an acceptance all the same.

I smiled at him.

He smiled back. His gaze raked over me, and his eyelids became heavy, staying at half-mast. "You look edible, by the way. You have no idea how badly I want under that skirt." His voice dipped huskily as he added, "I wish I had time to prove it."

Oh.

My.

"Nana said the hat is for you. I'm Alice in Wonderland, and you're the Mad Hatter."

With a laugh, he took the hat and settled it on his head.

"So, what are you doing that you don't have time to try and get under my skirt?" I moved my palms to measure the heavy beat of his heart.

His features closed up shop, displaying zero emotion. "*You* will just have to trust *me*."

A thousand questions sprang to instant life. I ignored them all. As his tone implied, I couldn't ask him to trust me about the vision if I couldn't extend him the same courtesy about this. Whatever "this" was. Besides, he could have lied and

made up an excuse for his behavior. He hadn't. He wasn't that kind of guy. He gave truth, or he gave nothing. I'd always liked that about him.

"Do you have a few minutes to spare?" I asked softly.

He fisted two handfuls of my hair, his grip hard and unyielding, holding me still for his perusal. "For you?" The panic I'd noticed last night returned for one second, two, before he gave me the softest of kisses and whispered, "Anything."

"Yo, Cole," a voice said. A head peeked around the corner. "I'm taking off with Kira and Jane and—"

I turned to look, and my gaze locked with Gavin's.

The world disappeared. Cole disappeared—

—there was only here, now, and Gavin, and we were back inside my bedroom, on my bed, my body on top of his. One of his hands was in my hair. The other was sliding down my back to cup my bottom and urge me to grind against him, hard…harder—

—a low snarl snapped me back to the present. To Cole. The growl had come from him.

"Yeah, uh, I'll just be going," Gavin said, and beat feet.

Cole and I stayed where we were for a long moment, silent.

"What I saw with him…" I began, fighting for calm. I'd said it wouldn't make a difference, and now had to pray I was right. "It was the first vision all over again." Only a bit more vivid.

"Don't tell me," he lashed out. "Not tonight."

"Cole—"

"Not tonight, Ali. Please." With that, he walked away from me for the second time that day.

He watched me from afar the rest of the night, but at least he continued to wear the hat.

As the days wore on, I had to admit my relationship with Cole was unraveling.

Every day he grew a little more distant with me. Anytime I tried to talk to him about Gavin and the vision, he would shut me down, saying, "I can't do this right now."

I was trying to trust him like he'd asked. I really was. But the hot-and-cold treatment was wearing me down. Even though he'd always been lavish with his praise of me, I hadn't spent the past few weeks mutating into a secure person. Especially with matters of the heart.

Should I call him again?

What was considered good girlfriend behavior? What delved into Stalkerville?

I knew something other than the vision was bugging him. The few times I'd seen him, his features had been withdrawn and pinched. And what had the panic been about? But again, when I tried to talk to him about it, he shut me down and walked away.

I wasn't sure how much longer I could wait for an explanation about his odd behavior without banging on my chest like a gorilla and screaming.

Eventually, he stopped returning my calls. His replies to my texts were short and abrupt—if he bothered to reply at all. He stopped coming by Mr. Ankh's, and he stopped working out at his own gym.

Maybe Gavin had told him about the vision, and he'd decided to wash his hands of me?

Oh, good glory. No! I bet that was it, though. Dang it! The admission should have come from me. I should have grown a pair of lady balls and forced Cole to listen to me. Then I could have assured him I would rather die than allow my lips to touch any part of that he-slut's body.

I hadn't seen the Georgian slayer since Halloween, and I had no idea what would happen the next time we locked eyes. Part of me didn't want to know. Part of me *needed* to know. If nothing happened, I could assure Cole wires had somehow gotten crossed—twice, yes—and I was meant to lick and grind on *him*.

What should I do next?

I couldn't talk to Kat about this. She had her own problems, and I wouldn't add to them.

I couldn't talk to Reeve. I couldn't risk a slipup.

I couldn't talk to Nana. She'd just lost her husband.

I couldn't even talk to Emma. To her, kissing was gross.

I missed the days when I'd thought the same. I was alone in this.

A bell rang, loud and shrill, signaling the end of class. I stood on shaky legs and gathered my notebook and pencil. Earlier today I'd met the new principal of Asher High, an older black man with kind eyes—a nice change considering the last one had been the queen of ice-cold hearts. I'd turned in all the work the teachers had sent to my sickbed. I was finally caught up.

"Glad to have you back and dominating my assignments, Ali Bell," called Ms. Meyers as I strode from the room.

That was right. In my turmoil over Cole, I'd lost my excitement for my grade. I palmed my cell and texted Nana.

Got an A on my Creative Writing paper! I'd been working on my own at home, and it was nice to know the time and attention I'd put into everything had paid off.

A few seconds later, her reply came in. WTF an A!

I blinked, sure I was misreading. But no, the letters didn't change.

Me: Nana, do U know what WTF means??

Her: Of course, silly. It means "well, that's fantastic."

I swallowed a laugh. I luv U!

Her: Love you, too! Now get back to work.

I stuffed my things in my locker and made my way to the cafeteria. Along the way I ran into Mackenzie. I was as happy to see her now as I'd been at the club but still grabbed her by the arm to stop her.

She looked at my fingers, curled her red lips in distaste and jerked away. But she didn't walk off, as per usual, and I was grateful.

"What do you want?" she snapped.

Such a sweet, sweet girl. "Where's Cole?"

"What am I? His keeper?"

"Just tell me where he is," I gritted.

"He's gone."

"What do you mean gone?" He'd left without saying goodbye? Again?

"Is there more than one meaning for the word?"

Don't punch her. You can't afford a suspension. "What's the deal with Veronica? She and Cole are on such great terms, I'm curious about how long they've known each other." I

should be discussing this with Cole, and only with Cole, but curiosity—and maybe a little anger—urged me onward.

"Cole dated her before me. I've heard rumors, but I'm not one hundred percent sure why they broke up. He never said."

Keep it together. Something about her tone... She knew something she wasn't telling me. "When he broke up with you, how did he do it?"

She stared at me as if I were a bug under a microscope—already dissected, ready to be sold for parts. Finally she averted her gaze, but not before I caught a glimmer of pity. "It was a few weeks after Bronx and I moved into his guesthouse, and a few months before you showed up. He got me alone, sat me down and told me we were over. I was absolutely blindsided. Even the day before, we were pretty into each other. Or so I thought."

Blindsided.

Into each other one day, but not the next.

Keep. It. Together.

Kat sidled up beside me, saying, "There you are."

She would help me, despite her problems.

"Well, well. Hello, Ally Kat." Mackenzie smiled with saccharine sweetness.

The two had never been friends, and probably never would be. Mackenzie, so protective of "her" boys, had tried to ruin Kat's relationship with Frosty a time or ten.

"Hello, Love Button," Kat replied, using the same tenor of falseness. Then she turned to me, putting her back to Mackenzie, as if the girl were of no consequence. Her cheeks were colorless, and her lips chapped from being chewed. "I'm blowing lunch and my last few hours and taking off. I'll pick

you up for tonight's game. And I know you want to spend a few minutes explaining why you can't go, but I'll save you the time since there's no way you can win this argument. You're going and that's final."

I opened my mouth, but she kissed my cheek and bounded off before I could get out a single word. "What if I have to, I don't know, help Cole?" I called. A few slayers had to patrol the streets nearly every night, just in case.

She never turned back.

"You don't. You haven't been put on rotation," Mackenzie said, and bounded off in the other direction.

Cole still hadn't added me.

Trembling, I entered the lunchroom and headed toward the table I shared with Reeve and the slayers. Halfway there, I slammed into a brick wall. Or rather, a brick wall that went by the name of Justin Silverstone.

"Move," I commanded.

Big brown puppy-dog eyes peered down at me, beseeching. "Why would I? I'm right where I want to be."

"That's odd, considering your location might just get your testicles knocked into your throat." I wasn't falling for his innocent act. Not again. He'd once used me for information to feed to Anima. He might even have helped them bomb my house. No telling what he'd do next.

"Give me a chance to explain my side of things, Ali. Please. I had nothing to do with—"

"Save it." I took a step to the side, intending to brush past him, then stopped as a thought occurred to me. "First, answer a question for me. Did you talk to Cole on the phone last Saturday night?"

An emotionless mask descended—the same one Cole had been donning lately. "No. Why?"

If he was to be believed, I'd dreamed their conversation. My mind really was a mess.

"Watch me as I don't discuss that with you." I marched to the table and sat with more of a slam than I'd intended.

"What did Justin want?" Frosty asked, looking ready to commit murder on my behalf.

"To chat about old times."

Bronx ran his tongue over his teeth. It was his way of telling me he would be at Frosty's side, inflicting major damage on the boy. With his spiked hair now dyed an electric blue rather than green, and the piercings in his eyebrow and lip—and, okay, the tattoo peeking from under the collar of his shirt—he didn't have to say anything to scare the crap out of most people.

Frosty crossed his arms over his chest. "Want me to break his face?"

"That's sweet of you to offer," I replied, liking that I had such fierce protectors, "but if there's going to be any face-breaking, I'm going to be the one to do it."

"Well, if you change your mind…"

"I'll let you know." I picked at the lunch I'd packed—a bagel with cream cheese—and wondered where Cole had gone, what he was doing and if this day could get any worse.

What a stupid question, I told myself later that evening. Of course the day could get worse.

By five, a cold front had swept into Birmingham, and by eight I felt like a Popsicle despite my winter wear. I huddled

on the stadium bleachers between Kat and Reeve. Neither girl seemed to notice the frigid temperatures. They were too busy bouncing up and down and celebrating. The Tigers had just scored their first touchdown of the game.

As the second quarter kicked off, Kat said, "So, get this. I'm, like, way more mad at Frosty than ever before. I may not ever forgive him."

"Why?" I asked. She was paler than she'd been at school, and despite her excitement over the game, her eyes were a little glassy. "What'd he do?"

"Last night he kissed some skank—right in my front yard."

"Oh, Kat. I'm so sorry."

"That snake!" Reeve exclaimed. "He deserves to die a thousand painful deaths."

Kat nodded, saying, "And that's not even the worst part. He put her on the back of his unicorn and rode off into the rainbow. He's *never* taken me to a rainbow."

Wait. "What are you talking about?"

"My dream last night," she said easily, then sipped her hot chocolate.

"Your dream." Reeve shook her head. "You're more mad at him than ever because of a dream?"

"Hey! I always behave myself in dreams," she said. "He should, too. And if he can't, he needs to apologize with more than my favorite flowers."

"He actually brought you flowers?" Stunned, I blinked at her. "For what he did in a dream?"

"Well, yeah. Wouldn't you?"

At the moment, I couldn't get Cole to say more than seven words to me. In real life.

Gavin suddenly plopped into the seat in front of me and though he grinned at me, he didn't look me in the eye.

Was this a nightmare?

A pretty brunette eased beside him, and she wasn't one of the girls from the club. She wrapped a possessive arm around his shoulders. A clear warning to me and my friends.

He had a girlfriend.

He frowned at the girl, removed her arm. *O-kay.* Maybe not a girlfriend.

"Ali Bell," he said with a nod of greeting. "It's good to see you again."

He hadn't shaved since the last time I'd seen him, and golden stubble now covered his jaw. Heart pounding unsteadily, I jerked my gaze to just over his shoulder, just in case he accidentally glanced up. "Uh, hi," I replied. "What are you doing here?"

"I came to see you."

"Hey, I remember you," Kat interjected. "From—" she caught herself before she admitted something she shouldn't and finished with a limp "—somewhere."

Reeve stiffened, as if she knew Kat was hiding something.

"You should," Gavin said. "I'm unforgettable."

"What a strange coincidence," Kat replied, fluffing her hair. "I am, too. So, are you a new member of the Asher High student body?"

The maybe/maybe-not-girlfriend snorted. "Does he look like he's in high school, kid?"

Her disdain irked.

Gavin, I'd discovered, had graduated last year. He was nineteen, not that much older than me, but he looked about

thirty. The finest of lines branched from his eyes—either laugh lines, scowl lines or both. With slayers, you couldn't be sure. Most of the guys were as mean as rattlesnakes, but they were also quite warped in the humor department.

"Hillary," Gavin admonished.

"It's Belinda," the girl corrected tightly.

"Whatever. I wanted one night, you wanted two. I agreed to give you the second night if you promised to behave. You're not behaving."

She pressed her lips together and remained silent.

Are you kidding me?

He was casually discussing sex with a woman he'd called by the wrong name. I had no words.

"Since no one is willing to make introductions," Reeve said to break up the tenser-by-the-second silence, "I'll do it. I'm Reeve Ankh."

Gavin looked her over with unabashed interest. "You the one dating Bronx?"

"Not dating, no. We're not even on friendly terms anymore."

I caught the bitterness in her tone. She had no idea her father had threatened to pull his support from the slayers if one of the boys made a play for her. Every day Bronx had to choose between the girl he wanted and the friends he was determined to protect.

"I'm actually seeing someone else," Reeve admitted quietly.

"What!" Kat gasped. "And you didn't tell me? Who is it? How long has this been going on?"

"I'll share if you will."

Kat's excitement deflated. "I'm not sure I know what you're talking about."

From the corner of my eye, I spotted Wren Kyler and Poppy Verdeck making their way toward the concession stand. They made a striking pair, the beautiful black girl and the delicate redhead. A few weeks ago, Kat, Reeve and I would have been with them.

The moment I'd started dating Cole and she'd gotten back together with Frosty, they'd dropped us. We were now considered troublemakers, a bad bet, and they'd thought their futures would be brighter without us.

They were probably right.

Justin was dating Wren, and he walked behind the pair. He looked up, his gaze landing on me as if he'd known where I was all along. Just like before, his eyes pleaded at me.

I broke the connection.

"Hey, can I talk to you?" Gavin asked me. "Alone?"

Hillary/Belinda opened her mouth to protest, quickly closed it.

My palms began to sweat. Gavin wanted to find out if we'd have another vision, didn't he?

I nodded, trying to sound normal as I said, "Sure. Why not?"

We stood in unison. He led me up the bleachers, his hand on my lower back, making me uncomfortable.

"Here's good." He stopped at a secluded spot overlooking the parking lot, then motioned to the section we'd just abandoned. "I need to be able to see the girls."

Agreed. Emma hadn't formed a rabbit cloud, so I wasn't

worried about an attack, but I'd learned to err on the side of caution.

"Before you ask," I said, still not meeting his gaze. "I don't know what causes the visions—or, apparently, what stops them. I thought building emotional walls was the key, but I'd built what I considered an impenetrable fortress against you before Hearts and yet we had another one."

He pushed out a heavy breath. "Note to self. Take Prozac before talking to Ali."

That probably wasn't a bad idea. "I don't think we should look at each other. Not here. Just in case."

"All right. Where? When?"

How about…never? I ignored the questions, saying, "Have you experienced a vision with anyone else?"

"No. But you have."

"Yes." And I was clearly the only unchanging variable. Somehow, this was all my fault. "What did you see in the barn?" Maybe he'd seen something different. Maybe—

"I saw you tasting my neck."

I gulped. No maybe. We'd seen the same thing. "That's never going to happen."

"That's not what Cole said."

Fury rose inside me, even though I'd already suspected Gavin had spilled the worst of the details. "You told him?"

"Of course. I had to. He's my friend. You're his girl."

Was I? I licked my lips. "When did you do it? What'd he say?"

"The day after the incident at the club. And nothing. He stormed off."

Why hadn't he called me?

I had to talk to him. I had to explain…what? What could I say to make this better?

"I feel the need to reiterate—I'm never going to lick you or throw you on my bed," I said.

Gavin fingered a lock of my hair. "Honey, I have to agree with you on that one. You're not even close to being my type."

"What type is that? Easy?"

"Among other things," he said unabashedly.

I stepped away from him and gripped the railing in front of me. In the parking lot, darkness was chased away by the occasional streetlamp, revealing car after car.

"I just want to figure out what's going on," he said.

"Me, too. And by the way, you're not my type, either."

"You don't like sexy?"

I rolled my eyes. "I just like Cole."

"So you like moody and broody."

I kind of wanted to smile at that. "I—" The scent of rot hit me, and I wrinkled my nose. Stiffening, I searched for any other sign of the zombies. They couldn't be here. They—

Were here.

Red eyes cut through the night, and my heart skittered into a wild beat. Anyone who wandered through the parking lot would be unable to see the evil lurking nearby, and the odds were good they'd become dinner.

"They're here," I said, trying not to panic. "The zombies are here."

BLOOD AND TEARS

I beat feet to my friends. "Stay here. No matter what you see or hear, don't leave the bleachers until I come back to get you, okay?" The zombies might have braved the parking lot, but their sensitive flesh would sizzle up here in the lights.

Kat paled—she knew what was happening. "Okay."

"What's going on?" Reeve demanded. "I've seen Bronx, Frosty and Cole act this way. Heard them say these things."

Unfazed, Gavin pointed a finger in her face. "Do as you've been told or I'll make sure you regret it." He switched his attention to his two-night stand. "You, too."

We didn't say anything else to the girls. There just wasn't time. Together, we pounded down the rest of the bleacher steps.

"You up for this, cupcake?" Gavin asked.

"Always. Jack-hole."

He laughed.

As I ran, I withdrew my phone and dialed Frosty. There was no reason to try to reach Cole right now. He'd just send me to voice mail. But Frosty failed to answer, as well. I left a message. "We're at the game. The enemy has entered the parking lot. Send backup ASAP."

Justin appeared at my side, keeping pace as we closed in on the darkness. "How many?" he demanded.

"Go home," I snapped. "We don't need your kind of help. You'll feed us to the Hazmats the moment we're distracted." He had before.

"I won't. Trust me."

Trust him, when I was struggling to trust Cole?

"He works with the Hazmats?" Gavin slowed down, moving behind us. Without any more warning than that, he punched Justin in the back of the head, knocking the boy forward. "Then he doesn't work with us."

Justin tripped over his own feet and went down, his hands and knees absorbing most of the impact. He could have recovered, but Gavin kicked him in the center of his back, sending him flying onto his stomach. Then Gavin stomped over his body and continued onward.

Part of me wanted to protest his methods. I wasn't Justin's friend, but wow. The other part of me was kind of impressed. He-slut had skills.

The moment we hit the parking lot, I withdrew my favorite daggers from the purse hanging at my side, then dropped the purse on the ground, not wanting to give the zombies anything extra to grab onto. There were streetlamps to my far left and right, illuminating sections of the lot. Four kids I recognized from school were climbing into a red truck.

Another two were standing in front of a sedan, a girl leaning against the hood, a boy leaning against her.

"Get out of here," I shouted, cruel to be kind. Contrary to popular opinion, stupidity did not make a less-than-delicious brain.

A strip of darkness consumed the center, and that was where we headed. I looked for the glow of the Blood Lines, but...found none. Very well. None of the cars would be solid to us when we entered the spirit realm. We could ghost through—and so could the zombies.

The closer we drew, the stronger the scent of rot became, and I gagged.

"Let's do this," Gavin said, and stepped out of his body as if it were a suit of armor he'd gotten tired of wearing.

As Cole had once told me, people were spirits. We had a soul, and we lived in a body. The spirit was the power source. The soul was the mind, will and emotions, and linked to the power. The body was the house.

I, too, forced my spirit and soul to split from my body, and my body froze in place, unable to move until I reentered it. If anyone stumbled upon the motionless shell, well, they'd get no response and I was sure there would be trouble. *Can't be helped.*

Instantly the air became colder, and the light I'd admired only a few seconds ago was too bright, making my eyes water. A typical reaction to leaving the natural realm and entering the spiritual.

"Shout if you get into trouble," Gavin called.

I didn't reply. Sometimes it was just better to remain silent. Whatever a slayer said while in spirit form came true.

Well, mostly. There were two caveats. We had to believe it, and we couldn't violate someone else's free will.

Some things happened instantly. Some took a while. As long as the words met the requirements, they happened. No exceptions.

Gavin picked up speed and moved in front of me. He extended both his arms, fired two SIG Sauers—and bonus points to me for knowing the type…or brand…whatever! Sparks exploded from the barrels, and the ensuing *boom, boom* made me cringe. Not that anyone around us would hear it.

The fight was on.

The two zombies closest to us went down. But a heartbeat later, they were climbing back to their feet, ready for more. I frowned. The bullets should have slowed them, at least a little. Zombies felt no pain, but their spiritual bodies *were* subject to injury, just like ours.

"I didn't miss," Gavin gritted. He fired the guns until they ran out of bullets.

He reached the creatures first, using the two he'd decorated with holes as punching bags.

I reached my own target and gave a wide slash of my dagger, clipping his spine, nearly removing his head. An action that would merely disable. There was only one thing that could forever end these creatures, and it was the fire from a slayer's hands. But I could have a lot of fun beforehand.

I kicked the next one in the stomach, knocking him backward and revealing the zombie coming in behind him. Too late. He moved too quickly. The new addition pushed me, and I pinwheeled over a body, landing with a hard thud, my side throbbing. I was jumped and pinned a second later, teeth

going for my neck. I broke his nose and his jaw and wiggled out from under him; he ended up gnawing on pavement.

As I stood, I swiped out my blades, the tips slashing into his neck once, twice, going deeper and deeper, into spinal cord, buying me a temporary reprieve. From him, at least.

I tried to summon my fire the same way I'd left my body, believing I could and thereby gaining the inner strength to actually do it, but I was so new to this, didn't have as much faith as the others and could only stretch myself so far. And multitask? Forget about it.

As expected, no flames.

Another zombie lunged at me, black-stained teeth bared. I spun and kicked, my booted heel slamming into his side. He stumbled away from me as yet another zombie lunged at me. I popped her in the nose and spun again, elbowing her in the temple when I lined up to her left. She went down, but quickly twisted and reached for my ankle.

I don't think so. I hopped up and stomped on her hand. Saw two more coming at me from the right. With a twirl of my dagger, I pressed the blade against my wrist, then punched one creature and kicked the other. At my side, a gnarled arm stretched out. I grabbed and bent it, forcing the zombie to hunch over as I jerked up my knee, barreling into his face. When I released him, he fell to the ground.

But like his brethren, he recovered in a rush. I performed another spin—*am getting so good at those!*—whipping out my leg to shove him back several feet. Before he could rise a second time, I swung my arm around and launched one of the daggers. The tip soared past his open mouth and embedded in the back of his throat.

Bull's-eye.

On instinct, I turned, realized a pack of zombies had launched a sneak attack. I arched left, right, narrowly avoiding nails and teeth, my blade constantly swinging, slicing through rotting flesh. Cold black goo dripped down my hands.

I grinned. Some people got off on drugs. I got off on this.

Something solid pressed against my back, and I threw an elbow, raised the blade. As I sliced in a downward arc, Justin ducked, barely avoiding impact.

"Idiot," I screamed. He knew better than to creep up on a slayer.

"Incoming." He motioned to just over my shoulder.

I drank in the scene as quickly as possible and decided what to do. A zombie had used my distraction to his advantage, stealing in close and preparing to sink his teeth in my upper arm. I could dive away, but Justin's nearness would put him in striking range. I could arch, but the creature's momentum would draw him back with me. We'd fall. His weight would cage me. I'd be more of a target, and he could go for my neck.

I had to take the bite in my arm and pray Justin or Gavin injected me with antidote right away, so I could jump back into battle.

Gonna sting.

"No!" Justin reached out, flames springing from the pores in his hand, the light shining as brightly as the streetlamps. The zombie bit into that light, and both Justin and the creature dropped.

The zombie frantically patted at his mouth, his throat, his

stomach, as if experiencing pain for the first time. But that wasn't possible. Was it? Even still, he hadn't been exposed to Justin's fire long enough to die.

On the opposite end of the spectrum, Justin *had* been exposed to enough toxin to die. A single drop was all it took. He writhed, the poison already pouring through him, a river, pulling him down, down, down, washing over him, drowning him.

I wanted to help him, meant to inject him, but there just wasn't time or opportunity. All I could do was stand over him and fight, protecting him from further harm, reeling that the boy I knew as a traitor had taken a blow meant for me. Maybe I should have been nicer to him.

Zombies, zombies, zombies, everywhere I looked; so many grotesque bodies I lost count. They were like a swarm of flies, moaning instead of buzzing. I hobbled one, and two more replaced him—and then the one I'd hobbled rejoined the party.

My inhalations were too shallow, my exhalations too quick. I trembled, the blades seeming to gain ten pounds with every move I made. I'd been without physical activity for too long. This was too much, too soon. I wasn't sure how much more I could take and still remain on my feet.

Can't let Justin's sacrifice be in vain.

Must avenge my family.

As I fought, I caught a glimpse of Gavin battling his own horde. He moved with the grace of a panther, his every action fluid, nothing without a purpose.

Should I call for help?

A clawed hand swiped at me. I barely managed to duck.

Teeth snapped at me. Hissing and snarls filled my ears. I swung, but an elbow jabbed into my middle, and I lost what little air I'd managed to take in. I doubled over. Fingers tangled in my hair, and hello, joyride to the ground.

"Gavin."

"Ali!" he shouted.

I kicked out, but two of the creatures managed to grab my ankles. I lashed out with my fists, but two others managed to grab my wrists. I bucked, but couldn't free myself.

Don't panic. Panic would prevent me from acting rationally. I could get out of this. I just had to... What?

"Ali!" another voice shouted.

Cole! Cole was here!

Cole, the light of my life.

Light. Yes.

"Light up, dang it," I commanded my hands. I could do this. I *would* do this. I believed. "Now!"

As Gavin ripped a zombie off me, flames at last burst from the ends of my fingertips.

The zombies still holding me instantly turned to ash.

"Help the kid," Gavin commanded, returning to finish off his own horde.

I looked over my shoulder—saw the creatures eating at Justin. Horrified, I scrambled over and performed an inelegant dance of touch and destroy, freeing him from grasping hands and too-sharp teeth.

Back on my feet, my arms glowing brightly, I ripped through the remaining zombies, touching this one, touching that one, destroying all. When the last one exploded into

tiny pieces of ash, my knees collapsed, and I fell. On impact, the flames vanished, and my skin returned to normal.

Victory.

Face splattered with black goo, Gavin closed the distance and grinned at me. "Now that's the kind of ability I can encourage."

Cole misted through the car beside me and stopped short. Fear radiated from him. Violet eyes I'd missed with every fiber of my being scanned me, searching for injury. "Were you bitten?"

"No, I'm good. But Justin isn't."

He frowned. "Justin?"

"He took a bite meant for me." I crawled to Justin's side and felt for a pulse. The beat thumped so swiftly I couldn't keep count. "He needs the antidote."

"I'll give him mine," Cole said, bending down as he withdrew a syringe from his back pocket.

"Justin," I said, patting his cheek. "We're here. We'll take care of you."

His eyelids split apart. Rivers of red ran through his irises. I gasped. Surely he wasn't... Couldn't... Not that quickly.

His head whipped toward me—and he sank his teeth into my wrist.

He quickly released me to curl into a ball and vomit, but the damage was done. I screamed. It was like electric paddles had been strapped to my chest, jump-starting a second heart, making it beat for the first time, but never in rhythm with the other one.

Suddenly there were two Alis, and both were in pain.

One hated it. One liked it.

That one was hungry. *So hungry.*

Cole loomed over me, his features tortured with concern. His mouth was moving, but I couldn't hear him. My attention caught on the pulse at the base of his neck. *Thump, thump. Thump, thump.*

Hypnotic.

Delicious.

Radiant light seeped through his pores. A light that didn't hurt my gaze. A light that drew me, every part of me. I licked my lips. If I could just get past his skin, I could reach that light. I could touch it. Taste it.

Consume it.

Desperate, I grabbed him by the shoulders and tugged him down, baring my teeth. Just before I could bite into him, a fist slammed into my temple. From the corner of my eye, I saw Gavin, raising his arm to deliver another blow. Cole stopped him.

It was the last thing I saw before darkness swept over me.

THE KING TAKES THE PAWN

I had spent the first sixteen years of my life under the watchful eye of a man who'd seen monsters no one else could see. I'd thought him insane, and part of me had resented him for the rules he'd enforced, the trouble he'd caused.

He'd built a house to protect us, a fortress of solitude, really, with iron behind the walls and bars over the windows. My sister and I had left our prison to attend school and church, and the occasional lunch date with our grandparents, but that was it. Every other second had been spent in confinement.

Now I knew more about the invisible world around me, more than Dad had ever known, and I knew the iron and the bars wouldn't have kept the monsters at bay. Only Blood Lines could. I knew zombies were drawn to life—the very thing they'd lost. I knew they hungered for slayers first, and

average Joes second. We were tastier dishes, I guess. I knew they found fear to be an aphrodisiac and fury to be a dessert.

Emotion added spice.

As miserable as I'd been back then, I missed the life I used to lead. I missed the hours I'd spent holding my sister while she drifted to sleep. I missed the hugs my mother had so freely given. Missed the smiles she and my dad used to share. The food she used to cook. The notes she used to leave under my pillow.

I love you, Alice Rose.
Thinking about you today, darling girl.
You're so strong and beautiful. How'd I get so lucky?

Remembering caused pain to scrape at my chest, over and over, again and again, razor-sharp claws tearing into flesh and muscle, even bone, leaving me raw and bleeding. I hurt. Oh, glory, I hurt with a hunger no one should ever have to endure. It was as if I'd never eaten. As if my body was destroying itself, cell by cell. And all the while, those two hearts pounded in my chest.

I unleashed a terrible scream.

The pain only expanded, razing my mind, pooling even in my toes. I tried to burrow my fingers past my skull, my chest, somewhere, anywhere, desperate to reach the pain and snatch it away, but I failed miserably.

My blood turned molten in my veins, burning me from the inside out. But a second later, a chill danced over my skin, causing me to shiver. *Cold.* My teeth chattered as I burrowed deeper under the blanket. *Hot.* I kicked the stupid

blanket away. *Cold.* I pulled my arms into my chest, trying to curl into myself for warmth. *Hot.* I tore at my clothing.

"Ali," called a voice I knew I should recognize. Male. Raspy with concern.

Cole, maybe. I inhaled deeply, and oh, he smelled so good. Pure and crisp and crackling with energy. The hunger overwhelmed me all over again. My mouth watered. "Feed me," I croaked.

Gentle hands smoothed over my cheeks, offering a comforting stroke.

My nerve endings went haywire, agonizing me further. I jerked away. "No. Don't."

"Ali."

Grab him. Devour him. You'll feel so much better.

"I administered a double dose of the antidote hours ago. Why isn't she better?"

Definitely Cole. He was here. He was with me.

"Give her another."

"Can she take it?"

"Do we have a choice?"

A sharp sting in my neck, a cool rush through my veins, and the pain and hunger at last died. The second heartbeat slowed, softened, but didn't disappear completely. Still, it was enough. I sagged into a boneless heap.

"Ali, I need you to wake up, okay?"

Anything for Cole. I ripped my way through the veil of darkness shrouding my conscious and pried open my eyelids. At first, I saw only a haze of white clouds.

Clouds.

Emma.

But…she wasn't here. Where was *here?* I frowned.

"Good girl, that's the way," Cole said. "Come back to me, sweetheart."

Sweetheart. An endearment.

He wasn't upset with me anymore.

Blinking rapidly shooed away the haze. Cole leaned over the side of the bed, peering down at me. Black hair shagged over a forehead furrowed with a mix of worry and relief. His eyes were glassy and bloodshot, making me think he'd been denied sleep. The shadow-beard he always sported was now thicker.

"Hey there," he said softly.

"Hey." My voice was damaged, as if my vocal cords had been cut and only recently sewn back together. "I'm glad you're speaking to me again."

He frowned, and suddenly I could see the storm brewing beneath his exhaustion. "I wasn't ever *not* speaking to you."

"You were avoiding me, then."

A stilted pause before he admitted, "Yes."

A second later, the world around me tunneled so that only Cole existed. Elation speared me—finally we were having a vision—

—in the Ankhs' game room, Cole stood across from me. He was smiling at something Veronica was saying. I stood in front of Gavin, my hands cupping his cheeks.

"You are a better man than I ever gave you credit for," I told him.

"I know," Gavin replied.

"And you're *so* modest."

He chuckled. "Are you happy with the way things turned out?"

My gaze strayed to Cole. The tension he'd worn like a second skin all these weeks had utterly vanished. "Yeah. Yeah, I am—"

—the vision vanished in a blink, right along with my elation, and Cole let his head drop into his upraised hands. He scrubbed his fingers through his already disheveled hair.

"Gavin's a man-whore, you know. Never been with the same girl twice. And he's never liked blondes. He won't stay with you for long."

There was ice in his tone, and it scared me. "I'm not interested in Gavin." I struggled to sit up. "Cole, you have to—"

"Don't say anything. Just…don't." Motions jerky, he shoved two pillows behind my back and reached over to lift a glass of water from the nightstand.

I was in my bedroom, I realized. Determined sunlight shoved its way through the curtains. The iPod Cole had given me was stationed in its dock on the desk and turned on. Soft music filled the room.

He placed the straw at my lips. "Drink."

I obeyed, the cool liquid sliding down my throat, soothing for a moment only to churn in my belly, frothing up acid. "Thank you."

He nodded stiffly and set the cup aside. "Let's talk about what happened with Justin."

Yes. Okay. A safe topic. "Has he recovered?"

"Yeah, and a lot quicker than you."

The accusation in his voice threw me, and I glowered at him. "Hey, don't blame me. I'm the victim here."

He massaged the back of his neck, somewhat contrite. "Yeah. I know. Sorry. It's been stressful, watching you suffer and not being able to help."

Slowly I relaxed. "Has a slayer ever bitten another slayer like that?"

"Not to my knowledge. Not while both are still human."

Why Justin? Why me? What had been different? "Did I try to bite anyone while I was...out of it?" The moment I asked, memories came flooding back to me. Cole. I'd tried to bite Cole.

"Just me," he said without any hint of emotion.

I soaked in horror like a sponge. "I'm sorry," I rushed out. "I know I failed. Wait. I failed, right?"

He gave one, sharp nod. "You did."

I relaxed again, but only slightly. "I'm so sorry, Cole. I don't know what came over me, but I do know I'm not going to do it again. I promise you."

He shrugged—and I wasn't sure whether he was trying to tell me he believed me...or that he didn't.

"I mean it," I insisted.

"You tried to bite me more than once," he said flatly.

Oh. I didn't remember the other times. "I'm so sorry," I repeated. "I didn't realize..."

"I know."

I gulped. Was he disgusted with me now? "Do you think Anima put Justin up to hurting me? Causing this kind of reaction, thinking we'd destroy each other?"

"Maybe, but like you, I don't think Justin knew what he was doing."

Agreed. The red I'd seen in his eyes… "Where is he now?"

"Ankh kept him below, in the dungeon, as you like to call it, for a few days to make sure the antidote was working and he wouldn't try to attack anyone else. Tests were run, and a strange toxin was found in his blood. Not zombie, but actually antizombie. Different than what's in the antidote. We think it's what made him vomit."

Wait. Hold everything. "A few days? How long have I been out? Did you check my blood, too?"

Used to my rapid-fire questions, he easily followed. "About a week. And yes. You had—have—the same anti-zombie toxin, only you have a lot more of it, which makes us think you shared it with him when he bit you."

Crap. I'd lost another week of my life. My poor Nana. Ugh, my poor grades. "How and where would I have gotten an antizombie toxin? And why is it in my blood, rather than my spirit?"

He shrugged. "Could be an ability, like the visions. And if it's in your spirit, it's in your blood. We have to test what we can."

Yes. Okay. All of that made sense.

When I'd first moved in with Nana, I'd found a journal written in a strange numbered code that always seemed to unravel by itself. Through it, I'd learned some slayers were born with strange abilities no one could explain. A poison-ous spirit, and thereby blood, had been on the list—which was actually a good thing. Like Justin, the zombies sickened soon after biting me.

"Just so you know, we told everyone you'd overdone it and reopened your wound," Cole said. "Both of which are true."

"Thank you."

He nodded, moved to the door.

He was...leaving me? Just like that?

"Cole," I called. "We need to talk."

"You need to rest."

"Cole." My voice lashed like a whip. I wasn't letting him get away. Not this time.

He paused, faced me. His features were blank.

"This has to stop."

He gave a single nod, and the formality of the action worried me.

"I tried not to push you, but you have to give me something. Your silence is driving me crazy."

He crossed his arms as if preparing for battle. "Some things aren't meant to be discussed, Ali."

Today, I just couldn't accept that. I'd come this far... "At Hearts, you couldn't spend time with me. Why?"

He ran his tongue over his teeth. "I've already told you all I'm willing to say on that subject."

"You asked me to trust you, and now I'm asking you to trust me with the truth. Why?"

Silence.

Argh! I tried a different approach, saying, "You told me you wanted me to stay away from Gavin, and yet you have been the one to stay away from me. Why?"

Again silence.

Dang him! I was giving, but he wasn't giving anything back. "What we just saw in the vision—"

"Will happen." Fury blazed in his eyes, making me miss the expressionless mask. "You know it will. It always does."

I'd denied it to myself, but I couldn't deny it to him. He'd call my bluff. "Maybe it doesn't mean what we think it means."

His head tilted to the side, and he studied me intently. Hopefully? "What do you think it means?"

"I...don't know." I wasn't at my best just then. But I knew that just because I'd stood with Gavin, and Cole had stood with Veronica, and just because I'd had my hands on Gavin and Cole had been smiling so peacefully at Veronica, didn't mean we belonged with Gavin and Veronica. "What do *you* think it means?"

Please tell me what I want to hear.

He would. He had to. Not many people were as layered as Cole. A hard outer shell covered razor blades, and razor blades covered steel. But for those willing to dig—and endure the injuries and bleeding—a soft, gooey center could be found. I'd dug. I'd found it. He wouldn't let me go, wouldn't turn to Veronica.

"I think it means...we're over," he said, and closed his eyes.

He would. He really would.

He might as well have slapped me. "No," I said, shaking my head. "No."

"Okay, let me rephrase. I *know* it means we're over. We have to be. I've almost lost you twice, and I'm going to lose you for good when the visions start coming true. I'm not going to hang on to a lost cause, Ali."

Panic set in. I had to make him understand. "I'm not a lost cause. *We're* not a lost cause. I don't like Gavin."

"But you will."

No! "Don't do this," I said. "Please. You have to trust me. Please," I said again, and I didn't care how desperate I sounded. "There are some things you can never take back, and this is one of them."

A terrible stillness came over him. I wasn't sure he was even breathing. Then he was stomping to the wall, throwing a fist.

Boom! I flinched. Plaster gave, leaving a hole. Dust mushroomed through the air.

Here was the dangerous boy I'd been warned about in the beginning. The one mothers wanted to hide from their daughters. The panty melter, I'd heard a few girls at school call him. The boy others feared. The violent criminal. The hard-hearted machine.

"I'm not going to look at Gavin and suddenly start wanting him," I whispered. I couldn't even imagine it. "You're the one for me. And this isn't like you," I added. "You never back down. You never walk away from a fight." *Fight for me.*

He pressed his forehead into the damaged wall.

"Cole," I said quietly. *Must get through to him.* "Do you want Veronica?"

"No," he said, and I could have sobbed with relief. "Not even a little."

"See!"

"Ali, I..." He straightened, turned toward me. I saw the panic a split second before a sheet of ice fell over his features, and that ice was far worse than the fury he'd displayed ear-

lier. "Our feelings right now aren't the problem. One day I hope you'll forgive me. I doubt I'll ever be able to forgive myself. But...we're done."

Done.

Just like that.

Over. Finished.

"Cole."

"We're done," he repeated more firmly. "We're done."

How finite he sounded. How sure.

For the second time in my life, my heart broke into thousands of pieces. I thought I would die. But this time, I had the second heart, the new one, whatever it was, to pick up the slack, to keep me alive.

Silent now, he backed up, away from me.

"I won't come crawling after you," I croaked.

"I don't want you to."

With those five words, he shredded the rest of me. Spirit, soul and body. I wouldn't give him the chance to do it again. I couldn't. "I won't take you back even if you come crawling back to *me*."

"I know," he said, despair creeping into his tone. "And I won't.... I can't...." He shook his head. "There's nothing I can say to make either of us feel better about this, and I'm sorry about that. You'll probably never know how much. But that's not going to change my mind. It has to be this way."

He turned and left.

WELCOME TO YOUR NIGHTMARE

I...

Broke...

Down.

Somehow I found the strength to stand. My legs shook. With fury. Sorrow. Helplessness. Regret.

Pain.

I wanted to chase after Cole and tear into him the way he'd just done to me. I wanted to hit him. I wanted to scream at him.

I wanted him to hurt the way I was hurting.

I wanted to cry and beg him to come back to me.

I wanted his arms around me.

I wanted to hate him.

Maybe I did hate him. Today he'd proved he wasn't the admirable boy I'd thought he was. How could he be? He'd cut me loose the same way he'd cut Mackenzie loose. As if

I meant nothing. Only difference was, I'd had a little warning. I just hadn't wanted to face the truth of it.

I wanted to avoid him forever.

I'd see him again. Of course I would. We would even talk to each other. We'd have to. In a way, he was my boss. He set the nightly rotation schedule. He headed up all training. But the easy camaraderie we'd shared was over. The bantering. The kissing. The touching.

Over.

He'd wanted to protect himself, and me, from further hurt, from fighting a losing battle, from whatever mystery he refused to discuss, from the devastation and shame of falling for other people while we were still together.

I'd been willing to risk it.

He'd decided I wasn't worth the effort.

I looked around the room that wasn't mine. It was only a loaner. The only things I owned were the clothes in the dresser and closet. I stumbled to the dresser without knowing why—until I felt my fingers curl around the edge and my arms push forward, sending the piece of furniture crashing into the floor.

I grabbed a drawer and tossed it, then another, and another. Socks and underwear went flying in every direction. Seeing them lying on the floor only made me madder. I was just like them. Tossed aside. In a place I didn't belong.

Cole had just changed the entire course of my life, and I'd been helpless to stop him. Just like I'd been helpless to stop the car crash.

How many other changes would I be forced to endure?

Everything changed. The world. The seasons. Time. Peo-

ple. Nothing and no one ever stayed the same. Accepting another change should be easy. After all, even I would change. One day, I would forget about Cole and the feelings I had for him. I would move on.

And so would he.

He would date another girl.

My gaze drifted to the picture I kept on my nightstand. Kat had snapped it when I'd been too distracted to know anyone else was around. In it, Cole stood behind me, his arms wrapped around me. His chin rested on top of my head, and he appeared utterly content. I was smiling with the dreamy confidence of a girl rushing headlong into love.

Love.

I refused to love him.

I picked up the photo and launched it across the room, my new heart racing with dangerous speed, my lungs burning, no longer able to pull in enough oxygen—as if something inside me was stealing it. My stomach curled into a ball and hardened into iron—but the iron was hollowed out and desperate to be filled. I was hungry again, so danged hungry...but not for food. For... I wasn't sure. But whatever it was, I needed it.

Now.

A high-pitched ringing scraped at my ears. Sweat broke out over my brow and my palms and trickled down my back. The room spun around and around, my equilibrium shot, and I flailed for balance...tilting anyway...and felt a sharp sting against my entire right side. I must have fallen to the floor.

Help me, I tried to call, but no words emerged. My heart

GENA SHOWALTER

sped up, faster and faster. My lungs constricted far more tightly, the burn intensifying. My hands and feet mutated into blocks of ice.

I...was dying? I had to be dying.

I crawled to the desk, reached blindly for my phone and knocked down the lamp. Glass shattered on the floor.

Had to text Co—no, Nana. Yes, Nana. She would come. She would take care of me—*she* loved me. But I couldn't see the keypad. The room was still spinning.

Hinges squeaked. "Ali? Are you okay? What happened to your room?"

Male voice. I recognized it. Mr. Ankh?

Help, I tried to say, but again, no sound emerged.

Footsteps. Strong arms slid underneath me, lifted me. I floated for a few seconds before the mattress pressed into my back.

"Is it the toxin?" he asked, even as he stuck me in the neck with a needle. Yes, it had to be Mr. Ankh. Like the rest of us, he carried the antidote in his pocket, just in case.

A cool stream raced through my veins, and the hunger simmered.

"Breathe," he said gently. "In. Out. Yes, just like that. Again. Again." Hands smoothed over my brow, offering comfort I so desperately needed. "Again."

At last, my heart...hearts...began to slow. My lungs began to fill. The sweat stopped pouring, and the chill kissed me goodbye.

I blinked open my eyes, and saw Mr. Ankh sitting at the side of my bed. Concern bathed his still-handsome features.

"That wasn't just about the toxin, was it?" he asked, the concern giving way to sympathy.

I remained silent.

"Has that ever happened before?"

"Wh-what?" Almost dying?

"A panic attack?"

Panic attack? No. "That's not what just happened." I'd weathered the death of my family. A breakup wouldn't ruin my mental stability. I wouldn't let it.

"Ali, sweetheart, I'm a doctor. More than that, for several years I was married to a woman with an anxiety disorder. I know a panic attack when I see one."

Anxiety disorder. No. Not that, either. "I'm fine," I said, my voice ragged. "Just tired."

His smile was sad. "Did something happen to trigger it?"

Something like losing the other part of me? "I told you I'm fine," I replied stiffly, then regretted my tone. He was being nice, trying to help me. He didn't deserve my rancor.

He sighed, pushed to his feet. "The more you know about the triggers, the better you'll handle the episodes. If you ever want to talk about it…"

"I don't. I won't. I'm fine, really."

"All right. Well, don't worry about the room. I'll send someone up to clean."

"No! No," I said more gently. "I'll take care of it."

A pause, then, "If that's what you prefer." Like Cole, he left the room.

Left me alone.

My new heart sped up all over again.

★ ★ ★

I righted the furniture and cleaned the room, even patched the hole in my wall. The one Cole had caused. It had reminded me of him, and I wasn't fond of reminders right now. I threw our picture in the trash.

The next week passed in a daze. Every day I had to bury my emotions as deep as they would go and pretend everything was peachy, just to make it through school. Kat and Reeve treated me the same; they had no idea Cole and I had broken up. I hadn't told anyone, and for some reason, neither had he. I think the girls were onto me, though, and I expected questions very, very soon.

I stayed away from Cole's gym and worked out with Kat in Mr. Ankh's. I still hadn't been put on rotation, but I hadn't pushed because the zombies hadn't made another appearance.

I wasn't eating, wasn't sleeping.

I couldn't go on like this.

"Emma," I said as I burrowed under my covers. "Emma." I needed my baby sister.

I wasn't sure how much time passed before she materialized in the center of my room.

"Oh, Ali." She stretched beside me on the bed, ghosting her hand through my hair. Somehow she calmed me, the weird heartbeat evening out, the hunger pains that always seemed to hover at the edge of my conscious ebbing. "I hate seeing you like this."

"I'm better now that you're here."

"I'm glad. And I'm glad you called me." Her dark eyes were luminous as she said, "Would it help to know I've been watching Cole? He's miserable, too."

"Maybe," I said with a sniffle. "Why have you been watching him?"

"I think he's spying on the other slayers."

Why would he do that? He trusted the people around him, everyone but me, that is, and—

Wait. "I don't care anymore." I changed the subject. "The night I was bitten, you didn't put a rabbit cloud in the sky. Why?"

"I had been watching the zombie nests, and none of them had stirred. The ones that attacked you came out of nowhere."

No, they'd had to come from somewhere. But where? And what did this mean…for the…future? *Can't concentrate. So tired.*

"I'm losing you," she said with a chuckle. "Rest now."

I must have fallen asleep at long last; the next time I opened my eyes, she was gone.

Thursday, Nana tried to talk to me about my sudden withdrawal. She was worried I was sick. I assured her I was the picture of health.

Friday, Mackenzie and Trina insisted on driving me home from school, and I buckled in back of a beat-up Jeep. They knew my situation without being told.

"I recognize the glaze in your eyes," Mackenzie said, twisting in the passenger seat. For once, there was no heat in her tone. No condescension or anger on her face. "I know we've never liked each other, but I do mean it when I say I'm sorry for what you're going through. And maybe I should have warned you. This is what he does. This is what he's always done."

I peered out the window. The sun was bright today, making my eyes water. "What do you mean? What does he always do?"

"He cuts and runs when things get serious, and I don't think he even realizes he's doing it. He just looks for an excuse, and then boom, it's over."

I remembered the panic I thought I'd seen in his eyes. I'd convinced myself I'd imagined each instance, but what if they had been the start of the demise of our relationship? *Not* the visions.

"Yesterday I asked Veronica straight-up," Trina said. "When he broke up with her, he told her he couldn't do the long-distance thing anymore."

I wondered what he would say about me, when he finally started talking.

"He's a great guy," Mackenzie said, "but he's never been in a relationship for the long haul."

"I think his friendships are the same way. Don't get me wrong, I know he loves us slayers." Trina maneuvered the car onto Reeve's street. "I'm never in doubt of that. But I'm always aware of the fact that he keeps me at a bit of an emotional distance. He does it with everyone but Frosty and Bronx—they're like brothers with other mothers or something. Frankly, I was shocked he let you get as close as you did, as fast as you did."

I thought I understood. Cole had lost his mom to the zombies. He knew he would lose his dad the next time his dad was bitten, since the man had developed an immunity to the antidote. If he let someone else all the way in, like,

say, a girlfriend, and then he lost her, too, he probably didn't think he would survive.

The fury returned—the roots had never withered. How dare he? How dare he lead me on, making me want more, when he'd never planned to see this thing through? And then to throw me away because of what might happen at some later date… Because of fear…

"There's the spirit we're used to seeing," Mackenzie said with a nod of approval.

No, this was something else. Something sharper. But I didn't correct her. "Has he ever gone back for seconds?"

"Never. Not even when we get desperate and try to steal his attention by messing around with someone else," she added bitterly.

There was a story there, but I wouldn't pry.

"So…what excuse did he give you?" Mackenzie asked.

"Have you heard about my vision with Gavin?"

She nodded. "Gavin has been soliciting advice."

"That's why."

Anger glazed her eyes. Anger on my behalf? "Someday some girl is going to come along, and he's not going to be able to let her go. Maybe she'll dump him, and he'll learn what rejection feels like."

Maybe. But that would mean he loved her. My nails dug into my thigh.

"I'm guessing your vision with Gavin is the reason Cole has stayed silent about the breakup," Trina said. She parked in Reeve's driveway. "He doesn't want Gavin coming to you for information about your ability, something he would do if he knew you and Cole were over."

"Which isn't like him," Mackenzie said, a little confused now. A lot intrigued. "Cole doesn't usually care what a girl does or who she does it with once he's done with her."

Part of me wanted to thrill over this knowledge. Maybe he still cared about me. The other part of me scoffed. I wasn't so pathetic…was I? "He and I are over, and that's that. I'll be fine," I said tightly. "Thanks for the ride, girls. And the conversation. I appreciate it."

Mackenzie grabbed my hand to stop me before I could emerge. "We're here if you need us."

I had the dream again.

My mother reached for me. Warmth spread through me.

She shook me, shouting, "Alice. Wake up!"

I didn't. Not this time.

The zombies came for her, dragged her off and threw her on the cold, hard ground next to my dad. Then they fell on her, disappearing inside her, eating her spirit right out of her body. At first, she screamed and fought. Then she quieted and writhed. Then she stilled. Black boils appeared all over her skin, the zombie toxin poisoning her from the inside out.

I watched, helpless, sobbing.

And when I woke up, my cheeks were actually wet.

Had she died that way? Even the thought filled me with a terrible, dark rage. She had been such a gentle, loving woman. She'd never knowingly hurt anyone. For those creatures to torture her that way…

Can't deal with the past. I crawled out of bed and into the shower, not leaving until my fingers and toes were like prunes. I towel-dried, swiped a shaky hand across the steam-

covered mirror. My gaze caught on my reflection, and I stumbled backward, shocked. I was… There was… *Impossible.*

Tick, tock. Tick, tock.

The sound whispered through my mind, keeping time to the beat of my new heart. I stepped as close to the mirror as I could get, until the round edge of the sink prevented me from going any farther. There were dark smudges under my eyes and around my lips, and a black dot the size of my thumb streaked over my heart. Though I scrubbed with all my strength, leaving welts and nearly peeling off my skin, the splotches remained.

Could stress do this?

Maybe. Probably.

I turned away from the glass, and the sound of the *tick-tocks* died. My hands shook as I dressed in a T-shirt, jeans and butt-kicking boots and sheathed a dagger at each ankle.

I picked up my cell and texted Kat.

Me: How soon can U get here? Time 2 work out.

It was just after noon on Saturday. I was done avoiding Cole. I was going to his gym, and I was moving on with my life. Self-inflicted incarceration had done me no good. Obviously.

Mad Dog: Like, NOW. I'm here! Come 2 Reeve's room.

Me: On my way.

Mad Dog: Walk faster. Reeve's annoying me.

Reeve: SHE LIES! I annoy no 1.

I stalked down the hall and up the stairs. Reeve occupied the entire top floor. I cleared the landing and sailed inside the first sitting room, an area decorated with pink, pink and more pink, coupled with mounds of lace and rows of ruffles.

Every time I came up here, I thought that maybe Valentine's Day had thrown up and this had been the result.

The bedroom door was open. The girls sat at the edge of the four-poster king (draped in pink satin). Reeve had her hand on Kat's forehead. Kat was shaking her head in denial of something, her cheeks pale, dark circles under her eyes.

"Are you okay?" I asked her.

Hazel eyes found me, only to skitter away. "Not you, too. I missed out on my beauty z's, that's all."

No. It was more than that. Lately, she'd had more bad days than good.

She returned her attention to me, looked me over and frowned. "But, uh, what's wrong with *you?* I mean, I know you've been going through something you haven't had the decency to share with us, but wow. You're like death walking."

"Kat!" Reeve said.

"What? It's true."

I attempted to scrub the discolorations from my skin. "I don't know what happened, but I can't get the smudges off."

"Smudges? What smudges? You're the same shade of snow-white as always—and that's a compliment, by the way. You're like a winter wonderland fairy, and I'd be eaten up with jealousy if—"

"You weren't so in love with yourself," Reeve interjected with a laugh.

"Exactly! You've seen me, right? God was on His A game when He made me, all, like, a dash of sexy here, a sprinkle of awesome there. It's just…your eyes," Kat said to me. "They're more haunted than usual."

The smudges had faded? That quickly? I stalked to the vanity mirror and leaned over, planting my palms on the surface scattered with makeup. My reflection stared back at me, the smudges just as dark as before. Disappointment hit me a split second before I realized something else was wrong. Something far worse.

I wasn't smiling—but my reflection was.

Tick, tock.

I shook my head, blinked, but the image remained the same. *Tick.* Reeling, I reached up and patted my lips. *Tock.* The corners hadn't somehow lifted without my knowledge. *Tick.*

No longer able to catch my breath, I straightened and turned away. What I'd just seen... The fault of my imagination, surely.

"I look normal to you?" I demanded.

"Sure. But you've lost a little weight your Nana's chocolate chip cupcakes would fix—hint, hint, I want chocolate chip cupcakes," Kat said at the same time Reeve said, "Totally."

Confirmation. My imagination *was* at fault.

No big deal, I decided. Everything would calm down once I'd dealt with my stress load.

I licked my lips. First step: I had to stop pretending. "So... Cole and I broke up. We're one hundred percent over. There's no hope of us ever getting back together."

"What?" Kat gasped, jolting to her feet. "What'd he do? And I know it's all his fault, the jerk! I'll kill him. I swear I will! Reeve, where are your Skittles?"

Reeve ignored her, her hand fluttering over her heart. "Oh, Ali. I'm so sorry."

I jutted my chin, somehow able to maintain my calm. "Don't be. That's life."

"But you guys were so happy. And he was spending the night with you," Kat said, clearly reeling. "Bronx told Frosty he caught Cole sneaking out to come see you multiple times."

I shook my head. "He might have snuck out and spent the night, but we never actually had sex." Not even before my injury.

Mom had told me to wait for someone special. Someone who loved and appreciated me for more than my body, and wouldn't run tattling to all his friends. Or hurt me. Or push for more than I was ready to give. Or abandon me if things got rough afterward. I'd thought Cole was that boy, but I must have sensed, deep down, he'd been holding a part of himself back.

Go me.

"He didn't think we'd last," I said, "and he didn't like me enough to fight for me. It hurts, I'm so mad I could do serious damage to him, but I'm not going to break down." Not again.

"Well, boys suck!" Kat flicked the length of her dark hair over one shoulder, truly angry on my behalf. "Ali, forget working out. Reeve, grab your keys and your dad's credit card. We're taking a girls' day, and since he's one of the enemy, he's paying."

"That seems fair. We just have to be back by six," Reeve replied, standing. "I have a date—I mean, uh, I'm sorry, Ali." Her dusky skin flushed, and her shoulders drooped

with shame. "I shouldn't have mentioned my date while you're suffering and…I'm just so sorry."

Oh, no, no, no. We weren't going down the pity road. "Don't you dare stop talking about your love life just because mine went up in flames."

"Yeah. What she said. Even though I have a feeling mine will be going up in flames, too." Kat toyed with the ends of her hair. "I don't think Frosty will be willing to become a girl for me, and right now I'm totally giving up on dudes."

Reeve shook her head in exasperation.

Me? I suddenly saw Kat through new eyes. She only ever talked about axing Frosty when she looked pale and withdrawn. In other words, when her kidneys were acting up. Fear was driving her, I realized, just like it had driven Cole. She probably felt vulnerable, desperate to protect herself.

Poor Kat. One day, Frosty might get tired of the hot-and-cold treatment and leave her.

Kat pointed a finger at Reeve. "Don't think I've forgotten you've been sidestepping my questions about your mystery guy."

"Maybe I'll tell you about him. Maybe I won't." Dark amber eyes gleamed with challenge. "You guys aren't the only ones who can keep secrets."

Kat backed down; what else could she do? "I don't know what you're talking about. I'm probably the most open and honest girl in the world," she muttered. "Just ask Ali."

Both girls peered over at me, expectant.

Kat wanted confirmation. Reeve wanted me to spill our secrets.

"Didn't someone mention a girls' day?" I asked.

★ ★ ★

We had our hair cut and styled, had facials and bought makeup, perfume, clothes and shoes. Or rather, they bought those things. I was still saving my money and refused to spend Mr. Ankh's. That didn't deter the girls. Every time my back was turned, they purchased something else for me and stuffed it in my bag.

Through it all, I avoided mirrors. I couldn't bring myself to look at my reflection, even though the girls raved about my appearance.

Sadly, I almost hyperventilated when Kat said, "A new you, for a new direction in life."

Fine. I did hyperventilate, and it freaked out both girls. It was just, terror had wrapped cold, clammy hands around my neck and squeezed, shutting off my airways. The second heartbeat had become more noticeable, and the intense hunger had returned.

Reeve splashed water in my face, but that wasn't what jolted me out of terror's grip. As close as she was, I could smell her—such a sweet, mouthwatering perfume—and I wanted to bite her. *So bad.* The desire threw me into another tailspin. I plopped into a chair, holding on to the arms for dear life…her life…again struggling to breathe.

Kat called Frosty, thinking I needed medical help only the slayers could provide.

Frosty, Bronx, Lucas and Cole—*please, anyone but Cole*—arrived at the store fifteen minutes later, and all heads turned in their direction. Eyes widened. Women muttered excitedly. Grown men backed away.

"What's he doing here?" Kat hissed.

The ringing in my ears was finally fading, allowing me to make out her words.

"Sheathe the claws, Kitten," Frosty said. "We weren't sure what we were dealing with. And what did you do to your hair?"

"Duh. I fixed it."

"But I liked it the way it was."

"Say one more word, I dare you, and I'll shave it all off. Your ex-girlfriend will be bald."

"You aren't my ex," he said flatly.

I'd never heard him use that tone with her. And yet, their familiar chatter helped soothe me, and the urge to bite Reeve at last diminished. What the heck was wrong with me?

Then Cole was crouching in front of my chair, and the rest of the world was forgotten. Embarrassment burned my cheeks. Wet strands of hair stuck to my forehead and cheeks. My T-shirt had a water ring around the collar.

I met his gaze, not expecting a vision this time and not getting one. I was careful to keep my features blank. Seconds…minutes…maybe hours passed…but he didn't do what I needed him to do and leave.

Please leave.

Then something happened. The same something that happened every time we were together.

The air around us came to life, thickening with awareness. My skin prickled in the most delicious way.

I didn't like it—because I liked it so much.

He must have felt it, too, because he looked away.

Thankful for the reprieve, I scrutinized his body language. His fingers were next to mine, twitching on the arms of

the chair, as if he wanted to reach for me but was fighting the impulse.

Did he want to reach for me?

My gaze lifted of its own accord.

He was staring at me again. Only he was staring far more intently, that violet gaze drilling into me, trying to burrow past skin and into soul to search for answers I didn't have.

"I didn't need the dark knight to race to my rescue," I sniped. "I'm fine."

"Ali," he said on a sigh. "You're not fine. Kat said you couldn't breathe."

"As you can see, I'm over it." I was proud of my seeming calm. "You can leave now."

Concern darkened his features, poking at my anger.

He had no right to feel concern for me.

"Why couldn't you breathe, Ali?"

"Does it really matter?"

At last he reached up, intending to cup my cheeks the way he used to. Just before contact he caught himself. His hands returned to the arms of the chair, caging me in, making me shiver—and hate myself. "Let Ankh run a few tests."

"No." I had been wrong to think I could face Cole today. It was too soon. Especially if he was going to be nice.

Why was he being nice?

"We're done here." I pushed him out of the way and stood on shaky legs. Frosty was scrubbing his knuckles into Kat's scalp while she laughed and batted at his arm. Bronx and Reeve were in the midst of a glaring contest.

"We have more to do," I said to the girls. Then I marched

away without another word, my coat and bags hanging at
my sides.

Both Kat and Reeve followed me, ditching the boys without hesitation.

"So...did you know that sleeping with twelve different
guys is the same thing as sleeping with, like, four thousand?"
Kat asked, breaking the silence, the tension.

I could have hugged her. She hadn't mentioned *our* guys,
and wasn't going to. She was trying to distract me.

"No way," Reeve said.

We cleared the doors of the mall, entered the coolness of
the day. I pulled on the coat.

Kat nodded. "I crunched the numbers myself. I'm eighty-
three percent sure that I'm one hundred percent sure that
my math is perfect. See, if you sleep with a guy, you've
then been with everyone he's been with and everyone his
other partners have been with and everyone their partners
have been with. It goes on and on." She held up one finger.
"Frosty is my only, but he's been with others and I'm sure
they've been with others, so, I'm guessing I've been with at
least fifty people—is there a scarlet letter on my forehead?"

"I wonder how many girls Bronx has gotten into bed,"
Reeve muttered.

"Bronx? Did you say Bronx? Because I could have sworn
you told me you're over him and seeing someone else," Kat
quipped.

Reeve pursed her lips.

I took a breath—held it. Exhaled, slowly. Mist formed in
front of my face. My first real post-breakup encounter with
Cole was now history. I'd survived with the tiniest shred of

dignity, and that was more than I'd expected. I was going to be okay.

A twentysomething guy stepped into our path, blocking us. We drew to a halt as he said, "Hey, pretty girl," with a wide, toothy grin aimed at Kat. "How about some company, hmm?"

Another guy pressed into his side. He eyed Reeve up and down as if she were a stick of cotton candy and he was dying from a sweet tooth.

"No, thanks," she said, and tried to inch around him.

He moved with her, continuing to block her. "Wait. You don't want to go until we've exchanged numbers, do you?"

The other guy leaned down to sniff Kat's neck. "My own personal brand of crack, right there."

"Quoting romance novels?" Scowling, she leaned back, out of reach. "Lesson of the day—you don't smell a girl until she gives you permission. Ever. It makes you a creeper."

He pouted.

I doubted the two were dangerous. I actually thought they were going for sexy and charming rather than disturbing. And maybe I could have tried to reach a verbal resolution with them. Maybe not.

Despite being "okay," anger still pulled at an already thin tether.

Nope. Wrong. The tether snapped.

I jabbed my palm into his nose, and cartilage shattered. Blood spurted. Cursing, his friend grabbed hold of my arm. To stop me from running—unnecessary—or to stop me from another attack, I wasn't sure. I only knew he'd made a mistake. I clamped onto his wrist and twisted with all of

my strength, forcing his body to turn with the motion to save the bone from breaking.

Before he could lurch free, I kicked the back of his knee, sending him to the ground. An elbow to the temple finished him off, and he collapsed the rest of the way. He sprawled on the concrete, motionless.

Satisfaction filled me, followed swiftly by guilt.

"Come on," I said. I tugged the lapels of my coat closer as I walked away.

"That was both cool and frightening," Kat said with a shudder, keeping pace with me. "I don't know whether to pat you on the back or run and hide."

"Where did you learn how to do that?" Reeve asked, her gaze darting back to the boys.

"Col— Around." My gaze landed on the tattoo shop across the street. Bright red letters—TATTIE'S INK— flashed on and off.

I stopped.

The girls backtracked.

"I want one," I found myself saying.

"One what?" Kat asked.

"A tattoo." The slayers marked themselves with the names of the loved ones they'd lost in the war against the zombies, or symbols to represent them. I had none, yet I'd lost my parents, my sister and my grandfather.

Bad Ali.

"I want one," I said again, more confident this time. I headed across the street.

The girls followed after me.

"What are you going to get?" Kat asked, clapping hap-

pily. "A skull and crossbones? Snake fangs dripping with blood? A unicorn?"

"This is a mistake," Reeve said.

A bell jingled over the door as I entered. The walls were covered with art, pictures of lions and tigers, dragons and aliens. Hearts. Stars. The sun, the moon, fish and lightning. Naked women. It was overwhelming.

A heavily tattooed man with piercings all over his face stood behind the counter, cleaning equipment. He glanced up, grunted with disdain. "You guys even close to eighteen?"

"No," Reeve and I said in unison.

"Yes," Kat said, and elbowed me.

He dried his hands on a rag. "You'll need a permission slip from your parents, and you'll need at least one parent present."

Kat offered her sweetest grin and wound her arm around my waist. "We knew that. That's why I'm here. I'm her mother, and I'll sign whatever form you've got."

A gleam of amusement in his eyes. "She must take after her father."

"All of my children do," Kat quipped.

His gaze landed on me. "Let me guess. You want a flower. Or a butterfly."

Not quite. "I want a white rabbit," I said.

He thought it over, shrugged and slid a pad and pen in Kat's direction. "Fill this out all properlike for your *daughter*, since I'm guessing your IDs will tell me you have different last names, and you," he said to me, "come on back. I think I have something you'll dig."

"Ali," Reeve said, latching onto my wrist. "A tattoo is permanent."

Yeah, and mine would be the only permanent thing in my life. Nana wouldn't live forever. And, as I'd been told time and time again by Mr. Ankh, the moment Reeve learned about the zombies she would be ripped out of my life. Not even the vivacious Kat was guaranteed a tomorrow.

"I have to do this." I pulled from her grip to trail Artist Guy behind a crimson curtain. There were several rooms, each blocked by one of those curtains. He led me to the one in back, swept the fabric aside and motioned to a lounge chair. I sat.

He flipped through an art book. When he found what he was searching for, he showed me the page. "What do you think?"

"I like the ears of this one," I said, pointing. "But the body of this one, and the tail of that one." Perfect for Emma. "Also, I'll want a second tattoo. Two daggers in the shape of a cross." I could think of no better representation of my parents. I wasn't sure what I'd get to represent Pops, though. His would have to wait.

Artist Guy frowned and set the book aside. "I'll have to draw both from scratch, and that's gonna cost extra."

"I'm fine with that." For the first time today, I wasn't going to worry about spending the allowance Nana had given me. I removed my coat, pushed up the sleeves of my shirt.

He peered at my pale, unmarked flesh and shook his head. "All right, then, where do you want them? Exactly?"

"One on each wrist. And I want them to face me, not the

people looking at me." I wanted to be able to see the designs without having to contort.

What would Nana say when she saw them?

"I've got to sketch what you want, so give me about...oh, half an hour." He left without another word.

An opportunity to leave. *Not going to happen.*

I closed my eyes and counted.

By the time he returned, I'd reached 1,532. I wondered what Kat and Reeve were doing in the lobby.

He gathered the necessary supplies and sat beside me.

"Still want to do this?" he asked. "Because once I start, there will be no backing out."

"Absolutely."

He used a piece of paper to transfer the first image onto my wrist. I saw big ears standing tall, a fat body and a bushy tail, just like the rabbits Emma had created in the sky time and time again to warn me of coming zombie attacks.

"Perfect," I said, a bit surprised.

"I only do perfect work." He sounded offended.

"Prove it."

My snark clearly surprised him, and he shook his head. "You know this will hurt, right?"

"I've known hurt. This will be nothing."

He snorted. "Sure, princess. Whatever you say."

Leaning over me, gun in hand, he got to work. And okay, it hurt more than I'd anticipated, stinging and throbbing, but a part of me welcomed the pain. I liked that I was feeling something other than anger and panic.

Panic. The word got stuck in my mind, echoing.

I'd panicked earlier.

I'd panicked big-time.

Mr. Ankh had been right, hadn't he? The episodes were panic attacks, triggered by...what? Emotion? Maybe. I was living with the guilt of knowing Emma's life would be forever unfulfilled. The ache of forging a new one for myself as the old one burned behind me. The uncertainty of navigating a spiritual world I'd been unprepared for. The fear of the unknown.

But emotions couldn't be the full story. Otherwise I'd never have moments of calm. I thought back. Lying in my bed, after Cole had walked out on me, I'd lamented about the new direction of my life. Then, boom, the panic had come. Then, later on, Kat had mentioned the newness of my appearance and boom, panic again.

New things.

Change, I realized. The thought of change had to be the trigger.

And okay. All right. Now that I knew, I could deal. But...

That wasn't the full story, either. It couldn't be. Panic failed to explain the double heartbeats...the hunger...and the fact that I'd wanted to bite Reeve. And what if I'd been wrong about the smudges? What if they weren't part of my imagination, but this...whatever *this* was?

That would mean...what?

I didn't know, but one thing was certain. More changes loomed on the horizon.

Just like that, perspiration beaded on my brow and upper lip, and an invisible elephant sat down on my chest. The pressure... I struggled to breath, barely even able to wheeze.

"Hey, are you okay?" the guy asked me.

"Fine," I managed to huff. "Just hurry."

"You don't rush quality. And I told you it would hurt."

My sister was my calming force, so I drew her image to the front of my mind, concentrating on her. I saw a mass of straight, dark hair. Sun-kissed skin. A mischievous gleam in her dark eyes.

"You're the prettiest girl in the whole world, Alice," she said, beaming up at me.

"No, brat, that would be you," I replied, gently tapping the tip of her nose.

"No way. A boy at my school told me he heard his dad say only blondes are worth doing."

"First, I never want to hear you say the words worth doing *again. Do you even know what that means? Second, that boy's dad is an idiot. And a pig!"*

So hungry... Must eat...

The whispery voice intruded on the memory, and I frowned at Artist Guy. "Did you say something?"

He didn't glance up, even as he moved to my other wrist. "Nope."

Hungry. Hungry! HUNGRY!

I shook my head, as if my mind had somehow locked on a different radio frequency and a little motion would change the channel back. But it didn't, and I found I couldn't tear my gaze away from the vulnerability of Artist Guy's now-glowing neck.

"Be still," he commanded.

"I'm sorry. I just... Did you hear that?"

"Hear what?"

"That voice. That whisper."

He paused long enough to dab at a bead of blood with a cotton ball. "Great. The pretty princess is one of the crazies. I should have known."

Bite him. Feed on him.

"Emma," I said.

"You want me to add a name?" he asked.

"No."

My sister appeared a few seconds later. "You're getting tattoos?" she squealed. Then she saw my face, and the excitement was replaced by concern. "Alice?"

"Something's wrong with me," I told her.

"I know." Artist Guy sighed. "That's what I just said."

"Cole?" she asked.

I snapped my teeth, then glanced at Artist Guy, trying to show her what the problem was.

"You want to bite him?"

I nodded.

Frowning, she traced her fingers through my hair, and the urge to bite instantly vanished, thrilling me...baffling me. "I'll ask around and return when I've learned something."

She disappeared. And maybe I passed out from relief. I don't know. One moment I was relaxed in my seat; the next Artist Guy was saying, "All right. All done. What do you think?"

I opened my eyes to see he was setting the equipment aside. I waited for the voice or urge to return, but...there was only silence. No hunger. I uttered a quiet prayer of thanks.

He crossed his arms and watched my expression. "Well?"

The ink was perfect, as promised, and exactly what I'd wanted. The white rabbit was on one side, and the daggers

on the other. The skin around the ink was red and swollen, though, and throbbed insistently.

"They're wonderful."

Grunting with satisfaction, he smothered each with ointment, then covered them with bandages. "Remove the dressing in about an hour and add more ointment. Keep the ink clean, but don't take long showers or baths for at least two weeks."

"Okay."

He ushered me to the front of the building, where Kat and Reeve waited.

Grinning when she spotted me, Kat jumped up and clapped. "Let me see, let me see!"

Reeve stood more slowly, as if she wanted to avoid looking at the tattoos as long as possible.

"Give me a minute to pay," I said.

The moment we were outside, I peeled back the bandages.

"Very cool! Cole will regret the day he let you get away," Kat said. As we climbed into Reeve's Porsche, she added, "I'm making it my life's mission. Well, that, and torturing Frosty."

I claimed the center of the backseat and buckled up. "Where are we going now?"

"To Reeve's. Then you and I are going to Cole's—uh, house, yes, to his house to work out," Kat said. "You're going to train me, as promised. No more treadmilling. And yes, I just turned a noun into a verb."

"Train you?" Reeve eased the car into traffic. "For what? I mean, I know you guys have been working out a lot, but I'd had no idea there was a purpose to it."

"Self-defense," I replied. "Like what I did today."

Kat nodded. "Only maybe not so hard-core."

"I promised I'd teach you," I said, flickers of dread light-ing me up, "and I will. Just…not today." I wanted to go home and wait for Emma.

"Well, I'd like to learn, too," Reeve said.

"Uh…hmm." I peered out the window, watching as cars whizzed past. Trees. Power lines. "I'd love to include you, but you'll have to get permission from your dad first."

Her brow furrowed. "He'll say yes."

Not even if she begged him.

"I mean, why would he say no? Especially after what hap-pened today," she added.

My gaze snagged on a cloud in the sky—a cloud cut in the shape of a rabbit. The zombies would invade tonight. I frowned. Was I ready?

Better question: Would I be invited to help?

"Uh, guys. I think someone's following us," Reeve said, her voice trembling with apprehension. "What if it's the guys from the mall? What should I do?"

I turned in my seat, peering out the back window. "Call—" I stopped myself before I said his name. "Which car?"

"A black SUV, dark-tinted windows."

It was two slots back, on the left. As big as it was, six peo-ple could be inside. The odds weren't great, but they weren't terrible, either. "Take the next exit ramp and pull over."

"What!" she and Kat demanded in unison.

"Just do it. Please." I was armed. I was also in a terrible mood. If Anima hoped to scare me, they'd soon learn the error

of such a fruitless endeavor. If the guys from the shopping center craved revenge, I'd give them something else to cry about. If this was just one big misunderstanding, I'd make sure it never happened again.

Reeve obeyed, reluctantly, and the moment the car came to a stop, I palmed my daggers and jumped out of the car. The SUV had tracked us off the highway and slowed down as it approached us. A window rolled down.

"Miss Bell," said a man I'd never before met. He was old enough to be my grandfather, with a full head of salt-and-pepper hair, thick glasses, an aquiline nose and dark brown skin. "I'd like a word with you."

He knew my name, and he'd come at me in the most secretive of ways. He had to be a Hazmat.

I didn't need to know any more than that. I threw one of my daggers, just as Cole had taught me, and the tip embedded in one of the SUV's tires. Air hissed out.

The man scowled at me. "Was that really necessary?"

"Probably not." I held up my other dagger. "I doubt what I do next will be, either, but I'm sure it'll be fun."

He flashed me a look full of disappointment. "Very well. When you're curious about your condition, you'll have to come to me." He tossed a card out the window, and as the paper floated to the ground, the SUV sped away.

OF ROTTING MONSTERS AND TASTY MEN

Normally, I would have hunted Cole down and told him what had happened. Today, I decided to tell Mr. Ankh.

On my way to his office, I ran into Nana. "Ali, honey, I have a surprise—"

"I'm sorry, Nana," I rushed out. "But I have to talk with Mr. Ankh about something. Rain check?"

Disappointment clouded her features. "All right. No problem."

Instant guilt. I'd hurry here and spend the rest of the day with her. I marched into the office without an invitation, a first for me, and shut and locked the door. He glanced up from the stack of papers on his desk.

He had dark hair and eyes, like Reeve, but he was almost always tense and formal, and I rarely left his presence feeling better about my circumstances. Right now, though, he was my only choice.

"Good," he said, "I've been wanting to talk to you. Sit down."

I obeyed, saying, "There's been an incident."

"All right," he acknowledged, folding his fingers together. "How bad is it? Does it need to be covered up?"

"No, nothing like that. It's just—"

"So there are no dead bodies?"

"No."

"No zombies?"

"No. Just—"

"Then listen," he said, once again cutting me off. "I've been told you've been cleaning up the house and only eating bagels and cream cheese. That isn't acceptable, Miss Bell. I pay someone to take care of the house, and I have enough food for an army."

"That's wonderful, but I'm not going to take advantage of you. Now. We went to a strip mall today and—"

"Does your grandmother know what you're doing? How you're starving yourself?"

"I'm *not* starving myself," I said. Then I told him what had gone down, described the SUV, the man who'd hoped to talk to me and what I'd done to his tire. The only detail I kept to myself was the business card currently burning a hole in pocket.

I'd grabbed it with every intention of handing it over to Mr. Ankh, but now, peering into his stern features, I just… couldn't.

When you're curious about your condition…

Did the man know what I didn't? Did he know what was wrong with me?

How could he know?

And what would Mr. Ankh say if I told him about the smudges and the heartbeat and the hunger? How many tests would he want to run? Would he lock me away?

He popped his jaw. "That is Anima's M.O. I'll put a security detail on—"

"Oh, no," I said, tugging at the sleeves of my shirt, making sure my bandages were covered. "No one's following me around." No telling what they'd see me do.

He frowned at me. "Privacy means nothing in the face of safety, Miss Bell. I'm sure your grandmother would agree with me."

Low blow. One I ignored. "No guards," I insisted. "Reeve might notice them and start asking more questions."

He relented. As I'd known he would.

He really did love his daughter.

For the first time, I began to wonder about this man's life...his past. "The woman you mentioned... The one who had the anxiety disorder... Was she Reeve's mom?"

"Yes." His tone was short, clipped, letting me know he'd said all he wanted to say on that subject.

We don't always get what we want. "Did she know about the zombies? Is that why she was afraid?"

He hammered his elbows into the desk, rattling the entire piece. "Yes, Miss Bell. Yes. She knew about them, but she couldn't see them, and so she began to imagine them around her every second of every day, and it was more than she could deal with. Finally she killed herself."

How awful. Poor Mrs. Ankh, to feel death was the only way. Poor Mr. Ankh, left to pick up the pieces. Poor Reeve,

a little girl drowning in sorrow and confusion. No wonder he insisted she be kept in the dark. He didn't want the same fate to befall her. "I'm sorry."

He waved my sympathy away. "The past is the past, Miss Bell."

Such easy words to offer—but was he actually living them? "Just so you know, I saw a rabbit cloud in the sky. Zombies could be coming out tonight."

He arched a brow, saying, "And you want in the rotation."

I'd told myself I wasn't ready to see Cole again. I'd even questioned my ability to fight. And still I found myself saying, "I do." I couldn't waste an opportunity to slay my enemy.

Mr. Ankh grilled me about my health. Was I feeling okay? Had I had any moments of weakness? Had I had another panic attack?

I answered the first two bluntly but sidestepped the last one. "Look, I was born to kill zombies. So, tonight, that's exactly what I'm going to do. Whether you're on board or not. And yes, that's a threat."

He grinned at me, but it wasn't a nice grin. "You can't do anything if you're unconscious."

He would drug me? "Try," was all I said.

He studied me for a long while before sighing, nodding stiffly. "Fine. You're determined. I get it. And this time, I'll let you have your way. You'll have to hurry, though. The slayers are at Cole's gym, and rotations are about to be decided for the week."

Crap. My day with Nana would have to wait. "Slight problem," I said. "I don't have a license or a car."

He released another sigh. "Be ready in five. My driver will be waiting out front."

"Thanks, Mr. Ankh." I stood and walked to the door.

"By the way, I wasn't teasing about the cleaning and the food."

"I didn't think you were." And he would learn I hadn't been teasing, either. I paused and glanced back at him. "I admire the way you're protecting Reeve, I do, but all our secrets are hurting her. She's already suspicious, and those suspicions are making her unhappy. There's got to be another way."

"Miss Bell," he said, slamming his pen on the desk.

I knew a very stern lecture was coming, so I hurried into the hall.

In my room, I changed into battle-ready clothing and gathered everything I'd need. More daggers, a syringe filled with the antidote, a pocketful of throwing stars and my phone.

I tucked the business card the man had given me in the bottom drawer of my desk and saw there was a note resting next to my computer.

I was going through the things that survived the fire, and I found my great-grandfather's journal. I had given it to your mother years ago. A few of the pages are now singed, but that's the only damage. I know it's weird, but I thought you might like to have a family heirloom.
Love, Nana

The journal!

I'd thought it had come from my dad, that *he'd* given it to my mom. How had my great-great-great-grandfather known to write it? I mean, the ability to see the zombies was passed through genes just as easily as blue eyes, but my mother had never seen them. Neither had Nana.

What could this mean?

No time for puzzles. Right.

But this had to be the surprise Nana had mentioned. And what an amazing surprise it was.

I owed that woman a million hugs.

I didn't mean to, but I glanced at the vanity mirror as I opened the door. A habit I'd developed after first meeting Cole. I'd always wanted to look my best for him. This time, my reflection caught me completely off guard.

Tick. The girl in the mirror—me!—had her hand lifted and pressed against the glass, as if reaching for me.

Tock. How could... How was... *Impossible.*

Tick. In a daze, I walked toward her—toward me.

Tock. She never moved. I mean, *my reflection* never moved.

Tick. I pressed a trembling hand against the coolness of the glass.

Tock. Her hand fell away.

A thousand different thoughts raced through my head.

I'd decided she was real rather than a figment. So...what was she? A part of me?

Another me?

The smudges under her eyes curved and seemed to drip onto her cheeks. A *dying* me?

Trembling, I swiped a tube of red lipstick from the bathroom and wrote over the glass. **Who Are You?**

I slammed the lipstick on the vanity surface and marched to the door. As I stepped into the hall, I glanced back. Breath caught in my throat. I read **Your Doom**.

Running back inside and smearing the words gave me no satisfaction, only increased my shock. Whatever she was, she didn't like me.

Can't worry about this right now.

I raced from the room, and this time, I didn't look back. I wouldn't think about anything I'd seen, about the change… the change… *No!* I wouldn't allow another panic attack to swoop in and carry me away. Mr. Ankh would find out, and I would be banned from the meeting at Cole's.

I checked the halls. Empty. Good. Reeve must be in her room, and I wasn't sure where Nana had gone. Even the housekeeper was nowhere to be seen. As promised, the driver was waiting for me at the front door. I sailed past him without a word and buckled into the backseat of the dark sedan. I held my breath as he slid into the driver's seat. He started the engine. Eased forward.

I exhaled.

Along the way, I checked the sky. The rabbit cloud was still there.

My phone rang, startling me. I recognized the number and experienced a conflicting tide of emotions, from uncertainty to gratitude. "Justin," I said. "I should have called you. Thank you for helping with the fight and taking what was meant for me."

"Hey, I owed you." Then, "How are you, Ali?" His voice

was low, as if he wasn't sure of his welcome and was determined not to spook me.

"I've been better."

He groaned. "Yeah, I'm sorry about that. I'm sorry I bit
you. I don't know what came over me. You were there, and
you smelled so good, so clean and pure, and my mouth was
watering, and the urge hit me, and it was so strong, so intense, I couldn't fight it." The words spilled from him with
barely a breath. "I didn't *want* to fight it."

Some of what he'd said really jelled with me. A clean, pure
scent. An unwillingness to fight. An unquenchable hunger.
"Has anything else happened to you since that night?"

A crackling pause that set my nerves on edge. "Like
what?"

Yeah, like I was really going to confide in him. "You tell
me," I said, using a tactic Cole had once used on me.

Cole. I ran my tongue over my teeth.

I had to stop thinking about him.

"To be honest, I've been normal," Justin said. "Nothing's
happened. To me, at least," he added. "I'm guessing something's happening with you, though."

The brakes on the car squeaked, and I peeked out the window to see we'd reached our destination. So soon?

"I have to go," I said.

"Don't want to talk about it?"

"I'm kind of busy." *And yes.*

Another pause. "We'll talk again, though?" he asked, hesitant.

"Yeah. I think so."

I hung up and stepped into the cold of the evening. The

sun would soon disappear, and the moon would take its place, full and golden in the sky. Even though darkness had yet to fall, the path to the barn was lit by small halogens meant to discourage any zombies from drawing near.

I used the code on the ID pad to open the door. Before our breakup, when I'd come here and he hadn't, Cole had finally broken down and given me the "key." I pushed my way inside, only to discover the meeting was already in full swing. A chair had been carried to the center of the boxing ring, where Cole was perched.

Veronica sat in his lap.

His arm was wrapped around her waist.

The girl was relaxed against him, completely at ease, as if she had no doubts about her reception.

Cole was disheveled, but also perfectly at ease. As if they'd messed around before settling down, and he'd never been happier.

The details hit me like bullets, one at a time, fast and sure. He'd always liked touching me. Sifting the ends of my hair through his fingers. Ghosting his knuckles across my jaw. Pulling me into the hard line of his body for a kiss. Seeing him act that way with someone else...

Pain? Yes, I felt pain. Betrayal? Jealousy? Yes, I felt those, too. Felt them so deeply I wasn't sure how I remained on my feet—or out of that ring. I think a part of me had hoped he would eventually come crawling back to me, no matter what I'd told him. No matter what I'd told my friends. But he wasn't going to, was he? We were done, just as he'd said. Just as I'd agreed. Only he'd already moved on.

Breathe. Just breathe.

I wouldn't freak out over this.

I'd come here to do a job. So I would do it.

I switched my focus. The rest of the crew leaned against the ropes. Frosty, Bronx, Mackenzie, Derek, Trina, Lucas, Collins, Cruz and Gavin, each hard bodied and dressed in black, ready for action. No one seemed to care that Cole—a guy who had only split from me a short while ago—had already forgotten about me.

Okay, so I hadn't exactly switched my focus.

Threads of fury joined an already toxic mix of emotions, whooshing through me. This wasn't right. This wasn't fair. How could he do this to me? Was he trying to punish me for the vision I'd had? A vision I couldn't control? A vision I wouldn't allow to come true?

No. This wasn't for my benefit and wasn't a punishment. He hadn't known I would show up. This was for him. He wanted that girl in his lap.

My hands fisted. I'd been wrong about his sense of honesty. He'd lied to me.

I remembered what he'd said to me.

Me: *Do you want Veronica?*

Him: *No. Not even a little.*

Liar! I longed to shout.

How easy it would be to stalk into the ring, sink my teeth into his spirit and—

His spirit?

Oh, good glory. Was I thinking like the zombies now?

I raised my chin, squared my shoulders. I'd rather die.

I forced myself to concentrate for real.

"—report every detail," Cole was saying. "I don't just

want to hear that you survived the night, or that you did or didn't see any zombies. I'm not kidding, I want every detail. In writing. From all of you. Two partners can't turn in one report. I want two from two, and I want you to write them separately. After what happened to Justin and Ali, I'm in an information-gathering mood." Shadows and light battled for dominance on his face, giving him a sinister bent. "Got me?"

He scanned the murmuring crowd, bypassed me and quickly returned. Guilt flashed in his eyes, only to be extinguished, leaving the cold, blank mask. He stood, forcing Veronica to stand as well, and dropped his arms to his sides. She remained only a whisper away and frowned when she noticed me.

I held Cole's gaze, again not expecting a vision, but wanting one—no, I didn't want one, shouldn't want one, but...

It never came.

Disappointment grew wings of sharply honed iron and flew through every inch of me, cutting at me.

Cole cleared his throat, clearly uncomfortable.

Don't give him a reaction.

He looked away. "From now on," he said, voice harder now, harsher, "if your partner gets bitten, administer the antidote the moment you're able. Don't wait until the fight is over. And if your partner bites you, don't try to hide it from us. We're not going to blame him."

"Or her," Mackenzie called, and snapped her teeth.

"Now you're just giving the girls permission to take a nibble anytime, anyplace," Frosty retorted. "I've got enough trouble keeping them off me as it is."

Chuckles resounded.

I couldn't force myself to laugh.

"You know who your partners are," Cole said, "and where you've been placed in the schedule. Do what you have to do to get ready."

The group broke apart; some kids were to walk the streets, hunting zombies; some were to go home and rest, catch up on schoolwork; some were to stay here and guard the bodies of the slayers, also waiting in case backup was needed.

Veronica rose on her tiptoes and whispered in Cole's ear.

The fury returned, expanded, but I managed to calmly say, "What about me?" and step up to the ring.

All eyes darted in my direction.

"Ali Bo Bali," Frosty said, throwing his arm over my shoulder. "I didn't think we'd see you tonight."

I appreciated the show of support.

"What about you?" Cole replied, hesitant.

Steady. "I want in."

A muscle ticked below his eye as he approached me. "After what happened today? No."

"What happened today?" Veronica asked, coming over to rest her head on his shoulder. Staking a claim? Digging the knife deeper?

If anyone told her what I'd gone through…

Cole eased away from her and massaged the back of his neck, a habit of his. Right now he was more than uncomfortable. He was discombobulated.

Good.

"You're injured," he said.

"I'm healed. Besides that, others have fought injured and you never complained."

"Others have had more training. And why do you have bandages on your wrists?"

He'd noticed them, even though I wore long sleeves?

Trying to control my sudden trembling, I pulled the bandages off for good. My skin was more reddened than before, and far more swollen, but the ink was still pretty.

Veronica leaned toward me, shrugged. "Don't take this the wrong way, but those are too big for your bone structure."

There was a right way to take that? I knew the tattoos were beautiful and just the right size for me.

I wouldn't give her the satisfaction of a response.

No, that wasn't true. I would. "I'm seconds away from giving *you* a brand-new bone structure."

She blinked at me as if I was missing a few screws. "I've been nothing but nice to you, and you want a go at me?"

That was *nice?*

"I think the tattoos are perfect." Cole stepped between us. His narrowed gaze roved over me, lingered in a few select places. I had to fight a shiver. "Tattoos. New hair. New makeup. I didn't notice it before. You were too wet. I'm noticing now."

"Wet?" Veronica said, the word almost strangled out of her. "Wet how?"

Scowling, Cole pushed her toward the rings. "Go. Now."

I kind of wished the floor would open up and swallow me.

She flicked me a confused glance over her shoulder but did as he'd commanded and left us alone.

Getting back on track. He had a problem with my makeover? "Are you saying I'm eye broccoli?"

Frosty barked out a laugh. "Where do girls get this stuff, man?"

"I'm not even sure what eye broccoli means," Cole said. "That you look bad, and I shouldn't want to eat you, or that you're loaded with vitamins and I should."

Kill me.

Please.

"That I look bad," I gritted.

"You don't. You never have." Cole lifted my wrists and traced his thumb around the designs. When he realized what he was doing, he scowled and dropped his arms. "So. Tell me. Why'd you make all these changes?"

Changes.

The C word overshadowed any pleasure I might have taken from his compliment...his touch. What would change tonight? Tomorrow?

Both hearts sped up, and my nasal passages seemed to clog with cotton.

"Easy, now," Frosty said.

Cole released my arms to cup my cheeks. "Breathe, Ali. Just like that. In and out. Good girl."

The moment I calmed, I pulled out of Cole's hold and shrugged away from Frosty's. Another rush of embarrassment washed through me. I couldn't allow myself to rely on these guys in any way.

"What was that about?" Cole asked.

"To answer your other question, the only one I'll acknowledge," I said tightly, "I made a few improvements. I wanted to look hot for the night my vision with Gavin comes true."

Direct hit—a shocker. Cole flinched, even paled. "You were hot the way you were," he said, staring deep into my eyes. "Whatever you think of me, whatever's happened between us, that was never up for debate."

Pretty words, nothing more, and yet the air between us charged, just like before, becoming electric with awareness. Every nerve ending in my body perked up, waiting for… something. Another visual caress. A hand on my shoulder. The nudge of his knee. *Anything.*

He backed up a few steps, and the charge fizzled. I could still smell his scent, though, soap and something woodsy, a hint of the animal he could sometimes be. Rough, wild, untamed. But underneath it all was the scent of roses… Veronica's scent.

Maybe I'd consume *both* their spirits.

"Did you really do all this for Gavin?"

His tone was dead. As if he didn't care.

As if he'd never cared.

"I did it for me," I said, and left it at that. I would never let him know how much he was hurting me.

He nodded, some of the tension leaving him.

Tension? I hadn't noticed it. I wonder what had calmed him. Because it certainly couldn't have been my admission. He didn't care, remember? "Where am I in the lineup?"

"You'll be on patrol tonight. Sunday you'll rest. Monday you'll stay here in the gym, in case you're needed. Tuesday, patrol again. Be ready to go in ten." He stalked into the locker room.

I remained in place, trying to control my inner turmoil.

Veronica stood in back, watching me.

I scowled at her, daring her to approach. No question she'd come to *my* Bama expecting to win Cole back by fair means or foul. Well, she'd done it. And she hadn't even had to work that hard.

"Enjoy him while it lasts," I called. "Apparently he has Girlfriend ADD."

She looked away, but not before I caught the blush staining her cheeks.

A blush from her. Why?

Frosty cleared his throat, a demand for my full attention. "Hate to stop you when you're going balls to the wall, but you need to talk to Reeve," he said. "Tell her to drop whoever she's seeing. This keeps up, and Bronx might just snap and play Prison Rules with the guy."

"How do you know about Reeve's new boyfriend, Ethan?" I demanded, searching for Bronx.

He hammered at the punching bag with so much force I was afraid his knuckles would crack. Dark hair streaked with blue was wet and plastered to his scalp. Sweat dripped from his temples to his bare shoulders, then down the ripped cords of his abs, and if I'd been with Cole, I wouldn't have watched those droplets, mesmerized.

Lucky Reeve.

Poor Ethan.

Frosty patted me on top of the head. "Aren't you cute? As if you don't know the answer to your own question."

Right. Kat. "Forget Reeve. Her life, her decisions. Your problem is the fact that Kat wants self-defense lessons, and I promised to give them to her. I know she would love it if

you helped." And with my new…urges, it would be better all the way around.

Uncomfortable with the new direction of the conversation, he shifted from one booted foot to the other. "No. And you're going to tell her you changed your mind."

"Are you kidding me? No, I'm not."

"It's not that I don't want her trained. It's that I want her stronger first. You could break her. I'd definitely break her."

"Cole didn't break me, and I'll be a much gentler teacher. So will you. I've seen you with her."

That earned me another head pat. "Cole went easy on you, sweet cakes. And I'm the worst coach the slayers have ever seen. Just ask them. I'm too impatient with failure, and I'd hurt Kat's feelings."

I got snagged on his first words. "Cole did not go easy on me."

He tsked. "Pretty, but delusional. A smoking-hot combination. No wonder all the boys want a go at you."

Hardly. "You're seconds away from a busted nose, Frosty."

He laughed. "Unlike Cole, I give back whatever's dished. Just remember what I said about Reeve." And he ambled away.

As if! "Who's on patrol tonight?" I called.

Frosty grinned over his shoulder. "There are two patrols going out. Gavin and Mackenzie, and Cole and Lucas. Want to guess who you'll end up with?"

A BEAUTIFUL DISASTER

For several minutes I stood where Frosty had left me, all by myself, feeling forgotten, abandoned. Finally the most unlikely source took pity on me and strode over.

"It won't always be this hard," Mackenzie said with a sad smile.

A show of compassion. One I didn't deserve. Not from her. I guess she'd meant what she'd told me before, about being there for me if I needed her.

I'd find a way to make up for every bad thing I'd ever said to her.

"Here's hoping," I replied.

She patted my shoulder before walking away.

A few seconds later, Trina took her place. "When you're ready, let me know and I'll take you out to meet someone outside our little circle. You'll have fun, I promise. It did wonders for Mac when she was in this same situation."

I nodded, and she was off. I wasn't sure I'd ever be ready.

Cole exited the locker room. He'd painted black half circles under his eyes and strapped weapons all over his body. I'd always loved seeing him like this. Strong. Ready for action. Just a little naughty, capable of any deed. Had we still been together, I would have thrown myself into his arms and kissed the breath out of him.

You know what wistful thinking gets you? A whole lot of nothing.

"What are my instructions?" I demanded.

He stopped in front of me. Avoiding my gaze, he withdrew a black bandanna from one of the pockets in his combat pants and covered my hair. "You'll stay with Gavin and Mackenzie, and you'll be careful."

"Wait. What?" Frosty called from the sidelines.

Yeah. What? Frosty had led me to believe Cole would want me to be with him.

Cole frowned at him, and I think the two somehow engaged in a silent argument with their eyes.

"Can't wait," I said, drawing Cole's attention back to me.

"I wish… Well, it doesn't matter." He rolled his shoulders, the tension back and clearly too much. "I have to be with Lucas tonight, and I have to be alone."

Something about his tone… It was the gruff one he used whenever he spoke about his secret. He had to be with Lucas because…he was spying on him? Emma had mentioned spying.

Or was I just giving him an excuse for not wanting to patrol with me?

Ugh. I hated this. Hated that I was taking everything he said, everything he did, and dissecting it, looking for hidden

meaning, trying to give myself a reason to hope for reconciliation I knew wasn't going to happen.

Stupid. Put your hope in the right thing, and it would be a lifeline. Put your hope in the wrong thing, and it would be a noose.

"I was serious. Be careful out there." He ghosted his knuckle across the curve of my jaw. "Stay alert."

I stepped back, out of reach. I wasn't sure what he'd meant by the touch—and I wasn't going to try to figure it out. I also wasn't allowing him to touch me like that anymore.

He frowned.

"By the way," I said, "I saw the rabbit cloud. I'm pretty sure the zombies will be out tonight."

His features hardened, chilled. "You tell me *now*, after I decide to send you on patrol?"

What, he'd thought the zombies would stay in tonight, and that was the only reason he'd opted to send me out? Anger sparked. "If you hadn't already broken up with me, I would absolutely be breaking up with you right this second. You're a grade-A douche bag, Cole Holland."

"According to your grandmother, it's douche purse. And if I'm going to do something, it's good to know I'm giving my best," he replied, unfazed by my insult. "You're a great fighter, and I have no problem throwing you into the heart of battle—when you're well—but you're still recovering from Justin's bite, on top of everything else. Tonight, you'll stay in."

I felt my hand curl into a fist. Felt my elbow draw back. Felt my arm dart forward, my knuckles crack into Cole's jaw. I couldn't stop myself.

His head whipped to the side, and blood leaked from a cut in his lip.

Behind me, gasps of shock abounded.

"I'm recovered," I said. "Believe me now?"

Those violet eyes slitted when they found me. "Assault and battery is illegal."

"So have me arrested."

He closed what little distance there was between us. Suddenly I could feel the warmth of his breath caressing my skin, could smell the decadence of his scent, the heat of his skin. "How about I put you over my lap and spank you instead?"

"How about I knee your balls into your throat?"

"If you're going to play with that particular area, I'd rather you use your hands."

"My hands aren't going near that area ever again."

A pause. Then, "I bet I could change your mind," he whispered huskily.

"I bet I could bash yours." I drew back another fist, but he was ready and caught me midswing. His pupils dilated, a sign of arousal. Another sign: he began to pant. He was acting like I'd just tried to unbuckle his jeans rather than smack the fire out of him.

"Hit me again," he said, still using that same whispered tone, "and I'll take it as an invitation."

I was just as bad. I trembled with longing I couldn't control and struggled to catch my breath. "An invitation to do what?"

His grip loosened, his fingers rubbing my skin. A caress, not a warning. "I guess we'll find out together."

What the heck are you doing?

The words screamed inside my head. This…whatever this was—flirting?—had to stop.

I dropped my arm and stepped back, only then noticing the silence inside the barn. Were the others watching, listening? My cheeks heated. "Look, I know you stayed friends with your other exes," I said, "and if you want to be friends with me, fine. I'll try. I just don't want to play this game. Understood?"

He opened his mouth, closed it with a snap. Then he nodded resolutely.

I spun away from him before I did or said something worse, and stalked to the wall of weapons. Gavin was there, weighing a semiautomatic in his hand.

"Nice right cross, Als," he said.

Finally. A cute nickname. Why did it have to come from *him?* "Thanks." I lifted an ax.

He took it from me. "Sorry, honey, but if you want a big boy's weapon, you'll have to fight me for it. Spoiler alert— I'll let you restrain me on the floor as long as you're straddling my waist."

I think my lips were curling at the corners. "I'm not straddling you," I muttered, selecting another, lighter ax.

"Too bad." He reached over and pressed a button on the bottom of my weapon. It was a lever of some sort and triggered metal spikes that popped out at the sides of the blade. "Do you know how to use this thing?"

"I have an arm, and I can swing. I figure that will do the trick."

"If you don't get yourself killed tonight, it'll be because

of a miracle," he said. "Good thing my middle name is Miracle."

"You've seen me fight. You know I'm good."

"True." He bumped my shoulder with his own. "So… have you ever thought about dyeing your hair punk-rocker-chick black? As I'm sure you've heard, I have a thing for brunettes and always avoid blondes."

"I've heard. And no."

"Too bad. Because you're making me rethink my stance about not doing my friends' exes."

I snorted, not even trying to hide my…incredulity? Surely I wasn't amused. "You're making me rethink my stance against cold-blooded homicide." I didn't wait for his reply but marched away.

Laughing, he followed me. "Are you always this on edge?"

"I didn't used to be, no." I sighed. "Look, I'm sorry if I hurt your feelings." I tried to sit down in one of the cushioned chairs in the back of the room, but he caught my arm in a gentle vise and forced me to face him.

"First, you didn't hurt my feelings. I doubt anyone could, considering the fact that I don't actually have any. Second, I believe we have some unfinished business."

I stared at his feet to avoid his gaze. Like Cole, he towered over me—which was not an easy feat. I had the legs of a giraffe.

"Cole assigned you to my team, and there's no way we'll be able to avoid each other. We can't risk having a vision during a fight with the zombies."

I nodded, but I still didn't look at him.

He placed two fingers under my chin and forced my head to lift. "Let's get this over with."

No, no, no…. But I couldn't avoid it, and our gazes locked. Annnd…nothing happened.

We both exhaled with relief.

"Well, that was certainly anticlimactic," he muttered.

"The on-and-off thing is kind of annoying, isn't it?" First with Cole, now Gavin.

"Maybe you need a tune-up."

I rolled my eyes. "I'll just pop into the supernatural ability repair shop sometime tomorrow."

He grinned, his fingertips tracing the line of my jaw. A patented Cole Holland move. The contact unnerved me, and I turned away.

"Sit down," Cole shouted. The harshness of his voice echoed off the walls.

I ignored him. It was either that, or tell him to suck it in a thousand different ways.

"Yeah, stop flirting. It sickens me," Mackenzie said loudly enough for everyone in the room to hear. She came up beside me and winked, and I realized she'd wanted Cole to hear, probably thinking he would erupt with jealousy.

Sweet of her, but she couldn't have been more wrong. I knew his attitude stemmed from my refusal to leave the fighting to the others.

Cole stomped past our group, viciously shouldering Gavin out of the way, and took his seat. Lucas blew me a kiss before taking his.

Frowning, Gavin sat. Mackenzie plopped into the chair next to his and motioned for me to take the one next to her.

"If there's any hint of trouble," Cole said to no one in particular, "I want to know about it immediately."

"Wow. Micromanage much?" Gavin muttered.

I tuned them out and closed my eyes. I could do this. A deep breath in, hold, hold, then release, and as the air left me, my spirit rose from my body. Chilly air wrapped cruel arms around me, squeezing me.

I turned and looked down. My body still reclined against the cushions, my eyes closed, my features relaxed.

Gavin tapped me on the shoulder.

My gaze lifted to his, and I arched a brow in question.

He motioned to the door with a tilt of his chin. I nodded. Right now, as emotional as I was, I would have to be more careful than usual about what I said.

Cole moved in front of Gavin and whispered a command, his expression fierce. I was able to make out the words *take care* but no others.

Take care of...me?

Gavin whispered something back, and I thought I heard the word *crazy*.

Me again?

Or was I being just a tad narcissistic? Not everything was going to be about me.

We left the barn using the door Frosty held open for us. Blood Lines surrounded the property, the house, the barn and everything inside it. Meaning all of it was solid to our touch.

Once we entered the forest, my group branched away from Cole's. Unable to help myself, I looked back. Cole's gaze was

already on me, watching me with confusion...longing...until he snaked the corner and the moment was lost.

I wasn't sure what the attention meant, or if I'd misread him, or how—

I slammed into a tree, ricocheting backward and landing on my butt.

Mackenzie laughed. "That, when she can see the Blood Lines."

"That true?" Gavin asked, helping me stand. "You can see the Blood Lines?"

"They glow," I replied through gritted teeth. I'd deserved to be pimp-slapped by a tree, I really had. No more Cole. Just. No. More.

Intrigued, Gavin said, "So...you, a girl who has never been on patrol before, a girl who has never been shown the proper path to take, could get us out of the forest using our preferred path?"

"Watch me." I took the lead, getting us out of the wheat fields and into the forest, maneuvering around every tree wiped with a Blood Line and ghosting through those that weren't. Within half an hour, we cleared the foliage to stand at the edge of a dirt road. I spread my arms in a look-at-me gesture.

"Impressive," Gavin said.

Even Mackenzie muttered her approval.

"Now what?" I asked. How much ground could we cover on foot like this?

"Now, we hunt." He took only two steps, but suddenly he was at the end of the road.

I whipped to Mackenzie, questions poised at the edge of

my tongue, but she followed Gavin, beside me one second, beside him the next. Shock beat through me. I took a step, then another, and...

I was only two steps away from where I'd started. What the heck?

I took another step, another and another, but I never gained extra ground. Frustration surpassed my shock.

"You will stop messing around," Gavin called. "Come on."

It was a command that did not violate my free will—I wanted to stop messing around. I stepped toward him and a second later, my surroundings blurred. A second after that, I was standing beside him.

"How did I do that?" I gasped out.

"Spirits are bound by spiritual laws, not physical," Mackenzie explained. "Just tell your feet to dash, and hello, they will."

"We're hitting neighborhoods tonight," Gavin said, pointing in the direction he wanted us to go.

He moved forward at that impossible speed, Mackenzie right behind him. I looked down at my booted feet and snapped, "You will move just as quickly!"

They obeyed, shocking me all over again. I quickly caught up with the twosome, and we soared through neighborhood after neighborhood, searching for any sign of zombie activity. I lasted one hour...two...three...before the swiftness of my movements began to take a dangerous toll.

My limbs trembled lightly at first, then more noticeably, then more violently. After a while, I was barely able to remain upright.

"Guys," I huffed, and stopped.

A mistake.

Suddenly I could feel the heaviness of my feet and could barely maintain my grip on the ax.

I hated to admit it, but Cole and Frosty were right. Stamina was important. I needed to up my training.

Gavin slowed and turned to face me.

"Rest," I said.

So hungry, a ragged voice whispered, claiming my attention.

I spun, but no one stood around me.

Will eat. Food will scream. Yes. Yes!

Hmm, what's that smell? Must have.

Hard bands wrapped around my upper arms. Instinct took over, and I raised my fist to attack the culprit. I turned.

Gavin ducked, avoiding impact. Straightening, he frowned. "What's wrong with you?"

"I—I don't know."

Your condition, the man in the car had said.

"The smell of rot is in the air." Excitement bubbled in Mackenzie's tone.

Smiling, Gavin released me. He shot a flare in the sky to alert Cole and Lucas, then palmed two daggers. "Yeah, baby. The zombies are nearby."

I inhaled deeply, but I smelled only the pine of the trees. And...Gavin. I smelled Gavin, and it was better than the pine. It was delicious. Mouthwatering.

"You able to fight?" he asked me.

I wasn't actually sure, wasn't even sure I cared. I leaned into him and sniffed. *Hmm. Snack time.*

He looked as if he wanted to question me, but a male with a hunched back and a twisted ankle ambled from the side of a house, drawing his attention.

The zombies weren't just nearby; they were here.

This one wore a dirty, ripped suit, and his tie was askew.

Three other zombies moseyed out behind him, and five more behind them.

Must have, must have, must have.

Mine, all mine.

Gonna be so good!

The voices stacked one on top of the other, insistent and loud. I shook my head and tugged at my ears, even as I licked my lips and stared at Gavin's neck.

He tossed something small and black at the zombies and shouted, "Down!"

He hit the ground. Confused, I remained standing.

Boom!

A minigrenade exploded, ripping through the first line of zombies. Arms flew one way and legs another, minus the bodies. A white-hot blast of air shoved me backward. When I landed, twigs and grass and body parts rained over me.

Gavin and Mackenzie hopped up and rushed headlong into battle, hacking and slashing at the creatures still standing.

I gritted my teeth and forced myself into motion. "I can do this. I can do this."

But...as I carved through the spine of a female zombie, she reached for Gavin, ignoring me. As I cut off the arm of another, he bit at Mackenzie, as if I wasn't even there.

WILL TASTE.

MINE, MINE, MINE.

HURT. MAIM. KILL.

GOOD, SO GOOD.

Argh! The voices. Louder now, screaming at me. I dropped the ax to clutch at my ears. *Stop. Please, stop.* But they didn't. They only grew louder. My knees gave out, and I collapsed to the ground. The zombies stepped over me, desperate to reach Gavin and Mackenzie.

What are you doing? Get up. Fight. Help your friends. You're better than this.

Finally Pep Talk Ali, a voice of reason. Barely discernible over the noise. I palmed a dagger with a trembling hand and stood. My legs quaked, and I swayed, but I somehow found the strength to lumber forward.

Splattered in black blood, Mackenzie presented a macabre picture as she spun and sliced the throats of the three zombies attempting to latch onto her arms. Gavin jumped over a pile of headless, writhing zombies, avoiding grasping hands, to press against Mackenzie's back.

I lifted my blade. I would help them...touch them. They glowed. Soft light pulsed from their pores. Such pretty light. Drawing me.

Mine.

I had to taste it. Them.

Taste. Yes. Mackenzie was closest, and she would be the first to feed me. I would gorge on her. She would scream, and I would laugh, because I would be full for the first time in my life.

"Ali," she growled. "There's one behind you!"

One…a zombie. Behind me. He didn't care about me. Bypassed me.

But she'd warned me. To help me…the way I was supposed to help her.

So many times I'd wanted to help the people I loved, and I'd failed. My dad, my mom, my sister, my grandfather. I couldn't fail again. I blinked, my wits returning. Realization—and horror—slammed into me. I'd come close to harming my friend.

I bit my tongue until I tasted blood, dropped the blade and backed away from her. How could I have entertained such dark thoughts?

"Ali, light up!" Cole called.

He was here. I turned, our gazes meeting. He was sprinting toward me, moving as quickly as I had done. And yet I easily tracked his movements. Could even see the concern on his face.

What if I decided to hurt him? What if I attacked him?

As much as I currently disliked him, I couldn't take the chance.

Panicked, I ran in the opposite direction, away from Cole, from the fight, from everyone and everything. I ran and never looked back.

DRINK ME

Gasping, I jolted upright. Panic cloaked me as I scanned surroundings I didn't remember stumbling upon. I was…

On the cold, hard ground in front of my old house. The house I'd lived in most of my life. The house my father had built. The house I hadn't visited since the death of my family.

Tremors rocked me. How had I gotten here? I'd run from Cole, from the zombies and the voices, yes, yes, that was right, and then I'd…blacked out, maybe. I remembered nothing else.

Now the sun was in the process of rising, though it was hidden behind a thick wall of clouds—one of which was shaped like a rabbit. I gulped. Looked away. The tree swing my dad had built for Emma had been removed. The rose garden my mom had poured her blood, sweat and tears into maintaining was now a pile of rocks.

Corrosive acid filled my veins, threatening to spill over.

Change, change, all around, here and there and everywhere, reminders that nothing and no one was safe from its clutches.

Familiar sensations pricked at me. The speeding up of my heartbeat—both of them—the beading of sweat on my brow, the constricting of my lungs. Knowing I was losing control of my body and my reactions only made everything worse.

Stop! Just stop. I wasn't this girl, wasn't some scared little mouse. I was stronger than this, forged from fire and sharpened by steel. *In*—I inhaled. *Out*—I exhaled. *In. Out. Good.*

Something soft shifted through my hair, tickling my scalp. "Oh, Alice. I hate to see you like this."

My gaze traveled up a pair of ballet slippers, stockings, a fluffy tutu and a glittery pink leotard. The remaining panic went head-to-head with a sudden burst of happiness, and, miracle of miracles, the happiness won.

"Emma." I leaped to my feet and gathered my baby sister in my arms. Wait. Something wasn't right. "I can touch you," I said. "I can actually touch you." Shock sent me careening backward. "How can I touch you? Am I dead?"

Golden eyes twinkled merrily, and perfect heart-shaped lips edged into a smile. "You're in spirit form, silly." She flicked the end of her pigtails over her shoulders, a familiar gesture. "Your body is waiting at Cole's barn, and your friends are, like, superworried."

The barn. That's right.

I didn't care. "I want to stay this way forever." I couldn't lose the feel of her again.

"You can't. Your body will die."

Just then, I didn't care about that, either. "Your point? We'll still be together."

Her smile slowly fell. "I don't think we would." Looking down at her ballet slippers, she said, "Once we promised never to lie to each other, and right now I'm going to keep that promise." A pause. A sigh. "You're in trouble, Alice, and it's getting worse every day."

"No." I shook my head. "I'm handling things."

Her gaze met mine. "I can see the smudges."

I gulped. "What are they?"

Expression filled with tenderness, she reached up and brushed one side of my face. "I told you I would talk to people, and I did. But, Alice...I don't think you're going to like what I learned."

"Tell me anyway." I had to know.

"Very well. Have you ever heard the story of the two hungry wolves living inside every man? One is good, one is evil and both are fighting for control. In the end, the one that's fed will end up the winner."

I shook my head.

"Well, that is what's happening. That night inside Anima Industries, when you were stabbed, you had so much zombie toxin inside you the antidote couldn't eradicate all of it. Your spirit was strong enough to fight it, though, keeping that part of you safe, but not your already weakened body. And the toxin, well, it was a mutated version and created something new, something born of you. Another spirit. That means there are now two spirits battling to the death for rights to live inside you. Yours, the human Alice. And the other...zombie Alice."

Pausing, she waited for those words to sink in.

I wrapped my arms around myself, as if I could protect

myself from such a terrible invasion. Zombie Alice. Fighting for control. My smudged reflection… The desperate whispering voices… The sickening urges… I nearly dropped to my knees.

"You're saying I've become a host to a…to a…zombie. But that can't be. I've had long moments without the darker urges. Like now. I don't want to bite you."

"That's true, but you have to think of this as a disease. Your human spirit is fighting the zombie spirit, even though you may not be aware of it, and the human one is mostly winning right now. But because your human spirit, and therefore your body, produces a poison for the zombies, and you now have a zombie inside you, you are basically poisoning yourself. You're allergic to yourself and weakening because of it."

"No," I said, shaking my head.

"You know I'm right," she said, and I could tell she was battling tears. "The darker side of you is sometimes strong enough to manifest *outside* you."

No. "I'll use more antidote."

"And that will help in the short term, but it's not a solution."

"What is?" I croaked.

"I…don't actually know. When Justin bit you, he woke this new side of you. Breathed life into it."

Finally I did fall to my knees. I couldn't deny her words anymore, could I? Seconds after Justin had bitten me, the new heart had started beating.

The new heart.

For the new me.

"What happens if she wins?" I asked.

"You know the answer to that."

I did. I just hadn't wanted to admit it.

I would become what I hated most.

"How long do I have?" I asked, trying not to sob.

"Longer than most. Do you remember when Mom put her hand on your leg after the crash?"

My eyes widened. I couldn't form words, could only nod. The dreams hadn't been dreams, then, but memories. Having it confirmed ripped me apart. She'd suffered. My mother had suffered.

"She didn't realize she was doing it, but she passed on her zombie-slaying abilities. Her…power, I guess is as good a word as any."

Hers. Not my father's. "But she never exhibited any abilities."

"You know better than anyone you don't have to see something for it to be there." She settled in front of me, squeezed my hand. "You inherited Dad's abilities, too. That's why you're so strong, and one of the reasons you can do things others can't. One of the reasons your body hasn't already died. If anyone can beat this, you can."

"How?"

"I don't know that, either," she said. Her shoulders drooped. "I'm sorry."

I tried to smile. I wasn't sure I succeeded. "Hey, don't worry about me. I'll find a way."

She nodded, and I could see that she wanted to believe me. And then she kissed my cheek, said, "I'm still searching for answers. I'll be back," and vanished.

I crouched there, breathing in and out, my hands fisted. No matter what, I wouldn't allow myself to become a zombie. I would fight this, and I would try to find a cure, but if I failed...

No. Not an option. I formulated a to-do list and calmed. *Find a way to decode the entire journal. Learn how to kill the zombie inside me. Actually kill her.*

Simple, yet amazingly complex. Whatever. I'd done worse.

"Ali!"

My brow furrowed. That was Cole's voice.

I stood and turned left, saw a car speeding through the neighborhood. I turned right, saw a woman walking to her car, a cup of coffee in hand.

"Ali!"

Suddenly a sharp sting pierced my cheek.

Had Cole just *slapped* me? I marched forward, setting a collision course for the barn and all my problems, annnd... the world around me blurred, only coming back into focus when I spotted the big red building where I'd left my body. Someone had left the door open for me. Inside, I caught a glimpse of Cole, Mr. Holland and all of the slayers crowding in front of my chair.

Cole lifted his arm, palm flat, ready.

He had. He really had.

I slipped into my body with a gasp. "I'm here."

He straightened. His gaze found mine and narrowed. It was a new day, but I was no longer surprised when a moment passed without a vision.

His father pushed a needle into my neck. "Antidote," he explained.

"Are you okay?" Cole demanded.

Okay? No. Even with my to-do list hovering in the back of my mind, I wanted to curl into a ball and cry. I wanted to tell him what I'd learned. I wanted…everything I couldn't have. His arms around me. His voice in my ear, telling me everything would be all right.

He was the only person I would believe.

It was odd, and probably just the moment, or my shock, but now that limits had been placed on my future, none of the fury I'd harbored for Cole remained. I was still hurt by what he'd done, and the way he'd been treating me, but none of that mattered just then.

A single night had changed me irrevocably.

Change.

I laughed without humor. Another change had come for me.

"Give the girl some breathing room." Mr. Holland shoved the slayers out of the way.

"I'm sorry," I said, my voice nothing more than a whisper.

Cole shrugged off his dad's attempts and planted his hands on the arms of my chair, leaning into me, putting us nose to nose. "Where were you? What the hell do you think you were doing out there? Do you have any idea how much worry you caused m—us?"

I blinked at him. Gone was the gentle Cole, the one who had tended me after my panic attack. The one who had sweetly covered my hair with the bandanna.

"I can guess about the worry," I said, and looked away from him. I was too raw, too susceptible to his concern and

his mood, torn to shreds all over again. "And I'm sorry," I repeated.

"Where were you?" he demanded a second time.

"At my old house."

"Why did you go there?"

"I don't know. I woke up, and there I was."

Mr. Holland opened his mouth, but Cole cut him off.

"You don't know?" Cole snorted, his anger far from assuaged. "How can you not know?"

What had brought about this transformation in him?

Gavin slapped him on the shoulder. "Dude. Let's give her a minute to explain."

Cole whipped to him, snarling, "You'd like that, wouldn't you?"

"Uh…yeah. We'd all like that." Confused, Gavin looked to me, probably expecting me to explain Cole's odd behavior. I couldn't.

And then I didn't want to. The world faded—

—Gavin was in my room, standing in front of me. I spun him and pushed him down on the bed, then climbed on top of him. I forced his head to the side, baring his neck. My tongue swiped over his skin as I tugged at his shirt, trying to pull it off his body and—

—*smack!*

I blinked into focus, the here and now returning just as quickly as it had vanished, only to realize Cole had just punched the partition over my head, leaving a gaping hole. Dust filled the air, making me cough. Then he pushed Gavin.

Gavin stumbled backward and scrubbed a hand down his face.

"What did you see?" Cole demanded. "Tell me, before I—"

"Get control of yourself, son." Mr. Holland grabbed him by the arm and thrust him toward the door. "If you can't, leave."

Cole took only a moment to decide. He stormed out of the barn, the door slamming shut behind him. Frosty and Bronx tossed me a sympathetic glance before following him. A few seconds later, I heard the squeal of tires and the spray of gravel.

"The rest of you need to leave, as well," Mr. Holland said. "Except you, Gavin. You stay."

All of the slayers filed out, except for Gavin. Mackenzie threw me a puzzled glance.

I'd left her in danger last night.

"I'm sorry," I said again, wrapping my arms around myself. Tears beaded in my eyes. "Did anyone get hurt?"

"No." Mr. Holland stared at me, his crystalline gaze boring into me like a laser. "I'm not going to ask what you and Gavin saw in your vision. Judging from your expression, I can guess. What I want to know is what happened to you last night."

Not too long ago, this man had found me utterly unreliable. He hadn't wanted me here. What would he do if he learned the truth, that I was rotting from the inside out?

Soon I could very well be a hazard to everyone we loved.

"I blacked out," I said.

"I was told the zombies wanted nothing to do with you."

"That's right." I shuddered with revulsion. They must already consider me one of their own.

"I want Ankh to check you out," Mr. Holland said.

I wouldn't protest. "Okay." Just what would he find? Would he discover the source of the problem? He hadn't yet.

"And I want you off rotation until this is figured out."

A denial rose immediately. One I quickly swallowed. I'd almost hurt Mackenzie and Gavin. I'd left my team to engage in battle without me. I deserved this, and worse.

I looked down, ashamed, and nodded.

Mr. Holland faced Gavin. "Drive her home." Then, having said his piece and issued his orders, he stomped out the door.

As soon we were trapped in his car, alone, Gavin said, "Why do we keep having the same vision?"

"I don't know. With Cole, we usually only had the same vision a few times before a new one took its place."

"Maybe this one is important."

I knew he didn't mean that in a conceited way. His tone was too confused. "Maybe we're not getting whatever it wants us to get."

"So the visions are alive? Sentient?"

"No," I said with a shake of my head. "But our minds are at work here, and they know what we get and what we don't."

He tapped his fingers against the steering wheel. "Let's forget the vision for a minute. You remember grabbing your ears during the fight, as if you were hearing something you shouldn't?"

I squirmed in my seat. I'd either heard Zombie Ali—

Z.A., I thought, because I hated pairing my name with that description—or the other zombies. Both options sickened me.

"Yeah." He turned the key, gunned the engine. "You remember. What'd you hear?"

"I'm not going to talk about it."

"Fine. Whatever. Just know I won't rat you out. You're a good girl, I can tell, and I'm sure you've got your reasons for keeping quiet about such an interesting development."

An unlikely ally. I desperately needed one. "Thank you."

He shrugged, and merged into traffic. "I guess I owe you."

"What do you mean?"

"After the way you were going at me, acting like you were on life support and my body had the oxygen you so desperately needed, I—"

Suddenly feeling a little more like my old self, I reached over and smacked him in the chest. "Shut up."

He grinned, his entire face lighting with amusement. "We have another vision like that, and Cole might just kill me in my sleep."

"Highly doubtful. I think he was just upset that I stayed out all night, making everyone worry."

His snort echoed through the cab. "Yeah, that's why he spent hours looking for you."

He had? Not for my benefit, surely, but for the team's. "Plus—and please hear me when I say this—I've been serious every time I've told you I have no interest in you."

His grin only widened. "You realize you're just making yourself more attractive to me, right? First, do you really not

understand how beautiful you are? Even to a guy like me. And second, there's never been a female I couldn't win over."

Me? Beautiful? "Maybe you've gotten the women you've wanted in the past, but there's always a first time for failure."

He clutched at his heart, as if in pain.

I rolled my eyes. "Don't pretend you like a challenge. I had you pegged at moment one, remember?"

His laughter proved to be infectious, and I reveled in the burst of hilarity with every fiber of my being. I wasn't sure I'd have many more opportunities.

"A guy can change, you know."

Change.

"Yeah. A guy can. So can a girl." I cast my attention to the hills outside and ignored him for the rest of the drive.

Gavin followed me inside the mansion, citing, "I was told to see you home safely, and I'd be remiss in my duties if I failed to walk you to your bedroom door. Who knows? Maybe you'll even try to kiss me goodbye."

"Stay away from my bedroom, you dirty he-slut."

He grabbed my hand and twirled me, as if we were dance partners. "I'm liking you more with every second that passes, Als. Maybe there's some truth to the visions, after all. Seriously. Think about it."

"Will you shut up about the you-knows? This isn't a conversation safe zone." I stalked to the staircase and found a note taped to the banister.

My office, Miss Bell. Now.

Guess I wouldn't be reading the journal right away. I balled up the paper and threw it at Gavin. "You're dismissed.

Apparently I already have a date." Mr. Holland must have called Mr. Ankh, and his other personality, Dr. Blood and Guts, must have jumped into action.

"Dismissed," he said. "That's another first."

"You're welcome." I switched directions and trudged inside Mr. Ankh's office.

"Shut the door," he commanded from the desk.

I obeyed without protest or comment.

"Take a seat."

Again, I obeyed, my nerves razed more with every second that passed.

He walked around the desk to claim the seat across from mine, then opened a black bag filled with needles, tubes, cotton balls and a ton of other paraphernalia I was sure I didn't want to know about. There was another black bag in the far corner of the room, filled with vials of the antidote. He kept it there for emergencies.

"Try not to scream," he muttered, reaching for the tourniquet.

"Sure. You try not to poke something you shouldn't."

"I'm a doctor. I know what I'm doing."

"You're a surgeon. You know how to cut and sew."

He pursed his lips the same way Reeve did. "After a thousand years of medical school, as my daughter says, I think I can do a little more than cut and sew."

He set the needle in place and pushed, and my vein rolled. My entire arm felt the sting, and I hissed in a breath.

"Sorry," he muttered, trying again. And wouldn't you know it, he missed a second time.

I could only bite my tongue and content myself with glaring at the top of his head.

"Sorry," he muttered. Finally he succeeded.

A few minutes later, he was labeling the packed tubes. "I'll have the results tomorrow."

What would he find? I rubbed my hand over the second heartbeat and forced myself to breathe. "Thanks."

My stomach growled, embarrassing me. I snuck into the kitchen and searched for my bagels. They weren't where I'd left them, and they weren't in the pantry. Someone must have eaten them. I gazed longingly at the boxed desserts and even the jars of vegetables, but still backed out without touching anything I shouldn't and made my way to Nana's room. I'd never thanked her for the journal. I knocked, waited.

"Your grandmother went to church," a soft voice said from behind me.

I turned and saw one of the maids dusting a side table. "Thanks."

Nana and I always went to church together. I hated that I'd missed. Especially since it probably seemed like I'd blown her off. Again. I hoped she wasn't upset.

I trudged to my room. Avoiding the mirrors, I sat at my desk and thumbed through the journal. I expected to start by rereading what had already been decoded. Instead, I found that every word was once again hidden from my understanding. But...how could that be?

Frowning, I went through every page slowly, line by line, studying every symbol, every number. Nope. No miraculous unveiling.

Must simplify the to-do list: *Learn how to kill the zombie inside me without the journal. Actually kill her.*

Where to start? My sister? Maybe she'd learned something else about my situation. "Emma. If you can swing another visit, I'd love to see you."

I had to wait longer than usual, but she did, eventually, arrive. "Hey there," she said.

I smiled at her. "You came."

"I told you. I'll always come." She stood beside the desk, fingering the ends of her skirt. "You look better."

"Thank you."

"So…whatcha doing?"

I lifted the book. "Apparently our great-great-great-grandfather wrote a journal about zombie slaying. Only he wrote it in some kind of code, and I can't decipher it. So I started to wonder whether you'd learned anything new."

"Not yet." She rubbed her hands together. "But let me take a crack at the journal."

Leaning over my shoulder, she scanned the pages and pouted with disappointment. "I was hoping to crack the code with my genius mind and rub it in your face forever, but I can read the words no problem."

I stared down at the still-coded pages. "How?"

"I don't know. I just can. Everything just looks normal to me."

"Read something to me, then."

"Okay…how about there?" She pointed. "The words are flashing at me."

Flashing? I nodded.

"'I've heard we need darkness to balance light,'" she read,

"'and light to balance darkness. I say we have no need of darkness, period. It confuses. It hurts. It tortures. It ruins. And really, darkness cannot remain with light. Light will always chase it away. Think about it. We kill the zombies with the fire from our hands—fire produces light. And they, the zombies, are the ultimate darkness. With a touch, they can be extinguished for eternity.'"

I let the words settle in my mind before turning them over again and again. Could Z.A. be killed by the fire the slayers produced? *My* fire? If so, if a slayer pressed his—or her—palm against my chest, would I die, too?

There was only one way to find out.

Was it worth the risk, though?

"Want me to read more?" Emma asked.

"Not right now." There was a tremor in my voice. *Crap.* I didn't want her to know what I was contemplating.

"Well, then, I better get back to my research."

I nodded, offering her as bright as smile as I could. Then she was gone.

Put-up or wuss-up time. I eased to the foot of the bed and rested the backs of my hands on my knees. My breathing was fast, too fast, as a bead of nervousness rolled through me, picking up steam.

I was a slayer. I could produce the fire.

I could kill Z.A.

And maybe myself...

Yeah, but maybe not.

I closed my eyes to concentrate. Before I could step out of my body, a thought bloomed, and I couldn't shake it.

Would Nana come in here and find a pile of ash, then blame someone else? One of the other slayers?

Should I leave a note?

Shaking, I scribbled a quick goodbye at my desk. *Did this to myself. Love you so much.* Just in case. And maybe I should have spent more time on it, explaining everything, but I didn't want to take a chance I'd talk myself out of such a necessary action.

So…without further ado, I forced my spirit to rise. I looked at my hands, and willed the fire to come. Little white flames sparked at the ends of my trembling fingertips. Not giving myself time to think, I turned and pressed those flames into my body's chest. Then I waited. I watched my own face as a muscle ticked under my eye…but nothing else happened.

Disappointed, a lot angry and just a little relieved, I dropped my arms to my sides.

Why hadn't that worked?

I rejoined spirit and body. Maybe…Z.A. had left my body with me?

Would she always?

I had to find out. But how?

Temples throbbing, I stalked out of my room and hunted for Reeve. I needed a distraction. Only, she wasn't in her room. Or the kitchen. I headed to the second floor, bypassing antique chairs and tables, each surrounded by colorful vases and paintings of flowers. The closer I got to my gym, the more grunts, groans and girlish laughter I heard. She was there.

I reached the open doorway and ground to a halt.

Veronica was in the process of teaching my friends how to defend themselves from an attack.

"—proper fist," she was saying. "Like this. That way, when you throw a punch, you won't break your thumb."

Reeve and Kat nodded eagerly.

"Show me," Veronica commanded.

The pair spent the next few minutes punching air.

"Excellent."

"I feel sorry for whoever makes a play for me," Kat said, flexing her arms. "Do you see the amazingly sick biceps I'm developing?"

Grinning, Reeve said, "So, how did you learn to fight like this, Ronny?"

Ronny. Just like that, I felt utterly betrayed. This was *my* home. They were *my* friends. And I'd had enough. Before the girl could reply, I stepped deeper into the room. "What are you doing here, Veronica?"

Three sets of eyes looked over at me.

"Frosty sent me," Veronica explained, tone now cold.

"He said you were fine with it, that you'd suggested he take care of it," Kat said with a frown. "But, uh, judging by your expression, I'm thinking he must have misunderstood."

Veronica glared at me. "Would you care to join us and learn something, Ali? A few skills could give you the confidence you need to actually engage in battle rather than run away."

I sucked in a breath. *Such* a low blow.

"What are you talking about?" Reeve demanded.

Kat threw the girl a dagger-sharp glare. "Oh, no, you didn't."

"You have no idea what went down, Veronica," I gritted. "Therefore, you have no right to comment."

"What went down?" Reeve asked. "And how do you know our self-defense instructor?"

My attention remained on Veronica. "You can leave now. I'm taking over."

"Uh, that would be a big fat no. Frosty wants these girls trained right."

Are you going to let her speak to you that way?

I didn't have to think about my answer. No. No, I wasn't.

Threatening her won't do you any good. You'll have to force her to zip her lips.

Yes. I could. I would.

Then do it. Here. Now.

A strange, almost stinging anticipation wound through me as I stalked forward. "I don't know about you, but I teach through demonstration."

MIRROR, MIRROR
ON THE BLOODY WALL

I'd been taunted by one of Cole's exes before, and there was no question I would be taunted again. I'd always—okay, mostly—chosen to walk away. I'd had what the other girls wanted: Cole. They'd just been lashing out, and I'd understood.

In that moment, I didn't understand anything but rage.

This girl thinks you're weak, someone to scare away.

She would learn better.

She probably spent the night with Cole.

She would suffer.

She probably laughs at you behind your back.

She would never laugh again.

I increased my speed. Kat and Reeve backpedaled, moving out of the way. Not Veronica. She met me in the middle. I threw a punch, but she leaned to the side, avoiding impact;

I swiped air. She returned the gesture, and I lifted my arm, blocking her, and went at her with my other fist.

Finally. Contact.

Impact sent her stumbling to the side. Unfortunately she recovered quickly and as I approached, threw a right. I ducked, and she nailed me with a left in the center of my scar, using my own trick against me.

As I struggled for purchase, she clipped my jaw with every bit of her strength—*as serious as I am*—and I whipped to the side. I stumbled back, but caught myself before I went down. Didn't matter. She threw herself at me, and we flew to the floor. I took most of the impact, and whatever oxygen I'd managed to suck in was once again stolen. *Don't care.* I rolled on top of her and landed a blow to her chin before she was able to kick me off. We stood.

Panting, she circled me.

"You've proven yourself to be toxic," she spat. "I'm not going to let you hurt my friends."

That stinging anticipation pulsed in my chest, almost as if it were a living thing. *Hurt...*

The rage magnified.

Hurt HER.

When she made her next move, I was ready. She launched at me, throwing another punch. I twisted to avoid her fist, moving behind her, and, with my back to her, kicked out my leg, buckling her knees. As she dropped, I elbowed her in the back of the head. Yeah. Forget honor. I'd go with dirty.

She attempted to rise. Grabbing a hank of her hair, I rolled her over, then wasted no time straddling her waist, pinning

her shoulders to the floor and whaling on her. Again and again...and again.

"Stop," Kat called. "Ali, you have to stop. She's bleeding. There's blood. Ali, stop. Please!"

"Ali," Reeve screamed. "Enough!"

I stilled only when Veronica's eyes closed, signaling she was out cold. Blood leaked from her nose. I might have broken it. Her teeth had cut into her lips, and had already swelled to three times the normal size.

Such a delicious buffet, unable to defend itself...

A wave of hunger hit me.

Kat ran over to push me away from the girl, but I batted at her hands and leaned down to sniff Veronica's neck. How sweet she smelled. Not as good as Cole or even Mackenzie, but she would do. I licked my lips.

One taste wouldn't hurt.

Muscled arms banded around me, jerking me backward. I struggled for freedom, desperate to return to the girl.

"Hey, now," Gavin said. "I've always thought there's nothing wrong with a little bloodshed between friends, but I draw the line at murder."

"Just want to—" *Bite her,* I realized. I wanted to bite her. Horror bathed me in ice, the hunger instantly forgotten.

"I'm so sorry," I said, my entire body beginning to tremble. "I wasn't thinking... Wasn't myself—" Oh, heaven help me, I'd been zombie. Almost fully zombie.

Want to die.

"Calm now?" Gavin set me aside and crouched beside his friend. Gently he smoothed the blood-soaked hair from her brow. "Veronica, honey. You okay?"

I backed out of the room, too ashamed to look anyone in the eye. In fact, I kept my gaze downcast until I reached my room. I shut and locked my door and tripped my way to the vanity. I closed my eyes. My chin wobbled, tears cascading down my cheeks.

I remembered what a sad little girl I'd once been, trapped inside my home, peering out my bedroom window while other kids played in their yards. Social Services had come once. They'd questioned my parents, questioned me, maybe even considered taking Emma and me away from the only home we'd ever known. Maybe we would have been separated from each other. Maybe not. I hadn't wanted to risk it, so I'd done something totally against my nature. I'd lied. I'd told them we were private people, that was all, and we enjoyed our family time and wouldn't sacrifice it. I'd laughed at their concerns of abuse.

In junior high, my friends had called me Nolice. *No, I can't go out with you. No, I can't stay the night. No, you can't stay the night with me.* One day, invitations had just stopped coming.

I'd wanted normal, give-and-take relationships more than anything. Now I had them, but I might have to walk away from them.

I was a menace. Dangerous.

Look. See who you're becoming.

Slowly I pried my eyelids apart. The mirror—and my reflection—came into view. Revulsion made me shudder. My eyes were red. The girl peering back at me wasn't me. Not anymore. Not in any way. She couldn't possibly be me. The smudges had spread, grown darker, and a black spiderweb of veins stretched over her forehead.

That. Quickly.

Her cheekbones were gaunt, her hair tangled.

Tick. She reached toward me with a smudge-stained hand, and I reared backward. Trembling, I waited for her next move, part of me expecting her to mist through the glass. But she merely pressed her palm against the surface, and I calmed enough to ease back into my seat.

Tock. "It is nice to finally have the strength to speak," she said.

Tick.

Oh. Good. Glory. I could hear her voice. *My* voice. But *I* wasn't speaking. "I know you're a zombie."

Tock. She lifted one shoulder in a shrug. "You say zombie, I say better half."

Tick. What *was* that? A clock? Yes, I realized. That was exactly what the strange *tick-tock* represented. A clock, and time was running out.

I steeled myself to ignore it.

"What do you want from me?" I demanded.

"What do you think?" she said with a grin. "I want *everything.*"

Everything. My body? My life? "I won't let you win." *I have a to-do list, and failure isn't on it.* Shaking, I reached out and pressed my fingers against the coolness of the glass.

She laughed. "You won't be able to stop me. I grow stronger every day."

"That means strength is measurable. So, if you can grow stronger, you can be made to grow weaker."

That wiped away her amusement. "Look how easily you gave in to my desires. Soon biting will be second nature."

"No." Never.

"Once your human spirit has been destroyed, I'll have control of your body. I'll be the first of my kind."

Breath crystallized in my lungs. "You can't—"

A knock sounded at the door, and a sweet, trembling voice said, "Ali. Is someone in there with you?"

Kat.

"No," I shouted a little too loudly.

A pause. "Will you let me in, then? Please. I need to know you're okay, and we need to talk about what just happened. I've never seen you act like that, not even when you were beating up those boys, and it scared me."

"I'm okay, and I'm sorry I scared you. But we'll talk about it later. I just… I need to be alone right now."

I heard her sigh even through the obstruction. "You're upset, and I want to comfort you—it's my specialty. Just don't hurt me, okay?"

I think she meant the words as a joke. I hoped she did. "I would never hurt you," I said, tears beading in my eyes.

"Ali, I know that, but you have to—"

"Please, Kat. Not now."

I waited several seconds, heard only silence. I turned back to the mirror.

My reflection was just as grotesque but no longer moved contrary to me. "Are you still there?" I whispered, watching my lips move.

My reflection offered no reply.

I bit my tongue as I injected myself with the antidote, just to be safe. Then I withdrew the business card from my desk drawer and peered down at the number. This man

knew something about what I was going through. Maybe he could save me.

How sad. Right now a stranger was my best shot.

Alter list: *however proves necessary, kill Z.A. ASAP.*

Though I didn't like the idea of using my cell and letting caller ID reveal my number, there was no other phone I could use. Not without alerting Mr. Ankh, and therefore Mr. Holland, and therefore Cole. I dialed before I could change my mind.

A man answered after the third ring. "Hello, Miss Bell."

He freaked me out, his welcome too much, too soon, and with a gasp, I hung up.

Stupid, stupid, stupid. I redialed.

He answered on the second ring. "I hope you'll actually say something this time."

"Who are you?" I demanded.

"Your new best friend," was the casual reply. "I am Dr. Bendari."

I wrapped my fingers around the edge of the vanity and squeezed, trying to relieve a little of the pressure building inside me. "Enough games. You should know straight-out that I don't trust you."

"Believe me, I received that message loud and clear when you slashed my tire," he replied drily.

"You're probably wondering why I called."

"No. I know. You're desperate."

Well, okay, then. We were on the same page. "How do I know you have the answers I seek?"

"Were you bitten by a slayer who'd been bitten by a zom-

bie? Are you now seeing things? Hearing things? Experi-encing unusual emotions and reactions?"

He knew. He really knew. "Yes," I whispered. "How did you know that?"

"I have a source on the inside. I also have the answers you seek."

"Tell me." A command. "And who is your source? Is he one of my friends?" Who would betray me?

"The source matters little. I will tell you everything else you wish to know, but I won't do it over the phone. You won't believe what I tell you. Not without pictures."

Anger infused every cell in my body. He could be lying, trying to draw me out, make me an easier target. "You want to meet," I said flatly.

"I do. Tonight. Midnight."

He could be playing me, could be planning to murder me. But honestly? I didn't care. Right now death was prefer-able to uncertainty. If I walked into my own personal hor-ror movie, oh, well. "All right. Where?"

"There's an all-night Chinese buffet in Birmingham called the Wok and Roll. Come alone, and I'll be there. Come with someone else, and I'll leave before you can spot me. That happens, and you will never hear from me again."

He hung up before I could agree. Or yell at him.

I paced my room for the rest of the day. Nana came to my door with lunch, then dinner, and both times I asked her to set the tray on the floor. Earlier I'd wanted to talk to her—I still did. Now just wasn't the right time. At the mo-ment, I couldn't trust myself to behave.

"You're going to tell me what's going on, Ali," she said

through the door. Never before had she spoken so sternly with me. "The boy, Gavin, he told me you beat another girl unconscious. How could you do something like that?"

"I'm asking myself that same question," I replied, my chin trembling.

A heavy pause. "Let me in the room. I want to look into your eyes while we talk about this."

She would see was my horror, my remorse. My tears.

My new nature?

"I...can't. I'm sorry."

"Is it the upcoming holiday?" she asked, hesitant. "Are you missing your parents?"

"No." To be honest, I hadn't given Thanksgiving a single thought.

Another pause, this one writhing with tension.

"Ali, you're shutting me out and it's hurting me."

Yes, I could hear the pain in her voice.

I stepped up to the door, reached for the knob, stopped myself. Hot tears cascaded down my cheeks. "I'm sorry," I repeated. "I would rather die than hurt you, but if I open that door I could hurt you worse. I just... I need a day to work through this, okay?"

Several minutes passed in silence before she said, "You've got one day." Footsteps resounded.

I picked up the tray, placed it inside my room, my stomach a twisted mess. I couldn't bring myself to eat.

Finally eternity came to an end and eleven-thirty arrived. I loaded myself with weapons and sneaked through the secret passages Mr. Ankh had built throughout the house. He'd

wanted his daughter to have an escape route if ever it proved necessary—not that she would know what chased her.

Reeve. I frowned. My nose wrinkled after I inhaled. I smelled her perfume. She must have used the passage, and quite recently.

Huh. The passage led to a hatch just beyond the front yard, seconds from the road. Still. I'd have to be careful. Mr. Ankh had cameras everywhere and—as I eased my out, I caught movement several yards away.

Gaze zooming in, I palmed a blade. Was that…Reeve? Had to be. Dark hair swished as a slender girl matching Reeve's height and build walked north. She'd sneaked out.

Dang you, Reeve! No matter how badly I wanted answers, no matter how dangerous I currently was, I couldn't let her wander the streets without backup.

As I followed her through the shadows, I dialed Bronx.

"What?" he snarled.

"Reeve snuck out. I'm a few yards behind her. I just thought you'd like to know."

He spewed a mouthful of curses. In the background, I heard a girl giggling.

"You're with someone?" I asked, shocked.

At the same time he said, "Where are you?"

I gave him our current location, and he hung up.

Thank you, Ali, I inwardly mocked. *I appreciate your help.*

A car drove past, and Reeve darted behind a tree trunk. I did the same, only to stiffen when the car slowed, stopped.

Reeve stepped from the shadows. "Ethan?"

"It's me, sweetheart."

Sweetheart. Hello, new boyfriend.

"Thank goodness! I realized the car was slowing down, and I almost peed my pants." She walked around the car and opened the passenger side door. "I thought you were meeting me at 7-Eleven."

"You were late, and I worried."

Bronx, who was in spirit form, moved through the trees and swept up beside me. The hair he'd dyed blue was now green, but it wasn't spiked. Tonight, it shagged over his forehead. There were several lipstick stains on the collar of his shirt—and not all of them were the same color.

"She just got into the car," I said, beyond grateful a slayer's ability to see spirits extended to human ones. Although...

Would this make my dark urges worse?

I tensed. Backed away.

No hunger pangs.

I stopped, unsure. I was...better? Once more safe to be around?

Look how easily you gave in to my desires.

That was what Z.A. had said. And she had been right. I did. Because I'd been mad at Veronica, my defenses weak. And every time before, I'd been a mess about Cole.

If I remained calm from now on, focused, I wouldn't have to ditch my friends or my grandmother. I could be around them without worry.

I wanted to shout with the force of my relief.

Scowling, Bronx waved me away. "Go home. I've got this."

His tone grated—my first test. *Calm.* "Are you sure you don't want to go back to bed and cuddle?" I asked sweetly.

He leveled me a look that would have frightened the most violent criminals. "The girls caught me at a bad time."

Girls. Plural, as I'd suspected. "Pig," I muttered. Could no guy stay faithful anymore? Sure, Bronx and Reeve weren't actually dating, and she was currently seeing another guy, but come the freak on.

"Whatever."

I heard the self-castigation in his voice and flinched.

"Sorry," I said on a sigh. "I didn't mean that."

He shrugged. "Do you really believe I'd be with anyone else if I could be with Reeve?"

No. I didn't. And when I thought about it, I understood. Sometimes the loneliness probably got to be too much and anyone seemed better than no one. He had no parents. They'd dropped him off in a forest, at night, when he was just a kid, hoping the wild animals would kill and dispose of him. He just wanted to be wanted, to have someone to call his own.

Earlier, as unstable as I'd been, I might even have settled on comfort from Gavin.

The driver—Ethan—turned the car around. Bronx stiffened, gearing to pursue.

He shouldn't do this on his own. I knew that. He could call for backup, but I also knew he wouldn't.

I looked behind me, in the direction I needed to go. I looked back at Bronx, at the anger and frustration shining from his features. He was distracted. He would probably get into trouble.

As the car sped away, Bronx arrowed forward.

I couldn't leave him.

With a mental push, my spirit left my body, which would remain hidden in the trees. I trailed after him, maintaining proper speed, just as Gavin and Mackenzie had taught me, keeping up without a problem.

We ghosted through other cars, and yeah, it freaked me out every time.

"Where's Cole?" I asked, barely panting.

"Taking care of Veronica."

I flinched as if I'd been punched.

"You really messed up, Ali," he continued, unaware of the pain his words had caused. "Beating on one of your own is never okay." His gaze raked over me, and he finally became aware. "He's not with her for that. He doesn't like her the way you think."

"It doesn't matter."

"To you, I think it does." But he offered no other words of encouragement.

About ten minutes later, the car parked in the driveway of a secluded house. Ethan emerged—leanly muscled, with blond hair and a handsome face—then rushed around to open Reeve's door.

"Thank you," she said with a grin.

He leaned down and kissed her cheek. "My pleasure, sweetheart."

Bronx growled low in his throat, a feral sound. He stalked forward, as if he planned to attack the guy, but crashed into a tree and ricocheted backward. He came up sputtering.

"Blood Lines." He looked left, right. "The guy has Blood Lines."

So…the guy knew about the zombies. And yet he couldn't

see them. Otherwise he would have seen us. And if he'd seen us, he would have reacted.

Ethan ushered Reeve into the house. Bronx trailed close to their heels, but the door closed before he could sweep inside, and he once again ricocheted backward. He cursed.

Bronx tried to bypass the walls and windows to no avail. We paced the front yard in unison, waiting for Reeve to come out, ticking off the nearly unbearable seconds.

"I have his address," Bronx snarled. "I'll find out who he is. Every detail. Every girl he's ever banged."

Only he didn't use the word *banged*.

"I'll know every secret."

Man. Bronx really liked Reeve, really wanted her. Her protection mattered to him. He was simply trying to respect her father's wishes, as well as the needs of the slayers.

Watching him, I knew this was how a boy should react to the idea of being separated from his girl. The way I'd wanted Cole to react.

The way Cole *hadn't* reacted.

Had he ever felt so strongly for a girl? Had it ever bothered him to walk away from one? Or was self-preservation wrapped so tightly around him it strangled any of the deeper feelings he had?

I wondered what he thought of me—if he thought of me at all.

"Ali," Bronx snapped, and I jolted back to awareness.

"Yes?"

"Go home. I've got this."

"No."

"You're making little growling noises in the back of your throat, and it's distracting me. Not in a good way."

Fear began to claw at me, because I knew what those growls meant. I had to do a better job of focusing—or else. I squared my shoulders. "I've already let one slayer down today. I'm not letting another. I'm staying."

He glanced at me, and I could see a new gleam of respect in his eyes. But all he said was "Whatever. Do what you want."

That respect...

It meant more to me than money.

And I knew how to get more. The list. *However proves necessary, kill Z.A. ASAP.*

You're going down, fiend.

When dark went against light, light always won. I was light—as long as I didn't let my fire get snuffed out.

I would win. Right?

Bronx bumped my shoulder. "You panicking over something, Bell?"

"No, I'm calm," I said. "From now on, I'm going to be a walking sedative."

ROT IN PEACE

The next morning, I climbed into Reeve's Porsche and bucked my seat belt. Our ten-minute drive to school couldn't end fast enough. I was ready to hide in the back of my first class and fall asleep.

She clearly concurred, gunning the engine as she shot from the garage. I wanted to rapid-fire questions at her, now that we were alone, but I was too tired. I leaned against the door instead, the sunlight streaming through the window warming me, lulling me.

Singing along to the radio, she merged into traffic. There were shadows under her eyes, and for once, she wore wrinkled clothing, as if she'd just rolled from bed and called it good.

I happened to know that she had.

As promised, I hadn't left Bronx alone. I'd waited for Reeve to exit Ethan's house. And she had, at 3:00 a.m. Ethan

had driven her home, dropped her off in the same spot he'd picked her up and kissed her on the mouth before driving away. Bronx hadn't said another word. His body language had said plenty, though.

Ethan was lucky to be alive.

The first moment I'd been alone, I'd called Dr. Bendari to reschedule, but the number had been unavailable. I had screeched with frustration, knowing I'd blown my best chance to talk with the only person with concrete answers.

Then I'd chastised myself for letting an emotion get the better of me.

Walking. Sedative.

"Wishing you hadn't gotten the tattoos?" Reeve asked.

"Of course not," I said. "Why?"

"Well, look at yourself."

I gazed down. I was absentmindedly rubbing my thumb over the daggers. *Oh. Well.* "They comfort me."

Reeve gasped and stomped on the brake. The car jerked to a stop, throwing me forward as much as the belt would allow.

"What the—"

"Bronx," she screeched, tearing off her belt and stepping into the daylight.

Just in front of her car, right in the middle of the road, was Bronx's old, rusted truck. He leaned against the hood, arms crossed.

I should have expected this.

"What do you think you're doing?" she demanded.

"What do you think *you're* doing?" he spat. "Sneaking out in the middle of the night, meeting some strange guy and going to his place. Do you know how dangerous that is?"

"How did you—argh! It doesn't matter." She grabbed a rock and threw it at him.

Reflexes honed, he ducked.

She shook her head, as if she couldn't believe what she'd just done. More calmly, she said, "He's not some strange guy, he's my boyfriend, and what I do with him isn't your business."

"Everything about you is my business."

Her back went ramrod straight. "Screw you. I'm not doing this with you, Bronx. Not anymore." She turned.

He grabbed her arm, spun her around. "Did you sleep with him?"

Very calmly, she said, "I told you. What I do with him is none of your business."

"And I told you everything about you is my business, but neither of us seems to be listening."

The forced calm vanished as she jerked away. "You can't do this to me. Can't pretend you care. Tomorrow, after I've dumped him, you'll change your mind." She shoved him, a puny action, really, when comparing a six-foot-five gigantor to a five-foot-five fairy princess, but he released her anyway.

"Does Daddy Dearest know about him?" he asked quietly.

She pointed her finger in his face. "No, and you won't say a word. You don't get to play any part in my love life. We've been sniffing around each other since junior high. You were so sweet to me at first. You made me things. You were my first kiss. Then suddenly you wouldn't look at me, wouldn't even talk to me—until I turned my sights to someone else and tried to move on. You'd come on strong, and I'd al-

ways fall back into your arms, but it wouldn't take long for you to start ignoring me all over again, and I'm tired of it."

I shouldn't be listening to this. I would have hated it if anyone had heard my arguments with Cole, especially the final one.

Trying to distract myself, I turned up the radio. Taylor Swift, "I Knew You Were Trouble." Fitting. I texted Nana. Can we talk later? Just U & me?

If my emotions started to go haywire, I'd adios.

Her: I would love that.

Me: I'm sorry I've been so weird lately, & I'm sorry about the fight w/the girl.

Her: We can talk about the reason at dinner. And just to make you happy, I promise I won't spend too much on groceries.

I laughed.

Her: BTW, do you want to tell me why I found a note in your room saying "Did this to myself"? WHAT DID YOU DO?

Uh-oh.

Me: Almost @ school. Gotta go. Love you!

Hey. Not a word of that was a lie.

"—can't be with you the way I want," Bronx was saying, drawing my attention back to the conversation.

"Why?" Reeve demanded. "For once, give me a straight answer. You do, and I'll never see Ethan again."

Bronx pressed his lips together.

"Yeah, that's what I thought." Bitterness tinged her tone.

Reeve stomped to the car. Bronx stomped to his. His tires squealed as he turned the vehicle around. Dirt sprayed as he shot forward.

"That boy," Reeve said, her body trembling.

"He cares about you."

"Yeah, just not enough."

I reached over, patted her hand. "Believe me, I get it."

She tossed me a sad smile before resuming the drive.

A few minutes later, she was parking in her usual spot. The lot could be overflowing, but no one, not even teachers, would dare encroach on her territory. Not because of her or her father's money, but because of Bronx. I heard someone made the mistake of parking here only once; Bronx had hot-wired the car and crashed it into the trees the students had spray-painted gold and black to proudly display our school colors.

Silent, we strode over the tiger paws mowed into the grass and headed inside the building.

Trina and Mackenzie were leaning against a locker, snarling at anyone stupid enough to approach them. When I walked past—*never said I was smart*—they pushed away from the wall and flanked my sides, shouldering Reeve out of the way.

"You have to talk to Cole," Trina began.

"I never thought I'd say this," Mackenzie said, "but I want you to do more than talk to him. I want you to seduce the hell out of him. I don't know how much more post-Ali drama I can take."

"O-kay. Cue my exit," Reeve said, branching away from us. "See you at lunch, Ali."

"Yeah. See ya." I sighed. "What's the problem?"

Trina twisted the ring in her eyebrow. "For starters, he's meaner than my stepdad's Yorkie."

"Your stepdad has a Yorkie?"

Mackenzie slashed a hand through the air. "Forget the tiny terror dog. Cole lashes out at everything we say, and has for weeks."

For weeks?

Until two nights ago, he'd shown me only his gentler side.

"He busted Lucas's nose during training," she continued. "Last night, he punched a window and needed eight stitches."

Last night? While he'd been with Veronica. "It has nothing to do with me," I assured them. If I'd had claws, I would have scraped them over the lockers.

Calm.

"I happen to think it has everything to do with you," Trina said. "I've seen the way he watches you when you're not looking."

"And I swear vessels burst in his forehead every time Gavin mentions your name," Mackenzie said, nodding.

"Guys. Cole broke up with me. I told him I'd work on being his friend, and I will, but that doesn't mean I'm going to stroke his…uh, ego and make him smile."

"Fine," Trina replied. "We'll stop trying to convince you to sex him up, but you still gotta talk to him. You're the only one he'll listen to."

"I don't think that's true."

She ignored me, saying, "He disappears for hours at a time. No one knows where he goes. He's paranoid we won't keep detailed records about what we find on patrol. He gets phone calls from blocked numbers and steps out of the room so no one will overhear his conversations. Before, he kept us in the loop about everything."

So he was still spying on the slayers. But what was it, exactly, that he was trying to uncover?

I reached my destination, freed the lock on my locker and stuffed my bag inside. "I'll talk to him about his weirdness, but that's all I can promise."

Mackenzie shocked me to my bones when she hugged me. "Thank you. We, like, seriously owe you one."

As if our conversation had summoned him, Cole turned the corner and strolled down the hall toward us. He was wearing a red baseball cap and had his hands in his pockets. I couldn't see his newest wound. He walked past us, nodding at Trina, then Mackenzie—avoiding me. My chest constricted.

"Or maybe I won't be talking to him," I muttered, and took off for my first class.

Just before Cole turned the corner, he looked back at me; our gazes locked. I tripped over my own feet. No vision. But I saw hunger. Fury. Regret. Remorse. Fear. Then he was gone.

Someone laughed, breaking me from the spell he'd woven. Dazed, a little angry with myself—*calm, dang it*—I looked to see what was so funny. Wren and Poppy stood with a group of girls making fun of a tall, skinny redhead with freckles and braces. Wren and Poppy weren't laughing, but they weren't stopping the taunts, either. The redhead was doing her best not to cry.

I stomped over and, to a chorus of "Hey" and "Watch it," shoved the girls out of the way. Glaring, I said, "You have five seconds to leave, and then I get mad."

I wasn't ever going to be a sedative, was I?

They might not know how good I was with my fists, but they certainly knew the people I ran with, and, paling, they left without another word. Poppy cast a remorseful look over her shoulder. Wren, too. Only she mouthed, *Thank you,* baffling me.

"Thank you," the redhead said, then swallowed a sob. "My shirt… I didn't bring a jacket today, so I can't cover up."

It was white and soaked with water, revealing every stitch on her bra. "Why don't we trade?" I didn't want her sitting in the cold and the wet and thinking about what had happened. "Your shirt goes better with my jeans."

"Really?"

"Really."

She brightened, and we raced to the bathroom.

"Thank you so much," she said after we'd made the switch.

"Don't worry about it." Shivering, I darted to class to avoid a tardy I couldn't afford.

To my surprise, Justin was waiting at the door. "Hey, Ali."

"Hey."

He opened his mouth to say more, closed it. Opened it. Snapped it closed. Finally he settled on "How are you?"

"I've been better." I headed toward my seat, and he followed me. "You?"

"Fine. I'm fine."

I studied him, saw dark circles under his eyes, gaunt cheekbones and lips that had clearly been chewed. He wasn't fine. "I know you told me nothing abnormal had been happening to you. Is that still the case?"

His brow furrowed, becoming a slash of anger. "Want to

tell me what's been happening to *you?* Because something has, right?"

I still wasn't sure what his motives were, but at the moment I had nowhere else to turn. "Possibly."

"Possibly?"

I sat down. "That's all I'm willing to say." *For now.*

He sat down beside me. "Okay, but I can't help you if I don't know what you're dealing with."

"*Will* you actually help me, though?"

His shoulders wilted, and he said, "I guess I deserved that."

Yeah, but I didn't have to be so crabby about it, did I? "Do you know someone by the name of Dr. Bendari?"

"No. Why?"

Crap. So…maybe Dr. Bendari wasn't with Anima, after all. Maybe Justin was lying. Or maybe Justin just hadn't met him. "Forget it."

"Ali. Please. Talk to me."

How many times was I going to hear those words?

The bell rang, saving me from having to reply. "Later," I said. *Maybe.*

Lunchtime arrived. I'd successfully managed to avoid Justin after first and second period. Trina and Mackenzie, too. But not Cole.

He cornered me in the girls' bathroom.

I was washing my hands as he stepped inside. A classmate of mine was in the process of closing a stall door when she spied him and squealed.

"Out," he said, and she took off, leaving me alone with him.

My heart thundered as I dried my hands with a paper towel. "If you plan to yell at me for hurting your girlfriend, let me save you the trouble. My anger got the best of me, but it's not going to happen again."

"She's not my girlfriend."

"It's okay if she is. You don't have to try and spare my feelings. I've moved on."

He did *not* appear grateful.

I tried to bypass him, deciding to talk to him about Trina and Mackenzie's allegations later, in a place without mirrors. He stepped into my path. "Stay," he said.

"Orders?" I glared up at him. "You know I'm not afraid to punch you, right?"

"Do what you want to me. I'm not leaving until you've listened to me."

Sometimes I really hated my curious nature. "What?"

When I backed off, he leaned against the sink, raked his gaze over me and frowned. "You're wearing a different shirt."

"Yes," was all I said, struggling with the sudden need to cover my chest.

"Why?"

Struggling—and failing. I covered my chest with my hands. "Is that why you're here? Because my reasons don't concern you."

His frown deepened. He shook his head, as if to get back on track. "I'm worried about you and want to discuss it like rational people."

"I don't have anything to say to you."

"Why? You said we could try and be friends."

Lesson learned: it was better to think before I spoke. "Fine. Discuss away."

He muttered something under his breath before saying to me, "Ankh told me you've been eating bagels at his house."

Wait. "This isn't about what happened on patrol? Or Veronica?"

"The bagels," he insisted.

What was with the freaking bagels? "Yes. I have been eating bagels. Last I heard, that wasn't a crime."

"It is when it's all you're eating."

I anchored my hands on my hips. "Why do you even care about this?"

He ignored the question, saying, "You didn't bring your lunch and you weren't planning on getting anything in the cafeteria today, were you? I know, because you didn't get anything last week, either. You're going to starve."

He made it sound worse than it was. "I'm saving to buy Nana a house of her own."

"Then bring food from Ankh's. He has more than enough."

"I'm living in his home free of charge. I'm not going to be any more of a burden and take more from him."

"You're not a burden."

"So you say."

"Ali."

"No," I said.

"Take from me, then." He withdrew a brown leather wallet with a chain at the end. "Please."

I violently shook my head. What the heck was happening here? "I don't want your money."

"Ali," he repeated, his tone ragged. "Friends share."

"We're not that close anymore."

He flinched. "You have to eat."

"I will. I promise."

"More than bagels," he insisted.

I nodded, anything to move this conversation along. After school, I'd walk to the convenience store close to the Ankhs' and buy bread and deli meat.

"Not just later, but now, at lunch," he said, as if he'd heard my thoughts. "Please."

Please.

His concern was doing something to me, weaving one of his spells around me, making me forget the world around me, the problems, taking me deeper and deeper into an obsession that had only gotten me hurt. I wanted out. I needed out.

"It's better that we broke up, you know." I said the words for my own benefit. "Our connection was so fast, we never took the time to get to know each other. Not really. And how would we ever have known if we truly cared about each other or if the visions had simply convinced us that we did?"

He smacked a hand against the mirror and leaned toward me. Glaring, he snapped, "I knew how I felt."

Past tense. Why did that hurt? "I know how you felt, too. Not strongly enough to fight for me."

A muscle ticked below his eye as he straightened, backed me into the black-and-gold-tiled wall. The warmth of his breath fanned over my face, as sure and sweet as a caress. His gaze took in every detail of my expression, lingering on my lips. Lips suddenly aching for the kisses he'd denied me during my recovery.

"We both know why I walked away," he said. "We both know what's going to happen."

"Yes, so what the heck do you think you're doing, closing in on me like this?" Good. I'd shaken off the melancholy and welcomed a bit of mettle.

"I don't know," he snarled, and I was suddenly face-to-face with Cole the Yorkie. "I never know anymore."

For my own good, I forced myself to say, "That's your problem, not mine." Then I angled around him and walked away.

This time, he let me go.

I was getting good at not looking back.

In the cafeteria, I spent three precious dollars on a mediocre hamburger. Cole was at the table by the time I eased beside Kat and Reeve, and he watched me eat half...and try to save the other half for later.

Scowling, he planted himself at my side, scooting Kat out of the way, then unwrapped the burger and put it back in my hand. I suspected he would try to force-feed me if I resisted, so I ate the rest. My stomach nearly wept with gratitude.

He pushed a Gatorade in my direction. His? Half the contents were already gone. I'd forgotten to buy a drink, I realized, and gratefully swallowed one mouthful, then another.

"Thank you," I said, trying not to care that he cared.

"That's what friends are for, right? Even if they're not close." He put his mouth where mine had been and drained the rest.

After school, Kat and I piled into Reeve's car. The three of us had one class together, and Mr. Toms, the teacher, had

allowed us to group up for a special humanitarian project. For it, we drove to Party Palace and bought a handful of Get Well Soon balloons.

"On a totally unrelated subject," Kat said, "do you guys want to go threezies on a gift for Aubrey Wilson's baby shower? And by threezies I mean your dad will pay the bulk of it, Reeve. We want to get her something totes amazeballs."

"She mentioned needing a crib," I said. Poor girl. She had just started showing, and her boyfriend had dumped her.

Reeve nodded. "Count me in."

As we meandered along back roads, searching for the next object we needed to complete Kat's "most brilliant idea ever," I checked the clouds. The sun glared at me, making my eyes water, but I still caught sight of a rabbit and moaned. *No, please no. Not tonight.* I wasn't ready to face the zombies—and my reaction to them—again.

Tonight I was supposed to stay at Cole's gym and guard the bodies the slayers left behind. But. Yeah, there was always a *but* with me, wasn't there? I'd be called out just as soon as the zombies were found—and they would most certainly be found.

Would I hear the voices again? Should I just call in sick?

"I'm sure we're going to get a terrible grade for this," Reeve said with a groan.

"If anything, we'll receive a certificate for awesomeness," Kat replied.

My phone beeped. I checked the screen and stiffened.

"What's wrong?" Kat asked.

"Cole wants to meet with me," I said without any inflection of emotion.

Inside, I churned.

I read the text again. My house. Five. Be there.

Dang it. I'd planned to have dinner with Nana before heading over.

"When? Where?" Reeve asked, and I gave her the details.

"Are you going to go?" Kat wondered.

Hands shaking, I texted Nana. Can we reschedule? I'm so sorry, but something's come up w/Cole.

I waited, but a response from her didn't come.

To Cole, I texted Why?

Cole (I'd deleted the part about McHottie): Do I really need a reason?

Me: 2 talk? Yes. We've said all we need 2 say.

Okay, so that wasn't exactly true. I still had to drum up the courage to mention his odd behavior, as promised.

Cole: Who runs this show? Just be there.

Me: Fine.

Cole: Your enthusiasm is humbling.

Me: Go screw yourself.

Cole: I have. I prefer 2 have a partner.

I think I gasped.

"Yeah. I'm going to go," I said. I wasn't going to call in sick. I had responsibilities. I'd keep them.

"Hold everything." Kat bounced up and down in her seat and clapped. "I think I see one."

"Where?" Reeve demanded.

Kat pointed. "Pull over."

Groaning, Reeve slowed the car, eased to the side of the

road and parked. I freed one of the balloons and exited. The girls joined me, and together we approached the centerpiece of our project—a dead raccoon, its arms and legs stiff and pointing in the air.

"Gloves," Kat said, holding out her hand.

Reeve dangled a pair just beyond her reach. "These are cashmere, you know."

"I'm sure the raccoon will be thrilled," she replied drily. "Even though I told you to buy latex."

"I thought you'd appreciate something softer." Sighing, Reeve relinquished the gloves, and Kat tugged them on. "I bought hand sanitizer instead."

"Balloon," she said next.

I handed it over.

Then Kat crouched over the poor dead animal and tied the ribbon to one of its wrists. There was no wind, so the Get Well Soon balloon stayed perfectly straight, flying proudly over the motionless animal.

"Your family will thank me for this one day," she said with a nod.

"As if we're really doing any good," Reeve said.

"Hello, we *so* are. People need to be more aware of the creatures crossing the road, thank you, and this is our way of helping. It's humorous—"

"And gross," Reeve interjected. "And cruel."

"And they'll remember," Kat finished.

We each snapped a few pictures with our phones, cleaned our hands, got back in the car and hunted the next Get Well Soon victim. I mean, recipient.

I couldn't help comparing myself to the animals. A car crash. A part of me dying.

I prayed I had a better end but had a feeling I was going to have to adjust my to-do list yet again.

DEADLY EYES BETRAY YOU

We dropped Kat off at the school parking lot, where her car waited, and drove home. Another note had been stuck to the bottom of the staircase railing. Sighing, I sailed into Mr. Ankh's office—only to find him in a heated discussion with Mr. Holland.

Interesting.

The moment the men spotted me, they zipped their lips. Mr. Holland had been leaning over the desk, putting himself nose to nose with Mr. Ankh. Now he eased back into his seat, and the two acted as friendly as ever.

Even more interesting.

I couldn't help thinking Mr. Holland was a portrait of Cole in twenty years. Both guys had dark hair and strong, chiseled features. Only difference was, Cole's eyes were that amazing violet and Mr. Holland's were an electric-blue.

"Miss Bell," Mr. Ankh acknowledged.

Did he ever go to work? I settled in the only available chair.

"Good. You're here." Mr. Holland massaged the back of his neck. "The three of us are due to have a discussion."

"Your newest blood work came in," Mr. Ankh said, "and the results have me confused."

I shifted uncomfortably.

"The toxin you and Justin shared, the one that is harmful to the zombies," he continued. "It disappeared in Justin, but it's now stronger in you. Also, your iron is lower than before, and your white blood cell count is higher."

I wasn't sure whether to laugh or cry. My human side was fighting, but my zombie side wasn't backing down. "What about the zombie toxin that is harmful to humans? Did I have any traces of that?"

He frowned. "No."

"Why would you ask that?" Mr. Holland said.

I wanted to tell him, I really did. But he'd killed his own wife when she'd turned zombie. No telling what he'd do to me, his son's unstable ex.

If these men left me alive, Mr. Ankh would for sure toss me out. Where I went, Nana went. I would not allow her to be homeless.

Then, of course, Mr. Holland would tell the others. How would Cole look at me then? He wouldn't worry about feeding me anymore, I knew that much.

"Curiosity," I hedged. In a way, it was the truth.

Mr. Holland sighed and twisted his chair to face mine. "Well, I'm curious about something, too. I know you and

my son broke up. What I don't know is why. He won't talk to me."

Instant downer. "And I won't, either," I said hollowly.

He began massaging the back of his neck again, a gesture of irritation or distress he and Cole shared. "He's been sneaking out, talking to people he shouldn't, making bad decisions, and I'm worried about him. Something's going on with him, but I don't know how to help."

"Who's he talking to?" I asked.

Silent, he ran his tongue over his teeth.

He wasn't going to share the information. Got it.

"Will you check on him?" Mr. Holland asked.

"Trina and Mackenzie noticed his odd behavior, too, and asked the same thing. I agreed to talk to him," I said. "I'm meeting him at five."

Mr. Holland pushed out a relieved breath. "Thank you."

I nodded, saying, "By the way, I saw a rabbit cloud today."

The two men shared an uneasy look.

I could guess what they were thinking. The zombies usually rested a week between feedings. Only once before had the creatures come out night after night, and that was to hunt me with the goal of turning me.

Were they focused on someone else now?

"I'll be called into action," I said. And I would find out, one way or another, if the other night had been an anomaly or not. If the zombies would once again ignore me. If I would hear crazed whispers. If I would black out and end up at my old home.

Mr. Holland replied, "I'll put everyone on patrol tonight

and make sure you have a partner who will whisk you to safety if you have another...episode."

"Thanks," I muttered. I left the office and shut myself inside my bedroom. Then I dialed Dr. Bendari. Again, a recording told me the carrier wasn't available. Dang it. Would he ever again activate it?

I thought about the journal, my other source of info. Light chased away darkness. Fire burned away evil. The words snagged me. I just couldn't let them go.

Sighing, I sat in front of the vanity and steeled myself to look in the mirror. I needed a status report, and this was the best way.

My gaze met hers. The smudges had actually spread, stretching from underneath her eyes to her cheeks, even delving down the plane of her neck. Shaking, I whipped my shirt over my head. She did the same...several beats after me. *Annnd* the smudges continued, branching from her neck to her shoulders. The largest smudge rested just over her heart. Once the size of my thumb, it was now the size of a giant's fist. I traced my fingertips over the skin there.

My reflection never moved.

Tick, tock. Tick, tock.

Louder than before.

She was stronger.

Fighting a wave of frustration, I injected myself with antidote, just to be safe, showered and dressed in my all-black fighting clothes. I opened my door to head to Nana's room. I needed a ride to Cole's. Kat caught me off guard, her hand posed as if she meant to knock.

"Everything okay?" I asked.

"Peachy. I came to offer you a ride to Cole's. Frosty texted. He asked me to meet him at the barn at five."

A coincidence? "I accept, thanks."

The barn was packed with slayers, and I realized I'd misunderstood Cole's intentions. We weren't going to talk. He was going to lecture. Not just me, but everyone.

I'd had too many highs and lows lately to let this disappoint me…much.

My gaze landed on Veronica, and I had to fight to keep my lunch. She had two black eyes, a slightly swollen nose and a busted lip, and she was peering up at Gavin, who was saying something to her. I quickly looked away.

"Kitty Kat," Frosty said.

"Jerk Face," she retorted, surprising me.

His eyes frosted over in tribute to his name. "What'd I do this time?"

"Nothing. I thought I'd be mad just to be mad and liven things up. We were getting stale."

In a snap, he lost his air of coldness. He barked out a laugh. "You're too sexy for words, you know that?"

"Actually, I do," she said, and ran to him, throwing herself in his arms.

He caught her, and as he spun her around, a sharp ache tore through my chest. I'd had that once. Would I die before I experienced it again?

Shut up, Downer Ali!

"What's going on?" I asked, hating the tremor in my voice.

Frosty set Kat on her feet but kept her tucked into his side,

acting as her shield, her sole support. "Don't know. Cole has something to tell everyone, but he's not here yet."

"Something to tell everyone...even me?" Kat asked, thumping a finger against her chest.

"Even you." He kissed her on the temple. "You're now an important member of our team."

"I am? I mean, of course I am. Duh." She beamed up at him.

He cupped her cheeks, ensuring that she couldn't look away. Tone serious, he said, "You can't go out at night and fight, since you can't see the zombies, so don't even ask. But you *can* patch me up if I come home injured."

"Dr. Kitty Kat," she said with a nod. "I approve."

"I hope you dole out kisses." He leaned down and pressed a soft one into her lips. "They're my medicine."

"Well, that kind of medicine will cost you. Just...don't come home injured. I'll be mad."

"You know I hate when my little kitty is mad. Her claws come out."

"They come out for other reasons, too," she purred.

In seconds, they were going at each other like wild beasts at mating season.

"Break it up before I break you in half, Frost," Bronx called, and he didn't sound like he was joking.

I found him in the crowd and pulled him into a shadowed corner. "Did you find out anything about Ethan?"

He nod was stiff. "Yeah, just not as much as I'd hoped. His name is Ethan Hamilton, he's twenty-one and a business major at Birmingham Southern. He has a fifteen-year-old sister who was diagnosed with leukemia last year."

How sad. "What are you going to do about him?"

Violence gleamed in his eyes. "Besides have a little chat with him?"

I knew that look. The chat would involve fists rather than words. "Are you sure you want to do that? He sounds like a pretty decent guy, and Blood Lines around his house isn't *that* uncommon. And I kind of understood Reeve's point today, about not being able to do the back-and-forth with you anymore. It might be time to let her go."

He peered at me for a long while before saying, "Do you really think you're in a good enough place to be throwing out advice? No, don't bother with a response. We both know the answer. So why don't I live my life, and you live yours?" With that, he stomped away.

Great. I doubted I could have messed that up more.

A chirp from my phone. I pulled the device from my pocket and read Dinner's ready! I made your favorite. Lasagna and garlic bread. I also asked Ankh if we could use his private balcony, and he said yes. I've got everything set and ready, so come out here as soon as you're able.

My heart twisted. *Oh, no.* She didn't know. She—

Another text came in a second later. I'm sorry, dear. I must have missed your text about canceling. Well, no worries. We'll do it another night.

Tears welled in my eyes. Nana had slaved in the kitchen, preparing my favorite meal. She'd probably decorated Mr. Ankh's balcony with twinkling Christmas lights, just because she knew I wasn't the biggest fan of the dark. That was how wonderful she was. And I'd canceled on her. For this.

I was a terrible person.

I moved back into the corner and called her. "Nana, I am so sorry. I'm at Cole's gym. He asked to meet. I thought it would be just the two of us, and I'd be able to find out what's wrong with him, but it's a meeting with all the slayers."

"Ali," she said on a sigh. "It's okay. I understand."

"I'll make it up to you, I swear."

Another sigh. "We'll have leftovers tomorrow, and we can talk then."

"Yes. I would love that."

We disconnected.

"Hey," a voice said from behind me.

Gavin. Every muscle in my body stiffened as I turned and faced him. I made sure to stare at my feet. "Hey."

"I came over to tell you I've got a date with a very hot chick tomorrow, but I'd be willing to do the unthinkable and break it. For you."

Uh, what? "Don't do that. And I thought you were mad at me for what I did to Veronica."

"I was never mad. That would require a range of emotions I never feel. I thought we'd covered that fact about me. So, about our date—"

I shook my head, oddly charmed. And now mad at *myself.* "We're not going out."

"Look at me and say that. Maybe then I'll believe you."

I responded automatically, glancing up. Our gazes locked, and...nothing. No vision.

My shoulders sagged with relief, but Gavin frowned.

Cole stalked out of the locker room, snagging everyone's attention. Conversations ceased.

His gaze snagged on me—no vision—skidded to Gavin and hardened. He climbed into the boxing ring and scanned the now silent, expectant crowd. He looked like he'd gotten in a fight since I'd last seen him. His features were tight with tension, his hair sticking out in spikes, and his clothing ripped.

I quashed my curiosity.

"All right, everyone," he called. "Listen up. We have a new member on our team. You will welcome him with open arms, and you will keep your fists—and weapons—to yourself."

Murmurs of astonishment surfaced.

A new member? Someone we'd want to hurt?

The locker-room door opened, and out stepped Justin Silverstone.

Gasps of shock replaced the murmurs.

Justin nodded stiffly, his puppy-dog eyes guarded. "Before you judge, hear me out. I made a mistake when I left, and I know it, and I'm sorry. What was done to Ali's grandfather... her home... I had no part in that, you have my word."

"Liar!" Trina spat. She pointed a finger at Cole. "He betrayed us once, and it cost us Boots and Ducky, and now you're going to give him the chance to do it again?"

"We need all the help we can get right now," Cole said, and I heard the rigidity in his voice.

Boots and Ducky. Cole bore their names on his chest.

Justin straightened his shoulders. "I'm back, and I'll do whatever it takes to prove my intentions are honorable."

"This is stupid," Lucas snapped. "I'm not working with him."

"You will." Cole eyed the crowd through narrowed lids. "You will or you're off the team."

LET THE DEAD HEADS ROLL

In a daze, I made my way to the back of the barn. The slayers had settled in the chairs, all of them cursing and preparing to push their spirits from their bodies. Justin included.

What a shocking turn of events.

Trina gave me a slitted look, and I knew she was commanding me to speak with Cole ASAP.

Soon, I mouthed.

Had Cole welcomed Justin because he hoped to keep his enemy close? Or did he actually trust Justin? Was he using Justin, pretending to trust him in the hopes of gaining information about Anima?

Was Justin sincere, or was he acting as a double agent?

So many possibilities.

One after the other, the slayers stood in spirit form. Except me. I tried, again and again, but each time I failed.

As I struggled, it felt as if someone was holding on to my spirit, forcing it to stay where it was.

Gavin and Veronica took off, followed by Trina and Collins, then Lucas and Mackenzie, Cruz and Bronx. Although it seemed otherwise, no one but me had a partner tonight— and I hadn't yet been told who that partner was. Everyone was to branch in different directions to cover as much ground as possible. However, no one was to engage until backup arrived.

"What's wrong?" Justin asked me, hanging back.

Was he my partner? No, surely not.

"Nothing. I'm fine. I can do this." I closed my eyes. Drawing on every ounce of my considerable determination, I imagined my spirit rising and felt my body respond. But when I opened my eyes, hard hands clamped around me and jerked me back into the chair. What the heck?

Justin shrugged, muttered, "Good luck," and took off.

Cole crouched in front of me, the only slayer left. *Oh, crap.* He was my partner, wasn't he? He looked at the door, then me. The door, me. Indecision played over his features. "Problem?" he asked.

Why not tell the truth? "Yeah, but I don't know what it is." Unless…was Z.A. now strong enough to hold me in place?

He looked relieved. "Stay here. I was supposed to be your sidekick, so we were going to cover the same area anyway. I'll just do it on my own."

And do it faster, his tone implied.

I scowled at him.

"Tomorrow," he continued, "Ankh can run a few more tests on you."

"That's your answer to everything. Test, test, test. He's run a thousand already, but hasn't found anything. There's nothing else to check."

"So? He'll do the same tests again. The results could be different."

Oh, really? "Do you know the definition of insanity? Doing the same thing over and over and expecting different results."

"Wrong. That's the definition of determination." Cole flattened his hands on my knees. Because he was in spirit form and I was in human, he ghosted through me, somehow leaving a trail of heat behind.

"Just go," I said, shivering. I motioned to the exit.

"Ali."

"Go," I repeated.

His gaze narrowed. "Despite everything, I am your boss, you know. You shouldn't talk to me that way."

Whatever. "You're my boss. My ex. My friend. Sometimes. Maybe. You can't be all of those things at once. You have to pick one."

His gaze narrowed further, until all I saw was the darkness of his pupils. "Today I'm picking boss. Tomorrow I might change my mind."

Frustrating boy. "Go!" Then, to be snotty, I added, "Sir."

He snapped his teeth at me, the same way he'd done when we first met, straightened and strode to the door. He used more force than necessary to push it open, and then he stomped into the night.

I gazed around the barn. Mr. Holland and Kat were locked in a conversation. Anger and frustration mixed, as powerful as a tsunami, and I banged my fist against the arm of my chair. Leaping to my feet, I paced to the end of the row of chairs, turned to pace back…and saw my body in the chair. Wait. I'd done it? But how? Why?

And why were my legs still burning?

Cole's touch… The burn…

Did Z.A. fear him? If so, I'd let him put those hot spirit hands all over me and hopefully scare her to death.

His hands…all over me… I shivered, then scowled.

I raced for the door. Because it was smeared with a Blood Line, I couldn't ghost through. Like Cole, I opened the obstruction and entered the night. I looked, but found no sign of the—

Wait. There was a streak of gold in the center of the yard, as if a tiny lightbulb had been dropped. A Blood Line. I closed the distance, saw flecks of red mixed with the gold and frowned. Or maybe *not* a Blood Line. I found another streak a few feet ahead and followed it, kept following, going deeper and deeper into the forest beyond the barn.

Trees knifed toward the starless sky, and branches clapped in the breeze. An owl hooted. The darkness was so thick it looked like a black blanket had been draped overhead. Cold air battered against me, and goose bumps doubled parked on my arms. Ahead, to my right, a shadow moved—and another smear was left on the ground. I frowned. The smears definitely weren't from Blood Lines, for sure, but from someone's shoes. How? Why?

I quickened my pace, whisking forward. The shadow had

stopped. I did the same. Tall, clearly muscled—a male. Black shirt, black pants, blending into the night. A dark bandanna covered his hair. Was he a slayer?

Frosty had worn a bandanna. So had Bronx. This guy pressed his chest into the base of a tree and leaned to the side.

"—can't believe Cole's doing this to us," I heard Trina say.

"I know," Lucas replied, his voice fading. He must be walking away.

So. The two hadn't left together, but they'd quickly found each other. Interesting.

"Ali better pony up and take care of this, or..."

After that, not even crickets could be heard.

The shadow moved, leaving another smear behind. I claimed the just vacated spot, then bounded forward, finding the shadow several feet ahead. I pressed into another tree.

"Seriously, what are we going to do?" Trina asked, her voice audible once again.

"Be careful. Guard our words and actions. I'm not giving Justin anything to take back to the Hazmats," Lucas replied, unaware of his tail.

The shadow was in spirit form, definitely, and he was... spying on the pair?

Sparks of anger burned through me. This wasn't Frosty or Bronx.

He darted around the tree, and I followed. This time he didn't linger to listen to anymore of Trina and Lucas's conversation. He branched off in another direction. I continued to follow, watching for the smears. The little traitor couldn't hide from me. I'd catch him in the act, and—

Something hard slammed into me, knocking me face-

first into the ground. Air exploded from my lungs, and dirt coated my tongue. Stars winked through my vision. I tried to crawl forward, but a heavy weight pinned me down. Fear threatened to overtake me, but I quickly rallied, twisting around and swinging out a fist.

Contact!

Pain cut through my knuckles. Maybe I'd broken one. I'd hit the guy in the jaw—a solid, intractable jaw.

"Let me go!" I demanded, expecting to see red eyes. Paper-thin, rotting skin. Hair, hanging in clumps. Instead, I saw familiar violet eyes…and my blood heated in the most delicious way. I stilled.

"Ali?"

"Cole? What are you doing? I…"

Was underneath him. My thoughts derailed. We'd lain like this before. Every other time, he'd been kissing me. Hands had wandered. My body had come alive. I didn't have my body this time, and yet I felt even more alive, as if I were connected to a generator, my nerve endings buzzing with energy.

His gaze drilled into mine…only to lower to my mouth and linger, everything about his expression softening. His breathing changed, emerging shallow and fast. "Are you okay? I couldn't see it in your body, but your spirit is gaunt. You've lost weight, and there are shadows under your eyes. I wasn't sure if you were a hiker who'd been lost for several days or a zombie."

I stiffened, trying not to panic. "I'm okay."

"Good. That's good." His thumbs traced the rise of my cheeks. "Ali…"

I knew that look, that tone, that touch, and knew where this was headed if I didn't put a stop to it. "Get off me," I said, ashamed of my sudden breathlessness.

He stayed right where he was. "What are you doing to me? How are you making me forget what's best for me... For you?"

"What's best?" Maybe, if he said it, I would finally believe him.

"Me...Ronny. You...Gavin."

No, I still wasn't convinced. "Wrong." I didn't worry about his words coming true later on, either—not in terms of spiritual law. My free will was not on board. I turned my head away, peering up at the sky. "I'm not attracted to Gavin, and you're not attracted to Veronica. Not anymore."

"You're right. I'm not." The perfect answer—until he added, "I don't think."

The addition stung. Pushed me over the edge of calm.

I gripped his jacket, shook him. "Do you really think you'll be happy with her?"

"I don't know."

"Heck, maybe you will be, at least for a little while, but if you're true to habit, it won't last and you won't stay with her."

He glared at me. "I don't have a habit."

Blind! "You seriously don't think you're so afraid of losing the people you care about that you cut them loose before they ever have a chance to get inside your heart?"

He took my hands and pressed them into the ground, over my head, forcing my back to arch and my chest to rub against his. "There are people in my heart," he gritted out.

What he didn't say but I heard anyway: *just not you.*

Have to stop setting myself up for this kind of rejection. "Maybe we're both wrong. Maybe you don't even have a heart."

"Oh, I have one." Eyes narrowing, he reached down with his free hand and parted my legs, giving himself a deeper cradle—a perfect cradle—and foolish, foolish Ali let him. Hardness against softness, male against female. "I just don't want it broken."

"So you go around breaking other people's?"

"I didn't break yours, and you know it," he snapped. "You got over me pretty fast, and I did my best to get over you."

That was all he said, but I knew. In that moment, I knew. "You've already done something with Veronica," I said flatly.

A dark curtain fell over his features. I waited for him to deny it.

He didn't deny it.

He nodded.

Even though I'd guessed, shock hit me with the force of a baseball bat. Shock and betrayal. I had no reason to entertain the betrayal. We'd broken up. But...but...here he was, on top of me, and here I was, loving every sensation, and meanwhile, the memory of messing around with Veronica was new and fresh and burning in the back of his mind.

I pushed him off and jerked upright. "I think I hate you."

"You aren't the only one. I think I hate myself."

I was done with this topic. It didn't matter. It couldn't matter.

What did you do with her? I almost shouted.

Shaking, I said, "Why did you tackle me if you thought I was a hiker?"

He drew in a deep breath, slowly released it. "A hiker sneaking around, as if looking for someone. I didn't want to take any chances." He scrubbed a hand down his face. "Everyone leaves and your ability to spirit walk magically starts working again? You got something to confess to me, Bell?"

I reeled for a moment. "Just what are you accusing me of, *Holland?*"

"Were you spying on me?"

He... Oh... I gasped and sputtered. "I was *not*. I was spying on a spy. Was that you I saw skulking after Trina and Lucas?"

A moment passed, the silence laced with incredulity. Cursing, he settled back on his haunches. "Someone was tailing them?"

"I think so, yes."

"What did he look like?"

"Like you, only not quite as tall. Strong. Wearing a bandanna." Cole wasn't wearing one. "His shoes left little golden smears behind."

Hope filled his eyes, softened his features. "Show me." He stood and helped me do the same.

Having his fingers intertwined with mine...the warmth, the comfort...I liked it, wanted more and hated myself far more than I hated him. The moment I was upright, I released him. My mouth dried as I backtracked, looking for that last smear I'd seen.

"There," I said, pointing. "Do you see it?"

"No."

No matter. He'd never been able to see the Blood Lines, either.

He examined the area. "Is there another one nearby?"

I searched and found another and another, but after a while the smears vanished. Either the guy had left the area or he'd overheard us and had known to take off his shoes.

"Okay. All right," Cole said. He pinched the bridge of his nose. "The spy has been verified, at least. And now I know he's male. That cuts my suspect list down."

"You suspected there was a spy." A statement, not a question. That was why *he'd* been spying.

He leaped into action, closing the distance between us. When he reached me, he grabbed me by the shoulders. "You will not tell a soul, Ali. Promise me."

Had I been a suspect, as well?

Anger returned, white-hot. "Why did you let Justin back in? I know he helped us before, but how do you know beyond any doubt he's not double-crossing you?"

He shook his head. "I'm not talking about this."

"Not with me, you mean. Have you discussed it with Veronica?" *Stop. Just stop.*

His nostrils flared. With anger? With relief? "Do you want to hear what happened with her?" he asked tightly.

Yes! "No." I don't know.

"I'll tell you. I think I actually want to tell you. Then you'll stay away from me, even when I'm stupid enough to come sniffing around. I'll finally stop wanting what I know I can't have."

I glared at him, saying, "You don't have to say another word for that to happen."

"I was at home," he began. "She came over."

I shook my head. "Shut up."

It was an order, but it wasn't his will. He continued. "I had been drinking. I never drink, but I was trying to forget about you."

"Shut up!"

"I had been drinking *a lot*. I kissed her. I thought about never being with you again, and I was angry with you, thinking about you with Gavin, and I kissed her with everything I had. I took off her shirt. I touched her."

"Shut up!" He was throwing the details at me as if they were weapons.

They were.

"She unbuckled my pants. I—"

"Shut up, shut up, shut up!" I was standing in front of him before I realized I'd moved. Both of my arms heated to a nearly unbearable degree, as if I was about to ash a zombie. But when I raised my hand and swiped at Cole's cheek, the flames crackling from my skin weren't white—they were red.

Cole tumbled to the ground as if he'd been hit by a Mack truck. He quickly jumped to his feet, now watching me warily. His cheek was split, but because he was in spirit form, the wound wasn't bleeding. His body would be, though. Back at the barn, I bet crimson streaked his face.

"What's going on with you?" he demanded.

Feed from him.

The words whispered through my mind, and I didn't care who had spoken them. Hunger gnawed at me, relentless. Yes, I would feed from him, would feast on his spirit. Scowling, I stalked forward. The red flames moved to my shoulders. I swung out my arm, but Cole ducked. He could

have launched a counterattack, could have kicked my feet out from under me. Instead, he straightened, his hands fisting.

"Don't do this," he said.

Not my will. Do it, I would. I circled him, our gazes locked together.

FEED!

"Go ahead, finish your story," I commanded, doing what he hadn't done and kicking out my leg. His ankles knocked together, and he tumbled to the ground a second time. The bottom of his pants burned away, revealing another gash in his skin. A gash I had caused. My feet were also covered in red flames. "Help me be sure I hate you."

"Is that what it will take?" He stood, saying, "She went down on me. And you know what? I liked it."

With a screech, I lashed out at him.

He dodged.

I would have done it again, but my gaze caught on the fireworks exploding in the sky. One after the other, the other slayers were shooting off their flares. Everyone, it seemed, had spotted a zombie.

Don't care.

A twig snapped.

My gaze whizzed to the left, and I saw red eyes peeking from the brittle wall of foliage.

Still don't care.

Cole moved closer to me, perhaps to protect me from the coming battle. When I scented him, my hunger spun out of control. I growled at him.

He looked at me.

I stepped forward… *When I'm done, there'll be nothing left of*

him… The world around me began to darken, until a black sheet enveloped me.

"No," I shouted.

Oh, yes.

I think…Z.A. was trying to take over.

I—she—continued forward in spite of the blindness, tripped.

"Ali," Cole said, concerned.

Time seemed to slow down as I fell, landed. Sound faded from my ears. Except for one.

Tick. Tock.

THE SLAUGHTER OF THE WHITE QUEEN

I blinked open my eyes and realized I couldn't catch my breath. Why couldn't I catch my breath?

I took stock. I was standing. My clothes were torn, and I was splattered in black goo from the top of my head to the soles of my feet. I had cuts on my arms and stomach. My entire body was shaking, as if I'd run the treadmill for hours, all uphill.

The forest around me had been torched. The trees were now naked, their leaves burned away, their branches covered with ash. Zombie ash? Or…slayer? The ground was just as bad, black and charred, no grass remaining.

Cole was on the ground, alive. Thank God! There were patches of black all over his skin. He'd been bitten multiple times, and his features were contorted with pain.

"Ali-gator," he gasped out.

I rushed to his side, and he flinched, as if he thought I meant to hurt him.

I frowned. I remembered...throwing a punch at him. Yes, I'd thrown a punch, and he'd ducked. He'd told me about kissing Veronica, about the other stuff they'd done—even now I choked on a well of pain. A need to feed from him had consumed me, and I'd attacked him in earnest. Then... nothing.

"I'm so, so sorry," I said, sliding my hands under the hem of his pant leg. The antidote was strapped to his ankle. I freed the syringe, and though I was trembling uncontrollably, managed to shove the needle into his neck.

He'd done this to me countless times, but I'd never had to do it to him. I remained by his side, watching, waiting. At last, the black began to fade from his skin, and he sagged into the decimated ground.

All of the cuts and gashes remained. At the barn, his body had to be covered in blood.

"What happened?" I asked.

"Do you not remember?"

I chewed on my bottom lip, shook my head. Z.A. had spoken to me—yes, that was right. Oh, good glory. She'd taken over.

Wincing, he sat up. He didn't meet my gaze as he said, "Your eyes went red, Ali, just like the zombies. The creatures arrived and ignored you, treating you as if you were one of their own. You burned the trees and—"

I gasped. "*I* burned the trees?"

"You touched them with the red flames, and the leaves instantly withered."

Tears welled in my eyes, and they stung, as if they had been fermenting, ready to spring for weeks, but I hadn't let them. "Did I do anything to you?" Was I responsible for any of the damage?

He fingered the gash in his cheek. "Something's going on with you, Ali," he said, ignoring my question.

I had. I'd hurt him.

"Yes," I whispered. I couldn't keep quiet anymore, whatever the consequences were for speaking out. I'd known I was a danger but hadn't taken enough precautions to protect my friends. "Mr. Ankh told me my blood work was fine, but, Cole, that can't be true. I'm filled with zombie toxin. It's there, inside me, and it's alive. A part of me. A new part. I've seen her—heard her."

I waited for hatred to gleam in his eyes.

I waited for a savage rage to be unleashed.

He had to kill me now. I was the enemy.

"What else?" he asked.

I blinked, confused. "Urges come, dark urges, and I find myself giving in. I never would have believed it unless—"

"What the hell happened?" Gavin demanded, cutting me off with his arrival.

I looked over in time to see him and Veronica stalk past the trees I'd burned. Z.A. might have done it, but she'd used my hands. The realization still flayed me.

The pair was as battle-wounded and dirty as Cole.

Cole reached out, squeezed my wrist. "I don't want you to say another word about this," he whispered.

He didn't plan to tell the others? Why? To protect me? Maybe. What would happen if the slayers learned what I'd

done to him? I'd be thrown out, no question. And they'd be smart to do it.

He lumbered to his feet, dragging me with him. "Let's get back to the barn," he said.

"Cole!" Veronica rushed to his side and cradled his battered face, tilting his head from one side to the other to study his injuries. "Sugar, you look like you've been mauled by a bear. Are you okay?"

Sugar.

"I'm fine." Clearly uncomfortable, he set Veronica away from him.

I was too wrung out to feel jealousy just then. Or anguish. Or longing. Yeah. Way too wrung out.

I swiped at the sting in my eyes with the back of my hand.

She tossed me a glare meant to slay me on the spot. "I thought you had special powers or something like that. You should have protected him."

"Yes," I said sadly, "I should have."

Gavin wrapped his arms around my shoulders in a surprising show of support, and I leaned against him. I was getting more and more comfortable with contact with him—and I wouldn't let myself think about what that meant. It wasn't romantic, I told myself, and that was all that mattered. "Catfight round two can wait. Cole's right. We need to get back to the barn."

Cole stepped toward us, the menace I'd expected earlier now radiating from him. His gaze moved from Gavin to me, then to Gavin again. He looked 100 percent capable of murder. Then he stopped himself and spun away.

So badly I wanted to follow him, to catch up to him. It

was utter anguish denying myself—fine, I was feeling it—but I couldn't risk another fight with him. Besides, I had a spy to catch.

He led the way through the forest, Veronica staying close to his heels. Along the way, we met up with Frosty and Justin, and I did some mental measuring. They were both about the size of the spy I'd seen. But then, so was Lucas. And Gavin.

Gavin also wore a bandanna.

The spy had to be someone close to our circle. I mean, the guy had known the location of Cole's barn and that we would be on patrol tonight. But...I didn't want to accuse any of the slayers. I might not be able to trust myself right now, but I did trust my friends. Even, surprisingly enough, Gavin.

In a lot of ways, he was like Cole. He got in your face with his with beliefs and opinions. He was fearless, cared nothing about consequences. But he was fierce when it came to the safety of his friends.

I had a lot to think about.

"What I'm about to say is true, so I'm not simply making it true in your life by speaking it, if you know what I mean, but she's a terrible enemy to have," Gavin said softly.

"Who? Veronica?"

He nodded.

I shrugged. I'd had enemies before, and I would make many more, I was sure. "What do guys see in her anyway? I mean, she's beautiful, but that's all she's got going for her." I think what I was really asking was—what did Cole see in her?

Gavin looked straight ahead. "She's actually a very nice

person, but envy has turned you both into raving— Well. Never mind. I want to keep my balls. As I was saying, she's smart, and she's funny, and the best part is, she puts out."

Was sex always on his mind? "Your words are like poetry."

He chuckled, saying, "I admit I'd like to take her to bed, have since the day I met her, and she'd let me, I think, if she weren't so determined to win back Cole, but unlike your Mr. Holland, I've never hooked up with another slayer. I like to keep business separate from pleasure. A cliché, I know, but there are far less complications that way. As I'm sure Cole is learning."

"I'm a slayer," I pointed out, "and yet you keep asking me out."

"You're also not my type. Or you weren't. I'm not sure what my type is anymore. You resist, and it drives me wild."

"That's sad."

"That's life."

I rolled my eyes, a common occurrence in his presence. "You might be the weirdest person I've ever met."

"Thank you."

"I don't think that was a compliment."

"Agree to disagree," he said.

We entered the barn, and my spirit jerked from Gavin's grip, flying forward as if tugged by an invisible cord. I skidded across the room and...boom!

Gasping, I pried open my eyes. I was sitting in the chair, spirit and body joined.

Mr. Ankh knelt in front of Cole, already patching up his injuries. Just as I'd suspected, he was covered in blood.

New to-do list: *Find a way to* disable *the zombie inside me. Kill the zombie inside me. Still do whatever proves necessary.*

He blinked open his eyes and grimaced.

Mr. Ankh said, "You need stitches, son," and began digging in his bag of supplies.

A lump grew in my throat as Cole's gaze met mine. Violet against blue. A cold mask against sorrow.

I'm sorry, I mouthed.

He nodded, looked away.

Would he cut me from his life now that he knew about Z.A.?

It was better than death, and yet almost as painful.

"Where's Kat?" Frosty demanded. Like Cole, he was covered in blood.

Without looking up from his task, Mr. Ankh replied, "When you started bleeding, she started screaming, and I insisted she go home."

I bet he'd had to threaten to ban her from the building forever to actually get her to go.

Frosty raced out.

"Everyone's been injected with the antidote?" Mr. Holland asked.

I hadn't, but then, I hadn't been bitten. Still, I requested a dose and received it a few minutes later. The cool stream came with a measure of strength, stopping my trembling.

"Zombies were everywhere, man," Gavin said, standing. "We couldn't contain them all."

"Yeah, and they seemed to know exactly where we'd be," Lucas threw at Justin.

Justin shot to his feet. "I didn't tell anyone about tonight.

I didn't know I'd be meeting with everyone until fifteen minutes ago, when Cole came and got me."

"Ever heard of a phone? Texting?"

"Cole watched me the entire time. And do you really think a zombie is capable of taking my calls?"

"You were in the locker room alone for several minutes. You could have gotten a message to someone at Anima," Trina spat. "They could have arranged this."

"You think I'm wearing a wire, too?" He ripped his shirt over his head, revealing a hard, cut physique I hadn't known he had.

A hand penetrated my line of sight, and I glanced up. Gavin stood in front of me, offering me assistance. I twined our fingers, and he tugged me to a stand. I wasn't as strong as I'd thought, because my knees almost buckled. He wound his arm around me and held me up.

A chair skidded. I saw Cole stand, brush Mr. Ankh aside and stalk into the locker room. The door slammed shut with a loud bang.

Of course, Veronica followed him.

I fell asleep thinking about ways to disable Z.A. Cut off my hands? Remove all my teeth? Then I'd live, and she'd have no way of hurting anyone.

Let's make that plan B.

The ring of my cell woke me. From the bed, I blindly reached out, patting my nightstand. "Hello," I rasped when the phone was at my ear. What time was it?

"You missed our appointment, Miss Bell."

Dr. Bendari?

I jolted upright. The fancy wall clock said it was 5:59 a.m. I'd set my alarm for six, and—my phone vibrated, right on cue. I needed to get ready for school.

"Something came up," I said. "I tried to call, but you shut off your phone."

"A necessary precaution."

"And why is that?"

"Do you expect me to believe you don't want your slayer friends to capture me?"

Reverse psychology? Please. "I'm the one with doubts, Dr. Bendari. You could be planning to murder me."

"I guess we're going to have to trust each other. Are you still interested in meeting?"

"I am."

"Good, because I'd like to hear about the trouble you had last night."

Had *he* sent the spy...his source? "How do you know about that?"

I imagined him shrugging as he said, "How else?"

"Well, the only way your source could have heard about last night's activities was if he was at the scene."

A chuckle devoid of humor crackled over the line. "Is that so? Well, you should check the morning news reports."

The news? I scrambled for the TV remote, pressed Power. Colors filled the screen. I switched channels and came to—

"—awoke to find twenty-six people had died from antiputrefactive syndrome," a reporter was saying. She stood on a street, the address of a neighborhood close to Cole's scrolling across the screen.

Antiputrefactive syndrome: when the human body was

infected with zombie toxin. Although civilians had no idea that was the cause.

The reporter continued. "Last year, two local high school boys died of this rare disease, and citizens were told it was not contagious. Just a month ago, an elderly man died. How and why are so many infected? The CDC has arrived, and the houses of the affected have been quarantined."

Dr. Bendari sighed with regret. "People were killed, Miss Bell. People who will rise again. Zombies entered their homes and ate every bit of their humanity, leaving only evil behind."

"Why?" The moisture in my mouth dried. "How?"

"Not every home has a Blood Line."

That would change, I thought, fisting the comforter. Soon.

For once, the C word actually empowered me.

"The zombies are mutating," he explained. "Just like you are mutating. They've become hungrier. They've become stronger. They—"

My door burst open and banged against the wall. Mr. Ankh and Mr. Holland strode inside. Both were scowling with a fury they'd never before directed at me. My heart drummed inside my chest, nearly cracking my ribs.

"What's going on?" I demanded. "What are you doing?"

Dr. Bendari said something, but I couldn't make out the words.

"Come with us, Ali," Mr. Holland said. "Now."

Dr. Bendari went quiet.

Last night, Gavin had dropped me off and I'd showered, dressed in a tank and boxer shorts and fallen into bed. The

men weren't seeing anything they shouldn't, but I was still embarrassed. "What's going on?" I repeated. "I'm not going anywhere until you tell me."

Mr. Ankh popped his jaw. "There's something you need to see."

I severed the connection with Dr. Bendari and stood. I was led down the hall, down the stairs, down another flight of stairs and into the basement. The air grew cooler and danker with every step, and I felt a layer of ice glaze my skin—one that matched the layer growing inside me. At the end of a hallway, we paused at the only door. It was closed and locked. Mr. Ankh pressed his hand against a new ID box, and a bright yellow light flashed.

The hinges on the door loosened, the entrance opening under its own steam.

We swept inside the laboratory. The floors were concrete, with drains in several locations. There were multiple curtained stalls, each containing a gurney with wrist and ankle straps.

I gulped.

Mr. Holland motioned to a chair in front of a TV screen. Shaking, I sat. "I've already seen the news."

"That has nothing to do with this moment. Now, I'm going to check your vitals." As he poked and prodded, he asked me one question. Only one. "Are you working for Anima?"

"No! Of course not." I had to tell him the truth, didn't I? Another to-do list: *Talk. Admit everything. Pray for the best.*

So, I did it. I poured out every Z.A. detail I'd been hoarding.

When I finished, Mr. Ankh shook his head. "Impossible. You're still human."

"For now."

He stared at me a long while, silent. Then he grimaced and pressed a button on a remote. Bright green colored the entire TV screen and—the forest! I saw the forest.

"This was taped through a night-vision lens," he said. "I have more cameras out there than any of you realized. I don't always check them, but the gash in Cole's cheek was strange, something I'd never seen before. When I asked him about it, he refused to answer."

I watched as a red line dove at another red line, knocking it to the ground. The two stayed in that position for several minutes, as though…talking. Cole and I, I realized.

"We're spirits. How did the camera pick us up?" I asked, dazed.

"Special camera. Special equipment."

"Did you happen to see the guy I was following?"

"Yes. But like you, he's just a line."

On the screen, Cole sat up. We talked some more. Stood. Walked around. A brighter red consumed my hands and I struck him. He fell. Stood again. We faced off. I came at him. He dodged.

Brighter pricks of red appeared at the tree line. The zombies?

A line—me—crashed into the ground.

That was when I'd fallen and blacked out. When Z.A. had taken over.

I watched myself stand and angle toward Cole. *Oh, no. Please, no.* I walked toward him. He ignored me and ran to

the zombies, attacking with a vengeance. I followed him. Rather than helping him, I struck him from behind.

I clutched my stomach, feeling as if I'd swallowed shards of glass. The zombies converged on him, yet still he managed to fight them off, working his way to his feet. I came at him again, obviously intending to hurt him, but he sidestepped me, putting his body between me and the zombies. He could have punched me, knocked me out, or even thrown me to the wolves. I'd left myself wide-open. Instead, he returned his focus to the zombies.

In that moment, I truly hated myself. How could I have attacked Cole in such a way? At such a critical time?

The zombies encircled him, reached for him. I grabbed two of the creatures by the arm, ripping them away from him, my target, and tossing them into the trees.

Wait. Maybe I'd been helping him, after all.

The red flames spread from my arms to the rest of my body, engulfing me. I grabbed two other zombies, repeating the toss. When they recovered, they paid me no heed, keeping their sights on Cole. I closed the distance and flattened one hand against a tree—the leaves turned to ash in an instant—and collared one of the zombies with the other. He didn't turn to ash but flopped around. I leaned down... and bit into his neck.

In the here and now, a scowling Mr. Ankh stepped in front of me. I stuttered around for the right words—found none. The horror of seeing myself do something like that... To know I'd ingested zombie rot...

"Miss Bell, I'm not sure I believe you about being both human and zombie, with the zombie part of you able to

manifest outside your body. But I do know I can no longer allow you to live in my home, with my daughter. I want you out within the hour."

YOU HAD
ME AT GOODBYE

I went into the bathroom and dressed, then packed up what few belongings I had. A couple of shirts, a couple of pairs of jeans, my daggers and the journal. That was it. Didn't take me long. Ten minutes, maybe. Tears burned at the backs of my eyes, but I blinked them away. No way I'd cry over this. I'd lost a home before, and one I'd loved with all my heart.

This? This was nothing.

Then why does it hurt so much?

I think a part of me had always known this day would come. I anchored the bag's strap over my shoulder and strode out of the room, bypassing the cold-blooded Mr. Ankh and the stone-hearted Mr. Holland.

Nana paced at the front entrance, her bag resting on the floor. Her anxious gaze landed on me as I pounded down the stairs, and she looked as if she'd aged ten years overnight.

Her hair was a mess. Her blouse and slacks were wrinkled. She wore no makeup.

Someone had woken her up and forced her to hurry.

I gnashed my teeth, noticed the second heart pounding ferociously in my chest and forced myself to breathe, to calm before the hunger had time to hit.

"Are you all right?" she asked me.

What had she been told? I forced a small smile. "I'm... stable. You?"

"Oh, I'm fine." Her gaze shifted to Mr. Ankh and narrowed. "What's going on? Why are you doing this to us?"

"I'll allow your granddaughter to explain. But there's no reason for you to fret. I'm not leaving you homeless. I've rented you a place in your old neighborhood. The address has already been programmed into your car's GPS."

I hated that he was paying our way and wanted to refuse. I didn't. Not yet. I'd let him spend his money only as long as it took me to find a new place—our place, one we could afford on our own. One he couldn't ever take away from us.

I picked up Nana's bag. As she struggled to understand what Mr. Ankh *hadn't* said, I ushered her outside. Her sedan was waiting in the driveway, the keys already in the ignition, the engine purring.

I threw the bags in the back of the car and buckled into the passenger seat. Nana claimed the driver's seat, and a few minutes later, we were soaring down the highway.

"Tell me what's going on," she said with a tremor. "Please. Lately I feel a lot like Reeve, desperate for answers but getting none. You're gone all the time, and I'm used to that, but when you're home, you're moody and distant, even

violent. And now the men who were supposed to help you with your cause want nothing to do with you."

"Nana, I'll talk to you about this, I promise. Just not in the car." What I had to say would upset her, more than she already was. Cars and emotional drivers were not a good combination.

"Ali."

"Please."

"All right. But the moment we're inside..."

Ten minutes later, we reached the house. She parked in the driveway. It was a two-story in the shape of a C, with red-brick and white shuttered windows. A step up from Nana's home, definitely newer, but colder—and a dump compared to Ankh's. *Keep it together.*

I carted the bags into the living room, surprised to see the place was empty, and surprised by my surprise. What? I'd expected the guy to keep us in style? The walls had been painted in bold, bright colors. Red. Blue. Green. I figured there was a Blood Line around the property, but I wouldn't be relying on a supposition. I'd talk to Nana, then get to work.

"Ali," Nana said, her voice breaking at the edges.

Calm. "I was bitten," I explained. "I was given the anti-dote, and that helped, but it didn't destroy the zombie toxin. I'm doing terrible things. Dangerous things. Becoming what I hate most. Mr. Ankh feared for Reeve. And Nana... I fear for you. I think it would be better if I—"

"No!" she said with a violet shake of her head. She closed the distance between us and grabbed me by the forearms. "You're not staying somewhere else, or whatever you were

going to say. You're my granddaughter and I love you. We will stay together and I will help you."

My chin trembled. I so did not deserve this woman.

"Why didn't you tell me sooner?"

"At first, I wasn't sure what was happening to me. Then…" Man, this was difficult to admit. "I was just too scared of what would happen."

"Oh, Ali."

I placed my hands over hers. "If ever I do something to frighten you, or my eyes turn red, or I stare at you too long, run. Run and don't look back."

She gave me a small shake. "You're not going to become a zombie, young lady. I won't let you."

A small laugh escaped me. I wish I had her confidence.

I leaned forward and enfolded her in a hug. "Thank you for loving me. And I really am sorry about dinner. If I'd kept our plans, last night wouldn't have… Well, it doesn't matter now. I'm just so, so sorry."

"Don't think another thing about it, A-diddy. You have responsibilities, and I know that."

A-diddy? I laughed again. Nana used to love to keep up with what she considered popular slang, but she'd stopped after Pops had died. Knowing she was finally picking up the pieces of her shattered life delighted me.

"Nana," I said, hopping on the counter that divided living room from kitchen. "Did you know the journal you gave me is all about zombie slaying?"

Her eyes grew wide. "No. I didn't."

"Has anyone in your family ever… I don't know, talked

about invisible monsters no one else could see? Or been committed to a crazy house, maybe?"

"Well," she said, peering down at her loafers. "My mother was an alcoholic, and she used to babble about creatures of the night desperate to steal her soul. My dad forbade us to discuss her condition with anyone, and as embarrassed as we were, we were more than happy to agree. Of course, when I was dating Pops, he would sneak over and…well…" She cleared her throat. "Never you mind. He witnessed one of her episodes."

Slayers. On my mom's side of the family. How could I not have known?

How many other slayers came from a double lineage?

"It's one of the reasons Pops and I were so adamant about your mother staying away from your father, and oh, Ali, I should have known, should have realized, the two were connected. In my mind, Mother was a drunk, pure and simple. And then, of course, your dad started drinking, and, well, you know the rest."

I did. She and Pops had hated my father, had never welcomed him over. I'd never blamed them, though, and still didn't. There'd been quite a few days I'd hated my father, too.

"How did your great-grandfather die?" I asked.

"He disappeared one day. At least, that's the story I was told when the journal was handed down to me."

Huh. Disappeared. I remembered a passage from the pages of his journal.

Some slayers have inklings of the future. Some can see the Blood Lines and recognize our sanctuaries. Some can destroy the zombies

one by one, then two by two, after being bitten a single time. Something in their spirit infects the zombies and spreads from one to another like a contagious disease, with no more action on the slayer's part. Some can do none of that. Some can do all of that. I can do all. That's how I know about the war that's coming. That's how I know that not a single slayer—or civilian—will survive unless something more is done. That's how I know what needs to be done.

I need to die.

Then, a few chapters later, he'd written, *Are you willing to give up your own life to save others? Have you realized that dying is the only way to truly live?*

Had he given up his life to save others? Had he died to truly live?

If so, great. Wonderful. But what did any of that mean? I hadn't known before, and I certainly didn't know now.

I tweaked my newest to-do list. *Pray for the best. Hope answers rain down.*

Outside, tires squealed. A door slammed.

I frowned and stalked to the window to peer out.

Because of the shape of the house, the driveway was hidden and I couldn't see the car. Or, apparently, the person who'd abandoned it to stomp to our porch and pound on the door.

"Ali," a voice called. "I just heard."

My heart nearly leaped into my throat. Cole? He hadn't cut me from his life?

I rushed to the entrance and opened up. He burst inside, paused in front of me. He looked me over, and I did the same to him. His eyes were bloodshot—clearly, he hadn't slept. His face was battered and bruised, his stitches stark.

His clothes were wrinkled and it was obvious he'd pulled them on hastily.

"I didn't say a word to them," he said.

"I know. They had a video."

One of his brows rose into an arch. "So you got to see what happened?"

I nodded, unable to hide my growing shame.

He cupped my cheeks as if he still had every right to touch me. My chin trembled—*no! no more tears*—and I battled the urge to lean into him, to rest my head on his shoulder and draw from his strength. I pulled away, severing contact.

His expression hardened.

"All right, well." Nana cleared her throat before gathering her purse and keys. "I'm headed to Target to pick up the things we're going to need. You two obviously have a few issues to work out."

"I don't need anything," I assured her.

She kissed me on the cheek, patted Cole on the arm and left us alone.

"I'll talk to Ankh," Cole said, shutting and locking the door.

"No. Don't. I'm furious for what he's done to Nana, but I do understand what he's done to me. I attacked you, Cole. Like, I planned to eat the life out of your spirit."

"I don't care about that."

"Well, I do."

He waved the words away. "You weren't in your right mind."

"What about the other thing? I bit a freaking zombie. No telling what other damage that's caused inside me, or just

how tainted I am now. I don't know what to do, or how to fix myself. Not really. I mean, the journal said I needed the fire, but I tried that and nothing happened, and now my fire is red. And did you hear the part about my being tainted?"

"Wait. You tried to fix yourself with your *fire?*"

Uh-oh.

"You actually tried to kill the zombie—you. And we were, what? Just supposed to find your ashes, never wonder what had happened and move on?"

"*You* had already moved on," I countered. "And you would have had answers." Sort of. "I left a note."

His sights narrowed on me as he walked toward me. I backed up. He was so much taller than me, so much wider, he dwarfed me in every possible way. "I am so angry with you right now, I don't even know what to say." He picked me up by the waist, unnerving me enough to swallow my protest, and hefted me onto the counter. Then he nudged my legs apart and edged closer to me, staring into my eyes with unmatched determination.

His heat surrounded me, irresistibly delicious. For the first time since Mr. Holland and Mr. Ankh had burst into my room, I felt warm.

Concentrate. "I thought I was doing the right thing."

"You thought wrong. And you're *not* tainted."

"I am." I flattened my hands on his shoulders. To push him away or draw him closer, I wasn't yet sure. I hadn't forgotten what he'd done with Veronica, and I wasn't sure I could ever forget. "Look. I'm trying to stay away from you. That's what you wanted, and that's what I'd like. You're making it difficult."

Anguish filled his eyes. "I know. But I'm not leaving until I know you're all right, and you understand you're not tainted."

This. This was the boy I'd dated. Concerned. Kind. Willing to fight to stay.

I wanted him back.

I couldn't have him back. Not permanently.

"Sorry, but I don't and won't understand any such thing. My dad was a slayer and apparently my mom was, too, though she didn't know it, and we've all heard the saying about being high and falling hard. With all my abilities..."

"Hey, I'm right there with you. My mom was a slayer, too."

Astonished, I said, "Both of your parents were slayers? Wow. Okay. I wasn't expecting that. Do you think it's why we had the visions?"

"Maybe. Gavin is the only other slayer I know with a double lineage. But then again, he and I never had a vision. Until you."

My breath caught in my throat. "You guys had a vision?"

He nodded stiffly.

My fingernails dug his shirt into his skin. "When? What did you see?"

He set his hands beside my thighs, as if he couldn't trust himself to touch me. "We saw...you. We came through a doorway, and you came running when you spotted us. You smiled and you jumped into his arms. His. Not mine. You chose him, and even kissed the hell out of him right in front of me."

"When did this vision happen?" I insisted.

"The morning I ended things with you. I was so worried about you, on edge, and then he came in the room, and our eyes met, and there it was. The vision." He pressed his forehead against my sternum. "It was terrible, Ali. I reacted the same way I would have if you'd just cheated on me. I wanted to kill Gavin, and I'm not talking figuratively. I wanted to shake you, then kiss you, then force you to make promises I was sure you couldn't keep."

Emotion clogged in my throat. I could imagine the pain and betrayal he must have felt—because I would have felt them, too. "Have you guys had another vision?"

"No."

I thought I'd nixed my wall theory, but…walls could have fallen amid his concern for me, and then gone back up amid his anger. If so, that would mean my walls kept falling, too. At least with Gavin. What did that mean?

"Why didn't you tell me this had happened?" I asked.

"I didn't tell you a lot of things," he replied darkly.

"Like?"

"Like…" He tangled his fingers in his hair, tugged on the strands, as if to rip them free. With a bitter laugh, he said, "Why not? What I've done so far has only made things worse. I'm miserable. You're miserable. Why not try a new path?"

"Cole! Please." My patience was already in tatters.

He closed his eyes, said flatly, "There's a spy among us."

"I know. I saw him—"

"No. In our group." He pinned me with a gaze that failed to hide the torment inside him. "It's one of us. Someone we trust. I've known for a while."

"I know that much, too. So I ask again, why didn't you tell me?"

"Wait. How did you know?"

"Emma."

"I should have guessed." He pushed out a breath. "I didn't tell you because I didn't want to ruin someone's good name before I had proof. And I didn't want to make you suspicious of everyone and ruin your relationship with the slayers who had only just begun to accept you. And what if the spy found out you suspected something? What would happen to you then? You'd be in constant danger, someone desperate to shut you up."

I couldn't argue with his logic. "Why tell me now?"

"Now your relationship with the others is ruined anyway. Ankh and my father will show everyone the video. They'll want the group to know why you're to be avoided."

That was for the best. And yet it still hurt, knowing I would lose so many people I cared about, all in one swoop. "How do you know there's a spy?"

"Justin called me, told me someone was feeding information to Anima Industries. Information only a person on the inside could have. Meeting times. Injuries we'd sustained. Snippets of conversation we'd had."

Justin *had* called him. I wondered what else Puppy Dog Eyes had lied to me about. "I just… I can't imagine any of the slayers doing it."

"Me, either. But someone is, and I have to find out who before this escalates and my friends get hurt."

"What if Justin is playing both sides? What if he told you

all of this, hoping you'd take him back? He could pretend to help and secretly sabotage."

"How would he have already known stuff he shouldn't before I welcomed him back?"

"Spying from the outside before spying from within."

Grim, he said, "I've been watching him, and have even fed him false information. So far, he hasn't taken the bait and moved on anything. And by the way, he mentioned you'd asked him if I'd talked to him and that he'd played dumb because he thought that's what I'd prefer."

A smart move, whether he was the spy or not. It covered all the bases. "Is that why you got so friendly with Veronica? You were spying on her?"

"At first, yes."

My eyes narrowed, even as my heart skipped a beat. "And then you began to believe you belonged with her."

His hands curved around my waist and held me tightly, as if he feared I would run away. "Yes."

Part of me did want to run. But I wouldn't. What he'd done had cut me and left a wound, and it needed to be cauterized. "And then you...made out with her."

He held my gaze unflinchingly, despite the pain now gleaming in those violet depths. "Yes. But I didn't tell you everything—"

"And I don't want you to," I interjected, placing a finger over his lips. His soft, soft lips. I shivered— No! No shivering. "There's no need. We're not together. So what are you still doing here, Cole?"

He pulled my finger away, held it, stared at it as if it

contained the cure for all of his ills. "I don't know." His head dropped, as if he was ashamed, but still he held on to that finger. "I just... I can't seem to stay away. You're like a magnet, and I'm drawn. And what about you? You're supposed to yell at me, scream profanities and tell me to go and never come back. Why aren't you yelling?" he asked almost bitterly.

Because, despite everything, I liked that he was here.

Foolish girl.

"You want me to yell?" I said, and drew in a deep breath, preparing. "I will."

He shook his head, looked up at me through the thick shield of those dark, dark lashes. "It's too late for that. I'm going to kiss you, Ali."

Kiss... Yes... No! "You made your bed."

"I know. But I still want you in it."

Just. Like. That. Every cell in my body woke up, stretching, reaching for him. Desperate for him. I had been thirsty for so long, and he was my water. Had always been my water.

One last time, I thought. Just one more. It would be closure. The end.

The very end.

"It...it won't mean anything," I whispered.

What are you doing?

Common Sense Ali poked out of the mire of my thoughts.

In that moment, I hated her. I needed this and wasn't going to argue with her.

"Let's hope," he said, the words nothing more than a low growl.

He meshed his lips against mine, infinitely tender, going

slowly, savoring every moment, as if he could draw out a response—or was willing to do anything necessary to earn one.

That was all it took.

The spark that had always burned between us exploded into a wild inferno. I thrust my tongue against his, and he thrust back. Neither of us was gentle. I clung to him with all of my strength, demanding more, taking more. Taking everything.

It wasn't enough.

I wasn't sure I would ever get enough.

He moved his hands through my hair, fisting the strands at the base of my neck and forcing my head to tilt, allowing him deeper access to my mouth. In that moment, he owned me.

The past ceased to matter. I was the girl who'd been starved, and he was more than the water. He was the honey. I devoured, unable to get enough of him.

"You feel so good," he rasped, "taste so good. I've missed you. Have to have you. Soon. Soon. Don't send me away."

"Stay." My blood fizzed with energy. I tore at his shirt, the force I used causing the fabric to rip. He stumbled backward. Separation. No. I jumped off the counter to follow after him, then pushed him to the floor and straddled his waist.

Our tongues met with even more force. I took more and I gave more, and it was wild, untamed, but it still wasn't enough for me. He tasted of mint and strawberries, my two favorite things—I needed more. He was firm where I was soft, and every point of contact was electric heat—I needed to be burned.

"Touch me," I demanded.

He rolled me over, pinning me to the carpet with his muscled weight, his hands frantic as they moved over me. I licked his neck, inhaled his scent.

Yes. Yes!

He came back down for another kiss, but paused just before contact, and frowned. "Your eyes. They're red."

In an instant, horror doused the flames. Horror and fear, such ugly fear. I wiggled out from under him, then crab-walked backward, widening the distance between us. "St-stay away from me. You have to stay away."

"Ali," he said, reaching for me. "I'm not going to hurt you. I want to help you."

Oh, glory. "Leave," I commanded, barely stopping myself from kicking his hand away. I had attacked him once. I wasn't going to give myself the opportunity to do it again. "Go to school before you get a tardy."

His hands fisted, fell to his sides. "School is closed today. Twenty-six people were found dead in their homes this morning, and three students were among their numbers. They aren't in your grade, so I don't think you ever met them," he added quickly. "Reports claim antiputrefactive syndrome is now contagious and sweeping through Birmingham, and precautions are being taken until it's known how it spreads."

He moved toward me, determined.

"No," I shouted, scrambling back until I hit the wall. Hot tears streamed down my cheeks. Guess I wasn't done crying, after all. "Go! Please!"

A long while passed before he stood. He peered down at

me, different emotions playing over his features. The anguish of before. Anger. Yearning. "I'm so confused right now."

The tears fell harder, faster. "Let me clear things up for you. I thought we could be friends. We can't. I don't want to see you again. Go away and never come back."

WE'RE ALL MAD HERE

The next few weeks passed in a blur. I no longer hung with the slayers, and I wasn't willing to patrol the streets on my own. So, I got a part-time job at the coffeehouse down the street, determined to make as much money as I could before I… Well. I worked Wednesday through Sunday, from five to ten. I walked there and back, and had yet to come across a zombie. My coworkers were nice—at first—but my distant attitude eventually got to them, and they soon stopped trying to be my friend.

Thanksgiving came and went, and I realized I was all out of to-do lists. I was living one minute at a time.

Nana tried to draw me out of my "protective shell," bless her heart, but I was too firmly entrenched. Besides, I hated the holiday. Emma visited for half an hour, but Mom, Dad and Pops didn't, couldn't, and celebrating without them sucked.

School started up just a few days after the "illness" hit. No one else had gotten sick, and doctors were still baffled. I wondered if the slain had turned into zombies. I wondered if the slayers had had to kill people they knew.

I wondered—but I never asked.

Reeve avoided me as if I'd contracted social leprosy, and though it was for the best—what I wanted, needed—it wounded me.

The slayers kept their distance, as well. Frosty especially. He couldn't get over what I'd done to Cole, and now he and Kat were at war because she refused to end our friendship.

For her safety, I confessed my problems to her, explained Frosty was simply concerned for her well-being, and that she would be better off listening to him and staying away from me, and for the first time in our acquaintance, she got mad at me.

"You're my friend," she said. "That means something to me."

"Yes, but *why* do you like me?" I asked. "I'm nothing special."

"Nothing special? Everyone makes fun of love at first sight, but, Ali, that's what I felt for you. Love, not like. You're the sister I never had, but always wanted. The day we met, when I walked into your hospital room, I saw a scared, pale girl with the most haunted eyes. You'd lost everyone, and I understood. I had to bury my mom, *my world,* too. So, why don't you do me a favor and think about why you love *me*—or if you do?"

"I don't have to think. I love your loyalty, your sense of humor, your smile, your courage, your total acceptance of

me, your support, your dedication, your positivity, your... everything."

She laughed and hugged me, and then she said ten little words I couldn't get out of my head. "Good. Now, what are you going to do about Cole?"

Cole...

Oh, that boy. What *was* I going to do with him? He'd come to my house a few times, and he'd come bearing gifts. A stuffed alligator. Dinner from my favorite hamburger joint located nearly an hour away. A protective cover for my great-great-great-grandfather's journal.

What the heck did he think he was doing?

I doubted even he knew.

Each time, he'd thrust the gifts at me, almost angrily, before stomping away.

Gavin had come over twice, but I hadn't opened the door. He'd want to talk about our vision, and I wasn't sure what to say to him.

I'd poured a Blood Line around the new house. I'd also turned the garage into a gym, using the treadmill and wrestling matt Nana had bought at a thrift store. The stronger I kept my human side, the longer I'd live. At least, that was my hope.

I hadn't heard any more whispers, thank God, but I also hadn't had the courage to look at my reflection. I'd tried to call Dr. Bendari, using the new number on my caller ID. Unavailable yet again, I inwardly cursed.

"—paying any attention to me?" Kat asked.

I blinked into focus. She stood on the other side of the wrestling matt. Today was my day off from the coffee shop,

so, after school, she'd driven me home and we'd decided to work on her self-defense. "Sorry," I mumbled. "I'm easily distracted lately. Maybe it would be better if Frosty took over your lessons."

Exasperated, she spread her arms to encompass the entire room. "Do you hear this?" she said to no one. "Ali, you know I'm not speaking to him ever again, right? Every day he commands me to stay away from you."

"He's just trying to protect you," I reminded her.

"Well, there are better ways." She unwound the tape from her knuckles. "Come on. Let's wash up and head out. I feel like punishing you for your continued negativity."

"And just how are you going to do that?"

"You'll see."

Well, all right, then. As if I could deny her anything—even the right to punish me. I used Nana's shower, and Kat used mine. Nowadays, we worked out so much she always brought a change of clothes with her.

We found Nana in the kitchen.

"You're getting Ali to go somewhere other than school and work?" she said to Kat. "It's a miracle."

I kissed her on the cheek. Her arms wrapped around me, and she held on for a long while, as if she couldn't bear to let go of me… As if she knew I was slipping away. When finally she released me, there were tears in her eyes.

"Nana…" I said, a lump growing in my throat. I hated that I was hurting her.

"Go," she said, waving me off. "Have fun. Be a teenager for once in your life."

Kat and I climbed into her car and headed north. The sky

was gray today, the sun shielded by heavy clouds. I didn't allow myself to search for a rabbit. I didn't want to know.

My phone rang. I checked the screen, but I didn't recognize the number. I chewed on my bottom lip, hopeful.

"Hello," I said, a tremor in my voice.

"Would you like to set up another meeting, Miss Bell?" Dr. Bendari.

I nearly whooped with relief. "Where have you been?"

"Out of the country, if you must know. Do you have an answer for me?"

"Yes. And yes, I would."

"Will you actually make this one?"

"Yes."

"Good. Now that you're away from the surgeon, I can pick you up at midnight."

He always knew my every move. How? His source, whoever it was, couldn't watch me 24/7...right? "Okay," I said. "I'll be ready."

"See you then." *Click.*

"Who was that?" Kat asked.

"Do you remember the SUV that followed us that day with Reeve?"

"The one you threw knives at? Nope. I've totally forgotten."

Har-har. "The old guy... He gave me his card. I called him. He called me back. And so on and so forth. We've now set up a meeting."

Paling, Kat tightened her hands on the steering wheel. "Ali, you don't know this man."

"Yeah, but I know I need answers and he might have them."

"Answers about...the dark side?"

"Yes," I replied softly.

She reached over and patted my knee. "You're going to overcome this. I just know it. You're strong. You've lost so much, and you're going to fight with everything you've got to keep from losing more."

I wanted to believe her, but I was fast losing hope.

She parked in front of—

Colluctor Park, I realized. It was a Tuesday, close to dinnertime and as cold as ice. No one walked the manicured lawn. The trees were barren, but there were benches, a swing set and monuments. There was also a creepy mausoleum.

"How is this punishment?" I asked as I unbuckled. "You planning to make me strip and streak?"

"You'll see," she said in a singsong tone.

We stepped into the harsh winter winds, and I shivered. Someone had staked Merry Christmas signs along the side of the cobbled path leading from the parking lot to the park.

Another holiday fast approaching. I'd do better with this one, I vowed, and make sure Nana had a fabulous time. Of course, I would need to buy her a present. And one for Kat. And maybe Cole.

No, not Cole.

Kat linked our arms at the elbows and tugged me forward. "Something wrong? Your face got all pinchy."

"Is *pinchy* even a word?"

"If it's not, it should be. And don't think I don't know you avoided my question. I know you're nervous about what I

have planned, and you totally should be. Behold." Over the hill, she pointed to—

A moan slipped from me. Reeve sat on a bench, Ethan beside her. The two were talking and laughing, happy to be together.

"You have to face her sometime," Kat said sternly.

"She has no interest in a reunion," I whispered.

"Only because her dad told her you hated living with them and had demanded your own space."

He'd *what?*

Well, that altered things, didn't it? I marched forward, determined.

"—you will love her," she was saying. "Everyone does. Just ask her yourself," she added with an affectionate chuckle.

Ethan glanced up, saw me and stiffened. "Can I help you?"

I ignored him, saying, "Hey, Reeve."

She twisted to look up at me and flinched. "Ali," she said with a reluctant nod. Then, as Kat moved up beside me, "Kat. You were supposed to come alone."

Kat shrugged. "I'm supposed to do a lot of things. That doesn't mean I do them."

Ethan stood. I was five-ten, and he was a few inches taller than me. His hair was disheveled from the breeze, and his features now closed off.

He held out his hand to shake. "I'm Ethan. It's nice to meet you."

His grip was weak, as if he was afraid he'd break me if he squeezed too hard. "You, too. I'm Ali."

He turned to Kat, shook her hand, as well. "Reeve's told me so much about you guys," he said as he sat back down.

Kat claimed the spot next to him, but I remained standing, suspecting Reeve would throw a fit if I encroached. "Look, I'm sorry I moved out without saying goodbye." I hated doing this in front of a guy I didn't know, but I wasn't sure when I'd have another opportunity. "And I didn't move out to get away from you. I loved living with you."

Dark fire snapped to life in her eyes. "Are you calling my father a liar?"

Yes! "I'm saying he was protecting you from the truth."

"And just what, exactly, is the truth?"

Ethan's attention zinged between us.

I remained silent. There were some things I still couldn't share.

"Of course. More secrets," she muttered, the fire in her dark eyes replaced by hurt. She looked at Ethan. "Do you see? This is what I have to deal with every day." She gathered her purse and stood. "Let's go, Ethan."

Stay calm. "Please, don't go."

Ethan reached out and tugged the lapels of Reeve's jacket closer, a total boyfriend move. "She's your friend, sweetheart. I've had to hold you while you've cried about her. Stay and hear her out."

The support surprised me.

"Hey, Eth—you don't mind if I call you Eth, do you?" Kat asked. "Why don't you escort me to the pond? I want to see the ducks, but I'll need someone to throw in their path if they turn violent."

He looked at Reeve, then looked at me. Reeve, me. As if he was considering every possible thing that could go wrong,

and wanted to take measures to prevent it. Finally he nodded. "It would be my pleasure," he said and offered his arm.

The two strode away, and Ethan only glanced back twice to check on his girlfriend.

Sighing, I took his seat and removed the bag from around my shoulder and waist. "Look, Reeve. I moved out because...I'm sick. Really, really sick, and I have these violent episodes.... We don't know a lot about what's going on, and your dad wants you safe. *I* want you safe. It's not contagious, or anything like that, but...it's just better this way."

Her features immediately softened, and she eased beside me. "Oh, Ali. I had no idea. I'm so sorry."

"I'm sorry, too."

"I just wish you'd told me. I would have told you not to go," she said, patting the top of my hand. "I don't care about any violent episodes, and I know my dad won't, either, if I talk to him."

"No," I said, shaking my head. "Please, don't talk to him. Don't talk to anyone about this."

"But—"

"Your dad will be mad that I told you this much, and—"

"Why would he be mad?" she interjected. "Unless something else is going on. And there must be. There's a reason Bronx runs so hot and cold. A reason so many of my friends go to bed without any injuries, but wake up covered with them. A reason my dad has a horror dungeon below the house. A reason he tolerates Cole's dad—a man he once hated."

Mr. Ankh and Mr. Holland had once hated each other? "Look, Reeve—"

"No. I'm tired of being in the dark, Ali. So very tired. I
need to be enlightened. I crave it. It's become an obsession."

Dark. Light.

Lies. Truth.

"If I tell you, you might long for the days of blissful ignorance, and I think that's what your father fears most." But
then, she'd finally know what was out there and would be
able to take measures to protect herself. Measures Mr. Ankh
would never be able to take from her.

"Please," she said.

"Let me think about it, okay?" I said. "I could get a lot
of people in trouble."

That was more than I'd ever offered before, and she nodded gratefully.

"So…Ethan seems nice," I said, taking the conversation
in another direction.

I was relieved when she said, "He is, he really is," without pressing me for more.

There was no dreamy sigh from her, no smile. "I sense a
but coming on."

Her shoulders sagged the slightest bit. "He really likes me.
He's sweet, attentive and last year his mother died, and now
his little sister is dealing with leukemia, so he's learned to
appreciate life and live every day to the fullest, but…I can't
get you know who out of my head."

Yeah. "Believe me, I get it. When it comes to Cole, I'm
the same way."

Kat cleared her throat. "We're, uh, back. Ethan was missing his girl."

Reeve jumped guiltily, her cheeks flushing.

"You guys make up?" Ethan claimed the seat on the other side of her and snuggled up, offering his warmth. If he'd heard Reeve's words about Bronx, he didn't act like it.

"We did," she replied.

"Thank God," Kat said. "It's about time, and seriously, go me for setting it up."

Ethan nodded, kissed Reeve's temple. "I agree."

It was obvious he cared for her, and I could see why she had chosen him. Despite her feelings for Bronx, they could have something normal. No secrets. No midnight battles with the undead. No suspecting everyone they met of foul play. No worrying if the other would come home every night—or be eaten.

Hungry...so hungry...

As the words whispered through my mind, I jolted to my feet and spun, searching, trying to squash a sudden bead of panic. My emotions had been under control. This shouldn't be happening.

"What's wrong?" Kat asked.

Hungry, hungry, hungry.

HUNGRY.

Hurt. Maim. Kill.

Soon...

"Ali, your eyes," she said.

No! I gasped for breath as I stumbled away from the group. Reeve stood, already reaching for me. Ethan grabbed her by the wrist and jerked her behind him, as if I'd sprouted horns, fangs and a tail. Maybe I had.

HUNGRYHURTMAIMKILLSOON.

The whispers... So loud... Blending together, somehow calling me, drawing me.

Kat withdrew her phone and started typing. Texting Frosty to come help me?

"No. Don't," I said, and tried to turn left. Somehow I'd lost control of my body and turned right. My feet moved one in front of the other without any command from my brain. I drew closer and closer to a creepy mausoleum, the whispers continuing to escalate. Surely my eardrums would burst, unable to withstand the chatter. "Syringe. Purse."

I halted at the double doors.

HUNGRYHURTMAIMKILLSOON!

I leaned forward—until I could go no further and my spirit separated from my body, ripping from me with painful force, as if pushed. Inside the building, cold air nearly flash-froze my skin.

HURTSOON!

HUNGRY!

The small enclosure was dark and dank, but smelled of wildflowers and sunshine. I shifted to the side, and what seemed to be a thousand red eyes opened to track the movement. A gasp of horror escaped me.

I'd just found a zombie nest.

THE ZOMBIES
ARE BACK IN TOWN

The shock must have brought me to my senses. As easily as my body had been dragged forward, it now whisked backward. Spirit and body collided, once again hooking up.

Kat was at my side, tugging at my arm. I tripped over her feet and fell, banging my knees into the cold, hard ground. The scent of rot clung to my nose, the wildflowers and sunshine gone.

"Frosty's on the way," she said. "He'll make everything better."

"Get back. Purse. Syringe. Throw."

"What's wrong with her?" Reeve asked with a tremor. "I know she's sick, but she was just comatose!"

"Sick?" Ethan demanded.

"Gets violent," Reeve said, distracted.

"Violent," he parroted hollowly.

"Back!" I shouted, pushing Kat away from me. If I helped

the zombies… If I hurt my friends… "Go! Please," I croaked. I no longer wanted her to take time to search for the anti- dote in my purse. *"Please."*

Ethan jerked a protesting Reeve away from me. She worked her way free and raced back to my side, but he quickly caught up with her, hefted her over his shoulder and took off for his car.

Maim. Kill.

Hungry.

Soon.

Cold.

The words played through my mind, a terrible song. I wanted to stand, but my vision was going dark. "Run, Kat," I commanded. "Run and don't look back. It's happening. The worst is happening."

The nearness of the zombies must have provoked Z.A. to rise.

"I'm not leaving you. I'm— Hmph! What are you doing, Ethan? Let me go!"

He was carting her to his car?

He must have. Tires squealed. Gravel sprayed. He had no idea what was going on, but he'd sensed the danger, had un- derstood the truth in Reeve's claim about violence and had reacted accordingly. I'd have to remember to thank him.

I lay on the ground, exactly where I'd fallen. Breath rasped from me, burning my lungs, my throat. Should I stay here and try to calm down?

Are you kidding? Stand up! Fight! Zombies had killed my family, and I had made it my life's mission to return the favor.

What was more, if the zombies emerged and innocents were around…

I pulled my knees into my chest and pushed, unfolding to my full height. I wobbled but managed to stay upright.

I curled stiff fingers around the dagger hilts sticking out of my boots; metal whistled against leather as I freed the blades. The darkness persisted, closing in on me, and I blinked rapidly. Little pricks of color suddenly appeared—all of them red.

The zombies *had* emerged.

Footsteps pounded at my side, and I stiffened. A hard breeze wafted over me, followed by another, and another. Unsure how close the monsters were, I swiped out an arm, encountered only air.

"Ali." Cole's voice registered a split second before I was tackled to the ground.

I lost my grip on the daggers, as well as what remained of my breath. My head thumped against a rock, and a sharp pain tore through my skull.

"Sorry, sorry," Cole rushed out.

I tried to sit up, but he pinned my arms to the ground, making any kind of movement impossible.

"You're staying right here. The others will take care of the zombies."

Around us, grunts and groans erupted. The fight was on, good against evil, light against dark.

I should be helping. I should—hmm, Cole smelled like heaven. The rot had faded, and his scent was crisp and clean, untainted, wonderfully pure, and the more I inhaled, the more I liked it. The more my mouth watered.

So. Hungry.

I could feel the utter emptiness of my stomach, could feel the pangs sharpening into little razor blades. My gaze locked on Cole's pulse. How it glowed and thumped, speaking to me. *Taste. Me. Taste. Me.*

Yes, I thought. I lifted my head, nuzzled my nose against the line of his neck. He was warm, and I was cold. Colder than I'd ever been, surely.

"What are you doing, Ali?" he demanded.

I bared my teeth, with every intension of biting him. *Gonna be so good.*

His strong fingers captured my jaw, keeping my mouth closed. "You don't want to do this. You're better than this."

Better? I wasn't better. I was hungry, and he was preventing me from eating. I wanted to eat! With a growl, I jerked from his grip.

"Ali. You once promised me you would never do this again. Do you remember?"

I stilled. I'd promised him all right, and I hated to lie.

Deep breath in. Out. Mind clearing.

"You can control this. You could control her."

Her. Z.A.

Remembering who—and what—she was gave me the wake-up call I'd needed.

Fight her.

This was a test of wills. Hers and mine. We were separate, and it was time to prove it. I was stronger. I had to be stronger.

"Good girl." He brushed his fingertips over my brow, and I felt a stream of warmth, a total evaporation of the hunger.

How did he do that?

Dark. Light.

The words struck me again.

Suddenly Cole went rigid. "Ow!" he spat, and released a tide of dark curses. I heard the rustle of clothing, the snap of metal hitting bone.

I struggled to sit up, only to realize Cole had left his body on top of me while his spirit slashed at the zombie determined to end him. One of his daggers lodged into the creature's collarbone, and Cole spun, slicing his opponent across the throat with the other.

As the zombie fell, its head detached from its body. Cole held out his hand, flames crackling over his fingers. He flattened his palm against the creature's chest. One second passed, two, three, I don't know how many more, I lost count, and the flames began to spread up and down, until they covered every inch of the zombie.

Boom.

The body exploded and ash rained through the air.

Cole did the same thing to the head, pressing the zombie face-first into the ground to hide the teeth. The creature was still alive, still trying to chomp on him.

Boom.

More ash sprayed.

He straightened, wavering on his feet. The fire had died from his hand. His knees buckled, and he hit the ground. I rallied my strength and bucked the weight of his body off me, then crawled to his spirit. He had no injuries—wait. His pants were ripped at the ankle. I twisted and saw the teeth

marks in his flesh, as well as the black goo the zombies always left behind.

I whimpered. He'd been bitten because he'd been distracted. By me.

"I'm so sorry," I said. I'd said those words a lot lately.

"Antidote," he rasped.

Yes, of course. I crawled back to his body, found the syringe in his back pocket and returned to him. Only the needle and my hand ghosted right through him. Why—because he was in spirit form, and I was in natural.

I tried to force my spirit out of my body, but the hard hands from before held on to me, keeping me inside. *Dang it!*

In the back of my mind, I thought I heard gleeful giggles.

Z.A. was laughing at me.

Maybe I could start a new to-do list. A small one, with only one task. *HURT HER.*

Scanning the area, I took note of the other slayers. Gavin slashed at two zombies at once. Veronica came in from behind and hobbled the zombies at the ankles. Frosty swooped in and pressed his glowing palm against the zombie's chest, just as Cole had done. Bronx fought every creature trying to reach the stationary Frosty.

I couldn't distract them. This was up to me, and there was only one solution. Back to Cole's body I went. I slid my hands under his shoulders and dragged him, one inch at a time, toward his now writhing spirit. He was so heavy, I stumbled with every step. Eventually I managed to drag him close enough to stretch out his arm and connect natural fingers with spiritual fingers, joining the two together.

Trembling, I rose to my knees and shoved the needle deep into his neck.

He arched, his back bowing off the ground. Then he sagged into place. "Thank you," he said, panting.

I crouched beside him, guarding him from further attack. But I'd taken so long to help him, the battle was over. Gavin straightened, ash from the last creature to die raining around him.

Veronica returned to her body, became one and rushed over to pull Cole up. "Are you okay, sugar?"

Sugar again. I wanted to push her away from him.

I didn't.

"I'm fine." Very gently, he added, "Don't...don't call me that. Okay?"

She blanched. Then she glared at me, spitting out, "You're the worst thing that's ever happened to him. Have you realized that yet?"

I couldn't, *wouldn't,* engage her. And I couldn't exactly refute her, could I?

"If you don't cut him loose, you're going to kill him, and I'm going to... I'll put you... Argh!" Clearly, she'd kept herself on a leash, and the leash had just broken. She launched at me, knocking me to my back and throwing a punch.

I took it, using what little energy I had left to work my legs between us and shove her away. She came back swinging and clipped me in the chin. I rolled with the impact, lumbered to my feet. We circled each other.

"I'm going to—"

"Nothing," Cole said, silencing her as he stood. "You're going to do nothing, Veronica."

Panting, she said, "Please tell me you don't still care about this girl. After everything she's done?" When he failed to reply, she paled and looked to me. "I don't know if you're human or zombie or both, Ali Bell, and I don't care. You're no good for Cole or anyone here, so why don't you do us all a favor and stay away? Or die. My vote is die."

"That's enough," Cole shouted.

I...*wanted* to die. Everything Veronica had said rang true. These people would have been far better off without me. Cole would have been able to fight. He wouldn't have gotten bitten. And what about tomorrow? What would happen then? I was nothing more than a living time bomb. I never knew what I would do next—or whom I would hurt. One day, I could detonate and take out everyone around me.

"The zombies are dead. Where's Kat?" Frosty demanded. He stood a few feet away from me, his clothes torn and splattered with black goo. Just then, his navy eyes did justice to his name—they were coated with ice.

Cole moved beside me and wrapped his arm around me in a shocking show of support. I loved his warmth and his scent and his strength and wanted nothing more than to bask in them, but I forced myself to move away from him.

He might support me in this right now, but it wouldn't last. He'd soon regret it and wish he'd kept me at a distance.

He lifted his chin, every muscle in his body tense.

I pretended to ignore him, marching over to grab my purse and inject myself with antidote.

"Kat," Frosty snapped.

"Ethan," I replied. "She's with Ethan Hamilton."

Frosty went still, a predator who'd just spotted the tastiest of prey. "Who's Ethan?"

"Reeve's…friend. I know where he lives." Bronx was just as disheveled, just as splattered, just as predatory. "Cole?"

"Go," he said, and the two boys needed no more prompting.

Gavin stepped to my side, saying, "You need a ride, Ali?"

"I'll take her." Cole approached me a second time, but I backpedaled toward Gavin.

"No. He'll take me," I rushed out. Avoiding Gavin had been stupid. He didn't tempt me to do things I shouldn't. I could remain calm with him.

I wouldn't become a menace.

Cole stopped abruptly, looking between us, his eyes narrowing. I wasn't sure of Gavin's reaction to this new turn of events, and I didn't care enough to switch my attention. My gaze remained locked with Cole's. My heart cracked.

"It's better this way, remember?" I said softly.

"For who?"

You. "Both of us."

He massaged the back of his neck and turned his now ice-cold focus to the others.

"I'll see you back at the barn," he said.

Trina nodded without looking up. Silent, Lucas flashed a thumbs-up. Veronica approached Cole, but he very gently shook her off and said, "We talked about this, Ronny."

Her features fell.

He stalked away. Twice he glanced back at me, and the crack in my heart widened.

Could *nothing* in my life go right?

TWEEDLEDEE AND TWEEDLEDUM DUMB

"Don't you need to get back out there?" I asked Gavin as I unlocked my front door. "There could be a flood of zombies tonight." Even though I hadn't noticed a rabbit cloud during the drive home. Yeah, I'd finally broken down and looked.

"It's doubtful. You woke a nest. That's the only reason those zombies came out when they did."

I paused in the open doorway and faced him, my arms spread to block his path. "Well, don't you need to be out there putting Blood Lines around the homes of the innocent?"

His lips curled at the corners. "Mr. Ankh and Mr. Holland have been taking care of that. Now, aren't you going to invite me in?"

Sure. In...never. "I don't want to be rude, but—"

"Good. Then don't be rude." He picked me up and set

me aside. "I'm spending the rest of the evening with you, then crashing on your couch."

Exasperated, I entered behind him. Did he think I'd leave and go on a killing rampage?

Like you can really blame him.

"Sorry, but we don't have a couch." We'd been buying one piece of furniture at a time, when we found cheap but reliable pieces, and so far had only managed to pick up two beds and a dining room table.

"Uh, are you sure about that?" He sounded amused.

"Maybe not," I said, my tone dry. "I only live here." I shut and locked the door before nailing him with a glare.

"Now, now. Don't look at me like that," he said, chucking me under the chin. "I saw the video, and I know what you're capable of, but I also know you wanted to bite Cole that night—and this one. The look in your eyes, the way you licked your lips… I've seen zombies do that. But the bottom line? You didn't do it. Before, you turned your hunger on the zombies, and today you somehow managed to snap yourself out of it. I respect the kind of strength that took."

He was…right, I realized. Z.A. had controlled me, darkened my mind, yet I'd had the strength to fight her. Hope bloomed brighter than it had in days, as pretty as a flower opening in the sun. Maybe I wasn't such a terrible menace after all.

"If you aren't afraid of what I'll do, why do you want to stay here?" I asked, waving my hand at—

A furnished and decorated living room. I frowned and bustled forward. "Nana," I called.

"Ali, dear. You're home." Dusting her hands together, she

snaked around the hallway corner. "Oh, no. You're injured. What happened?"

"The usual," I said, then motioned to the new furnishings. "How much did all of this cost?"

She fidgeted with the hem of her shirt. "Don't you worry about that. I gave myself a budget and stuck to it."

"Nana," I said.

My expression must have betrayed my thoughts, because she said, "I know you want to save to buy a house of our own, but I don't want us living like paupers while we do it."

Okay. All right. If she wanted this stuff, then I wanted her to have it.

I hugged her tight and kissed her on the temple. "Everything looks amazing, Nana. Seriously."

"I'm so glad you think so. Wait till you see your bedroom," she said with a smile.

Gavin cleared his throat, and Nana peeked around me.

"Oh, I'm so sorry, Gavin. I didn't realize you were here. It's lovely to see you again." Her gaze moved over him, widened. "I'm guessing you ran into the same bit of *usual* trouble my Ali did."

"Yes, ma'am, I sure did."

She gulped. "There were others with you? And everyone…survived?"

"More than. We thrived." He shook off his coat and draped the fabric over his arm. "I don't know about you, but I'm starving. I'd love a chance to cook you dinner to thank you for allowing me to sleep on your couch."

Wait. The he-slut of the great South knew how to cook?

Nana's gaze met mine for a split second, her mouth forming a small O. "You're staying the night?"

"If it's all right with you. I'll behave, you have my word."

"Are you two…"

"No," I rushed out, at the same time Gavin said, "We're debating it."

I glared at him. "We're better off as friends."

"In that case, it'll be nice having a man around," Nana said, once again dusting her hands together. "I bought a bookcase I wasn't looking forward to putting together."

"I'll do it," he said. "I'm always ready for a chance to be a hero."

She giggled like a schoolgirl—a dirty, dirty schoolgirl—and I did a double take. "You already are. The bookcase can wait until after dinner, though. I've got a few more things to arrange in my room."

The moment we were alone, I anchored my hands on my hips. "Will you please stop forgetting you're into brunettes?"

"I realized I can't see hair color in the dark."

Oh, wow. "However will I continue to resist such wondrous flattery?"

Smiling, he swept around me and entered the kitchen. "What can't be manufactured is attitude, and I happen to like yours."

I came in behind him and opened the fridge to grab something to drink. It was now fully stocked with all my favorites. Orange juice, milk, protein shakes, fruits, vegetables and even the chocolate cupcakes I liked to eat cold. I groaned.

"What?" Gavin said.

"She spent too much money on me."

"Most girls wouldn't complain about that."

I selected one of the shakes. "Most girls don't have my Nana. I want to pamper her, not the other way around."

Gavin reached in behind me to snag a juice. Our arms brushed, and I scowled up at him.

"Stop trying to seduce me," I said.

"Why? Is it working?"

"If you like to be stabbed, yes."

"I've let girls do a lot worse to me."

I shook my head, exasperated.

"Look, I don't want to go home. I've been dividing my time between Cole's house, a crappy motel and the homes of the women I'm fu...screwing."

"You can say it. My ears won't melt off."

He snorted. "Cole says we're not to cuss around you. Potty mouth is contagious, I guess. *Anyway*. A guy can only take so much. I'm desperate for a break."

Well, I couldn't exactly kick him out now. I wasn't that cruel.

I nodded my agreement before moving around him.

He grinned at me, his eyes alight with mischief. "You act all proper now, but in the visions, you've definitely got a lady boner for me."

I choked on a laugh. "Lady boner?"

He shrugged. "I kinda like knowing there are two sides to you and I'm the one responsible."

Two sides to me. He had no idea one of those sides was the enemy. "Gavin."

"Nah. You don't need to put me in my place again. Whether you admit it or not, you're softening toward me."

Absolutely, but not in the way he wanted.

A knock sounded at the door, and I stiffened.

"I bet that's Cole," he said with a sigh. "I expected him sooner."

No way. Cole wouldn't come after me. Not after the public rejection I'd just dished. And yet I was trembling as I opened the door. Annnd…sure enough, tall, strong and impossibly beautiful Cole waited on the other side.

Sweet mercy.

"Kat and Reeve are both fine," he said, one arm propped against the wooden frame. "They're with Frosty and Bronx."

"Did the guys hurt Ethan?"

"No. He was pretty freaked out by what he'd seen. They questioned him, nothing more."

I covered my throat with my hand, a protective action. "What did he see?"

"Apparently you looked as if you wanted to eat Kat and Reeve at one point, and not in the good way."

I wasn't going to touch that statement. "Well." I cleared my throat. "Thank you for the update, but it's getting late and you're probably wanted at home."

He shook his head. "Sorry, babe, but I'm not leaving."

What, was this disagree with Ali day? "It's for your own good, Cole."

"Right now I'd rather be bad and deal with the consequences later."

Please be bad. Very, very bad. Downright naughty.

I shivered, and the shiver made me mad. So did my treacherous mind. "You might not survive these particular con-

sequences." I smiled with saccharine sweetness—and tried to shut the door in his face.

He shouldered his way inside. "I'm willing to risk it."

Argh!

"Hey, Cole," Gavin called from the kitchen. "You staying for dinner?"

Cole would have seen his car in the driveway and known Gavin was here, but still his back went iron-bar straight at the sound of the other guy's voice. "Are you the chef?"

"I am."

Cole marched forward and settled into a bar stool as if he owned it. "Good. I'm starved."

This could not be happening.

"We've got the stuff for enchiladas or roast beef sandwiches," Gavin said, glancing at me.

"Enchiladas," Cole replied.

"Sandwiches it is, then," Gavin said.

Cole offered him a chilling smile.

Oh, glory. If they decided to play Animal Planet, I'd… let them, I decided. Both would end up unconscious and I would no longer be trapped in this tug-of-war. Sure, I'd have to clean a pool of blood, but just then that actually seemed like the better choice. We had plenty of baking soda and vinegar.

While Gavin puttered around the kitchen, Cole swiveled in the chair to face me. "How are you feeling?"

"Fine," I said, taking the seat next to him. I could be polite. "How about you?

"Better." He reached out, pinched a lock of my hair. "I'm not afraid of you, you know."

"You should be." I was. I tugged my hair from his grip. Softly, I added, "But we both know that's not our only problem."

He blanched, and I felt guilty. I shouldn't feel guilty.

"I know what you're thinking, and that's not what I meant," I said and sighed.

"Then what?"

"I'll…have to show you." I motioned to the hall—my bedroom—with a tilt of my chin.

He nodded, something hot and dark in his eyes.

"Once again it's not what you're thinking," I said drily.

I think he…pouted.

What do you know—here was yet another side to Cole.

"Don't you want to show me, too?" Gavin said, his tone a little tight. He chopped the lettuce with more force.

"Not this," I replied, trying to be gentle. "I'm sorry."

"Don't apologize to him," Cole snapped.

O-kay. The ice was back.

"He's my guest," I said, "and I like him, and *he's* acting civil. He deserved an apology from me, so I gave it, and now he deserves one from you. I'm not leaving this spot until he gets it."

Gavin smirked.

Cole gritted out a very mean "Sorry."

"Good. Let's go." As Cole and I stood, another knock sounded at my door. Dang it, who was *that?* Considering my luck, it was probably Veronica. "Just a sec." I stomped to the door. This time, I found Justin waiting on the other side. "You've got to be kidding me."

Cole came up behind me, the intense heat he radiated a caress against my skin. "What are you doing here?"

A bundle of energy, Justin couldn't seem to stand still. "You told me to contact you if I had news. Well, I have news, and besides that, I thought you told Ali what's going on."

Cole glanced over his shoulder, saying, "You should have called."

"No way. This was too big."

"What is?" I asked at the same time Gavin called, "Who is it?"

Justin pressed his lips into a thin line. He backed up, saying, "Sorry. Didn't realize. I'll text you as soon as I get inside my car."

The door shut with a soft click. He'd better hurry. Curiosity was now in the process of eating me alive.

"You were going to show me something," Cole prompted.

I nodded, and led him past the kitchen. Gavin glanced up from the loaf of potato bread he was slicing, frowned. "Seriously? You're abandoning me?"

"Only for a few minutes."

"You don't owe him an explanation, either," Cole said, dragging me away. "And I'm not apologizing again."

I think Gavin flipped him off, but I couldn't be sure. In the hall, I heard Nana humming under her breath.

"We have another guest," I called.

She stuck her head out of the door and brightened. "Cole. It's wonderful to see you."

"You, too."

She arched a brow when she noticed my hand on the knob of my door. "You're going in there…alone?"

"Just for a few minutes," I said.

Her eyes narrowed, but she nodded. "I'll be watching the clock."

I stepped inside—only to gasp. She had decorated my room with everything she knew I'd love. The furnishings were a dark cherrywood and polished to a glossy shine. Wispy white curtains covered my window, and a framed picture of Emma and me hung on the wall. She was in front of me, wrapped in my arms, and we were both smiling our biggest smiles.

There was a note taped to the border.

Angels must have held this photo in their hands, because that's the only way it could have survived the bomb. I had it framed weeks ago, but wanted to wait to give it to you at Christmas. This seemed like a better time.
Love, Nana

Oh, Nana, I thought as tears welled in my eyes.

"You're both adorable," Cole said, stepping up behind me to study the photo. "You look so happy."

"We were. We'd just finished playing hide-and-seek in the house, and of course, she had won. She always won. My legs were too long to fit anywhere. She was gloating in that sweet way she had—*nah, nah, nah, I'm the crown champion again*—so I snatched her up to tickle her. Mom demanded we pose."

He squeezed my shoulder. "I have one of my mom and

me, taken a few weeks before she died. It's more valuable to me than my heart and lungs."

I liked when he shared something from his past. He didn't do it often. I turned, met his gaze.

He hooked a strand of hair behind my ear. I could feel myself getting lost in the moment, in him, so when his phone beeped a few seconds later, I jumped. I also sighed with relief.

"Go ahead," I said. "Check it."

He hesitated a moment before scrolling through the message, his features darkening as he read. "Justin says the spy is someone who was at the park tonight. Information about the fight has already hit Anima."

"So…that rules out Collins and Cruz. And Frosty and Bronx were too busy rescuing Kat and Reeve to hand out any details."

"Not necessarily, but I know them better than I know myself, and they'd never help the enemy. I've never suspected them."

Had he ever suspected me? "You can rule out Lucas and Trina, too. I watched the spy watch them, remember? So that leaves…Veronica."

"You saw a male in the forest."

"Yes, and she could be working with him."

"Maybe." His gaze locked with mine and searched. "There's also Gavin."

My hand fluttered to my throat, rubbed. Gavin… He had to be innocent. And yet he wanted to stay the night here, no matter how uncomfortable he'd be on the couch. Maybe not because he hated the motel, after all, but to keep tabs on me and my dark metamorphosis.

"Anyway, they weren't the only ones there," Cole reminded me.

"Me?" I squeaked.

He rolled his eyes. "I never suspected you. I mean Kat. Reeve."

"Girl. Girl."

"Like you said, a girl could be working with a boy."

"Besides," I continued, "there's no way Kat would betray us, and Reeve doesn't know anything."

"Kat has no filter. She—"

"Isn't responsible," I insisted.

"What about Ethan?"

"Bronx has already looked into him. Found nothing suspicious."

After a short pause, he nodded. "That leaves us with… yeah, Gavin and Veronica. But I've already checked, and they came out clean. As you know, that's the reason I spent so much time with her. I was going through her stuff, checking everything she said. Nothing dubious came up. More than that, the problems started before the pair got here."

"Maybe you didn't dig deep enough. Maybe one or both were working for Anima before they got here and asked to be assigned to your team. Talk to Mr. Ankh and your dad. They'll have ideas about what to—"

"No way. My reasons for staying quiet are still the same. I won't blacken someone's name without at least a little proof."

"Yeah, but once the truth comes to light, whoever you've accused will be vindicated. Or not."

He shook his head, saying, "The problem is, my closest friends will know I didn't trust them. Maybe they'll forgive

me, maybe not, but from that moment on, no matter what I do, what I say, they'll always wonder at my motives. That stuff doesn't leave a person."

Had he ever been accused of something he hadn't done?

I must have asked the question aloud because he said, "When Justin started working with Anima, he hung around my team for information, just like the newest spy. I knew something was going on and stupidly blamed Boots and Ducky, members of the team you never got to meet." As he spoke, he rubbed the tattoos of their names. "They were so mad at me, so hurt, they went hunting that night, I guess to prove their loyalty, and they found a nest of zombies. That's the night they were killed. I can't go through something like that again."

"Cole—" I said, but he stopped me with another shake of his head.

"I'll do more digging with Gavin and Veronica. And now let's close this subject and revisit at another date. You said you had something to show me. Was it a kiss?" He backed me into the door, putting his body in front of me, and the hardwood in back of me, effectively caging me. And oh, good glory, had I just used the word *hardwood?* "Lately I haven't been able to think about anything else."

"Cole. No."

"Just one more," he said raggedly. "Then we'll stop. Then maybe the madness will finally end and we'll be able to be friends. I know you said we couldn't be, but I don't like the thought of being without you. I need you in my life, at least in some way."

"Friends don't kiss." Besides, I'd already had my *one more.*

Whimper. "Nana would hear us, we aren't always quiet. She'll come to the door, knock. I'll be hugely embarrassed."

"Okay." He anchored his palms at my temples. "Okay."

I had to stop breathing. He smelled too good, the scent of him invading my senses, making me dizzy with need and want and breaking through whatever new walls I'd managed to build against him. "You're not acting like it's okay."

"When is the madness going to end?" he asked. "I must be obsessed with you, Ali. Addicted. Whatever I feel is definitely unhealthy. Without you, I'm having trouble eating and sleeping. I think about you all the time, wonder what you're doing, and who you're doing it with. Do you know how many times I've been tempted to hunt you down and just carry you away?"

"Cole—"

He wasn't done. "You're smart, fierce, brave. You have a habit of staring off into space, your mind lost to your memories. When you love, you love with your whole heart. And your compassion... When Holly Dumfries went on a date with Chad Stevens, Kerry Goldberg—Chad's ex— dumped a bottle of water on Holly the next day at school. You helped Holly clean up, even switched shirts with her. Yeah. I checked into the shirt thing. Then, when everyone made fun of Aubrey Wilson for getting pregnant, you offered to throw her a baby shower."

My eyes were so wide they had to look like saucers. I'd had no idea he'd known about Holly and Aubrey, and the fact that he did, that he'd kept tabs on me... My knees were threatening to buckle.

"What am I going to do with you?" he asked softly. He

pressed his forehead into mine. "I've thought about sending Gavin back to Georgia, but then I feared something would happen to force you to follow him, and I wouldn't be able to see you."

"Cole—"

"You were right to call me a coward before. I'm afraid of the future, Ali. I can't stand the thought of you with him, so how am I going to survive the reality of it?"

I wanted to wrap my arms around him, which is exactly why I pushed him away. "You don't trust me when I say I'm not interested in him in a romantic way, and that I'm not ever going to be interested in him. You trust the visions more than you trust me and my feelings, and I deserve better."

There was torment in his eyes as he muttered, "You're right."

And like that, something seemed to break inside him.

He fell onto the bed, put his elbows on his knees and his head in his hands. He stayed like that for a long while, simply breathing.

"Are you okay?" I asked softly.

"Not yet, but I will be." He looked up, and I saw determination swimming in his eyes.

Determination to what?

It kind of…scared me.

I turned my back on him. Trembling, I said, "By the way, some of your friends aren't happy with you lately. You've been really mean, apparently." There. A safer topic.

"You want me to be nicer to them?" he asked almost carefully.

"Yes."

He pushed out a breath. "Then I'll be nicer."

That easily? "Thank you." I drew him toward the vanity. I sat down, keeping my gaze downcast. "Now, what I wanted to show you. Take a look at my reflection."

"All right." He remained at my back, his hands steady on my shoulders. "Is there something specific you want me to notice?"

"Watch what happens," I said, and opened my eyes.

Z.A. grinned at me, and there was blood on her teeth. My blood?

"What do you see?" I asked Cole, trying not to fidget.

He lifted my hair, bent down and placed a soft kiss at the curve of my neck. I stiffened, and his grip hardened, as did his gaze; he straightened. "I see you."

A dangerous shiver stole through me. "No," I said. "What do you see in the mirror?"

In the glass, his gaze met *hers*. He frowned. "I still see you."

My brow furrowed with confusion. "You don't see the black smudges?"

"No," he said.

"Please. Introduce us." She chuckled, the sound low and creepy. "He might prefer me."

"Did you hear that?" I asked, clutching my stomach.

"Hear what?"

"Her."

Comprehension dawned. "The dark presence you mentioned?"

I nodded.

"I didn't."

Dang it. Why? He could see and hear spirits in any form. He could see and hear Emma. Why not Z.A., too?

A hard knock pounded at my door. "Dinner's ready," Gavin called.

Scowling, Cole straightened. I stood, a little relieved.

"We'll continue this later," he said. A promise.

"All right." An evasion.

We were silent as we headed into the kitchen.

GO TO SLEEP, MY DARLINGS

Gavin stayed the night, as promised. But then, so did Cole.

Cole took the couch, and Gavin made a pallet on the floor. I tossed and turned, knowing they were both out there, so close. Gavin, perhaps watching over me; Cole, definitely watching over Gavin. Testosterone charged the air.

I couldn't sneak out to meet Dr. Bendari—even though I'd promised I wouldn't renege on him again. The boys would catch me. All I could do was lie in bed and think.

Was Gavin the spy?

Was Veronica, via someone else?

Were they working together?

I...didn't think so. At least, when I really thought about it, I still believed in Gavin's innocence.

Was I right about him? Could I trust myself with this, when I couldn't trust myself with anything else?

You had better. You scolded Cole for not trusting you.

True.

Okay, so I'd take my own advice, no muss, no fuss. I would believe in Gavin.

That left Veronica. She had to be working with the spy. And, sure, there was a good chance my jealousy was coloring my perception of her. But what if it wasn't?

How were we going to find out the truth? It was too late for me to try and be friends with her and learn more about her. That ship had sailed, and the storm had already beaten us down, left us adrift. I wouldn't be able to fake a change of heart. No matter what I did, she would never believe me.

Cole would have to feel her out—or up. Would he decide to continue his romance with her? Maybe. Just how far would he allow himself to go with her? Exactly what would he have to do to soften her enough to catch her in the act?

A few kisses? A few caresses?

Sex?

I had no right to feel hurt by the thought of Veronica and him getting together again. No matter the reason. I had no right to be upset. And we desperately needed answers. But…

Like every time before, I *was* hurt. I *was* upset.

I forced myself to think about something else. Something less painful. Like Z.A. I snorted. In what world was the creature trying to take over my body a safer topic?

Simple. Mine.

Did she have any weaknesses?

I couldn't think of one.

By the time the sun rose, my nerves were frayed. I lumbered out of bed, showered and dressed in jeans and a T-shirt that read Always Be Yourself Unless You Can Be

a Kat Then Always Be a Kat. A housewarming gift from, surprise, surprise, Kat.

In the living room, I discovered the blankets Gavin and Cole had used were folded, and the couch cushions were pushed back into place. Both boys were gone, and neither had left a note.

Had Cole rushed off to see Veronica?

Biting the inside of my cheek, I stomped into the kitchen.

"Good morning," Nana said, having just finished off an egg sandwich.

"Morning."

"I hope you're hungry. Cole did all of this, and he made you a plate before he left." Nana slid a massive pile of scrambled eggs, bacon and biscuits in my direction. "He told me to tell you to eat every crumb or else. Oh, and he also left you a note."

She handed me a folded piece of paper.

Don't give up on me the way I gave up on you. Please. Somehow I'll find a way to make it up to you.
X Cole

Was he saying what I thought he was saying?

Did I *want* him to say what I thought he was saying?

I would have asked him, but he never made it to school. Where was he? What was he doing?

As the day eked by, I thought about calling him, then decided against it. Thought about texting him, then decided against it. I was a mess of uncertainty by the time Kat dropped me off at home.

Nana was gone. I changed into my work clothes and stuffed a few necessities into a backpack. My favorite weapons, a change of clothes, my cell and a little of the money I'd saved. I liked to stay prepared. I donned my coat, hat and gloves and left the house.

The air was bitterly cold, misting in front of my face as I breathed. Frost covered the grass, making me slip a few times. I set off down the street, walking fast. When I cleared the neighborhood, I came to a busy intersection. I passed the light and the convenience store and began to shiver. And yet the exposed skin on my face burned as if I'd crawled inside an oven. I frowned.

Sensitivity to the sun was a zombie trait.

Tires squealed. I palmed a dagger as I searched for the reason. An unfamiliar sedan with dark-tinted windows parked at the curb.

A door in back opened. "Get in," Dr. Bendari commanded.

I stepped toward him, froze. If I did this, I would be late for work, maybe even miss my shift entirely. And if I missed my shift without calling in—would he let me call in or threaten to bail if I tried?—I could lose the job. But could I really pass up this opportunity?

Anticipation, nervousness and dread filled me all at once, propelling me the rest of the way. I jumped into the car, keeping the blade hidden but at the ready. Dr. Bendari moved to the side, giving me space. Even before I'd shut the door, the vehicle was speeding away.

Warm air blew from the vents, enveloping me as I buckled my seat belt.

Dr. Bendari studied me. "Face-to-face at last, Miss Bell."

"I'm sorry I didn't come out last night."

"You had guests. I know." He looked to the driver. "Alert me if there's even a hint of a tail."

"Yes, sir," the driver said.

"How did you know?" I demanded. "How do you always know?"

"I told you," Dr. Bendari said, reaching for something on the floorboard. "My source."

"I'm loaded with weapons," I rushed out, waving the dagger. "Sudden movements aren't an option for you. If you try anything..."

Dr. Bendari straightened without grabbing anything and, looking at me as if I were a wounded animal, gently said, "You need me too much to dispose of me, Miss Bell."

"Yeah? And why is that?"

"I told you. I have the answers you seek."

"If that's so, why would you *want* to help me? Who are you? What's your purpose? Your endgame? Why the veil of secrecy? Who do you work for? Do you have someone spying on my friends? Who is your source, dang it? I want to know!"

He rubbed his temples as if trying to ward off an intense ache. "Are you always this inquisitive?"

"Always."

"It's quite off-putting."

"Well, I'm quite desperate."

He studied me, frowned with a hint of sadness. "I bet you are." Sighing, he very slowly reached for...whatever it was. A pile of folders. He settled them in his lap. "I'm sure

you will be less than thrilled to learn this, but I worked for Anima Industries for many years."

Even though I'd suspected, I found my fingers tightening around the hilt of my weapon.

Keeping his eyes on the road, the driver extended an arm, a gun now in his hand, the barrel pointed at my face. "I gave you a chance to put that thing away. You didn't. Now I'm telling you straight-up. If you make a move against my employer, little girl, I'll end you."

"Now, now," Dr. Bendari chided. "Let's calm down, everyone. I said I *worked* with Anima, Miss Bell. In case you missed it, that's past tense. I have since left the company. My source is still working for them, however, and that's where he gets his intel. Whatever I know, they know, too. They are, apparently, watching you closely."

I relaxed, but only slightly, considering what I'd just learned. I set the dagger on my thigh.

The driver lowered his gun.

"I was growing increasingly upset with their...business practices, I guess you could say," Dr. Bendari continued. "Lately, they've been using cancer patients as lab rats, and I couldn't take it anymore. I left the company, but you see, no one with my security clearance leaves Anima alive."

"You seem to be breathing just fine."

"Yes, and I've had to take drastic measures to keep it that way."

Fair enough. "Do you know Justin Silverstone?"

"I know *of* him. I also know he's playing a very dangerous game, and I'm not sure whose side he's on. He reports to Anima, but he also reports to Cole Holland. So he's

either betraying both parties or playing one, and it's going to get him killed. It did his twin sister."

"What?" Jaclyn was dead?

He flipped open one of the files. I looked at the page on top—and gagged. It was a photo of Jaclyn sprawled on a bed of grass, her body twisted at an odd angle and splattered with blood. There was a hole the size of a fist in her chest.

I'd never liked her, and she'd never liked me, but seeing her body like that... A well of sympathy bubbled up inside me. "There have been no reports of her body being found."

"I wasn't there. I don't know what happened. But I discovered the pictures and can only suppose someone carted her away and destroyed her. If I know Anima—and I do—there will *never* be a report about her."

Poor Jaclyn. Poor Justin. I had witnessed the deaths of my family, and it had been tragic and terrible, but at least I knew what had happened. "Does Justin have any idea?"

"I'm not sure. The powers that be could have shown him the photos and threatened him with the same fate, hoping to get him to do something they wanted. Or they could have shown him the photos and blamed your group, thinking he'd seek revenge. Or they could be pretending ignorance. They are very good at all three."

I believed him. Justin could be the spy, out to avenge his sister and the part he thought Cole had played in her death.

"I see the wheels in your head spinning. However, my source is not getting his information from Justin's reports. There is someone else spying on your group, Miss Bell, but I don't know the male's identity."

Male, he'd said. Not a girl paying a boy.

Trusting myself, remember. It's not Gavin. "What do you know about me?" I asked. "About my…condition. And how do you know? Or maybe a better question is, how does *your source* know?"

"At first, my source knew only that you had been bitten and begun to act strangely. I deduced the rest. Then you were seen producing a red fire rather than a white one." His expression was sad as he flipped through another folder, showing me photo after photo of people trapped in cages. Human people, not zombies. Only the more photos he showed me, the more zombielike those people became. I was horrified.

"These people are nothing more than guinea pigs," he said. "They were diagnosed with cancer, but without the medical insurance to pay for treatment. They were desperate enough to try anything. They've been experimented on— with my formula." There at the end, shame dripped from his voice. "I first came to work for Anima with the hope of creating a medication to increase life expectancy. A fountain of youth, if you will. Then I learned I was supposed to do it through the zombies."

"You can see them?"

He shook his head. "My staff and I weren't able to see into that other realm like you slayers, and we can't leave our bodies without help, so we can't see or touch the creatures until they are ringed."

Without help? What help? First, I concentrated on the most important thing he'd revealed. "Ringed?"

"Our version of your Blood Line." He showed a picture of a large metal band. "It goes around their necks and sends out electrical pulses that make the creatures tangible, but the

pulse does something to the zombies... Eventually works them into a frenzy, and that frenzy makes them stronger. I've had more coworkers have to be killed because they'd been bitten during a frenzy than for any other reason."

"Are you planning to put me down?" I asked with a tremor.

"No. Of course not." He frowned. "Tell me exactly what happened to you, Miss Bell."

I was surprised he didn't already know every stinking detail. "Justin was bitten by a zombie. He then bit me. We were both given the antidote. He recovered, but I got worse. And now I'm slowly turning into a zombie, which sucks more than you probably realize, because my spirit is toxic to zombies—and that means I'm toxic to myself."

He sighed. "I knew you were becoming a zombie, but I hoped I was wrong."

"How did you know?"

"I recognized the signs."

"You also know I'm seeing things. Hearing whispers."

"Yes. As the essence of the zombie takes over your body, you begin to see into both the spiritual and natural realm at the same time."

"I could already see into both realms."

"Not to this degree. One realm will always be more real than the other. Right now you're in transition."

I gulped. "Have you ever saved someone like me? Someone infected with the zombie toxin, after it's too late to be cured by the antidote?"

He played with the wedding ring on his finger. Ignoring my question, he said, "I had no idea you were dealing with

the other problem. The allergy. So, all right. Let's break this down piece by piece."

I took that as a no and swallowed my cry of distress.

"I have heard of a few other people having a spirit that is toxic to zombies."

One of them was my great-great-great-grandfather, I would bet.

"Justin reacted as he did because he was bitten by zombies Anima had experimented on and released. Their toxin is stronger, works faster."

"But Justin went back to normal and I didn't."

"Justin isn't allergic to himself." He lifted a small, dark case from the floor and popped open the lid, revealing stacks of prefilled, plastic syringes. "I created different types of the antidote for all the different reactions I had heard about."

"How many different kinds are there?"

"Eight. I took the formulas with me when I left Anima, and I've made several batches of each. Let's give you a dose of the antihistamine antidote now and see what happens."

I should say no. I shouldn't let a strange man inject me with a strange substance.

Common Sense Ali screamed it was foolish. And yet Survivalist Ali shouted it was currently my best chance of winning this.

"Okay," I said and nodded.

He selected a vial from the case. I shrugged my coat off my shoulder and tugged my shirt collar out of the way. He pushed the needle into the upper part of my arm. There was a sting, and a cool river moved through the muscle and spread.

For the first time in weeks, the double heartbeat seemed to vanish. The pressure eased from my chest, and the darkness thinned from my mind.

A burst of relief had me grinning. *Suck it, Common Sense!*

I wasn't out of the game. The new antidote bought me what I needed most. Time.

"I'll send all I've got with you," he said. "Whenever you start to feel zombielike urges, give yourself a dose. It's not a cure, but it's a start. You'll also be safer to be around."

"Thank you."

He removed fifteen of the vials and handed them to me, and I stuffed them in my pack. "I'll make more. But I should warn you... I'm sorry, Miss Bell, but there will come a point when your body will no longer respond to this antidote or any other. The more you use it, the faster you will develop an immunity to it."

Yeah, I knew that. "I was told there actually *is* a cure, that the essence of the zombie is darkness, and that the light chases that darkness away."

He frowned. "The light from a slayer's hand?"

"Exactly." I told him what I'd done, how my spirit had left my body, how I'd summoned the flames and touched my chest, but nothing had happened.

"I'm surprised you didn't kill yourself."

Dying is the only way to truly live.

Maybe that was the point. Maybe I *needed* to die.

Disappointment rose. Before, I might have been willing to risk death. Now I knew I wasn't ready for the end.

"This will require further study and thought," he said.

"Uh, sir. I hate to break up the party," the driver interjected, "but we've got a tail."

Dr. Bendari stiffened, looked back. "Can you lose it?"

"We're on a deserted road. There's nowhere—"

Crunch!

Metal slammed against metal. Our car swerved and then flipped. I screamed, mentally returning to the night my family died. Tires squealed as we hit the ground; metal crumpled as we flipped again, and glass shattered. I was jostled forward and back, forward and back, my brain banging against my skull.

Then everything stopped. Everything but me. *Dizzy...*

"Dr. Bendari." We were hanging upside down. Blood was rushing to my head. "Are you okay?"

He moaned.

I struggled to unlatch my belt. The moment it was free, I dropped, hitting the roof of the car—now the floor—my backpack slapping me in the face. I grunted as a lance of pain tore through me. No time to check for injuries.

"Help," he gurgled. His chest was covered in blood—blood dripping onto his face, filling his mouth. His shirt was ripped, and a jagged edge of his collarbone peeked past his skin.

Can't panic. "I can't release you. You'll drop." As wounded as he was, he might not survive the landing.

As I anchored my backpack in place, trying to decide what to do with the doctor, a pair of leather boots appeared. A shadow moved, and then a man was crouched in front of the shattered window. I was too disoriented to make out his features. "Help us," I pleaded.

"Dr. Bendari," he said, and a sense of self-preservation sent me scrambling as far from him as possible. "I was told to bring you back to Anima—unless you were sharing our secrets with the very people seeking to destroy us. Guess what you were doing?" He pointed a gun, fired a shot.

Pop.

Something warm and wet splattered over me, and Dr. Bendari went lax. His blood…everywhere, all around, all over me. I screamed, too shocked to react any other way.

The shooter grabbed the scattered files, then me, and dragged me out of the vehicle.

BLOOD IS THE NEW BLACK

Dr. Bendari was dead. Shot and killed in front of me.

Pain and panic threatened to overwhelm me as I scanned my surroundings. We were on an abandoned road, just as the doctor's driver had said, thick patches of trees on either side. There was another car behind ours—and the shooter was dragging me toward it.

If I could get to the trees, I could hide.

I was as good as dead if Shooter managed to stuff me inside that car.

Time for a new to-do list: *Get the guy to release me, race to the trees, hide. Use my phone to call Cole.*

I jerked against his hold, adrenaline giving me strength—just not enough to be effective. "Let go!"

"You want to die, sweetness?" he asked casually, making his words that much more frightening. "They've got plans for you, but if you continue to give me problems, you won't arrive in one piece."

They, he'd said. The people at Anima.

I fought that much harder, kicking out my leg, tripping the guy. Down he went, crashing into the gravel road. His hold on me loosened, and the photos he held scattered in the wind.

Shooter reached out to catch one, leaving himself wide open; I sucker punched him in the kidney, a very sensitive area. Grunting, he curled into himself. I grabbed as many files and pictures as I could before jolting to my feet.

I meant to run, I did, but a door slammed, and the driver of Shooter's car raced around the area, trying to gather up the rest of the photos while keeping a gun trained on me.

"Don't even think about it," he growled. He had bright red hair, a shade I'd never before seen. "I'll shoot you in the back without a moment's pause."

He'd shoot me anyway.

I spun and ran, moving in a zigzag to make myself less of a target, my backpack slamming against me again and again. Soon I was huffing and puffing, my lungs burning.

Pop!

I cringed, expecting an explosion of pain. But...I felt nothing and looked back. The driver of Dr. Bendari's car had crawled out from the rubble to shoot Red.

I slowed down and tried to catch my breath.

My only remaining ally faced me, shouting, "Keep running, more will come," before limping forward and pointing his weapon at the first guy, Shooter.

Pop!

Pop!

Dr. Bendari's driver collapsed, and my eyes went wide.

Why… How… Then I watched as Shooter fought to get vertical; despite his obvious pain, his focus was sharp as it landed on me. That was why. That was how. One pop had come from Shooter, and the other had come from Dr. Bendari's driver.

Shooter stumbled forward, taking something small, round and black out of his pocket, biting something off it and throwing it at Dr. Bendari's car. Grenade!

I spun and ran—

Boom!

The world went eerily quiet as a violent gust of white-hot air picked me up and threw me into a tree. I bounced backward, losing what little breath I had, shaking my head to clear the fresh surge of dizziness. Smoke filled the air, choking me, turning my line of sight to a hazy black and white.

A slight ringing erupted in my ears, growing louder, louder still, until it stopped as quickly as it had begun, and the world around me came back into focus.

I stood, almost fell. From the corner of my eye, I could see flames engulfing both cars—and Shooter still standing. Swallowing bile, I rushed into the forest.

Rearrange list: *call Cole, then hide.*

I stuffed the photos into my backpack and grabbed my phone. I was careful to alternate between watching the path ahead of me and looking at the names in my contact list. Around a thick tree trunk. The *C*s. Over a rock. *CO*s. Ragged breath scraped my nose and lungs.

I almost shouted with relief when I found *COLE*.

"Answer," I muttered when I heard the first ring. "Please answer."

"Ali," he said a moment later.

A sob left me. "Cole."

His concern came immediately. "Baby, what's wrong?"

"There was a car crash. They shot him. *Shot him.* He's dead. A bomb. Now they're after me, and I don't know what to do."

I could hear the static over the line, knew he was running as quickly as I was. "Where are you?"

"What's going on?" I heard Veronica ask in the background. "Where are we going?"

He was with *her.*

"I don't know," I said, too numb from the shock of everything that had happened to react. "I didn't watch."

"What's around you?"

"An abandoned road. A forest. I'm in the forest."

"Where were you before? What direction were you headed before the crash?"

"Nana's house." The words left me, barely audible as I panted. "Walked out of neighborhood. South, toward coffee shop. Picked me up. Farther south. Followed. Crash. Smoke. There's so much smoke."

"I'll find you," he vowed. An engine roared to life. Tires squealed.

"Cole," Veronica called.

That was the last thing I heard. I tripped over a limb and hit the ground with all the grace of a china shop bull, my cell skidding out of my grip. Frantic, I threw a glance over my shoulder for Shooter. No sign. Maybe he'd passed out from blood loss. Maybe he'd died. Fingers crossed.

I clambered to my feet, searched, but couldn't find my phone. Decided to leave it behind. My legs stiffened even as

I trudged deeper into the woods, and all too soon, I could barely chug forward an inch at a time. I scanned the area.

Bad news: as naked as the trees were, they wouldn't offer much coverage if I climbed.

Good news: Shooter would have to look up to see me.

Bad news: he could easily look up.

I had no other option. Using pieces of bark as handrails and stepstools, I shimmied my way up the tallest I could find. Every inch was agony. Finally I reached a large enough limb to support my weight and stopped, pressing my back against the trunk. I palmed the two daggers sheathed at my ankles and drew my knees up to my chest, trembling...waiting.

A horde of birds flew overhead, and a gentle wind whistled, hopefully masking the thunderous beat of my heart and the wheeze in my lungs. In a battle to the death, what would I do? I had no problem fighting zombies, ending them. They weren't people. He was.

He wanted to kill me. I should have no problem ending him, too. And there he was, inching from one tree to the other, using the trunks as a shield. He scanned one way, then the other, before moving on. He scanned up, and he scanned down, and—

Our gazes locked.

Instinct kicked in, and I launched a dagger before he could aim his gun. The tip embedded in his shoulder, flinging him backward.

Pop! He'd managed to squeeze off a shot. The bullet hit just above my shoulder, and bark flew in every direction. Some of it landed in my mouth, and I spat it out as I jumped.

Impact banged my teeth together. I tasted old pennies.

Go, go, go. I took several steps, intending to run—then I stopped. If I ran, he would probably find me again. There wasn't anywhere to hide. I could throw another knife and maybe stop him, maybe not. He could just shoot at me again.

It might be better to face him here and now.

Trembling, I turned and approached him. He was lying on the ground, his chest rising and falling in quick succession as he struggled to sit up. His gun had been knocked out of his hand and rested a few feet away.

He dived for it when he spotted me, but then, so did I. I beat him by a fraction of a second, straightening and pointing the barrel at him.

He glared at me. "You wouldn't."

"You're still wearing my dagger like it's this year's must-have accessory. Of course I'll shoot you." My trembling became more pronounced, the weight of the gun almost too much for me to handle.

He replaced the glare with a smug smile, saying sweetly, "You want to go to prison for murder, sweetness?"

"I want to survive, and we both know this would be self-defense." My finger twitched on the trigger. *Come on, Cole.* "Why do you work for Anima?" I asked to stall.

"Why not? The pay is good."

"You don't care that the company isn't interested in destroying the zombies? That they hope to make money off them?"

The look he gave me was pitying. "No need to give me a speech about right and wrong. I'd fight for your side if the price was right." As he spoke, he slowly angled to the side.

He was planning something.

I fired the gun, my arms jerking up with the recoil.

He grunted and pulled his leg into his chest.

"Move again," I said, "and I'll put a hole in the other one."

A mouthful of curses was hurtled at me. "I'm going to make you pay for this, little girl."

Threats? Seriously?

I shot his other leg. Just. Because.

As he writhed in pain, the bushes to my left rustled. Footsteps pounded. I backed away, intending to run. Or hide. Or both.

"Ali!" Cole called.

"Here!" I shouted back, overjoyed.

Cole and Veronica burst into my line of sight.

He'd brought her with him.

Cole seemed to take in the entire scene with only a glance. He dived on top of the man and whaled, throwing punch after punch. The gun fell out of my hand, and my knees gave out.

Now that I was safe, the surge of strength abandoned me completely. As my eyes closed, I saw Veronica watching Cole beat the man senseless. There was no recognition on her face. No remorse over what was happening to Anima's employee.

Maybe she wasn't the spy, either.

WEEP SOME MORE

Boom!

The sound reverberated in my head. Panting, I jolted upright. Sweat poured from me, every one of my pulse points pounding to the beat of a riotous drum.

"You're all right. I'm here."

Cole's voice. Strong hands urged me back onto the mattress.

I blinked to clear my vision, but only darkness greeted me. "Where am I?" I croaked, the words scraping against a throat gone raw.

"Ankh's. He looked you over. Said you'd bruised a few ribs, had a few cuts, but were otherwise fine."

As the surge of panic eased, aches and pangs battled for my attention, and memories surfaced. I'd survived another car crash, but others had died. I'd been hunted, nearly killed. I

might have killed another human being. Tears burned the backs of my eyes, and I gave a humiliating sniffle—or six.

Cole linked our fingers and squeezed.

The crack in my heart widened a little more, and warmth seeped through…until I remembered something else. He'd come to the forest with Veronica. I tugged my hand free.

"Ali," he said. A pause. Then, "Can you give us a minute?" he snarled.

Whoa. Where had—

"Tell us what happened, Miss Bell," Mr. Ankh said, and I realized Cole hadn't been talking to me.

I peered beyond his shoulder. Or tried to. The darkness was too thick to penetrate.

"Am I blind?" I shrieked.

"What?" Cole said. "No. Of course not. If you're having trouble seeing, it's because your eyes are a little swollen from the smoke and we put some salve on them. Don't worry. You'll heal."

Okay. Okay, then. "I have to call the coffee shop. Tell them I won't be in."

"Already taken care of," Cole said. "I told them you'd been in an accident."

"Nana—"

"Knows you're alive and well. I've stayed in contact with her and told her I'd try to have you home by eleven."

"What time is it?"

"Eight."

Three more hours; then I'd go home. Could I keep it together?

"Miss Bell," Mr. Ankh prompted.

I still wasn't his biggest fan, but the story poured out of me. I told him about Dr. Bendari. I told him about the photos and what I'd learned about my condition and the antidote. I told him about Justin and his sister. About the shooter, and the two drivers, and the chase through the forest.

I wished I could see his face, judge his expression.

"We found the photos in your pack," he said. "The others must have burned in the fire."

Some were better than none. "Which ones did I grab?"

"One of Justin's sister. Four of an Anima facility, and two of a computer screen with a formula they used for what I'm guessing is an improvement on the antidote."

Not a bad haul.

Mr. Holland cleared his throat, alerting me to his presence. "The shooter Cole brought in escaped his cage in this facility—the dungeon—and we have no idea how. He was weakened from blood loss. We don't think he could have survived for long out on his own without medical attention, but to our knowledge no dead bodies have been found. He could still be out there."

What Mr. Holland was trying to say without panicking me: the guy could still be after me. Just then, in the safety of the room, I didn't care.

"Now I'm going to check your eyes," Mr. Ankh said.

Footsteps. He gently wiped my eyes with a tissue, then flashed a muted light in front of my face. "I don't understand—ah, there we go. You're finally responding." As he continued to shine that light, the darkness began to thin at last.

"It's getting better already," I said.

"Good. We ran some more tests and found your antizombie toxin is significantly lower."

"The new antidote helped, then."

"New?"

"There are vials of it in my pack."

"I'll take one and see if I can replicate it. I'll send the others home with you."

"Thank you."

He stepped back, and Cole stepped forward. Our eyes locked, violet against blue. Need against... I wasn't sure what I was projecting at him. We—

—were standing in my bedroom. His expression was tortured, even sad, as he aimed a crossbow at my chest.

"I'm sorry," he said.

"Cole—"

—We were back inside Mr. Ankh's basement dungeon.

I blinked in surprise. Nothing had distracted us or gotten in our way, the usual reasons for a vision to end. This one had stopped all on its own.

Because he'd shot me and I'd died? Whatever. At least we'd had one. That meant a part of me was back to normal. I *was* better.

How long would it last, though?

Apparently I was going to do something so terrible Cole would feel his only recourse was to kill me. I couldn't even process that.

"I have no plans to aim my crossbow at you," he said tightly. "I won't. Ever."

I nodded. Really, what could I say?

That wasn't good enough for him. "You had to be right before. The visions have to mean something else."

I really, really hoped so.

"I'm not going to hurt you. Trust me. Please."

The very words I'd once—four times?—given him. "Okay," I said, and he exhaled with relief. I just didn't have room for another worry.

"Cole, call Justin and tell him to come by," Mr. Holland said. "I need to tell him about his sister."

I looked and found him standing beside the curtain separating my "room" from the others.

"I'll tell him." My pronouncement was quickly met with inquiring glances. "I know what it's like to lose your family. And I know you guys do, too," I added in a rush. They'd all lost someone in the war. "But with me, the loss is fresh. Jaclyn was his twin, and he loved her more than he loved himself. I felt the same way about Emma."

Mr. Ankh sighed. "Very well."

Cole made the call.

It wasn't long before Mr. Holland was escorting Justin to my bedside. He sat down opposite Cole, his expression closed off. He had no idea why he was here. My chin trembled as I said, "Justin, I met with a man named Dr. Bendari."

He nodded. "You've mentioned him before."

"Yes. He was...he was killed in front of me." Tears streamed down my cheeks, burning, leaving track marks, I was sure.

Justin softened. "I'm sorry."

"Before he died, he told me that your sister—"

With a pained groan, he jumped up, the chair skidding behind him. "I know. Don't say it. Don't you dare say it."

"You know?" Cole asked.

Justin closed his eyes, drew in a shaky breath. But that was it, his only reaction. And yet my heart broke for him. I knew what he was doing, because I'd done the same thing. I'd boxed up my grief and shoved it deep, deep inside.

He would feel better for a little while. Then, one day, someone would come along and say something, or he would see something, and the box would begin to open. All of those negative emotions would come pouring out, and he'd be helpless to stop them. He would break down.

"The leader, Mr. K, showed me pictures."

"Mr. K?" Mr. Holland said. "What does the K stand for?"

"I don't know. It's all anyone ever calls him." He lifted his chin. "Mr. K told me you were responsible, and it was my job to exact revenge. But I couldn't kill you, he said. Just had to spy on you." He offered us a cold smile. "He didn't realize I knew you better than that and knew you'd never hurt my sister—that he was responsible. So I've given him information, but nothing damaging. Just enough to make him think I'm playing his game."

"So you're the spy," Cole gritted out. "And you dared to send me on a wild chase? Why? To distract me?"

"Spy?" Mr. Ankh and Mr. Holland said in unison.

"No." Justin shoved his hands into his pockets. "You've got a traitor in your midst. I never lied about that, I just don't know who it is. Every bit of information I gave you is true. I want Anima taken down, and I want to help you do it."

The fierceness of his expression...the chilling determina-

tion in his voice…the hatred oozing off him all combined to scream *I'm telling the truth.*

"Spy," Mr. Holland repeated.

"I'll talk to you about it later." Cole nodded stiffly to Justin, a silent command to continue.

"My parents think Jace ran away. They worry about her, my mom even cries, but I can't bring myself to tell them that she's…that she's… Because I can't prove it, and I can't answer their questions. And now you know everything I know. So we're done here." Justin turned and stalked from the room.

Cole stepped forward, intending to chase, but I grabbed his arm. "Let him go. He needs to be alone right now."

Mr. Ankh and Mr. Holland watched as Cole settled back in his seat.

"Some privacy," Cole said, waving them away.

Mr. Holland rolled his eyes and left. Mr. Ankh opened his mouth, closed it. Then he, too, took off.

"I know you probably have more questions, but I want to talk to you about Veronica first. About what happened with her after our breakup."

"No," I said, anger suddenly rising.

He continued anyway. "I told you she went down on me, and I wasn't lying, but I didn't tell you that I stopped her before…just before. And I don't think you have any idea how difficult that was. With something like that, it doesn't always matter if a guy likes the girl or wants someone else."

"Should I give you a medal?" I snapped. I still hated the image of what they'd done.

"Yes. No." He banged his head against the side of my bed. "I'm screwing this up. Again."

"There's no reason to hash this out—"

He looked up, his gaze beseeching me. "There *is*. When you called me, I was with her." He latched onto my hand, holding tight enough to ensure I couldn't break free. "Nothing was going on, I promise you. I was telling her I wasn't over you, I wouldn't be getting over you and that I would be with no one but you."

My heart dropped into my feet.

I wanted to give in—so bad. *Can't give in.*

I'd warned him.

Take your refusal one step at a time. Otherwise I'd crumble like a cookie.

First step. "Cole," I said, plucking at the sheet covering me. "No. We're not going there. You're a relationship runner, not a sticker, and I can't go through another breakup."

He held me tighter. "Correction. I *was* a runner. I'm now a sticker. I get it now. I was letting fear make my decisions for me. I was so afraid of losing someone else, I was always looking for the expiration date. Not just with you, but with all my girlfriends."

Could a girl dance for joy and sob with despair at the same time?

Second step. "I'm glad you realize that, and that you're determined to move forward, but what happens if you also realize you never got over some of those other girls?"

"That's not possible. I want *you*. And I know you warned me, told me not to even think about crawling back. I know I messed up in the worst possible way, something I can promise you will never happen again. I know, but I'm still coming after you with everything I've got."

I might have sobbed.

Third step, the hardest. "Cole—"

"Shh, baby. Please. Listen to me. You're a part of me, and I'll take whatever you're willing to give me, for however long you're willing to give it." He rushed on, adding, "I've walked away from a lot of girls. Sometimes it hurt. Sometimes it didn't. But I always got over it, and thought I was better for it. I haven't gotten over you, Ali, and I'm definitely not better. I need you. Please," he repeated.

Another attempt at that third step. "No," I whispered. Together, we were a roller coaster. Up and down, up and down. Sometimes you just had to stay off the ride. "My answer is no."

He wasn't deterred. "I gave up too easily, and I'm not making that mistake again. I should have fought for you, just like you said. I realize that now. I didn't trust you. Well, I'm going to trust you now, because I can't live with the results of *not* trusting you."

As he spoke, every word wrapped in longing, he leaned forward, toward me. I absorbed the words, such beautiful, needed words. Soothing words. I wanted so badly to meet him halfway.

Tears filled my eyes, spilled over. Fourth step. The final. "I'm sorry. I can't. I just can't."

"Baby, don't cry. It hurts me to know I've upset you." He wiped the droplets away with his thumb. "Okay, we won't talk about this right now." He drew in a breath, released it. "Let's talk about the spy."

Definitely sobbed. "Yes. Okay."

"I know we suspect Gavin and Veronica—"

"I don't," I said, doing my best to remain calm. "Everything inside me says they're innocent."

He nodded. "Okay. I told you I trust you, and I do. I will. In everything, in every way."

I...didn't know what to say.

I gulped.

"That leaves Kat, Reeve and Ethan," he added, filling the silence.

"Ethan is the only unknown."

"Then we'll start with him."

We, he'd said.

A waft of air hit me, and I shivered with cold.

"May I hold you?" he asked.

I tried to say no, I really did. "Yes." I'd had a last kiss. Now I would have a last embrace.

He climbed into bed with me, gathered me against him.

I'd missed him. I'd missed *this*. His warmth enveloped me, and his strength soothed me.

Meaningless...

Right.

"We found your phone in the woods when we swept the area for more photos. You can text your grandmother." He pulled the device from his pocket.

I accepted gratefully and shot Nana a text to tell her I was okay, I loved her and I would be home by eleven, just as Cole had promised. Her response was immediate. Don't ever worry me like that again.

Me: Will try my best.

"Ask me something," Cole said after I'd set the phone on the cart beside the bed.

"Like what?" I said, confused.

"Anything you want to know. You ask, and I'll answer. I want you to get to know me better. Before, you said we didn't know each other well enough, that the vision brought us together."

Carte blanche? Yes, please. *So sure this is meaningless?* "Who was your first time?" I asked.

He snorted, saying, "Wow, okay. You aren't messing around, are you? And just so you know, I don't usually discuss these kinds of details with anyone. For you, though... I was fifteen, and she was twenty-one, the daughter of one of my mother's friends. I lasted about five seconds."

I tried to swallow my giggles, failed. "Ugh, I shouldn't be laughing at your extremely poor seduction skills. Because, Cole, that pervy woman totally took advantage of your childhood innocence."

He barked out a laugh, the sound rusty but so danged welcome. "You are too adorable for words."

"Why? It's true."

"Maybe."

Not maybe. "If a twenty-one-year-old man had sex with me when I was fifteen, would you be laughing?"

He instantly sobered. "Okay. Point taken."

"Tell me her name. I'm going to track her down and knock her teeth down her throat."

"As hot as that is, no. She's part of a past I'd now like to forget. But...I'm glad you never slept with anyone. I don't like the thought of you with anyone else, probably would have fed the fuc—uh, the *guys* more than teeth."

Must resist this possessive, charming side of him. "Do I get another question?"

"You get as many as you want."

He sounded determined.

I'd probably make him regret that.

"Did you sleep with Veronica?"

He stiffened, but he didn't hesitate to answer. "Yes. But it was over a year ago, when we were dating."

"Mackenzie?"

"Yes. Months ago, for a little while after we'd stopped dating. Then I met you, and that was over."

"Others?"

"Yes. You want the exact number?"

"No," I grumbled. *Yes.* Maybe. "Am I the only girlfriend not to go all the way with you?"

"No," he said. "But I wouldn't change anything about what we've done—and haven't done. I wanted—want—you ready for me, not sleeping with me because it's supposedly expected. I would wait forever for you."

Oh, glory, this totally meant something.

Are you sure you need to resist him? "Yes, well. You might have to." I cleared my throat. "Next, I have an observation rather than a question."

His arms tightened around me. "Go on."

"Sometimes you call Mackenzie and Veronica by cutesy nicknames. Kenz and Ronny. It's hurtful to the girl you're with."

"Do I?" He toyed with the ends of my hair. "I hadn't realized. It's a habit, I guess. We all parted as friends."

"Well, we didn't," I pointed out, now a little hurt by that, too. "I mean, we tried, but it clearly wasn't working."

He pressed his lips together to cut off a...frown? Smile? "A. Dor. A. Bull. Baby, I still wanted you, still considered you mine and didn't want to share you with Gavin. There was no way I could be friendly about it."

Dying here...

He kissed my temple. "Enough chatting. We've got two and a half hours before I have to drive you home, and I want you rested. If you're feeling better by Thursday night, I plan to take you to a party to celebrate the Tigers' winning football season. Since we don't have school on Friday, everyone always kicks off the four-day weekend early."

A chance to act normal. "I'll go to the party, one way or another. And I'm not tired."

He chuckled. "Sure you're not. Your eyelids are already half-closed."

"No, they're..."

I don't remember finishing that sentence.

I woke up in Cole's arms.

The alarm on my phone had gone off. He must have set it before he'd fallen asleep. He never even twitched, his expression relaxed, almost boyish, and I smiled as a deep well of affection spilled over. Looking at him now, no one would ever suspect his violent nightly activities.

Trina sat beside the bed, reading a book. When I stirred, she glanced up and said, "About time," and closed the cover. *Dare You To,* by Katie McGarry. "I want you to know I was upset when I saw the video of you going after Cole so vi-

ciously. I still don't understand it, but I'm sorry I never gave you a chance to explain."

"Thank you," I said, and I meant it.

Mackenzie strode into the room. "Heard voices," she said. Then, "Hey."

"Hey," I replied.

"You look better."

"Thanks."

Cole stirred, stretched.

"Okay, time for us to go bye-bye." Trina stood.

"But I just got here," Mackenzie complained.

Trina gave her a push toward the exit. "Ali, do yourself a favor and take a shower before he wakes up. Like, seriously."

Was I that bad?

The two strode from the room. I eased from the bed and nearly toppled to the floor as my knees shook under my weight. There was a bathroom around the corner, and though I was nervous about looking into the mirror, I did it.

Yeah, I was that bad.

There was no hint of Z.A., thank God, but my hair was styled in what could only be dubbed Last Year's Ugliest Rat's Nest. There was a big black bruise on my cheek, a slice in my lip, a knot on my jaw. *So pretty.*

Someone had cut away my blood-splattered clothing and put me in a paper-thin hospital gown. Three possible suspects. Cole, Mr. Ankh and Mr. Holland. There wasn't a front-runner, each equally bad. When Cole first saw me naked, I didn't want it to be like this.

Wait. *When?*

I'd just told him we weren't getting back together.

I'd meant it. Hadn't I?

Now, looking back on the conversation without the fog of anger and pain…and need…I wasn't so sure. What I did know? Staying away from him didn't actually have anything to do with a roller coaster. I'd never actually ridden on one, but I bet they were exciting. They had to be; people kept going back for more.

Was I punishing him for the hurt he'd caused me? Or was I simply afraid of losing him again and doing exactly as he had done?

Pensive, I took a quick shower, dressed in the T-shirt and sweatpants Mr. Ankh kept in the drawers. The first fit just fine. The second barely came to my ankles. Unfortunately Mr. Ankh did not keep a drawer stocked with bras and panties, so I had to go commando—the alternative to slipping back into my dirty underwear. I brushed my teeth twice and then my hair, wincing from the pain. Finally I emerged on a cloud of steam.

Cole hadn't moved from the bed, but now he was sitting up, watching me, his eyelids heavy. His gaze moved over me, lingering in certain places. "Com'ere," he said, his voice low and husky with want.

"We should probably leave," I hedged.

"We will. I want to kiss you first."

"You shouldn't… I shouldn't…"

"I'll make you glad we did," he said softly, almost…shyly.

How could I resist this new side of him?

Yet another one. How many did he have? Would I fall for each of them?

I crawled on top of him.

His big hands tenderly cupped my cheeks, the calluses on his fingers abrading my skin in the most delicious way. Moving slowly, giving me time to stop him, he lifted his head and pressed his lips against mine.

The cut stung a little, but I didn't care. I kissed him with all the pent-up need inside me. The need to taste him. The need to take from him and give to him. The need to brand him, to make him mine. All mine.

As our tongues thrust together, he shifted, rolling me to my side and hooking my leg over his hip. With the new angle, he'd created the perfect cradle and was able to scoot closer to me, practically fusing our bodies…rubbing against me, once, twice.

"You feel good enough for this?" he rasped.

"Stop talking and keep kissing."

He chuckled softly, and I nipped at his bottom lip. "Tell me if I hurt you."

"Still. Talking." I slid my hands under his shirt, tugged the material over his head. He fisted the hem of my mine, and the next thing I knew, the entire thing was being tossed over his shoulder.

Cool air brushed my skin, but the heat radiating from him quickly chased it away, even turned my blood to lava. I wrapped my arms around him, scraped my nails along his back. All the while he continued rubbing against me, back and forth, pressing, easing, pressing again…oh, yes…just… like…*that.*

"Ali," he gasped out.

The most amazing scent wafted from him. Pure, crisp. Familiar.

The urge to bite would follow.

"Ali," he said again.

I licked my lips. "Cole." If I could chew my way past skin, vein and bone, I could get to what I wanted. The heart of him. The—

No! I reared back and tumbled from the bed. "I need the antidote from my pack," I rushed out, crab-walking to the wall, widening the distance. "Now. Please."

He asked no questions. He hopped up, dug through the pack and rushed back to my side. There was a sharp sting in my neck before a cool river washed through my veins. And yet the river couldn't wash away the horror of what I wanted to do.

Cole stayed by my side, and I could still smell him. My gaze snagged on his hammering pulse, and there was a flood of moisture in my mouth.

"More," I said.

"That's too much."

"Just do it."

With a growl, he returned to the pack, found another syringe. He stuck me with more force, and another cool burst cascaded through me. My fascination with his pulse finally ebbed. The delicious smell faded. I sagged into the cold, hard floor, already crying.

"Better?" Cole asked.

"Better."

"Then why the tears?" He traced his fingers over the slope of my nose. "I'll get Ankh. He can—"

"No. No more tests." We already knew what was wrong. "I just want to go home." I'd give Nana a hug. I'd rest some

more, get stronger. By the time Cole picked me up for the party, I'd be as good as new. *Please.*

"All right, but we'll need to put a shirt on you first," he said, and I heard the thread of humor in his voice.

Oh, spank me. As Kat would say. I was sprawled out, shirtless. Braless.

My cheeks flushed, and I covered my chest with my hands. "Good idea."

"Not my best," he said drily, "but I think your grandmother would approve."

"I think you're right."

He smiled, and for a moment, I felt as if everything really would be okay. "Come on. I'll take you home."

CAN'T GO BACK TO YESTERDAY

Nana had waited up for me, and I hugged her as planned. She looked me over and twittered over each of my bruises and abrasions.

"I'm so glad you're okay. When Cole called and told me you'd been in a car accident, my heart almost stopped."

"I'm sorry," I said.

"Ali, I don't know what I'd do if I lost you."

"Nana, I…" Didn't know what to say.

"I know you're fighting for a good cause, but it's hard on me sometimes. Waiting and worrying."

"I'm sorry," I repeated, but I couldn't promise to morph into a normal teenager with normal problems, and we both knew it.

"Yes, well, enough about that for now." As she bustled around the kitchen to make me a sandwich, she changed the subject and said, "Are you and Cole back together? Or

are you seeing two hot totties at the same time? Or are you single and just playing the court?"

Hot totties? Playing the court? "No, Cole and I aren't back together, but we *are* going to a party on Thursday. And Gavin... Well, he and I will only ever be friends."

"I think maybe you need to rethink things with Cole. He's good for you. You light up when you see him, and he can actually get you to smile. It's an honor few people receive."

I smiled so rarely? I hadn't noticed.

She slid the sandwich in front of me, and after I'd eaten every crumb, she put the plate in the sink and patted my shoulder. "Ali, bear, I know your mom talked to you about, you know, sex, so there's no need for me to mention STDs and babies."

Someone kill me. "Right. No need," I managed to croak.

"But I'm going to mention them anyway. I read that a lot of teens are too embarrassed to buy condoms, and that's one of the reasons teen pregnancy is so high, so, if you ever want me to, you know, buy you some, please just let me know. Not that I'm condoning sex at your age. I'm not. I really think you should wait until your emotions are as ready as your body."

Seriously. A gun to the head. A knife in the gut. Either would work. "Cole and I haven't had sex."

"But judging by the way you look at him, you've considered it and I'd guess you've come pretty close—"

"Nana. Please."

"Oh, all right. I just don't want to see you get hurt. Sex can be a commitment for a girl, and a mere moment for a boy and—"

"Nana!"

"Okay, okay. Go on to bed," she said, kissing my temple. "You look ready to fall over."

Cheeks burning, I stood and gave her another hug. "Love you."

"Love you, too. I'll see you in the morning before school."

I drifted to sleep the moment I was snuggled in the softness of my covers.

I wasn't sure how many hours passed before I noticed the light streaming through the curtains. A new day. I lumbered out of bed, my body far more sore than it had been last night. A hot, steaming shower helped, but not enough to keep me from wincing as I dressed in a pink T-shirt and jeans and dried my hair, leaving it down.

My door opened, the hinges loud. "Ali?" Nana said. "You awake?"

"Yes, ma'am."

"Good. You've got a visitor."

I frowned. "Who?"

Gavin stepped beside her and grinned. "Me."

Nana arched a brow at me.

I shrugged—I wasn't sure why he was here—then nodded to let her know I'd be okay with him.

For a moment, she wrestled with indecision. And I think if the situation had been any different—if I hadn't been a slayer, used to taking care of myself, if I hadn't been dealing with Z.A., fearing for my life—she would have forced us to go into the living room.

"You have ten minutes," she finally said, and walked away.

Gavin stepped inside and I was grateful he didn't shut the

door. Curious, I motioned for him to sit at the desk, then eased onto the side of the bed, across from him.

He laughed. "Afraid the vision will come true?"

Yes. No. Maybe. "What are you doing here?"

"Thought I'd drive you to school today."

"That's nice of you."

"Well, I'm a nice guy."

"I guess that depends who you ask," I said drily, and he grinned.

"Funny girl." He sobered. "I heard about the crash and explosion and wanted to check on you. You okay?"

"I'm sore and upset a man was killed in front of me, but yeah. I'm dealing."

"I'm sorry."

I nodded to acknowledge the words. My nose wrinkled as I caught a peculiar scent, distracting me. "What is it I'm smelling?"

"My manliness?"

I crossed my arms. "Seriously. What?"

"What do you mean?"

"It's like you couldn't decide on an air freshener, so you decided to use them all."

He gave another exuberant laugh. "Maybe that's exactly what happened."

"Or...you were with another girl or six last night? Oh, my gosh. That's it!"

He shrugged, unabashed.

"How do you get the girls to flock to you like that?"

"Besides this beautiful face?" he said, rubbing his jaw. "I can speak French, and they like it."

I gaped. "You speak French?"

His eyelids dipped to half-mast, as if they were too heavy to hold up. *"Je peux casser trois briques avec ma main."*

Grinning, I fanned myself.

He wiggled his brows. "Sexy, right?"

"Not going to answer that. So, what'd you say?"

"I can break three bricks with my hand."

I couldn't help it. I laughed.

He stood, drawing my gaze to the band of skin revealed as the hem of his shirt lifted from his jeans. Tanned muscles underneath. Beautiful. But I was happy to note I still felt nothing romantic for him.

"We should go." He held out his hand, waved his fingers.

His scent wafted to me once again. This time, hunger pangs followed.

Feed.

I moaned. Not again. Not here, not now. Not with him. *Fight this.*

"Ali?" Concerned, he closed the distance.

Even though I told myself not to, I gripped him by the forearms. I rose to my tiptoes and put my nose at his neck, breathing deeply. *So. Good.*

"Ali?" Curiosity this time.

"You should run." Even as I warned him, I swung him around and pushed, sending him to the bed, on his back. As he bounced, I climbed on top of him. "Don't run. I need you," I said, only I wasn't speaking this time. *She* was.

She'd used my voice, putting everything she had into taking me over.

Gavin's brows furrowed with confusion, but he didn't pro-

test as I leaned down…down…and pressed my lips against his neck. One of his hands actually tangled in my hair, holding me close, helping her.

"Let me shut the door," he whispered.

Stop! I inwardly screamed. *Please, stop.*

She laughed with glee. "No." Gripping his chin, she forced his head to the side for better access. He allowed it, his lower body arching into mine. He ran his fingers down my spine, cupped my butt.

She ran my tongue up the length of his throat.

He shuddered. "Yeah. I like that, but one of us really should shut the door."

"Forget the stupid door." She bared my teeth.

Hard bands wrapped around my upper arms and jerked me backward.

She struggled to free my body and get back to Gavin. So close! His eyes were wide. He was panting from exertion, his pulse thumping wildly. He was confused—no, now he was afraid. She'd made him afraid, and she knew the fear would taste so sweet.

"Her eyes are red," he gasped out.

"Ali! Snap out of it."

Cole's voice.

I tried to speak. I gurgled.

He tossed me on the floor and pinned me with his knees. She continued to struggle against him, turning my head in an effort to bite into his inner thigh.

He barked something. I don't know what. Then Gavin was there, placing something in Cole's hand. A needle. A

needle Cole jabbed into my neck. A familiar cool stream bathed me.

I sagged into the carpet. Cole glared down at me, violet eyes crackling.

"Ali," he said.

"Yes," I croaked.

He eased off me. "You were trying to feed from him."

I rolled to my side and curled into a ball. "Leave. Please."

"Ali." Gavin this time.

"Get out of here." Cole scooped me up in his arms and carried me toward the bed.

Gavin was trying to lead my Nana away.

"Is she going to be okay?" she whispered.

"Yeah. I've got her now." Cole lay down with me still locked tight in his embrace.

He held me for a long while, whispering to me, smoothing his hands through my hair.

"I hate this," I said.

"I know."

"She took over, Cole. She used my voice, controlled my actions."

"The new antidote stopped her."

"For now. But we both know I can't take the antidote forever."

He kissed my temple.

"Cole."

"Yes?"

"If she takes over and the antidote doesn't work, I need you to—"

"Don't say it," he growled.

"—kill me," I finished anyway. "Please."

"That's not going to happen, Ali."

That wasn't what my instincts said. Maybe it was time to bring back my original to-do list, version two, but with a slight tweak. *Find a way to disable the zombie inside me. Kill the zombie inside me.* Addendum: *even if I have to die, too.*

I made it through the school day without incident. I hadn't wanted to go, but Cole had insisted, citing I couldn't afford another absence. He watched over me, making sure my zombie side didn't try to take over.

He even dropped me off at work, only to return an hour later and remain inside the coffeehouse for the rest of my shift. My coworkers stared at him, the guys frightened, the girls excited. Everyone whispered, speculating about who he was, and why he was there.

I think I blew their minds when I left with him.

"Any zombie sightings tonight?" I asked. The moon was high, full.

"So far, none."

"Shouldn't you be out there searching?"

"I traded nights with Gavin." His voice tightened. "He owed me."

"Don't fight him over me. Over what happened."

"I want to, but I won't," he said tightly. "You aren't mine. Not officially. Technically he didn't do anything wrong."

He dropped me off at home but didn't try to kiss me. I couldn't blame him.

I received a text from him the next day. No party tonight,

I'm sorry & I'm not ditching U this time, promise. My dad is sending me out of town. Will U miss me?

Me: I plead the 5th.

Him: I will definitely miss U.

Sappy girl. My heart soared.

I could have gone to the party with Kat, but after what had happened with Gavin, I wasn't going to risk it. And, to be honest, I was kind of bummed that I wouldn't be seeing Cole.

As the week passed, I received at least one text a day from him.

Friday.

Him: I can't stop thinking about our last kiss. U were topless.

Me (blushing): Thanks 4 the reminder.

Him: If U needed a reminder, I need 2 work on my technique.

Saturday.

Him: Are U eating properly?

Me: Yes, Dad.

Him: I kind of like the sound of that. How about a spanking??

Sunday.

Him: I actually watched the Hallmark channel 2day & thought of U. The main couple went at it like monkeys.

Where was he? Who was he with?

The questions began to plague me, but I never asked. I wanted him to offer the information freely.

Monday.

Him: I hear Z's were out last night in Bama. U being careful? I know U walk home from work—when I get back I'm teaching U how 2 drive, no more excuses from U.

Me: I'm being careful, swear. Are U?

Him: When I've got something precious 2 come home 2? YES.

How did all caps make me feel so warm and fuzzy?

Tuesday.

Him: I'm in a bunkhouse with six other guys, & 3 of them snore. Am considering offering myself 2 the Z's on silver platter just 2 escape.

Me: No girls there 2 soothe UR pains?

What a subtle hint.

Him: Why, Ali B, is that jealousy I detect??

Me: NO!

It was. It so was. Lying? Really? Over this? I kind of sucked.

He didn't respond, and I reeled with guilt.

Wednesday.

Him: There's only 1 girl 4 me.

After that, the texts stopped coming. Another week passed. I couldn't allow myself to worry. The more stressed I was, the weaker my body was, and I needed my body at top strength.

Mr. Ankh had managed to duplicate the antidote, so I had an unlimited supply. And as long as I injected myself three times a day, all signs of Z.A. were kept at bay.

Check off the list: *disabled.*

Side note: *for now.*

How long would the reprieve last? Not much longer, I didn't think.

But I wasn't going to worry about that today. Nana and I stood on Kat's doorstep, a glass partition between us and

warmth. Just as Nana raised her hand to ring the bell, an apron-wearing Kat stepped into view. She smiled when she spotted us.

She was pale today. I'd gone to a few of her dialysis appointments and knew she'd had one late last night. She had three a week, sometimes four, and they were grueling on her, but she never complained—more than a dozen times.

"Hurry up before you freeze us all!" she said, waving us in. Flour streaked her cheek, and there was a smear of something red on her chin. "Oh, and Merry Christmas."

This morning, I'd called for Emma, needing her face to be the first I saw on Christmas, just as it had been when she was alive. She'd arrived with a huge smile and hadn't seemed to mind that she was dead (in body) and that our family wasn't together. I was trying not to mind, as well.

Nana had given me a glass heart, with tiny pictures of my mom, dad, grandfather and sister peppered throughout. I would cherish it forever. I'd given Nana a bracelet with a charm to represent every member of our family.

Two guys sat in the living room with Kat's dad, Gary. All three guys stared at the TV, riveted by the football game. *My* attention became riveted on one of the guys and I stumbled to a halt, nearly dropping the pumpkin pie I held.

"Cole," I gasped. He was back. He was here.

He hadn't called or texted me.

Three pairs of eyes swung in my direction.

Gary stood and grinned. "Nice to see you again, Ali."

"You, too," I said with a distracted nod.

My gaze remained locked with Cole's, my heart careening

out of control. I waited for a vision, hoping, praying, but…
no. Not this time. "When did you get back?"

"Three days ago," he admitted through tight lips.

Three days. Why had he stopped texting? Had he met
someone else? I swallowed the questions I clearly had no
right to ask, but couldn't swallow my hurt. "Well, I'm glad
you're okay."

Kat patted me on the butt. "After I explained to Cole the
consequences of not coming, he was more than happy to
show up."

"Threatening people again, Katherine?" Gary tsked.

"Always, Daddy."

"It's one of the things I like best about her," Frosty said.

Gary ignored him and looked to Cole. "I'm sorry about
that, son."

"Don't be." Cole looked me over, seeming to drink me
in, and I shivered. "I wanted to be here."

Then why hadn't he contacted me? Why a renewal of the
hot-and-cold treatment?

Nana swept into the living room, taking a seat between
the two boys. "I've missed you guys, and it hurts my heart
that you never come by anymore. So, now you're going to
make it up to me and tell me what's been going on in your
lives."

"Come on," Kat whispered to me.

I followed her to the kitchen. "What did you threaten
Cole with?" I asked when we were alone.

"I told him I'd set you up with my cousin Rick."

"And that worked?"

"Like magic."

I fit the pie between the giant turkey and the stuffing. The rest of the counter was covered with bowls of broccoli and rice casserole, cranberry sauce, green beans, corn, gravy, mashed potatoes and to my surprise, spaghetti.

"You did all of this?" I asked.

"Everything but the spaghetti."

"Which you have because...?"

"Of my rules. I only eat what I'm craving, and I was craving my dad's spaghetti. He got up earlier and made it for me so he'd be out of my way when I needed the kitchen."

How sweet was that? "Well, what can I do to help?"

"Exactly what you're doing. Stand there and look pretty. The rolls are baking, and as soon as they're done, we'll be ready to consume like the manimals we are."

Cole stalked into the room. He didn't say a word, but grabbed my hand and led me away, much like he'd done Halloween night. I glanced back at Kat. Just as she had at the club, she gave me a thumbs-up.

He didn't stop until we were on the front porch, the cold surrounding us.

"You have to stop doing that," I said.

"What?"

"Tugging me around without a word."

"And give you a chance to refuse?"

Good point.

"How are you?" he asked, peering deep into my eyes, searching for...what?

"I'm good." I licked my lips. "How have you been?"

"Busy. My dad was upset that I didn't tell him about the spy sooner."

"Is that why he sent you away?"

"One of the reasons. By the way, he's been following Ethan and so far hasn't found anything suspicious."

Were we on the wrong track? "What's another reason?"

He sighed. "He thought I needed to take a break from… Well, it doesn't matter."

From me, then. I did my best to mask my wounded feelings.

"Don't," Cole said, brushing his fingertips over my cheek. "He thought I needed some perspective, so he sent me to Georgia to help Gavin and Veronica's usual crew."

"They went with you?" I shrieked. Then I cringed.

He actually smiled. "No. They stayed here." He tugged at the hem of my shirt, causing me to stumble into him. "So…I got you a Christmas present."

My eyes widened. "But I didn't get you anything. I mean, I thought about it, but I didn't—"

"That's okay," he said, his grin widening. "I can't give yours to you now. I have to wait till you come over to my house. Having you there is all the gift I need."

What could he have gotten me?

His expression suddenly darkened, surprising me, reminding me of a storm about to break. "About Gavin, and what happened with him."

Guilt pierced me, and my gaze dropped to my feet. That was right, we hadn't talked about it. Not really. "I'm sorry. He came over. We were in the middle of a conversation, an innocent conversation, and the hunger hit."

"Don't be sorry. I came over, too, hoping to drive you to school. Your grandmother mentioned Gavin was there, so

I sprinted back to your room. I was planning to clean the floor with his face. Then I saw you on the bed with him, and I admit, it looked bad. But then it hit me. I know you. You wouldn't kiss me one day, and another guy the next, and you wouldn't kiss a guy with the door open while your grandmother was in the other room. The truth hit me a second later, and I grabbed you before you could bite him."

"You trusted me," I said, shocked to my soul, "despite what you saw." That was absolutely, utterly *huge.*

"Yes," he said. He fit his hands against my jaw. "I told you I did. I'm in this thing, Ali. All the way."

"But…why did you stop texting me?"

I saw the ice frost over his eyes, and I shuddered. "My dad was monitoring my phone feed."

Oh. The ice wasn't for me, but for his father.

I looked away from him, trying to give myself time to think, and caught a glance of my reflection in the glass. I stumbled backward.

Zombie Ali was back.

Flickers of red burned in her eyes, and the black smudges on her cheeks were thicker. She smiled at me, waved—and then, through the reflection, I watched her step out of my body, away from the glass.

THE RAIN OF BROKEN GLASS

With the tick of a clock loud in my ears, I watched Z.A. glide off the porch and into the driveway. She paused to look back at me and crook her finger, a silent command for me to follow. A need to know her purpose consumed me, and I stepped off after her.

Uncheck from list: *disabled.*

"Ali," Cole called.

"Tell Nana I'll be back as soon as possible. And don't come after me." Who knew where she was leading me?

Z.A. continued moving forward, across the street, into someone else's yard. The sun was hidden behind thick gray clouds, creating a dreary backdrop. Any moment, I expected fat raindrops to fall, soaking and freezing me. I wondered how she would react—if the water would even touch her.

"Food's ready," Kat called. She must have stuck her head outside the door.

I never heard Cole's reply.

Z.A. ghosted through a fence, and I was forced to climb it. Thankfully, no one was in the backyard to accuse me of trespassing. We repeated this process three more times before coming to a creek with tall, brittle grass.

She glanced back at me and giggled.

"What are you doing?" I demanded.

"You'll see," came the singsong reply. She continued on.

I stayed in place, debating the wisdom of my actions. But then, the farther away she moved, the more I felt pulled toward her. Compelled. My feet kicked into gear without any prompting.

She reached another front yard, another fence. Again she ghosted through. Again I climbed. We exited the backyard, came to a street, and she stopped to once again crook her finger at me. I closed the distance, putting us nose to nose.

"How are you doing this?" I snapped.

She reached up, traced her fingers over my cheek. I couldn't feel the pressure of her touch, but I could feel the coldness of her skin—a cold far worse than the air around us.

I shuddered.

"So pretty," she said.

I jerked away from her reach. "I can't return the compliment."

Her lips curled in a slow smile. She leaned forward and whispered, "If I can't have your body, I'll have to get rid of it and free myself from our connection."

In the distance, I heard the honk of a car. A second later, something hard slammed into me, throwing me a good distance. I landed, lost my breath and then the "something"

slammed on top of me, pushing out any air that had managed to remain in my lungs. As pain tore through me, the sound of squealing tires registered.

"Are you trying to kill yourself?" Cole shouted.

I glanced up. A car zoomed past the place I'd just been standing, swerving, finally managing to straighten out. I looked across the road, my gaze colliding with Z.A.'s.

I saw fury.

"You disappeared for a moment," Cole said. "I couldn't see you. I don't think the driver could see you. Then you reappeared and the car honked, but you just stood there."

"I…" Wasn't sure what to say. Z.A. had just tried to kill me.

"That's it. I'm officially signing on as your keeper." He stood, hefted me over his shoulder as if I were a bag of potatoes and carried me toward Kat's house.

"Let me go, Cole. I'm going to *murder* her!" I beat at his back, not to hurt him but to gain his attention. He never slowed.

Z.A. watched us warily as we closed in on her.

"Murder who?" he asked casually.

"Her! My tormentor." I would force my own spirit out of my body, and I would summon the fire and burn her to ash—whether the fire was white or red. If she could survive without me, I could survive without her. Surely.

He turned a corner, and she stretched out her arm. He had no idea. I, however, felt her as she was sucked back inside me.

Argh! "Why can't you see her? You can see other spirits."

"I don't know. Maybe, like you, she has special abilities. Maybe she can cloak herself."

That…made sense. Terrible, scary sense.

"Tell me everything that just happened, Ali. Give me the long version, but make it short. I want the full story before we reach Kat's."

"She left my body, and she tried to kill me, and now she's back inside me, and she'll be more careful, because she's smart and she knows I can't get to her until she leaves me again." Frustration overwhelmed me, and I banged my fists into his back with more force. "I hate this. I hate her!" I accidentally kneed him in the stomach, but he held firm.

"Ali, calm down."

No. I was done with calm. I twisted my upper body, sliding off his shoulder. He couldn't stop me, but he made sure to catch me before I hit the ground. I came up fast, trying to avoid him, intending to run. The moment I was alone, I was going to freaking *kill the zombie inside me!*

He grabbed my wrist and kept me in place. "Calm down," he repeated. "I mean it."

Calm? Calm! I. Utterly. Exploded.

I launched myself at him, throwing a left, right, left. He ducked, then arched, then swung in the other direction, but I never managed to land a blow and that angered me all the more.

"What's wrong with you?" he demanded.

"My life is changing again, and just when I think I'm on the right road, something else happens to prove me wrong, and I'm so tired of being wrong and I think I'm mad at you because you stayed away an extra three days, and now you're back but I know it would be best if I stayed away from you

and everyone else because I could hurt you, seriously hurt you, and I just don't know how much more I can take!"

I swung at him. Again he ducked.

"You think it was easy to stay away from you?"

"Yes."

"My dad told me he'd keep his nose out of my relationship with you if I'd keep away from you for ten days. Just ten. No contact. I think he hoped the craving would fade. Do you know what day this is, Ali? Nine. I couldn't make it one more damn night."

I stilled, panting. I didn't know what to say to that.

He stared over at me. "I love you, Ali. Do you understand? I love you."

Wait. What? "You love me?"

"I've never said those words to another girl." He lifted his chin, squared his shoulders and braced his legs apart, as if preparing for a real battle. "You're stubborn, too curious for your own good and you've become a wild card, but yes, I love you."

He.

Loved.

Me.

"And that's how you tell me?" Snarling, I kicked out my leg and knocked his ankles together. He fell backward, and I followed him down, throwing more punches—but these lacked any heat. My heart was too busy doing somersaults.

He rolled me to my back and pinned my arms over my head. I bucked, but he weighed more than me, and I couldn't dislodge him. Our gazes met, and tension smoldered between us, hot and strong and undeniable.

"Let me go," I rasped.

"Never again," he replied.

I was breathing so heavily my chest rubbed against his. Our legs were tangled, and I could feel every inch of him. I ran my tongue over the seam of my mouth, anger giving way to need.

"Tell me how you feel about me," he croaked.

"No," I said, shaking my head. I couldn't. I wouldn't. If I said the words—*I love you, Cole, love you so much I ache*—he would keep his word to never let me go, and he had to let me go. "I told you. I'm no good for you right now. That's the only thing that hasn't changed, and I'm not going to risk—"

"So you're not ready. Okay. I get it. We'll revisit this subject later." He lowered his head, until his nose brushed mine.

I breathed him in. "No. Not later."

"Fine. We'll finish it now. I want you, and you want me. For now, that'll have to be enough." He smashed his mouth against mine, his tongue thrusting deep, and I moaned at the perfection of it. His taste, his heat, his strength, his… everything. This was what I'd missed. This was what I'd craved. Us…together. Not out of anger or hurt. Just need.

I wrapped my legs around his waist and arched up, unable to help myself. He released my hands, and I immediately tangled my fingers in his hair.

"This doesn't mean we're back together," I said.

"Whatever you say, Ali-gator."

The pressure escalated, almost unbearable, yet not enough—*not enough, must have more*—as his hands roamed over me, kneading my breasts, doing things to the centers…such thrilling things. With all the different emotions

still rampaging through me, my skin became more sensitive, my blood all the hotter; my nerve endings hummed. I loved it. I hated it.

I loved him. Had to tell him. Couldn't tell him. I had to stop this, but I wanted more. So much more. Desperate for as much skin-to-skin contact as I could get, I slid my hands under his shirt and scoured my nails over the ridges of his spine. He hissed in a breath.

"I love it when you touch me," he said.

I did it again, and the kiss spun out of control, until we were nipping at each other, and he was pulling at my clothes, and I was pulling at his, and oh, this was going to happen, wasn't it? Here and now, outside, in the cold. I wasn't sure how much time I had left, so nothing would stop me from stealing this moment.

"O-kay. I should have guessed this was why you both took off so unexpectedly."

Nothing except Frosty.

Dang it! I was so sick of interruptions!

Cole sprang away from me, assuming a battle-ready position.

Frosty rolled his shoulders, hard and intractable, and just as ready. "Don't bother trying to get rid of me. I'm not leaving without Ali. Nana is worried."

"Fine. But you will turn around," Cole snapped.

Though he looked as if he wanted to protest, Frosty obeyed.

My cheeks burned, and my heart pounded as I sat up. Cole helped me right my disheveled clothing before righting his own. Our gazes locked for a long, strained moment,

and we both knew there were a million things we needed to say, but couldn't. Not now.

Later, he mouthed, hooking a strand of hair behind my ear.

I should tell him no again, that this was it, the end. I might be dangerous to his health, but he was dangerous to my self-control. Instead, I found myself nodding.

Cole kept his arm around me while we walked back to the house.

"So, listen, Ali," Frosty said. "I know I haven't been your biggest fan lately, and I'm sorry. I like you, I do, and I know you're going through something tough right now, but I saw what you did to Cole and I imagined you doing it to Kat. I can't let you do it to Kat," he said raggedly. "She isn't strong enough to survive."

"I understand," I replied. "I've been so careful around her. If ever I feel even the slightest urge come upon me, I leave her and dose up on the antidote. I don't want to see her hurt, either."

His nod was stiff, but it was a start.

"Ali, honey."

Nana's voice pulled me from a deep sleep.

"I'm headed to the grocery. Is there anything you need?"

"What time is it?" I asked on a moan.

"Eight."

Too early. It was the day after Christmas and I didn't have anywhere to be until five. I would have liked to sleep till four. I'd stayed up late, trying to taunt Z.A. into leaving my body and fighting me. She'd ignored me, and I'd finally fallen into bed. Now I was tired. So very tired.

"I'm good. Thanks, though."

"All right, then. I'll be back in an hour or so."

I put a pillow over my head. Heard footsteps. The whine of my door as it shut.

I wasn't sure how much time actually passed before I heard cabinet doors banging shut, then silence, then the slam of the front door, as if Nana had left again.

I wanted to get up and investigate, but I just didn't have the energy.

The doorbell rang.

I rolled out of bed, pulled a robe over my tank and shorts and stalked into the living room. Expecting Kat and a thousand questions about what had happened with Cole, since we hadn't had a moment alone to talk, I opened the door. Gavin leaned against the frame, a formidable sight with his pale hair spiked back from his face and his eyes glinting ice.

He'd come over several others times, but I'd reverted to ignoring him.

"You need to stop avoiding me, and we need to talk about what happened the last time I was here," he said.

"Okay," I said, and moved aside. I could be brave. "Fine."

He stomped his way inside, and I shut the door.

"Just…give me a few minutes first. I just got out of bed." I raced into my room, brushed my teeth and hair, then threw on a T-shirt and jeans. I glanced at the mirror as I raced back out and gritted my teeth when I saw Z.A. grinning smugly at me.

I scowled at her. "Soon," I told her. "We're going to have a showdown."

She smirked.

"You hungry?" I asked Gavin when I reached the living room. "You want some breakfast?"

He eyed me suspiciously, but said, "Sure."

I put biscuits in the oven, fried bacon and whisked up some gravy. He watched me, but didn't speak (or try to help). I didn't push him. When everything was ready, I slid a plate in his direction.

"No eggs?" he asked.

"Wow. Your gratitude is humbling."

A smile teased the corners of his mouth. "What? I like eggs."

My lips twitched, as well. I hadn't liked seeing him so formal. I sat beside him, and we dug into the food.

Finally he said, "I've been thinking about things, and I'm sorry I didn't realize what was going on with you sooner... sorry I put my hands on you and tried for more than a few licks. I've gotten to know you over the past few months, and I should have realized you never would have made a move on me while your grandmother was a few feet away. And you *did* try to warn me."

Wait. *He* was apologizing to *me*? Not what I'd expected. "Well, I'm sorry I tried to eat you."

His lips stretched in a full-blown smile this time. "From anyone else, those words would be a turn-on. You, not so much."

I laughed. "I have to admit, I'm a little surprised you didn't kill me the moment you realized what was happening."

"I won't lie. I thought about it. I mean, I know you had pulled out of similar crazes before, but this was the first time one had been directed at me. Problem was, I would have

had to go through Cole to get to you, and I would have had to kill him to get through him, because he wouldn't have stopped shielding you any other way. That boy really loves you."

I turned away to hide the elation surely shining in my eyes; someone else had noticed his feelings for me—and came face-to-face with Zombie Ali.

She stood beside me, and she was still grinning.

Looked like our showdown was today.

Heart slamming against my ribs, I pushed my spirit out of my body without any hindrance; chilly air enveloped me. As I shivered, I reached for her, but she giggled and darted behind the couch.

"You're gonna get it now," I said.

"Ali?" Gavin said.

"Do you see her?" I pointed.

"See who?"

Cole thought she could shield herself, and maybe she could. "Stay here. You can't see or hear the zombie in the room. She cloaks herself, and I don't want her to hurt you."

"Can't catch me," she sang.

"I can't wait to prove you wrong." I dived for her, and slammed into the top of the couch. Had we not doused all of our furniture with the Blood Lines, I would have ghosted through. But we had, and now everything was as solid to my spirit was it was to my body. Couldn't forget again.

As I threw my legs over the edge of the couch, I summoned the fire. Small red flames began to crackle at the ends of my fingers. Red? Why red? Z.A. was no longer inside my body.

Maybe her toxin was still there. Maybe—

The cushions beneath my palms burned to ash. What the heck?

Z.A. zoomed past me, and I reached for her. I missed, popped to my feet and gave chase. In the kitchen, she circled the granite-topped island. I threw myself on top, sliding...falling...the entire structure crashed into the floor, taking me with it.

"Stop," Gavin shouted. "Ali, you have to stop this."

Laughing, Z.A. raced down the hall, into Nana's bedroom. She jumped on the bed. Again I dived for her. When I hit the pillows, the bed disintegrated, and I toppled to the floor.

Dang her!

She slipped out of Nana's room and into mine. I was right behind her. She knocked a chair into my path. I picked it up and threw it across the room, aiming for her head.

The chair burned midway, ash drifting through the air.

Can't blow this chance.

"Nah, nah, nah, nah, you can't catch me."

"—happening?" I heard Nana say. "How? Her body is in the kitchen. She can't be doing this! No one can! There's no one in here."

Her voice penetrated the dark determination urging me on. I blinked, forcing myself to focus on the natural world. Nana stood in the doorway, pale and trembling, gazing around the room I'd destroyed. Gavin and Cole stood beside her.

I took a step toward her.

The boys moved in front of her, blocking her from my path.

"Get her grandmother out of here," Cole said to Gavin.

Gavin took Nana by the arm and drew her back. I reached for her again, realized my hands were still ablaze with the red flames and froze with horror.

Had contact been made, I would have reached past flesh and burned her spirit—and what happened in the spirit always manifested in the flesh. She would have died.

I would have killed her.

Exactly what Z.A. must have wanted. She'd failed to kill me, so she'd gone after my loved one *through* me. And I'd let her. I hadn't stopped to think about the wisdom of my actions.

"You're worse, Ali," Cole said, holding out his hands in the most nonthreatening gesture he could manage, approaching me. "I'm afraid we won't be able to control you if something like this happens again."

"Cole."

"Don't agree with me," he interjected. "Don't say anything. Just think about what you're doing right now, all right?"

But I had to tell him—no, I couldn't. He was right. If I believed it, I would receive whatever I said.

I looked behind me, unsure what to do about Z.A.

She wasn't there.

My gaze darted to the mirror. There. She was there.

Back inside me. Scowling.

"Put the fire out for me, okay?" Cole said gently.

I tried, I really did, but the flames only grew hotter, only spread faster.

"I'm sorry, Ali," Cole said, and reached for the minicross-bow he kept stashed at his ankle. Rather than load it with

an arrow, he loaded it with a syringe. Then he stepped out of his body, so that we were spirit to spirit.

He paused, then said, "I thought about the vision, and stopped carrying arrows. Realized I might need antidote instead." A second later, a sharp pain hit my neck.

In a blink, he had another syringe loaded and flying at me. I experienced another sharp sting. Warmth rushed through me, and yet the flames began to wane…finally vanished.

He loaded a third. "This is a sedative."

I felt a third sting, and whatever the sedative was, it worked quickly. Darkness fell over me, and my knees collapsed. I knew nothing more.

My head pounded as I blinked open my eyes. I lay on… my bed? No, the mattress beneath me was too narrow to be mine. Gingerly I sat up. Dizziness struck me, and I moaned.

"Hey, Ali-gator."

Cole's voice. I breathed deep in an effort to clear my head, saw the haunting beauty of his face. I hated to look away, but curiosity got to me. We…were in a small bedroom I didn't recognize, with log walls and planked floors.

"You're in a secluded home Ankh owns. It's twenty miles from my house," he said, "but they aren't highway miles, so it takes me forty minutes to get here."

I'd been banished.

My expression must have fallen to reflect my dismay, even though I knew this was for the best, because he added, "You're too dangerous to be around others right now, sweetheart."

Acid eroded my throat, and I choked. "I know, and I prob-

ably should have been sent here weeks ago. But, um, how long will I be allowed to stay?"

"As long as it takes."

To heal…or to die, whichever came first. "Cole…"

"You have to quit your job, I'm sorry. Your grandmother is going to call your boss. And when school starts back up, she plans on speaking to the principal about allowing us to set up a computer so that you can remotely attend your classes. If they won't let you, you'll have to quit the district for a home school program."

"Cole," I said, trying again. What did I want to say to him? I wasn't sure.

He shook his head, dark hair falling and hanging in his eyes. "I took your journal," he continued. "I'll go through every page, every passage. Emma told me the key to saving you is in there."

"When did you talk to her?"

"This morning. She came to see me, and I think I freaked out my dad. He wanted to know why I was talking to air."

I smiled.

Cole pushed out a breath. "Better."

"What?"

He cupped my cheek. I reached up, wrapped my fingers around his wrists. "I hate that you've been hurt by all of this, I *needed* to see you smile."

No wonder I was drawn to this boy. "How can you still like me after everything I've done?"

His thumb brushed away a tear that had seeped from the corner of my eye. "It isn't that I like you, Ali, it's that I can't

stop liking you. And I don't want to stop. Besides, you were trying to end a zombie. That's admirable."

"You saw her?"

"I did. Her shield slipped for just a second when Gavin and I stepped in front of your grandmother. She was so angry her eyes glowed bright red. When I met her gaze I think it scared her, because she raced back into you."

"We haven't seen the end of her." I could still feel her, a presence in the back of my mind. A heartbeat I had failed to stop.

"We'll find a way to beat her," he said, and I nodded despite my fears.

Emma had said the same.

Nana had said the same.

Heck, I had said the same.

Now...I wasn't so sure.

"You know," Cole said, "my mom once told me a boy would know he'd become a man when he stopped putting himself first. She said a girl would come along and I wouldn't be able to get her out of my mind. She said this girl would frustrate me, confuse me and challenge me, but she would also make me do whatever was necessary to be a better man—the man she needed. With you, I want to be better. I want to be what you need. Tell me what you need."

I need...you, I thought.

Mackenzie had told me she hoped Cole would meet a girl he couldn't live without. In that moment, I was pretty certain I was that girl. And it was odd to me. So much had happened. So much had yet to happen. But this...thing between us *hadn't* changed.

"Will you get on the bed with me?" I asked.

His smile was wry. "I will give you anything but that. I know us, and I know what happens when we kiss and if I get up there, we're going to kiss. And I'm good with that, crave it, but there's no one here to stop us."

"You think Zombie Ali will take over again?"

"Maybe she will, maybe she won't, but it's not that."

"Good. Because I don't think I'll want you to stop," I admitted softly.

He brought my hand to his mouth, kissed my knuckles. "And you don't know how happy that makes me. But I don't have a condom and I refuse to risk you, even by pulling out. I don't have a disease or anything like that," he added in a rush. "I've never been with a girl without a condom, but getting you pregnant is a very real concern."

For once I wasn't embarrassed to talk about this with him. "Oh. Well, that sucks."

"Believe me. I know." He stood and looked down at me. "I stocked the fridge with all the food I know you like. I expect you to eat it."

"I will."

"I'll come back tomorrow. And every day after."

"I'll miss you," I said.

He reached for me. Balled his hand just before contact. And then he walked away.

This time, he looked back more times than I could count.

I'M LATE FOR A
KILLER DATE

I felt sorry for lab rats. Like, really sorry. Every morning, Mr. Ankh came to the small house in the woods and drew my blood, checked my vitals. I'd been poked and prodded so much I had to look like a junkie.

I'd told him all the testing was unnecessary.

I was going to die here, and I knew it. All I could do now was enjoy the time I had left.

And I was. Because of Cole. But deep down, I admitted this wasn't the way I wanted to go out. I wanted to die fighting, taking as many zombies as possible with me.

I sighed. Cole visited me every afternoon, and he always brought Nana. I could tell she'd asked him for a ride and he'd been unable to tell her no, because there was always a gleam of frustration in his eyes. But even though he wanted to be alone with me, he never complained.

Once, he pulled me aside and said, "Your grandmother is the toughest coc—uh, sex block I've ever come across."

I'd giggled.

On New Year's, the three of us sat on the couch, watching a movie Nana had brought. I was too distracted by Cole's heat and scent and general deliciousness to care what it was. I occupied the middle, he had my right, with my head on his shoulder, and Nana had my left.

When the credits finally rolled, I said, "I really am sorry about the new furniture you bought, Nana." I'd said the same words every day. Guilt hadn't left me.

"I told you. Furniture is replaceable. You aren't."

"But the money—"

"Ali Bell," she said, wagging a finger at me, the charms on her bracelet slapping together. "If I hear one more word about money, I'm going to scream. I mean it."

"Good luck with that," Cole said. "Ali is the most stubborn person I've ever met."

"Hey," I said.

"It's not an insult if it's true." He kissed my temple. "I wish we could stay longer, but my dad is expecting me back."

And he probably had some zombie hunting to do.

Nana kissed my cheek.

Cole gave me a long, searching look that told me he would be on me if we were alone. Then the two of them were in his Jeep, driving away. I watched from the window, trying not to cry.

Needing a distraction, I walked through the home, my bare feet thumping against the wooden floors. All of the mirrors had been removed. There were hundreds of books—

romances, mysteries, science fiction and fantasy, nonfiction, a Bible—plus a TV and a fully stocked refrigerator. Cole had made sure I had my own clothes, an iPod loaded with Thousand Foot Krutch and Krystal Meyers, two new favorites, and the picture of Emma and me that Nana had found.

A chirp sounded from my phone. I check the screen, and smiled widely as I read Cole's text.

I'm coming back after I check in w/my Dad. If U could B naked by the time I get there, U would really save me some time.

He was coming back.

To-do list: *kiss him. Touch him. Own him.*

Hinges creaked, jerking me out of my dreamy elation.

I frowned. I knew the sound well. Someone had just opened the front door, but it couldn't have been Cole. I grabbed a knife from the kitchen counter and pressed my back against the wall. Slowly moving forward, I peeked around the corner. My heart hammered erratically.

Footsteps closed in.

Squeezing the weapon's handle, I jumped out, prepared to attack.

A girl screamed. Her hand flattened over her heart as she scrambled backward, away from me.

"Kat?" I asked, lowering my arm.

"Don't you dare stab me, Ali Bell." She stepped from the shadows, moonlight washing in from the window and spilling over her. She anchored her hands on her hips, becoming the very picture of ire, despite the paleness of her skin and the bruises under her eyes. She wasn't well. "You have

some explaining to do. We finally figure out where you are and come to your rescue, and you almost murder me before we can complete the job."

We?

Shock barreled through me at an alarming rate. "I have missed you so, so much, Mad Dog, but you shouldn't have come."

"Like I could really leave you out here once I learned Ankh had you deported to Siberia."

"I'm only twenty miles away, and he did me a favor. I like it here. And how did you learn about it?"

She ignored my question, saying, "Of course you don't like it here. There are bars on the doors and window."

Those bars were meant to protect people *from* me. "I don't want to leave."

Her eyes narrowed. "Are you suffering from Stockholm or something? Because I know my Ali, and she would never move away without saying goodbye, and she would never choose to live here."

I wasn't going to get through to her, was I? "Seriously, how did you find me? And who is *we?*"

"I can answer that." Ethan moved to her side, watching me warily.

Ethan? The potential spy?

Great. Wonderful. This couldn't get any worse. "Fill me in before I have a panic attack."

"Well, for starters," said another female, "I found out about the zombies."

Reeve stepped up to Kat's other side.

Okay. It was officially worse.

"My dad doesn't know that I know," Reeve said.

"When you disappeared, Reeve did some investigating, and told me what she learned," Ethan said, "and that's when we discovered the zombies, and your whereabouts, and decided to bring Kat in to help us save you. You're welcome, by the way. Do you have any idea what we had to do to hack into Mr. Ankh's computer and get the coordinates to this place?"

I hoped that was rhetorical.

"In other astonishing news," Kat said before I could process everything I'd been told, "Frosty and I broke up—of course. He wouldn't tell me where you were being held."

"I doubt he knows."

She waved away my words, and I noted her hand was trembling. "Semantics."

"You have to stop pushing that boy away every time you're feeling vulnerable," I said. "One day he's going to stop coming back."

Her mouth opened, closed.

"Enough chatting," Ethan said. "Let's get out of here."

"Wait." The three of them weren't safe with me, not without a trained slayer nearby, but if there were zombies out there tonight, they wouldn't be safe without me. I'd have to escort them to their car, wherever it was. "Give me a minute."

I stalked to my bedroom, dressed in a black shirt, camo pants and combat boots. Then I strapped blades to my ankles and wrists, sheathed a larger revolver at my waist and stuffed two smaller ones in my pockets.

I phoned Cole but immediately went to voice mail. Ei-

ther his phone was now turned off or it was in use. Probably in use. "Ethan, Kat and Reeve just showed up at the cabin. I'm going to walk them back to their car. I'll also try to do a little detective work on Ethan. Call me."

When I returned, Kat wouldn't meet my gaze. Dang it. I shouldn't have stepped into her business. I thought I'd learned my lesson in the butt-in department.

"I'm sorry," I said, and squeezed her hand.

She nodded, the action stiff.

I read the fine print: not forgiven. I sighed. "Follow me." When we reached the front door, I drew in a deep breath for strength. My hand trembled as I twisted the knob, and my knees knocked as I walked outside. Cold air enveloped me, hugging me with unwelcoming arms of ice.

A forest loomed around me. A dusting of snow had fallen, leaving the slightest glaze of white. It was pretty. I stiffened, searched the darkness…but saw nothing out of the ordinary.

"Where's your car?" I asked.

"On the road outside the forest," Ethan replied. "We didn't want your captors to hear us coming."

I'd talked to Cole about the area, and knew we had a two-mile hike.

"I'll take the lead," I said. "You guys will do what I say, when I say, without any argument. I'm serious. I love you girls with all my heart, but if you question me out here, I'll knock out your teeth, I swear I will."

Kat finally cracked a grin. "Look at you, all forceful."

Ethan stepped in front of Reeve, protecting her from my supposed wrath. Did he understand I'd do what I'd threatened—and so much worse—to him?

"Stay behind me." I entered the forest, listening. Footsteps crunched behind me. No sound in front of me. Good. We maneuvered around trees, going downhill, minute after minute ticking past.

"So, Ethan," I said, "have you ever heard of Blood Lines?"

"No."

"Then why do you have them around your house?"

"Your friends asked me the same question, and I'll tell you what I told them. I don't know."

He was lying. He had to be lying.

"How did you and Reeve meet?"

"Can we not do this now?" he asked tightly.

"You're right. We'll wait till we get to the car. We'll put the girls inside, and then you and I will walk away for a little chat." Afterward, there was a chance only one of us would be walking back.

"Ali?" Reeve said. "What's going on?"

He nodded readily. Too readily? "The car."

"I'll let Ethan explain it later." We reached a small, round clearing, the sky no longer shielded by the tops of the trees. A big white cloud shaped like a rabbit appeared to be… pulsing. There. Gone. There. Gone. There.

I stopped, stiffened. Smelled nothing I shouldn't.

Hungry, a voice whispered. *So hungry.*

Hmm. Smells so good.

Must have.

Want.

Mine. Mine, mine, mine.

The zombies *were* out, and they were nearby.

"What is it?" Ethan whispered, his voice trembling.

"Kat, Reeve, climb the trees behind you," I demanded, palming a dagger and a gun. "Now!" I scanned the line of trees in front of us. At the far right, a bush shook, snow dancing to the ground.

A second later, Emma burst through, even though I hadn't summoned her.

Panic bathed her expression as she ran, her tiny arms pumping quickly at her sides. "They're coming!" she screamed. "Leave! Alice, leave now! It's a trap!"

A trap? I couldn't leave *and* protect my friends. What was more, I wasn't going anywhere without my sister. I launched into motion. As I raced, I tried to push my spirit from my body, but Z.A. wrapped her hands around me and anchored me inside.

"Let go," I screamed at her.

She laughed.

Behind Emma, zombies broke through the thicket.

They were chasing her?

Oh, heck no. She was a spirit. They were spirits.

They would be able to touch her.

Not on my watch.

The closer we drew together, the faster we both pushed ourselves. Then she darted *through* me, the contact shoving my spirit out of my body, making Z.A. shriek in pain.

I stumbled backward, my body remaining in front of me. The cold should have thickened. Instead, I felt embraced by warmth. I looked back. Emma had finally stopped—in front of Ethan. She swung her fists at him, but no contact was made. He stood beside a tree, his hand resting on the bark. He was unaware of what was happening around him,

watching me, his expression grim. The girls were nowhere to be seen. They must have obeyed me and climbed.

I turned back to the zombies, aimed the gun and squeezed the trigger. *Boom, boom, boom! Boom, boom, boom!*

Bodies fell…only to crawl back up. I threw down the gun, the clip empty, and grabbed a second dagger. The creatures came closer and closer, moving faster than ever before. Almost within reach… For the first time in weeks, those red, evil eyes were utterly focused on me. Eager for a go at me? Oh, yeah. Whatever the reason—had Emma done more than freak out Z.A.?—I was once again a target. I pounced.

My daggers slashed through one throat, two, six, then severed a spine, two, eight, rotted arms continually reaching for me. Blackened teeth chomped at me. At least no other whispers bombarded me. I arched backward, forward, avoiding being grabbed. I turned, stabbed. Turned, stabbed, staying in constant motion, knowing a single moment of hesitation would lose the battle for me.

I swung a zombie in front of me, using him as a shield as I spun around and stabbed his partner in the side. Black goo sprayed in every direction. Then I decapitated my shield.

No one else made a play for me, and I realized a wall of writing bodies had formed, blocking the others.

I climbed out, on alert, and my new targets stalked around me as if pondering the best course of action.

Some were mindless. These were not. And they weren't just stalking around me, but were inching closer and closer, closing in. I exploded into motion—*crap, I'd lost my daggers.* I slammed the heel of one hand into the jaw of the zombie

on my left, and the heel of the other into the throat of the zombie on my right.

As multiple other arms stretched out, I rolled to the ground, knocking several of the creatures off their feet. Coming up with two new guns, I aimed, fired, aimed, fired, taking no more than a second for each action, but always swinging my arms to ensure that I got the zombies closest to me.

I shot a zombie in the face, and both guns clicked. Out of bullets.

As a new horde approached me, I pressed the button on the side of the handles, causing blades to extend from under the barrel of the guns. Gnarled arms reached for me. I crossed the weapons in front of me and hit two creatures in the temple, twisted, hit two more, twisted, hit two more—

A hard fist slammed into my jaw.

Stupid stars, winking at me. Still I managed to duck, missing a second blow and forcing the zombie behind me to take the brunt of the impact. I straightened, grabbing another zombie, intending to use him as a shield, but his arm detached. I stumbled to the side, my momentum jacked. One of the creatures shackled my wrist and tugged me to the ground. Jerking free, but losing my hold on the weapons, I rolled, once again knocking down several of the zombies.

"Light up!" I shouted.

The smallest of flames flickered across my knuckles, and it was white. Relief speared me.

Footsteps behind me.

I twisted, reached out to brush my fingertips against the

zombie closest to me. He didn't ash, but he did hiss and stumble away from me.

He came back for more, the fool, and I did it again. This time, he batted my hand away, determined. Someone stepped up behind him, stopping him, attaching a metal collar to his neck. He sagged to the ground, motionless.

I looked around, confused.

Hazmats surrounded me, and they were snapping collars on the rest of the zombies.

Realization sent me backpedaling, but I ran into something solid. I turned, already swinging, and nailed a Hazmat in the chin. He stumbled to the side and would have given me a clear shot to my friends, but three other Hazmats took his place.

Before I realized what was happening, a collar was being snapped around *my* neck, sharp electrical pulses shooting through me. Suddenly I couldn't move, could barely breathe. Panic filled me, joining the adrenaline rushing through me, and my body wasn't sure how to react. Keep fighting, or shut down.

"What are you doing?" I heard Kat scream. "Let her go!"

She could see me? The collar, maybe…

Keep fighting. Definitely keep fighting. I tried to stand, but my legs refused to cooperate.

"You want me docile? Leave the girls out of this," I tried to shout, but only gurgles escaped.

"Ethan?" Reeve gasped. "Help us!"

"You told me you wouldn't hurt Reeve," Ethan shouted.

Instant comprehension. He knew the Hazmats, because he was one of them.

He was the spy—no doubts about that now—and he had gotten some of his information from Reeve. When I'd lived with her, she'd known my schedule. The rest he must have gotten by watching me.

He'd covered his tracks very well. I still felt stupid. I should have known.

Someone crouched in front of me and removed the clear panel from his mask. He had to be in his fifties, with salt-and-pepper hair and thick lines around gunmetal-gray eyes.

He offered me a sad smile. "I hate that matters have come to this, Miss Bell, I really do, but my daughter is sick, and I suspect you're going to be her cure."

WHO STOLE THE POISONED TARTS?

My spirit was dragged to my body, the collar removed by one Hazmat while several others forced the two halves of me to join. At the moment of connection, I jolted into motion, determined to fight these people with everything I had. Some of the Hazmats were not in spirit form, however, and one of them managed to slam a hard fist into my temple.

Dizzy…

Slowing…

Still I fought.

I heard a whoosh of air, felt a sharp stab of pain in my arm. I patted blindly at the spot and dislodged a small dart.

The dizziness spun out of control, helped along by…a drug? I swayed, bones liquefying, knees buckling. When I hit the ground, I was roughly hauled to my feet, my hands tied behind my back, and there was nothing I could do about it. A black hood was draped over my head, and I was stuffed

into a vehicle, driven I don't know how many miles. Time ceased to exist. There was only here, now. Darkness, rising panic. Where was Kat? Reeve?

I listened for movement—or whimpers—but heard only the wet slosh of tires, the zoom of passing cars and the soft hum of the radio.

Stay calm.

Easy to think, so difficult to do. Tremors racked me, and sweat beaded over my skin. The blood in my veins was somehow a dangerous mix of too hot and too cold.

After we parked, I was towed outside with the *kind* aid of two guards. We ascended a flight of steps and entered a pool of warmth. A heated building? I heard footsteps. A *ding.* We stopped, and the world around me jostled. We were in an…elevator?

Another *ding.* Again I was towed forward. We stopped several more times, and I imagined my surrounding went far beyond grim. A dungeon, like Mr. Ankh's. A torture chamber, with wall after wall of deadly weapons once found in the Middle Ages.

We entered a room with a deluge of new sounds. Moans, groans, rattling metal.

Other prisoners?

Can't stay here. Act! Gathering every ounce of strength I possessed, I struggled for freedom. I managed to head-butt one of my captors and trip another, and we all tumbled to the floor. Before I could run, someone fisted the back of my shirt and lifted me to my feet. The ties were cut from my wrists, and I was thrust forward. As I tripped to my hands and knees, I thought I heard Kat and Reeve gasp. Hinges

groaned, and a door slammed. Trembling, I ripped off the hood and blinked as the bright light in the room stung my eyes.

We were in a laboratory. There were computers, strange equipment I didn't recognize and a handful of humans wearing lab coats. There were also cages, with collared, frenzied zombies locked inside.

Locked inside—like me.

And in the cage next door to ours was a girl I'd thought dead. Jaclyn Silverstone.

She was dirty, her hair in tangles, her far-too-thin body stretched out on a cot. But she was alive, and in that moment, she stopped being my enemy and became my best ally.

"They're not allowed to talk to or look at us," she said weakly. "Mr. K is too afraid they'll start feeling guilty and set us free."

The horror of the situation struck me, followed by rage, and I lumbered to my feet. I had to know if she was right, and threw myself into the bars, shaking the entire cage. "Let us out!"

As Jaclyn had promised, everyone ignored me.

"Hey!" Kat called, stepping up to my side. There was a tremor in her voice. "She's talking to you. You better listen or you're gonna regret it."

Again we were ignored.

Soft sobs echoed behind me. I turned to see Reeve standing in the center of the cell, her arms wrapped around her middle. Tears streamed down her cheeks, little pink track marks left behind.

"He betrayed me," she said with a sniffle. "I caused this.

I talked to him, told him everything I discovered. I just...
I never suspected he already knew what was going on, that
he was pushing me to find out more for him, that he was
using me. *Using me.*"

Kat raced to her side.

I threw one last look at the lab coats—no one met my
gaze—before striding to my friends. Reeve verged on the
edge of a breakdown; I recognized the signs.

"You couldn't have known his plan," I said, doing my best
to sound calm, rational. But when my words registered, I
realized I'd lied. She *could* have known—if I'd told her what
was going on when she'd first expressed interest. "Your dad
has cameras everywhere. He will have seen what happened
in that forest. He'll find us."

He had better find us.

Kat nibbled on her bottom lip. "I'm so sorry, Ali, but
Ethan helped us disable all the cameras. He said he didn't
want anyone to be able to see or stop us from rescuing you."

The brightest hope I'd had died a quick death, and I
pinched the bridge of my nose. This was bad. Really, really bad.

But I had three small hopes left. The first, Emma. She
could warn Cole. The second, the message I'd left him. The
third, Justin. He might know the truth about what had happened to us. But...was he truly on our side?

I did my best to keep my expression neutral as I urged the
girls to the back of the cage and onto the cold, concrete floor.

"What are we going to do?" Reeve whispered.

"Yeah, Ali, what?" Kat asked, her usual bravado gone.

"Right now we're going to rest," I said with a small smile.
I glanced over at Jaclyn. "I'll think of something. Promise."

Hour after hour ticked by with agonizing slowness. I
summoned Emma, but she didn't appear. I studied my surroundings, taking in every detail. The same glow I'd seen
in the forest, when I'd tracked the spy, streaked the floor
and walls in here. Zombie toxin, maybe?

There was a camera posted at the top right corner of our
cage, recording our every move and word.

There were no beds for us, no blankets and the toilet was
out in the open. The number of lab coats thinned out in
an unhurried but continuous stream, until only two people remained. The others would be back, though. I knew
they would.

I stepped up to the bars blocking me from Jaclyn. Up
close, I could see the gauntness of her cheeks.

"How long have you been here?" I asked.

"A little over a month, I think. I lost track of time."

"We thought you were dead."

"Only in my favorite dreams." She shrugged, the action
weak. "Mr. K wanted a way to control Justin, to force him
back to Cole...to you. Rather than tell him I was a prisoner,
and risk him spending his time searching for me, he told my
brother Cole killed me."

Mr. K. The guy running this show. Ms. Wright's replacement. The man whose daughter was sick—the girl I was
somehow supposed to help.

"I've tried to escape," she said. "I think that's why they
keep me undernourished now. So I stay pathetic and feeble."

Good plan. Fatigue had added weight to each of my limbs, and my eyelids felt as if they'd been replaced by sandpaper. Blinking was a terrible chore. *Can't allow myself to fall asleep.* An opportunity to do something, *anything,* might present itself.

"People come in, but they never walk out," she continued. "Mr. K likes to experiment on cancer patients. I think maybe he's trying to cure them, because he's always upset when they die, but he's sucked it up worse than a Hoover. The patients are now the zombies that you see here."

He'd made an army of zombies out of cancer patients? The man was seriously unbalanced.

"What kind of security does he have?" I asked.

"There are always guards outside the room, monitoring us. I don't know how many. And they've got their version of the Blood Lines all over the place, even the bars, so our spirits can't leave and alert another slayer."

No wonder Emma hadn't shown.

Another hope withered.

At 7:58 a.m. the doors at the far end of the room slid open, and the grinning man from the forest entered. Two tall, armed men flanked his sides, and the group approached my cage. Kat and Reeve were huddled together, leaning on each other, their eyes closed and their breathing even. Their adrenaline had crashed, I think, and when sleep had finally come, they'd been unable to resist.

"You're coming with us, Miss Bell."

Jaclyn reached through the bars and squeezed my wrists. "It's going to hurt. I'm sorry."

Metal rattled against metal as the cage door was unlocked.

The armed men pounded inside, and my heart beat in tune with their angry steps. I wouldn't leave my friends easily and threw a punch. My knuckles connected with the nose of the guy on the left. Blood spurted, and he howled with pain. Before I could do the same to the other guy, he grabbed my arm and twisted it behind my back, pain exploding through my shoulder.

Cuffs were slapped on me and I was shoved out of the cage. That. Easily.

"Hey! What are you doing? Let her go!" Kat called, the commotion having roused her.

The zombies erupted into a flurry of motion and sound. Grunts, groans, shuffling footsteps.

Hungry…

Feed…

Soon…

Now…

As the whispers reached my conscious, making me tremble, I was led into another room. There was a chair; something usually found in a dentist's office. Beside it was a padded stool, a table with different-sized blades and syringes strewn across the surface and some kind of machine that looked like a car engine.

As I was strapped to the chair, I fought for freedom.

"Calm down, Miss Bell," Forest Guy said. "We're going to talk, you and I."

"Screw you."

He ignored me. "I'm Kelly Hamilton. I don't usually share my name—I prefer the anonymity of Mr. K—but you and

I are going to be closer than most. You, my dear, may call me Kelly."

Hamilton. Like Ethan Hamilton. Kelly had to be his father.

More of a betrayal than I'd realized.

And oh, glory, I wasn't meant to leave this laboratory, was I? That was why he felt so comfortable sharing his full name, his link to Ethan. It had nothing to do with closeness.

He sat on the stool and tugged on a pair of latex gloves. "I must admit, you have been a difficult girl to find. Just when I decided you could help me, you disappeared."

"For good reason."

"And what would that be?"

"I'm dangerous." *You better believe it, jerk.*

"Yes. I was told you'd developed a few zombielike tendencies. The fact that you're still alive, your body healthy and whole, intrigues me."

I snapped my teeth at him. "If you aren't careful, I'll show you those tendencies firsthand."

He gave my shoulder a comforting pat. "I know you're scared, and I'm sorry for that, but you can rest assured that what happens in here is for a very worthy cause. My daughter is dying, Miss Bell, and I must find a cure."

Ethan's sister. Leukemia. "Exactly how do you think I can help?"

"Unless you slayers use your fire to ash, the zombies possess the ability to live forever. It is my hope to harness that ability for humans."

"That's ridiculous. The zombies live, in their way, but they never stop rotting."

"And even that, in itself, is a miracle, Miss Bell. Think about the possibilities. If we can figure out how, and why, the rotting occurs, then we can figure out how to eliminate it as a side effect and save human beings from death."

"Zombies *are* death, in every sense of the word. Those tendencies you mentioned make me want to kill people."

"A small price to pay for eternal life." He held up an empty syringe and waved the needle in front of my face, making sure he had my attention. "Just think. Your actions in this laboratory will help save countless lives."

Maybe. One day. But what about the countless lives lost in the meantime?

He wanted to save his daughter. I got that. I did. I'd want to help Nana, Cole, Kat and all of my friends if the situation were reversed. I'd be desperate to help, actually—I already was. Watching Kat's decline was a true horror. But this wasn't the right way.

"You love your daughter," I said, "and I'm betting she loves you. Would she want you to do this? To hurt people in order to help her?"

His lips compressed into a thin line. "This is going to sting, but I'll be as gentle as I can." Leaning over me, he wound a tourniquet around my upper arm and stuck the needle in the soft tissue of my inner elbow.

I cringed, watching as crimson filled the belly of the tube.

"We're going to figure out what caused your body to embrace the zombie toxin, and yet not actually kill you or even cause you to rot." He removed the tourniquet and bandaged the puncture wound.

He's too determined. You're not going to talk any sense into him.

Gotta work with what you've got. "You don't need the girls for this. Let them go. They have nothing to do with our war."

"Your concern is admirable, but we actually do need the girls. We want to keep you malleable, and they are our insurance card."

I knew that wasn't all Kat and Reeve were to him. They were witnesses.

I had to get them out of here.

"I'll promise malleability if you let them go."

"You'll give it anyway. Now, are you light-headed?" he asked. "I've got a cookie with your name on it if so."

I would have preferred evil straight-up, with no dash of kindness.

"Very well. We'll move on. What comes next is going to be far more painful for you, and I'm sorry for that, but I need to know what your body can take...and what it can't. Your strengths and your weaknesses, if you will. I also need to know what happens to the zombie toxin when your body is placed under tremendous stress." He held up another syringe; this one had a thick green liquid swirling inside the tube.

My bonds stretched taut as I tried to scramble away. "What's that?" I demanded, unable to mask my tremble.

"An isotope of adrenaline and other goodies meant to speed your body into a fight-or-flight response, to put you under that tremendous stress I mentioned. My hope is that you'll recover swiftly, and the toxin won't be able to overtake you and harm you."

I had nowhere to go, no way to twist, as he jabbed the needle in my arm and injected me with fire. Molten lava spread through me, burning me up, melting all of my organs.

Sweat suddenly poured from me. Maybe blood. I couldn't tell—my vision hazed. Muscles I hadn't known I possessed jerked painfully, and both of my hearts kicked into a dangerously swift rhythm. *Boom, boom, boom, boom,* no pausing, no slowing, just pound after pound against my ribs. I bit my tongue to keep from screaming.

"Stop it," I gasped out, my lungs squeezing tight. "Stop it right now."

"Don't worry. It won't last long. Just a few minutes." He smoothed a hand over my brow. "I'm not a terrible person, and I don't like to see you worked up. But I'm also a determined person. I have to save my daughter, Miss Bell, and if that means destroying the world and everyone in it to do so, I will."

"Criminal," I managed. "Deserve...prison."

"That's the pain talking. I take no offense." He stood and taped electrodes to my temples, neck, wrists, belly and ankles. "We're going to keep track of what happens to your spirit, too."

He grabbed another syringe of green liquid. Before I could protest, he'd injected me a second time. Another stream of lava blazed through me.

My back bowed of its own accord. This time, my heart thumped with so much force I expected to hear my ribs crack. I couldn't stop my screams. They came, one after the other, scraping along my throat, until fists seemed to wrap around my neck and squeeze.

"Interesting," Kelly said, pressing his fingers into my carotid. "Your body and spirit are weakening at a rapid rate, and yet there's something inside you that's strengthening."

My eyesight blurred, but I think I saw Zombie Ali standing in the corner of the room, watching me.

"Why won't you die?" she snapped.

Yes. She was here. Was she the thing that was strengthening?

One step, two, she approached me. Floated, really. Pale hair tangled around a face now completely smudged. She grinned, revealing teeth still stained with blood. "It's just a matter of time now."

I closed my eyes to block her image.

"There, there," Kelly said. "That's enough. We'll take a break."

I felt another sharp sting in my neck, though this one was accompanied by ice rather than fire. My heartbeat slowed, and I sagged into the chair, a wet, soggy mess.

"I must admit," Kelly said, as he made a notation in a notebook, "I was hoping to see the red fire. I was told it hurt the slayers *and* the zombies, yet not you. And that makes me wonder…what did it do to you?"

Z.A. stood just behind him, and I was careful not to meet her gaze.

"What would you have done if you'd seen it, huh?" I panted. "I would have burned the chair and, fingers crossed, you."

"There's an extinguisher in the ceiling, directly above you." He motioned to it with the tip of his pen. "With the press of a button, I would have you doused."

"Maybe."

"Definitely." He tapped the pen against his chin. "I know. We'll see if the red fire makes an appearance when I intro-

duce more zombie toxin to your system." He set the note-book aside and held up another syringe, this one filled with black goo.

What? "No!" I struggled against the leather straps. They tore into my wrists and ankles—held steady. Blood dripped onto the chair, the floor.

Z.A. clapped. "You'll never be able to stop me now!"

"You'll kill me," I said, snubbing her, "and you won't learn anything new. Won't help your daughter."

Kelly shook his head. "I've done this to others, Miss Bell. I know what I can give, and what I can't, and still keep a person alive."

He didn't understand. The words rushed from me, desperate. "I'm different. Don't do this. Please, don't do this."

"Calm down. This is an engineered version of the toxin, made not to infect you permanently but to burn through you in about half an hour. You won't even need the anti-dote to improve."

"No, you don't understand. I—"

He stuck me with the needle.

ALL THE MONSTERS WANT TO PLAY

Many times, as a little girl, I'd looked at the home my father had built and considered it a prison. Only twice had I fought my forced incarceration, screaming and yelling at my parents about the unfairness of it all. Not just for me, but for Emma. She had no life, no friends.

And maybe that was why the two of us had been so close. We'd only ever had each other. We understood each other, because we'd been trapped in the same boat, in the middle of the same storm.

Then my dad had begun to train me in the art of self-defense, and I'd discovered I had a talent for it. It had given me something to do, something to think about, something to look forward to. But when it had come to the zombies, he hadn't known many tricks.

Those I'd learned from Cole. Under his tutelage, I'd

begun to feel confident, maybe, at times even undefeatable. But none of that training helped me now.

Though I struggled with all my might against the hold of the guards, they managed to drag me back to the cage.

HUNGRY!

NEED!

SOON!

MINE!

No longer whispering, the zombie thoughts now shouted through my mind—an echo of my own thoughts. I could smell the sweetest, purest perfume in the air...wafting from the guards, from Kat and Reeve, from Jaclyn.

Mmm...so good...

Z.A. had stepped back inside me, and I could feel her hunger. Why she hadn't attacked Kelly while she was out of my body, I didn't know. Unless she couldn't. She hadn't gone after Cole or Gavin, either. Maybe, as long as she was tethered to me, she was bound somewhat to my will.

"Stand at the back wall," one of the guards yelled. Kat and Reeve had rushed to the bars upon spotting me. "Now!"

The girls obeyed, probably desperate and willing to do anything to get to me, and the door was opened. I was thrust inside, the door slammed behind me. Strength had long since abandoned me, and I fell to my hands and knees.

The girls rushed to my side, the sweetness of their scents so strong I had to be drooling.

"Get away," I croaked. "You have to get away."

"Do what she says," I heard Jaclyn demand. "It's for your own good."

What would one taste hurt?

"What did they do to you?" Kat demanded.

"Oh, Ali," Reeve breathed.

"Now!" I crawled away from the girls and huddled in the far corner of the cell. I wrapped my arms around my middle, my entire body trembling from residual pain. From cold and weakness and fear and dread and hunger...oh, the hunger...

I banged my head into the brick. *Can't think about the girls. Can't think about how easy it would be to overpower them, to hold them down and work my teeth past skin and muscle and into—*

No! Can't think.

I banged harder, faster. So much harder. Black spots appeared behind my eyelids, and I smiled with my first wave of relief. The end of my torment was coming, sneaking in... would soon arrive... I sighed happily as I sank into blissful unconsciousness.

When I woke up, the world was, strangely enough, a much brighter place. I hadn't hurt my friends. I'd been at my worst, hunger-ravaged and desperate, but I'd kept to myself.

Some part of me—my love for Kat and Reeve, maybe— was stronger than Z.A.

I could do this, win this. I could fight and overcome.

This time, I actually believed it.

I put together a new to-do list. *Do whatever's necessary to escape with Kat, Reeve and Jaclyn. Come back with Cole and the other slayers. Destroy Anima—start with Kelly.*

To escape, I needed strength.

For strength, I needed food.

We were each given a small, dry sandwich and told to

392   GENA SHOWALTER

make it last—it was supposed to be our breakfast, lunch and dinner.

Amendment. *First convince someone to feed us.*

A little while later, I was escorted to Kelly's chamber of horrors and strapped to the chair, electrodes taped all over me.

Kelly sat beside me. "See. I told you the toxin wouldn't kill you." Grinning proudly, he patted my hand like Pops used to do. "Now, let's talk before we begin today's testing."

"Let's not. I'm too hungry."

He ignored me, saying, "We know where each of your friends lives, but what we don't know is if they possess any unusual abilities, like you. More specifically, I'd like to know if any of them are able to heal supernaturally fast."

"I'll trade answers for food." False answers.

His expression hardened. "I admire your spirit, Miss Bell, but it's going to get you into trouble. I told you I would do whatever was necessary to help my daughter and I meant it."

"Cheeseburger. Fries. Chocolate shake."

He stickered me with more electrodes, these attached to the funny-looking machine, and flipped a switch. Volts of electricity shot through me, sharp and hot and carnivorous. I opened my mouth to scream.

The pain stopped as swiftly as it had begun.

Desperately trying to suck oxygen into deflated lungs, I glared up at my tormentor.

"Now, I'm sorry I had to do that, but you brought it on yourself. Thankfully for you, I'm willing to try again. Do any of your friends possess the ability to heal supernaturally fast?"

"Pizza," I rasped.

Frowning, Kelly flipped the switch.

The pain lasted longer this time, my heart actually stopping in my chest before restarting on its own.

On and on we continued. He would ask a question about the slayers and their abilities, and I would name a food—if I could speak. I was pretty sure my brain had turned into a cherry Slushie.

"Pay attention, Miss Bell."

My head rolled in Kelly's direction. He thought to break me, and with my body, he was succeeding, but he was only strengthening my resolve.

"If you don't want to talk about the slayers right now, we won't, but we're not quite done with today's session. You see, I sent a man to capture you. He shot Halim Bendari, and someone else shot his driver. I haven't seen or heard from him since. Do you happen to know where he is?"

"Try looking...up your butt."

He popped his jaw—and flipped the switch.

The chair shook with the force of my shudders, the pain acute, gut-wrenching and soul-zapping. Kelly was going to kill me. How could he not? After a while, even my skin began to vibrate, and it didn't stop when he turned off the machine. My bones felt brittle, as if they would break at any second. My lungs had to be filled with glass rather than air. Every breath was agony.

I...came to as Kelly tapped my cheek. I must have passed out.

"That's enough for today," he said with a sigh. "We'll pick

this up again tomorrow. I hope you'll be in a more agree-
able mood."

I think he'd pushed me harder than he'd intended.

"Lasagna. Spaghetti. Garlic bread."

He scowled. "I don't want to do it, but I'll strap your
friend Kat to the table. I'll make you watch as I infect her.
Will you talk before I inject the first needle?"

Monster! I bared my teeth at him, wishing so badly I could
do more.

He smoothed the soaked hair from my forehead, knowing
he'd reached me on a level the machine hadn't. "Tomorrow
we'll have another chat. If you fail me as you've done today,
I'll use the already sick Katherine Parker."

He knew. He knew she was sick, and he was still going
to use her.

I was unable to support a single pound of my own weight
and had to be carted back to the cage. I wanted to assure Kat
and Reeve I was okay, but the moment the guards dumped
me on the floor, darkness swallowed me.

"—so sorry," a male was saying. I recognized his voice.
It made me angry. Angry enough to force myself out of my
deep sleep, the only thing preventing me from feeling the
pain still lingering in my body.

I blinked, looked through eyes glassy from the strain
they'd endured. Ethan stood at the bars of our cage, pleading with Reeve to forgive him for the part he'd played in
our capture.

The anger magnified, giving me strength. Snarling like
the very animal I might be becoming, I launched myself at

the bars. I reached for Ethan, intending to choke the life out of him—and laugh while doing it.

He reared backward, out of reach.

Two of the lab coats rushed toward him, to protect and shield him, most likely, but he held up his hand and they stopped, quickly returning to their stations. He tugged at the collar of his sweater, keeping enough distance between us to prevent a repeat of what had just happened.

"You did this," I shouted, surprised at the sound of my voice. I'd shouted, but only a whisper could be heard. "I'll kill you. I'll kill you so dead."

"Let me explain," he said, expression as tormented as his tone. "Please."

"Save your words. There's no explanation good enough."

His gaze slid to Reeve for a second, as if seeking some kind of softness. "The man who runs this place is my father. He's worked for Anima for two decades and was finally promoted to one of the top positions."

A family legacy. How sweet. "I'm going to cut out your eyes, stop you from ever doing this again! You were the one in the forest that night, spying on Trina and Lucas."

Ethan's head dropped. With shame? He nodded. "My dad and I can't afford failure, not if my sister is going to survive. So we wanted all the bases covered. That's why he sent me to Reeve and why I agreed. That's why he sent Justin to the slayers."

"You used me," Reeve said quietly. "And you expect me to forgive and forget?"

Reminded of her presence, I turned to her. I waited for the scent of her to hit me, to unnerve and obsess me, but

encountered only a soft waft of the expensive perfume probably embedded in her skin. The darker urges were at bay.

I squeezed her hand in reassurance, and she offered me a small smile of thanks.

"I didn't use you," Ethan said with a shake of his head. "I mean, at first, yes, I did, but even then I was attracted to you. The more time I spent with you, the harder I fell. You were never supposed to get hurt."

"With your dad, everyone is expendable," I said hotly. "You should have known that."

Ethan popped his jaw. Ignoring me, he said, "I love you, Reeve. I never lied about that."

She raised her chin, and I knew her stubborn side was about to kick in. "I never said those three little words back to you because I never felt the same. I still don't."

He closed his eyes, released a heavy breath. "I don't care. I think I love you enough for both of us. I won't let them do anything else to you."

"Like you'll be able to stop them. They're already starving us. And one day, when I've outgrown my use—" or died "—your dad will kill her and you know it." I knew I was scaring her, but I considered the results worth it. If Ethan feared for her life, he might aid in our escape. And with his aid, food was of little consequence. "She knows too much, has seen too much."

"No," he said, again shaking his head.

"Oh, yes."

"I'll talk to my father."

"And you'll believe whatever he says? You'll believe the

man who's already betrayed you and locked up the girl you love?"

Ethan's mouth opened and closed, and I knew he was searching for a response. When he found none, he turned on his heel and marched out of the laboratory.

"Good riddance," Kat muttered.

I turned and found her in the spot she'd occupied for the past several hours. Her skin was pale—too pale—and her body shaky. Her eyes were glazed, as if she were in tremendous pain.

"Kat," Reeve said, concerned.

"I look terrible, I know. I got myself a set of bad kidneys. Sorry I never told you."

"What?" Reeve rushed to her side.

"What can I do?" I asked.

"I'm okay," she assured me. "Really. I'm just so hungry I'm considering having Paula Deen tattooed on my stomach when this is all over. She makes these scallop sliders I'd stab my dad to have."

She needed dialysis, like, now, and I knew it. From this point on, she was only going to get worse. And with kidneys, there was no recovering from the damage. I'd checked.

"This is my fault," Reeve said with a trembling chin. "I never should have trusted Ethan."

"We all made mistakes," Kat said, and with a confident smile added, "But Frosty will come. He'll save the day. He won't let anything happen to me. Or us. Mostly me."

Reeve played along, saying, "Maybe he'll bring Bronx and I can beg for his forgiveness."

"Beg while naked," Kat suggested. "He'll agree to anything then."

I patted Kat's hand. It was limp, cold. I couldn't wait for Ethan to grow a conscience or a pair of balls. Couldn't wait for the boys to find us, or food to strengthen me. I had to act now.

How?

I moved to Jaclyn's side of the cage and studied the lab, searching for things I might have missed. Anyone coming or going had to flash an ID badge over the box on the door. There was a glass case on the far wall with several tranq guns inside. I'd seen the lab coats use those weapons on the collared zombies.

The guards had the keys to the cells. Maybe the lab coats did, maybe they didn't, but I couldn't see evidence either way. The guards were the sure thing.

I needed to steal a key the next time they came for me.

"What are you thinking?" Jaclyn asked.

"Probably the same thing you are."

"Yeah. Blueberry pancakes would be awesome."

I almost grinned. "No. I'm thinking it's time to go."

We both looked at Kat. She yawned and rested her head on Reeve's shoulder.

"She shouldn't be this bad this quickly," Jaclyn whispered, unable to mask her worry.

"It's the stress of the situation," I replied. "It's making everything worse."

"I can hear you, you know," Kat said. Then, "What are we going to do?"

"Let me worry about that." I held Jaclyn's stare until she nodded.

"I wish there was something I could do," she said, "but they don't even open my cage anymore. I could try, but they're used to me, expect my tricks and just ignore me, whatever I say."

I motioned Reeve over.

She eased Kat's head to the floor and closed the distance. I put my mouth to her ear and whispered, "When the guards come for me, and they will, I want you to attack one. He might hit you, and I'm sorry for that, because it's going to hurt, but I need him out of the way for just a few seconds. Can you do it? Can you remember what Veronica taught you?"

She gave a determined nod.

"Enough of that, you two," a hard voice snapped. A stick was rubbed against the bars.

I looked over. One of the guards stood at the door of our cage.

"We're hungry and thirsty," I spat at him. "Why don't you reduce the number of crimes you've committed against us and fix that?"

He looked us over, lingering a bit too long on Reeve, before pivoting on his booted heel. "Get them something to eat and drink," he commanded one of the lab coats. "Now."

We were each given a bag of peanut butter crackers and a bottle of water, even Jaclyn.

As hungry as I was, it was like a four-star meal. How sad was that?

"Protein isn't good for me right now," Kat mumbled. "Makes my kidneys have to work too hard."

"We'll scrape off the peanut better and you can eat the crackers," I replied, "because you're eating *something*." Words Cole had once spoken to me. I got it now.

Kat and Reeve fell asleep soon after they'd eaten, and I paced the cell, watching the clock. As the day wore on, the labs coats thinned out, just as before. By 2:00 a.m., there were only two people left in the lab. Again, just as before. By six, the others returned. Hello, pattern.

I'd have a four-hour window to act.

I wondered how many guards were stationed at the monitors at 2:00 a.m. One or two I could take. Any more than that, and I'd have big-time problems.

I'd have to risk it. Tonight.

Tomorrow, Kelly would try to use Kat against me.

The guards returned for me at 10:00 a.m.

"You two," said the one who—pressed his thumb into a keypad. *Crap!* No actual key to steal. "Get against the back wall." His attention moved to me. "You, stand in the middle."

"Forget my plan," I whispered to Reeve, and she blinked with surprise.

Her eyes were wide, her body quivering as I was cuffed and led out of the cell. I knew she wanted to help me in some way, any way, but I couldn't cut off the guy's thumb, so there wasn't anything to do.

I was escorted into the torture chamber. Kelly was already there, sitting, waiting for me.

"How are you feeling?" he asked.

"Gotta admit I've had better days." As I looked him over, another plan took shape. It was dangerous. It was stupid. But there was no other way.

"I'm sure you have," he said, and nodded to the guards.

Have to act now. The moment I was uncuffed, I lunged for Kelly, purposely slamming my body into the cart of syringes and scalpels along the way.

We hit the floor, and I grabbed the first thing my fingers found and shoved it into his neck. As the guards scrambled to catch me, I grabbed the second thing my fingers found and shoved it into my pocket.

Everything happened in two, maybe three seconds.

A hard fist slammed into my temple, throwing my body to the side. Stars. Pain. A heavy weight crashed into me, forcing me to my stomach. My arms were roughly twisted behind my back and the cuffs reapplied.

"Get her...out of here..." Kelly gasped.

As I was hauled to my feet, I watched him sit up and pull a syringe out of his neck. Only a syringe. Too bad.

The guard shoved me forward, and I tripped my way back to the cage. Once inside, I did the same thing I'd done yesterday. I threw myself into the far corner, hiding my face—and my actions. As stealthily as possible, I reached into my pocket. Felt...a scalpel.

Perfect.

Whatever's necessary.

Reeve approached, placed a soft hand on my shoulder. "Are you okay? Your hand is bleeding."

I looked down and realized the scalpel had sliced through my palm. My adrenaline must be riding high, because I

didn't feel it. "I'll take care of it." My shirt was already torn and easy to rip with my teeth. I tied a strip of material around the wound, applying pressure.

"Get some rest," I told her. For what came next, she was going to need it.

As I paced the cage, watching the clock yet again, waiting, waiting, I felt as if my sanity…my emotions…my *everything* hung at the end of a horribly frayed rope. Any second the threads would snap, and I would fall, crack open and all the darkness inside me would spill out.

Death and destruction would ensue.

No one would be safe.

I just… I had to hold it together for Kat, Reeve and Jaclyn.

Fatigue rode me harder than ever, but I forced myself to look past the burning eyes, the quivering limbs and the aches and pangs. I could sleep when the girls were safe.

Finally 2:00 a.m. arrived. The moment of truth.

All but one lab coat had left. The straggler was a heavyset man around forty years old. I could take him in a fight, no problem. The only unknown was how many guards were monitoring the camera feeds.

Actually, no, that wasn't true. I also didn't know how many people were in the building. Or how many security clearances I'd have to go through to reach the front doors.

That wasn't going to stop me. *Whatever's necessary.*

I glanced back at the girls. Kat was asleep, though not at rest. Her eyes rolled behind her lids, and violent shivers racked her body.

Though Reeve was awake and watching me, she lay behind Kat, arms curled around her, offering warmth.

Jaclyn sat at the edge of her cot.

Now, I mouthed, then faced Lab Coat.

"Let us out," I shrieked, the sound startling the guy enough that he actually glanced over at me. I rattled the bars with every bit of my strength. "My friend needs help. Where's your heart? How can you leave us like this? To starve? To face torture?"

The shrillness of my voice awakened the zombies. Moans and groans erupted all around me.

Hungry.

Eat. Must eat.

Lab Coat pushed to his feet and stomped from the room. If he failed to bring back a guard…

The side door opened, and Lab Coat stalked inside with a tired-looking guard at his side.

I did my best to hide my relief.

Frowning, the guard pointed a finger at me. "Be quiet," he barked.

Smells so good.

Him. Want him.

Must eat…drain…empty…

Zombie thoughts…or Z.A.'s?

"I'm through being quiet," I shouted. *Bang, bang, bang.* I punched at the bars, unconcerned by the sting in my already sore hands. "I'll never be quiet again. You'll have to make me."

Reeve rushed to my side, her voice harmonizing with mine. "We want out. Let us out. Let us out."

I laughed, but it wasn't a nice sound. "So brave out there, aren't you?" I taunted the guard. "Doubt you'd be so confident in here. I could take you down in seconds."

"This is your last chance to be quiet," he snarled, hand curling around the stick hanging at his waist. Then his gaze landed on Reeve and narrowed. He licked his lips. "But please, do me a favor and refuse it. I'll come in there and show you just how brave I can be."

"Let us out. Let us out." Reeve.

"Coward!" Me.

Grinning a terrible grin, he pressed his thumb against the lock. When he pulled the door open, I shoved Reeve behind me and backed her toward Kat, who had woken up and now leaned against the far wall. All the while, I gripped the scalpel I'd stolen, the blade hidden by my arm.

He stomped toward us, his eagerness to get his hands on Reeve making him stupid. He grabbed me, probably intending to toss me to the side, but I struck without hesitation, stabbing him in the neck.

Howling, eyes going wide, he stumbled away from me. His knees buckled before he could exit the cage, and he went down. Blood gushed from the wound, leaking through his knuckles as he applied pressure.

Whatever's necessary, remember?

"Scalpel," Jaclyn shouted, jerking me out of the daze.

I tossed it to her, wondering why she needed it, then rushed out of the cage, closing in on Lab Coat. He remained on his feet, as if frozen.

"Don't hurt me," he pleaded.

"Like you didn't hurt me?" I punched him in the throat

with a blood-covered hand, and he, too, went down. I tore the badge from around his neck before stalking to the glass case where the tranq guns were stored.

In the hallway, an alarm erupted, screeching through the airways. *Dang it.* There was at least one more guard.

"Get Kat and get out of here," I instructed Reeve, and pounded my fist into the glass. "I'll get Jaclyn."

Shards rained to the floor; my knuckles stung and bled. I grabbed the gun as the side door burst open, a single guard rushing through. Just before he reached me, I managed to turn and squeeze the trigger. He fell—right on top of me.

Struggling to breathe, I wiggled out from under him and turned to finish off Lab Coat, only to realize he'd already regained his bearings, found another badge to use on the door and rushed out of the room.

"Ali." In the cage, Reeve was struggling to hold up Kat. I pocketed as many tranq darts as I could hold and rushed over to help, passing Jaclyn along the way.

She'd freed herself.

I looked around and computed how. The guard's arm had been close enough for her to reach through the bars, and she had removed his thumb with the scalpel. *We think alike.* Then she'd used what she'd taken to unlock the door.

The guard had stopped writhing, was motionless in a pool of his own blood. Unblinking eyes stared off in the distance.

I'd taken a life.

WHATEVER'S NECESSARY.

A sob escaped me, a testament to the still-fraying rope holding back my emotions. It wouldn't last much longer now.

Shaking, I removed his badge and handed it to Reeve, just in case we were separated.

"Got another tranq gun." Jaclyn came up beside me and gently removed Kat from my hold, wrapping her arm around the girl's waist to remove half the burden from Reeve.

"You're strongest. You lead the way."

"I'm just going to slow you guys down," Kat panted. "Leave me here and come back for me later."

"Don't be ridiculous," I said. "I'd rather stay here than leave without you."

"Seriously, Ally Kat," Jaclyn said. "Shut it."

"Now follow me."

I used Lab Coat's badge to open the door to the hallway. We entered a long, narrow passage I was relieved to find empty. Maybe I'd disabled the only guards. *Please, please.*

"Where should we go?" Reeve asked, her voice strained.

I ripped the emergency exit map from the wall, considered the corridors and said, "This way."

Down the hall. Around a corner. Another hall, another corner. In the stairwell, our breathing and footsteps echoed off the walls. But those were the only sounds. No one was following us. Others would be here soon, though. I was certain the alarm had already been reported to Kelly, wherever he was.

Kat's head lolled to the side as the girls carried her down, down, down the steps. As fatigued as I was, as undernourished, as wounded, my trembling seemed to magnify with every new inch of ground I gained.

Finally we reached the end of the well, and I used the key card to open the door.

"—remote camera show they entered the stairwell." Kelly's voice rose above a symphony of pounding footsteps.

Dang it! How had he gotten here so quickly?

Jaclyn and I shared a look of absolute, utter panic.

"I want you six to comb every inch of it. And I want a man posted on every floor. We're dealing with four half-starved teenage girls. You should have no trouble finding and subduing them."

As yet unnoticed, we dragged Kat to the side of the now-abandoned security desk.

Perfect timing. A group of men whisked past us. Six entered the door we'd just left, and one muttered, "We aren't paid enough for this." Some entered the elevators. They were all dressed haphazardly, as if they'd been roused from sleep and had had to hurry. There must be a facility close by. Like army barracks, maybe. We'd have to be careful to avoid it.

I gazed longingly at the wall of glass doors leading outside.

"You two," Kelly said as he entered the elevator, "wait here." There was a white bandage wrapped around his neck. He was pale, almost as shaky as I was. "Call me if they make it this far."

The doors closed on him.

The two men he'd left behind assumed their positions, forcing us to inch our way around the desk to continue to hide our presence. I sat for a moment, trying to decide on our next move.

There was only one thing to do, really.

"Wait here," I whispered, and crawled to the end of the desk. I peeked around the edge, noting the exact positions

of the guards. Then I set a dart beside my thigh, readied my gun, aimed.

Deep breath in…hold…ouuut…I squeezed the trigger.

There was a gasp, a rustle of clothing—then a heavy thump. The first guard had just gone down.

Yes!

"What's wrong?" the other asked, racing to his side.

He saw the dart in the man's thigh, frowned and glanced up.

Before I could finish loading the gun for round two, he was placing a walkie-talkie at his mouth.

"Mr. K, I found—"

I fired.

His knees buckled, and he went silent.

"Found what?" Kelly demanded over the walkie-talkie.

So close! "Come on," I said, and Jaclyn and Reeve tugged Kat to her feet.

Together, we rushed forward. We stepped on the guards, too tired to leap over them, and shoved our way past the glass doors. Frigid air enveloped us, worse because we were without coats, hats and gloves. We wore only T-shirts and jeans.

Since our captivity, the snow had continued to fall, and there were now several inches covering the sidewalk and parking lot. Kat wouldn't last long. "Hang on," I said, going back inside the building, meaning to take a coat from one of the guards. But pulling the garment off a deadweight proved to be too much for me. *Failure!*

Plop.

A cell phone had just fallen out of one of the pockets. *Silver lining.* I picked it up and rushed outside. With Kat tucked

between us, Reeve and I angled away from the lamps in the parking lot and toward the darkness of the landscape.

A treacherous-looking hill loomed ahead. It was covered in ice, but there were also trees. We could hide there. Maybe we'd freeze to death. Maybe we wouldn't. I didn't care anymore, as long as we were out of Kelly's clutches.

As we ran, I dialed Cole's number. Or rather, I tried to. The motion—on top of my trembling—caused me to misdial. *Come on, come on. You can do this.* I tried again, succeeded.

He answered on the third ring, demanding harshly, "Who is this?"

"Cole," I panted.

"Ali!"

"That's Ali?" I heard Frosty say in the background. "Ask her about Kat."

"Ask her about Reeve," Bronx rushed out.

"Help us," I interjected. "Have to...help us."

"We are, sweetheart," Cole said, and I heard the worry in his voice. "We are. We finally tracked your location, and we're almost there. Hang on just a little longer."

"Escaped building...headed for...hill. Kat, medical attention. Kelly...after us. Cold. Jaclyn...alive."

"Faster," he commanded whoever was driving. "We're two minutes away, baby. Just hang on," he repeated.

"Miss Bell," Kelly suddenly called out, and in my panic, I dropped the phone. "I know you're out here."

Reeve gasped.

Jaclyn growled.

Forget the phone. I picked up the pace, soon bypassing the

first line of trees. Wind gusted, and, I thought, sliced at my skin. Two minutes. I could outwit my enemy for two minutes. Actually, one minute, forty-five seconds now.

We settled Kat against the tree trunk.

I whispered, "Guard them," to Jaclyn. To Reeve, "Keep Kat warm."

"Where are you going?" Reeve wrapped herself around Kat, offering what heat she could. "What are you going to do?" Terror glazed her moon-darkened features.

"Let her do what needs doing, and ask questions later," Jaclyn said, already in position, gaze scanning. She would shoot anyone who approached, without hesitation.

I squeezed Reeve's hand and tiptoed away without another word. When I reached the edge of the forest, I pressed against another trunk, peering out at the building. Lights spilled from the windows, illuminating the area around it. Kelly stood just outside the doors, his hands on his hips, his breath misting in front of his face every time he exhaled.

Just how far would the tranq gun shoot?

Just how good was my aim?

While staying at the cabin, I'd continued my training. Nowadays, I hit more than I missed, as proven by the guards in the lobby. But just then, I was shaking so badly I couldn't hold the gun steady.

Gotta try. I set the scalpel in front of me on a rock, just in case, and stretched out flat on my belly, my elbow beside the blade. No matter what I tried, however, my hand couldn't be steadied.

A crunch of snow at my left. Instinct kicked in, and I had the scalpel palmed and thrown in the next second. A man

fell to the ground, gasping for breath, the blade sticking out of his throat.

How many other guards were already out here?

In the distance, I heard a crash. Metal against metal. A second later, a Jeep skidded into the lot, the tires locked. The moment it stopped, Cole, Justin, Frosty and Bronx hopped out.

A second vehicle arrived, and out came Trina, Gavin, Veronica and Lucas.

A third vehicle pulled in, and out came Mr. Ankh, Mr. Holland and the rest of the slayers.

I wanted to… Was about to have… *Hold it together. Just a little longer.* They were here. They were here, and the girls would be saved, and all of the pain and suffering would have been worth it, and oh, glory, I was crying, the tears hazing my eyesight and freezing on my cheeks.

"Where are they?" Mr. Holland demanded.

Every slayer unsheathed a gun and aimed at Kelly.

Every guard around him unsheathed a gun and aimed at the slayers.

Kelly's hands fisted. "I don't know what you're talking about. I do, however, know that this is private property and you were not invited. Leave, before I'm forced to take measures you won't appreciate."

"We know they're here," Cole growled. "Ali!"

"You're surrounded," Kelly gritted out. "Are you sure you want to go this route?"

"Are you sure that you do?" Mr. Ankh said, as calm as ever. "I'm sure a dozen dead bodies in your parking lot would be too difficult for even you to explain away or hide."

"We want the girls," Cole spat. "Now."

"Here," I called. "We're here."

Kelly stiffened.

Frosty and Bronx followed the echo of my voice. They reached me in seconds.

"Where's Kat?" Frosty demanded.

"Back here," Reeve called, and I knew she was doing her best to sound brave and unaffected.

"Jaclyn, lower the weapon," I said.

"Jaclyn?" Justin took off in a run.

Frosty and Bronx, too. It wasn't long before Frosty was carrying Kat, Bronx was carrying Reeve and Justin was carrying Jaclyn. I think every one of them was crying. I forced myself to stand, to inch forward, toward the slayers.

Cole kept his gun trained on Kelly, his finger twitching over the trigger. He wanted to kill the man. Like, bad. I saw it in the posture of his body. Felt it in the rage radiating from him.

"I know you hate the man and want him dead for taking Ali, but you need to go get your girl," Gavin said, wrapping his fingers around the barrel of the gun. "Or I will."

Cole cursed under his breath but relinquished the weapon without tapping the trigger; he rushed to my side. His gaze swept over me, and his expression hardened. He swept me up in his arms, and I could only rest my head on his shoulder.

"I've got you, sweetheart," he whispered, "and I'm not ever letting you go again."

My chin trembled, a fresh round of tears threatening to fall.

"Go ahead, take them," Kelly said, his body trembling

with rage of his own. "You'll find no evidence that they were ever here. In fact, I should call the authorities and let them know four teenage girls were sneaking around the premises."

"Shoot him," I said, my voice weak, strained.

Of course, no one obeyed. They'd begun to back up, heading for the cars. Well, sorry, but I couldn't let Kelly walk away unscathed, no matter how noble he considered his cause. I had to do something. Now, while I had the chance.

With Cole's body heat surrounding me, some of my tremors waned. So, with my last burst of energy, I lifted the tranq gun and squeezed the trigger.

A dart sank into Kelly's cheek.

I'd aimed for his eye. Oh, well.

His knees buckled and he went down.

Some of the guards rushed to him. The others cocked their weapons, ready to retaliate. I was shoved into a car as shots rang out, Cole using his body as a shelter.

"Sorry," I mumbled. "Couldn't resist."

"Don't be sorry. Ali, I don't know what I would have done… I couldn't stand…" His arms tightened around me, squeezing me. "You have to tell me what happened in there."

"Not now," I said, even the thought threatening to immobilize me. "Please."

"Okay. All right. But soon."

"Soon," I promised.

The first two days back at Mr. Ankh's, I slept, my body doing its best to recover from the abuse it had suffered—but its best wasn't quite good enough. My strength continued

to diminish. I was vaguely aware of Nana coming to see me and clutching my hand, Emma pacing beside my bed and Mr. Ankh checking my vitals.

Where was Cole?

It wasn't until the third day that I discovered he'd been sleeping in a chair in the corner of my room the entire time. I woke up crying and couldn't stop. I cried until my tear ducts dried from overuse, and he rushed over, gathering me in his arms, whispering the sweetest words into my ear.

I missed you so much.

I tore the world apart looking for you. I wasn't going to stop until I had you back.

You are so special to me. I need you.

I clung to him as if he were my only lifeline.

Just then, he was.

He told me Kat and Reeve were on the mend. That he knew Reeve had been the unwitting spy, and because of her, Ethan. He'd told the slayers everything that had been going on; they were eager to see me, he said.

"How is Jaclyn?" I asked.

"She's at home with Justin, and he says she's healing physically but not mentally. She refuses to leave the house."

"They were terrible to her," I said with a shudder.

"The were terrible to you, too. To all of you. Will you tell me now?"

"Tomorrow," I whispered, not wanting the taint of dark memories to intrude upon this moment.

Then tomorrow came. My fourth day back. Mr. Ankh and Mr. Holland strode into the room, asked for details, and I told them everything I'd learned…and suffered. Cole

held me then, too, and I was glad. Though he stiffened and cursed, he remained tender with me, sifting his fingers through my hair, whispering how brave I was when I thought I'd have another breakdown, telling me how sorry he was.

The adults were pale by the time I finished.

"Well," Mr. Ankh said, then cleared his throat. Were his eyes gleaming with tears? "I'm sorry for everything you endured, Miss Bell."

I nodded to let him know I'd heard him.

"But I'm afraid you're not in the clear yet," he added. "The antizombie toxin in your blood is higher than ever. We gave you more antidote, and it helped...for a while. You burned through it so quickly I believe you're already developing an immunity to it. You'll be able to use it another few weeks, is my guess, but not much more than that."

So little time.

I gulped.

When the adults left the room, Cole parted my hair and held on to the pigtails he'd created, peering into my eyes. "Kelly isn't going to get away with this. You have my word."

He was so beautiful. So fierce. "Cole."

"No, don't say anything. You're still recovering, and I want you focused on that. I just... I want to show you something." He rolled to his back, leaving me on my side, and lifted the hem of his T-shirt to reveal the entire expanse of his muscled chest.

His tattoos were—*oh, glory.*

In big, bold letters, my name had been added among his plethora of tattoos.

ALI BELL arched from one nipple to the other, the pierced one, taking up far more real estate than any other.

"Cole," I repeated with a tremor.

"I wanted to give you more than words. I wanted to *show* you that you're it for me, that there is no one else, that there will never be anyone else. I don't care what happens. I don't care what the visions tell us. I just want you."

No boy had ever made such a finite gesture for me. No boy had ever looked at me like this one did, as if I were the most important part of his life. As if he couldn't *not* look at me. "I love you," I whispered, my heavy eyelids drifting closed and my mind falling into a pool of black.

I think I was smiling.

My fifth day back, Cole moved me into Reeve's suite. With both Mr. Ankh's and Mr. Parker's permission, Kat had moved in as well, and the two girls had been asking for me—needing me. An unbreakable bond had formed inside that cell, one that would last as long as we lived.

The men in our lives weren't willing to upset us, so, regardless of the danger I still presented, three twin beds now dominated the sleeping area.

But...

On the sixth day, I began to feel Z.A. stirring. She was angry. Hungry. Determined. I fought her with all that I was, doing my best to keep her on a tight leash, and it cost me. What little strength I'd won, I lost again, confining me to the bed.

Reeve recovered from the trauma first, and that was when her father pounced.

He strode into the room, sat at her bedside and held her

hand. Uncaring about his audience, he said, "I'm going to talk, and you're going to listen without saying a word until I'm done." He waited for her to nod before he continued. "I want to send you abroad. I never wanted you to know what was going on here, didn't want you to live your life in fear and danger—"

"I'm not going anywhere," she interjected. "And are you trying to tell me the zombie problem is isolated to this area?"

"No, it's not," he gritted out. "But I don't want you around the people who fight in the war. They're targets. Magnets. If you're here, you'll cave and hang out with them. Then, as you see the injuries they receive, you'll start to fear and stop living your life."

"I've seen the injuries, and I'm not afraid. I'm ready and willing to help. Those guys carry a huge burden, and I need to step up and take on my share."

I lay on my side, and Kat, who had the middle bed, lay on hers. We peered at each other, remaining quiet, listening to the conversation over the beeps and hums of medical equipment.

"What can you do?" Mr. Ankh demanded. "You can't see the monsters."

"Neither can you, and yet you manage just fine."

"I'm a doctor."

"And I'm a healthy girl with two arms and two legs, capable of taking orders to assist the doctor tending to the slayers."

He shook his head. "The zombies could bite you."

"And I could be given the antidote," she sniped. "Look, Dad. I'm going to help the cause whether I do it here or somewhere else. That's not something you can stop. I caused

the mess we're currently in. Me. And I want to make amends. I *need* to make amends."

"No, you—"

"Dad," she insisted. "We both know the truth. I've been spying on everyone, trying to figure out what's going on and why the people I love, the people who profess to love me, kept lying to me. In my quest for answers, Ethan was able to encourage me and teach me how to be a better spy. I told him everything I learned. *I caused this.*"

His shoulders drooped, and he scrubbed a hand down his face.

I yawned, my eyelids growing heavy.

"If you want to stay, stay," he said softly. "If you want to help, help. But you will not go near that boy." There at the end, his tone had hardened. "Do you understand me?"

Reeve scowled at him. "He has a name."

"Bronx," the doctor gritted. "You'll not go near him."

"Why? Why do you hate him so much?"

"I don't hate him. I just hate the thought of you with him. He's too…rough for you, honey. You haven't read his file, and you don't know his past or the trouble he's been in, the things he's done or the things he'll do."

Her smile was sad. "And I don't care. I know the boy he is now, and that's all that matters to me."

"Reeve—"

"No! I'm not Mom. I didn't understand her breakdowns before, or what they did to you, but I do now. I get it. But you don't get to control this part of my life. And if you try to punish him and the slayers because I want to be with him, then you will lose me. I will move out. And who do you think will be there to take me in?"

I gave another yawn, this one nearly cracking my jaw. My eyelids drifted closed, and the rest of the conversation faded from my awareness.

Not over… Will try again… You're not going to win… Z.A.'s voice filled my head, oozing past the barriers I'd managed to build.

I wanted to reply, but there was a strange fog in my head, muddying up my words.

"—still sleeping," Kat said.

"Yes," Cole said. "She sleeps all the time."

I tried to open my eyes but couldn't quite manage it.

"I'm worried about her." Kat said. "I've never seen her look so…fragile."

Were they talking about me?

"She'll recover," Nana said. "I'm not going to lose her."

Nana was here, too?

If Cole replied, I missed it.

I wasn't sure how much time passed before I felt warm fingers brush through my hair. At last the fog dissipated. I pried open my eyes as sparks of energy bloomed. Nana was gone, I realized. Kat and Reeve were asleep. Cole was next to me, his eyes closed. He absently stroked my scalp.

I smiled. I needed more of this, more of him.

I thought about the journal. The answer. Light. Fire. Clearly, he was a light to me. Just as clear, I burned for him. But there was more, something I was missing.

To-do: *figure it out, and fast.* Time was running out.

"—I've always known," Frosty was saying to Kat.

My eyelids fluttered open, and I realized two things at

once. I'd fallen asleep while Cole stroked me, and morning had arrived.

Frosty sat beside Kat's bed, holding her hand. Her other had tubes sticking out of it—tubes attached to a dialysis machine.

Her eyes widened with shock. "You have?"

"Well, yeah. Kitty Kat, I'm, like, a master black ops agent man, and not just when it comes to Call of Duty. To hang around you, and to let you hang around my friends, I had to know all about you. I never said anything about your illness because I wanted you to trust me enough to admit the truth on your own."

Oh, wow. He'd always known.

"Well, that didn't stop you from asking a bazillion questions about what I was doing each day," she grumbled.

"I was giving you the opportunity to come clean," he said with an unrepentant grin.

"It was entrapment, you turd, plain and simple. I should be furious with you."

He arched a brow. "Should?"

She sighed. "For some reason, I've never found you sexier. And you know I have trouble staying mad at anything sexy."

He barked out a laugh, but sobered only a few seconds later. His gaze pierced her, intense and demanding. "I want you healed, Kat. I want you around, tormenting me, forever."

"I want that, too," she whispered. "More than anything. And I'm sorry I've broken up with you so much. I just didn't want you to see me while I was sick. I didn't want your sym-

pathy or pity, or worse, you staying with me because you felt obligated."

"You have nothing to be sorry for. You made me chase you, and I loved it. And I stayed with you because I love you, no other reason."

My heart constricted. I shouldn't be listening to this. It was private. A moment of vulnerability and longing I wasn't meant to share. I rolled to my other side, giving the pair as much privacy as possible, and came face-to-face with Cole.

He was watching me.

"You look better," he said.

"You're still here," I replied. I wasn't sure why I was surprised.

"Of course I am. There's nowhere I'd rather be."

My heart leaped into my threat. "Cole," I breathed. "Thank you for coming to find me. Thank you for everything."

He nodded, but a hard gleam appeared in his eyes. "I dropped your grandmother off, checked in with my dad and went back to the cabin. You weren't there, but your tracks were outside. Then I got your message. I think I was an hour and a half behind you, and by then it was too late. And *I'm* sorry for that. No," he added when I opened my mouth to respond. "You don't get to tell me I have no reason to feel guilty. I love you, and I'll feel guilty if I want."

He'd once told me he was coming after me with everything he had. This. This was all I needed.

Though I tried, I couldn't find the strength to lift my arms and hug him. All I could do was lean forward and press my forehead against his chest. His heart beat fast but steady.

"How did you track us?" I asked.

"Justin had the address for several Anima facilities in the area. I nearly shouted my house down trying to get your sister's attention. She showed up, I gave her the addresses and she was better than a camera."

"But she couldn't get into the building to see us. There was a block."

"Yeah, but she could see and hear everyone who entered and left. You were mentioned."

Oh. Thank you, sweet sister.

He kissed my temple. "Will you tell me what I want to hear now? Without falling asleep on me while you're doing it?"

"Totally. But what do you want to hear?"

Two of his fingers gently pinched my chin and lifted my head until my gaze locked on his. He searched me for a long while, silent, before grinning wryly. "Never mind. I'll wait."

"For what?"

"You." He tucked my head against his chest—against the final *L* in my last name—breaking eye contact. Toying with the ends of my hair, he said, "I know you like to ask a thousand questions. Is there anything you're dying to know about what's been happening around here?"

I was confused by the exchange—seriously, what did he want me to say?—yet caught up in the seduction of him. Everything about him lulled me into a deep sense of relaxation. "Do you know where Nana is?"

"Earlier she was walking by, heard you talking in your sleep and decided to spend the rest of the night by your side, just in case you needed her. I came in a few hours ago. I'd

left to shower, and sent her to her old room to rest. She refused to go until I promised to call her when you woke up."

Darling Nana. She'd seen so much death lately. "I want to kill Zombie Ali *so* bad."

"Urges?"

I knew what he was asking. "I can feel them, the desires to attack and feed, waiting at the edges of my conscious. I need more light."

"Yes. That's what the journal says."

Surprised, I said, "You were you able to read it?"

"I was. I sat with that thing for hours, getting nowhere, thinking about the numbers and the symbols, about what they could mean, rolling them around in my head, and finally, all of a sudden, the words began to clear. I was so startled I looked around to make sure I wasn't dreaming and caught a glimpse of my reflection. My eyes were silver."

"Silver?"

"Yeah. Like mirrors."

Mirrors. Interesting. "If eyes are the windows to the soul, I guess they can be mirrors, too." I paused. "What was the catalyst, do you think?"

"Maybe my utter absorption with it. We are what we eat, right? My brain was definitely eating that journal."

"What were you able to read?"

"A passage about some slayers having gifts others do not, like the visions, and your ability to see the Blood Lines."

Yes, I'd read that part, too.

"Then there was a section about dying to really live, and the fact that you need fire to burn the toxin out of you." He arms tightened around me. "I know you tried that on

yourself, but I'm thinking your fire was already compromised. Either that or Zombie Ali is as immune to your fire and toxin as you're becoming to the antidote."

That one, I thought. That second one. That was the answer. "I wonder what will happen if you use *your* fire on me."

"I've thought about that, and I'm not willing to risk it. What if it kills you? Ashes you? I would never forgive myself."

What if Z.A. died, and I lived? "Just...don't take it off the table, okay?"

He sighed. "All right, but it'll be a last resort. It's risky, and I'm not happy with the idea of risking you."

"Great risk comes with great reward."

"Yo, Muhammad *Ali,*" a female voice said before he could reply.

I peeked up from my position against Cole's chest and watched as Trina, Mackenzie and Lucas approached the side of my bed.

Trina said, "You got yourself and three wimps out of Anima. I'm not sure I've ever been prouder of you."

"Hey," Kat huffed.

"Yeah! Who are you calling a wimp?" Reeve demanded.

"I believe she was talking about you," Bronx said.

He was here? I looked over and found him seated beside Reeve's bed, and the two were...oh, glory...the two were holding hands. Openly. Unashamedly.

Happily.

Mr. Ankh must have relented.

"Ali Bell doesn't play hide-and-seek," Lucas said. "She plays hide-and-pray-I-don't-find-you."

Mackenzie smiled. "When Ali Bell gives you the finger, she's telling you how many seconds you have to live."

Cole chuckled, saying, "Fear of spiders is arachnophobia, and fear of tight spaces is claustrophobia, but fear of Ali Bell is just called logic."

"Oh, oh." Kat clapped excitedly. "There used to be a street named after Ali Bell, but it was changed because nobody crosses Ali Bell and lives. True story."

I snorted.

"I heard Ali Bell once got bitten by a rattlesnake," Lucas said, deadpan, "but after three days of pain and agony, the rattlesnake died."

"Well, I heard that when Ali Bell wants to laugh," Reeve exclaimed, "she reads the *Guinness Book of World Records*."

Giggles spilled out of me, but they quickly turned to coughs. I wasn't sure how many minutes passed before the hacking stopped. I only knew I'd spewed blood all over my hands. *Awkward*.

"Ankh told me this might happen," Cole said. "The zombie toxin and the antizombie toxin you produce are going head-to-head."

Trina tossed me a rag.

"Thanks." As Cole cleaned me up, he kicked her, Mackenzie and Lucas out of the room. "You, too," he said to Frosty and Bronx.

"Sorry, bro," Frosty replied, sounding anything but apologetic. "I'm not leaving Kat."

Bronx gave him the finger. "And yes, I'm telling you how long you've got to live if you try and make me go."

Cole opened his mouth to protest. I knew he wanted to

limit the scope of my embarrassment, and I fell a little deeper under his spell.

"They can stay," I said. How could I deprive my friends of their boyfriends? I'd hate anyone who tried to take mine away.

Cole rested his chin on the top of my head, petted my hair. "Okay. For you."

Bronx leaned forward in his seat and buried his face in his hands. "I don't think I'll ever leave your side again. You were so close to death, Reeve, and there was nothing I would have been able to do to stop it from happening."

Reeve traced her fingers over the shell of his ear. "I survived. We all survived."

The way he looked up and stared at her caused the air in the room to crackle with awareness.

It was the same stare Cole often gave me. Needy. Confused. Resolute. A little savage.

"We have to bring Anima down," Cole said, determined and cold. "We can't allow such a threat to remain."

"What are we going to do?" I asked.

A pause as the three boys shared a look fraught with promise.

"Go to war," Cole said.

BLOOD BATH AND BEYOND

The boys lived up to their promise.

A few days later, after I'd gotten caught up on my school-work, a grinning Cole strode into the bedroom. It was Tuesday afternoon, and Kat and Reeve were in class. Nana was downstairs making cookies.

She hadn't wanted to leave my side, but she'd started to cry every time she'd looked at me, and her worry had pricked at the darkness writhing and frothing at the back of my mind, banging at the barely standing barriers.

I'd told her I had a craving for something sweet.

Cole leaned down and kissed my forehead, his lips soft and perfect. I wished I'd had the energy to fix my hair and slap on a thousand pounds of makeup.

Maybe it was a good thing all the mirrors had been removed from the room.

"You should be at school," I said.

His grin only widened. "School shmool. I've got a surprise for you." He swept me into his arms and carried me through the house...then down the stairs and into the basement.

I sniffed, expecting to smell rot. There was a good chance he had a zombie down here. But no. I smelled copper. Dried blood. I frowned. Then I heard the rattle of bars.

Frosty, Gavin and Bronx formed a wall of menace in front of one of the cages, and Cole shouldered his way past them to give me a front-row look at—

Ethan.

If I had been standing, I would have fallen from the shock.

One of his eyes was swollen, and there were several cuts on his bottom lip. Someone—or four someones—had beaten the crap out of him.

Gavin winked at me. "We did good, yeah?"

Frosty cracked his battered knuckles. "Hunting him down was easy. Taking him captive was easier. Still. You're welcome, world. Now, who wants to watch me get a little information out of this douche purse?"

I would never live that down.

"You didn't capture me," Ethan spat. "I gave myself up."

"Sure you did," Bronx said. "After we pounded your face into the dirt."

Ethan shook his head. "Just listen. The same way my father got the zombies to enter people's homes, he's sending the zombies to Cole Holland's barn tonight." He drew in a breath. "My father captures and collars the creatures, and lets some of them go. The collars have GPS, and he's able to monitor their whereabouts. Then, through electrical im-

pulses, he's able to lead the zombies to where he wants them to go."

Remote control zombies. Nice.

"If that's true, why haven't the zombies entered any other houses?" Cole demanded.

"The night they entered the houses was a test to see if it would work. Tonight isn't a test. My father wants Ali back. He thinks she's the key to saving my sister. Izzy only has a few more months to live—if she's lucky."

"Which gives you motive to pretend to help us," Cole said.

Ethan shook his head, sad. "Believe me. I learned my lesson. I can't save someone I love by hurting someone else I love."

Like Cole, I remained suspicious.

Cole returned me to the bedroom and tucked me back into bed.

"What are we going to do about the supposed zombie attack?" I asked.

His knuckles ghosted along the curve of my cheek. "I'll plan my own attack. Meanwhile, you'll rest and regain your strength."

Translation: I wasn't to be involved.

"I have to go," he said. "But I'll come back after... I'll come back."

Then he was gone. And I was alone.

I didn't worry about the outcome of the coming battle.

I drafted a new to-do list.

Only one item: *don't let my friends go into the danger zone without me.*

When I was at my best, I was an asset. I could be at my best again, if only for a little while. So, when Nana came in with cookies and milk, I thanked her and kissed her and sent her on another errand. I told her Mr. Ankh was at work (finally), and his PMS—personal male secretary—wasn't here to guard the office, then asked if she would grab the bag filled with vials of antidote.

He wouldn't mind, I assured her. And I needed it.

She didn't understand I was developing an immunity to it, and the more antidote I used, the faster that immunity would build, so she found nothing suspicious about the request. To her, it was medicine, and I was entitled to medicine.

"Found it," Nana said as she strolled inside the room. She lifted the black medical bag for my perusal before setting it beside me on the bed. She was smiling, always smiling. Until she looked at me.

Nowadays, no one but Cole smiled when they looked at me.

"You're the best, Nana."

"Of course I am. I'm partly responsible for your creation." Tapping a fingertip against my wrist, she said, "Ali, darling, when were you going to tell me about your tattoos?"

Uh-oh. "Are you mad?" I asked softly.

"No, but you're a minor and I would have liked to be a part of the decision."

"Well." If I survived the coming events, and I would… *confidence matters*…I might as well warn her about tattoos three and four. "I would like to get two more."

"What? And why?"

I explained about the slayers, and the memorials they had

etched on their bodies, and her expression softened. I told her how badly I wanted to honor Pops, but left the details of the fourth tattoo vague. It had to do with Cole…

"All right," she said with a sigh. "I give my permission. But next time, I'm going with you. Now, should I inject you with the medicine? I've never used a needle before, but I've watched a lot of TV, so I'm just sure I'll do it right."

"Sure, just—" My gaze had locked on her neck…on her pulse, glowing so prettily, beating so softly, wafting the sweetest scent to my nose.

Shuddering, I closed my eyes. When it came to the protection of the people I loved, I was stronger than I'd ever realized. But right now I wasn't going to take any chances.

"Are you all right, dear?" she asked, flattening her hand over my brow. "You do feel warm."

I hissed at the moment of contact.

Bite her, Z.A. whispered.

"I'll be fine, don't worry. Just… Nana, I love you so much, but I need to be alone right now. I'm going to inject myself, okay?"

"I love you, too," she said, but I heard the hurt in her tone. "And I'll give you your privacy, but please don't shut me out." She kissed my cheek before striding from the room.

My hand shook as I dug through the bag, withdrawing one, three, six specially marked syringes. The ones with the antiallergy antidote. I stuck myself in the arm, again and again, and felt the familiar warm tide. Z.A. screeched, then quieted. The urge to bite and feed left me. And, with the massive amount of the dose, Z.A. was no longer able to

feed off *me,* and energy returned to my body. The trembling faded from my limbs.

Testing my range of motion, I threw my legs over the side of the bed and stood. I remained steady, my knees rock-solid. I stretched my arms over my head, then twisted from the left to the right. No pain. No weakness.

It had worked.

For the past few days, I'd had to suffer through the humiliation of Nana's sponge baths. Once, when I had been whining about my desire for a shower, Cole had picked me up and carried me into the stall. He'd gotten in with me, holding me up, and we'd washed with our undergarments on.

All I could say about that: if I'd been well, I wouldn't be a virgin.

Today, though, I showered on my own. After drying off, I dressed in my fighting clothes. Long-sleeve black top, camo pants and combat boots. My weapons had been moved into Reeve's room with me, more for my peace of mind than anything, and I loaded up with daggers and throwing stars.

There was a mirror in the hall, and I meant to bypass it, I did, but I found myself stopping and peering into the glass. I saw…me. Just me. My face a little too thin for my liking, and there were bruises under my eyes, cracks in my lips, but my color was good, rosy, all health and no sickness.

I found Nana in the kitchen, cleaning up the mess she'd made while baking the cookies.

"Ali!" she exclaimed, running over and throwing her arms around me. "You look… Wow! The medicine worked."

"Thank you." I took a moment to absorb her love and

warmth, basking in the sense of home. "Now, I need to borrow your car."

She pulled back, frowned. "My car?"

"I'll be careful with it, I promise."

"I know you will, but you've never shown an interest in driving before. And I know you've had a few lessons, but you still only have your permit, and—"

I cupped her cheeks. "Trust me, Nana. I need to do this." It was time. A girl on her way to war had no room for fear. I wasn't going to tolerate this one anymore.

"I can drive you anywhere—"

"Please, Nana. Please. I'm not shutting you out. I just want to prove to myself that I can do this." I needed to start this new journey with a victory.

"All right." She nodded. "I'll get the keys."

Perspiration dotted my brow, and I struggled to draw air past the lump growing in my throat. On the wheel, my knuckles were bleached of color. Cars zoomed past me, and horns blared.

Someone gave me the finger.

What was the problem? I was only going ten miles an hour under the speed limit. If ten was the new word for twenty. And twenty was the new word for thirty. Whatever. I was motoring forward, and that should be good enough.

I managed to double the usual fifteen-minute drive before reaching Cole's barn—and miracle of miracles, I didn't crash. Several other vehicles were parked in the gravel driveway, so I knew a handful of slayers were already here, preparing for the night's activities.

As I stalked to the door, I glanced at the sky and found a rabbit-shaped cloud directly overhead.

Emma was still looking out for me.

I smiled as I entered the building. Cole, Frosty, Gavin and Veronica were bent over a table, talking, probably planning as they looked over a stack of papers.

I took a moment to enjoy the utter normalcy of the moment. The savage beauty of Cole. The bond between the four. The determination they radiated.

Anima should run and hide.

"Ali," Veronica gasped out.

All eyes lasered straight to me. I cared only about Cole, and—

—he had me draped over his shoulder. Blood dripped from both of us, and I couldn't tell if it belonged to us or someone else. I was panting, struggling to free myself from his hold.

"Let me go," I demanded.

"Never again."

"You keep saying that. What do you want with me—"

—as quickly as the vision had appeared, it vanished.

I blinked, shook my head. I'd asked Cole Holland...*what do you want with me?* As if he were a stranger?

Why?

"What'd you see?" Gavin asked, and I looked to him—

—we stood in the middle of a night-darkened road. Zombie ash was piled at our feet, twirling into the air, dancing away, and Hazmats surrounded us.

Kelly raised his mask. He was scowling. "Where is he? What have you done with him—"

"—this again," I heard Veronica say, jerking me back into the present.

Gavin scowled at her. "Next time, shut your mouth and let the vision finish. We saw tonight's battle. At least, what I think is going to be tonight's battle, and it wasn't pretty."

She sputtered for a response.

Cole closed the distance between us. "How?"

I knew what he was asking and I wanted to lie. "Antidote." No lies. I jutted my chin. "What we saw—"

"I don't know what it means, and I'm not going to try to guess. I've never been right before. What matters—you were told not to use the antidote unless absolutely necessary. Today, it wasn't necessary." His eyes narrowed, and he took my hand, tugging me into the locker room. I expected him to turn and lecture me the moment the door closed, shutting us inside, alone.

He did turn.

But he didn't lecture.

He meshed his lips onto mine, feeding me a bone-melting kiss I'd never forget. I responded immediately, wrapping myself around him, drawing him closer, drinking him in.

Backing me up, he pinned me against the wall and caged me in. His body enveloped me, pressing, rubbing, seeking. All the while his hands roamed, stopping to knead here and there and oh…glory. I shivered with the force of the pleasure.

"You feel so good," he rasped. "Taste so good. You're ready for me, right? You told me you were ready."

"So ready."

"We have to stop, though. We can't do this here."

Whimper. "I know."

Panting, we broke apart.

A hard knock sounded at the door. "Cole," Frosty called. "Your dad just walked in."

Cole pressed his forehead into mine. "We'll be out in a sec."

Murmuring. Fading footsteps.

"One day," he said to me, "we're taking off, just the two of us."

One day. I wanted that—wanted a future.

Cole's eyes narrowed. "What you did was stupid, Ali."

"Sometimes the wisest decision seems like the most foolish."

"I should spank you."

"Try. Please."

He chuckled. "You thinking you'll end up spanking *me?*"

"Knowing it."

Before I realized what was happening, he was spinning me around and smacking me on the butt. "Come on. You can help us figure out the best course of action for tonight. In the morning, we'll talk about our latest vision…and what you did with the antidote. And more about you being ready for me."

I heard the husky promise in his voice. "Cole," I began.

He shook his head. "Later."

Yeah. That was probably for the best. I nodded.

GAME...SET...DEATH MATCH

The rest of the slayers arrived at different times throughout the day, and all of them had the same reaction upon spotting me. Absolute, utter shock. I was hugged. I was patted on top of the head. I was met with sad little smiles because everyone knew the situation wouldn't last.

Took us a few hours, but we all finally agreed on a plan of attack.

I kinda felt sorry for the Hazmats.

When the sun began to set, Cole gave me a quick kiss and took his place among the chairs lining the far wall. "You see a zombie," he said, "you light up and start ashing. Don't waste your energy trying to fight. That's what we're here to do."

"Sir, yes, sir." I eased beside him.

"If your flames are red—"

"I know. Inject myself with the antidote, then run far, far away."

He tweaked the end of my nose, a gesture of affection. "When it's over, I'll come find you. You better not have a single injury."

"Same to you."

Veronica walked toward us, and I watched her purse her lips as she noticed our easy banter.

You should see his chest, Ronny dear.

She sat across from me. The rest of the slayers joined us, and one by one we forced our spirits out of our bodies. The antidote continued to do its job, and I was able to stand with only the slightest resistance from Z.A.

The chill in the air was more pronounced than usual. Cole wrapped me in his arms, sharing his warmth, before leading the way out of the barn.

Night was in full swing, the sun completely gone, the moon in its place, and the halogens Mr. Holland kept around the property glowing brightly, illuminating our way. My eyes burned and watered against the glare.

We passed the gate at the property line, each of us on alert.

In the sky, Emma's rabbit cloud pulsed, as though agitated.

I remembered the last time that had happened and gulped. "They're close," I said.

"No." Cole's expression was menacing. "The zombies are already here."

They sure were. I looked, and saw multiple sets of red eyes glowing in the distance. Moans resounded, and the scent of rot drifted. I hadn't expected things to kick off so fast, but that didn't stop anticipation from firing me up.

Ethan had told the truth.

"Go, go, go," Cole commanded.

As one cohesive mass we rushed forward. Cole fired his crossbow, the arrow sprouting four points at the end and slicing through a zombie's throat. Trina picked up speed, surging ahead, already swinging her ax. Frosty and Bronx tag-teamed two zombies, whipping around the creatures and binding the pair with rope before slicing here, slicing there. The creatures could only endure the violence—before their legs were removed and they toppled to the ground.

Gavin stayed close to Veronica. She was in the process of shoving a row of zombies into the swing of his sword. Lucas, Derek and Cruz hacked through the second and third line of monsters. I stopped in the thick of it and spread my arms. A zombie tried to grab me, but Cole was there, swinging a short sword and removing the limb just before contact.

Another zombie made a play for me, but this time I was ready, filled with power—I could do this. Fire leaped from the tips of my fingers. It was white and tipped with gold, thank God, and in an instant it spread to my shoulders. I could have whooped with joy.

The zombie touched me and burst into ash.

I was grinning as the fire continued to spread to my head, then down my chest, to my waist, down my legs and over my ankles and feet. I gave myself up to the heat, basking in it, empowered by it, and marched forward, ghosting my fingertips over the spine of the zombie chomping at Cole.

Ash.

I moved to the next and the next. Ash. Ash. One touch, that was all that was needed. Soon there were no creatures

left standing. The slayers were panting, watching me with rapt fascination.

"Dibs on being Ali's partner," Gavin said with a fist pump to the sky. "For, like, infinity."

Veronica jabbed him in the stomach.

"What?" he said, frowning. "I believe it. I say it. I receive it. Right? That's a spiritual law."

"Not if you violate my free will." I stuck my tongue out at him. "Was anyone bitten?"

"No," echoed a welcome chorus.

"Good." Cole nodded with satisfaction. "All right. It's time to split up." He looked to me. "You still good?"

My pores seemed to open up and suck the flames inside, but the heat stayed just under the surface, ready and eager for more. "I am. You?"

"Yeah."

We held hands for a moment, only a moment, offering silent assurances, before I moved to Gavin's side. The two of us parted from the group, heading for the road we'd seen in our vision, maintaining a normal, natural pace.

"You and Veronica seem awfully close," I said to him. "Closer than usual."

"Makes sense. We hooked up last night."

"You did not."

"It was good, but not great." Amusement dripped from his tone. "Practically a pity fu—screw."

"Ugh. You shouldn't be telling me this."

"Why not?"

"Telling people who you've banged is so low class."

He shrugged. "Lucas walked in on us. It's not like it's some big secret."

Still.

"You jealous?" he asked.

I rolled my eyes and made sure he noticed. "Gavin, I suddenly find you repulsive."

"Funny. That's what she said after I told her sex is sex, and I'd be willing to make myself available to her anytime she wanted it, but not to expect anything more. And you know what? She still jumped me."

"Some girls have no taste."

"In this case, you're the one without it."

That earned him another eye roll. "While she's making herself available to you, you're going to be seeing other women, aren't you?"

"I thought I'd made that clear. Was that not clear?"

"The fact that I've had my tongue on your body…" I shuddered.

His grin was slow but full-wattage. "So we can joke about that now?"

"Why not?" I said, mocking him. It felt good to tease him, to act like the girl I used to be. "As terrible as it was, I don't think there's anything else we can do about it."

"Terrible?"

"You practically checked my tonsils for infection, Gavin."

He barked out a laugh. "Ha! If you were lucky enough to be kissed by me, you'd still be screaming with pleasure."

"You say pleasure, I say—" I spotted the telltale red eyes in the distance. Inhaling sharply, I smelled the putrid stink

of rot. My ears twitched, and I heard the grunts and groans of a hunger never to be satisfied. "They're here."

He got serious in a snap, and we picked up the pace.

Seconds before I reached the creatures, I summoned the fire, and just like that, my entire body erupted with flames. Then contact, contact, contact. Ash, ash, ash. The fight wasn't even fair anymore, I thought with a surge of satisfaction.

The zombies had no defense.

But then, they weren't the ones we were after tonight.

The remaining monsters branched off, half surrounding me, half surrounding Gavin. The air was so fetid it clogged my nose and tickled my throat. I gagged, felt the flames begin to sputter and practically danced through the ranks to fell as many monsters as possible before it was too late.

I focused on Gavin and realized he hadn't had the same level of success. Around twenty of the mutated zombies still encompassed him as he sliced and hacked with his blades. I moved toward him, but not fast enough. One managed to crawl up behind him and bite into his calf. Howling with pain, Gavin dropped to the knees.

I dived for the creature, and at the moment of contact my flames licked over him. *Buh-bye now.*

"Others," Gavin rasped, the toxin already working through his bloodstream.

I destroyed the remaining zombies and crouched at Gavin's side, whipping the antidote from my pocket and sticking him in the neck. The white-gold flames hadn't dissipated, I realized too late. They licked over his throat and face, and he howled, his entire body bowing.

"I'm sorry!" I hadn't meant… Might have… Crap! What if I'd just signed his death warrant?

He screamed as the flames disappeared under his skin. I fell backward, panting, praying, trying not to panic, and then, babbling, "Thank you, thank you, thank you," as he quieted and sagged against the brittle grass, still breathing.

He would live.

As the flames at last left me, I looked around and realized piles of ash surrounded us.

Piles I'd seen in our vision.

Excited, and trying not to give way to a rise of dread, I reached out and slapped Gavin across the cheek. "Wake up!"

"I am. Jeez, woman! That hurt."

There was enough derision in his voice to scare the bravest of men, but I could only laugh.

"What just happened?" he demanded.

"I think the flames burned through the toxin." Chased away the darkness, like the journal had promised. "Is the toxin still active?"

He thought for a moment, blinked. A sense of amazement radiated from him. "No. It's gone."

Would his flames have the same affect on me? Or, because I was part zombie, would his flames destroy me? Either way, I now knew without a doubt this was the solution I'd been hoping for; there just wasn't time to explore it.

I climbed to my feet and helped him do the same. "Stay aware."

"Sir, yes, sir," he said, mocking me as I'd mocked Cole.

Footsteps suddenly beat into my awareness. I spun, my

heart drumming swiftly. Hazmats. Coming at us from every angle, soon surrounding us. Guns aimed at our heads.

Because they weren't slayers, but could see us, I knew they were in spirit form. They must have used the mechanical device Dr. Bendari mentioned.

Gavin and I pressed back to back.

"Where is he?" Kelly demanded as he removed his mask. "What have you done with him?"

The vision.

"Who? Your precious son?" I grinned. *Payback sucks, doesn't it?* "I think I'll keep that information to myself."

A cock of a gun. "Actually, why don't I show you where he is?" Cole said from behind him.

Kelly paled.

The slayers were still in spirit form, and they had come out of the darkness to circle the Hazmats.

Our hope was that they would be so intimidated by having our weapons trained on them, they would submit to us. We would lock them up in Mr. Ankh's basement until we figured out our next move. But that best-case scenario wasn't what we'd planned for—and I was glad.

Without further ado, the Hazmats exploded into action, and the battle was on.

Some of the slayers' guns were knocked away. Some weren't, and the sound of gunfire filled the night, reminiscent of firecrackers. *Pop. Pop. Pop.*

Two suited bodies fell.

Punches were thrown. Grunts abounded. Bones cracked. Screams joined the chorus. For several heartbeats, I stood there, pinned by uncertainty—I was supposed to step back,

wait. Forget being benched. I marched toward Kelly as he watched the madness.

From the corner of my eye I saw Cole knock the mask off one of the Hazmats. Trina took a punch to the chin, but quickly recovered, swung her ax and hit her mark. Another suited body fell. This one didn't get back up. Frosty played with his prey, grinning as he sliced through his opponent's suit. Bronx whaled on two men at the same time, punching one and kicking the other.

Justin backhanded the guy in front of him. Mackenzie vaulted on a man's shoulders, wrapped her thighs around his neck and arched back, forcing him to his back. Somehow she maintained her hold when they hit, choking him until he passed out. Veronica blocked a punch to the head only to take one to the side from another Hazmat. Impact stunned her, but she recovered quickly, and oh, was she angry! Growling, she threw herself into the culprit, and the two hurtled to the ground in a tangle of limbs. Two of the suits had Lucas's arms trapped behind him while another suit tried to fit a metal collar around his neck.

In front of Kelly, I punched him in the cheek. He stumbled, caught himself and glared, fury blazing in his eyes.

"You won't stop us," he said. "I won't let my daughter die."

"We *will* stop you—and you'll have no one but yourself to blame."

He made to flee. I kicked out my leg and knocked his ankles together. As he fell, flailing for an anchor, I dived on him. We hit the ground, and he lost his mask.

He swung at me, but I shifted out of the way. Then I

broke his nose. Cracked his eye socket. Split his lip. His teeth shredded the skin on my knuckles, but I didn't care.

He wiggled his legs between us, flattened his feet on my belly and pushed. I sailed backward, and he jumped to his feet, stumbling away from me. As I stood, I searched the crowd for him, but one white suit bled into another, hiding him.

Someone grabbed me by the hair and flung me in the opposite direction. I recovered, rolling and kicking my legs into the culprit's stomach. I straightened as he tripped over one of his fallen comrades.

I heard the whistle of metal against air and turned to see a man swinging a blade at me. I arched out of the way, but not quickly enough. Impact—

Never came. Gavin had swooped in and removed the guy's wrist, saving me.

"Thank you!" I called over the screams.

"Anytime, cupcake."

Movement at my other side. I turned.

Another Hazmat came at Gavin, gun already aimed. I grabbed hold of his arm, his momentum strong enough to pull me to my feet. The moment I was balanced I used all of my strength to twist the guy's arm behind his back. The gun dropped as bone snapped. He unleashed a wail of agony as his knees buckled.

I caught sight of Trina a few feet away, a collar now clasped firmly around her neck. It was the same collar these people had once used on me, the same collar they used on the zombies to send electrical impulses through their bod-

ies. At least Lucas had escaped the same fate. He savagely fought anyone who dared approach the girl.

I tried to pry the metal from her neck, but the clamp held steady. She peered up at me with hazel eyes now dark with pain. Her lips parted, but no sound emerged.

Anger rose. "Hold on. I'll find a way to help you."

"Yes, help her," Lucas gritted, ducking to avoid a punch.

I looked around the field, found what I needed. I stalked to a motionless suit and dragged the guy to Trina's side. After cutting away his glove, I pressed his thumb into the small ID pad that acted as a key. Nothing happened.

Maybe Kelly had learned from his mistakes. Maybe his print was the only one that would work.

I searched one more time. Still no sign. Coward that he was, he'd probably left the battle. But he wouldn't have gone far. He would want to watch, to see whether his men succeeded or failed.

I panned the darkness, watching for movement rather than a silhouette. There! A bush swayed. Kelly? Only one way to find out.

"I have a plan." Needing a boost, I dosed up on antidote before racing off, staying in the heart of the shadows, heading for the line of trees. The moment I broke the first, I changed direction, heading for the trembling bush.

I kept my steps as light as possible, but a twig snapped. Though I tensed, I didn't allow myself to stop or slow. I palmed two daggers, and just before I reached the bush, I raised them. Ready.

But he wasn't there.

A few feet away, another bush danced, and I figured he'd

heard me and moved on. I picked up the pace, charging after him.

I smelled the rot before I passed the wall of brittle foliage. The moment I stood in the small clearing, I saw the zombies surrounding him. Six creatures, reaching for him, snapping teeth at him.

What happened next happened quickly. Within three seconds, at the most. I could only watch.

One of the creatures bit into his arm. The suit protected his skin, but he felt the pressure of the action and grunted. He swung with his other arm, hitting the zombie in the head. The creature bit down with more vigor, like a bulldog with a bone, refusing to give up the prize. Another zombie latched onto his other arm, jerking to the ground.

"Let go," he commanded. "Stop. Stop!"

Another creature fell upon him, sinking teeth into his unprotected cheek. Kelly released a high-pierced shriek.

I launched into action, willing the fire to come as I moved. White-gold flames spread. They weren't as wild and consuming as before, nor as weak as they'd been with Gavin, but they would do. I reached the zombies and got to work. Contact. Ash. Contact. Ash. Contact. Ash.

Victorious, I peered down at the writhing Kelly.

"Antidote," he rasped. "Please. In my pocket."

Strapped to a chair… Injected with poison… Electric shocks tearing through me… "I'll help you, but then you're going to help my friend." I slid my hand into the pocket of his suit. Placed the needle at his neck.

Just like with Gavin, my flames licked over him, and his back bowed.

"Don't worry. It'll fade in—"

Kelly burst into ash.

Shocked, I fell to my butt, my flames dying. Like Kelly. I stared down at the pile of blackened dust he'd left behind, wide-eyed. I had...I had just...

Hard hands dug into my shoulders and jerked me backward. I hit my head on a rock, and dizziness took advantage, consuming me. Two collared zombies circled me, peering down at me with abject hunger. Their red eyes were bright, no more than a blur to me.

What were they doing? Why hadn't they attacked?

The collars?

I tried to sit up and fight, but my body had thrown in the towel. I should...oh, pretty...stars swirled overhead, spinning round and round, hypnotizing me. *Think. Concentrate.* "Emma." Yes. She would help. "Get...Cole." He could see her. She could tell him where I was.

I thought I saw a wall of clouds part and my little sister float down to me. Worry contorted her features, and she opened her mouth to speak, but I couldn't hear the words.

Zombie Ali rose from my body and grabbed her by the arm. The two faced off.

"Don't...touch...her," I tried to shout.

The zombies bared black-stained teeth.

The zombies!

How could I have forgotten?

Done waiting, the pair fell on me, biting into me. The pain was intense, white-hot yet freezing cold. I needed to summon the flames...flames...*flames*...but they remained at bay, out of reach.

All of a sudden, the zombies sprang away from me, sickened by the antitoxin, seizing, clutching at their throats.

Emma raced out of the area, and I tried to call her back, to tell her never mind, it wasn't safe, she needed to leave.

Where was Z.A.? Back inside me?

Flames...flames...still nothing. All I could do was lie there, a bone-deep hunger growing inside me.

I wasn't sure how much time passed before I felt a warm caress against my cheek. My eyelids fluttered open. Cole loomed over me, his features bathed in red. Red...from my eyes? He was speaking, but just like with Emma, I couldn't hear him. He stuck me with a syringe, then another, and another.

How many doses had I had today?

I felt a rushing river of strength, and some of the pain faded. The cold and heat evened out.

Careful of my injuries, I sat up. How much trauma could I endure? "I broke your rules," I said. "Got bitten."

"Don't care." Cole kissed me hard and fast. "You're okay now. That's what matters."

"I'm okay," I agreed. "You? Everyone?"

"I'm fine. Some of the guys are cut up pretty bad, and Trina..."

"I know. She's collared. I think Kelly's print would have opened the metal, but I...I killed him. Cole, I killed him with my fire. He was full of zombie toxin, and I touched him, and just like the zombies, he ashed."

He traced his thumbs over my cheeks. "Baby, he needed to die. As for Trina, we'll find another way. Come on."

As he helped me to my feet, I said, "How did you find me?"

"Emma. She said she had to fight Zombie Alice to get to me."

That was right. Z.A. had tried to hurt my little sister.

No one hurt my little sister and lived to tell about it.

We left the clearing, hand in hand. When I tried to hurry him, he shook his head.

"It's over." He grinned, violet eyes glowing with triumph. "We won."

We decided to leave the Hazmats in the forest, both surviving and dead, rather than taking the time to cart them to the dungeon. Our main concern was Trina, and our own injured. We hooked up with our bodies and rushed to Mr. Ankh's basement. There, Ethan was able to remove Trina's collar with his thumbprint.

After everyone had been bandaged up, Mr. Holland, Cole, Frosty and Gavin shoved Ethan into the back of a car and drove off...somewhere. They planned to release him into the wild. With his father gone, Ethan was the only one left to take care of his sister, Isabelle. I hoped the girl recovered, I really did. Just not at our expense.

Despite our ragged condition, the rest of us ended up congregating in Mr. Ankh's game room. Some played pool. Some Ping-Pong. Some darts. Anima wasn't out for the count, we knew that, but the entire company had been severely crippled tonight, and we were flooded with the intoxicating taste of victory.

Reeve and Kat heard the commotion and hurried down the stairs. They looked for Frosty and Bronx, and when they didn't see them, raced to me and H-bombed me with

a thousand questions about what had happened. I explained as best I could, and they relaxed.

"You should have seen our girl, the Ali-nator," Justin said, coming up to my side and putting his arm around my shoulders. "I've never seen anything like it."

I smiled at him. "You weren't so bad yourself."

"Probably the second best out there," he said with a nod.

"Please. Your skills aren't even close to mine, Justin," Lucas called. He had his front pressed against Trina's back as she lined up a shot at the pool table, and she didn't seem to mind.

Were they a couple?

"You looked like a beginner compared to me," Justin said.

Lucas flipped him off, and Trina laughed, her stick digging into the table.

"Concentrate on the game, Rina," Collins commanded. "Seriously, my mom plays better than you. And she's blind!"

"Maybe Trina's just that poor of a player," Justin said as if sticking up for her. "Ever think of that?"

Trina blew him a raspberry.

I liked that the group was so relaxed around Justin now. He'd proved himself. He was one of us.

"See you girls around. I'm going to dominate that pool table," he called, moving off.

Reeve's gaze continually darted to the entrance. "The second Bronx gets here, I'm going to corner him and we're going to talk. We haven't discussed anything that's happened, haven't dared broach the subject of a future together. We've just hung out without fighting—which is a first for us, yes, but it's not enough."

"Good for you," Kat said. "If he doesn't tell you every-thing you want to hear, I'll have Frosty beat him up."

"But…" Reeve shifted from one bare foot to the other. "What if he doesn't want me? What if he liked having an excuse to stay away from me?"

"Please tell me I don't get silly ideas like this," I said to Kat.

"Well, do you want me to lie?" she replied.

I fought a grin. "He wants you," I said to Reeve. "There's no question about that. I mean, you weren't there the night we discovered you sneaking out to meet Ethan. Wait. You *were* there, you just didn't know *we* were. He freaked out. Like, hard-core."

"Really?" she asked hopefully.

"Really."

"Ali-Kat Bell," Kat said, putting her hands on her hips. "You caught Reeve sneaking out and you never thought to share the information with me?"

"Or me," Mr. Ankh said from behind us, and we all stiff-ened. "I brought up a tray of snacks. Ali, why don't you and Kat go eat and give me a few moments alone with Miss Prison Break?"

I mouthed an apology and headed to the table, Kat at my side.

I smacked into Veronica.

We both ricocheted a few steps back. "Sorry," I mumbled.

"Yeah," she replied. Neither of us moved away.

Kat hadn't noticed the interruption and rooted around the tray Mr. Ankh had brought.

"I'm not sure what Cole sees in you," Veronica said softly.

Cole and I hadn't made anything official yet, but he *was* committed to me. I could tell her to stay away from him, but I didn't want to be that girl. If I couldn't trust him with Veronica, even if she came sniffing around, I shouldn't be with him.

"It's safe to say he sees something he likes." I tried to step around her, but she moved with me. "Do you really want to do this here, now, and ruin everyone's night?"

"You're right," she said, and I could tell she was fighting tears. "I've finally accepted that's not going to change. I guess I'm sorry I made a play for him."

I…wasn't sure how to respond. *Gee, thanks* seemed like a mistake.

"Cole and I wouldn't have lasted long anyway."

Was this a trick? This had to be a trick? "Why do you say that?"

"Other than his massive obsession with you?" she said, and my heart fluttered. "I've never argued with him. I've always acquiesced. But you…you beat him up and call him names, and he can't stop panting for more. I want no part of that kind of relationship."

Poor girl had no idea what she was missing.

"Well, I hope you find what you do want," I said, and that was about as gracious as I could manage considering the circumstances.

She closed her eyes for a moment. When she refocused, her vulnerability was replaced by anger. "Just don't hurt him, or I'll do more than make another play for him. I'll reveal my ace and bury you." With that, she was gone.

Her ace? What was her ace?

Why did I even care? He'd tattooed my name on his chest. He was mine, period.

I joined Kat at the snack tray and nearly moaned at the bounty spread out before me. Crab cakes, mini egg rolls, some kind of cream puffs. Slices of chocolate cake, apple and cinnamon scones.

Only the Ankhs could create such a feast on such short notice.

For once, I was going to let myself sponge. I ate my fill, and as my stomach rejoiced, a sense of fatigue began to plague me. I yawned, and maybe even swayed as my head lolled forward.

"Come on," Kat said, leading me toward the couch. "You look dead on your feet."

I sprawled out, and Reeve appeared to cover me with a blanket.

"How'd the conversation with your dad go?" I asked after another yawn.

"He's decided not to ground me for the rest of my life."

"Oh…good…." After that, I dozed on and off, the rest of the gang continuing to celebrate around me.

"Finally! They're here," Kat said minutes…hours…days… later, clapping with excitement.

I sat up with a jolt, and as I peered through the window, I saw Cole, Frosty and Gavin exit Mr. Holland's dark SUV and enter the night. Morning hadn't yet come. When they reached the porch, I lost sight of them.

Heart beating wildly, I eased to my feet. My knees held steady. Good. The fatigue had left me, too. I waited. And waited. And then Gavin strode through the game-room

door, tall and strong, a commanding presence that drew the eye. But his clothes were dirtier than when he'd left, and he had a scrape on his cheek he hadn't had before.

I'd find out why. First, I owed him a big, fat thank-you. He'd saved my life tonight.

I raced over and threw my arms around him, hugging him and planting a grateful kiss right smack on his mouth. "You," I said. For some reason, that was all I could manage.

Knowing what I meant, he hugged me back, kissed my cheek. "My pleasure, Blondie."

I found my wits and added, "You're a better man than I ever gave you credit for." I frowned, the words familiar to me somehow.

"I know."

"And you're *so* modest."

He chuckled.

"You...went to him first," Cole said, an odd note in his voice as he stepped up beside us.

Seeing him, I grinned and threw myself at him. "You're back."

"You went to him first," he repeated.

I pulled back and blinked, a little unsure now. "I didn't see you."

"I came in right behind him."

"Cole?" I asked, a *lot* unsure now.

"The vision," he said, and I noticed he, too, had a few extra scrapes.

Like me, Gavin blinked. "Yeah. That was it. The one we had. Part of it anyway."

And there'd been nothing romantic about it. "He saved my life. I owed him. I was just saying thank you."

"I know. Now." Cole massaged the back of his neck. "I broke up with you for nothing," he said softly.

"That wasn't the only reason. You were afraid I'd—"

"Don't make excuses for me. I'm sorry. I'm so sorry." He grabbed me up and meshed his lips onto mine.

Cheers quickly abounded, soon joined by whistles. I didn't care. I took and gave and took some more. All that he was. All that I was. The past, the present and the future.

When he lifted his head, I could only sag into him.

"I missed you," he said, rubbing his nose against mine.

"I missed you, too."

"How are you feeling?"

"Better now."

He chuckled softly, but the spurt of humor didn't last long. "I'm sorry for everything, Ali."

"Hey. It's done. It's over. We're here now. But why are you and Gavin sporting new injuries?"

"The guy who shot and bombed your Dr. Bendari showed up and tried to take Ethan away from us. He must not have realized we were letting the guy go. Anyway, he was back on his feet, and stronger than he should have been, so there was a fight. We won, but he got away again."

The cheers seeped back into my awareness, and I looked around.

"Sweet fancy," Nana said, fanning herself. When had she gotten here? "The hormones in this room."

Frosty and Kat were engaged in a similar kiss. Bronx and

Reeve had claimed the couch and were talking softly. Everyone else watched us unabashedly and grinned.

"Give me five minutes to check on everyone," Cole whispered to me, "and then I want some time alone with you."

I nodded, already counting down the seconds.

He gave me another kiss before joining his friends at the Ping-Pong table, and they each clasped palms before punching each other in the shoulder. It was like a secret handshake or something.

Nana ruffled my hair, saying, "Oh, to be young again."

"You're still young enough to go on the prowl," I said, then immediately wished I could snatch back the words.

She smiled, and suddenly she looked ten years younger. "Speaker's remorse?" she asked with a laugh. "No worries. I might enjoy looking, but I'm not interested in taming one." Rising on her tiptoes, she kissed my cheek. "I'm headed back to bed. I just came down to find out what was going on. Have fun…but not too much."

"Love you, Nana."

"Love you, too." She flittered away.

I munched on a crab cake and watched as Cole went from friend to friend, talking and laughing. He epitomized beauty, everything right in the world…in *my* world. He moved to Veronica's side, and said something that made her frown. There wasn't a single spark of jealousy inside me. *Good Ali.*

"By the way, I want you to know I'm done coming on to you, Ali Bell," Gavin said as he approached me. "You've never looked at me the way you look at Cole, and I'm starting to think that's a look I'd like to receive."

"Aw. This means my little boy is growing up. I'll even help you out with rock-solid tip to get you started."

"And that is?"

"Give up your ho-bag ways."

Grinning, he bumped my shoulder with his own. "Has anyone ever told you that you're a brat?"

"I'm just certain Cole has mentioned it a time or twelve."

"Smart boy." He enfolded me in his arms, giving me another hug.

I hugged him back.

"Are you happy with the way things worked out?" he asked.

I cupped his cheeks, and the action reminded me of the vision. I looked at Cole, still with Veronica. The tension he'd worn like a second skin had fallen away. "I am. But what about you?"

"Never better. Veronica and I have decided to move here. I don't know her reasons, but mine are simple. Alabama is an ocean of untapped, horny fish and daddy likes his seafood."

I laughed. "I'm glad you're staying. I would have missed you." My gaze returned to Cole. He was watching me now. There was no suspicion in his eyes, no anger. He still trusted me, the same way I trusted him.

He closed the distance between us.

"I'm more certain by the second that the visions don't always mean what we think they do. And now your five minutes are up," he said, taking my hand. "It's time for our talk."

"Talk? That's what we're calling it these days?" Gavin said with a laugh.

We passed Mr. Ankh, and then Mr. Holland, and my cheeks heated.

"Where are you going?" Mr. Holland demanded.

"Ali's old room."

"You have ten minutes. And then I come up to get you."

From the corner of my eye, I think I saw Cole flip off his dad.

"Fine, fifteen minutes," Mr. Holland grumbled.

"You give them fifteen. I'm giving them five," Mr. Ankh said. "Her grandmother has a temper and I don't want to face it again."

Nana had a temper?

The moment we entered my old room and shut the door, I turned to him and wrapped my arms around him. We were kissing in the next instant, and it was electric, consuming, the force of it so great I felt as if I became a part of him.

"Ali," he said, when he finally came up for air. "People are always throwing the word *love* around, but before you, I never did. And I'd never needed to hear it, either. Then, the other night, you uttered those words to me, and it's okay if you don't remember, but I heard them, and it affected me, and now I want to hear the words for real because I love you so much it hurts. I *need* to hear the words. If you're ready to give them."

Huge step. The one that would send me over the cliff.

He took my hand and shoved it under his shirt, placing my palm on his skin, just over his heart, where the last part of my name was etched. "You're a part of me, and you'll always be a part of me, and if you need more time, that's all right, too."

"Cole…"

He shook his head. "Don't say anything. Not yet. I want to get the rest of this out."

My eyes widened. There was more?

"I think I've told you how stubborn you are, how curious and now, even jealous, and you're also quick tempered, and you've got the meanest right cross of all time."

"Hey," I said, losing a little of my happy buzz.

"But I get more joy from your smiles than anything else," he continued. "I look at you, and I want you. Actually, I have only to think about you to want you. There's a sweetness to you, a vulnerability you allow so few people to see, but I'm one of the lucky ones and I'll be forever grateful."

Oh.

Who was I kidding? I'd already leaped off the cliff.

"You're mine, Ali Bell."

Silence.

"Can I talk now?" I asked.

He nodded stiffly.

Did he fear what I had to say? "Breaking up with you was the toughest thing I've ever gone through. At least I thought so at the time. Staying away from you proved tougher. From the moment our eyes first met, I've been drawn to you. Not just because you're the hottest guy I've ever met, but also because you have a core of courage and honor and when I'm with you, I feel safe and protected, and even cherished. I might be yours, but you are certainly mine, and I'm never letting you go. I love you, too, Cole Holland."

"Thank God." His hold on me tightened.

Now for the bad news. "When I'm no longer able to use the antidote," I said softly, "I want to use the flames on me."

"No."

"Yes," I said. "You must."

"I can't lose you."

"Maybe you won't." To-do: *survive.*

"Maybe I will."

"Faith," I said. "Have faith in me, in this. The last time you didn't, we fell apart."

"Ali—"

"Light will chase away the darkness," I interjected.

"Ali," he repeated again.

"I know. I know it's hard." I kissed him and said nothing more. But I didn't change my mind.

I never would.

END AT A NEW BEGINNING

For the next week, I floated on clouds of bliss. I stayed dosed
up on the antidote, so I stayed somewhat strong, though I
had moments of utter weakness and moments of depraved
hunger.

Z.A. was fighting.

Cole rarely left my side. He showed me the Christmas
present he'd gotten for me—a drawer in his bedroom. I'd
jumped into his arms, wound my legs around his waist and
whooped like a madwoman. He'd broken up with Mackenzie when she moved in, citing things were getting too
serious. For me, he said, things couldn't get serious enough.

Afterward, he'd taken me to visit Jaclyn. Poor girl. Since
our rescue, she had turned away every visitor. Me, she'd let
inside her bedroom, and she'd hugged me and sobbed until
she'd passed out from exhaustion.

I was now determined to draw her back into the world.

Wren and Poppy had been there, hanging out with Justin. They knew he and Cole were friends once again, so I was a little surprised to learn Wren and Justin were still dating. I was also surprised when the girls talked to me, as if we were still on decent terms, and promised to call.

Change. No matter where we were, it always showed up.

Right now all of the slayers and those in the know were in Cole's barn, gathered around a huge TV screen, watching a video of five-year-old Cole being trained by his father to fight zombies.

He was beyond adorable—Cole, not his father—with a mop of black hair and big violet eyes. He got a little over-eager with the nunchaku and nailed his dad between the legs. The crowd burst into laughter.

I was perched on his lap. He grinned at me, saying, "Yeah. I'm just that good."

I loved this playful side of him.

Who was I kidding? I loved every side of him.

Kat, who sat beside us, shouted, "Rewind that!" and threw popcorn at the screen. "Mr. Holland's expression was all, like, oh, no, I'm going to need my balls reattached, and Cole's was all, you're about to lose something else, sucka."

She and Frosty had not broken up once since she'd confessed her illness. And Reeve's talk with Bronx had gone better than she'd dreamed—and exactly as Kat and I had expected. He was fully committed to her and demanded exclusivity.

Everyone was so happy. Even Veronica seemed to be at peace. (I wondered if she'd made use of Gavin again.)

I rested my head on Cole's shoulder, and he hugged me

tight. We still hadn't had sex. As much time as he'd spent with me, Nana had spent with me. And if not Nana, Mr. Holland or Mr. Ankh. Or Kat and Reeve. We were never left alone, and I got it, I did. Everyone knew Cole's kisses sometimes overwhelmed me, allowing Z.A. to take over my body.

Sometimes not even a kiss was necessary. And oh, glory, now was one of those times. I was rubbing my nose against the length of his neck, I realized, barely even conscious of it, getting caught up in the sweetness of his scent. My mouth watered.

Hungry, I thought.

No. Oh, no.

Smell so good.

No! Never.

Must feed!

No.

Shaking, I held my breath and stood. "I…have to go," I said.

"Something wrong?" he asked, looking up at me and frowning. He held on to my waist, keeping me in place.

"I need another dose."

The frown intensified. "But you had one only half an hour ago."

"I know." A sickening heat swept over me, causing me to both sweat and shiver. A sensation I knew well. Only this one was far more intense. A strange buzz replaced the noise in the room. "I…I…" I backed away from him, shaking my head. "It's worse this time."

"Ali?" Kat reached out to grab me, only to shriek in pain and jerk back.

Frosty jumped up and threw her behind him.

Cole jumped to his feet, as well. I glanced down. The red flames had returned, crackling over my hands. My *human* hands. The fire was so strong it had breached my spirit and seeped out of my flesh. As I fought to douse it, the blaze spread.

Everyone but Cole scrambled away from me. "Ali," he said, approaching.

"Don't touch me," I croaked. "I'm going to walk out of here, and give myself a final dose. Then someone is going to use their flames on me. Please."

He violently shook his head. "They'd have to get through me, and that's not happening."

Z.A. whispered inside my head. *You think you could have lasted this long if I hadn't let you? I've been waiting for this moment, when the antidote would no longer help you. So go ahead. Dose yourself again. See what happens.*

I watched in horror as the flames spread even farther, to my elbows. And it hurt. Oh, it hurt. Pain shot through me, undeniable, agony in its purest form. "Have to...go," I panted. "Go. Everyone."

Not heeding my command, Cole picked me up. I was careful to keep my hands pressed against my middle, away from him, and my ankles straight out. He stopped at the table piled with food and drinks and anchored me against his chest to sweep everything to the floor. Then he gently laid me down.

I heard the gurgle of spilling liquid as he peered at me.

"Fight it," he commanded.

The flames spread to my shoulders. "Trying."

"Try harder."

The rest of the slayers surrounded me. I saw pity. I saw fear. I saw dread.

They hadn't left. They needed to leave.

You're going to die, and I'm going to rise.

"Don't let her live," I said. "Kill her. Kill her through me."

Impossible now, she gloated. *I'm going to feast on him. Empty him.*

"No," he said, his voice breaking at the end. "Anything but that."

"Cole, have to…kill her…*please.*" She wouldn't stop with him. She would destroy *everyone.* "She's here… Wants you."

"No," he insisted. "There has to be another way."

Tears fell down my cheeks, and even those burned. "Please," I begged. "Hurt. I hurt. The pain. Too much." And like the flames, it was only growing stronger.

"You'll just have to bear it, because I can't bear to lose you. If you die, I'll go with you."

"No," I shouted, and I think the other slayers did the same.

"Fight, then," he demanded. "With everything you've got, fight."

Didn't he understand? That was what I'd been doing.

I tried to scoot away from him, my gaze scanning the faces of those around me. "Help."

"I survived it," Gavin rushed out. "She accidentally touched me with her flames, and I survived. The zombies had bitten me, and she had to give me the antidote, and she burned me. Afterward, I felt stronger than ever before."

over both, glowing brightly. He was shaking as he pressed his palm over my chest—inside my chest.

I released another scream.

No! Z.A. shouted.

The red intensified, and though Cole hissed from the pain of it, he didn't back off.

Lucas left his body, too, and jerked him away from me, shouting, "She might not mean to, but she'll kill you, my man."

Cole fought him, throwing the boy backward. I sagged against the table, the red flames spreading faster, as if to compensate for what Cole had tried to do. Then Cole was once again beside me, once again touching me.

The pain magnified a thousand degrees, shooting through me, eating at me, consuming me, and another scream burst free. My back arched, coming up off the table, all of my weight settling in my shoulders and toes. I'd shatter. Any second, I would shatter.

What if Cole died because of this?

"S-stop," I managed. "Stop."

He snarled, but never severed contact.

"Cole!" Frosty yelled. "Stop this. We won't let you do this."

"Help me pull him away," Bronx gritted.

My skin felt as if it were snapping and popping and ripping away. The agony... Nothing compared to this. Now it was too much, too much, far too much. I *wanted* to die.

"The red is fading now," I heard Gavin shout. "She's healing. Help Cole. Light up and put your hands on her."

I wasn't sure how many seconds—minutes?—passed before

everyone obeyed. I couldn't see past the pain, but I eventually felt pressure on my ankles, knees, thighs, belly, arms and shoulders. A terrible heat filled me up and split me apart.

No! Zombie Ali shrieked. *No, make them stop, make them stop!*

No longer on…my to-do…list, I tried to tell her.

Her voice grew quiet, quieter…until it evaporated altogether.

And then the pain was…leaving?

Yes, I realized a few seconds later. It was. The heat was becoming bearable, almost pleasant. I sagged against the table, finally able to breathe.

My eyesight cleared, and I could see flames dancing all over me; they were no longer red, but gold, like they were supposed to be.

The slayers had saved me.

Their hands fell away from me. Someone held a mirror in front of my face, and I looked, seeing no sign of Z.A. Then the mirror was gone, and I was staring at Cole, marveling that I experienced only a desire to hug and kiss him, not to bite.

Excitement, relief and undiluted joy filled me, and I found the strength to lift my arms and encircle his neck. "Cole," I sobbed.

His hands shook as he brushed the hair from my face. "You're still here. You're still here!"

I was, and he was, though there were blisters all the way up his arm—blisters I had caused. "I'm so sorry I hurt you."

"Don't be. I'm not."

"Well, don't ever do anything like that again, do you hear me?"

"Don't ever scare me like that again."

"Don't worry."

He pressed a swift kiss into my mouth. "The light chased away the darkness."

Yes. I'd finally died to the evil and lived to the light.

"But your father. Your grandfather. Kelly. They ashed when you touched them with the flames."

True. I'd put my glowing hands on all three men, and they'd ashed. "My dad and grandfather were fully zombie, with no humanity left. And Kelly had destroyed his own humanity with his actions. I was still fighting." A thought occurred to me. "Have you ever put your hands on another slayer like that?"

"No. Never. We were too afraid we'd burn each other."

I sat up, surprised to find there was no ensuing dizziness, no weakness. Just pure, unadulterated strength. Actually, I'd never felt better.

Check off list: *kill Z.A., survive.*

I flexed my fingers, popped the bones in my neck. "There isn't a trace of the zombie toxin," I said, marveling. "I don't need the antidote. I don't need anything. I'm one hundred percent racer ready."

His violet gaze studied my face. "You look it. The bruises have fled. The chapped lips are gone. The gauntness has even left you."

We'd had the power to do this all along; we just hadn't known it. Now I suspected none of us would ever need the antidote again. We wouldn't have to worry about develop-

ing an immunity to it. We wouldn't ever have to stop fighting the zombies. We could help each other. Strengthen each other.

Someone would have to get bitten, and we would have to try this again to be sure, but deep down I knew I was right. Even Mr. Holland would be able to fight the zombies again.

Kat shoved her way through the crowd, shoved Cole aside and threw her arms around me. "You're healed!"

I hugged her back.

And there was Reeve, wrapping her arms around me, and then the three of us were jumping up and laughing. I wanted this for Kat, couldn't stand the thought of losing her to kidney disease. What would the fire do to her, though? Would we kill her if we touched her, a nonslayer, with the flames?

What I knew: she was going to die if we didn't.

I bet I could read the journal now. The answer might be inside it.

"Okay. My turn." Cole pried me out of the girls' arms and pulled me into the locker room. He faced me.

Before he could speak, I stood on my tiptoes and pressed my mouth into his.

His hands wrapped around my waist and lifted me, even as he pressed my back into the wall. I wound my legs around him and drew him ever closer. The kiss deepened, our tongues rolling together, sure and confident, driving me crazy with heat and sweetness and sensation.

His strength surrounded me. He was all that I knew, all that I wanted to know. We were the only two people alive. And we were together. Now, always.

"You need to sleep in your old bedroom tonight," he said. "I'm sending everyone home and sneaking in."

"Don't want Kat and Reeve to hear your best moves?"

"Don't want Kat and Reeve to hear the way you respond to my best moves."

Oh, my.

"Are we officially back together?" I asked.

"I should spank you for even saying that. We've been together this whole time. You were just being stubborn." He kissed his way down my neck. "I've never been so scared in my life, Ali. I've been trying to hold it together, but watching you spiral, then watching you fade and not knowing what to do..." He shuddered.

"I told you to have faith." I nibbled on the lobe of his ear. "We survived and we learned. We're stronger than ever now."

He moaned, tilting his head to allow me better access. "Against the zombies, yes. But what about Anima? They're still out there, and they have to be stopped for good."

"We'll figure it out," I said. "Right now you're going to kiss me until I have a permanent impression of your lips on mine. Then you're going to send everyone home. Then you're going to sneak into my room, as promised. *Then* you're going to show me just how much you love me."

"Consider it done. But if someone interrupts us tonight, I'm going to... I'm not sure there's an action violent enough."

I laughed.

He softened. "I love when you laugh. It's the perfect birthday present."

My eyes widened. "Today's your birthday?"

"No. January ninth."

A few days ago. I'd missed it, I realized, and frowned. "Cole—"

"No. You were sick, and I wasn't going to celebrate without you."

"Well, you're eighteen. Legal. You're getting a party," I said. "A surprise party."

He was the one to laugh this time. "Then why are you telling me about it?"

"Oh, just shut up and kiss me."

★ ★ ★ ★ ★

A NOTE FROM COLE

I'd rather not write this. You want to know how I feel. You want to know, in minute detail, why I did what I did, what happened behind the scenes, what I think of my mistakes, the outcome and what I plan to do next. You want me to describe the things I'm desperate to do with Ali.

Why don't you just take my sac, instead? The result will be the same.

I'm not a bare-your-heart-to-strangers kind of guy, and that's not going to change, so I'm not going to give you what you want. No, I'm not sorry.

I know this proves everything you've heard whispered about me. I'm too hard-core. I'm only nice to a select few. I'm mean, bossy. I'm not an easy guy to like. Some people can take me, but most would rather leave me.

I don't really care.

I am what life has made me.

Besides, you're wrong about all of it—I'm worse.

Here's what I *will* tell you: I've seen and done things that would make you vomit. I spend the majority of my time in the shadows, and sometimes darkness clings. Sometimes it's hard to shake off. But most important, I will die to protect what's mine—better yet, I will kill.

Ali is mine.

If you're out there, Anima—and I know that you are—if you're planning to make another move against my girl, you had better be prepared to battle the beast you'll wake. I will hunt you, and I will not stop. I will take you out one by one, until the last of you is gone.

You may look at me and see a teenager. An afterthought. I will look at you and see a target. A dead one.

I'm very good at hitting my targets.

So, think long and hard before you decide to take me on. There is nothing I won't do—*nothing*—to ensure the health and wellness of those I love. If you're smart, you'll run and hide before it comes to that.

This is the only warning you will receive.

Cole Holland

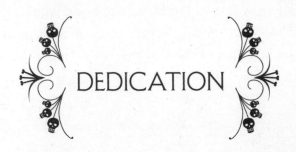

DEDICATION

To the two best kids any mother could ever have—my kids. R and V. I'm blessed to have you, blessed to have raised you and blessed to know you. May your lives be everything you dream. Mommy loves you.

To a wonderful husband who, after almost twenty years of marriage, still makes me feel pretty…even though I wear the same sweatpants almost every day of the week. Washed smoshed.

To my best friend Jill Monroe, who still takes my calls, even at the most inopportune times. What a treasure you are! One of my favorite divine connections.

To my "totes amazeballs" editor Natashya Wilson, who goes above and beyond for me every time. Your support means more to me than I can possibly say. And I don't think I can ever thank you enough for your notes on this book. Talk about nailing it! Woman, you make me smile.

To my mother, who, when I called crying, picked me up, dusted me off and helped me stand back on my feet.

To my agent, Deidre Knight, who supports me every step of the way. I'm excited to march into the future with you!

To Alyshea Rains. I'm blessed to know you!

And to God, because at one of the lowest points in my life, I looked up and there You were with Isaiah 43:1-2.